Forever Rumpole

Forever Rumpole

The Best of the Rumpole Stories

JOHN MORTIMER

VIKING

an imprint of

PENGUIN BOOKS

VIKING

Published by the Penguin Group
Penguin Books Ltd, 80 Strand, London WC2R 0RL, England
Penguin Group (USA) Inc., 375 Hudson Street, New York, New York 10014, USA
Penguin Group (Canada), 90 Eglinton Avenue East, Suite 700, Toronto, Ontario, Canada M4P 2Y3
(a division of Pearson Penguin Canada Inc.)
Penguin Ireland, 25 St Stephen's Green, Dublin 2, Ireland (a division of Penguin Books Ltd)
Penguin Group (Australia), 250 Camberwell Road,
Camberwell, Victoria 3124, Australia (a division of Pearson Australia Group Pty Ltd)
Penguin Books India Pvt Ltd, 11 Community Centre,
Panchsheel Park, New Delhi – 110 017, India
Penguin Group (NZ), 67 Apollo Drive, Rosedale, Auckland 0632, New Zealand
(a division of Pearson New Zealand Ltd)
Penguin Books (South Africa) (Pty) Ltd, 24 Sturdee Avenue,
Rosebank, Johannesburg 2196, South Africa

Penguin Books Ltd, Registered Offices: 80 Strand, London WC2R 0RL, England

www.penguin.com

This collection first published 2011

1

Set in Dante MT Std 12/14.75 pt
Typeset by Jouve (UK), Milton Keynes
Printed in Great Britain by Clays Ltd, St Ives plc

A CIP catalogue record for this book is available from the British Library

ISBN: 978–0–670–91936–9

www.greenpenguin.co.uk

Contents

Introduction by Ann Mallalieu

I first met John Mortimer in the early seventies when he was a practising barrister, just before he created Horace Rumpole. We were in the Bar Mess at the Old Bailey, then as now a long gloomy room rather reminiscent of the lounge of some two-star hotel. That is where barristers congregate to gossip, have lunch and innumerable coffee breaks during long trials and to sit anxiously reading old copies of *Country Life* while waiting for the jury to return with a verdict.

He was then a distinguished QC and playwright and I was to be his junior for the defence in a case under the Obscene Publications Act involving what John was later to describe to the jury as 'a little spanking mag'.

'Is there anything I can do for my leader?' I asked, expecting to be instructed to prepare a schedule of seized documents, a draft detailed argument on the law or to go through the thousands of pages of unused material looking for hidden nuggets which might assist the defence. 'A little cup of coffee would be nice,' was the reply.

John Mortimer, like Horace Rumpole, was not really interested in the finer points of law. If he had to conduct legal argument he did so with skill but without relish. What really interested him about being a barrister were the people and jury advocacy at which he truly excelled. There was no help that I could give or that he needed with that.

During our case, the prosecutor made a fatal error of describing our magazine as not depicting 'upright sex'. John was on to his phrase like a terrier on to a rat. During his final speech a number of jurors were crying with laughter. Even the judge had his fist in his mouth. His portrayal of counsel for the Crown as a man stuck in a Victorian time warp, a literary philistine and probably a tool of the thought police, when contrasted by him with their own modern, urbane, liberal sophistication was totally compelling. After the inevitable acquittal, a number of jurors came up to John outside the courtroom to ask for his autograph!

That case was the start of a friendship, at first professional, then personal, with John and his family which was to last for forty years until his death.

He led me in cases many times after that, always defending. I think John only ever prosecuted once and that case involved a corrupt police officer. Like Rumpole, he did not believe that the rules of the profession should be followed to the letter. The 'cab rank' principle which obliges criminal barristers, if available, to accept cases as they come, on whichever side, was not one which attracted John. His heart would not have been in putting people into prisons, which were places to be hated.

Being led in a case by John was one of the great treats of being a junior barrister, though it was often nerve-wracking in the mornings as he would tend to arrive just as the judge came into court. He would have completed several hours writing, having usually begun by 6 a.m. Then during the lunch break we would always repair to one of the local wine bars where John would entertain, with 'a little glass of champagne', actors, producers and publishers; people from the other life he was even then leading. At 4.30 p.m., when the court rose for the day, John would often be racing off to what he described as 'the real world' of the theatre for a read-through, rehearsal or meeting.

It was at one of those wine bar lunches that I remember a discussion as to whether his new television series should be called 'Rumpole of the Old Bailey' or just 'The Bailey' as the Bar knew it, then and now. Would a TV audience understand what it meant? The risk was taken, and they did.

Horace Rumpole was John's best-known and I think finest literary creation – part fiction, part observation of others and part self-portrait.

John was more successful at the Bar than Rumpole ever was, taking silk, being head of chambers, a Bencher of his Inn and instructed in some of the highest profile cases of his day. But the two of them shared many traits. Both were never part of the establishment.

John's left-wing inclinations and his less than total commitment to the Bar and its accepted career path to the Bench made him slightly suspect to his colleagues and, I think, the object of some jealousy.

Rumpole had a thicker skin, less tact and little ability to suffer fools gladly, which no doubt put a brake on his ambition. He was probably frightened of women too, which John was not. John hated criticism, minded intensely if people disliked him, which they rarely did, and had enormous natural charm. What the two men shared most powerfully were a love of literature and a fundamental belief in the importance of civil liberties and, above all, trial by jury.

The early Rumpole stories were written while John was still in practice. He would have liked to stop going to court and write full time but something of his father's influence kept him at it. The Bar was a 'proper job', writing too hazardous, and a wish to earn his father's posthumous approval seemed to lurk in the back of his mind and prevent his early retirement. When he did eventually leave, he said his only regret was not having done so earlier.

The beneficiaries of this were the Rumpole stories. All the earlier ones were written against a background which John knew intimately because he was a part of it. The criminal law and the way successive governments changed it, usually for the worse to curry favour with popular opinion, was something he saw happening at first hand. Personal experiences provided many storylines, and the characters, in chambers and on the Bench, were drawn so closely from people he encountered that one member of the judiciary threatened legal action. At least two Bailey regulars thought they were Rumpole and many of us recognize descriptions of events in which we played some part reappearing in connection with Miss Phillida Trant, Claude Erskine-Brown, Uncle Tom and the others.

Later, when he had left the Bar, John would often telephone in mid-Rumpole story-writing with questions about new laws and how things were now done. Anecdotes relayed to him would reappear, honed, polished and generally improved but with no acknowledge-ment of their origins. John was still in touch with the Bar. The public who enjoyed his writing still thought of him as a barrister, but he was no longer part of that world. He did not see at first hand the changes which started creeping into the legal system, steadily undermining the independent Bar of which he and Horace were a part. In addition, a tide of equal opportunities, ethnic awareness and political correctness changed the profession out of recognition in many respects and, in doing so, much reduced the scope for one-off eccentricity such as both John and Rumpole possessed. After he left, for many reasons, both Bench and Bar became less colourful.

John went on writing Rumpole stories until the very end. They were interspersed with autobiography, novels, plays and screenplays and trenchant political journalism. His second career was in fact his vocation. Any day, even on holiday in Tuscany, in which he did not manage to do some writing he regarded as having been wasted. By contrast, Horace Rumpole could not live without the Bar and, after being made to retire by Hilda, he found a way to return.

As a writer John had an endearing lack of self-confidence which was never apparent in court. He was terrified of bad reviews of his work and bore lifelong resentment towards any critic who said his writing was not up to scratch. He needed approval and praise. If he thought them in short supply he would say mournfully, 'My career is at an end.' If however, as was more usual, a rave notice appeared, he would say quietly, 'I think things are going really rather well.' Life was therefore something of a roller-coaster for those close to him.

Increasingly in demand as an after-dinner speaker, John continued his contacts with the law. Each year the London Criminal Solicitors Association held an annual dinner at the Savoy where leading firms entertained barristers with whom they worked. Known at the Bar as 'The Touts Ball', invitations to it were, unsurprisingly, desperately sought by barristers at every level keen to make new contacts and impress their hosts. John's speech as guest of honour one year broke every rule of the new PC code. As he told a story about the sentencing of a vertically challenged defendant in which the judge had begun his sentencing remarks with the words 'Stand up, midget!', barristers and solicitors alike hugged their stomachs with the pain of uncontrollable laughter. Such was the helplessness of his audience that if John had told us to leave by the rear entrance of the hotel and jump into the Thames, to a man and woman we would have done it. To have an audience of over a thousand people in the palm of one's hand is a gift given to very few.

Smaller audiences were equally captivated. On another occasion, John and his wife, Penny, were present at a small dinner party held in a well-known restaurant, whose chef could well have been the template for Jean-Pierre O'Higgins into whose establishment Hilda once forced Rumpole. To a man who considered a lamb chop the limit of fine dining, it was not a success.

During the evening it was noticeable that diners at other tables at this temple to food spoke to one another not at all. They just listened as John told his stories at ours, pretending not to do so and stifling their laughter in their napkins. John seldom lost his temper, but waiter after waiter that evening interrupted his stories to deliver lengthy descriptions of the gastronomic miracles being delivered to our table. At last the cheese arrived, unfortunately just as he was about to deliver the punch line of his favourite anecdote. With the cheese came an interminable description of what it was, where it came from and how it had been made. Finally John snapped. 'Just go away!' he cried. The entire restaurant broke into spontaneous applause. The story was resumed and no further pretence was made by anyone that they were not listening in and loving every moment.

John's stories were often repeated but grew better and better each time until the original was no longer recognizable. Sometimes they were loosely based on something which had happened to him, but The Truth for John was a very flexible concept. What mattered was to entertain and gain the approval of an audience, however large or small. He loved to please others. Horace Rumpole pleased himself.

It is sometimes said that barristers are frustrated actors. In later years, John became an actor in reality, taking his one-man show *Mortimer's Miscellany*, an evening of poetry and prose interspersed with those stories, on the road to theatres, village halls and churches in aid of charities such as the Howard League for Penal Reform, for which he cared greatly.

As he became increasingly frail, wheelchair-bound and with a growing list of painful disabilities, he would say that the only time he was free from pain was when he was on stage performing. He suffered from nerves beforehand as in the old days at court when he would be sick before a big speech to a jury, but once performing at one of his 'gigs' as he called them, before an audience, both nerves and physical suffering vanished.

John has gone now and there will be no new Rumpoles. Two champions of liberty, one actual and one fictional, are no more.

In many ways the courts, chambers and the Bar have already changed beyond recognition. Neither John nor Horace used a computer, preferring pencil and paper. They were not required to attend Continuing Professional Development courses each year. Nor would it have been proper for clerks to hand out football and theatre tickets to solicitors to encourage work for chambers as they now do. There were no chambers' marketing committees or arguments about the chambers' logo.

Neither saw the extension of rights of audience and repeated legal aid cuts making it increasingly difficult for criminal solicitors and junior barristers to make a living.

But there are still independent barristers who care, as they did, about justice, that an accused should be properly represented because he is innocent until proved guilty and who still regard trial by jury as 'the lamp that shows that freedom lives'. Thank goodness for them.

Ann Mallalieu
March 2011

Publisher's Note

In 1993 John Mortimer published a selection of his favourite Rumpole stories called *The Best of Rumpole*: 'These are the stories I have enjoyed writing most, those which made me laugh a little when I was writing them (the only reliable test of a successful piece of work) and which drew some laughter from the actors when they read through the television versions.'

This new volume consists of those seven stories chosen by the author himself, together with a further seven stories representing the best of the later work. In addition, there is a fragment of a novel – 'Rumpole and the Brave New World' – which he had just embarked upon when he died in January 2009.

Author's Introduction

About seventeen years ago I thought I needed a character like Maigret or Sherlock Holmes to keep me alive in my old age. I wanted a sort of detective, who could be the hero of a number of stories but whose personality and approach to life were more important than the crimes with which he was concerned. He would have to be a comic character, as well as being courageous and more than usually astute, because I believe life to be best portrayed as comedy.

I spent most of my life following two professions. I was first and last a writer, an inventor of stories. I also practised as a lawyer and I defended many people accused of crimes at the Old Bailey, London's Central Criminal Court. There I was concerned with stories, many of which were too fantastic and improbable for even the most gifted writer to persuade his readers to believe. An English criminal trial is a very theatrical occasion – the barristers and judges wear wigs and gowns, some of the judges are in scarlet and ermine and, on state occasions, carry bunches of flowers (once necessary to protect their noses from prison stench). I often left court to go to a rehearsal of a play I had written and felt I had left the world of fantasy and make-believe at the Old Bailey for the harsh reality of the world of art.

So, when I looked for a character to be my detective I found him very near at hand. I thought of all the old defenders in criminal trials I had known – rumpled, untidy men, fond of claret and steak and kidney pie, who often called the most unattractive judges and the most hardened bank robbers 'old darling' but never called their wives 'old darling'. I thought of my father, who was also a barrister, and his costume, which was rather like that which Mr Churchill used to wear in the war: a black jacket and waistcoat across which stretched a gold watch-chain, often smothered in cigar ash, a stand-up collar and a bow-tie. My father also had Rumpole's habit of quoting poetry at very inapposite moments. When I was about four when he saw me he would say, 'Is execution done on Cawdor?' which, when you're four, is a pretty tough question to have to answer. Barristers are meant to be polite to solicitors, who bring them work, but when he was displeased with one of them my father often said, 'The devil damn thee black, thou cream-faced loon,' thinking they'd be glad of another quotation from *Macbeth*.

So, from a collection of characters, Horace Rumpole was born. He is very unlike me, being a far more stoic and single-minded person than I am. However, he has this great advantage – he does say a good many of the things I think and if I said them they might sound rather leftish and off-putting, but when given voice by Rumpole they become crusty, conservative and much more appealing. He is, after all, the great defender of muddled and sinful humanity, the man who believes in never pleading guilty. He is, in its most admirable form, the archetypal Old Bailey hack.

Although the defence in a criminal case has a number of rights, many judges tend to favour the prosecution, and old defenders such as Rumpole are often treated as though they were criminals themselves. Some judges do this with great subtlety; others, like Rumpole's old enemy Judge Bullingham, are given to head-on confrontations. When summing up, judges are bound to remind the jury of the defence case, but there are various ways of doing this. An Australian judge is said to have held his nose and pulled an imaginary lavatory chain after reading out the evidence given on behalf of the accused. His Honour Judge Bullingham and his like content themselves with sighing heavily, raising their eyes to heaven and saying, 'Of course you *can* believe that if you want to, members of the jury. It's a matter entirely for you.' Over the years Rumpole has learnt to fight this snorting and purple-faced member of the judiciary with the skill of a toreador, sometimes emerging with a figurative ear or a tail. But such days in court are hard for Rumpole.

He also has a number of fights on his hands in his chambers, where his total lack of respect for authority gets him into perpetual trouble with the more pompous legal hacks. Throughout these stories I have been anxious to make it clear that judges and lawyers are not all wise, infallible and trustworthy but as vain, insecure, sometimes as prejudiced and often as foolish as the rest of us.

And then there is Rumpole's home life, which I wanted to make as testing an experience for him as his days in court. The particular term of endearment he uses for the formidable Hilda – 'She Who Must Be Obeyed' – comes from *She* by Rider Haggard, a book Rumpole remembers having read as a boy. The 'She' in that story was kept alive in a cave for about a thousand years and may have even once been Queen Cleopatra. Hilda simply calls her husband 'Rumpole', but their adversarial relationship springs from a deep mutual need. Although the Rumpoles sometimes feel they can't stand living together, they couldn't, I'm sure, contemplate living apart. Their differences may come from the fact that Hilda might not mind a bit of sex but Rumpole's amorous experiences wouldn't fill one wet weekend in Weston-super-Mare. In writing about them I have found that any incident in married life, between a large assortment of people, fits easily into the mansion flat in the Gloucester Road where the Rumpoles argue their various causes.

I wrote the first Rumpole story as a one-off *Play For Today* on BBC television. When I had written it I looked around for an actor to play Rumpole and I thought of the magnificent Alastair Sim. However Mr Sim was dead and unable to take on the part. In a happy moment Leo McKern was approached and in an even happier moment he agreed to play the role. He is a superb actor of endless invention and instinctive taste. He brought Rumpole wholly and wonderfully to life, and it would now be impossible to think of anyone else playing the part. After our one-off play the BBC was a little slow to commission the series so we went off to commercial television, for which I have written about thirty-six Rumpole stories. After the initial play, Rumpole's chambers filled with characters – the opera-loving and susceptible Claude Erskine-Brown; the beautiful Phillida Erskine-Brown, née Trant, the 'Portia of our chambers'; the accident-prone Guthrie Featherstone, QC, MP, soon to become one of Her Majesty's most haunted judges; Uncle Tom, the briefless old barrister who practises putting in the clerk's room and has a head full of legal anecdotes and music-hall songs; Mizz Liz Probert, the fearless young radical lawyer; Henry the clerk and the intolerably pompous Sam Ballard, QC, leading light of the Lawyers As Christians Society and well-trained husband of the ex-matron at the Old Bailey. It has been a great pleasure to weave their stories in with the crimes and the trials and the Rumpoles' domestic life, but doing so has meant that every Rumpole story has had to have at least three plots, so I must have invented well over a hundred stories. I hope this makes them more enjoyable to read, although it doesn't make them any easier to write.

The first Rumpole on the BBC was fairly well received, but nothing prepared me for his long life or, indeed, for his popularity abroad. He is as resolutely English as boiled beef and carrots and yet perhaps his greatest success has been in America and Australia. In the vast Gas and Electricity Building in San Francisco the ever-growing Rumpole Society holds its meetings. Californian judges in 'She Who Must Be Obeyed' T-shirts serve out Château Thames Embankment in a mock-up of Pommeroy's Wine Bar. There is a character in the stories called Dodo Mackintosh who makes 'cheesy bits' for the chambers' parties; the proceedings in San Francisco start with a blind tasting of Dodo's cheesy bits. They also include such events as a Hilda Rumpole look-alike competition and the compilation of a Rumpole cookbook. As I write the stories quite fast, my hero's address in Froxbury Mansions has appeared in somewhat different forms. This gives the Rumpolians much to speculate about and discuss. Apart from having a number of societies to his name, Rumpole has several pubs, an office building and an excellent restaurant in Brisbane which, however, serves none of his favourite food.

He also has to suffer the indignity of having me mistaken for him. Criminals I defended often said, 'That Mr Rumpole could have got me off this one, I don't know why you couldn't.' Passing through Australian airports, I am often greeted with cries of 'G'day Rumpole!' When I did my last case, which happened to be in Singapore, I staggered into the robing-room of that country's Central Court, jet-lagged, hungover, with no clear idea of what the case was all about, in the usual position of a leading counsel at the beginning of an important criminal trial. This particular oriental robing-room was presided over by an elderly Chinese woman who was busy brewing up Nescafé and pouring out cough mixture for barristers with sore throats. At the sight of me, she called out gleefully, 'Ah, there you are, Lumpore of the Bairey!' I knew I didn't want to spend my declining years trudging around the Far East being called Lumpore, so I gave up my legal practice. All the same, I am not at all ashamed of having been mistaken for the great man.

It is said that Conan Doyle grew tired of his creation and, for that reason, arranged for him to be pushed off the Reichenbach Falls, although he had to bring him back to life by popular request. I have never felt tempted to push Rumpole under a train at the Temple station. Although I can imagine an author tiring of Holmes's dry and ascetic character, Rumpole stories have the great advantage, for me, of moving with the times. Whatever's happening in the world, and needs mocking – the power of social workers, the fallibility of judges, euthanasia, political correctness and the ghastliness of our penal system – can all be dealt with in a Rumpole story. So each one doesn't only need three plots, it also needs a theme, a basic idea and something, I hope something unsettling, to think about while you laugh.

And in creating Rumpole I did have another purpose in mind. On the whole, lawyers are as unpopular as income tax collectors and traffic wardens. People think they tell lies and make a great deal of money. In fact, old criminal defenders like Rumpole don't make much money and they stand up for our great legal principles – free speech, the idea that people are innocent until someone proves them guilty to the satisfaction of twelve ordinary members of a jury, and the proposition that the police should not invent more of the evidence than is absolutely necessary. They protect the rights for which we have fought and struggled over the centuries, and do so at a time when jury trials and the rights of an accused person to silence are under constant attack from the government. So Rumpole has always been popular with lawyers, although it's embarrassing to go into the wine bars round the Old Bailey and see a lot of fat, elderly barristers with cigar ash on their watch-chains drinking bad claret and pretending to be the original Rumpole. Writing Rumpole plays had another great advantage for me when I worked in the courts: if the judge did something especially silly I could always write him into a Rumpole.

John Mortimer
Turville Heath
October 1992

Acknowledgements

'Rumpole and the Younger Generation' first appeared in *Rumpole of the Bailey*, 1978. 'Rumpole and the Showfolk' first appeared in *The Trials of Rumpole*, 1979. 'Rumpole and the Tap End' and 'Rumpole and the Bubble Reputation' first appeared in *Rumpole and the Age of Miracles*, 1988. 'Rumpole à la Carte' first appeared in *Rumpole à la Carte*, 1990. 'Rumpole and the Children of the Devil' and 'Rumpole on Trial' first appeared in *Rumpole on Trial*, 1992. 'Rumpole and the Way through the Woods' and 'Rumpole and the Angel of Death' first appeared in *Rumpole and the Angel of Death*, 1995. 'Rumpole and the Old Familiar Faces' and 'Rumpole Rests His Case' first appeared in *Rumpole Rests His Case*, 2001. 'Rumpole and the Primrose Path' and 'Rumpole Redeemed' first appeared in *Rumpole and the Primrose Path*, 2002. 'Rumpole and the Christmas Break' first appeared in *The Strand Magazine* and *Woman's Weekly* in 2004, and was republished in *Rumpole at Christmas*, 2009. 'Rumpole and the Brave New World' first appeared in the *Guardian*, 24 January 2009. All the books were first published by Penguin or Viking Penguin; and all the stories are copyright © Advanpress Ltd.

Rumpole and the Younger Generation

I, Horace Rumpole, barrister at law, sixty-eight next birthday, Old Bailey hack, husband to Mrs Hilda Rumpole (known to me only as She Who Must Be Obeyed) and father to Nicholas Rumpole (lecturer in social studies at the University of Baltimore, I have always been extremely proud of Nick); I, who have a mind full of old murders, legal anecdotes and memorable fragments of the *Oxford Book of English Verse* (Sir Arthur Quiller-Couch's edition) together with a dependable knowledge of bloodstains, blood groups, fingerprints and forgery by typewriter; I, who am now the oldest member of my chambers, take up my pen at this advanced age during a lull in business (there's not much crime about, all the best villains seem to be off on holiday in the Costa Brava), in order to write my reconstructions of some of my recent triumphs (including a number of recent disasters) in the courts of law, hoping thereby to turn a bob or two which won't be immediately grabbed by the taxman, or my clerk, Henry, or by She Who Must Be Obeyed, and perhaps give some sort of entertainment to those who, like myself, have found in British justice a lifelong subject of harmless fun.

When I first considered putting pen to paper in this matter of my life, I thought I must begin with the great cases of my comparative youth, the Penge Bungalow Murders, where I gained an acquittal alone and without a leader, or the Great Brighton Benefit Club Forgery, which I contrived to win by reason of my exhaustive study of typewriters. In these cases I was, for a brief moment, in the public eye, or at least my name seemed almost a permanent feature of the *News of the World*, but when I come to look back on that period of my life at the Bar it all seems to have happened to another Rumpole, an eager young barrister whom I can scarcely recognize and whom I am not at all sure I would like, at least not enough to spend a whole book with him.

I am not a public figure now, so much has to be admitted; but some of the cases I shall describe, the wretched business of the Honourable Member, for instance, or the charge of murder brought against the youngest, and barmiest, of the appalling Delgardo brothers, did put me back on the front page of the *News of the World* (and even got me a few inches in *The Times*). But I suppose I have become pretty well known, if not something of a legend, round the Old Bailey, in Pommeroy's Wine Bar in Fleet Street, in the robing room at London Sessions and in the cells at Brixton Prison. They know me there for never pleading guilty, for chain-smoking small cigars, and for quoting Wordsworth when they least expect it. Such notoriety will not long survive my not-to-be-delayed trip to Golders Green Crematorium. Barristers' speeches vanish quicker than Chinese dinners, and even the greatest victory in court rarely survives longer than the next Sunday's papers.

To understand the full effect on my family life, however, of that case which I have called 'Rumpole and the Younger Generation', it is necessary to know a little of my past and the long years that led up to my successful defence of Jim Timson, the sixteen-year-old sprig, the young hopeful, and apple of the eye of the Timsons, a huge and industrious family of South London villains. As this case was, by and large, a family matter, it is important that you should understand my family.

My father, the Reverend Wilfred Rumpole, was a Church of England clergyman who, in early middle age, came reluctantly to the conclusion that he no longer believed any one of the Thirty-nine Articles. As he was not fitted by character or training for any other profession, however, he had to soldier on in his living in Croydon and by a good deal of scraping and saving he was able to send me as a boarder to a minor public school on the Norfolk coast. I later went to Keble College, Oxford, where I achieved a dubious third in law – you will discover during the course of these memoirs that, although I only feel truly alive and happy in law courts, I have a singular distaste for the law. My father's example, and the number of theological students I met at Keble, gave me an early mistrust of clergymen, whom I have always found to be most unsatisfactory witnesses. If you call a clergyman in mitigation, the old darling can be guaranteed to add at least a year to the sentence.

When I first went to the Bar, I entered the chambers of C. H. Wystan. Wystan had a moderate practice, acquired rather by industry than talent, and a strong disinclination to look at the photographs in murder cases, being particularly squeamish on the fascinating subject of blood. He also had a daughter, Hilda Wystan as was, now Mrs Hilda Rumpole and She Who Must Be Obeyed. I was ambitious in those days. I did my best to cultivate Wystan's clerk, Albert, and I started to get a good deal of criminal work. I did what was expected of me and spent happy hours round the Bailey and Sessions and my fame grew in criminal circles; at the end of the day I would take Albert for a drink in Pommeroy's Wine Bar. We got on extremely well and he would always recommend 'his Mr Rumpole' if a solicitor rang up with a particularly tricky indecent assault or a nasty case of receiving stolen property.

There is no point in writing your memoirs unless you are prepared to be completely candid, and I must confess that, in the course of a long life, I have been in love on several occasions. I am sure that I loved Miss Porter, the shy and nervous, but at times liberated daughter of Septimus Porter, my Oxford tutor in Roman Law. In fact we were engaged to be married, but the engagement had to be broken off because of Miss Porter's early death. I often think about her, and of the different course my home life might have taken, for Miss Porter was in no way a girl born to command, or expect, implicit obedience. During my service with the ground staff of the RAF I undoubtedly became helplessly smitten with the charms of an extremely warm-hearted and gallant officer in the WAAFs by the name of Miss Bobby O'Keefe, but I was no match for the wings of a pilot officer, as appeared on the chest of a certain Sam 'Three Fingers' Dogherty. During my conduct of a case, which I shall describe in a later chapter which I have called 'Rumpole and the Alternative Society', I once again felt a hopeless and almost feverish stirring of passion for a young woman who was determined to talk her way into Holloway Prison. My relationship with Hilda Wystan was rather different.

To begin with, she seemed part of life in chambers. She was always interested in the law and ambitious, first for her widowed father, and then, when he proved himself unlikely Lord Chancellor material, for me. She often dropped in for tea on her way home from shopping, and Wystan used to invite me in for a cup. One year I was detailed off to be her partner at an Inns of Court ball. There it became clear to me that I was expected to marry Hilda; it seemed a step in my career like getting a brief in the Court of Appeal, or doing a murder. When she proposed to me, as she did over a glass of claret cup after an energetic waltz, Hilda made it clear that, when old Wystan finally retired, she expected to see me head of chambers. I, who have never felt at a loss for a word in court, found absolutely nothing to say. In that silence the matter was concluded.

So now you must picture Hilda and me twenty-five years later, with a son at that same east-coast public school which I just managed to afford from the fruits of crime, in our matrimonial home at 25B Froxbury Mansions, Gloucester Road. (A mansion flat is a misleading description of that cavernous and underheated area which Hilda devotes so much of her energy to keeping shipshape, not to say Bristol fashion.) We were having breakfast, and, between bites of toast, I was reading my brief for that day, an Old Bailey trial of the sixteen-year-old Jim Timson charged with robbery with violence, he having allegedly taken part in a wage snatch on a couple of elderly butchers: an escapade planned in the playground of the local comprehensive. As so often happens, the poet Wordsworth, that old sheep of the Lake District, sprang immediately to mind, and I gave tongue to his lines, well knowing that they must only serve to irritate She Who Must Be Obeyed: ' "Trailing clouds of glory do we come From God, who is our home; Heaven lies about us in our infancy!" '

I looked at Hilda. She was impassively demolishing a boiled egg. I also noticed that she was wearing a hat, as if prepared to set out

upon some expedition. I decided to give her a little more Wordsworth, prompted by my reading the story of the boy Timson:
' "Shades of the prison house begin to close Upon the growing boy." '

Hilda spoke at last.

'Rumpole, you're not talking about your son, I hope. You're
never referring to Nick . . .'

' "Shades of the prison house begin to close"? Not round our son,
of course. Not round Nick. Shades of the public school have grown
round him, the thousand-quid-a-year remand home.'

Hilda always thought it indelicate to refer to the subject of school
fees, as if being at Mulstead were a kind of unsolicited honour for
Nick. She became increasingly businesslike.

'He's breaking up this morning.'

'Shades of the prison house begin to open up for the holidays.'

'Nick has to be met at 11.15 at Liverpool Street and given lunch.
When he went back to school you promised him a show. You haven't
forgotten?'

Hilda was clearing away the plates rapidly. To tell the truth I had
forgotten the date of Nick's holidays; but I let her assume I had a
long-planned treat laid on for him.

'Of course I haven't forgotten. The only show I can offer him is a
robbery with violence at the Old Bailey. I wish I could lay on a murder. Nick's always so enjoyed my murders.'

It was true. On one distant half-term Nick had sat in on the Peck-
ham Billiard Hall Stabbing, and enjoyed it a great deal more than
Treasure Island.

'I must fly! Daddy gets so crotchety if anyone's late. And he does
love his visits.'

Hilda removed my half-empty coffee cup.

'Our father which art in Horsham. Give my respects to the old
sweetheart.'

It had also slipped my mind that old C. H. Wystan was laid
up with a dicky ticker in Horsham General Hospital. The hat was,
no doubt, a clue I should have followed. Hilda usually goes shopping in a headscarf. By now she was at the door, and looking
disapproving.

'"Old sweetheart" is hardly how you used to talk of the head of your chambers.'

'Somehow I can never remember to call the head of my chambers "Daddy".'

The door was open. Hilda was making a slow and effective exit.

'Tell Nick I'll be back in good time to get his supper.'

'Your wish is my command!' I muttered in my best imitation of a slave out of *Chu Chin Chow*. She chose to ignore it.

'And try not to leave the kitchen looking as though it's been hit by a bomb.'

'I hear, oh Master of the Blue Horizons.' I said this with a little more confidence, as she had by now started off on her errand of mercy, and I added, for good measure, 'She Who Must Be Obeyed'.

I had finished my breakfast, and was already thinking how much easier life with the Old Bailey judge was than marriage.

Soon after I finished my breakfast with Hilda, and made plans to meet my son at the start of his holidays from school, Fred Timson, star of a dozen court appearances, was seeing *his* son in the cells under the Old Bailey as the result of a specially arranged visit. I know he brought the boy his best jacket, which his mother had taken specially to the cleaners, and insisted on his putting on a tie. I imagine he told him that they had the best 'brief' in the business to defend him, Mr Rumpole having always done wonders for the Timson family. I know that Fred told young Jim to stand up straight in the witness-box and remember to call the judge 'my Lord' and not show his ignorance by coming out with any gaffe such as 'your Honour', or 'Sir'. The world, that day, was full of fathers showing appropriate and paternal concern.

The robbery with which Jim Timson was charged was an exceedingly simple one. At about 7 p.m. one Friday evening, the date being 16 September, the two elderly Brixton butchers, Mr Cadwallader and Mr Lewis Stein, closed their shop in Bombay Road and walked with their week's takings round the corner to a narrow alleyway known as Green's Passage, where their grey Austin van was parked. When they got to the van they found that the front tyres had been deflated. They stooped to inspect the wheels and, as they did so, they were attacked by a number of boys, some armed with knives and one flourishing a cricket stump. Luckily, neither of the butchers was hurt, but the attaché case containing their money was snatched.

Chief Inspector 'Persil' White, the old darling in whose territory this outrage had been committed, arrested Jim Timson. All the other boys got clean away, but no doubt because he came from a family well known, indeed almost embarrassingly familiar, to the chief inspector, and because of certain rumours in the school playground, he was charged and put on an identity parade. The butchers totally failed to identify him; but, when he was in the remand centre, young Jim, according to the evidence, had boasted to another boy of having 'done the butchers'.

As I thought about this case on my way to the Temple that morning, it occurred to me that Jim Timson was a year younger than my son, but that he had got a step further than Nick in following his father's profession. I had always hoped Nick would go into the law, and, as I say, he seemed to thoroughly enjoy my murders.

In the clerk's room in chambers Albert was handing out the work for the day: rather as a trainer sends his string of horses out on the gallops. I looked round the familiar faces, my friend George Frobisher, who is an old sweetheart but an absolutely hopeless advocate (he can't ask for costs without writing down what he's going to say), was being fobbed off with a nuisance at Kingston County Court. Young Erskine-Brown, who wears striped shirts and what I believe are known as 'Chelsea boots', was turning up his well-bred nose at an indecent assault at Lambeth (a job I'd have bought Albert a double claret in Pommeroy's for at his age) and saying he would prefer a little civil work, adding that he was sick to death of crime.

I have very little patience with Erskine-Brown.

'A person who is tired of crime,' I told him quite candidly, 'is tired of life.'

'Your dangerous and careless at Clerkenwell is on the mantelpiece, Mr Hoskins,' Albert said.

Hoskins is a gloomy fellow with four daughters; he's always

7

lurking about our clerk's room looking for cheques. As I've told him often enough crime doesn't pay, or at any rate not for a very long time.

When a young man called MacLay had asked in vain for a brief I invited him to take a note for me down at the Old Bailey. At least he'd get a wig on and not spend a miserable day unemployed in chambers. Our oldest member, Uncle Tom (very few of us remember that his name is T. C. Rowley), also asked Albert if there were any briefs for him, not in the least expecting to find one. To my certain knowledge, Uncle Tom hasn't appeared in court for fifteen years, when he managed to lose an undefended divorce case, but, as he lives with a widowed sister, a lady of such reputed ferocity that she makes She Who Must Be Obeyed sound like Mrs Tiggy-winkle, he spends most of his time in chambers. He looks remarkably well for seventy-eight.

'You aren't actually *expecting* a brief, Uncle Tom, are you?' Erskine-Brown asked. I can't like Erskine-Brown.

'Time was,' Uncle Tom started one of his reminiscences of life in our chambers. 'Time was when I had more briefs in my corner of the mantelpiece, Erskine-Brown, than you've seen in the whole of your short career at the Bar. Now,' he was opening a brown envelope, 'I only get invitations to insure my life. It's a little late for that.'

Albert told me that the robbery was not before 11.30 before Mr Justice Everglade in Number One Court. He also told me who was prosecuting, none other than the tall, elegant figure with the silk handkerchief and gold wristwatch, leaning against the mantelpiece and negligently reading a large cheque from the Director of Public Prosecutions, Guthrie Featherstone, MP. He removed the silk handkerchief, dabbed the end of his nose and his small moustache and asked in that voice which comes over so charmingly, saying nothing much about any important topic of the day in *World at One*, 'Agin me Rumpole? Are you agin me?' He covered a slight yawn with the handkerchief before returning it to his breast pocket. 'Just come from an all-night sitting down at the House. I don't suppose your robbery'll be much of a worry.'

'Only, possibly, to young Jim Timson,' I told him, and then gave Albert his orders for the day. 'Mrs Rumpole's gone down to see her father in Horsham.'

'How is Wystan? No better, is he?' Uncle Tom sounded as gently pleased as all old men do when they hear news of illness in others.

'Much the same, Uncle Tom, thank you. And young Nick, my son . . .'

'Master Nick?' Albert had always been fond of Nick, and looked forward to putting him through his paces when the time came for him to join our stable in chambers.

'He's breaking up today. So he'll need meeting at Liverpool Street. Then he can watch a bit of the robbery.'

'We're going to have your son in the audience? I'd better be brilliant.' Guthrie Featherstone now moved from the fireplace.

'You needn't bother, old darling. It's his dad he comes to see.'

'Oh, *touché*, Rumpole! *Distinctement touché!*'

Featherstone talks like that. Then he invited me to walk down to the Bailey with him. Apparently he was still capable of movement and didn't need a stretcher, even after a sleepless night with the Gas Mains Enabling Bill, or whatever it was.

We walked together down Fleet Street and into Ludgate Circus, Featherstone wearing his overcoat with the velvet collar and little round bowler hat, I puffing a small cigar and with my old mac flapping in the wind; I discovered that the gentleman beside me was quietly quizzing me about my career at the Bar.

'You've been at this game a long while, Rumpole,' Featherstone announced. I didn't disagree with him, and then he went on.

'You never thought of taking silk?'

'Rumpole, QC?' I almost burst out laughing. 'Not on your Nelly. Rumpole "Queer Customer". That's what they'd be bound to call me.'

'I'm sure you could, with your seniority.' I had no idea then, of exactly what this Featherstone was after. I gave him my view of QCs in general.

'Perhaps, if I played golf with the right judges, or put up for

Parliament, they might make me an artificial silk, or, at any rate, a nylon.' It was at that point I realized I had put up a bit of a black. 'Sorry. I forgot. You *did* put up for Parliament.'

'Yes. You never thought of Rumpole, QC?' Featherstone had apparently taken no offence.

'Never,' I told him. 'I have the honour to be an Old Bailey hack! That's quite enough for me.'

At which point we turned up into Newgate Street and there it was in all its glory, touched by a hint of early spring sunshine, the Old Bailey, a stately law court, decreed by the city fathers, an Edwardian palace, with an extensive modern extension to deal with the increase in human fallibility. There was the dome and the Blindfold Lady. Well, it's much better she doesn't see *all* that's going on. That, in fact, was our English version of the *palais de justice*, complete with murals, marble statues and underground accommodation for some of the choicest villains in London.

Terrible things go on down the Bailey – horrifying things. Why is it I never go in the revolving door without a thrill of pleasure, a slight tremble of excitement? Why does it seem a much *jollier* place than my flat in Gloucester Road under the strict rule of She Who Must Be Obeyed? These are questions which may only be partly answered in the course of these memoirs.

At the time when I was waving a cheerful umbrella at Harry, the policeman in the revolving door of the Old Bailey extension, my wife Hilda was at her daddy's bedside at the Horsham General arranging her dozen early daffs and gently probing, so she told me that evening, on the subject of his future, and mine.

'I'll have to give up, you know. I can't go on for ever. Crocked up, I'm afraid,' said Wystan.

'Nonsense, Daddy. You'll go on for years.'

I imagine Hilda did her best to sound bracing, while putting the daffs firmly in their place.

'No, Hilda. No. They'll have to start looking for another head of chambers.'

This gave Hilda her opportunity. 'Rumpole's the senior man. Apart from Uncle Tom and he doesn't really practise nowadays.'

'Your husband the senior man.' Wystan looked back on a singularly uneventful life. 'How time flies! I recall when he was the junior man. My pupil.'

'You said he was the best youngster on bloodstains you'd ever known.' Hilda was doing her best for me.

'Rumpole! Yes, your husband was pretty good on bloodstains. Shaky, though, on the law of landlord and tenant. What sort of practice has Rumpole now?'

'I believe . . . Today it's the Old Bailey.' Hilda was plumping pillows, doing her best to sound casual. And her father showed no particular enthusiasm for my place of work.

'It's always the Old Bailey, isn't it?'

'Most of the time. Yes. I suppose so.'

'Not a frightfully good *address*, the Old Bailey. Not exactly the SW1 of the legal profession.'

Sensing that Daddy would have thought better of me if I'd been in the Court of Appeal or the Chancery Division, Hilda told me she thought of a master stroke.

'Oh, Rumpole only went down to the Bailey because it's a family he knows. It seems they've got a young boy in trouble.'

This appealed to Daddy, he gave one of his bleak smiles which amount to no more than a brief withdrawal of lips from the dentures.

'Son gone wrong?' he said. 'Very sad that. Especially if he comes of a really good family.'

That really good family, the Timsons, was out in force and waiting outside Number One Court by the time I had got on the fancy dress, yellowing horse-hair wig, gown become more than a trifle tattered over the years, and bands round the neck that Albert ought to have sent to the laundry after last week's death by dangerous driving. As I looked at the Timson clan assembled, I thought the best thing about them was the amount of work of a criminal nature they had brought into chambers. They were all dressed for the occasion, the men in dark blazers, suede shoes and grey flannels; the ladies in tight-fitting suits, high heels and elaborately piled hairdos. I had never seen so many ex-clients together at one time.

'Mr Rumpole.'

'Ah, Bernard! You're instructing me.'

Mr Bernard, the solicitor, was a thirtyish, perpetually smiling man in a pinstriped suit. He regarded criminals with something of the naïve fervour with which young girls think of popular entertainers. Had I known the expression at the time I would have called him a grafters' 'groupie'.

'I'm always your instructing solicitor in a Timson case, Mr Rumpole.' Mr Bernard beamed and Fred Timson, a kindly man and most innocent robber, stepped out of the ranks to do the honours.

'Nothing but the best for the Timsons, best solicitor and best barrister going. You know my wife Vi?'

Young Jim's mother seemed full of confidence. As I took her hand, I remembered I had got Vi off on a handling charge after the Croydon Bank Raid. Well, there was really no evidence.

'Uncle Cyril.' Fred introduced the plumpish uncle with the small moustache whom I was sure I remembered. What was *his* last outing exactly? Carrying house-breaking instruments by night?

'Uncle Dennis. You remember Den, surely, Mr Rumpole?'

I did. Den's last little matter was an alleged conspiracy to forge log books.

'And Den's Doris.'

Aunty Doris came at me in a blur of henna-ed hair and darkish perfume. What was Doris's last indiscretion? Could it have been receiving a vast quantity of stolen scampi? Acquitted by a majority, at least I was sure of that.

'And yours truly. Frederick Timson. The boy's father.'

Regrettable, but we had a slip-up with Fred's last spot of bother. I was away with flu, George Frobisher took it over and he got three years. He must've only just got out.

'So, Mr Rumpole. You know the whole family.'

A family to breed from, the Timsons. Must almost keep the Old Bailey going single-handed.

'You're going to do your best for our young Jim, I'm sure, Mr Rumpole.'

I didn't find the simple faith of the Timsons that I could secure acquittals in the most unlikely circumstances especially encouraging. But then Jim's mother said something which I was to long remember.

'He's a good boy. He was ever so good to me while Dad was away.'

So that was Jimbo's life. Head of the family at fourteen, when Dad was off on one of his regular visits to Her Majesty.

'It's young Jim's first appearance, like. At the Old Bailey.' Fred couldn't conceal a note of pride. It was Jim boy's bar mitzvah, his first communion.

So we chatted a little about how all the other boys got clean away, which I told them was a bit of luck as none of them would go into the witness-box and implicate Jim, and Bernard pointed out that the identification by the butchers was pretty hopeless. Well, what did he expect? Would you have a photographic impression of the young hopeful who struck you a smart blow on the back of the head with a cricket stump? We talked with that curious suppressed excitement there always is before a trial, however disastrous the outcome may be, and I told them the only thing we had to worry about, as if that were not enough, was Jim's confession to the boy in the remand centre, a youth who rejoiced in the name of Peanuts Molloy.

'Peanuts Molloy! Little grass.' Fred Timson spoke with a deep contempt.

'Old Persil White fitted him up with that one, didn't he?' Uncle Cyril said it as if it were the most natural thing in the world, and only to be expected.

'Detective Chief Inspector White,' Bernard explained.

'Why should the chief inspector want to fit up your Jimbo?' It was a question to which I should have known what their answer would be.

'Because he's a Timson, that's why!' said Fred.

'Because he's the apple of our eye, like,' Uncle Den told me, and the boy's mother added:

'Being as he's the baby of the family.'

'Old Persil'd fit up his mother if it'd get him a smile from his super.' As Fred said this the chief inspector himself, grey-haired and avuncular, walked by in plain clothes, with a plain-clothes sergeant.

'Morning, Chief Inspector,' Fred carried on without drawing breath.

'Morning, Fred. Morning, Mrs Timson.' The chief inspector greeted the family with casual politeness – after all, they were part of his daily work – and Vi sniffed back a 'Good morning, Chief Inspector.'

'Mr Timson. We'll shift our ground. Remove, good friends.'

Like Hamlet, after seeing the ghost, I thought it was better to continue our conference in private. So we went and sat round a table in the canteen, and, when we had sorted out who took how many lumps, and which of them could do with a choc roll or a cheese sandwich, the family gave me the lowdown on the chief prosecution witness.

'The chief inspector put that little grass Peanuts Molloy into Jim's painting class at the remand centre.' Fred had no doubt about it.

'Jim apparently poured out his soul to Peanuts.' The evidence sounded, to my old ears, completely convincing, and Bernard read us a snatch from his file.

'We planned to do the old blokes from the butcher's and grab the wages . . .'

'That,' I reminded the assembled company, 'is what Peanuts will say Jim told him.'

'You think I'd bring Jim up to talk in the nick like that? The Timsons ain't stupid!' Fred was outraged, and Vi, pursing her lips in a sour gesture of wounded respectability, added, 'His dad's always told him. Never say a word to anyone you're banged up with – bound to be a grass.'

One by one, Aunty Doris, Uncle Den and Uncle Cyril added their support.

'That's right. Fred's always brought the boy up proper. Like the way he should be. He'd never speak about the crime, not to anyone he was banged up with.'

'Specially not to one of the Molloys!'

'The Molloys!' Vi spoke for the Timsons, and with deep hatred. 'Noted grasses. That family always has been.'

'The Molloys is beyond the pale. Well known for it.' Aunty Doris nodded her henna-ed topknot wisely.

'Peanuts's grandad shopped my old father in the Streatham Co-op Robbery. Pre-war, that was.'

I had a vague memory then of what Fred Timson was talking about. The Streatham Co-op case, one of my better briefs – a long case with not much honour shown among thieves, as far as I could remember.

'Then you can understand, Mr Rumpole. No Timson would ever speak to a Molloy.'

'So you're sure Jimbo never said anything to Peanuts?' I was wondering exactly how I could explain the deep, but not particularly creditable, origins of this family hostility to the jury.

'I give you my word, Mr Rumpole. Ain't that enough for you? No Timson would ever speak to a Molloy. Not under any circumstances.'

There were not many matters on which I would take Fred Timson's word, but the history of the Streatham Co-op case came back to me, and this was one of them.

It's part of the life of an Old Bailey hack to spend a good deal of his time down in the cells, in the basement area, where they keep the old door of Newgate, kicked and scarred, through which generations of villains were sent to the treadmill, the gallows or the whip. You pass this venerable door and ring a bell, you're let in and your name's taken by one of the warders who bring the prisoners from Brixton. There's a perpetual smell of cooking and the warders are snatching odd snacks of six inches of cheese butties and a gallon of tea. Lunch is being got ready, and the cells under the Bailey have a high reputation as one of the best caffs in London. By the door the screws have their pinups and comic cartoons of judges. You are taken to a waiting room, three steel chairs and a table, and you meet the client. Perhaps he is a novice, making his first appearance, like

Jim Timson. Perhaps he's an old hand asking anxiously which judge he's got, knowing their form as accurately as a betting-shop proprietor. Whoever he is, the client will be nervously excited, keyed up for his great day, full of absurd hope.

The worst part of a barrister's life at the Old Bailey is going back to the cells after a guilty verdict to say 'goodbye'. There's no purpose in it, but, as a point of honour, it has to be done. Even then the barrister probably gets the best reaction, and almost never any blame. The client is stunned, knocked out by his sentence. Only in a couple of weeks' time, when the reality of being banged up with the sour smell of stone walls and his own chamber-pot for company becomes apparent, does the convict start to weep. He is then drugged with sedatives, and Agatha Christies from the prison library.

When I saw the youngest Timson before his trial that morning, I couldn't help noticing how much smaller, and how much more experienced, he looked than my Nick. In his clean sports jacket and carefully knotted tie he was well dressed for the dock, and he showed all the carefully suppressed excitement of a young lad about to step into the limelight of Number One with an old judge, twelve jurors and a mixed bag of lawyers waiting to give him their undivided attention.

'Me speak to Peanuts? No Timson don't ever speak to a Molloy. It's a point of honour, like,' Jim added his voice to the family chorus.

'Since the raid on the Streatham Co-op. Your grandfather?'

'Dad told you about that, did he?'

'Yes. Dad told me.'

'Well, Dad wouldn't let me speak to no Molloy. He wouldn't put up with it, like.'

I stood up, grinding out the stub end of my small cigar in the old Oxo tin thoughtfully provided by HM's government. It was, I thought, about time I called the meeting to order.

'So Jim,' I asked him, 'what's the defence?'

Little Jim knitted his brows and came out with his contribution. 'Well. I didn't do it.'

'That's an interesting defence. Somewhat novel – so far as the Timsons are concerned.'

'I've got my alibi, ain't I?'

Jim looked at me accusingly, as at an insensitive visitor to a garden who has failed to notice the remarkable display of gladioli.

'Oh, yes. Your alibi.' I'm afraid I didn't sound overwhelmed with enthusiasm.

'Dad reckoned it was pretty good.'

Mr Bernard had his invaluable file open and was reading from that less-than-inspiring document, our Notice of Alibi.

'Straight from school on that Friday September 2nd, I went up to tea at my aunty Doris's and arrived there at exactly 5.30. At 6 p.m. my uncle Den came home from work accompanied by my uncle Cyril. At 7 p.m. when this alleged crime was taking place I was sat round the television with my aunty and two uncles. I well remember we was watching *The Newcomers*.'

All very neat and workmanlike. Well, that was it. The family gave young Jim an alibi, clubbed together for it, like a new bicycle. However, I had to disappoint Mr Bernard about the bright shining alibi and we went through the swing doors on our way into court.

'We can't use that alibi.'

'We can't?' Mr Bernard looked wounded, as if I'd just insulted his favourite child.

'Think about it, Bernard. Don't be blinded by the glamour of the criminal classes. Call the uncles and the aunties? Let them all be cross-examined about their records? The jury'll realize our Jimbo comes from a family of villains who keep a cupboard full of alibis for all occasions.'

Mr Bernard was forced to agree, but I went into my old place in court (nearest to the jury, furthest from the witness-box) thinking that the devilish thing about that impossible alibi was that it might even be true.

So there I was, sitting in my favourite seat in court, down in the firing line, and there was Jim boy, undersized for a prisoner, just peeping over the edge of the dock, guarded, in case he ran amok and started attacking the judge, by a huge dock officer. There was the jury, solid and grey, listening dispassionately as Guthrie Featherstone spread out his glittering mass of incriminating facts before them. I don't know why it is that juries all look the same; take twelve good men and women off the street and they all look middle-aged, anonymous, slightly stunned, an average jury, of average people trying an average case. Perhaps being a jury has become a special profession for specially average people. 'What do you want to do when you grow up, my boy?' 'Be a jury man, Daddy.' 'Well done, my boy. You can work a five-hour day for reasonable expenses and occasionally send people to chokey.'

So, as the carefully chosen words of Guthrie Featherstone passed over our heads like expensive hair oil, and as the enthusiastic young MacLay noted it all down, and the Rumpole Supporters Club, the Timsons, sat and pursed their lips and now and then whispered, 'Lies. All lies' to each other, I sat watching the judge rather as a noted toreador watches the bull from the barrier during the preliminary stages of the corrida, and remembered what I knew of Mr Justice Everglade, known to his few friends as 'Florrie'. Everglade's father was Lord Chancellor about the time when Jim's grandfather was doing over the Streatham Co-op. Educated at Winchester and Balliol, he always cracked *The Times* crossword in the opening of an egg. He was most happy with international trust companies suing each other on nice points of law, and was only there for a fortnight's slumming down the Old Bailey. I wondered exactly what he was going to make of Peanuts Molloy.

'Members of the Jury, it's right that you should know that it is alleged that Timson took part in this attack with a number of other youths, none of whom have been arrested,' Featherstone was purring to a halt.

'"The boy stood on the burning deck whence all but he had fled,"' I muttered, but the judge was busy congratulating learned counsel for Her Majesty the Queen who was engaged that morning in prosecuting the pride of the Timsons.

'It is quite right you should tell the jury that, Mr Featherstone. Perfectly right and proper.'

'If your Lordship pleases.' Featherstone was now bowing slightly, and my hackles began to rise. What was this? The old chums' league? Fellow members of the Athenaeum?

'I am most grateful to your Lordship for that indication.' Feather-stone did his well-known butler passing the sherry act again. I wondered why the old darling didn't crawl up on the Bench with Mr Justice Everglade and black his boots for him.

'So I imagine this young man's defence is – he wasn't *ejusdem generis* with the other lads?' The judge was now holding a private conversation, a mutual admiration society with my learned friend. I decided to break it up, and levered myself to my feet.

'I'm sorry. Your Lordship was asking about the defence?'

The judge turned an unfriendly eye on me and fumbled for my name. I told you he was a stranger to the Old Bailey, where the name of Rumpole is, I think, tolerably well known.

'Yes, Mr . . . er . . .' The clerk of the court handed him up a note on which the defender's name was inscribed. 'Rumpole.'

'I am reluctant to intrude on your Lordship's confidential conversation with my learned friend. But your Lordship was asking about the defence.'

'You are appearing for the young man . . . Timson?'

'I have that honour.'

At which point the doors of the court swung open and Albert came in with Nick, a boy in a blazer and a school tie who passed the boy in the dock with only a glance of curiosity. I always thank God, when I consider the remote politeness with which I was treated by the Reverend Wilfred Rumpole, that I get on extremely well with Nick. We understand each other, my boy and I, and have, when he's at home, formed a strong but silent alliance against the almost invincible rule of She Who Must Be Obeyed. He is as fond as I am of the Sherlock Holmes tales, and when we walked together in Hyde Park and Kensington Gardens, young Nick often played the part of Holmes whilst I trudged beside him as Watson, trying to deduce the secret lives of those we passed by the way they shined their shoes, or kept their handkerchiefs in their sleeves. So I gave a particularly welcoming smile to Nick before I gave my attention back to Florrie.

'And, as Jim Timson's counsel,' I told his Lordship, 'I might know a little more about his case than counsel for the prosecution.'

To which Mr Justice Everglade trotted out his favourite bit of Latin. 'I imagine,' he said loftily, 'your client says he was not *ejusdem generis* with the other lads.'

'*Ejusdem generis*? Oh yes, my Lord. He's always saying that. *Ejusdem generis* is a phrase in constant use in his particular part of Brixton.'

I had hit a minor jackpot, and was rewarded with a tinkle of laughter from the Timsons, and a smile of genuine congratulation from Nick.

Mr Justice Everglade was inexperienced down the Bailey – he gave us a bare hour for lunch and Nick and I had it in the canteen. There is one thing you can say against crime, the catering facilities aren't up to much. Nick told me about school, and freely confessed, as I'm sure he wouldn't have done to his mother, that he'd been in some sort of trouble that term. There was an old deserted vicarage opposite Schoolhouse and he and his friends had apparently broken in the scullery window and assembled there for poker parties and the consumption of cherry brandy. I was horrified as I drew up the indictment which seemed to me to contain charges of burglary at common Law, house breaking under the Forcible Entries Act, contravening the Betting, Gaming, Lotteries Act and serving alcohol on unlicensed premises.

'Crabtree actually invited a couple of girls from the village,' Nick continued his confession. 'But Bagnold never got to hear of that.'

Bagnold was Nick's headmaster, the school equivalent of Persil White. I cheered up a little at the last piece of information.

'Then there's no evidence of girls. As far as your case goes there's no reason to suppose the girls ever existed. As for the other charges, which are serious . . .'

'Yes, yes, I suppose they are rather.'

'I imagine you were walking past the house on Sunday evening and, attracted by the noise . . . You went to investigate?'

'Dad. Bagnold came in and found us – playing poker.'

Nick wasn't exactly being helpful. I tried another line.

'I know, "My Lord. My client was only playing poker in order not to look too pious whilst he lectured his fellow sixth-formers on the evils of gambling and cherry brandy."'

'Dad. Be serious.'

'I am serious. Don't you want me to defend you?'

'No. Bagnold's not going to tell the police or anything like that.'

I was amazed. 'He isn't? What's he going to do?'

'Well . . . I'll miss next term's exeat. Do extra work. I thought I should tell you before you got a letter.'

'Thank you, Nick. Thank you. I'm glad you told me. So there's no question of . . . the police?'

'The police?' Nick was laughing. 'Of course not. Bagnold doesn't want any trouble. After all, we're still at school.'

I watched Nick as he finished his fish and chips, and then turned my thoughts to Jim Timson, who had also been at school, but with no kindly Bagnold to protect him.

Back in court I was cross-examining that notable grass, Peanuts Molloy, a skinnier, more furtive edition of Jim Timson. The cross-examination was being greatly enjoyed by the Timsons and Nick, but not much by Featherstone or Detective Chief Inspector Persil White who sat at the table in front of me. I also thought that Mr Justice Florrie Everglade was thinking that he would have been happier snoozing in the Athenaeum, or working on his *grospoint* in Egerton Terrace, than listening to me bowling fast inswingers at the juvenile chief witness for the prosecution.

'You don't speak. The Molloys and the Timsons are like the Montagues and the Capulets,' I put it to Peanuts.

'What did you say they were?' The judge had, of course, given me my opportunity. I smacked him through the slips for a crafty single. 'Not *ejusdem generis*, my Lord,' I said.

Nick joined in the laughter and even the ranks of Featherstone had to stifle a smile. The usher called 'Silence'. We were back to the business in hand.

'Tell me, Peanuts . . . How would you describe yourself?'

'Is that a proper question?' Featherstone uncoiled himself gracefully. I ignored the interruption.

'I mean artistically. Are you a latter-day Impressionist? Do all your oils in little dots, do you? Abstract painter? White squares on a white background? Do you indulge in watches melting in the desert like dear old Salvador Dali?'

'I don't know what you're talking about.' Peanuts played a blocking shot and Featherstone tried a weary smile to the judge.

'My Lord, neither, I must confess, do I.'

'Sit quietly, Featherstone,' I muttered to him. 'All will be revealed to you.' I turned my attention back to Peanuts. 'Are you a dedicated artist? The Rembrandt of the remand centre?'

'I hadn't done no art before.' Peanuts confirmed my suspicions.

'So we are to understand that this occasion, when Jim poured out his heart to you, was the first painting lesson you'd ever been to?'

Peanuts admitted it.

'You'd been at the remand centre how long?'

'Couple of months. I was done for a bit of an affray.'

'I didn't ask you that. And I'm sure the reason you were on remand was entirely creditable. What I want to know is, what inspired you with this sudden fascination for the arts?'

'Well, the chief screw. He suggested it.'

Now we were beginning to get to the truth of the matter. Like his old grandfather in the Streatham Co-op days, Jim had been banged up with a notable grass.

'You were suddenly told to join the painting class, weren't you . . . and put yourself next to Jim?'

'Something like that, yeah.'

'What did he say?' Florrie frowned. It was all very strange to him and yet he was starting to get the hint of something that wasn't quite cricket.

'Something like that, my Lord,' I repeated slowly, giving the judge a chance to make a note. 'And you were sent there, not in the pursuit of art, Peanuts, but in the pursuit of evidence! You knew that and you supplied your masters with just what they wanted to hear – even though Jim Timson didn't say a word to you!'

Everyone in court, including Nick, looked impressed. DCI White bit hard on a polo mint and Featherstone oozed to his feet in a rescue bid.

'That's great, Dad!'

'Thanks, Nick. Sorry it's not a murder.'

'I don't know quite what my learned friend is saying. Is he suggesting that the police . . .'

'Oh, it's an old trick,' I said, staring hard at the chief inspector. 'Bang the suspect up with a notable grass when you're really pushed for evidence. They do it with grown-ups often enough. Now they're trying it with children!'

'Mr Rumpole,' the judge sighed, 'you are speaking a language which is totally foreign to me.'

'Let me try and make myself clear, my Lord. I was suggesting that Peanuts was put there as a deliberate trap.'

By now, even the judge had the point. 'You are suggesting that Mr Molloy was not a genuine "amateur painter"?'

'No, my Lord. Merely an amateur witness.'

'Yes.' I actually got a faint smile. 'I see. Please go on, Mr Rumpole.'

Another day or so of this, I felt, and I'd get invited to tea at the Athenaeum.

'What did you say first to Jim? As you drew your easel alongside?'

'Don't remember.'

'Don't you?'

'I think we was speaking about the Stones.'

'What "stones" are these?' The judge's ignorance of the life around him seemed to be causing him some sort of wild panic. Remember, this was 1965, and I was in a similar state of confusion until Nick, whispering from behind me, gave me the clue.

'The Rolling Stones, my Lord.' The information meant nothing to him.

'I'm afraid a great deal of this case seems to be taking place in a foreign tongue, Mr Rumpole.'

'Jazz musicians, as I understand it, my Lord, of some notoriety.' By courtesy of Nick, I filled his Lordship in on 'the scene'.

'Well, the notoriety hasn't reached me!' said the judge, providing the obedient Featherstone with the laugh of the year, if not the century. When the learned prosecuting counsel had recovered his solemnity, Peanuts went rambling on.

'We was talking about the Stones concert at the Hammersmith Odeon. We'd both been to it, like. And, well . . . we talked about that. And then he said . . . Jim said . . . Well, he said as how he and the other blokes had done the butchers.'

The conversation had now taken a nasty turn. I saw that the judge was writing industriously. 'Jim said . . . that he and the other blokes . . . had done the butchers.' Florrie was plying his pencil. Then he looked up at me, 'Well, Mr Rumpole, is that a convenient moment to adjourn?'

It was a very convenient moment for the prosecution, as the evidence against us would be the last thing the jury heard before sloping off to their homes and loved ones. It was also a convenient moment for Peanuts. He would have his second wind by the morning. So there was nothing for it but to take Nick for a cup of tea and a pile of crumpets in the ABC, and so home to She Who Must Be Obeyed.

So picture us three that evening, finishing dinner and a bottle of claret, celebrating the return of the Young Master at Hack Hall, Counsel's Castle, Rumpole Manor, or 25B Froxbury Mansions, Gloucester Road. Hilda had told Nick that his grandpa had sent his love and expected a letter, and also dropped me the encouraging news that old C. H. Wystan was retiring and quite appreciated that I was the senior man. Nick asked me if I was really going to be head of chambers, seeming to look at me with a new respect, and we drank a glass of claret to the future, whatever it might be. Then Nick asked me if I really thought Peanuts Molloy was lying.

'If he's not, he's giving a damn good imitation.' Then I told Hilda as she started to clear away, 'Nick enjoyed the case. Even though it was only a robbery. Oh, Nick . . . I wish you'd been there to hear me cross-examine about the bloodstains in the Penge Bungalow Murders.'

'Nick wasn't born when you did the Penge Bungalow Murders.'

My wife is always something of a wet blanket. I commiserated with my son. 'Bad luck, old boy.'

'You were great with that judge!'

I think Nick had really enjoyed himself.

'There was this extraordinary judge who was always talking Latin and Dad was teasing him.'

'You want to be careful,' Hilda was imposing her will on the pudding plates. 'How you tease judges. If you're to be head of chambers.' On which line she departed, leaving Nick and me to our claret and conversation. I began to discuss with Nick the horrifying adventure of *The Speckled Band*.

'You're still reading those tales, are you?' I asked Nick.

'Well . . . not lately.'

'But you remember. I used to read them to you, didn't I? After She had ordered you to bed.'

'When you weren't too busy. Noting up your murders.'

'And remember we were Holmes and Watson? When we went for walks in Hyde Park.'

'I remember *one* walk.'

That was odd, as I recall it had been our custom ever at a weekend, before Nick went away to boarding school. I lit a small cigar and looked at the Great Detective through the smoke.

'Tell me, Holmes. What did you think was the most remarkable piece of evidence given by the witness Peanuts Molloy?'

'When he said they talked about the Rolling Stones.'

'Holmes, you astonish me.'

'You see, Watson, we were led to believe they were such enemies – I mean, the families were. They'd never spoken.'

'I see what you're driving at. Have another glass of claret – stimulates the detective ability.' I opened another bottle, a clatter from the kitchen telling me that the lady was not about to join us.

'And there they were chatting about a pop concert. Didn't that strike you as strange, my dear Watson?'

'It struck me as bloody rum, if you want to know the truth, Holmes.' I was delighted to see Nick taking over the case.

'They'd both been to the concert . . . Well, that doesn't mean anything. Not necessarily . . . I mean, *I* was at that concert.'

'Were you indeed?'

'It was at the end of the summer holidays.'

'I don't remember you mentioning it.'

'I said I was going to the Festival Hall.'

I found this confidence pleasing, knowing that it wasn't to be shared with Hilda.

'Very wise. Your mother no doubt feels that at the Hammersmith Odeon they re-enact some of the worst excesses of the Roman Empire. You didn't catch sight of Peanuts and young Jimbo, did you?'

'There were about two thousand fans – all screaming.'

'I don't know if it helps . . .'

'No.'

'If they were old mates, I mean. Jim might really have confided in him. All the same, Peanuts is lying. And *you* noticed it! You've got the instinct, Nick. You've got a nose for the evidence! Your career at the Bar is bound to be brilliant.' I raised my glass to Nick. 'When are you taking silk?'

Shortly after this She entered with news that Nick had a dentist's appointment the next day, which would prevent his reappearance down the Bailey. All the same, he had given me a great deal of help and before I went to bed I telephoned Bernard, the solicitor, tore him away from his fireside and instructed him to undertake some pretty immediate research.

Next morning, Albert told me that he'd had a letter from old C. H. Wystan, Hilda's Daddy, mentioning his decision to retire.

'I think we'll manage pretty well, with you, Mr Rumpole, as head of chambers,' Albert told me. 'There's not much you and I won't be able to sort out, sir, over a glass or two in Pommeroy's Wine Bar . . . And soon we'll be welcoming Master Nick in chambers?'

'Nick? Well, yes.' I had to admit it. 'He is showing a certain legal aptitude.'

'It'll be a real family affair, Mr Rumpole . . . Like father, like son, if you want my opinion.'

I remembered Albert's words when I saw Fred Timson waiting for me outside the court. But before I had time to brood on family tradition, Bernard came up with the rolled-up poster for a pop concert. I grabbed it from him and carried it as unobtrusively as possible into court.

'When Jim told you he'd done up the butchers . . . He didn't tell you the date that that had happened?' Peanuts was back, facing the bowling, and Featherstone was up to his usual tricks, rising to interrupt.

'My Lord, the date is set out quite clearly in the indictment.'

The time had come, quite obviously, for a burst of righteous indignation.

'My Lord, I am cross-examining on behalf of a sixteen-year-old boy on an extremely serious charge. I'd be grateful if my learned friend didn't supply information which all of us in court know – except for the witness.'

'Very well. Do carry on, Mr Rumpole.' I was almost beginning to like Mr Justice Everglade.

'No. He never told me when, like. I thought it was sometime in the summer.' Peanuts tried to sound co-operative.

'Sometime in the summer? Are you a fan of the Rolling Stones, Peanuts?'

'Yes.'

'Remind me . . . they were . . .' Still vaguely puzzled, the judge was hunting back through his notes.

Sleek as a butler with a dish of peas, Featherstone supplied the information. 'The musicians, my Lord.'

'And so was Jim a fan?' I ploughed on, ignoring the gentleman's gentleman.

'He was. Yes.'

'You had discussed music, before you met in the remand centre?'

'Before the nick. Oh yes.' Peanuts was following me obediently down the garden path.

'You used to talk about it at school?'

'Yes.'

'In quite a friendly way?' I was conscious of a startled Fred Timson looking at his son, and of Jim in the dock looking, for the first time, ashamed.

'We was all right. Yes.'

'Did you ever go to a concert with Jimbo? Please think carefully.'

'We went to one or two concerts together,' Peanuts conceded.

'In the evening?'

'Yes.'

'What would you do? . . . Call at his home and collect him?'

'You're joking!'

'Oh no, Peanuts. In this case I'm not joking at all!' No harm, I thought, at that stage, in underlining the seriousness of the occasion.

'Course I wouldn't call at his home!'

'Your families don't speak. You wouldn't be welcomed in each other's houses?'

'The Montagues and the Capulets, Mr Rumpole?' The old sweetheart on the Bench had finally got the message. I gave him a bow, to show my true love and affection.

'If your Lordship pleases . . . Your Lordship puts it extremely aptly.' I turned back to Peanuts. 'So what would you do, if you were going to a concert?'

'We'd leave school together, like – and then hang around the caffs.'

'Hang around the caffs?'

'Caf*ays*, Mr Rumpole?' Mr Justice Everglade was enjoying himself, translating the answer.

'Yes, of course, the caf*ays*. Until it was time to go up West? If my Lord would allow me, up to the "West End of London" together?'

'Yes.'

'So you wouldn't be separated on these evenings you went to concerts together?' It was one of those questions after which you hold your breath. There can be so many wrong answers.

'No. We hung around together.'

Rumpole breathed a little more easily, but he still had the final question, the great gamble, with all Jim Timson's chips firmly piled on the red. *Faites vos jeux, M'sieurs et Mesdames* of the Old Bailey jury. I spun the wheel.

'And did that happen . . . When you went to the Rolling Stones at the Hammersmith Odeon?'

A nasty silence. Then the ball rattled into the hole.

Peanuts said, 'Yes.'

'That was this summer, wasn't it?' We were into the straight now, cantering home.

'In the summer, yeah.'

'You left school together?'

'And hung around the caffs, like. Then we went up the Odeon.'

'Together . . . All the time?'

'I told you – didn't I?' Peanuts looked bored, and then amazed as I unrolled the poster Bernard had brought, rushed by taxi from Hammersmith, with the date clearly printed across the bottom.

'My Lord. My learned friend might be interested to know the date of the only Rolling Stones concert at the Hammersmith Odeon this year.' I gave Featherstone an unwelcome eyeful of the poster.

'He might like to compare it with the date so conveniently set out in the indictment.'

When the subsequent formalities were over, I went down to the cells. This was not a visit of commiseration, no time for a 'sorry old sweetheart, but . . .' and a deep consciousness of having asked one too many questions. All the same, I was in no gentle mood, in fact, it would be fair to say that I was bloody angry with Jimbo.

'You had an alibi! You had a proper, reasonable, truthful alibi, and, joy of joys, it came from the prosecution! Why the hell didn't you tell me?'

Jim, who seemed to have little notion of the peril he had passed, answered me quite calmly, 'Dad wouldn't've liked it.'

'Dad! What's Dad got to do with it?' I was astonished.

'He wouldn't've liked it, Mr Rumpole. Not me going out with Peanuts.'

'So you were quite ready to be found guilty, to be convicted of robbery, just because your dad wouldn't like you going out with Peanuts Molloy?'

'Dad got the family to alibi me.' Jim clearly felt that the Timsons had done their best for him.

'Keep it in the family!' Though it was heavily laid on, the irony was lost on Jim. He smiled politely and stood up, eager to join the clan upstairs.

'Well, anyway. Thanks a lot, Mr Rumpole. Dad said I could rely on you. To win the day, like. I'd better collect me things.'

If Jim thought I was going to let him get away as easily as that, he was mistaken. Rumpole rose in his crumpled gown, doing his best to represent the majesty of the law. 'No! Wait a minute. I didn't win the day. It was luck. The purest fluke. It won't happen again!'

'You're joking, Mr Rumpole.' Jim thought I was being modest. 'Dad told me about you . . . He says you never let the Timsons down.'

I had a sudden vision of my role in life, from young Jim's point of view, and I gave him the voice of outrage which I use frequently in court. I had a message of importance for Jim Timson.

'Do you think that's what I'm here for? To help you along in a career like your dad's?' Jim was still smiling, maddeningly. 'My God! I shouldn't have asked those questions! I shouldn't have found out the date of the concert! Then you'd really be happy, wouldn't you? You could follow in Dad's footsteps all your life! Sharp spell of Borstal training to teach you the mysteries of house-breaking, and then a steady life in the nick. You might really do well! You might end up in Parkhurst maximum security wing, doing a glamorous twenty years and a hero to the screws.'

At which the door opened and a happy screw entered, for the purpose of springing young Jim – until the inevitable next time.

'We've got his things at the gate, Mr Rumpole. Come on, Jim. You can't stay here all night.'

'I've got to go,' Jim agreed. 'I don't know how to face Dad, really. Me being so friendly with Peanuts.'

'Jim,' I tried a last appeal. 'If you're at all grateful for what I did . . .'

'Oh I am, Mr Rumpole, I'm quite satisfied.' Generous of him.

'Then you can perhaps repay me.'

'Why – aren't you on legal aid?'

'It's not that! Leave him! Leave your dad.'

Jim frowned, for a moment he seemed to think it over. Then he said, 'I don't know as how I can.'

'You don't know?'

'Mum depends on me, you see. Like when Dad goes away. She depends on me then, as head of the family.'

So he left me, and went up to temporary freedom and his new responsibilities.

My mouth was dry and I felt about ninety years old, so I took the lift up to that luxurious eatery, the Old Bailey canteen, for a cup of tea and a Penguin biscuit. And, pushing his tray along past the urns, I met a philosophic Chief Inspector Persil White. He noticed my somewhat lugubrious expression and tried a cheering 'Don't look so miserable, Mr Rumpole. You won, didn't you?'

'Nobody won, the truth emerges sometimes, Inspector, even down the Old Bailey.' I must have sounded less than gracious. The wily old copper smiled tolerantly.

'He's a Timson. It runs in the family. We'll get him sooner or later!'

'Yes. Yes. I suppose you will.'

At a table in a corner, I found certain members of my chambers, George Frobisher, Percy Hoskins, and young Tony MacLay, now resting from their labours, their wigs lying among cups of Old Bailey tea, buns and choccy bics. I joined them. Wordsworth entered my head, and I gave him an airing: ' "Trailing clouds of glory do we come." '

'Marvellous win, that. I was telling them.' Young MacLay thought I was announcing my triumph.

'Yes, Rumpole. I hear you've had a splendid win.' Old George, ever generous, smiled, genuinely pleased.

'It'll be *years* before you get the cheque,' Hoskins grumbled.

> 'Not in entire forgetfulness,
> And not in utter nakedness,
> But trailing clouds of glory do we come
> From God, who is our home.'

I was thinking of Jim, trying to sort out his situation with the help of Wordsworth.

'You don't get paid for years at the Old Bailey. I try to tell my grocer that. If you had to wait as long to be paid for a pound of sugar, I tell him, as we do for an armed robbery . . .' Hoskins was warming to a well-loved theme, but George, dear old George, was smiling at me.

'Albert tells me he's had a letter from Wystan. I just wanted to say, I'm sure we'd all like to say, you'll make a splendid head of chambers, Rumpole.'

> 'Heaven lies about us in our infancy!
> Shades of the prison-house begin to close
> Upon the growing boy,
> But he beholds the light, and whence it flows,
> He sees it in his joy.'

I gave them another brief glimpse of immortality. George looked quite proud of me and told MacLay, 'Rumpole quotes poetry. He does it quite often.'

'But does the growing boy behold the light?' I wondered. 'Or was the old sheep of the Lake District being unduly optimistic?'

'It'll be refreshing for us all, to have a head of chambers who quotes poetry,' George went on, at which point Percy Hoskins produced a newspaper which turned out to contain an item of news for us all.

'Have you seen *The Times*, Rumpole?'

'No, I haven't had time for the crossword.'

'Guthrie Featherstone. He's taken silk.'

It was the apotheosis, the great day for the Labour-Conservative Member for wherever it was, one time unsuccessful prosecutor of Jim Timson and now one of Her Majesty's counsel, called within the Bar, and he went down to the House of Lords tailored out in his new silk gown, a lace jabot, knee breeches with *diamanté* buckles, patent shoes, black silk stockings, lace cuffs and a full-bottomed wig that made him look like a pedigree, but not over-bright, spaniel. However, Guthrie Featherstone was a tall man, with a good calf in a silk stocking, and he took with him Marigold, his lady wife, who was young enough, and I suppose pretty enough, for Henry, our junior clerk, to eye wistfully, although she had the sort of voice that puts me instantly in mind of headscarves and gymkhanas, that high-pitched nasal whining which a girl learns from too much contact with the saddle when young, and too little with the Timsons of this world in later life. The couple were escorted by Albert, who'd raided Moss Bros for a top hat and morning coat for the occasion and when the Lord Chancellor had welcomed Guthrie to that special club of Queen's Counsel (on whose advice the Queen, luckily for her, never has to rely for a moment) they came back to chambers where champagne (the NV cooking variety, bulk-bought from Pommeroy's Wine Bar) was served by Henry and old Miss Patterson, our typist, in Wystan's big room looking out over Temple Gardens. C. H. Wystan, our retiring head, was not among those present as the party began, and I took an early opportunity to get stuck into the beaded bubbles.

After the fourth glass I felt able to relax a bit and wandered to where Featherstone, in all his finery, was holding forth to Erskine-Brown about the problems of appearing *en travesti*. I arrived just as he was saying, 'It's the stockings that're the problem.'

'Oh yes. They would be.' I did my best to sound interested.

'Keeping them up.'

'I do understand.'

'Well, Marigold. My wife Marigold . . .' I looked across to where Mrs QC was tinkling with laughter at some old legal anecdote of Uncle Tom's. It was a laugh that seemed in some slight danger of breaking the wine glasses.

'*That* Marigold?'

'Her sister's a nurse, you know . . . and she put me in touch with this shop which supplies suspender belts to nurses . . . among other things.'

'Really?' This conversation seemed to arouse some dormant sexual interest in Erskine-Brown.

'Yards of elastic, for the larger ward sister. But it works miraculously.'

'You're wearing a suspender belt?' Erskine-Brown was frankly fascinated. 'You sexy devil!'

'I hadn't realized the full implications,' I told the QC, 'of rising to the heights of the legal profession.'

I wandered off to where Uncle Tom was giving Marigold a brief history of life in our chambers over the last half-century. Percy Hoskins was in attendance, and George.

'It's some time since we had champagne in chambers.' Uncle Tom accepted a refill from Albert.

'It's some time since we had a silk in chambers,' Hoskins smiled at Marigold who flashed a row of well-groomed teeth back at him.

'I recall we had a man in chambers once called Drinkwater – oh, before you were born, Hoskins. And some fellow came and paid Drinkwater a hundred guineas – for six months' pupillage. And you know what this Drinkwater fellow did? Bought us all champagne – and the next day he ran off to Calais with his junior clerk. We never saw hide nor hair of either of them again.' He paused. Marigold looked puzzled, not quite sure if this was the punch line.

'Of course, you could get a lot further in those days – on a hundred guineas,' Uncle Tom ended on a sad note, and Marigold laughed heartily.

'Your husband's star has risen so quickly, Mrs Featherstone. Only ten years' call and he's an MP *and* leading counsel.' Hoskins was clearly so excited by the whole business he had stopped worrying about his cheques for half an hour.

'Oh, it's the PR you know. Guthrie's frightfully good at the PR.'

I felt like Everglade. Marigold was speaking a strange and incomprehensible language.

'Guthrie always says the most important thing at the Bar is to be polite to your instructing solicitor. Don't you find that, Mr Rumpole?'

'Polite to solicitors? It's never occurred to me.'

'Guthrie admires you so, Mr Rumpole. He admires your style of advocacy.'

I had just sunk another glass of the beaded bubbles as passed by Albert, and I felt a joyous release from my usual strong sense of tact and discretion.

'I suppose it makes a change from bowing three times and offering to black the judge's boots for him.'

Marigold's smile didn't waver. 'He says you're most amusing out of court, too. Don't you quote poetry?'

'Only in moments of great sadness, madam. Or extreme elation.'

'Guthrie's so looking forward to leading you. In his next big case.'

This was an eventuality which I should have taken into account as soon as I saw Guthrie in silk stockings; as a matter of fact it had never occurred to me.

'Leading *me*? Did you say, *leading* me?'

'Well, he has to have a junior now . . . doesn't he? Naturally he wants the best junior available.'

'Now he's a leader?'

'Now he's left the Junior Bar.'

I raised my glass and gave Marigold a version of Browning. 'Just for a pair of knee breeches he left us . . . Just for an elastic suspender belt, as supplied to the nursing profession . . .' At which the QC himself bore down on us in a rustle of silk and drew me into a corner.

'I just wanted to say, I don't see why recent events should make the slightest difference to the situation in chambers. You *are* the senior man in practice, Rumpole.'

Henry was passing with the fizzing bottle. I held out my glass and the tide ran foaming in it.

' "You wrong me, Brutus," ' I told Featherstone. ' "I said an elder soldier, not a better." '

'A quotation! *Touché*, very apt.'

'Is it?'

'I mean, all this will make absolutely no difference. I'll still support you, Rumpole, as the right candidate for head of chambers.'

I didn't know about being a candidate, having thought of the matter as settled and not being much of a political animal. But before I had time to reflect on whatever the Honourable Member was up to, the door opened letting in a formidable draught and the head of chambers, C. H. Wystan, She's Daddy, wearing a tweed suit, extremely pale, supported by Albert on one side and a stick on the other, made the sort of formidable entrance that the ghost of Banquo stages at dinner with the Macbeths. Wystan was installed in an armchair, from which he gave us all the sort of wintry smile which seemed designed to indicate that all flesh is as the grass, or something to that effect.

'Albert wrote to me about this little celebration. I was determined to be with you. And the doctor has given permission, for no more than one glass of champagne.' Wystan held out a transparent hand into which Albert inserted a glass of non-vintage. Wystan lifted this with some apparent effort, and gave us a toast.

'To the great change in chambers! Now we have a silk. Guthrie Featherstone, QC, MP!'

I had a large refill to that. Wystan absorbed a few bubbles, wiped his mouth on a clean, folded handkerchief, and proceeded to the oration. Wystan was never a great speech maker, but I claimed another refill and gave him my ears.

'You, Featherstone, have brought a great distinction to chambers.'

'Isn't that nice, Guthrie?' Marigold proprietorially squeezed her master's fingers.

'You know, when I was a young man. You remember when we were young men, Uncle Tom? We used to hang around in chambers for weeks on end.' Wystan had gone on about these distant hard times at every chambers meeting. 'I well recall we used to occupy ourselves with an old golf ball and mashie-niblick, trying to get chip shots into the waste-paper baskets. Albert was a boy then.'

'A mere child, Mr Wystan,' Albert looked suitably demure.

'And we used to pray for work. *Any* sort of work, didn't we, Uncle Tom?'

'We were tempted to crime. Only way we could get into court,' Uncle Tom took the feed line like a professional. Moderate laughter, except for Rumpole who was busy drinking. And then I heard Wystan rambling on.

'But as you grow older at the Bar you discover it's not having any work that matters. It's the *quality* that counts!'

'Hear, hear! I'm always saying we ought to do more civil.' This was the dutiful Erskine-Brown, inserting his oar.

'Now Guthrie Featherstone, QC, MP will, of course, command briefs in all divisions – planning, contract,' Wystan's voice sank to a note of awe, 'even Chancery! I was so afraid, after I've gone, that this chambers might become known as merely a criminal set.' Wystan's voice now sank in a sort of horror. 'And, of course, there's no doubt about it, too much criminal work does rather lower the standing of a chambers.'

'Couldn't you install pit-head baths?' I hadn't actually meant to say it aloud, but it came out very loud indeed.

'Ah, Horace.' Wystan turned his pale eyes on me for the first time.

'So we could have a good scrub down after we get back from the Old Bailey?'

'Now, Horace Rumpole. And I mean no disrespect whatever to my son-in-law.' Wystan returned to the oration. From far away I heard myself say, 'Daddy!' as I raised the hard-working glass. 'Horace does practise almost exclusively in the criminal courts!'

'One doesn't get the really fascinating points of *law*. Not in criminal work,' Erskine-Brown was adding unwanted support to the motion. 'I've often thought we should try and attract some really lucrative tax cases into chambers.'

That, I'm afraid, did it. Just as if I were in court I moved slightly to the centre and began my speech.

'Tax cases?' I saw them all smiling encouragement at me. 'Marvellous! Tax cases make the world go round. Compared to the wonderful world of tax, crime is totally trivial. What does it matter? If some boy loses a year, a couple of years, of his life? It's totally unimportant! Anyway, he'll grow up to be banged up for a good five, shut up with his own chamber-pot in some convenient hole we all prefer not to think about.' There was a deafening silence, which came loudest from Marigold Featherstone. Then Wystan tried to reach a settlement.

'Now then, Horace. Your practice no doubt requires a good deal of skill.'

'Skill? Who said "skill"?' I glared round at the learned friends. 'Any fool could do it! It's only a matter of life and death. That's all it is. Crime? It's a sort of a game. How can you compare it to the real world of offshore securities? And deductible expenses?'

'All you young men in chambers can learn an enormous amount from Horace Rumpole, when it comes to crime.' Wystan now seemed to be the only one who was still smiling. I turned on him.

'You make me sound just like Fred Timson!'

'Really? Whoever's Fred Timson?' I told you Wystan never had much of a practice at the Bar, consequently he had never met the Timsons. Erskine-Brown supplied the information.

'The Timsons are Rumpole's favourite family.'

'An industrious clan of South London criminals, aren't they, Rumpole?' Hoskins added.

Wystan looked particularly pained. 'South London criminals?'

'I mean, do we want people like the Timsons forever hanging about in our waiting room? I merely ask the question.' He was not bad, this Erskine-Brown, with a big future in the nastier sort of breach of trust cases.

'Do you? Do you merely ask it?' I heard the pained bellow of a distant Rumpole.

'The Timsons . . . and their like, are no doubt grist to Rumpole's mill,' Wystan was starting on the summing up. 'But it's the balance that *counts*. Now, you'll be looking for a new head of chambers.'

'Are we still looking?' My friend George Frobisher had the decency to ask. And Wystan told him, 'I'd like you all to think it over carefully. And put your views to me in writing. We should all try and remember, it's the good of the chambers that matters. Not the feelings, however deep they may be, of any particular person.'

He then called on Albert's assistance to raise him to his feet, lifted his glass with an effort of pure will and offered us a toast to the good of chambers. I joined in, and drank deep, it having been a good thirty seconds since I had had a glass to my lips. As the bubbles exploded against the tongue I noticed that the Featherstones were holding hands, and the brand-new artificial silk was looking particularly delighted. Something, and perhaps not only his suspender belt, seemed to be giving him special pleasure.

Some weeks later, when I gave Hilda the news, she was deeply shocked.

'*Guthrie Featherstone*! Head of chambers!' We were at breakfast. In fact Nick was due back at school that day. He was neglecting his cornflakes and reading a book.

'By general acclaim.'

'I'm sorry.' Hilda looked at me, as if she'd just discovered that I'd contracted an incurable disease.

'He can have the headaches – working out Albert's extraordinary book-keeping system.' I thought for a moment, yes, I'd like to have been head of chambers, and then put the thought from me.

'If only you could have become a QC.' She was now pouring me an unsolicited cup of coffee.

'QC? CT. That's enough to keep me busy.'

'CT? Whatever's CT?'.

'Counsel for the Timsons!' I tried to say it as proudly as I could. Then I reminded Nick that I'd promised to see him off at Liverpool Street, finished my cooling coffee, stood up and took a glance at the book that was absorbing him, expecting it to be, perhaps, that spine-chilling adventure relating to the Footprints of an Enormous Hound. To my amazement the shocker in question was entitled simply *Studies in Sociology*.

'It's interesting,' Nick sounded apologetic.

'You astonish me.'

'Old Bagnold was talking about what I should read if I get into Oxford.'

'Of course you're going to read law, Nick. We're going to keep it in the family.' Hilda the barrister's daughter was clearing away deafeningly.

'I thought perhaps PPE and then go on to sociology.' Nick sounded curiously confident. Before Hilda could get in another word I made my position clear.

'PPE, that's very good, Nick! That's very good indeed! For God's sake. Let's stop keeping things in the family!'

Later, as we walked across the barren stretches of Liverpool Street station, with my son in his school uniform and me in my old striped trousers and black jacket, I tried to explain what I meant.

'That's what's wrong, Nick. That's the devil of it! They're being

39

born around us all the time. Little Mr Justice Everglades . . . Little Timsons . . . Little Guthrie Featherstones. All being set off . . . to follow in father's footsteps.' We were at the barrier, shaking hands awkwardly. 'Let's have no more of that! No more following in father's footsteps. No more.'

Nick smiled, although I have no idea if he understood what I was trying to say. I'm not totally sure that I understood it either. Then the train removed him from me. I waved for a little, but he didn't wave back. That sort of thing is embarrassing for a boy. I lit a small cigar and went by tube to the Bailey. I was doing a long firm fraud then; a particularly nasty business, out of which I got a certain amount of harmless fun.

Rumpole and the Showfolk

I have written elsewhere of my old clerk, Albert Handyside, who served me very well for a long term of years, being adept at flattering solicitors' clerks, buying them glasses of Guinness and enquiring tenderly after their tomato plants, with the result that the old darlings were inclined to come across with the odd dangerous and careless, indecent assault or take and drive away, which Albert was inclined to slip in Rumpole's direction. All this led to higher things such as robbery, unlawful wounding and even murder; and in general to that body of assorted crimes on which my reputation is founded. I first knew Albert when he was a nervous office boy in the chambers of C. H. Wystan, my learned father-in-law; and when he grew to be a head clerk of magisterial dimensions we remained firm friends and often had a jar together in Pommeroy's Wine Bar in the evenings, on which relaxed occasions I would tell Albert my celebrated anecdotes of Bench and Bar and, unlike She Who Must Be Obeyed, he was always kind enough to laugh no matter how often he had heard them before.

Dear old Albert had one slight failing, a weakness which occurs among the healthiest of constitutions. He was apt to get into a terrible flurry over the petty cash. I never enquired into his bookkeeping system; but I believe it might have been improved by the invention of the abacus, or a monthly check-up by a primary-school child well versed in simple addition. It is also indubitably true that you can't pour drink down the throats of solicitors' managing clerks without some form of subsidy, and I'm sure Albert dipped liberally into the petty cash for this purpose as well as to keep himself in the large Bells and sodas, two or three of which sufficed for his simple lunch. Personally I never begrudged Albert any of this grant in aid, but ugly words such as embezzlement were uttered by Erskine-Brown and others, and, spurred on by our second clerk, Harry, who clearly thirsted for promotion, my learned friends were induced to part with Albert Handyside. I missed him very much. Our new clerk, Henry, goes to Pommeroy's with our typist, Dianne, and tells her about his exploits when on holiday with the Club Méditerranée in Corfu. I do not think either of them would laugh at my legal anecdotes.

After he left us Albert shook the dust of London from his shoes and went up North, to some God-lost place called Grimble, and there joined a firm of solicitors as managing clerk. No doubt northerly barristers' clerks bought him Guinness and either he had no control of the petty cash or the matter was not subjected to too close an inspection. From time to time he sent me a Christmas card on which was inscribed among the bells and holly 'Compliments of the Season, Mr Rumpole, sir. And I'm going to bring you up here for a nice little murder just as soon as I get the opportunity. Yours respectfully, A. Handyside.' At long last a brief did arrive. Mr Rumpole was asked to appear at the Grimble Assizes, to be held before Mr Justice Skelton in the Law Courts, Grimble: the title of the piece being *The Queen* (she does keep enormously busy prosecuting people) versus *Margaret Hartley*. The only item on the programme was wilful murder.

Now you may have noticed that certain theatrical phrases have crept into the foregoing paragraph. This is not as inappropriate as it may sound, for the brief I was going up to Grimble for on the Intercity train (a journey about as costly as a trip across the Atlantic) concerned a murder which took place in the Theatre Royal, East Grimble, a place of entertainment leased by the Frere-Hartley Players: the victim was one G. P. Frere, the leading actor, and my client was his wife, known as Maggie Hartley, co-star and joint director of the company. And as I read on into *R. v. Hartley* it became clear that the case was like too many of Rumpole's, a born loser: that is to say that unless we drew a drunken prosecutor or a jury of anarchists there seemed no reasonable way in which it might be won.

One night after the performance, Albert's instructions told me, the stage-door keeper, a Mr Croft, heard the sound of raised voices and quarrelling from the dressing-room shared by G. P. Frere and his wife Maggie Hartley. Mr Croft was having a late cup of tea in his cubbyhole with a Miss Christine Hope, a young actress in the company, and they heard two shots fired in quick succession. Mr Croft went along the passage to investigate and opened the dressing-room door. The scene that met his eyes was, to say the least, dramatic.

It appeared from Mr Croft's evidence that the dressing-room was in a state of considerable confusion. Clothes were scattered round the room, and chairs overturned. The long mirror which ran down the length of the wall was shattered at the end furthest from the door. Near the door Mr G. P. Frere, wearing a silk dressing-gown, was sitting slumped in a chair, bleeding profusely and already dead. My client was standing halfway down the room still wearing the long white evening-dress she had worn on the stage that night. Her make-up was smudged and in her right hand she held a well-oiled service revolver. A bullet had left this weapon and entered Mr Frere's body between the third and fourth metacarpals. In order to make quite sure that her learned counsel didn't have things too easy, Maggie Hartley had then opened her mouth and spoken, so said Croft, the following unforgettable words, here transcribed without punctuation.

'I killed him what could I do with him help me.'

In all subsequent interviews the actress said that she remembered nothing about the quarrel in the dressing-room, the dreadful climax had been blotted from her mind. She was no doubt, and still remained, in a state of shock.

I was brooding on this hopeless defence when an elderly guard acting the part of an air hostess whispered excitedly into the intercom, 'We are now arriving at Grimble Central. Grimble Central. Please collect your hand baggage.' I emerged into a place which seemed to be nestling somewhere within the Arctic Circle, the air bit sharply, it was bloody cold, and a blue-nosed Albert was there to meet me.

'After I left your chambers in disgrace, Mr Rumpole . . .'

'After a misunderstanding, shall we say.'

'My then wife told me she was disgusted with me. She packed her bags and went to live with her married sister in Enfield.'

Albert was smiling contentedly, and that was something I could understand. I had just had, *à côté de* chez Albert Handyside, a meal which his handsome, still youngish second wife referred to as tea, but which had all the appurtenances of an excellent cold luncheon with the addition of hot scones, Dundee cake and strawberry jam.

'Bit of luck then really, you getting the petty cash so "confused".'

'All the same. I do miss the old days clerking for you in the Temple, sir. How are things down South, Mr Rumpole?'

'Down South? Much as usual. Barristers lounging about in the sun. Munching grapes to the lazy sounds of plucked guitars.'

Mrs Handyside the Second returned to the room with another huge pot of dark brown Indian tea. She replenished the Rumpole cup and Albert and I fell to discussing the tea-table subject of murder and sudden death.

'Of course it's not the Penge Bungalow Job.' Albert was referring to my most notable murder and greatest triumph, a case I did at Lewes Assizes alone and without the so-called aid of leading counsel. 'But it's quite a decent little case, sir, in its way. A murder among the showfolk, as they terms them.'

'The showfolk, yes. Definitely worth the detour. There is, of course, one little fly in the otherwise interesting ointment.'

Albert, knowing me as he did, knew quite well what manner of insect I was referring to. I have never taken silk. I remain, at my advanced age, a 'junior' barrister. The brief in R. v. *Hartley* had only one drawback, it announced that I was to be 'led' by a local silk, Mr Jarvis Allen, QC. I hated the prospect of this obscure North Country Queen's Counsel getting all the fun.

'I told my senior partner, sir. I told him straight. Mr Rumpole's quite capable of doing this one on his own.' Albert was suitably apologetic.

'Reminded him, did you? I did the Penge Bungalow Murders alone and without a leader.'

'The senior partner did seem to feel . . .'

'I know. I'm not on the Lord Chancellor's guest list. I never get invited to breakfast in knee breeches. It's not Rumpole, QC. Just Rumpole, Queer Customer . . .'

'Oo, I'm sure you're not,' Mrs Handyside the Second poured me another comforting cup of concentrated tannin.

'It's a murder, sir. That's attracted quite a lot of local attention.'

'And silks go with murder like steak goes with kidney! This Jarvis Allen, QC . . . Pretty competent sort of man, is he?'

'I've only seen him on the Bench . . .'

'On the what?'

The Bench seemed no sort of a place to see dedicated defenders.

'Sits as Recorder here. Gave a young tearaway in our office three years for a punch-up at the Grimble United ground.'

'There's no particular *art* involved in getting people into prison, Albert,' I said severely. 'How is he at keeping them out?'

After tea we had a conference fixed up with my leader and client in prison. There was no women's prison at Grimble, so our client was lodged in a room converted from an unused dispensary in the hospital wing of the masculine nick. She seemed older than I had expected as she sat looking composed, almost detached, surrounded by her legal advisers. It was, at that first conference, as though the case concerned someone else, and had not yet engaged her full attention.

'Mrs Frere.' Jarvis Allen, the learned QC started off. He was a thin, methodical man with rimless glasses and a general rimless appearance. He had made a voluminous note in red, green and blue biro: it didn't seem to have given him much cause for hope.

'Our client is known as Maggie Hartley, sir,' Albert reminded him. 'In the profession.'

'I think she'd better be known as Mrs Frere. In court,' Allen said firmly. 'Now, Mrs Frere. Tommy Pierce is prosecuting and of course I know him well . . . and if we went to see the judge, Skelton's a perfectly reasonable fellow. I think there's a sporting chance . . . I'm making no promises, mind you, there's a sporting chance they might let us plead to manslaughter!'

He brought the last sentence out triumphantly, like a Christmas present. Jarvis Allen was exercising his remarkable talent for getting people locked up. I lit a small cigar, and said nothing.

'Of course, we'd have to accept manslaughter. I'm sure Mr Rumpole agrees. You agree, don't you, Rumpole?' My leader turned to me for support. I gave him little comfort.

'Much more agreeable doing ten years for manslaughter than ten years for murder,' I said. 'Is that the choice you're offering?'

'I don't know if you've read the evidence . . . Our client was found with the gun in her hand.' Allen was beginning to get tetchy.

I thought this over and said, 'Stupid place to have it. If she'd actually *planned* a murder.'

'All the same. It leaves us without a defence.'

'Really? Do you think so? I was looking at the statement of Alan Copeland. He is . . .' I ferreted among the depositions.

'What they call the "juvenile", I believe, Mr Rumpole,' Albert reminded me.

'The "juvenile", yes.' I read from Mr Copeland's statement. ' "I've worked with G. P. Frere for three seasons . . . G. P. drank a good deal. Always interested in some girl in the cast. A new one every year . . ." '

'Jealousy might be a powerful motive, for our client. That's a two-edged sword, Rumpole.' Allen was determined to look on the dreary side.

'Two-edged, yes. Most swords are.' I went on reading. ' "He quarrelled violently with his wife, Maggie Hartley. On one occasion, after the dress rehearsal of *The Master Builder*, he threw a glass of milk stout in her face in front of the entire company . . ." '

'She had a good deal of provocation, we can put that to the judge. That merely reduces it to manslaughter.' I was getting bored with my leader's chatter of manslaughter.

I gave my bundle of depositions to Albert and stood up, looking at our client to see if she would fit the part I had in mind.

'What you need in a murder is an unlikeable corpse . . . Then if you can find a likeable defendant . . . you're off to the races! Who knows? We might even reduce the crime to innocence.'

'Rumpole.' Allen had clearly had enough of my hopeless optimism. 'As I've had to tell Mrs Frere very frankly, there is a clear admission of guilt – which is not disputed.'

'What she said to the stage-door man, Mr . . .'

'Croft.' Albert supplied the name.

'I killed him, what could I do with him? Help me.' Allen repeated the most damning evidence with great satisfaction. 'You've read that, at least?'

'Yes, I've read it. That's the trouble.'

'What *do* you mean?'

'I mean, the trouble is, I read it. I didn't *hear* it. None of us did. And I don't suppose Mr Croft had it spelt out to him, with all the punctuation.'

'Really, Rumpole. I suppose they make jokes about murder cases in London.'

I ignored this bit of impertinence and went on to give the QC some unmerited assistance. 'Suppose she said . . . Suppose our client said, "I killed him" and then,' I paused for breath, ' "What could I do with him? Help me!"?'

I saw our client look at me, for the first time. When she spoke, her voice, like Cordelia's, was ever soft, gentle and low, an excellent thing in woman.

'That's the reading,' she said. I must admit I was puzzled, and asked for an explanation.

'What?'

'The reading of the line. You can tell them. That's exactly how I said it.'

At last, it seemed, we had found *something* she remembered, I thought it an encouraging sign; but it wasn't really my business.

'I'm afraid, dear lady,' I gave her a small bow, 'I shan't be able to tell them anything. Who am I, after all, but the ageing juvenile? The reading of the line, as you call it, will have to come from your QC, Mr Jarvis Allen, who is playing the lead at the moment.'

After the conference I gave Albert strict instructions as to how our client was to dress for her starring appearance in the Grimble Assize

Court (plain black suit, white blouse, no make-up, hair neat, voice gentle but audible to any OAP with a National Health deaf-aid sitting in the back row of the jury, absolutely no reaction during the prosecution case except for a well-controlled sigh of grief at the mention of her deceased husband) and then I suggested we met later for a visit to the scene of the crime. Her Majesty's counsel for the defence had to rush home to write an urgent, and no doubt profitable, opinion on the planning of the new Grimble Gas Works and so was unfortunately unable to join us.

'You go if you like, Rumpole,' he said as he vanished into a funereal Austin Princess. 'I can't see how it's going to be of the slightest assistance.'

The Theatre Royal, an ornate but crumbling Edwardian music hall, which might once have housed George Formby and Rob Wilton, was bolted and barred. Albert and I stood in the rain and read a torn poster.

A cat was rubbing itself against the poster. We heard the North Country voice of an elderly man calling 'Puss . . . Puss . . . Bedtime, pussy.'

The cat went and we followed, round to the corner where the stage-door man, Mr Croft, no doubt, was opening his door and offering a saucer of milk. We made ourselves known as a couple of lawyers and asked for a look at the scene.

'Mr Derwent's round the front of the house. First door on the right.'

I moved up the corridor to a door and, opening it, had the unnerving experience of standing on a dimly lit stage. Behind me flapped a canvas balcony, and a view of the Mediterranean. As I wandered forward a voice called me out of the gloom.

'Who is it? Down here, I'm in the stalls bar.'

There was a light somewhere, a long way off. I went down some steps that led to the stalls and felt my way towards the light with Albert blundering after me. At last we reached the open glass door of a small bar, its dark red walls hung with photographs of the company, and we were in the presence of a little gnome-like man,

**The Theatre Royal,
East Grimble**

The Frere-Hartley Players

present

G. P. Frere and Maggie Hartley

in

'Private Lives'

by

Noël Coward

with

**Alan Copeland
Christine Hope**

Directed by Daniel Derwent

**Stalls £1.50 and £1. Circle £1 and 75p
Matinées and Senior Citizens 50p**

wearing a bow-tie and a double-breasted suit, and that cheerily smiling but really quite expressionless apple-cheeked sort of face you see on some ventriloquist's dolls. His boot-black hair looked as if it had been dyed. He admitted to Albert that he was Daniel Derwent and at the moment in charge of the Frere-Hartley Players.

'Or what's left of them. Decimated, that's what we've been! If you've come with a two-hander for a couple of rather untalented juveniles, I'd be delighted to put it on. I suppose you *are* in the business.'

'The business?' I wondered what business he meant. But I didn't wonder long.

'Show business. The profession.'

'No . . . Another . . . profession altogether.'

I saw he had been working at a table in the empty bar, which was smothered with papers, bills and receipts.

'Our old manager left us in a state of total confusion,' Derwent said. 'And my ear's out to *here* answering the telephone.'

'The vultures can't hear of an actor shot in East Grimble but half the character men in *Spotlight* are after me for the job. Well, I've told everyone. Nothing's going to be decided till after Maggie's trial. We're not reopening till then. It wouldn't seem right, somehow. *What* other profession?'

'We're lawyers, Mr Derwent,' Albert told him. 'Defending.'

'Maggie's case?' Derwent didn't stop smiling.

'My name's Handyside of instructing solicitors. This is Mr Rumpole from London, junior counsel for the defence.'

'A London barrister. In the sticks!' The little thespian seemed to find it amusing. 'Well, Grimble's hardly a number one touring date. All the same, I suppose murder's a draw. Anywhere . . . Care for a tiny rum?'

'That's very kind.' It was bitter cold, the unused theatre seemed to be saving on central heating and I was somewhat sick at heart at the prospect of our defence. A rum would do me no harm at all.

'Drop of orange in it? Or as she comes?'

'As she comes, thank you.'

'I always take a tiny rum, for the cords. Well, we depend on the cords, don't we, in our professions.'

Apart from a taste for rum I didn't see then what I had in common, professionally or otherwise, with Mr Derwent. I wandered off with my drink in my hand to look at the photographs of the Frere-Hartley Players. As I did so I could hear the theatre manager chattering to Albert.

'We could have done a bomb tonight. The money we've turned away. You couldn't buy publicity like it,' Derwent was saying.

'No . . . No, I don't suppose you could.'

'Week after week all we get in the *Grimble Argus* is a little para: "Maggie Hartley took her part well." And now we're all over the front page. And we can't play. It breaks your heart. It does really.' I heard him freshen his rum with another slug from the bottle. 'Poor old G. P. could have drawn more money dead than he ever could when he was alive. Well, at least he's sober tonight, wherever he is.'

'The late Mr G. P. Frere was fond of a drink occasionally?' Albert made use of the probing understatement.

'Not that his performance suffered. He didn't act any worse when he was drunk.'

I was looking at a glossy photograph of the late Mr G. P. Frere, taken about ten years ago I should imagine: it showed a man with grey sideburns and an open-necked shirt with a silk scarf round his neck and eyes that were self-consciously quizzical. A man who, despite the passage of the years, was still determined to go on saying 'Who's for tennis?'

'What I admired about old G. P.,' I heard Derwent say, 'was his selfless concern for others! Never left you with the sole responsibility of entertaining the audience. He'd try to help by upstaging you. Or moving on your laugh line. He once tore up a newspaper all through my long speech in *Waiting for Godot* . . . Now you wouldn't do that, would you, Mr Rumpole? Not in anyone's long speech. Well, of course not.'

He had moved, for his last remarks, to a point rather below, but still too close to, my left ear. I was looking at the photographs of a moderately pretty young girl, wearing a seafaring sweater, whose lips were parted as if to suck in a quick draft of ozone when out for a day with the local dinghy club.

'Miss Christine Hope?' I asked.

'Miss Christine Hopeless I called her.' This Derwent didn't seem to have a particularly high opinion of his troupe. 'God knows what G. P. saw in her. She did that audition speech from *St Joan*. All breathless and excited . . . as if she'd just run up four flights of stairs because the angel voices were calling her about a little part in *Crossroads*. "We could *do* something with her," G. P. said. "I know what," I told him. "Burn her at the stake."'

I had come to a wall on which there were big photographs of various characters, a comic charlady, a beautiful woman in a white evening-dress, a duchess in a tiara, a neat secretary in glasses, and a tattered siren who might have been Sadie Thompson in *Rain* if my theatrical memory served me right. All the faces were different, and they were all the faces of Maggie Hartley.

'Your client. My leading lady. I suppose *both* our shows depend on her.' Derwent was looking at the photographs with a rapt smile of appreciation. 'No doubt about it. She's good. Maggie's good.'

I turned to look at him, found him much too close and retreated a step. 'What do you mean,' I asked him, 'by good, exactly?'

'There is a quality. Of perfect truthfulness. Absolute reality.'

'Truthfulness?' This was about the first encouraging thing we'd heard about Maggie Hartley.

'It's very rare.'

'Excuse me, sir. Would you be prepared to say that in court?' Albert seemed to be about to take a statement. I moved tactfully away.

'Is that what you came here for?' Derwent asked me nervously.

I thought it over, and decided there was no point in turning a friendly source of information into a hostile witness.

'No. We wanted to see . . . the scene of the crime.'

At which Mr Derwent, apparently reassured, smiled again.

'The Last Act,' he said and led us to the dressing-room, typical of a provincial Rep. 'I'll unlock it for you.'

The dressing-room had been tidied up, the cupboards and drawers were empty. Otherwise it looked like the sort of room that would have been condemned as unfit for human habitation by any decent local authority. I stood in the doorway, and made sure that the mirror which went all along one side of the room was shattered in the corner furthest away from me.

'Any help to you, is it?'

'It might be. It's what we lawyers call the *locus in quo*.'

Mr Derwent was positively giggling then.

'Do you? How frightfully camp of you. It's what we actors call a dressing-room.'

So I went back to the Majestic Hotel, a building which seemed rather less welcoming than Her Majesty's Prison, Grimble. And when I was breaking my fast on their mixed grill consisting of cold greasy bacon, a stunted tomato and a sausage that would have looked ungenerous on a cocktail stick, Albert rang me with the unexpected news that at one bound put the Theatre Royal Killing up beside the Penge Bungalow Murders in the Pantheon of Rumpole's forensic triumphs. I was laughing when I came back from the telephone, and I was still laughing when I returned to spread, on a slice of blackened toast, that pat of margarine which the management of the Majestic were apparently unable to tell from butter.

Two hours later we were in the judges' room at the law court discussing, in the hushed tones of relatives after a funeral, the unfortunate event which had occurred. Those present were Tommy Pierce, QC, counsel for the prosecution, and his junior, Roach, the learned judge, my learned leader and my learned self.

'Of course these people don't really live in the real world at all,' Jarvis Allen, QC, was saying. 'It's all make-believe for them. Dressing up in fancy costumes . . .'

He himself was wearing a wig, a tailed coat with braided cuffs and a silk gown. His opponent, also bewigged, had a huge stomach from which a gold watch-chain and seal dangled. He also took snuff and blew his nose in a red spotted handkerchief. That kind and, on the whole, gentle figure Skelton J. was fishing in the folds of his scarlet gown for a bitten pipe and an old leather pouch. I didn't think we were exactly the ones to talk about dressing up.

'You don't think she appreciates the seriousness,' the judge was clearly worried.

'I'm afraid not, Judge. Still, if she wants to sack me . . . Of course it puts Rumpole in an embarrassing position.'

'Are you embarrassed, Rumpole?' his Lordship asked me.

As a matter of fact I was filled with a deeper inner joy, for Albert's call at breakfast had been to the effect that our client had chosen to dismiss her leading counsel and put her future entirely in the hands of Horace Rumpole, BA, that timeless member of the Junior Bar.

'Oh yes. Dreadfully embarrassed, Judge.' I did my best to look suitably modest. 'But it seems that the lady's mind is quite made up.'

'Very embarrassing for you. For you both.' The judge was understanding. 'Does she give any reason for dispensing with her leading counsel, Jarvis?'

'She said . . .' I turned a grin into a cough. I too remembered what Albert had told us. 'She said she thought Rumpole was "better casting".'

' "Better casting"? Whatever can she mean by that?'

'Better in the part, Judge,' I translated.

'Oh dear.' The judge looked distressed. 'Is she very actressy?'

'She's an actress,' I admitted, but would go no further.

'Yes. Yes, I suppose she is.' The judge lit his pipe. 'Do you have any views about this, Tommy?'

'No, Judge. When Jarvis was instructed we were going to ask your views on a plea to manslaughter.'

The portly Pierce twinkled a lot and talked in a rich North Country accent. I could see we were in for a prosecution of homely fun, like one of the comic plays of J. B. Priestley.

'Manslaughter, eh? Do you want to discuss manslaughter, Rumpole?'

I appeared to give the matter some courteous consideration.

'No, Judge, I don't believe I do.'

'If you'd like an adjournment you shall certainly have it. Your client may want to think about manslaughter . . . Or consider another leader. She should have leading counsel. In a case of this . . .' the judge puffed out smoke '. . . seriousness.'

'Oh, I don't think there's much point in considering another leader.'

'You don't?'

'You see,' I was doing my best not to look at Allen, 'I don't honestly think anyone else would get the part.'

When we got out of the judges' room, and were crossing the imposing Victorian Gothic hallway that led to the court, my learned ex-leader, who had preserved an expression of amused detachment up to that point, turned on me with considerable hurt.

'I must say I take an extremely dim view of that.'

'Really?'

'An extremely dim view. On this circuit we have a tradition of loyalty to our leaders.'

'It's a local custom?'

'Certainly it is,' Allen stood still and pronounced solemnly. 'I can't imagine anyone on this circuit carrying on with a case after his leader has been sacked. It's not in the best traditions of the Bar.'

'Loyalty to one's leader. Yes, of course, that is extremely important . . .' I thought about it. 'But we must consider the other great legal maxim, mustn't we?'

'Legal maxim? What legal maxim?'

' "The show must go on." Excuse me. I see Albert. Nice chatting to you but . . . Things to do, old darling. Quite a number of things to do . . .' So I hurried away from the fired legal eagle to where my old clerk was standing, looking distinctly anxious, at the entrance of the court. He asked me hopefully if the judge had seen fit to grant an adjournment, so that he could persuade our client to try another silk, a course on which Albert's senior partner was particularly keen.

'Oh dear,' I had to disappoint him. 'I begged the judge, Albert. I almost went down on my knees to him. But would he grant me an adjournment? I'm afraid not. "No, Rumpole," he told me, "the show must go on." ' I put a comforting hand on Albert's shoulder. 'Cheer up, old darling. There's only one thing you need say to your senior partner.'

'What's that, sir?'

'The Penge Bungalow Murders.'

I sounded supremely confident of course; but as I went into court

I suddenly remembered that without a leader I would have absolutely no one to blame but myself when things went wrong.

'I don't know if any of you ladies and gentlemen have actually attended *performances* at the Theatre Royal . . .' Tommy Pierce, QC, opening the case for the prosecution, chuckled as though to say 'Most of us got better things to do, haven't we, Members of the Jury?' 'But we all have passed it going up the Makins Road in a trolleybus on the way to Grimble football ground. You'll know where it is, Members of the Jury. Past the Snellsham roundabout, on the corner opposite the Old Britannia Hotel, where we've all celebrated many a win by Grimble United . . .'

I didn't know why he didn't just tell them: 'The prisoner's represented by Rumpole of the Bailey, a smart alecky lawyer from London, who's never ever heard of Grimble United, let alone the Old Britannia Hotel.' I shut my eyes and looked uninterested as Tommy rumbled on, switching, now, to portentous seriousness.

'In this case, Members of the Jury, we enter an alien world. The world of the showfolk! They live a strange life, you may think. A life of make-believe. On the surface everyone loves each other. "You were wonderful, darling!" said to men and women alike . . .'

I seriously considered heaving myself to my hind legs to protest against this rubbish, but decided to sit still and continue the look of bored indifference.

'But underneath all the good companionship,' Pierce was now trying to make the flesh creep, 'run deep tides of jealousy and passion which welled up, in this particular case, Members of the Jury, into brutal and, say the Crown, quite cold-blooded murder . . .'

As he went on I thought that Derwent, the little gnome from the theatre, whom I could now see in the back of the pit, somewhere near the dock, was perfectly right. Murder is a draw. All the local nobs were in court including the judge's wife, Lady Skelton, in the front row of the stalls, wearing her special matinée hat. I also saw the Sheriff of the County, in his fancy dress, wearing lace ruffles and a sword which stuck rather inconveniently between his legs, and Mrs Sheriff of the County, searching in her handbag for something which might well have been her opera glasses. And then, behind me, the star of the show, my client, looking as I told her to look. Ordinary.

'This is not a case which depends on complicated evidence, Members of the Jury, or points of law. Let me tell you the facts.'

The facts were not such that I wanted the jury to hear them too clearly, at least not in my learned friend's version. I slowly, and quite noisily, took a page out of my notebook. I was grateful to see that some of the members of the jury glanced in my direction.

'It simply amounts to this. The murder weapon, a Smith and Wesson revolver, was found in the defendant's hand as she stood over her husband's dead body. A bullet from the very weapon had entered between the third and fourth metacarpals!'

I didn't like Pierce's note of triumph as he said this. Accordingly I began to tear my piece of paper into very small strips. More members of the jury looked in my direction.

'Ladies and gentlemen. The defendant, as you will see on your abstract of indictment, was charged as "Maggie Hartley". It seems she prefers to be known by her maiden name, and that may give you some idea of the woman's attitude to her husband of some twenty years, the deceased in this case, the late Gerald Patrick Frere . . .'

At which point, gazing round the court, I saw Daniel Derwent. He actually winked, and I realized that he thought he recognized my paper-tearing as an old ham actor's trick. I stopped doing it immediately.

'It were a mess. A right mess. Glass broken, blood. He was sprawled in the chair. I thought he were drunk for a moment, but he weren't. And she had this pistol, like, in her hand.' Mr Croft, the stage-door-man, was standing in the witness-box in his best blue suit. The jury clearly liked him, just as they disliked the picture he was painting.

'Can you remember what she said?' The learned prosecutor prompted him gently.

'Not too fast . . .' Mr Justice Skelton was, worse luck, preparing himself to write it all down.

'Just follow his Lordship's pencil . . .' said Pierce, and the judicial pencil prepared to follow Mr Croft.

'She said, "I killed him, what could I do with him?" '

'What did you understand that to mean?'

I did hoist myself to my hind legs then, and registered a determined objection. 'It isn't what this witness understood it to mean. It's what the jury understands it to mean . . .'

'My learned friend's quite wrong. The witness was there. He could form his own conclusion . . .'

'Please, gentlemen. Let's try and have no disagreements, at least not before luncheon,' said the judge sweetly, and added, less charmingly, 'I think Mr Croft may answer the question.'

'I understood her to say she was so fed up with him, she didn't know what else to do . . .'

'But to kill him . . . ?' Only the judge could have supplied that and he did it with another charming smile.

'Yes, my Lord.'

'Did she say anything else? That you remember?'

'I think she said, "Help me." '

'Yes. Just wait there, will you? In case Mr Rumpole has some questions.'

'Just a few . . .' I rose to my feet. Here was an extremely dangerous witness whom the jury liked. It was no good making a head-on attack. The only way was to lure Mr Croft politely into my parlour. I gave the matter some thought and then tried a line on which I thought we might reach agreement.

'When you saw the deceased, Frere, slumped in the chair, your first thought was that he was drunk?'

'Yes.'

'Had you seen him slumped in a chair drunk in his dressing-room on many occasions?'

'A few.' Mr Croft answered with a knowing smile, and I felt encouraged.

'On most nights?'

'Some nights.'

'Were there some nights when he *wasn't* the worse for drink? Did he ever celebrate with an evening of sobriety?'

I got my first smile from the jury, and the joker for the prosecution arose in full solemnity.

'My Lord . . .'

Before Tommy Pierce could interrupt the proceedings with a speech I bowled the next question.

'Mr Croft. When you came into the dressing-room, the deceased Frere was nearest the door . . .'

'Yes. Only a couple of feet from me . . . I saw . . .'

'You saw my client was standing halfway down the room?' I asked, putting a stop to further painful details. 'Holding the gun.'

Pierce gave the jury a meaningful stare, emphasizing the evidence.

'The dressing-room mirror stretches all the way along the wall. And it was broken at the far end, away from the door?'

'Yes.'

'So to have fired the bullet that broke that end of the glass, my client would have had to turn away from the deceased and shoot behind her back . . .' I swung round, by way of demonstration, and made a gesture, firing behind me. Of course I couldn't do that without bringing the full might of the prosecution to its feet.

'Surely that's a question for the jury to decide.'

'The witness was there. He can form his own conclusions.' I quoted the wisdom of my learned friend. 'What's the answer?'

'I suppose she would,' Croft said thoughtfully and the jury looked interested.

The judge cleared his throat and leant forward, smiling politely and being, as it turned out, surprisingly unhelpful.

'Wouldn't that depend, Mr Rumpole, on where the deceased was at the time that particular shot was fired . . . ?'

Pierce glowed in triumph and muttered, 'Exactly!' I did a polite bow and went quickly on to the next question.

'Perhaps we could turn now to the little matter of what she said when you went into the room.'

'I can remember that perfectly.'

'The words, yes. It's the reading that matters.'

'The *what*, Mr Rumpole?' said the judge, betraying theatrical ignorance.

'The stress, my Lord. The intonation . . . It's an expression used in show business.'

'Perhaps we should confine ourselves to expressions used in law courts, Mr Rumpole.'

'Certainly, my Lord.' I readdressed the witness. 'She said she'd killed him. And then, after a pause, "What could I do with him? Help me."'

Mr Croft frowned. 'I . . . That is, yes.'

'Meaning "What could I do with his dead body?" and asking for your help . . . ?'

'My Lord. That's surely . . .' Tommy Pierce was on his hind legs, and I gave him another quotation from himself.

'He was there!' I leant forward and smiled at Croft trying to make him feel that I was a friend he could trust.

'She never meant that she had killed him because she didn't know what to do with him?'

There was a long silence. Counsel for the prosecution let out a deep breath and subsided like a balloon slowly settling. The judge nudged the witness gently. 'Well? What's the answer, Mr Croft? Did she . . . ?'

'I . . . I can't be sure how she said it, my Lord.'

And there, on a happy note of reasonable doubt, I left it. As I came out of court and crossed the entrance hall on my way to the cells I was accosted by the beaming Mr Daniel Derwent, who was, it seemed, anxious to congratulate me.

'What a performance, Mr Rumpole. Knock-out! You were wonderful! What I admired so was the timing. The pause, before you started the cross-examination.'

'Pause?'

'You took a beat of nine seconds. I counted.'

'Did I really?'

'Built-up tension, of course. I could see what you were after.'

He put a hand on my sleeve, a red hand with big rings and polished fingernails. 'You really must let me know. If ever you want a job in Rep.'

I dislodged my fan club and went down the narrow staircase to the cells. The time had clearly come for my client to start remembering.

Maggie Hartley smiled at me over her untouched tray of vegetable pie. She even asked me how I was; but I had no time for small talk. It was zero hour, the last moment I had to get some reasonable instructions.

'Listen to me. Whatever you do or don't remember . . . it's just impossible for you to have stood there and fired the first shot.'

'The first shot?' She frowned, as if at some distant memory.

'The one that *didn't* kill him. The one that went behind you. He must have fired that. He *must* . . .'

'Yes.' She nodded her head. That was encouraging. So far as it went.

'Why the hell . . . why in the name of sanity didn't you tell us that before?'

'I waited. Until there was someone I could trust.'

'Me?'

'Yes. You, Mr Rumpole.'

There's nothing more flattering than to be trusted, even by a confirmed and hopeless villain (which is why I find it hard to dislike a client), and I was convinced Maggie Hartley wasn't that. I sat down beside her in the cell and, with Albert taking notes, she started to talk. What she said was disjointed, sometimes incoherent, and God knows how it was going to sound in the witness-box, but given a few more breaks in the prosecution case and a following wind I was beginning to get the sniff of a defence.

One, two, three, four . . .

Mr Alan Copeland, the juvenile lead, had just given his evidence-in-chief for the prosecution. He seemed a pleasant enough young man, wearing a tie and a dark suit (good witness-box clothing) and his evidence hadn't done us any particular harm. All the same I was trying what the director Derwent had admired as the devastating pause.

Seven . . . eight . . . nine . . .

'Have you any questions, Mr Rumpole?' The judge sounded as if he was getting a little impatient with 'the timing'. I launched the cross-examination.

'Mr Alan . . . Copeland. You know the deceased man owned a Smith and Wesson revolver? Do you know where he got it?'

'He was in a spy film and it was one of the props. He bought it.'

'But it was more than a bit of scenery. It was a real revolver.'

'Unfortunately, yes.'

'And he had a licence for it . . . ?'

'Oh yes. He joined the Grimble Rifle and Pistol Club and used to shoot at targets. I think he fancied himself as James Bond or something.'

'As James who . . . ?' I knew that Mr Justice Skelton wouldn't be able to resist playing the part of a mystified judge, so I explained carefully.

'A character in fiction, my Lord. A person licensed to kill. He also spends a great deal of his time sleeping with air hostesses.' To Tommy Pierce's irritation I got a little giggle out of the ladies and gentlemen of the jury.

'Mr Rumpole. We have quite enough to do in this case dealing with questions of *fact*. I suggest we leave the world of fiction . . . outside the court, with our overcoats.'

The jury subsided into serious attention, and I addressed myself to the work in hand. 'Where did Mr Frere keep his revolver?'

'Usually in a locker. At the rifle club.'

'Usually?'

'A few weeks ago he asked me to bring it back to the theatre for him.'

'He asked *you*?'

'I'm a member of the club myself.'

'Really, Mr Copeland.' The judge was interested. 'And what's your weapon?'

'A shotgun, my Lord. I do some clay pigeon shooting.'

'Did Frere say *why* he wanted his gun brought back to the theatre?' I gave the jury a puzzled look.

'There'd been some burglaries. I imagine he wanted to scare any intruder . . .'

I had established that it was Frere's gun, and certainly not brought to the scene of the crime by Maggie. I broached another topic. 'Now, you have spoken of some quarrels between Frere and his wife.'

'Yes, sir. He once threw a drink in her face.'

'During their quarrels, did you see my client retaliate in any way?'

'No. No, I never did. May I say something, my Lord . . .'

'Certainly, Mr Copeland.'

I held my breath. I didn't like free-ranging witnesses, but at his answer I sat down gratefully.

'Miss Hartley, as we knew her, was an exceptionally gentle person.'

I saw the jury look at the dock, at the quiet almost motionless woman sitting there.

'Mr Copeland. You've told us you shot clay pigeons at the rifle club.' The prosecution was up and beaming.

'Yes, sir.'

'Nothing much to eat on a clay pigeon, I suppose.'

The jury greeted this alleged quip with total silence. The local comic had died the death in Grimble. Pierce went on and didn't improve his case.

'And Frere asked for this pistol to be brought back to the theatre. Did his wife know that, do you think . . . ?'

'I certainly didn't tell her.'

'May I ask why not?'

'I think it would have made her very nervous. I certainly was.'

'Nervous of what, exactly?'

Tommy Pierce had broken the first rule of advocacy. Never ask your witness a question unless you're quite sure of the answer.

'Well . . . I was always afraid G. P.'d get drunk and loose it off at someone . . .'

The beauty of that answer was that it came from a witness for the prosecution, a detached observer who'd only been called to identify the gun as belonging to the late-lamented G. P. Frere. None too soon for the health of his case Tommy Pierce let Mr Copeland leave the box. I saw him cross the court and sit next to Daniel Derwent, who gave him a little smile, as if of congratulation.

In the course of my legal career I have had occasion to make some study of firearms; not so intensive, of course, as my researches into the subject of blood, but I certainly know more about revolvers than I do about the law of landlord and tenant. I held the fatal weapon in a fairly expert hand as I cross-examined the inspector who had recovered it from the scene of the crime.

'It's clear, is it not, Inspector, that two chambers had been fired?'

'Yes.'

'One bullet was found in the corner of the mirror, and another in the body of the deceased, Frere?'

'That is so.'

'Now. If the person who fired the shot into the mirror pulled back this hammer,' I pulled it back, 'to fire a second shot . . . the gun is now in a condition to go off with a far lighter pressure on the trigger?'

'That is so. Yes.'

'Thank you.'

I put down the gun and as I did so allowed my thumb to accidentally press the trigger. I looked at it, surprised, as it clicked. It was a moderately effective move, and I thought the score was fifteen – love to Rumpole. Tommy Pierce rose to serve.

'Inspector. Whether the hammer was pulled back or not, a woman would have no difficulty in firing this pistol?'

'Certainly not, my Lord.'

'Yes. Thank *you*, Inspector.' The prosecution sat down smiling. Fifteen – all.

The last witness of the day was Miss Christine Hope who turned her large *ingénue* eyes on the jury and whispered her evidence at a sound level which must have made her unintelligible to the audiences at the Theatre Royal. I had decided to cross-examine her more in sorrow than in anger.

'Miss Hope. Why were you waiting at the stage-door?'

'Somehow I can never bear to leave. After the show's over . . . I can never bear to go.' She gave the jury a 'silly me' look of girlish enthusiasm. 'I suppose I'm just in love with the Theatre.'

'And I suppose you were also "just in love" with G. P. Frere?'

At which Miss Hope looked helplessly at the rail of the witness-box, and fiddled with the Holy Bible.

'You waited for him every night, didn't you? He left his wife at the stage-door and took you home.'

'Sometimes . . .'

'You're dropping your voice, Miss Hope.' The judge was leaning forward, straining to hear.

'Sometimes, my Lord,' she repeated a decibel louder.

'Every night?'

'Most nights. Yes.'

'Thank you, Miss Hope.'

Pierce, wisely, didn't re-examine and La Belle Christine left the box to looks of disapproval from certain ladies on the jury.

I didn't sleep well that night. Whether it was the Majestic mattress, which appeared to be stuffed with firewood, or the sounds, as of a giant suffering from indigestion, which reverberated from the central heating, or mere anxiety about the case, I don't know. At any rate Albert and I were down in the cells as soon as they opened, taking a critical look at the client I was about to expose to the perils of the witness-box. As I had instructed her she was wearing no make-up, and a simple dark dress which struck exactly the right note.

'I'm glad you like it,' Maggie said. 'I wore it in *Time and the Conways*.'

'Listen to the questions, answer them as shortly as you can.' I gave her her final orders. 'Every word to the North Country comedian is giving him a present. Just stick to the facts. Not a word of criticism of the dear departed.'

'You want *them* to like me?'

'They shouldn't find it too difficult.' I looked at her, and lit a small cigar.

'Do I have to swear on . . . the Bible?'

'It's customary.'

'I'd rather affirm.'

'You don't believe in God?' I didn't want an obscure point of theology adding unnecessary difficulties to our case.

'I suppose He's a possibility. He just doesn't seem to be a very frequent visitor to the East Grimble Rep.'

'I know a Grimble jury,' Albert clearly shared my fears. 'If you *could* swear on the Bible?'

'The audience might like it?' Maggie smiled gently.

'The jury,' I corrected her firmly.

'They're not too keen on agnostic actresses. Is that your opinion?'

'I suppose that puts it in a nutshell.'

'All right for the West End, is that it? No good in Grimble.'

'Of course I want you to be *yourself* . . .' I really hoped she wasn't going to be difficult about the oath.

'No, you don't. You don't want me to be myself at all. You want me to be an ordinary North Country housewife. Spending just another ordinary day on trial for murder.' For a moment her voice had hardened. I looked at her and tried to sound as calm as possible as I pulled out my watch. It was nearly time for the curtain to go up on the evidence for the defence.

'Naturally you're nervous. Time to go.'

'Bloody sick to the stomach. Every time I go on.' Her voice was gentle again, and she was smiling ruefully.

'Good luck.'

'We never say "good luck". It's bad luck to say "good luck". We say "break a leg" . . .'

'Break a leg!' I smiled back at her and went upstairs to make my entrance.

Calling your client, I always think, is the worst part of any case. When you're cross-examining, or making a final speech, you're in control. Put your client in the witness-box and there the old darling is, exposed to the world, out of your protection, and all you can do is ask the questions and hope to God the answers don't blow up in your face.

With Maggie everything was going well. We were like a couple of ballroom dancers, expertly gyrating to Victor Silvester and certain to walk away with the cup. She seemed to sense my next question, and had her answer ready, but not too fast. She looked at the jury, made herself audible to the judge, and gave an impression, a small, dark figure in the witness-box, of courage in the face of adversity. The court was so quiet and attentive that, as she started to describe that final quarrel, I felt we were alone, two old friends, talking intimately of some dreadful event that took place a long time ago.

'He told me . . . he was very much in love with Christine.'

'With Miss Hope?'

'Yes. With Christine Hope. That he wanted her to play Amanda.'

'That is . . . the leading lady? And what was to happen to you?'

'He wanted me to leave the company. To go to London. He never wanted to see me again.'

'What did you say to that?'

'I said I was terribly unhappy about Christine, naturally.'

'Just tell the ladies and gentlemen of the jury what happened next.'

'He said it didn't matter what I said. He was going to get rid of me. He opened the drawer of the dressing-table.'

'Was he standing then?'

'I would say, staggering.'

'Yes, and then . . . ?'

'He took out the . . . the revolver.'

'This one . . . ?'

I handed the gun to the usher, who took it to Maggie. She glanced at it and shuddered.

'I . . . I think so.'

'What effect did it have on you when you first saw it?'

'I was terrified.'

'Did you know it was there?'

'No. I had no idea.'

'And then . . . ?'

'Then. He seemed to be getting ready to fire the gun.'

'You mean he pulled back the hammer . . . ?'

'My Lord . . .' Pierce stirred his vast bulk and the judge was inclined to agree.

He said: 'Yes. Please don't lead, Mr Rumpole.'

'I think that's what he did,' Maggie continued without assistance. 'I didn't look carefully. Naturally I was terrified. He was waving the gun. He didn't seem to be able to hold it straight. Then there was a terrible explosion. I remember glass, and dust, everywhere.'

'Who fired that shot, Mrs Frere?'

'My husband. I think . . .'

'Yes?'

'I think he was trying to kill me.' She said it very quietly, but the jury heard, and remembered. She gave it a marked pause and then went on. 'After that first shot. I saw him getting ready to fire again.'

'Was he pulling . . . ?'

'Please don't lead, Mr Rumpole.' The trouble with the great comedian was that he couldn't sit still in anyone else's act.

'He was pulling back . . . that thing.' Maggie went on without any help.

Then I asked the judge if we could have a demonstration and the usher went up into the witness-box to play the scene with Maggie. At my suggestion he took the revolver.

'We are all quite sure that thing isn't loaded?' The judge sounded nervous.

'Quite sure, my Lord. Of course, we don't want *another* fatal *accident!*'

'Really, my Lord. That was quite improper!' Pierce rose furiously. 'My learned friend called it an accident.'

I apologized profusely, the point having been made. Then Maggie quietly positioned the usher. He raised the gun as she asked him. It was pointed murderously at her. And then Maggie grabbed at the gun in his hand, and forced it back, struggling desperately, against the usher's chest.

'I was trying to stop him. I got hold of his hand to push the gun away . . . I pushed it back . . . I think . . . I think I must have forced back his finger on the trigger.' We heard the hammer click, and now Maggie was struggling to hold back her tears. 'There was another terrible noise . . . I never meant . . .'

'Yes. Thank you, Usher.'

The usher went back to the well of the court. Maggie was calm again when I asked her: 'When Mr Croft came you said you had killed your husband?'

'Yes . . . I had . . . By accident.'

'What else did you say?'

'I think I said . . . What could I do with him? I meant, how could I help him, of course.'

'And you asked Mr Croft to help you?'

'Yes.'

It was time for the curtain line.

'Mrs Frere. Did you ever at any time have any intention of killing your husband?'

'Never . . . ! Never . . . ! Never . . . !' Now my questions were finished she was crying, her face and shoulders shaking. The judge leaned forward kindly.

'Don't distress yourself. Usher, a glass of water?'

Her cheeks hot with genuine tears, Maggie looked up bravely.

'Thank you, my Lord.'

'Bloody play-acting!' I heard the cynical Tommy Pierce mutter ungraciously to his junior, Roach.

If she was good in chief Maggie was superb in cross-examination. She answered the questions courteously, shortly, but as if she were genuinely trying to help Tommy clear up any doubt about her innocence that might have lingered in his mind. At the end he lost his nerve and almost shouted at her:

'So according to you, you did nothing wrong?'

'Oh yes,' she said. 'I did something terribly wrong.'

'Tell us. What?'

'I loved him too much. Otherwise I should have left him. Before he tried to kill me.'

During Tommy's final speech there was some coughing from the jury. He tried a joke or two about actors, lost heart and sat down upon reminding the jury that they must not let sympathy for my client affect their judgment.

'I agree entirely with my learned friend,' I started my speech. 'Put all sympathy out of your mind. The mere fact that my client clung faithfully to a drunken, adulterous husband, hoping vainly for the love he denied her; the terrible circumstance that she escaped death at his hands only to face the terrible ordeal of a trial for murder; none of these things should influence you in the least . . .' and I ended with my well-tried peroration. 'In an hour or two this case will be over. You will go home and put the kettle on and forget all about this little theatre, and the angry, drunken actor and his wretched infidelities. This case has only been a few days out of your lives. But for the lady I have the honour to represent . . .' I pointed to the dock, '*all* her life hangs in the balance. Is that life to be broken and is she to go down in darkness and disgrace, or can she go back into the glowing light of her world, to bring us all joy and entertainment and laughter once again? Ask yourselves that question, Members of the Jury. And when you ask it, you know there can only be one answer.'

I sank back into my seat exhausted, pushing back my wig and mopping my brow with a large silk handkerchief. Looking round the court I saw Derwent. He seemed about to applaud, until he was restrained by Mr Alan Copeland.

There is nothing I hate more than waiting for a jury to come back. You smoke too much and drink too many cups of coffee, your hands sweat and you can't do or think of anything else. All you can do is to pay a courtesy visit to the cells to prepare for the worst. Albert Handyside had to go off and do a touch of dangerous driving in the court next door, so I was alone when I went to call on the waiting Maggie.

She was standing in her cell, totally calm.

'This is the bad part, isn't it? Like waiting for the notices.'

I sat down at the table with my notebook, unscrewed my fountain pen.

'I had better think of what to say if they find you guilty of manslaughter. I think I've got the facts for mitigation, but I'd just like to get the history clear. You'd started this theatrical company together?'

'It was my money. Every bloody penny of it.' I looked up in some surprise. The hard, tough note was there in her voice; her face was set in a look which was something like hatred.

'I don't think we need go into the financial side.'

I tried to stop her but she went on: 'Do you know what that idiotic manager we had then did? He gave G. P. a contract worth fifty per cent of the profits: for an investment of nothing and a talent which stopped short of being able to pour out a drink and say a line at the same time. Anyway I never paid his percentage.' She smiled then, it was quite humourless. 'Won't need to say that, will we?'

'No,' I said firmly.

'Fifty per cent of ten years' work! He reckoned he was owed around twenty thousand pounds. He was going to sue us and bankrupt the company . . .'

'I don't think you need to tell me any more.' I screwed the top back on my fountain pen. Perhaps she had told me too much already.

'So don't feel too badly, will you? If we're not a hit.'

I stood up and pulled out my watch. Suddenly I felt an urgent need to get out of the cell.

'They should be back soon now.'

'It's all a game to you, isn't it?' She sounded unaccountably bitter. 'All a wonderful game of "let's pretend". The costume. The bows. The little jokes. The onion at the end.'

'The onion?'

'An old music-hall expression. For what makes the audience cry. Oh, I was quite prepared to go along with it. To wear the make-up.'

'You didn't wear any make-up.'

'I know, that was brilliant of you. You're a marvellous performer, Mr Rumpole. Don't let anyone tell you different.'

'It's not a question of performance.' I couldn't have that.

'Isn't it?'

'Of course it isn't! The jury are now weighing the facts. Doing their best to discover where the truth lies.' I looked at her. Her face gave nothing away.

'Or at least deciding if the prosecution has proved its case.'

Suddenly, quite unexpectedly, she yawned, she moved away from me, as though I bored her.

'Oh, I'm tired. Worn out. With so much *acting*. I tell you, in the theatre we haven't got time for all that. We've got our livings to get.'

The woman prison officer came in.

'I think they want you upstairs now. Ready, dear?'

When Maggie spoke again her voice was low, gentle and wonderfully polite.

'Yes thanks, Elsie. I'm quite ready now.'

'Will your foreman please stand? Mr Foreman. Have you reached a verdict on which you are all agreed?'

'Not guilty, my Lord.'

Four words that usually set the Rumpole ears tingling with delight and the chest swelling with pleasure. Why was it, that at the end of what was no doubt a remarkable win, a famous victory even, I felt such doubt and depression? I told myself that I was not the judge of fact, that the jury had clearly not been satisfied and that the prosecution had not proved its case. I did the well-known shift of responsibility which is the advocate's perpetual comfort, but I went out of court unelated. In the entrance hall I saw Maggie leaving; she didn't turn back to speak to me, and I saw that she was holding the hand of Mr Alan Copeland. Such congratulations as I received came from the diminutive Derwent.

'Triumph. My dear, a total triumph.'

'You told me she was truthful . . .' I looked at him.

'I meant her acting. That's quite truthful. Not to be faulted. That's all I meant.'

At which he made his exit and my learned friend for the prosecution came sailing up, beaming with the joy of reconciliation.

'Well. Congratulations, Rumpole. That was a bloody good win!'

'Was it? I hope so.'

'Coming to the circuit dinner tonight?'

'Tonight?'

'You'll enjoy it! We've got some pretty decent claret in the Mess.'

If my judgement hadn't been weakened by exhaustion I would never have agreed to the circuit dinner which took place, as I feared, in a private room at the Majestic Hotel. All the gang were there – Skelton J., Pierce, Roach and my one-time leader Jarvis Allen, QC. The food was indifferent, the claret was bad, and when the port was passed an elderly silk whom they called 'Mr Senior' in deference to his position as leader of the Circuit, banged the table with the handle of his knife and addressed young Roach at the other end of the table.

'Mr Junior, in the matter of Rumpole.'

'Mr Senior,' Roach produced a scribble on a menu. 'I will read the indictment.'

I realized then that I had been tricked, ambushed, made to give myself up to the tender mercies of this savage northerly circuit. Rumpole was on trial: there was nothing to do but drink all the available port and put up with it.

'Count one,' Roach read it out. 'Deserting his learned leader in his hour of need. That is to say on the occasion of his leader having been given the sack. Particulars of offence . . .'

'Mr Senior. Have five minutes elapsed?' Allen asked.

'Five minutes having elapsed since the loyal toast, you may now smoke.'

Tommy Pierce lit a large cigar. I lit a small one. Mr Junior Roach continued to intone.

'The said Rumpole did add considerably to the seriousness of the offence by proceeding to win in the absence of his learned leader.'

'Mr Junior. Has Rumpole anything to say by way of mitigation?'

'Rumpole.' Roach took out his watch – clearly there was a time limit in speeches. I rose to express my deepest thoughts, loosened by the gentle action of the port.

'The show had to go on!'

'What? What did Rumpole say?' Mr Justice Skelton seemed to have some difficulty in hearing.

'Sometimes. I must admit, sometimes . . . I wonder why,' I went on, 'what sort of show is it exactly? Have you considered what we are *doing* to our clients?'

'Has that port got stuck to the table?' Allen sounded plaintive and the port moved towards him.

'What are we *doing* to them?' I warmed to my work. 'Seeing they wear ties, and hats, keep their hands out of their pockets, keep their voices up, call the judge "my Lord". Generally behave like grocers at a funeral. Whoever they may be.'

'One minute,' said Roach, the time-keeper.

'What do we tell them? Look respectable! Look suitably serious! Swear on the Bible! Say nothing which might upset a jury of lay-preachers, look enormously grateful for the trouble everyone's taking before they bang you up in the nick! What do we find out about our clients in all these trials, do we ever get a fleeting glimpse of the truth? Do we . . . ? Or do we put a hat on the truth. And a tie. And a serious expression. To please the jury and my Lord the judge?' I looked round the table. 'Do you ever worry about that at all? Do you *ever*?'

'Time's up!' said Roach, and I sat down heavily.

'All right. Quite all right. The performance is over.'

Mr Senior swigged down port and proceeded to judgment.

'Rumpole's mitigation has, of course, merely added to the gravity of the offence. Rumpole, at your age and with your experience at the Bar you should have been proud to get the sack, and your further conduct in winning shows a total disregard for the feelings of an extremely sensitive silk. The least sentence I can pass is a fine of twelve bottles of claret. Have you a cheque-book on you?'

So I had no choice but to pull out a cheque-book and start to write. The penalty, apparently, was worth thirty-six quid.

'Members of the Mess will now entertain the company in song,' Roach announced to a rattle of applause.

'Tommy!' Allen shouted.

'No. Really . . .' The learned prosecutor was modest but was

74

prevailed upon by cries of 'Come along, Tommy! Let's have it. "The Road to Mandalay" . . . etc. etc.'

'I'm looking forward to this,' said Mr Justice Skelton, who was apparently easily entertained. As I gave my cheque to young Roach, the stout leading counsel for the Crown, rose and started in a light baritone:

> 'On the Road to Mandalay . . .
> Where the old Flotilla lay . . .
> And the dawn came up like thunder
> Out of China 'cross the Bay!'

Or words to the like effect. I was not really listening. I'd had quite enough of show business.

Rumpole and the Tap End

There are many reasons why I could never become one of Her Majesty's judges. I am unable to look at my customer in the dock without feeling 'There but for the grace of God goes Horace Rumpole.' I should find it almost impossible to order any fellow citizen to be locked up in a Victorian slum with a couple of psychopaths and three chamber-pots, and I cannot imagine a worse way of passing your life than having to actually listen to the speeches of the learned friends. It also has to be admitted that no sane Lord Chancellor would ever dream of the appointment of Mr Justice Rumpole. There is another danger inherent in the judicial office: a judge, any judge, is always liable to say, in a moment of boredom or impatience, something downright silly. He is then denounced in the public prints, his resignation is called for, he is stigmatized as malicious or at least mad and his Bench becomes a bed of nails and his ermine a hair-shirt. There is, perhaps, no judge more likely to open his mouth and put his foot in it than that, on the whole well-meaning old darling, Mr Justice Featherstone, once Guthrie Featherstone, QC, MP, a member of Parliament so uninterested in politics that he joined the Social Democrats and who, during many eventful years of my life, was head of our chambers in Equity Court. Now, as a judge, Guthrie Featherstone had swum somewhat out of our ken, but he hadn't lost his old talent for giving voice to the odd uncalled-for and disastrous phrase. He, I'm sure, will never forget the furore that arose when, in passing sentence in a case of attempted murder in which I was engaged for the defence, his Lordship made an unwise reference to the 'tap end' of a matrimonial bathtub. At least the account which follows may serve as a terrible warning to anyone contemplating a career as a judge.

I have spoken elsewhere, and on frequent occasions, of my patrons the Timsons, that extended family of South London villains for whom, over the years, I have acted as attorney-general. Some of you may remember Tony Timson, a fairly mild-mannered receiver of stolen video-recorders, hi-fi sets and microwave ovens, married to that April Timson who once so offended her husband's male chauvinist prejudices by driving a getaway car at a somewhat unsuccessful bank robbery. Tony and April lived in a semi on a large housing estate with their offspring, Vincent Timson, now aged eight, who I hoped would grow up in the family business and thus ensure a steady flow of briefs for Rumpole's future. Their house was brightly, not to say garishly, furnished with mock tiger-skin rugs, Italian-tile-style linoleum and wallpaper which simulated oak panelling. (I knew this from a large number of police photographs in various cases.) It was also equipped with almost every labour-saving device which ever dropped off the back of a lorry. On the day when my story starts this desirable home was rent with screams from the bathroom and a stream of soapy water flowed out from under the door. In the screaming, the word 'murderer' was often repeated at a volume which was not only audible to young Vincent, busy pushing a blue-flashing toy police car round the hallway, but to the occupants of the adjoining house and those of the neighbours who were hanging out their washing. Someone, it was not clear who it was at the time, telephoned the local cop shop for assistance.

In a surprisingly short while a real, flashing police car arrived and the front door was flung open by a wet and desperate April Timson, her leopard-skin-style towelling bathrobe clutched about her. As Detective Inspector Brush, an officer who had fought a running battle with the Timson family for years, came up the path to meet her she sobbed out, at the top of her voice, a considerable voice for so petite a redhead, 'Thank God, you've come! He was only trying to bloody murder me.' Tony Timson emerged from the bathroom a few seconds later, water dripping from his earlobe-length hair and his gaucho moustache. In spite of the word RAMBO emblazoned across his bathrobe, he was by no means a man of formidable physique. Looking down the stairs, he saw his wife in hysterics and his domestic hearth invaded by the Old Bill. No sooner had he reached the hallway than he was arrested and charged with attempted murder of his wife, the particulars being that, while sharing a bath with her preparatory to going to a neighbour's party, he had tried to cause her death by drowning.

In course of time I was happy to accept a brief for the defence of Tony Timson and we had a conference in Brixton Prison where the alleged wife-drowner was being held in custody. I was attended, on that occasion, by Mr Bernard, the Timsons' regular solicitor, and that up-and-coming young radical barrister, Mizz Liz Probert, who had been briefed to take a note and generally assist me in the *cause célèbre*.

'Attempted murderer, Tony Timson?' I opened the proceedings on a somewhat incredulous note. 'Isn't that rather out of your league?'

'April told me,' he began his explanation, 'she was planning on wearing her skin-tight leatherette trousers with the revealing halter-neck satin top. That's what she was planning on wearing, Mr Rumpole!'

'A somewhat tasteless outfit, and not entirely *haute couture*,' I admitted. 'But it hardly entitles you to drown your wife, Tony.'

'We was both invited to a party round her friend Chrissie's. And that was the outfit she was keen on wearing . . .'

'She says you pulled her legs and so she became submerged.' Bernard, like a good solicitor, was reading the evidence.

'The Brides in the Bath!' My mind went at once to one of the classic murders of all times. 'The very method! And you hit on it with no legal training. How did you come to be in the same bath, anyway?'

'We always shared, since we was courting.' Tony looked surprised that I had asked. 'Don't all married couples?'

'Speaking for myself and She Who Must Be Obeyed the answer is, thankfully, no. I can't speak for Mr Bernard.'

'Out of the question.' Bernard shook his head sadly. 'My wife has a hip.'

'Sorry, Mr Bernard. I'm really sorry.' Tony Timson was clearly an attempted murderer with a soft heart.

'Quite all right, Mr Timson,' Bernard assured him. 'We're down for a replacement.'

'April likes me to sit up by the taps.' Tony gave us further particulars of the Timson bathing habits. 'So I can rinse off her hair after a shampoo. Anyway, she finds her end that much more comfortable.'

'She makes you sit at the tap end, Tony?' I began to feel for the fellow.

'Oh, I never made no objection,' my client assured me. 'Although you can get your back a bit scalded. And those old taps does dig into you sometimes.'

'So were you on friendly terms when you both entered the water?' My instructing solicitor was quick on the deductions.

'She was all right then. We was both, well, affectionate. Looking forward to the party, like.'

'She didn't object to what you planned on wearing?' I wanted to cover all the possibilities.

'My non-structured silk-style suiting from Toy Boy Limited!' Tony protested. 'How could she object to that, Mr Rumpole? No. She washed her hair as per usual. And I rinsed it off for her. Then she told me who was going to be at the party, like.'

'Mr Peter Molloy,' Bernard reminded me. 'It's in the brief, Mr Rumpole.'

Now I make it a rule to postpone reading my brief until the last possible moment so that it's fresh in my mind when I go into court, so I said, somewhat testily, 'Of course I know that, but I thought I'd like to get the story from the client. Peanuts Molloy! Mizz Probert, we have a defence. Tony Timson's wife was taking him to a party attended by Peanuts Molloy.'

The full implications of this piece of evidence won't be apparent to those who haven't made a close study of my previous handling of the Timson affairs. Suffice it to say the Molloys are to the Timsons as the Montagues were to the Capulets or the Guelphs to the Ghibellines, and their feud goes back to the days when the whole of South London was laid down to pasture, and they were quarrelling about stolen sheep. The latest outbreak of hostilities occurred when certain Molloys, robbing a couple of elderly Timsons as *they* were robbing a bank, almost succeeded in getting Tony's relatives convicted for an offence they had not committed. Peter, better known as 'Peanuts', Molloy was the young hopeful of the clan Molloy and it was small wonder that Tony Timson took great exception to his wife putting on her leatherette trousers for the purpose of meeting the family enemy.

Liz Probert, however, a white-wig at the Bar who knew nothing of such old legal traditions as the Molloy–Timson hostility, said, 'Why should Mrs Timson's meeting Molloy make it all right to drown her?' I have to remind you that Mizz Liz was a pillar of the North Islington women's movement.

'It wasn't just that she was meeting him, Mr Rumpole,' Tony explained. 'It was the words she used.'

'What did she say?'

'I'd rather not tell you if you don't mind. It was humiliating to my pride.'

'Oh, for heaven's sake, Tony. Let's hear the worst.' I had never known a Timson behave so coyly.

'She made a comparison like, between me and Peanuts.'

'What comparison?'

Tony looked at Liz and his voice sank to a whisper. 'Ladies present,' he said.

'Tony,' I had to tell him, 'Mizz Liz Probert has not only practised in the criminal courts, but in the family division. She is active on behalf of gay and lesbian rights in her native Islington. She marches, quite often, in aid of abortion on demand. She is a regular reader of the woman's page of the *Guardian*. You and I, Tony, need have no secrets from Mizz Probert. Now, what was this comparison your wife made between you and Peanuts Molloy?'

'On the topic of virility. I'm sorry, Miss.'

'That's quite all right.' Liz Probert was unshocked and unamused.

'What we need, I don't know if you would agree, Mr Rumpole,' Mr Bernard suggested, 'is a predominance of *men* on the jury.'

'Under-endowed males would condone the attempted murder of a woman, you mean?' The Probert hackles were up.

'Please. Mizz Probert.' I tried to call the meeting to order. 'Let us face this problem in a spirit of detachment. What we need is a sympathetic judge who doesn't want to waste his time on a long case. Have we got a fixed date for this, Mr Bernard?'

'We have, sir. Before the Red Judge.' Mr Bernard meant that Tony Timson was to be tried before the High Court judge visiting the Old Bailey.

'They're pulling out all the stops.' I was impressed.

'It *is* attempted murder, Mr Rumpole. So we're fixed before Mr Justice Featherstone.'

'Guthrie Featherstone.' I thought about it. 'Our one-time head of chambers. Now, I just wonder . . .'

We were in luck. Sir Guthrie Featherstone was in no mood to try a long case, so he summoned me and counsel for the prosecution to his room before the start of the proceedings. He sat robed but with his wig on the desk in front of him, a tall, elegant figure who almost always wore the slightly hunted expression of a man who's not entirely sure what he's up to – an unfortunate state of mind for a fellow who has to spend his waking hours coming to firm and just decisions. For all his indecision, however, he knew for certain that he didn't want to spend the whole day trying a ticklish attempted murder.

'Is this a long case?' the judge asked. 'I am bidden to take tea in the neighbourhood of Victoria. Can you fellows guess where?'

'Sorry, Judge. I give up.' Charles Hearthstoke, our serious-minded young prosecutor, seemed in no mood for party games.

'The station buffet?' I hazarded a guess.

'The station buffet!' Guthrie enjoyed the joke. 'Isn't that you all over, Horace? You will have your joke. Not far off, though.' The joke was over and he went on impressively. 'Buck House. Her Majesty has invited me – no, correction – "commanded" me to a royal garden party.'

'God Save the Queen!' I murmured loyally.

'Not only Her Majesty,' Guthrie told us, 'more seriously, one's lady wife would be extremely put out if one didn't parade in grey top-hat order!'

'He's blaming it on his wife!' Liz Probert, who had followed me into the presence, said in a penetrating aside.

'So naturally one would have to be free by lunchtime. Hearthstoke, is this a long case from the prosecution point of view?' the judge asked.

'It is an extremely serious case, Judge.' Our prosecutor spoke like a man of twice his years. 'Attempted murder. We've put it down for a week.' I have always thought young Charlie Hearthstoke a megasized pill ever since he joined our chambers for a blessedly brief period and tried to get everything run by a computer.

'I'm astonished,' I gave Guthrie a little comfort, 'that my learned friend Mr Hearthrug should think it could possibly last so long.'

'Hearth*stoke*,' young Charlie corrected me.

'Have it your own way. With a bit of common sense we could finish this in half an hour.'

'Thereby saving public time and money.' Hope sprang eternal in the judge's breast.

'Exactly!' I cheered him up. 'As you know, it is an article of my religion never to plead guilty. But, bearing in mind all the facts in this case, I'm prepared to advise Timson to put his hands up to common assault. He'll agree to be bound over to keep the peace.'

'Common assault?' Hearthstoke was furious. 'Binding over? Hold on a minute. He tried to drown her!'

'Judge.' I put the record straight. 'He was seated at the tap end of the bath. His wife, lying back comfortably in the depths, passed an extremely wounding remark about my client's virility.'

It was then I saw Mr Justice Featherstone looking at me, apparently shaken to the core. 'The *tap end*,' he gasped. 'Did you say he was seated at the *tap end*, Horace?'

'I'm afraid so, Judge.' I confirmed the information sorrowfully.

'This troubles me.' Indeed the judge looked extremely troubled. 'How does it come about that he was seated at the tap end?'

'His wife insisted on it.' I had to tell him the full horror of the situation.

'This woman insisted that her husband sat with his back squashed up against the taps?' The judge's voice rose in incredulous outrage.

'She made him sit in that position so he could rinse off her hair.'

'At the *tap end*?' Guthrie still couldn't quite believe it.

'Exactly so.'

'You're sure?'

'There can be no doubt about it.'

'Hearthrug . . . I mean, *stoke*. Is this one of the facts agreed by the prosecution?'

'I can't see that it makes the slightest difference.' The prosecution was not pleased with the course its case was taking.

'You can't see! Horace, was this conduct in any way typical of this woman's attitude to her husband?'

'I regret to say, entirely typical.'

'Rumpole . . .' Liz Probert, appalled by the chauvinist chatter around her, seemed about to burst, and I calmed her with a quiet 'Shut up, Mizz.'

'So you are telling me that this husband deeply resented the position in which he found himself.' Guthrie was spelling out the implications exactly as I had hoped he would.

'What married man wouldn't, Judge?' I asked mournfully.

'And his natural resentment led to a purely domestic dispute?'

'Such as might occur, Judge, in the best bathrooms.'

'And you are content to be bound over to keep the peace?' His Lordship looked at me with awful solemnity.

'Reluctantly, Judge,' I said after a suitable pause for contemplation, 'I would agree to that restriction on my client's liberty.'

'Liberty to drown his wife!' Mizz Probert had to be 'shushed' again.

'Hearth*stoke*.' The judge spoke with great authority. 'My compliments to those instructing you and in my opinion it would be a gross waste of public funds to continue with this charge of attempted murder. We should be finished by half past eleven.' He looked at his watch with the deep satisfaction of a man who was sure that he would be among those present at the royal garden party, after the ritual visit to Moss Bros to hire the grey topper and all the trimmings. As we left the sanctum, I stood aside to let Mizz Probert out of the door. 'Oh, no, Rumpole, you're a man,' she whispered with her fury barely contained. 'Men always go first, don't they?'

★

So we all went into court to polish off *R. v. Timson* and to make sure that Her Majesty had the pleasure of Guthrie's presence over the tea and strawberries. I made a token speech in mitigation, something of a formality as I knew that I was pushing at an open door. While I was speaking, I was aware of the fact that the judge wasn't giving me his full attention. That was reserved for a new young shorthand writer, later to become known to me as a Miss (not, I'm sure in her case, a Mizz) Lorraine Frinton. Lorraine was what I believe used to be known as 'a bit of an eyeful', being young, doe-eyed and clearly surrounded by her own special fragrance. When I sat down, Guthrie thanked me absent-mindedly and reluctantly gave up the careful perusal of Miss Frinton's beauty. He then proceeded to pass sentence on Tony Timson in a number of peculiarly ill-chosen words.

'Timson,' his Lordship began harmlessly enough. 'I have heard about you and your wife's habit of taking a bath together. It is not for this court to say that communal bathing, in time of peace when it is not in the national interest to save water, is appropriate conduct in married life. *Chacun à son goût*, as a wise Frenchman once said.' Miss Frinton, the shorthand writer, looked hopelessly confused by the words of the wise Frenchman. 'What throws a flood of light on this case,' the judge went on, 'is that you, Timson, habitually sat at the tap end of the bath. It seems you had a great deal to put up with. And your wife, she, it appears from the evidence, washed her hair in the more placid waters of the other end. I accept that this was a purely domestic dispute. For the common assault to which you have pleaded guilty you will be bound over to keep the peace . . .' And the judge added the terrible words, '. . . in the sum of fifty pounds.'

So Tony Timson was at liberty, the case was over and a furious Mizz Liz Probert banged out of court before Guthrie was halfway out of the door. Catching up with her, I rebuked my learned junior. 'It's not in the best traditions of the Bar to slam out before the judge in any circumstances. When we've just had a famous victory it's quite ridiculous.'

'A famous victory.' She laughed in a cynical fashion. 'For men!'

'Man, woman or child, it doesn't matter who the client is. We did our best and won.'

'Because he was a man! Why shouldn't he sit at the tap end? I've got to do something about it!' She moved away purposefully.

I called after her. 'Mizz Probert! Where're you going?'

'To my branch of the women's movement. The protest's got to be organized on a national level. I'm sorry, Rumpole. The time for talking's over.'

And she was gone. I had no idea, then, of the full extent of the tide which was about to overwhelm poor old Guthrie Featherstone, but I had a shrewd suspicion that his Lordship was in serious trouble.

The Featherstones' two children were away at university, and Guthrie and Marigold occupied a flat which Lady Featherstone found handy for Harrods, her favourite shopping centre, and a country cottage near Newbury. Marigold Featherstone was a handsome woman who greatly enjoyed life as a judge's wife and was full of that strength of character and quickness of decision his Lordship so conspicuously lacked. They went to the garden party together with three or four hundred other pillars of the establishment: admirals, captains of industry, hospital matrons and drivers of the royal train. Picture them, if you will, safely back home with Marigold kicking off her shoes on the sofa and Guthrie going out to the hall to fetch that afternoon's copy of the *Evening Sentinel*, which had just been delivered. You must, of course, understand that I was not present at the scene or other similar scenes which are necessary to this narrative. I can only do my best to reconstruct it from what I know of subsequent events and what the participants told me afterwards. Any gaps I have been able to fill in are thanks to the talent for fiction which I have acquired during a long career acting for the defence in criminal cases.

'There might just be a picture of us arriving at the Palace.' Guthrie brought back the *Sentinel* and then stood in horror, rooted to the spot by what he saw on the front page.

'Well, then. Bring it in here,' Marigold, no doubt, called from her reclining position.

'Oh, there's absolutely nothing to read in it. The usual nonsense. Nothing of the slightest interest. Well, I think I'll go and have a bath and get changed.' And he attempted to sidle out of the room, holding the newspaper close to his body in a manner which made the contents invisible to his wife.

'Why're you trying to hide that *Evening Sentinel*, Guthrie?'

'Hide it? Of course I'm not trying to hide it. I just thought I'd take it to read in the bath.'

'And make it all soggy? Let me have it, Guthrie.'

'I told you . . .'

'Guthrie. I want to see what's in the paper.' Marigold spoke in an authoritative manner and her husband had no alternative but to hand it over, murmuring the while, 'It's completely inaccurate, of course.'

And so Lady Featherstone came to read, under a large photograph of his Lordship in a full-bottomed wig, the story which was being enjoyed by every member of the legal profession in the Greater London area. CARRY ON DROWNING screamed the banner headline. TAP END JUDGE'S AMAZING DECISION. And then came the full denunciation:

Wives who share baths with their husbands will have to be careful where they sit in the future. Because 29-year-old April Timson of Bexley Heath made her husband Tony sit at the tap end the judge dismissed a charge of attempted murder against him. 'It seems you had a good deal to put up with,' 55-year-old Mr Justice Featherstone told Timson, a 36-year-old window cleaner. 'This is male chauvinism gone mad,' said a spokesperson of the Islington Women's Organization. 'There will be protests up and down the country and questions asked in Parliament. No woman can sit safely in her bath while this judge continues on the Bench.'

'It's a travesty of what I said, Marigold. You know exactly what these court reporters are. Head over heels in Guinness after lunch,' Guthrie no doubt told his wife.

'This must have been in the morning. We went to the Palace after lunch.'

'Well, anyway. It's a travesty.'

'What do you mean, Guthrie? Didn't you say all that about the tap end?'

'Well, I may just have mentioned the tap end. Casually. In passing. Horace told me it was part of the evidence.'

'Horace?'

'Rumpole.'

'I suppose he was defending.'

'Well, yes . . .'

'You're clay in the hands of that little fellow, Guthrie. You're a Red Judge and he's only a junior, but he can twist you round his little finger,' I rather hope she told him.

'You think Horace Rumpole led me up the garden?'

'Of course he did! He got his chap off and he encouraged you to say something monumentally stupid about tap ends. Not, I suppose, that you needed much encouragement.'

'This gives an entirely false impression. I'll put it right, Marigold. I promise you. I'll see it's put right.'

'I think you'd better, Guthrie.' The judge's wife, I knew, was not a woman to mince her words. 'And for heaven's sake try not to put your foot in it again.'

So Guthrie went off to soothe his troubles up to the neck in bathwater and Marigold lay brooding on the sofa until, so she told Hilda later, she was telephoned by the Tom Creevey Diary Column on the *Sentinel* with an enquiry as to which end of the bath she occupied when she and her husband were at their ablutions. Famous couples all over London, she was assured, were being asked the same question. Marigold put down the instrument without supplying any information, merely murmuring to herself, 'Guthrie! What have you done to us now?'

Marigold Featherstone wasn't the only wife appalled by the judge's indiscretions. As I let myself into our mansion flat in the Gloucester Road, Hilda, as was her wont, called to me from the living-room, 'Who's that?'

'I am thy father's spirit,' I told her in sepulchral tones.

> 'Doomed for a certain term to walk the night,
> And for the day confined to fast in fires,
> Till the foul crimes done in my days of nature
> Are burnt and purged away.'

'I suppose you think it's perfectly all right.' She was, I noticed, reading the *Evening Sentinel*.

'What's perfectly all right?'

'Drowning wives!' she said in the unfriendliest of tones. 'Like puppies. I suppose you think that's all perfectly understandable. Well, Rumpole, all I can say is, you'd better not try anything like that with me!'

'Hilda! It's never crossed my mind. Anyway, Tony Timson didn't drown her. He didn't come anywhere near drowning her. It was just a matrimonial tiff in the bathroom.'

'Why should *she* have to sit at the tap end?'

'Why indeed?' I made for the sideboard and a new bottle of Pommeroy's plonk. 'If she had, and if she'd tried to drown him because of it, I'd have defended her with equal skill and success. There you are, you see. Absolutely no prejudice when it comes to accepting a brief.'

'You think men and women are entirely equal?'

'Everyone is equal in the dock.'

'And in the home?'

'Well, yes, Hilda. Of course. Naturally. Although I suppose some are born to command.' I smiled at her in what I hoped was a soothing manner, well designed to unruffle her feathers, and took my glass of claret to my habitual seat by the gasfire. 'Trust me, Hilda,' I told her. 'I shall always be a staunch defender of women's rights.'

'I'm glad to hear that.'

'I'm glad you're glad.'

'That means you can do the weekly shop for us at Safeway's.'

'Well, I'd really love that, Hilda,' I said eagerly. 'I should regard that as the most tremendous fun. Unfortunately I have to earn the boring stuff that pays for our weekly shop. I have to be at the service of my masters.'

'Husbands who try to drown their wives?' she asked unpleasantly.

'And vice versa.'

'They have late-night shopping on Thursdays, Rumpole. It won't cut into your worktime at all. Only into your drinking time in Pommeroy's Wine Bar. Besides which I shall be far too busy for shopping from now on.'

'Why, Hilda? What on earth are you planning to do?' I asked innocently. And when the answer came I knew the sexual revolution had hit Froxbury Mansions at last.

'Someone has to stand up for women's rights,' Hilda told me, 'against the likes of you and Guthrie Featherstone. I shall read for the Bar.'

Such was the impact of the decision in *R. v. Timson* on life in the Rumpole home. When Tony Timson was sprung from custody he was not taken lovingly back into the bosom of his family. April took her baths alone and frequently left the house tricked out in her skintight, wet-look trousers and the exotic halter-neck. When Tony made so bold as to ask where she was going, she told him to mind his own business. Vincent, the young hopeful, also treated his father with scant respect and, when asked where he was off to on his frequent departures from the front door, also told his father to mind his own business.

When she was off on the spree, April Timson, it later transpired, called round to an off-licence in neighbouring Dalton Avenue. There she met the notorious Peanuts Molloy, also dressed in alluring leather, who was stocking up from Ruby, the large black lady who ran the 'offey', with raspberry crush, Champanella, crème de cacao and three-star cognac as his contribution to some party or other. He and April would embrace openly and then go off partying together. On occasion Peanuts would ask her how 'that wally of a husband' was getting on, and express his outrage at the lightness of the sentence inflicted on him. 'Someone ought to give that Tony of yours a bit of justice,' was what he was heard to say.

Peanuts Molloy wasn't alone in feeling that being bound over in the sum of fifty pounds wasn't an adequate punishment for the attempted drowning of a wife. This view was held by most of the newspapers, a large section of the public, and all the members of the North Islington Women's Organization (Chair, Mizz Liz Probert). When Guthrie arrived for business at the judges' entrance of the Old Bailey, he was met by a vociferous posse of women, bearing banners with the following legend: WOMEN OF ENGLAND, KEEP YOUR HEADS ABOVE WATER, GET JUSTICE FEATHERSTONE SACKED. As the friendly police officers kept these angry ladies at bay, Guthrie took what comfort he might from the thought that a High Court judge can only be dismissed by a bill passed through both houses of Parliament.

Something, he decided, would have to be done to answer his many critics. So Guthrie called Miss Lorraine Frinton, the doe-eyed shorthand writer, into his room and did his best to correct the record of his ill-considered judgment. Miss Frinton, breathtakingly decorative as ever, sat with her long legs neatly crossed in the judge's armchair and tried to grasp his intentions with regard to her shorthand note. I reconstruct this conversation thanks to Miss Frinton's later recollection. She was, she admits, very nervous at the time because she thought that the judge had sent for her because she had, in some way, failed in her duties. 'I've been living in dread of someone pulling me up about my shorthand,' she confessed. 'It's not my strongest suit, quite honestly.'

'Don't worry, Miss Frinton,' Guthrie did his best to reassure her. 'You're in no sort of trouble at all. But you are a shorthand writer, of course you are, and if we could just get to the point when I passed sentence. Could you read it out?'

The beautiful Lorraine looked despairingly at her notebook and spelled out, with great difficulty, 'Mr Hearthstoke has quite wisely . . .'

'A bit further on.'

'Jackie a saw goo . . . a wise Frenchman . . .' Miss Frinton was decoding.

'*Chacun à son goût!*'

'I'm sorry, my Lord. I didn't quite get the name.'

'*Ça ne fait rien.*'

'How are you spelling that?' She was now lost.

'Never mind.' The judge was at his most patient. 'A little further on, Miss Frinton. Lorraine. I'm sure you and I can come to an agreement. About a full stop.'

After much hard work, his Lordship had his way with Miss Frinton's shorthand note, and counsel and solicitors engaged in the case were assembled in court to hear, in the presence of the gentlemen of the press, his latest version of his unfortunate judgment.

'I have had my attention drawn to the report of the case in *The Times*,' he started with some confidence, 'in which I am quoted as saying to Timson, "It seems you had a great deal to put up with. And your wife, she, it appears from the evidence, washed her hair in the more placid waters" etc. It's the full stop that has been misplaced. I have checked this carefully with the learned shorthand writer and she agrees with me. I see her nodding her head.' He looked down at Lorraine, who nodded energetically, and the judge smiled at her. 'Very well, yes. The sentence in my judgment in fact read: "It seems you had a great deal to put up with, and your wife." Full stop! What I intended to convey, and I should like the press to take note of this, was that both Mr and Mrs Timson had a good deal to put up with. At different ends of the bath, of course. Six of one and half a dozen of the other. I hope that's clear?' It was, as I whispered to Mizz Probert sitting beside me, as clear as mud.

The judge continued. 'I certainly never said that I regarded being seated at the tap end as legal provocation to attempted murder. I would have said it was one of the facts that the jury might have taken into consideration. It might have thrown some light on this wife's attitude to her husband.'

'What's he trying to do?' *sotto voce* Hearthstoke asked me.

'Trying to get himself out of hot water,' I suggested.

'But the attempted murder charge was dropped,' Guthrie went on.

'He twisted my arm to drop it,' Hearthstoke was muttering.

'And the entire tap end question was really academic,' Guthrie told us, 'as Timson pleaded guilty to common assault. Do you agree, Mr Rumpole?'

'Certainly, my Lord.' I rose in my most servile manner. 'You gave him a very stiff binding over.'

'Have you anything to add, Mr Hearthstoke?'

'No, my Lord.' Hearthstoke couldn't very well say anything else, but when the judge had left us he warned me that Tony Timson had better watch his step in future as Detective Inspector Brush was quite ready to throw the book at him.

Guthrie Featherstone left court well pleased with himself and instructed his aged and extremely disloyal clerk, Wilfred, to send a bunch of flowers, or, even better, a handsome pot plant to Miss Lorraine Frinton in recognition of her loyal services. So Wilfred told me he went off to telephone Interflora and Guthrie passed his day happily trying a perfectly straightforward robbery. On rising he retired to his room for a cup of weak Lapsang and a glance at the *Evening Sentinel*. This glance was enough to show him that he had achieved very little more, by his statement in open court, than inserting his foot into the mud to an even greater depth.

BATHTUB JUDGE SAYS IT AGAIN screamed the headline. *Putting her husband at the tap end may be a factor to excuse the attempted murder of a wife.*

'Did I say that?' the appalled Guthrie asked old Wilfred who was busy pouring out the tea.

'To the best of my recollection, my Lord. Yes.'

There was no comfort for Guthrie when the telephone rang. It was old Keith from the Chancellor's office saying that the Lord Chancellor, as head of the judiciary, would like to see Mr Justice Featherstone at the earliest available opportunity.

'A bill through the houses of Parliament.' A stricken Guthrie put down the telephone. 'Would they do it to me, Wilfred?' he asked, but answer came there none.

' "You do look," my clerk, "in a moved sort, as if you were dismayed." ' In fact, Henry, when I encountered him in the clerk's room, seemed distinctly rattled. 'Too right, sir. I am dismayed. I've just had Mrs Rumpole on the telephone.'

'Ah. She Who Must wanted to speak to me?'

'No, Mr Rumpole. She wanted to speak to me. She said I'd be clerking for her in the fullness of time.'

'Henry,' I tried to reassure the man, 'there's no immediate cause for concern.'

'She said as she was reading for the Bar, Mr Rumpole, to make sure women get a bit of justice in the future.'

'Your missus coming into chambers, Rumpole?' Uncle Tom, our oldest and quite briefless inhabitant, was pursuing his usual hobby of making approach shots to the waste-paper basket with an old putter.

'Don't worry, Uncle Tom.' I sounded as confident as I could. 'Not in the foreseeable future.'

'My motto as a barrister's clerk, sir, is anything for a quiet life,' Henry outlined his philosophy. 'I have to say that my definition of a quiet life does not include clerking for Mrs Hilda Rumpole.'

'Old Sneaky MacFarlane in Crown Office Row had a missus who came into his chambers.' Uncle Tom was off down Memory Lane. 'She didn't come in to practise, you understand. She came in to watch Sneaky. She used to sit in the corner of his room and knit during all his conferences. It seems she was dead scared he was going to get off with one of his female divorce petitioners.'

'Mrs Rumpole, Henry, has only just written off for a legal course in the Open University. She can't yet tell provocation from self-defence or define manslaughter.' I went off to collect things from my tray and Uncle Tom missed a putt and went on with his story.

'And you know what? In the end Mrs MacFarlane went off with a co-respondent she'd met at one of these conferences. Some awful fellow, apparently, in black and white shoes! Left poor old Sneaky high and dry. So, you see, it doesn't do to have wives in chambers.'

'Oh, I meant to ask you, Henry. Have you seen my Ackerman on *The Causes of Death?*' One of my best-loved books had gone missing.

'I think Mr Ballard's borrowed it, sir.' And then Henry asked, still anxious, 'How long do they take then, those courses at the Open University?'

'Years, Henry,' I told him. 'It's unlikely to finish during our lifetime.'

When I went up to Ballard's room to look for my beloved Ackerman, the door had been left a little open. Standing in the corridor I could hear the voices of those arch-conspirators, Claude Erskine-Brown and Soapy Sam Ballard, QC. I have to confess that I lingered to catch a little of the dialogue.

'Keith from the Lord Chancellor's office sounded *you* out about Guthrie Featherstone?' Erskine-Brown was asking.

'As the fellow who took over his chambers. He thought I might have a view.'

'And have you? A view, I mean.'

'I told Keith that Guthrie was a perfectly charming chap, of course.' Soapy Sam was about to damn Guthrie with the faintest of praise.

'Oh, perfectly charming. No doubt about that,' Claude agreed.

'But as a judge, perhaps, he lacks judgement.'

'Which is a pretty important quality in a judge,' Claude thought.

'Exactly. And perhaps there is some lack of . . .'

'Gravitas?'

'The very word I used, Claude.'

'There was a bit of lack of gravitas in chambers, too,' Claude remembered, 'when Guthrie took a shine to a temporary typist . . .'

'So the upshot of my talk with Keith was . . .'

'What was the upshot?'

'I think we may be seeing a vacancy on the High Court Bench.' Ballard passed on the sad news with great satisfaction. 'And old Keith was kind enough to drop a rather interesting hint.'

'Tell me, Sam?'

'He said they might be looking for a replacement from the same stable.'

'Meaning these chambers in Equity Court?'

'How could it mean anything else?'

'Sam, if you go on the Bench, we should need another silk in chambers!' Claude was no doubt licking his lips as he considered the possibilities.

'I don't see how they could refuse you.' These two were clearly hand in glove.

'There's no doubt Guthrie'll have to go.' Claude pronounced the death sentence on our absent friend.

'He comes out with such injudicious remarks.' Soapy Sam put in another drop of poison. 'He was just like that at Marlborough.'

'Did you tell old Keith that?' Claude asked and then sat open-mouthed as I burst from my hiding-place with 'I bet you did!'

'Rumpole!' Ballard also looked put out. 'What on earth have you been doing?'

'I've been listening to the Grand Conspiracy.'

'You must admit, Featherstone J. has made the most tremendous boo-boo.' Claude smiled as though he had never made a boo-boo in his life.

'In the official view,' Soapy Sam told me, 'he's been remarkably stupid.'

'He wasn't stupid.' I briefed myself for Guthrie's defence. 'As a matter of fact he understood the case extremely well. He came to a wise decision. He might have phrased his judgment more elegantly, if he hadn't been to Marlborough. And let me tell you something, Ballard. My wife, Hilda, is about to start a law course at the Open University. She is a woman, as I know to my cost, of grit and determination. I expect to see her Lord Chief Justice of England before you get your bottom within a mile of the High Court Bench!'

'Of course you're entitled to your opinion.' Ballard looked tolerant. 'And you got your fellow off. All I know for certain is that the Lord Chancellor has summoned Guthrie Featherstone to appear before him.'

The Lord Chancellor of England was a small, fat, untidy man with steel-rimmed spectacles which gave him the schoolboy look which led to his nickname 'the Owl of the Remove'. He was given to fits of teasing when he would laugh aloud at his own jokes and unpredictable bouts of biting sarcasm during which he would stare at his victims with cold hostility. He had been, for many years, the captain of the House of Lords croquet team, a game in which his ruthless cunning found full scope. He received Guthrie in his large, comfortably furnished room overlooking the Thames at Westminster, where his long wig was waiting on its stand and his gold-embroidered purse and gown were ready for his procession to the woolsack. Two years after this confrontation, I found myself standing with Guthrie at a Christmas party given in our chambers to members past and present, and he was so far gone in *Brut* (not to say *Brutal*) Pommeroy's *Méthode Champenoise* as to give me the bare bones of this historic encounter. I have fleshed them out from my knowledge of both characters and their peculiar habits of speech.

'Judgeitis, Featherstone,' I hear the Lord Chancellor saying. 'It goes with piles as one of the occupational hazards of the judicial profession. Its symptoms are pomposity and self-regard. It shows itself by unnecessary interruptions during the proceedings or giving utterance to private thoughts far, far better left unspoken.'

'I did correct the press report, Lord Chancellor, with reference to the shorthand writer.' Guthrie tried to sound convincing.

'Oh, I read that.' The Chancellor was unimpressed. 'Far better to have left the thing alone. Never give the newspapers a second chance. That's my advice to you.'

'What's the cure for judgeitis?' Guthrie asked anxiously.

'Banishment to a golf club where the sufferer may bore the other members to death with recollections of his old triumphs on the Western Circuit.'

'You mean, a bill through two houses of Parliament?' The judge stared into the future, dismayed.

'Oh, that's quite unnecessary!' The Chancellor laughed mirthlessly. 'I just get a judge in this room and say, "Look here, old fellow. You've got it badly. Judgeitis. The press is after your blood and quite frankly you're a profound embarrassment to us all. Go out to Esher, old boy," I say, "and improve your handicap. I'll give it out that you're retiring early for reasons of health." And then I'll make a speech defending the independence of the judiciary against scurrilous and unjustified attacks by the press.'

Guthrie thought about this for what seemed a silent eternity and then said, 'I'm not awfully keen on golf.'

'Why not take up croquet?' The Chancellor seemed anxious to be helpful. 'It's a top-hole retirement game. The women of England are against you. I hear they've been demonstrating outside the Old Bailey.'

'They were only a few extremists.'

'Featherstone, all women are extremists. You must know that, as a married man.'

'I suppose you're right, Lord Chancellor.' Guthrie now felt his position to be hopeless. 'Retirement! I don't know how Marigold's going to take it.'

The Lord Chancellor still looked like a hanging judge, but he stood up and said in businesslike tones, 'Perhaps it can be postponed in your case. I've talked it over with old Keith.'

'Your right-hand man?' Guthrie felt a faint hope rising.

'Exactly.' The Lord Chancellor seemed to be smiling at some private joke. 'You may have an opportunity some time in the future, in the not-too-distant future, let us hope, to make your peace with the women of England. You may be able to put right what they regard as an injustice to one of their number.'

'You mean, Lord Chancellor, my retirement is off?' Guthrie could scarcely believe it.

'Perhaps adjourned. *Sine die.*'

'Indefinitely?'

'Oh, I'm so glad you keep up with your Latin.' The Chancellor patted Guthrie on the shoulder. It was an order to dismiss. 'So many fellows don't.'

So Guthrie had a reprieve and, in the life of Tony Timson also, dramatic events were taking place. April's friend Chrissie was once married to Shaun Molloy, a well-known safe-breaker, but their divorce seemed to have severed her connections with the Molloy clan and Tony Timson had agreed to receive and visit her. It was Chrissie who lived on their estate and had given the party before which April and Tony had struggled in the bath together; but it was at Chrissie's house, it seemed, that Peanuts Molloy was to be a visitor. So Tony's friendly feelings had somewhat abated, and when Chrissie rang the chimes on his front door one afternoon when April was out, he received her with a brusque 'What you want?'

'I thought you ought to know, Tony. It's not right.'

'What's not right?'

'Your April and Peanuts. It's not right.'

'You're one to talk, aren't you, Chrissie? April was going round yours to meet Peanuts at a party.'

'He just keeps on coming to mine. I don't invite him. Got no time for Peanuts, quite honestly. But him and your April. They're going out on dates. It's not right. I thought you ought to know.'

'What you mean, dates?' As I have said, Tony's life had not been a bed of roses since his return home, but now he was more than usually troubled.

'He takes her out partying. They're meeting tonight round the offey in Dalton Avenue. Nine-thirty time, she told me. Just thought you might like to know, that's all,' the kindly Chrissie added.

So it happened that at nine-thirty that night, when Ruby was presiding over an empty off-licence in Dalton Avenue, Tony Timson entered it and stood apparently surveying the tempting bottles on display but really waiting to confront the errant April and Peanuts Molloy. He heard a door bang in some private area behind Ruby's counter and then the strip lights stopped humming and the off-licence was plunged into darkness. It was not a silent darkness, however; it was filled with the sound of footsteps, scuffling and heavy blows.

Not long afterwards a police car with a wailing siren was screaming towards Dalton Avenue; it was wonderful with what rapidity the Old Bill was summoned whenever Tony Timson was in trouble. When Detective Inspector Brush and his sergeant got into the off-licence, their torches illuminated a scene of violence. Two bodies were on the floor. Ruby was lying by the counter, unconscious, and Tony was lying beside some shelves, nearer to the door, with a wound in his forehead. The sergeant's torch beam showed a heavy

cosh lying by his right hand and pound notes scattered around him.
'Can't you leave the women alone, boy?' the detective inspector said
as Tony Timson slowly opened his eyes.

So another Timson brief came to Rumpole, and Mr Justice Featherstone got a chance to redeem himself in the eyes of the Lord
Chancellor and the women of Islington.

Like two knights of old approaching each other for combat, briefs
at the ready, helmeted with wigs and armoured with gowns, the
young black-haired Sir Hearthrug and the cunning old Sir Horace,
with his faithful page Mizz Liz in attendance, met outside Number
One Court at the Old Bailey and threw down their challenges.

'Nemesis,' said Hearthrug.

'What's that meant to mean?' I asked him.

'Timson's for it now.'

'Let's hope justice will be done,' I said piously.

'Guthrie's not going to make the same mistake twice.'

'Mr Justice Featherstone's a wise and upright judge,' I told him,
'even if his foot does get into his mouth occasionally.'

'He's a judge with the Lord Chancellor's beady eye upon him,
Rumpole.'

'I wasn't aware that this case was going to be decided by the Lord
Chancellor.'

'By him and the women of England.' Hearthstoke smiled at Mizz
Probert in what I hoped she found a revolting manner. 'Ask your
learned junior.'

'Save your breath for court, Hearthrug. You may need it.'

So we moved on, but as we went my learned junior disappointed
me by saying, 'I don't think Tony Timson should get away with it
again.'

'Happily, that's not for you to decide,' I told her. 'We can leave
that to the good sense of the jury.'

However, the jury, when we saw them assembled, were not a particularly cheering lot. For a start, the women outnumbered the men
by eight to four and the women in question looked large and severe.
I was at once reminded of the mothers' meetings that once gathered

round the guillotine and I seemed to hear, as Hearthstoke opened the prosecution case, the ghostly click of knitting-needles.

His opening speech was delivered with a good deal of ferocity and he paused now and again to flash a white-toothed smile at Miss Lorraine Frinton, who sat once more, looking puzzled, in front of her shorthand notebook.

'Members of the Jury,' Hearthrug intoned with great solemnity. 'Even in these days, when we are constantly sickened by crimes of violence, this is a particularly horrible and distressing event. An attack with this dangerous weapon' – here he picked up the cosh, Exhibit One, and waved it at the jury – 'upon a weak and defence-less woman.'

'Did you say a *woman*, Mr Hearthstoke?' Up spoke the anxious figure of the Red Judge upon the Bench. I cannot believe that pure chance had selected Guthrie Featherstone to preside over Tony Timson's second trial.

Our judge clearly meant to redeem himself and appear, from the outset, as the dedicated protector of that sex which is sometimes called the weaker by those who have not the good fortune to be married to She Who Must Be Obeyed.

'I'm afraid so, my Lord,' Hearthstoke said, more in anger than in sorrow.

'This man Timson attacked a *woman*!' Guthrie gave the jury the benefit of his full outrage. I had to put some sort of a stop to this so I rose to say, 'That, my Lord, is something the jury has to decide.'

'Mr Rumpole,' Guthrie told me, 'I am fully aware of that. All I can say about this case is that should the jury convict, I take an extremely serious view of any sort of attack on a woman.'

'If they were bathing it wouldn't matter,' I muttered to Liz as I subsided.

'I didn't hear that, Mr Rumpole.'

'Not a laughing matter, my Lord,' I corrected myself rapidly.

'Certainly not. Please proceed, Mr Hearth*stoke*.' And here his Lordship whispered to his clerk, Wilfred, 'I'm not having old Rumpole twist me round his little finger in *this* case.'

'Very wise, if I may say so, my Lord,' Wilfred whispered back as he sat beside the judge, sharpening his pencils.

'Members of the Jury,' an encouraged Hearthstoke proceeded. 'Mrs Ruby Churchill, the innocent victim, works in an off-licence near the man Timson's home. Later we shall look at a plan of the premises. The prosecution does not allege that Timson carried out this robbery alone. He no doubt had an accomplice who entered by an open window at the back of the shop and turned out the lights. Then, we say, under cover of darkness, Timson coshed the unfortunate Mrs Churchill, whose evidence you will hear. The accomplice escaped with most of the money from the till. Timson, happily for justice, slipped and struck his head on the corner of the shelves. He was found in a half-stunned condition, with the cosh and some of the money. When arrested by Detective Inspector Brush he said, "You got me this time, then." You may think that a clear admission of guilt.' And now Hearthstoke was into his peroration. 'Too long, Members of the Jury,' he said, 'have women suffered in our courts. Too long have men seemed licensed to attack them. Your verdict in this case will be awaited eagerly and hopefully by the women of England.'

I looked at Mizz Liz Probert and I was grieved to note that she was receiving this hypocritical balderdash with starry-eyed attention. During the mercifully short period when the egregious Hearthrug had been a member of our chambers in Equity Court, I remembered, Mizz Liz had developed an inexplicably soft spot for the fellow. I was pained to see that the spot remained as soft as ever.

Even as we sat in Number One Court, the Islington women were on duty in the street outside bearing placards with the legend JUSTICE FOR WOMEN. Claude Erskine-Brown and Soapy Sam Ballard passed these demonstrators and smiled with some satisfaction. 'Guthrie's in the soup again, Ballard,' Claude told his new friend. 'They're taking to the streets!'

Ruby Churchill, large, motherly, and clearly anxious to tell the truth, was the sort of witness it's almost impossible to cross-examine effectively. When she had told her story to Hearthstoke, I rose and felt the silent hostility of both judge and jury.

'Before you saw him in your shop on the night of this attack,' I asked her, 'did you know my client, Mr Timson?'

'I knew him. He lives round the corner.'

'And you knew his wife, April Timson?'

'I know her. Yes.'

'She's been in your shop?'

'Oh, yes, sir.'

'With her husband?'

'Sometimes with him. Sometimes without.'

'Sometimes without? How interesting.'

'Mr Rumpole. Have you many more questions for this unfortunate lady?' Guthrie seemed to have been converted to the view that female witnesses shouldn't be subjected to cross-examination.

'Just a few, my Lord.'

'Please. Mrs Churchill,' his Lordship gushed at Ruby. 'Do take a seat. Make yourself comfortable. I'm sure we all admire the plucky way in which you are giving your evidence. *As a woman.*'

'And as a woman,' I made bold to ask, after Ruby had been offered all the comforts of the witness-box, 'did you know that Tony Timson had been accused of trying to drown his wife in the bath? And that he was tried and bound over?'

'My Lord. How can that possibly be relevant?' Hearthrug arose, considerably narked.

'I was about to ask the same question.' Guthrie sided with the prosecution. 'I have no idea what Mr Rumpole is driving at!'

'Oh, I thought your Lordship might remember the case,' I said casually. 'There was some newspaper comment about it at the time.'

'Was there really?' Guthrie affected ignorance. 'Of course, in a busy life one can't hope to read every little paragraph about one's cases that finds its way into the newspapers.'

'This found its way slap across the front page, my Lord.'

'Did it really? Do you remember that, Mr Hearthstoke?'

'I think I remember some rather ill-informed comment, my Lord.' Hearthstoke was not above buttering up the Bench.

'Ill-informed. Yes. No doubt it was. One has so many cases before one . . .' As Guthrie tried to forget the past, I hastily drew the witness back into the proceedings.

'Perhaps your memory is better than his Lordship's?' I suggested to Ruby. 'You remember the case, don't you, Mrs Churchill?'

'Oh, yes. I remember it.' Ruby had no doubt.

'Mr Hearthstoke. Are you objecting to this?' Guthrie was looking puzzled.

'If Mr Rumpole wishes to place his client's previous convictions before the jury, my Lord, why should I object?' Hearthstoke looked at me complacently, as though I were playing into his hands, and Guthrie whispered to Wilfred, 'Bright chap, this prosecutor.'

'And can you remember what you thought about it at the time?' I went on plugging away at Ruby.

'I thought Mr Timson had got away with murder!'

The jury looked severely at Tony, and Guthrie appeared to think I had kicked a sensational own goal. 'I suppose that was hardly the answer you wanted, Mr Rumpole,' he said.

'On the contrary, my Lord. It was exactly the answer I wanted! And having got away with it then, did it occur to you that someone . . . some avenging angel, perhaps, might wish to frame Tony Timson on this occasion?'

'My Lord. That is pure speculation!' Hearthstoke arose, furious, and I agreed with him.

'Of course it is. But it's a speculation I wish to put in the mind of the jury at the earliest possible opportunity.' So I sat down, conscious that I had at least chipped away at the jury's certainty. They knew that I should return to the possibility of Tony having been framed and were prepared to look at the evidence with more caution.

That morning two events of great pith and moment occurred in the case of the Queen against Tony Timson. April went shopping in Dalton Avenue and saw something which considerably changed her attitude. Peanuts Molloy and her friend Chrissie were coming out of the off-licence with a plastic bag full of assorted bottles. As Peanuts held his car door open for Chrissie they engaged in a passionate and public embrace, unaware that they were doing so in the full view of Mrs April Timson, who uttered the single word 'Bastard!' in the hearing of the young hopeful Vincent who, being on his school holidays, was accompanying his mother. The other important matter was that Guthrie, apparently in a generous mood as he saw a chance of re-establishing his judicial reputation, sent a note to me and Hearthstoke asking if we would be so kind as to join him, and the other judges sitting at the Old Bailey, for luncheon.

Guthrie's invitation came as Hearthstoke was examining Miss Sweating, the schoolmistress-like scientific officer, who was giving evidence as to the bloodstains found about the off-licence on the night of the crime. As this evidence was of some importance, I should record that blood of Tony Timson's group was traced, on the floor and on the corner of the shelf by which he had fallen. Blood of the same group as that which flowed in Mrs Ruby Churchill's veins was to be found on the floor where she lay and on the cosh by Tony's hand. Talk of blood groups, as you will know, acts on me like the smell of greasepaint to an old actor, or the cry of hounds to John Peel. I was pawing the ground and snuffling a little at the nostrils as I rose to cross-examine.

'Miss Sweating,' I began. 'You say there was blood of Timson's group on the corner of the shelf?'

'There was. Yes.'

'And from that you assumed that he had hit his head against the shelf?'

'That seemed the natural assumption. He had been stunned by hitting his head.'

'Or by someone else hitting his head?'

'But the detective inspector told me . . .' the witness began, but I interrupted her with 'Listen to me and don't bother about what the detective inspector told you!'

'Mr Rumpole!' That grave protector of the female sex on the Bench looked pained. 'Is that the tone to adopt? The witness is a woman!'

'The witness is a scientific officer, my Lord,' I pointed out, 'who pretends to know something about bloodstains. Looking at the photograph of the stains on the corner of the shelf, Miss Sweating, might not they be splashes of blood which fell when the accused was struck in that part of the room?'

Miss Sweating examined the photograph in question through her formidable horn-rims and we were granted two minutes' silence which I broke into at last with 'Would you favour us with an answer, Miss Sweating? Or do you want to exercise a woman's privilege and not make up your mind?'

'Mr Rumpole!' The newly converted feminist judge was outraged.

But the witness admitted, 'I suppose they might have got there like that. Yes.'

'They are consistent with his having been struck by an assailant. Perhaps with another weapon similar to this cosh?'

'Yes,' Miss Sweating agreed, reluctantly.

'Thank you. "Trip no further, pretty sweeting . . ."' I whispered as I sat down, thereby shocking the shockable Mizz Probert.

'Miss Sweating' – Guthrie tried to undo my good work – 'you have also said that the bloodstains on the shelf are consistent with Timson having slipped when he was running out of the shop and striking his head against it?'

'Oh, yes,' Miss Sweating agreed eagerly. 'They are consistent with that, my Lord.'

'Very well.' His Lordship smiled ingratiatingly at the women of the jury. 'Perhaps the ladies of the jury would like to take a little light luncheon now?' And he added, more brusquely, 'The gentlemen too, of course. Back at five past two, Members of the Jury.'

When we got out of court, I saw my learned friend Charles Hearthstoke standing in the corridor in close conversation with the beautiful shorthand writer. He was, I noticed, holding her lightly and unobtrusively by the hand. Mizz Probert, who also noticed this, walked away in considerable disgust.

A large variety of judges sit at the Old Bailey. These include the Old Bailey regulars, permanent fixtures such as the Mad Bull Bullingham and the sepulchral Graves, judges of the lower echelon, who

wear black gowns. They also include a judge called the Common
Sergeant, who is neither common nor a sergeant, and the Recorder,
who wears red and is the senior Old Bailey judge – a man who has
to face, apart from the usual diet of murder, robbery and rape, a
daunting number of City dinners. These are joined by the two visiting High Court judges, the Red Judges of the Queen's Bench, of
whom Guthrie was one, unless and until the Lord Chancellor
decided to put him permanently out to grass. All these judicial figures trough together at a single long table in a back room of the
Bailey. They do it, and the sight comes as something of a shock to
the occasional visitor, wearing their wigs. The sight of Judge Bullingham's angry and purple face ingesting stew and surmounted
with horse-hair is only for the strongest stomachs. They are joined
by various City aldermen and officials wearing lace jabots and tailed
coats and other guests from the Bar or from the world of business.

Before the serious business of luncheon begins, the company is
served sherry, also taken while wearing wigs, and I was ensconced
in a corner where I could overhear a somewhat strange preliminary
conversation between our judge and counsel for the prosecution.

'Ah, Hearth*stoke*,' Guthrie greeted him. 'I thought I'd invite both
counsel to break bread with me. Just want to make sure neither of
you had anything to object to about the trial.'

'Of course not, Judge!' Hearthstoke was smiling. 'It's been a very
pleasant morning. Made even more pleasant by the appearance of
the shorthand writer.'

'The . . . ? Oh, yes! Pretty girl, is she? I hadn't noticed,' Guthrie
fibbed.

'Hadn't you? Lorraine said you'd been extraordinarily kind to
her. She so much appreciated the beautiful pot plant you sent her.'

'Pot plant?' Guthrie looked distinctly guilty, but Hearthstoke
pressed on with 'Something rather gorgeous she told me. With pink
blooms. Didn't she help you straighten out the shorthand note in
the last Timson case?'

'She corrected her mistake,' Guthrie said carefully.

'*Her* mistake, was it?' Hearthstoke was looking at the judge. 'She
said it'd been yours.'

'Perhaps we should all sit down now.' Guthrie was keen to end this embarrassing scene. 'Oh and, Hearthstoke, no need to mention that business of the pot plant around the Bailey. Otherwise they'll all be wanting one.' He gave a singularly unconvincing laugh. 'I can't give pink blooms to everyone, including Rumpole!'

'Of course, Judge.' Hearthstoke was understanding. 'No need to mention it at all *now*.'

'*Now?*'

'Now,' the prosecutor said firmly, 'justice is going to be done to Timson. At last.'

Guthrie seemed thankful to move away and find his place at the table, until he discovered that I had been put next to him. He made the best of it, pushed one of the decanters in my direction and hoped I was quite satisfied with the fairness of the proceedings.

'Are *you* content with the fairness of the proceedings?' I asked him.

'Yes, of course. I'm the judge, aren't I?'

'Are you sure?'

'What on earth's that meant to mean?'

'Haven't you asked yourself why you, a High Court judge, a Red Judge, have been given a paltry little robbery with violence?' I refreshed myself with a generous gulp of the City of London's claret.

'I suppose it's the luck of the draw.'

'Luck of the draw, my eye! I detect the subtle hand of old Keith from the Lord Chancellor's office.'

'Keith?' His Lordship looked around him nervously.

'Oh, yes. "Give Guthrie *Timson*," he said. "Give him a chance to redeem himself by potting the fellow and sending him down for ten years. The women of England will give three hearty cheers and Featherstone will be the Lord Chancellor's blue-eyed boy again." Don't fall for it! You can be better than that, if you put your mind to it. Sum up according to the evidence and the hell with the Lord Chancellor's office!'

'Horace! I don't think I've heard anything you've been saying.'

'It's up to you, old darling. Are you a man or a rubber stamp for the Civil Service?'

Guthrie looked round desperately for a new subject of conversation and his eye fell on our prosecutor who was being conspicuously bored by an elderly alderman. 'That young Hearthstoke seems a pretty able sort of fellow,' he said.

'Totally ruthless,' I told him. 'He'd stop at nothing to win a case.'

'Nothing?'

'Absolutely nothing.'

Guthrie took the decanter and started to pour wine into his own glass. His hand was trembling slightly and he was staring at Hearthstoke in a haunted way.

'Horace,' he started confidentially, 'you've been practising at the Old Bailey for a considerable number of years.'

'Almost since the dawn of time.'

'And you can see nothing wrong with a judge, impressed by the hard work of a court official, say a shorthand writer, for instance, sending that official some little token of gratitude?'

'What sort of token are you speaking of, Judge?'

'Something like' – he gulped down wine – 'a pot plant.'

'A plant?'

'In a pot. With pink blossoms.'

'Pink blossoms, eh?' I thought it over. 'That sounds quite appropriate.'

'You can see nothing in any way improper in such a gift, Horace?' The judge was deeply grateful.

'Nothing improper at all. A "busy Lizzie"?'

'I think her name's Lorraine.'

'Nothing wrong with that.'

'You reassure me, Horace. You comfort me very much.' He took another swig of the claret and looked fearfully at Hearthstoke. Poor old Guthrie Featherstone, he spent most of his judicial life painfully perched between the horns of various dilemmas.

'In the car after we arrested him, driving away from the off-licence, Tony Timson said, "You got me this time, then."' This was the evidence of that hammer of the Timsons, Detective Inspector Brush. When he had given it, Hearthstoke looked hard at the jury to emphasize the point, thanked the officer profusely and I rose to cross-examine.

'Detective Inspector. Do you know a near neighbour of the Timsons named Peter, better known as "Peanuts", Molloy?'

'Mr Peter Molloy is known to the police, yes,' the inspector answered cautiously.

'He and his brother Greg are leading lights of the Molloy firm? Fairly violent criminals?'

'Yes, my Lord,' Brush told the judge.

'Have you known both Peanuts and his brother to use coshes like this one in the course of crime?'

'Well. Yes, possibly . . .'

'My Lord, I really must object!' Hearthstoke was on his feet and Guthrie said, 'Mr Rumpole. Your client's own character . . .'

'He is a petty thief, my Lord.' I was quick to put Tony's character before the jury. 'Tape-recorders and freezer-packs. No violence in his record, is there, Inspector?'

'Not up to now, my Lord,' Brush agreed reluctantly.

'Very well. Did you think he had been guilty of that attempted murder charge, after he and his wife quarrelled in the bathroom?'

'I thought so, yes.'

'You were called to the scene very quickly when the quarrel began.'

'A neighbour called us.'

'Was that neighbour a member of the Molloy family?'

'Mr Rumpole, I prefer not to answer that question.'

'I won't press it.' I left the jury to speculate. 'But you think he got off lightly at his first trial?' I was reading the note Tony Timson had scribbled in the dock while listening to the evidence as DI Brush answered, 'I thought so, yes.'

'What he actually said in the car was "I suppose you think you got me this time, then?"'

'No.' Brush looked at his notebook. 'He just said, "You got me this time, then."'

'You left out the words "I suppose you think" because you don't want him to get off lightly this time?'

'Now would I do a thing like that, sir?' Brush gave us his most honestly pained expression.

'That, Inspector Brush, is a matter for this jury to decide.' And the jury looked, by now, as though they were prepared to consider all the possibilities.

Lord Justice MacWhitty's wife, it seems, met Marigold Featherstone in Harrods, and told her she was sorry that Guthrie had such a terrible attitude to women. There was one old judge, apparently, who made his wife walk behind him when he went on circuit, carrying the luggage, and Lady MacWhitty said she felt that poor Marigold was married to just such a tyrant. When we finally discussed the whole history of the Tony Timson case at the chambers party, Guthrie told me that Marigold had said that she was sick and tired of women coming up to her and feeling sorry for her in Harrods.

'You see,' Guthrie had said to his wife, 'if Timson gets off, the Lord Chancellor and all the women of England will be down on me like a ton of bricks. But the evidence isn't entirely satisfactory. It's just possible he's innocent. It's hard to tell where a fellow's duty lies.'

'Your duty, Guthrie, lies in keeping your nose clean!' Marigold had no doubt about it.

'My nose?'

'Clean. For the sake of your family. And if this Timson has to go inside for a few years, well, I've no doubt he richly deserves it.'

'Nothing but decisions!'

'I really don't know what else you expected when you became a judge.' Marigold poured herself a drink. Seeking some comfort after a hard day, the judge went off to soak in a hot bath. In doing so, I believe Lady Featherstone made it clear to him, he was entirely on his own.

Things were no easier in the Rumpole household. I was awakened at some unearthly hour by the wireless booming in the living-room and I climbed out of bed to see Hilda, clad in a dressing-gown and hairnet, listening to the device with her pencil and notebook poised while it greeted her brightly with 'Good morning, students. This is first-year Criminal Law on the Open University.

I am Richard Snellgrove, law teacher at Hollowfield Polytechnic, to help you on this issue . . . Can a wife give evidence against her husband?'

'Good God!' I asked her. 'What time does the Open University open?'

'For many years a wife could not give evidence against her husband,' Snellgrove told us. 'See *R. v. Boucher* 1952. Now, since the Police and Criminal Evidence Act 1984, a wife can be called to give such evidence.'

'You see, Rumpole.' Hilda took a note. 'You'd better watch out!' I found and lit the first small cigar of the day and coughed gratefully. Snellgrove continued to teach me law.

'But she can't be compelled to. She has been a competent witness for the defence of her husband since the Criminal Evidence Act 1898. But a judgment in the House of Lords suggests she's not compellable . . .'

'What's that mean, Rumpole?' she asked me.

'Well, we could ask April Timson to give evidence for Tony. But we couldn't make her,' I began to explain, and then, perhaps because I was in a state of shock from being awoken so early, I had an idea of more than usual brilliance. 'April Timson!' I told Hilda. 'She won't know she's not compellable. I don't suppose she tunes into the "Open at Dawn University". Now I wonder . . .'

'What, Rumpole? What do you wonder?'

'Quarter to six.' I looked at the clock on the mantelpiece. 'High time to wake up Bernard.' I went to the phone and started to dial my instructing solicitor's number.

'You see how useful I'll be to you' – Hilda looked extremely pleased with herself – 'when I come to work in your chambers.'

'Oh, Bernard,' I said to the telephone, 'wake you up, did I? Well, it's time to get moving. The Open University's been open for hours. Look, an idea has just crossed my mind . . .'

'It crossed *my* mind, Rumpole,' Hilda corrected me. 'And I was kind enough to hand it on to you.'

When Mr Bernard called on April Timson an hour later, there was no need for him to go into the nice legal question of whether she was a compellable witness or not. Since she had seen Peanuts and her friend Chrissie come out of the 'offey', she was, she made it clear, ready and willing to come to court and tell her whole story.

'Mrs April Timson,' I asked Tony's wife when, to the surprise of most people in court including my client, she entered the witness-box, as a witness for the defence, 'some while ago you had a quarrel with your husband in a bathtub. What was that quarrel about?'

'Peanuts Molloy.'

'About a man called Peter "Peanuts" Molloy. What did you tell your husband about Peanuts?'

'About him as a man, like . . . ?'

'Did you compare the virility of these two gentlemen?'

'Yes, I did.' April was able to cope with this part of the evidence without embarrassment.

'And who got the better of the comparison?'

'Peanuts.' Tony, lowering his head, got his first look of sympathy from the jury.

'Was there a scuffle in your bath then?'

'Yes.'

'Mrs April Timson, did your husband ever try to drown you?'

'No. He never.' Her answer caused a buzz in court. Guthrie stared at her, incredulous.

'Why did you suggest he did?' I asked.

'My Lord. I object. What possible relevance?' Hearthrug tried to interrupt but I and everyone else ignored him.

'Why did you suggest he tried to murder you?' I repeated.

'I was angry with him, I reckon,' April told us calmly, and the prosecutor lost heart and subsided.

The judge, however, pursued the matter with a pained expression. 'Do I understand,' he asked, 'you made an entirely false accusation against your husband?'

'Yes.' April didn't seem to think it an unusual thing to do.

'Don't you realize, madam,' the judge said, 'the suffering that accusation has brought to innocent people?'

'Such as you, old cock,' I muttered to Mizz Liz.

'What was that, Rumpole?' the judge asked me.

'Such as the man in the dock, my Lord,' I repeated.

'And other innocent, innocent people.' His Lordship shook his head sadly and made a note.

'After your husband's trial did you continue to see Mr Peanuts Molloy?' I went on with my questions to the uncompellable witness.

'We went out together. Yes.'

'Where did you meet?'

'We met round the offey in Dalton Avenue. Then we went out in his car.'

'Did you meet him at the off-licence on the night this robbery took place?'

'I never.' April was sure of it.

'Your husband says that your neighbour Chrissie came round and told him that you and Peanuts Molloy were going to meet at the off-licence at nine-thirty that evening. So he went up there to put a stop to your affair.'

'Well, Chrissie was well in with Peanuts by then, wasn't she?' April smiled cynically. 'I reckon he sent her to tell Tony that.'

'Why do you reckon he sent her?'

Hearthstoke rose again, determined. 'My Lord, I must object,' he said. 'What this witness "reckons" is entirely inadmissible.' When he had finished, I asked the judge if I might have a word with my learned friend in order to save time. I then moved along our row and whispered to him vehemently, 'One more peep out of you, Hearthrug, and I lay a formal complaint on your conduct!'

'What conduct?' he whispered back.

'Trying to blackmail a learned judge on the matter of a pot plant sent to a shorthand writer.' I looked across at Lorraine. 'Not in the best traditions of the Bar, that!' I left him thinking hard and went back to my place.

After due consideration he said, 'My Lord. On second thoughts, I withdraw my objection.'

Hearthstoke resumed his seat. I smiled at him cheerfully and continued with April's evidence. 'So why do you think Peanuts wanted to get your husband up to the off-licence that evening?'

'Pretty obvious, innit?'

'Explain it to us.'

'So he could put him in the frame. Make it look like Tony done Ruby up, like.'

'So he could put him in the frame. An innocent man!' I looked at the jury. 'Had Peanuts said anything to make you think he might do such a thing?'

'After the first trial.'

'After Mr Timson was bound over?'

'Yes. Peanuts said he reckoned Tony needed a bit of justice, like. He said he was going to see he got put inside. Course, Peanuts didn't mind making a bit hisself, out of robbing the offey.'

'One more thing, Mrs Timson. Have you ever seen a weapon like that before?'

I held up the cosh. The usher came and took it to the witness.

'I saw that one. I think I did.'

'Where?'

'In Peanuts's car. That's where he kept it.'

'Did your husband ever own anything like that?'

'What, Tony?' April weighed the cosh in her hand and clearly found the idea ridiculous. 'Not him. He wouldn't have known what to do with it.'

When the evidence was complete and we had made our speeches, Guthrie had to sum up the case of R. v. *Timson* to the jury. As he turned his chair towards them, and they prepared to give him their full attention, a distinguished visitor slipped unobtrusively into the back of the court. He was none other than old Keith from the Lord Chancellor's office. The judge must have seen him, but he made no apology for his previous lenient treatment of Tony Timson.

'Members of the Jury,' he began. 'You have heard of the false accusation of attempted murder that Mrs Timson made against an innocent man. Can you imagine, Members of the Jury, what misery that poor man has been made to suffer? Devoted to ladies as he may be, he has been called a heartless "male chauvinist". Gentle and harmless by nature, he has been thought to connive at crimes of violence.

Perhaps it was even suggested that he was the sort of fellow who would make his wife carry heavy luggage! He may well have been shunned in the streets, hooted at from the pavements, and the wife he truly loves has perhaps been unwilling to enter a warm, domestic bath with him. And then, consider,' Guthrie went on, 'if the unhappy Timson may not have also been falsely accused in relation to the robbery with violence of his local "offey". Justice must be done, Members of the Jury. We must do justice even if it means we do nothing else for the rest of our lives but compete in croquet competitions.' The judge was looking straight at Keith from the Lord Chancellor's office as he said this. I relaxed, lay back and closed my eyes. I knew, after all his troubles, how his Lordship would feel about a man falsely accused, and I had no further worries about the fate of Tony Timson.

When I got home, Hilda was reading the result of the trial in the *Evening Sentinel*. 'I suppose you're cock-a-hoop, Rumpole,' she said.

'Hearthrug routed!' I told her. 'The women of England back on our side and old Keith from the Lord Chancellor's office looking extremely foolish. And a miraculous change came over Guthrie.'

'What?'

'He suddenly found courage. It's something you can't do without, not if you concern yourself with justice.'

'That April Timson!' Hilda looked down at her evening paper. 'Making it all up about being drowned in the bathwater.'

' "When lovely woman stoops to folly" ' – I went to the sideboard and poured a celebratory glass of Château Thames Embankment – ' "And finds too late that men betray, What charm can soothe her melancholy . . ." '

'I'm not going to the Bar to protect people like her, Rumpole.' Hilda announced her decision. 'She's put me to a great deal of trouble. Getting up at a quarter to six every morning for the Open University.'

' "What art can wash her guilt away?" *What* did you say, Hilda?'

'I'm not going to all that trouble, learning Real Property and Company Law and eating dinners and buying a wig, not for the likes of April Timson.'

'Oh, Hilda! Everyone in chambers will be extremely disappointed.'

'Well, I'm sorry.' She had clearly made up her mind. 'They'll just have to do without me. I've really got better things to do, Rumpole, than come home cock-a-hoop just because April Timson changes her mind and decides to tell the truth.'

'Of course you have, Hilda.' I drank gratefully. 'What sort of better things?'

'Keeping you in order for one, Rumpole. Seeing you wash up properly.' And then she spoke with considerable feeling. 'It's disgusting!'

'The washing-up?'

'No. People having baths together.'

'Married people?' I reminded her.

'I don't see that makes it any better. Don't you ever ask me to do that, Rumpole.'

'Never, Hilda. I promise faithfully.' To hear, of course, was to obey.

That night's *Sentinel* contained a leading article which appeared under the encouraging headline BATHTUB JUDGE PROVED RIGHT.

Mrs April Timson [*it read*] has admitted that her husband never tried to drown her and the jury have acquitted Tony Timson on a second trumped-up charge. It took a judge of Mr Justice Featherstone's perception and experience to see through this woman's inventions and exaggerations and to uphold the law without fear or favour. Now and again the British legal system produces a judge of exceptional wisdom and integrity who refuses to yield to pressure groups and does justice though the heavens fall. Such a one is Sir Guthrie Featherstone.

Sir Guthrie told me later that he read these comforting words while lying in a warm bath in his flat near Harrods. I have no doubt at all that Lady Featherstone was with him on that occasion, seated at the tap end.

Rumpole and the Bubble Reputation

It is now getting on for half a century since I took to crime, and I can honestly say I haven't regretted a single moment of it.

Crime is about life, death and the liberty of the subject; civil law is entirely concerned with that most tedious of all topics, money. Criminal law requires an expert knowledge of bloodstains, policemen's notebooks and the dark flow of human passion, as well as the argot currently in use round the Elephant and Castle. Civil law calls for a close study of such yawn-producing matters as bills of exchange, negotiable instruments and charter parties. It is true, of course, that the most enthralling murder produces only a small and long-delayed legal aid cheque, sufficient to buy a couple of dinners at some Sunday supplement eaterie for the learned friends who practise daily in the commercial courts. Give me, however, a sympathetic jury, a blurred thumbprint and a dodgy confession, and you can keep *Mega-Chemicals Ltd* v. *The Sunshine Bank of Florida* with all its fifty days of mammoth refreshers for the well-heeled barristers involved.

There is one drawback, however, to being a criminal hack: the judges and the learned friends are apt to regard you as though you were the proud possessor of a long line of convictions. How many times have I stood up to address the tribunal on such matters as the importance of intent or the presumption of innocence only to be stared at by the old darling on the Bench as though I were sporting a black mask or carrying a large sack labelled SWAG? Often, as I walk through the Temple on my way down to the Bailey, my place of work, I have seen bowler-hatted commercial or revenue men pass by on the other side and heard them mutter, 'There goes old Rumpole. I wonder if he's doing a murder or a rape this morning?' The sad truth of the matter is that civil law is regarded as the Harrods and crime the Tesco's of the legal profession. And of all the varieties of civil action the most elegant, the smartest, the one which attracts the best barristers like bees to the honey-pot, is undoubtedly the libel action. Star in a libel case on the civilized stage of the High Court of Justice and fame and fortune will be yours, if you haven't got them already.

It's odd, isn't it? Kill a person or beat him over the head and remove his wallet, and all you'll get is an Old Bailey judge and an Old Bailey hack. Cast a well-deserved slur on his moral character, ridicule his nose or belittle his bank balance and you will get a High Court judge and some of the smoothest silks in the business. I can only remember doing one libel action, and after it I asked my clerk, Henry, to find me a nice clean assault or an honest break and entering. Exactly why I did so will become clear to you when I have revealed the full and hitherto unpublished details of *Amelia Nettleship* v. *The Daily Beacon and Maurice Machin*. If, after reading what went on in that particular defamation case, you don't agree that crime presents a fellow with a more honourable alternative, I shall have to think seriously about issuing a writ for libel.

You may be fortunate enough never to have read an allegedly 'historical' novel by that much-publicized authoress Miss Amelia Nettleship. Her books contain virginal heroines and gallant and gentlemanly heroes and thus present an extremely misleading account of our rough island story. She is frequently photographed wearing cotton print dresses, with large spectacles on her still pretty nose, dictating to a secretary and a couple of long-suffering cats in a wisteria-clad Tudor cottage somewhere outside Godalming. In the interviews she gives, Miss Nettleship invariably refers to the evils of the permissive society and the consequences of sex before marriage. I have never, speaking for myself, felt the slightest urge to join the permissive society; the only thing which would tempt me to such a course is hearing Amelia Nettleship denounce it.

Why, you may well ask, should I, whose bedtime reading is usually confined to *The Oxford Book of English Verse* (the Quiller-Couch edition), Archbold's *Criminal Law* and Professor Ackerman's *Causes of Death*, become so intimately acquainted with Amelia Nettleship? Alas, she shares my bed, not in person but in book form, propped up on the bosom of She Who Must Be Obeyed, alias my wife, Hilda, who insists on reading her far into the night. While engrossed in *Lord Stingo's Fancy*, I distinctly heard her sniff, and asked if she had a cold coming on. 'No, Rumpole,' she told me. 'Touching!'

'Oh, I'm sorry.' I moved further down the bed.

'Don't be silly. The book's touching. Very touching. We all thought Lord Stingo was a bit of a rake but he's turned out quite differently.'

'Sounds a sad disappointment.'

'Nonsense! It's ending happily. He swore he'd never marry, but Lady Sophia has made him swallow his words.'

'And if they were written by Amelia Nettleship I'm sure he found them extremely indigestible. Any chance of turning out the light?'

'Not yet. I've got another three chapters to go.'

'Oh, for God's sake! Can't Lord Stingo get on with it?' As I rolled over, I had no idea that I was soon to become legally involved with the authoress who was robbing me of my sleep.

My story starts in Pommeroy's Wine Bar to which I had hurried for medical treatment (my alcohol content had fallen to a dangerous low) at the end of a day's work. As I sipped my large dose of Château Thames Embankment, I saw my learned friend Erskine-Brown, member of our chambers at Equity Court, alone and palely loitering. 'What can ail you, Claude?' I asked, and he told me it was his practice.

'Still practising?' I raised an eyebrow. 'I thought you might have got the hang of it by now.'

'I used to do a decent class of work,' he told me sadly. 'I once had a brief in a libel action. You were never in a libel, Rumpole?'

'Who cares about the bubble reputation? Give me a decent murder and a few well-placed bloodstains.'

'Now, guess what I've got coming up?' The man was wan with care.

'Another large claret for me, I sincerely hope.'

'Actual bodily harm and affray in the Kitten-A-Go-Go Club, Soho.' Claude is married to the Portia of our chambers, the handsome

Phillida Erskine-Brown, QC, and they are blessed with issue rejoicing in the names of Tristan and Isolde. He is, you understand, far more at home in the Royal Opera House than in any Soho Striperama. 'Two unsavoury characters in leather jackets were duelling with broken Coca-Cola bottles.'

'Sounds like my line of country,' I told him.

'Exactly! I'm scraping the bottom of your barrel, Rumpole. I mean, you've got a reputation for sordid cases. I'll have to ask you for a few tips.'

'Visit the *locus in quo*,' was my expert advice. 'Go to the scene of the crime. Inspect the geography of the place.'

'The geography of the Kitten-A-Go-Go? Do I have to?'

'Of course. Then you can suggest it was too dark to identify anyone, or the witness couldn't see round a pillar, or . . .'

But at that point we were interrupted by an eager, bespectacled fellow of about Erskine-Brown's age who introduced himself as Ted Spratling from the *Daily Beacon*. 'I was just having an argument with my editor over there, Mr Rumpole,' he said. 'You do libel cases, don't you?'

'Good heavens, yes!' I lied with instant enthusiasm, sniffing a brief. 'The law of defamation is mother's milk to me. I cut my teeth on hatred, ridicule and contempt.' As I was speaking, I saw Claude Erskine-Brown eyeing the journalist like a long-lost brother.

'Slimey Spratling!' he hallooed at last.

'Collywobbles Erskine-Brown!' The hack seemed equally amazed. There was no need to tell me that they were at school together.

'Look, would you join my editor for a glass of Bolly?' Spratling invited me.

'What?'

'Bollinger.'

'I'd love to!' Erskine-Brown was visibly cheered.

'Oh, you too, Colly. Come on, then.'

'Golly, Colly!' I said as we crossed the bar towards a table in the corner. 'Bolly!'

So I was introduced to Mr Maurice – known as 'Morry' – Machin, a large silver-haired person with distant traces of a Scots accent, a blue silk suit and a thick gold ring in which a single diamond winked sullenly. He was surrounded with empty Bolly bottles and a masterful-looking woman whom he introduced as Connie Coughlin, the features editor. Morry himself had, I knew, been for many years at the helm of the tabloid *Daily Beacon*, and had blasted many precious reputations with well-aimed scandal stories and reverberating 'revelations'.

'They say you're a fighter, Mr Rumpole, that you're a terrier, sir, after a legal rabbit,' he started, as Ted Spratling performed the deputy editor's duty of pouring the bubbly.

'I do my best. This is my learned friend, Claude Erskine-Brown, who specializes in affray.'

'I'll remember you, sir, if I get into a scrap.' But the editor's real business was with me. 'Mr Rumpole, we are thinking of briefing you. We're in a spot of bother over a libel.'

'Tell him,' Claude muttered to me, 'you can't do libel.'

'I never turn down a brief in a libel action.' I spoke with confidence, although Claude continued to mutter, 'You've never been offered a brief in a libel action.'

'I don't care,' I said, 'for little scraps in Soho. Sordid stuff. Give me a libel action, when a reputation is at stake.'

'You think that's important?' Morry looked at me seriously, so I treated him to a taste of *Othello*. '"Good name in man or woman, dear my lord"' (I was at my most impressive),

'Is the immediate jewel of their souls.
Who steals my purse, steals trash; 'tis something, nothing;
'Twas mine, 'tis his, and has been slave to thousands:
But he that filches from me my good name
Robs me of that which not enriches him
And makes me poor indeed.'

Everyone, except Erskine-Brown, was listening reverently. After I had finished there was a solemn pause. Then Morry clapped three times.

'Is that one of your speeches, Mr Rumpole?'

'Shakespeare's.'

'Ah, yes . . .'

'Your good name, Mr Machin, is something I shall be prepared to defend to the death,' I said.

'Our paper goes in for a certain amount of fearless exposure,' the *Beacon* editor explained.

'The "*Beacon* Beauties".' Erskine-Brown was smiling. 'I catch sight of it occasionally in the clerk's room.'

'Not that sort of exposure, Collywobbles!' Spratling rebuked his old schoolfriend. 'We tell the truth about people in the public eye.'

'Who's bonking who and who pays,' Connie from Features explained. 'Our readers love it.'

'I take exception to that, Connie. I really do,' Morry said piously. 'I don't want Mr Rumpole to get the idea that we're running any sort of a cheap scandal-sheet.'

'Scandal-sheet? Perish the thought!' I was working hard for my brief.

'You wouldn't have any hesitation in acting for the *Beacon*, would you?' the editor asked me.

'A barrister is an old taxi plying for hire. That's the fine tradition of our trade,' I explained carefully. 'So it's my sacred duty, Mr Morry Machin, to take on anyone in trouble. However repellent I may happen to find them.'

'Thank you, Mr Rumpole.' Morry was genuinely grateful.

'Think nothing of it.'

'We are dedicated to exposing hypocrisy in our society. Wherever it exists. High or low.' The editor was looking noble. 'So when we find this female pretending to be such a force for purity and parading her morality before the Great British Public . . .'

'Being all for saving your cherry till the honeymoon,' Connie Coughlin translated gruffly.

'Thank you, Connie. Or, as I would put it, denouncing premarital sex,' Morry said.

'She's even against the *normal* stuff!' Spratling was bewildered.

'Whereas her own private life is extremely steamy. We feel it our duty to tell our public. Show Mr Rumpole the article in question, Ted.'

I don't know if they had expected to meet me in Pommeroy's but the top brass of the *Daily Beacon* had a cutting of the alleged libel at the ready. THE PRIVATE LIFE OF AMELIA NETTLESHIP BY BEACON GIRL ON THE SPOT, STELLA JANUARY I read, and then glanced at the story that followed. 'This wouldn't be *the* Amelia Nettleship?' I was beginning to warm to my first libel action. 'The expert bottler of pure historical bilge-water?'

'The lady novelist and hypocrite,' Morry told me. 'Of course I've never met the woman.'

'She robs me of my sleep. I know nothing of her morality, but her prose style depraves and corrupts the English language. We shall need a statement from this Stella January.' I got down to business.

'Oh, Stella left us a couple of months ago,' the editor told me.

'And went where?'

'God knows. Overseas, perhaps. You know what these girls are.'

'We've got to find her,' I insisted and then cheered him up with 'We shall fight, Mr Machin – Morry. And we shall conquer! Remember, I never plead guilty.'

'There speaks a man who knows damn all about libel.' Claude Erskine-Brown had a final mutter.

It might be as well if I quoted here the words in Miss Stella January's article which were the subject of legal proceedings. They ran as follows:

Miss Amelia Nettleship is a bit of a puzzle. The girls in her historical novels always keep their legs crossed until they've got a ring on their fingers. But her private life is rather different. Whatever lucky young man leads the 43-year-old Amelia to the altar will inherit a torrid past which makes Mae West sound like Florence Nightingale. Her home, Hollyhock Cottage, near Godalming, has been the scene of one-night stands and longer liaisons so numerous that the neighbours have given up counting. There is considerably more in her jacuzzi than bath salts. Her latest Casanova, so far unnamed, is said to be a married man who's been seen leaving in the wee small hours.

From the style of this piece of prose you may come to the conclusion that Stella January and Amelia Nettleship deserved each other.

One thing you can say for my learned friend Claude Erskine-Brown is that he takes advice. Having been pointed in the direction of the Kitten-A-Go-Go, he set off obediently to find a cul-de-sac off Wardour Street with his instructing solicitor. He wasn't to know, and it was entirely his bad luck, that Connie Coughlin had dreamt up a feature on London's Square Mile of Sin for the *Daily Beacon* and ordered an ace photographer to comb the sinful purlieus between Oxford Street and Shaftesbury Avenue in search of nefarious goings-on.

Erskine-Brown and a Mr Thrower, his sedate solicitor, found the Kitten-A-Go-Go, paid a sinister-looking myrmidon at the door ten quid each by way of membership and descended to a damp and darkened basement where two young ladies were chewing gum and removing their clothes with as much enthusiasm as they might bring to the task of licking envelopes. Claude took a seat in the front row and tried to commit the geography of the place to memory. It must be said, however, that his eyes were fixed on the plumpest of the disrobing performers when a sudden and unexpected flash preserved his face and more of the stripper for the five million readers of the *Daily Beacon* to enjoy with their breakfast. Not being a particularly observant barrister, Claude left the strip joint with no idea of the ill luck that had befallen him.

While Erskine-Brown was thus exploring the underworld, I was closeted in the chambers of that elegant Old Etonian civil lawyer Robin Peppiatt, QC, who, assisted by his junior, Dick Garsington, represented the proprietors of the *Beacon*. I was entering the lists in the defence of Morry Machin, and our joint solicitor was an anxious little man called Cuxham, who seemed ready to pay almost any amount of someone else's money to be shot of the whole business. Quite early in our meeting, almost as soon, in fact, as Peppiatt had poured Earl Grey into thin china cups and handed round the *petits beurres*, it became clear that everyone wanted to do a deal with the other side except my good self and my client, the editor.

'We should work as a team,' Peppiatt started. 'Of which, as leading counsel, I am, I suppose, the captain.'

'Are we playing cricket, old chap?' I ventured to ask him.

'If we were it would be an extremely expensive game for the *Beacon*.' The QC gave me a tolerant smile. 'The proprietors have contracted to indemnify the editor against any libel damages.'

'I insisted on that when I took the job,' Morry told us with considerable satisfaction.

'Very sensible of your client, no doubt, Rumpole. Now, you may not be used to this type of case as you're one of the criminal boys . . .'

'Oh, I know' – I admitted the charge – 'I'm just a juvenile delinquent.'

'But it's obvious to me that we mustn't attempt to justify these serious charges against Miss Nettleship's honour.' The captain of the team gave his orders and I made bold to ask, 'Wouldn't that be cricket?'

'If we try to prove she's a sort of amateur tart the jury might bump the damages up to two or three hundred grand,' Peppiatt explained as patiently as he could.

'Or four.' Dick Garsington shook his head sadly. 'Or perhaps half a million.' Mr Cuxham's mind boggled.

'But you've filed a defence alleging that the article's a true bill.' I failed to follow the drift of these faint-hearts.

'That's our bargaining counter.' Peppiatt spoke to me very slowly, as though to a child of limited intelligence.

'Our what?'

'Something to give away. As part of the deal.'

'When we agree terms with the other side we'll abandon all our allegations. Gracefully,' Garsington added.

'We put up our hands?' I contemptuously tipped ash from my small cigar on to Peppiatt's Axminster. Dick Garsington was sent off to get 'an ashtray for Rumpole'.

'Peregrine Landseer's agin us.' Peppiatt seemed to be bringing glad tidings of great joy to all of us. 'I'm lunching with Perry at the Sheridan Club to discuss another matter. I'll just whisper the thought of a quiet little settlement into his ear.'

'Whisper sweet nothings!' I told him. 'I'll not be party to any settlement. I'm determined to defend the good name of my client Mr Maurice Machin as a responsible editor.'

'At our expense?' Peppiatt looked displeased.

'If necessary. Yes! He wouldn't have published that story unless there was some truth in it. Would you?' I asked Morry, assailed by some doubt.

'Certainly not' – my client assured me – 'as a fair and responsible journalist.'

'The trouble is that there's no evidence that Miss Nettleship has done any of these things.' Clearly Mr Cuxham had long since thrown in the towel.

'Then we must find some! Isn't that what solicitors are for?' I asked, but didn't expect an answer. 'I'm quite unable to believe that anyone who writes so badly hasn't got *some* other vices.'

A few days later I entered the clerk's room of our chambers in Equity Court to see our clerk, Henry, seated at his desk looking at the centre pages of the *Daily Beacon*, which Dianne, our fearless but somewhat hit-and-miss typist, was showing him. As I approached, Dianne folded the paper, retreated to her desk and began to type furiously. They both straightened their faces and the smiles of astonishment I had noticed when I came in were replaced by looks of legal seriousness. In fact Henry spoke with almost religious awe when he handed me my brief in *Nettleship* v. *The Daily Beacon and anor*. Not only was a highly satisfactory fee marked on the front but refreshers, that is the sum required to keep a barrister on his feet and talking, had been agreed at no less than five hundred pounds a day.

'You *can* make the case last, can't you, Mr Rumpole?' Henry asked with understandable concern.

'Make it last?' I reassured him. 'I can make it stretch on till the trump of doom! We have serious and lengthy allegations, Henry. Allegations that will take days and days, with any luck. For the first time in a long career at the Bar I begin to see . . .'

'See what, Mr Rumpole?'

'A way of providing for my old age.'

The door then opened to admit Claude Erskine-Brown. Dianne and Henry regarded him with solemn pity, as though he'd had a death in his family.

'Here comes the poor old criminal lawyer,' I greeted him. 'Any more problems with your affray, Claude?'

'All under control, Rumpole. Thank you very much. Morning, Dianne. Morning, Henry.' Our clerk and secretary returned his greeting in mournful voices. At that point, Erskine-Brown noticed Dianne's copy of the *Beacon*, wondered who the 'Beauty' of that day might be, and picked it up before she could stop him.

'What've you got there? The *Beacon*! A fine crusading paper. Tells the truth without fear or favour.' My refreshers had put me in a remarkably good mood. 'Are you feeling quite well, Claude?'

Erskine-Brown was holding the paper in trembling hands and had gone extremely pale. He looked at me with accusing eyes and managed to say in strangled tones, '*You* told me to go there!'

'For God's sake, Claude! Told you to go where?'

'The *locus in quo*!'

I took the *Beacon* from him and saw the cause of his immediate concern. The *locus in quo* was the Kitten-A-Go-Go, and the blown-up snap on the centre page showed Claude closely inspecting a young lady who was waving her underclothes triumphantly over her head. At that moment, Henry's telephone rang and he announced that Soapy Sam Ballard, our puritanical head of chambers, founder member of the Lawyers As Christians Society (LACS) and the Savonarola of Equity Court, wished to see Mr Erskine-Brown in his room without delay. Claude left us with the air of a man climbing up into the dock to receive a stiff but inevitable sentence.

I wasn't, of course, present in the head of chambers' room where Claude was hauled up. It was not until months later, when he had recovered a certain calm, that he was able to tell me how the embarrassing meeting went and I reconstruct the occasion for the purpose of this narrative.

'You wanted to see me, Ballard?' Claude started to babble. 'You're looking well. In wonderful form. I don't remember when I've seen you looking so fit.' At that early stage he tried to make his escape from the room. 'Well, nice to chat. I've got a summons, across the road.'

'Just a minute!' Ballard called him back. 'I don't read the *Daily Beacon*.'

'Oh, don't you? Very wise,' Claude congratulated him. 'Neither do I. Terrible rag. Half-clad beauties on page four and no law reports. So they tell me. Absolutely no reason to bother with the thing!'

'But, coming out of the Temple tube station, Mr Justice Fishwick pushed this in my face.' Soapy Sam lifted the fatal newspaper from his desk. 'It seems he's just remarried and his new wife takes in the *Daily Beacon*.'

'How odd!'

'What's odd?'

'A judge's wife. Reading the *Beacon*.'

'Hugh Fishwick married his cook,' Ballard told him in solemn tones.

'Really? I didn't know. Well, that explains it. But I don't see why he should push it in your face, Ballard.'

'Because he thought I ought to see it.'

'Nothing in that rag that could be of the slightest interest to you, surely?'

'Something is.'

'What?'

'You.'

Ballard held out the paper to Erskine-Brown, who approached it gingerly and took a quick look.

'Oh, really? Good heavens! Is that me?'

'Unless you have a twin brother masquerading as yourself. You feature in an article on London's Square Mile of Sin.'

'It's all a complete misunderstanding!' Claude assured our leader.

'I'm glad to hear it.'

'I can explain everything.'

'I hope so.'

'You see, I got into this affray.'

'You got into what?' Ballard saw even more cause for concern.

'This fight' – Claude wasn't improving his case – 'in the Kitten-A-Go-Go.'

'Perhaps I ought to warn you, Erskine-Brown.' Ballard was being judicial. 'You needn't answer incriminating questions.'

'No, *I* didn't get into a fight.' Claude was clearly rattled. 'Good heavens, no. I'm doing a case, about a fight. An affray. With Coca-Cola bottles. And Rumpole advised me to go to this club.'

'Horace Rumpole is an *habitué* of this house of ill-repute? At *his* age?' Ballard didn't seem to be in the least surprised to hear it.

'No, not at all. But he said I ought to take a view. Of the scene of the crime. This wretched scandal-sheet puts the whole matter in the wrong light. Entirely.'

There was a long and not entirely friendly pause before Ballard proceeded to judgment. 'If that is so, Erskine-Brown,' he said, 'and I make no further comment while the matter is *sub judice*, you will no doubt be suing the *Daily Beacon* for libel?'

'You think I should?' Claude began to count the cost of such an action.

'It is quite clearly your duty. To protect your own reputation and the reputation of this chambers.'

'Wouldn't it be rather expensive?' I can imagine Claude gulping, but Ballard was merciless.

'What is money,' he said, 'compared to the hitherto unsullied name of number 3 Equity Court?'

Claude's next move was to seek out the friend of his boyhood, 'Slimey' Spratling, whom he finally found jogging across Hyde Park. When he told the *Beacon* deputy editor that he had been advised to issue a writ, the man didn't even stop and Erskine-Brown had to trot along beside him. 'Good news!' Spratling said. 'My editor seems to enjoy libel actions. Glad you liked your pic.'

'Of course I didn't like it. It'll ruin my career.'

'Nonsense, Collywobbles.' Spratling was cheerful. 'You'll get briefed by all the clubs. You'll be the strippers' QC.'

'However did they get my name?' Claude wondered.

'Oh, I recognized you at once,' Slimey assured him. 'Bit of luck, wasn't it?' Then he ran on, leaving Claude outraged. They had, after all, been at Winchester together.

When I told the helpless Cuxham that the purpose of solicitors was to gather evidence, I did so without much hope of my words stinging him into any form of activity. If evidence against Miss Nettleship were needed, I would have to look elsewhere, so I rang up that great source of knowledge, 'Fig' Newton, and invited him for a drink at Pommeroy's.

Ferdinand Isaac Gerald, known to his many admirers as 'Fig' Newton, is undoubtedly the best in the somewhat unreliable band of professional private eyes. I know that Fig is now knocking seventy; that, with his filthy old mackintosh and collapsing hat, he looks like a scarecrow after a bad night; that his lantern jaw, watery eye and the frequently appearing drip on the end of the nose don't make him an immediately attractive figure. Fig may look like a scarecrow but he's a very bloodhound after a clue.

'I'm doing civil work now, Fig,' I told him when we met in Pommeroy's. 'Just a big brief in a libel action which should provide a bit of comfort for my old age. But my instructing solicitor is someone we would describe, in legal terms, as a bit of a wally. I'd be obliged if you'd do his job for him and send him the bill when we win.'

'What is it that I am required to do, Mr Rumpole?' the great detective asked patiently.

'Keep your eye on a lady.'

'I usually am, Mr Rumpole. Keeping my eye on one lady or another.'

'This one's a novelist. A certain Miss Amelia Nettleship. Do you know her works?'

'Can't say I do, sir.' Fig had once confessed to a secret passion for Jane Austen. 'Are you on to a winner?'

'With a bit of help from you, Fig. Only one drawback here, as in most cases.'

'What's that, sir?'

'The client.' Looking across the bar I had seen the little group from the *Beacon* round the Bollinger. Having business with the editor, I left Fig Newton to his work and crossed the room. Sitting myself beside my client I refused champagne and told him that I wanted him to do something about my learned friend Claude Erskine-Brown.

'You mean the barrister who goes to funny places in the afternoon? What're you asking me to do, Mr Rumpole?'

'Apologize, of course. Print the facts. Claude Erskine-Brown was in the Kitten-A-Go-Go purely in pursuit of his legal business.'

'I love it!' Morry's smile was wider than ever. 'There speaks the great defender. You'd put up any story, wouldn't you, however improbable, to get your client off.'

'It happens to be true.'

'So far as we are concerned' – Morry smiled at me patiently – 'we printed a pic of a gentleman in a pinstriped suit examining the goods on display. No reason to apologize for that, is there, Connie? What's your view, Ted?'

'No reason at all, Morry.' Connie supported him and Spratling agreed.

'So you're going to do nothing about it?' I asked with some anger.

'Nothing we *can* do.'

'Mr Machin.' I examined the man with distaste. 'I told you it was a legal rule that a British barrister is duty-bound to take on any client however repellent.'

'I remember you saying something of the sort.'

'You are stretching my duty to the furthest limits of human endurance.'

'Never mind, Mr Rumpole. I'm sure you'll uphold the best traditions of the Bar!'

When Morry said that I left him. However, as I was wandering away from Pommeroy's towards the Temple station, Gloucester Road, home and beauty, a somewhat breathless Ted Spratling caught up with me and asked me to do my best for Morry. 'He's going through a tough time.' I didn't think the man was entirely displeased by the news he had to impart. 'The proprietor's going to sack him.'

'Because of this case?'

'Because the circulation's dropping. Tits and bums are going out of fashion. The wives don't like it.'

'Who'll be the next editor?'

'Well, I'm the deputy now . . .' He did his best to sound modest.

'I see. Look' – I decided to enlist an ally – 'would you help me with the case? In strict confidence, I want some sort of a lead to this Stella January. Can you find out how her article came in? Get hold of the original. It might have an address. Some sort of clue . . .'

'I'll have a try, Mr Rumpole. Anything I can do to help old Morry.' Never had I heard a man speak with such deep insincerity.

The weather turned nasty, but, in spite of heavy rain, Fig Newton kept close observation for several nights on Hollyhock Cottage, home of Amelia Nettleship, without any particular result. One morning I entered our chambers early and on my way to my room I heard a curious buzzing sound, as though an angry bee were trapped in the lavatory. Pulling open the door, I detected Erskine-Brown plying a cordless electric razor.

'Claude,' I said, 'you're shaving!'

'Wonderful to see the workings of a keen legal mind.' The man sounded somewhat bitter.

'I'm sorry about all this. But I'm doing my best to help you.'

'Oh, please!' He held up a defensive hand. 'Don't try and do anything else to help me. "Visit the scene of the crime," you said. "Inspect the *locus in quo!*" So where has your kind assistance landed me? My name's mud. Ballard's as good as threatened to kick me out of chambers. I've got to spend my life's savings on a speculative libel action. And my marriage is on the rocks. Wonderful what you can do, Rumpole, with a few words of advice. Your clients must be everlastingly grateful.'

'Your marriage, on the rocks, did you say?'

'Oh, yes. Philly was frightfully reasonable about it. As far as she was concerned, she said, she didn't care what I did in the afternoons. But we'd better live apart for a while, for the sake of the children. She didn't want Tristan and Isolde to associate with a father dedicated to the exploitation of women.'

'Oh, Portia!' I felt for the fellow. 'What's happened to the quality of mercy?'

'So, thank you very much, Rumpole. I'm enormously grateful. The next time you've got a few helpful tips to hand out, for God's sake keep them to yourself!'

He switched on the razor again. I looked at it and made an instant deduction. 'You've been sleeping in chambers. You want to watch that, Claude. Bollard nearly got rid of me for a similar offence.'

'Where do you expect me to go? Phillida's having the locks changed in Islington.'

'Have you no friends?'

'Philly and I have reached the end of the line. I don't exactly want to advertise the fact among my immediate circle. I seem to remember, Rumpole, when you fell out with Hilda you planted yourself on us!' As he said this I scented danger and tried to avoid what I knew was coming.

'Oh. Now. Erskine-Brown. Claude. I was enormously grateful for your hospitality on that occasion.'

'Quite an easy run in on the Underground, is it, from Gloucester Road?' He spoke in a meaningful way.

'Of course. My door is always open. I'd be delighted to put you up, just until this mess is straightened out. But . . .'

'The least you could do, I should have thought, Rumpole.'

'It's not a sacrifice I could ask, old darling, even of my dearest friend. I couldn't ask you to shoulder the burden of daily life with She Who Must Be Obeyed. Now I'm sure you can find a very comfortable little hotel, somewhere cheap and cosy, around the British Museum. I promise you, life is by no means a picnic in the Gloucester Road.'

Well, that was enough, I thought, to dissuade the most determined visitor from seeking hospitality under the Rumpole roof. I went about my daily business and, when my work was done, I thought I should share some of the good fortune brought with my brief in the libel action with She Who Must Be Obeyed. I lashed out on two bottles of Pommeroy's bubbly, some of the least exhausted flowers to be found outside the tube station and even, such was my reckless mood, lavender water for Hilda.

'All the fruits of the earth,' I told her. 'Or, let's say, the fruits of the first cheque in *Nettleship* v. *The Beacon*, paid in advance. The first of many, if we can spin out the proceedings.'

'You're doing that awful case!' She didn't sound approving.

'That awful case will bring us in five hundred smackers a day in refreshers.'

'Helping that squalid newspaper insult Amelia Nettleship.' She looked at me with contempt.

'A barrister's duty, Hilda, is to take on all comers. However squalid.'

'Nonsense!'

'What?'

'Nonsense. You're only using that as an excuse.'

'Am I?'

'Of course you are. You're doing it because you're jealous of Amelia Nettleship!'

'Oh, I don't think so,' I protested mildly. 'My life has been full of longings, but I've never had the slightest desire to become a lady novelist.'

'You're jealous of her because she's got high principles.' Hilda was sure of it. 'You haven't got high principles, have you, Rumpole?'

'I told you. I will accept any client, however repulsive.'

'That's not a principle, that's just a way of making money from the most terrible people. Like the editor of the *Daily Beacon*. My mind is quite made up, Rumpole. I shall not use a single drop of that corrupt lavender water.'

It was then that I heard a sound from the hallway which made my heart sink. An all-too-familiar voice was singing '*La donna è mobile*' in a light tenor. Then the door opened to admit Erskine-Brown wearing my dressing-gown and very little else.

'Claude telephoned and told me all his troubles.' Hilda looked at the man with sickening sympathy. 'Of course I invited him to stay.'

'You're wearing my dressing-gown!' I put the charge to him at once.

'I had to pack in a hurry.' He looked calmly at the sideboard. 'Thoughtful of you to get in champagne to welcome me, Rumpole.'

'Was the bath all right, Claude?' Hilda sounded deeply concerned.

'Absolutely delightful, thank you, Hilda.'

'What a relief! That geyser can be quite temperamental.'

'Which is your chair, Horace?' Claude had the courtesy to ask.

'I usually sit by the gas fire. Why?'

'Oh, do sit there, Claude,' Hilda urged him and he gracefully agreed to pinch my seat. 'We mustn't let you get cold, must we, after your bath?'

So they sat together by the gas fire and I was allowed to open champagne for both of them. As I listened to the rain outside the window my spirits, I had to admit, had sunk to the lowest of ebbs. And around five o'clock the following morning, Fig Newton, the rain falling from the brim of his hat and the drop falling off his nose, stood watching Hollyhock Cottage. He saw someone – he was too far away to make an identification – come out of the front door and get into a parked car. Then he saw the figure of a woman in a nightdress, no doubt Amelia Nettleship, standing in the lit doorway waving goodbye. The headlights of the car were switched on and it drove away.

When the visitor had gone, and the front door was shut, Fig moved nearer to the cottage. He looked down at the muddy track on which the car had been parked and saw something white. He stooped to pick it up, folded it carefully and put it in his pocket.

On the day that *Nettleship* v. *The Beacon* began its sensational course, I breakfasted with Claude in the kitchen of our so-called mansion flat in the Gloucester Road. I say breakfasted, but Hilda told me that bacon and eggs were off as our self-invited guest preferred a substance, apparently made up of sawdust and bird droppings, which he called muesli. I was a little exhausted, having been kept awake by the amplified sound of grand opera from the spare bedroom, but Claude explained that he always found that a little Wagner settled him down for the night. He then asked for some of the goat's milk that Hilda had got in for him specially. As I coated a bit of toast with Oxford marmalade, the man only had to ask for organic honey to have it instantly supplied by She Who Seemed Anxious to Oblige.

'And what the hell,' I took the liberty of asking, 'is organic honey?'

'The bees only sip from flowers grown without chemical fertilizers,' Claude explained patiently.

'How does the bee know?'

'What?'

'I suppose the other bees tell it. "Don't sip from that, old chap. It's been grown with chemical fertilizers."'

So, ill-fed and feeling like a cuckoo in my own nest, I set off to the Royal Courts of Justice, in the Strand, that imposing turreted château which is the Ritz Hotel of the legal profession, the place where a gentleman is remunerated to the tune of five hundred smackers a day. It is also the place where gentlemen prefer an amicable settlement to the brutal business of fighting their cases.

I finally pitched up, wigged and robed, in front of the court which would provide the battleground for our libel action. I saw the combatants, Morry Machin and the fair Nettleship, standing a considerable distance apart. Peregrine Landseer, QC, counsel for the plaintiff, and Robin Peppiatt, QC, for the proprietors of the *Beacon*, were meeting on the central ground for a peace conference, attended by assorted juniors and instructing solicitors.

'After all the publicity, my lady couldn't take less than fifty thousand.' Landseer, Chairman of the Bar Council and on the brink of becoming a judge, was nevertheless driving as hard a bargain as any second-hand car dealer.

'Forty and a full and grovelling apology.' And Peppiatt added the bonus. 'We could wrap it up and lunch together at the Sheridan.'

'It's steak and kidney pud day at the Sheridan,' Dick Garsington remembered wistfully.

'Forty-five.' Landseer was not so easily tempted. 'And that's my last word on the subject.'

'Oh, all right,' Peppiatt conceded. 'Forty-five and a full apology. You happy with that, Mr Cuxham?'

'Well, sir. If you advise it.' Cuxham clearly had no stomach for the fight.

'We'll chat to the editor. I'm sure we're all going to agree' – Peppiatt gave me a meaningful look – 'in the end.'

While Landseer went off to sell the deal to his client, Peppiatt approached my man with 'You only have to join in the apology, Mr Machin, and the *Beacon* will pay the costs and the forty-five grand.'

' "Who steals my purse, steals trash," ' I quoted thoughtfully. ' "But he that filches from me my good name . . ." You're asking my client to sign a statement admitting he printed lies.'

'Oh, for heaven's sake, Rumpole!' Peppiatt was impatient. 'They gave up quoting that in libel actions fifty years ago.'

'Mr Rumpole's right.' Morry nodded wisely. 'My good name – I looked up the quotation – it's the immediate jewel of my soul.'

'Steady on, old darling,' I murmured. 'Let's not go *too* far.' At which moment Peregrine Landseer returned from a somewhat heated discussion with his client to say that there was no shifting her and she was determined to fight for every penny she could get.

'But Perry . . .' Robin Peppiatt lamented, 'the case is going to take two weeks!' At five hundred smackers a day I could only thank God for the stubbornness of Amelia Nettleship.

So we went into court to fight the case before a jury and Mr Justice Teasdale, a small, highly opinionated and bumptious little person who is unmarried, lives in Surbiton with a Persian cat, and was once an unsuccessful Tory candidate for Weston-super-Mare North. It takes a good deal of talent for a Tory to lose Weston-super-Mare North. Worst of all, he turned out to be a devoted fan of the works of Miss Amelia Nettleship.

'Members of the Jury,' Landseer said in opening the plaintiff's case, 'Miss Nettleship is the authoress of a number of historical works.'

'Rattling good yarns, Members of the Jury,' Mr Justice Teasdale chirped up.

'I beg your Lordship's pardon.' Landseer looked startled.

'I said "rattling good yarns", Mr Peregrine Landseer. The sort your wife might pick up without the slightest embarrassment. Unlike so much of the distasteful material one finds between hard covers today.'

'My Lord.' I rose to protest with what courtesy I could muster.

'Yes, Mr Rumbold?'

'Rum*pole*, my Lord.'

'I'm so sorry.' The judge didn't look in the least apologetic. 'I understand you are something of a stranger to these courts.'

'Would it not be better to allow the jury to come to their own conclusions about Miss Amelia Nettleship?' I suggested, ignoring the Teasdale manners.

'Well. Yes. Of course. I quite agree.' The judge looked serious and then cheered up. 'And when they do they'll find she can put together a rattling good yarn.'

There was a sycophantic murmur of laughter from the jury, and all I could do was subside and look balefully at the judge. I felt a pang of nostalgia for the Old Bailey and the wild stampede of the mad Judge Bullingham.

As Peregrine Landseer bored on, telling the jury what terrible harm the *Beacon* had done to his client's hitherto unblemished reputation, Ted Spratling, the deputy editor, leant forward in the seat behind me and whispered in my ear.

'About that Stella January article,' he said. 'I bought a drink for the systems manager. The copy's still in the system. One rather odd thing.'

'Tell me . . .'

'The log-on – that's the identification of the word processor. It came from the editor's office.'

'You mean it was written there?'

'No one writes things any more.'

'Of course not. How stupid of me.'

'It looks as if it had been put in from his word processor.'

'That is extremely interesting.'

'If Mr Rum*pole* has quite finished his conversation!' Peregrine Landseer was rebuking me for chattering during his opening speech.

I rose to apologize as humbly as I could. 'My Lord, I can assure my learned friend I was listening to every word of his speech. It's such a rattling good yarn.'

So the morning wore on, being mainly occupied by Landseer's opening. The luncheon adjournment saw me pacing the marble corridors of the Royal Courts of Justice with that great source of information, Fig Newton. He gave me a lengthy account of his observation on Hollyhock Cottage, and when he finally got to the departure of Miss Nettleship's nocturnal visitor, I asked impatiently, 'You got the car number?'

'Alas. No. Visibility was poor and weather conditions appalling.' The sleuth's evidence was here interrupted by a fit of sneezing.

'Oh, Fig!' I was, I confess, disappointed. 'And you didn't see the driver?'

'Alas. No, again.' Fig sneezed apologetically. 'However, when Miss Nettleship had closed the door and extinguished the lights, presumably in order to return to bed, I proceeded to the track in front of the house where the vehicle had been standing. There I retrieved an article which I thought might just possibly have been dropped by the driver in getting in or out of the vehicle.'

'For God's sake, show me!'

The detective gave me his treasure trove, which I stuffed into a pocket just as the usher came out of court to tell me that the judge was back from lunch, Miss Nettleship was entering the witness-box, and the world of libel awaited my attention.

If ever I saw a composed and confident witness, that witness was Amelia Nettleship. Her hair was perfectly done, her black suit was perfectly discreet, her white blouse shone, as did her spectacles. Her features, delicately cut as an intaglio, were attractive, but her beauty was by no means *louche* or abundant. So spotless did she seem that she might well have preserved her virginity until what must have been, in spite of appearances to the contrary, middle age. When she had finished her evidence-in-chief the judge thanked her and urged her to go on writing her 'rattling good yarns'. Peppiatt then rose to his feet to ask her a few questions designed to show that her books were still selling in spite of the *Beacon* article. This she denied, saying that sales had dropped off. The thankless task of attacking the fair name of Amelia was left to Rumpole.

'Miss Nettleship,' I started off with my guns blazing, 'are you a truthful woman?'

'I try to be.' She smiled at his Lordship, who nodded encouragement.

'And you call yourself an historical novelist?'

'I try to write books which uphold certain standards of morality.'

'Forget the morality for a moment. Let's concentrate on the history.'

'Very well.'

One of the hardest tasks in preparing for my first libel action was reading through the works of Amelia Nettleship. Now I had to quote from Hilda's favourite.

'May I read you a short passage from an alleged historical novel of yours entitled *Lord Stingo's Fancy*?' I asked as I picked up the book.

'Ah, yes.' The judge looked as though he were about to enjoy a treat. 'Isn't that the one which ends happily?'

'Happily, all Miss Nettleship's books end, my Lord,' I told him. 'Eventually.' There was a little laughter in court, and I heard Landseer whisper to his junior, 'This criminal chap's going to bump up the damages enormously.'

Meanwhile I started quoting from *Lord Stingo's Fancy*. '"Sophia had first set eyes on Lord Stingo when she was a dewy eighteen-year-old and he had clattered up to her father's castle, exhausted from the Battle of Nazeby,"' I read. '"Now at the ball to triumphantly celebrate the gorgeous, enthroning coronation of the Merry Monarch King Charles II they were to meet again. Sophia was now in her twenties but, in ways too numerous to completely describe, still an unspoilt girl at heart." You call that an *historical* novel?'

'Certainly,' the witness answered unashamed.

'Haven't you forgotten something?' I put it to her.

'I don't think so. What?'

'Oliver Cromwell.'

'I really don't know what you mean.'

'Clearly, if this Sophia . . . this girl . . . How do you describe her?'

'"Dewy", Mr Rumpole.' The judge repeated the word with relish.

'Ah, yes. "Dewy". I'm grateful to your Lordship. I had forgotten the full horror of the passage. If this dew-bespattered Sophia had been eighteen at the time of the Battle of Naseby in the reign of Charles I, she would have been thirty-three in the year of Charles II's coronation. Oliver Cromwell came in between.'

'I am an artist, Mr Rumpole.' Miss Nettleship smiled at my pettifogging objections.

'What kind of an artist?' I ventured to ask.

'I think Miss Nettleship means an artist in words,' was how the judge explained it.

'Are you, Miss Nettleship?' I asked. 'Then you must have noticed that the short passage I have read to the jury contains two split infinitives and a tautology.'

'A what, Mr Rumpole?' The judge looked displeased.

'Using two words that mean the same thing, as in "the enthroning coronation". My Lord, t-a-u . . .' I tried to be helpful.

'I can *spell*, Mr Rumpole.' Teasdale was now testy.

'Then your Lordship has the advantage of the witness. I notice she spells Naseby with a "z".'

'My Lord. I hesitate to interrupt.' At least I was doing well enough to bring Landseer languidly to his feet. 'Perhaps this sort of cross-examination is common enough in the criminal courts, but I cannot see how it can possibly be relevant in an action for libel.'

'Neither can I, Mr Landseer, I must confess.' Of course the judge agreed.

I did my best to put him right. 'These questions, my Lord, go to the heart of this lady's credibility.' I turned to give the witness my full attention. 'I have to suggest, Miss Nettleship, that as an historical novelist you are a complete fake.'

'My Lord. I have made my point.' Landseer sat down then, looking well pleased, and immediately whispered to his junior, 'We'll let him go on with that line and they'll give us four hundred thousand.'

'You have no respect for history and very little for the English language.' I continued to chip away at the spotless novelist.

'I try to tell a story, Mr Rumpole.'

'And your evidence to this court has been, to use my Lord's vivid expression, "a rattling good yarn"?' Teasdale looked displeased at my question.

'I have sworn to tell the truth.'

'Remember that. Now let us see how much of this article is correct.' I picked up Stella January's offending contribution. 'You do live at Hollyhock Cottage, near Godalming, in the county of Surrey?'

'That is so.'

'You have a jacuzzi?'

'She has *what*, Mr Rumpole?' I had entered a world unknown to a judge addicted to cold showers.

'A sort of bath, my Lord, with a whirlpool attached.'

'I installed one in my converted barn,' Miss Nettleship admitted. 'I find it relaxes me, after a long day's work.'

'You don't twiddle round in there with a close personal friend occasionally?'

'That's worth another ten thousand to us,' Landseer told his junior, growing happier by the minute. In fact the jury members were looking at me with some disapproval.

'Certainly not. I do not believe in sex before marriage.'

'And have no experience of it?'

'I was engaged once, Mr Rumpole.'

'Just once?'

'Oh, yes. My fiancé was killed in an air crash ten years ago. I think about him every day, and every day I'm thankful we didn't' – she looked down modestly – 'do anything before we were married. We were tempted, I'm afraid, the night before he died. But we resisted the temptation.'

'Some people would say that's a very moving story,' Judge Teasdale told the jury after a reverent hush.

'Others might say it's the story of *Sally on the Somme*, only there the fiancé was killed in the war.' I picked up another example of the Nettleship *œuvre*.

'That, Mr Rumpole,' Amelia looked pained, 'is a book that's particularly close to my heart. At least I don't do anything my heroines wouldn't do.'

'He's getting worse all the time,' Robin Peppiatt, the *Beacon* barrister, whispered despairingly to his junior, Dick Garsington, who came back with 'The damages are going to hit the roof!'

'Miss Nettleship, may I come to the last matter raised in the article?'

'I'm sure the jury will be grateful that you're reaching the end, Mr Rumpole,' the judge couldn't resist saying, so I smiled charmingly and told him that I should finish a great deal sooner if I were allowed to proceed without further interruption. Then I began to read Stella January's words aloud to the witness.

' "Her latest Casanova, so far unnamed, is said to be a married man who's been seen leaving in the wee small hours." '

'I read that,' Miss Nettleship remembered.

'You had company last night, didn't you? Until what I suppose might be revoltingly referred to as "the wee small hours"?'

'What are you suggesting?'

'That someone was with you. And when he left at about five-thirty in the morning you stood in your nightdress waving goodbye and blowing kisses. Who was it, Miss Nettleship?'

'That is an absolutely uncalled-for suggestion.'

'You called for it when you issued a writ for libel.'

'Do I have to answer?' She turned to the judge for help. He gave her his most encouraging smile and said that it might save time in the end if she were to answer Mr Rumpole's question.

'That is absolutely untrue!' For the first time Amelia's look of serenity vanished and I got, from the witness-box, a cold stare of hatred. 'Absolutely untrue.' The judge made a grateful note of her answer.

'Thank you, Miss Nettleship. I think we might continue with this tomorrow morning, if you have any further questions, Mr Rumpole?'

'I have indeed, my Lord.' Of course I had more questions and by the morning I hoped also to have some evidence to back them up.

I was in no hurry to return to the alleged mansion flat that night. I rightly suspected that our self-invited guest, Claude Erskine-Brown, would be playing his way through *Die Meistersinger* and giving Hilda a synopsis of the plot as it unfolded. As I reach the last of a man's seven ages I am more than ever persuaded that life is too short for Wagner, a man who was never in a hurry when it came to composing an opera. I paid a solitary visit to Pommeroy's well-known watering-hole after court in the hope of finding the representatives of the *Beacon*; but the only one I found was Connie Coughlin, the features editor, moodily surveying a large gin and tonic.

'No champagne tonight?' I asked as I wandered over to her table, glass in hand.

'I don't think we've got much to celebrate.'

'I wanted to ask you' – I took a seat beside the redoubtable Connie – 'about Miss Stella January. Our girl on the spot. Bright, attractive kind of reporter, was she?'

'I don't know,' Connie confessed.

'But surely you're the features editor?'

'I never met her.' She said it with the resentment of a woman whose editor had been interfering with her page.

'Any idea how old she was, for instance?'

'Oh, young, I should think.' It was the voice of middle age speaking. 'Morry said she was young. Just starting in the business.'

'And I was going to ask you . . .'

'You're very inquisitive.'

'It's my trade.' I downed what was left of my claret. '. . . About the love life of Mr Morry Machin.'

'Good God. Whose side are you on, Mr Rumpole?'

'At the moment, on the side of the truth. Did Morry have some sort of a romantic interest in Miss Stella January?'

'Short-lived, I'd say.' Connie clearly had no pity for the girl if she'd been enjoyed and then sacked.

'He's married?'

'Oh, two or three times.' It occurred to me that at some time, during one or other of these marriages, Morry and La Coughlin might have been more than fellow hacks on the *Beacon*. 'Now he seems to have got some sort of steady girlfriend.' She said it with some resentment.

'You know her?'

'Not at all. He keeps her under wraps.'

I looked at her for a moment. A woman, I thought, with a lonely evening in an empty flat before her. Then I thanked her for her help and stood up.

'Who are you going to grill next?' she asked me over the rim of her gin and tonic.

'As a matter of fact,' I told her, 'I've got a date with Miss Stella January.'

Quarter of an hour later I was walking across the huge floor, filled with desks, telephones and word processors, where the *Beacon* was produced, towards the glass-walled office in the corner, where Morry sat with his deputy, Ted Spratling, seeing that all the scandal that was fit to print, and a good deal of it that wasn't, got safely between the covers of the *Beacon*. I arrived at his office, pulled open the door and was greeted by Morry, in his shirt-sleeves, his feet up on the desk.

'Working late, Mr Rumpole? I hope you can do better for us tomorrow,' he greeted me with amused disapproval.

'I hope so too. I'm looking for Miss Stella January.'

'I told you, she's not here any more. I think she went overseas.'

'I think she's here,' I assured him. He was silent for a moment and then he looked at his deputy. 'Ted, perhaps you'd better leave me to have a word with my learned counsel.'

'I'll be on the back bench.' Spratling left for the desk on the floor which the editors occupied.

When he had gone, Morry looked up at me and said quietly, 'Now then, Mr Rumpole, sir. How can I help you?'

'Stella certainly wasn't a young woman, was she?' I was sure about that.

'She was only with us a short time. But she was young, yes,' he said vaguely.

'A quotation from her article that Amelia Nettleship "makes Mae West sound like Florence Nightingale". No young woman today's going to have heard of Mae West. Mae West's as remote in history as Messalina and Helen of Troy. That article, I would hazard a guess, was written by a man well into his middle age.'

'Who?'

'You.'

There was another long silence and the editor did his best to smile. 'Have you been drinking at all this evening?'

I took a seat then on the edge of his desk and lit a small cigar. 'Of course I've been drinking *at all*. You don't imagine I have these brilliant flashes of deduction when I'm perfectly sober, do you?'

'Then hadn't you better go home to bed?'

'So you wrote the article. No argument about that. It's been found in the system with your word processor number on it. Careless, Mr Machin. You clearly have very little talent for crime. The puzzling thing is, why you should attack Miss Nettleship when she's such a good friend of yours.'

'Good friend?' He did his best to laugh. 'I told you. I've never even met the woman.'

'It was a lie, like the rest of this pantomime lawsuit. Last night you were with her until past five in the morning. And she said goodbye to you with every sign of affection.'

'What makes you say that?'

'Were you in a hurry? Anyway, this was dropped by the side of your car.' Then I pulled out the present Fig Newton had given me outside court that day and put it on the desk.

'Anyone can buy the *Beacon*.' Morry glanced at the mud-stained exhibit.

'Not everyone gets the first edition, the one that fell on the editor's desk at ten o'clock that evening. I would say that's a bit of a rarity around Godalming.'

'Is that all?'

'No. You were watched.'

'Who by?'

'Someone I asked to find out the truth about Miss Nettleship. Now he's turned up the truth about both of you.'

Morry got up then and walked to the door which Ted Spratling had left half-open. He shut it carefully and then turned to me. 'I went down to ask her to drop the case.'

'To use a legal expression, pull the other one, it's got bells on it.'

'I don't know what you're suggesting.'

And then, as he stood looking at me, I moved round and sat in the editor's chair. 'Let me enlighten you.' I was as patient as I could manage. 'I'm suggesting a conspiracy to pervert the course of justice.'

'What's that mean?'

'I told you I'm an old taxi, waiting on the rank, but I'm not prepared to be the get-away driver for a criminal conspiracy.'

'You haven't said anything? To anyone?' He looked very frightened.

'Not yet.'

'And you won't.' He tried to sound confident. 'You're my lawyer.'

'Not any longer, Mr Machin. I don't belong to you any more. I'm an ordinary citizen, about to report an attempted crime.' It was then I reached for the telephone. 'I don't think there's any limit on the sentence for conspiracy.'

'What do you mean, "conspiracy"?'

'You're getting sacked by the *Beacon*; perhaps your handshake is a bit less than golden. Sales are down on historical virgins. So your steady girlfriend and you get together to make half a tax-free million.'

'I wish I knew how.' He was doing his best to smile.

'Perfectly simple. You turn yourself into Stella January, the unknown girl reporter, for half an hour and libel Amelia. She sues the paper and collects. Then you both sail into the sunset and share the proceeds. There's one thing I shan't forgive you for.'

'What's that?'

'The plan called for an Old Bailey hack, a stranger to the civilized world of libel who wouldn't settle, an old war-horse who'd attack La Nettleship and inflame the damages. So you used me, Mr Morry Machin!'

'I thought you'd be accustomed to that.' He stood over me, suddenly looking older. 'Anyway, they told me in Pommeroy's that you never prosecute.'

'No, I don't, do I? But on this occasion, I must say, I'm sorely tempted.' I thought about it and finally pushed away the telephone. 'Since it's a libel action I'll offer you terms of settlement.'

'What sort of terms?'

'The fair Amelia to drop her case. You pay the costs, including the fees of Fig Newton, who's caught a bad cold in the course of these proceedings. Oh, and in the matter of my learned friend Claude Erskine-Brown . . .'

'What's he got to do with it?'

'. . . Print a full and grovelling apology on the front page of the *Beacon*. And get them to pay him a substantial sum by way of damages. And that's my last word on the subject.' I stood up then and moved to the door.

'What's it going to cost me?' was all he could think of saying.

'I have no idea, but I know what it's going to cost me. Two weeks at five hundred a day. A provision for my old age.' I opened the glass door and let in the hum and clatter which were the birth-pangs of the *Daily Beacon*. 'Goodnight, Stella,' I said to Mr Morry Machin. And then I left him.

So it came about that next morning's *Beacon* printed a grovelling apology to 'the distinguished barrister Mr Claude Erskine-Brown' which accepted that he went to the Kitten-A-Go-Go Club purely in the interests of legal research and announced that my learned friend's hurt feelings would be soothed by the application of substantial, and tax-free, damages. As a consequence of this, Mrs Phillida Erskine-Brown rang chambers, spoke words of forgiveness and love to her husband, and he arranged, in his new-found wealth, to take her to dinner at Le Gavroche. The cuckoo flew from our nest, Hilda and I were left alone in the Gloucester Road, and we never found out how *Die Meistersinger* ended.

In court my one and only libel action ended in a sudden outburst of peace and goodwill, much to the frustration of Mr Justice Teasdale, who had clearly been preparing a summing-up which would encourage the jury to make Miss Nettleship rich beyond the dreams of avarice. All the allegations against her were dropped; she had no doubt been persuaded by her lover to ask for no damages at all and the *Beacon*'s editor accepted the bill for costs with extremely bad grace. This old legal taxi moved off to ply for hire elsewhere, glad to be shot of Mr Morry Machin.

'Is there a little bit of burglary around, Henry?' I asked our clerk, as I have recorded. 'Couldn't you get me a nice little gentle robbery? Something which shows human nature in a better light than civil law?'

'Good heavens!' Hilda exclaimed as we lay reading in the matrimonial bed in Froxbury Mansions. I noticed that there had been a change in her reading matter and she was already well into *On the Make* by Suzy Hutchins. 'This girl's about to go to Paris with a man old enough to be her father.'

'That must happen quite often.'

'But it seems he *is* her father.'

'Well, at least you've gone off the works of Amelia Nettleship.'

'The way she dropped that libel action. The woman's no better than she should be.'

'Which of us is? Any chance of turning out the light?' I asked She Who Must Be Obeyed, but she was too engrossed in the doings of her delinquent heroine to reply.

Rumpole à la Carte

I suppose, when I have time to think about it, which is not often during the long day's trudge round the Bailey and more down-market venues such as the Uxbridge Magistrates' Court, the law represents some attempt, however fumbling, to impose order on a chaotic universe. Chaos, in the form of human waywardness and uncontrollable passion, is ever bubbling away just beneath the surface and its sporadic outbreaks are what provide me with my daily crust, and even a glass or two of Pommeroy's plonk to go with it. I have often noticed, in the accounts of the many crimes with which I have been concerned, that some small sign of disorder – an unusual number of milk bottles on a doorstep, a car parked on a double yellow line by a normally law-abiding citizen, even, in the Penge Bungalow Murders, someone else's mackintosh taken from an office peg – has been the first indication of anarchy taking over. The clue that such dark forces were at work in La Maison Jean-Pierre, one of the few London eateries to have achieved three Michelin stars and to charge more for a bite of dinner for two than I get for a legal aid theft, was very small indeed.

Now my wife, Hilda, is a good plain cook. In saying that, I'm not referring to She Who Must Be Obeyed's moral values or passing any judgement on her personal appearance. What I can tell you is that she cooks without flights of fancy. She is not, in any way, a woman who lacks imagination. Indeed some of the things she imagines Rumpole gets up to when out of her sight are colourful in the extreme, but she doesn't apply such gifts to a chop or a potato, being quite content to grill the one and boil the other. She can also boil a cabbage into submission and fry fish. The nearest her cooking comes to the poetic is, perhaps, in her baked jam roll, which I have always found to be an emotion best recollected in tranquillity. From all this, you will gather that Hilda's honest cooking is sufficient but not exotic, and that happily the terrible curse of *nouvelle cuisine* has not infected Froxbury Mansions in the Gloucester Road.

So it is not often that I am confronted with the sort of fare photographed in the Sunday supplements. I scarcely ever sit down to an octagonal plate on which a sliver of monkfish is arranged in a composition of pastel shades, which also features a brush stroke of pink sauce, a single peeled prawn and a sprig of dill. Such gluttony is, happily, beyond my means. It wasn't, however, beyond the means of Hilda's cousin Everard, who was visiting us from Canada, where he carried on a thriving trade as a company lawyer. He told us that he felt we stood in dire need of what he called 'a taste of gracious living' and booked a table for three at La Maison Jean-Pierre.

So we found ourselves in an elegantly appointed room with subdued lighting and even more subdued conversation, where the waiters padded around like priests and the customers behaved as though they were in church. The climax of the ritual came when the dishes were set on the table under silvery domes, which were lifted to the whispered command of '*Un, deux, trois!*' to reveal the somewhat mingy portions on offer. Cousin Everard was a grey-haired man in a pale grey suiting who talked about his legal experiences in greyish tones. He entertained us with a long account of a takeover bid for the Winnipeg Soap Company which had cleared four million dollars for his clients, the Great Elk Bank of Canada.

Hearing this, Hilda said accusingly, 'You've never cleared four million dollars for a client, have you, Rumpole? You should be a company lawyer like Everard.'

'Oh, I think I'll stick to crime,' I told them. 'At least it's a more honest type of robbery.'

'Nonsense. Robbery has never got us a dinner at La Maison Jean-Pierre. We'd never be here if Cousin Everard hadn't come all the way from Saskatchewan to visit us.'

'Yes, indeed. From the town of Saskatoon, Hilda.' Everard gave her a greyish smile.

'You see, Hilda. Saskatoon as in *spittoon*.'

'Crime doesn't pay, Horace,' the man from the land of the igloos told me. 'You should know that by now. Of course, we have several fine dining restaurants in Saskatoon these days, but nothing to touch this.' He continued his inspection of the menu. 'Hilda, may I make so bold as to ask, what is your pleasure?'

During the ensuing discussion my attention strayed. Staring idly round the consecrated area I was startled to see, in the gloaming, a distinct sign of human passion in revolt against the forces of law and order. At a table for two I recognized Claude Erskine-Brown, opera buff, hopeless cross-examiner and long-time member of our chambers in Equity Court. But was he dining tête-à-tête with his wife, the handsome and successful QC, Mrs Phillida Erskine-Brown, the Portia of our group, as law and order demanded? The answer to that was no. He was entertaining a young and decorative lady solicitor named Patricia (known to herself as Tricia) Benbow. Her long golden hair (which often provoked whistles from the cruder junior clerks round the Old Bailey) hung over her slim and suntanned shoulders and one generously ringed hand rested on Claude's as she gazed, in her usual appealing way, up into his eyes. She couldn't gaze into them for long as Claude, no doubt becoming uneasily aware of the unexpected presence of a couple of Rumpoles in the room, hid his face behind a hefty wine list.

At that moment an extremely superior brand of French head waiter manifested himself beside our table, announced his presence with a discreet cough, and led off with, '*Madame, messieurs*. Tonight Jean-Pierre recommends, for the main course, *la poésie de la poitrine du canard aux céleris et épinards crus.*'

'*Poésie* . . .' Hilda sounded delighted and kindly explained, 'That's poetry, Rumpole. Tastes a good deal better than that old Wordsworth of yours, I shouldn't be surprised.'

'Tell us about it, Georges.' Everard smiled at the waiter. 'Whet our appetites.'

'This is just a few wafer-thin slices of breast of duck, marinated in a drop or two of Armagnac, delicately grilled and served with a celery *rémoulade* and some leaves of spinach lightly steamed . . .'

'And mash . . . ?' I interrupted the man to ask.

'*Excusez-moi?*' The fellow seemed unable to believe his ears.

'Mashed spuds come with it, do they?'

'Ssh, Rumpole!' Hilda was displeased with me, but turned all her charms on Georges. 'I will have the *poésie*. It sounds delicious.'

'A culinary experience, Hilda. Yes. *Poésie* for me too, please.' Everard fell into line.

'I would like a *poésie* of steak and kidney *pudding*, not pie, with mashed potatoes and a big scoop of boiled cabbage. *English* mustard, if you have it.' It seemed a reasonable enough request.

'Rumpole!' Hilda's whisper was menacing. 'Behave yourself!'

'This . . . "pudding"' – Georges was puzzled – 'is not on our menu.'

'"Your pleasure is our delight." It says that on your menu. Couldn't you ask Cookie if she could delight me? Along those lines.'

'"Cookie"? I do not know who M'sieur means by "Cookie". Our *maître de cuisine* is Jean-Pierre O'Higgins himself. He is in the kitchen now.'

'How very convenient. Have a word in his shell-like, why don't you?'

For a tense moment it seemed as though the looming, priestly figure of Georges was about to excommunicate me, drive me out of the temple, or at least curse me by bell, book and candle. However, after muttering, '*Si vous le voulez. Excusez-moi,*' he went off in search of higher authority. Hilda apologized for my behaviour and told Cousin Everard that she supposed I thought I was being funny. I assured her that there was nothing particularly funny about a steak and kidney pudding.

Then I was aware of a huge presence at my elbow. A tall, fat, red-faced man in a chef's costume was standing with his hands on his hips and asking, 'Is there someone here wants to lodge a complaint?'

Jean-Pierre O'Higgins, I was later to discover, was the product of an Irish father and a French mother. He spoke in the tones of those Irishmen who come up in a menacing manner and stand far too close to you in pubs. He was well known, I had already heard it rumoured, for dominating both his kitchen and his customers; his phenomenal rudeness to his guests seemed to be regarded as one of the attractions of his establishment. The gourmets of London didn't feel that their dinners had been entirely satisfactory unless they were served up, by way of a savoury, with a couple of insults from Jean-Pierre O'Higgins.

'Well, yes,' I said. 'There is someone.'

'Oh, yes?' O'Higgins had clearly never heard of the old adage about the customer always being right. 'And are you the joker that requested mash?'

'Am I to understand you to be saying,' I enquired as politely as I knew how, 'that there are to be no mashed spuds for my delight?'

'Look here, my friend. I don't know who you are . . .' Jean-Pierre went on in an unfriendly fashion and Everard did his best to introduce me.

'Oh, this is Horace Rumpole, Jean-Pierre. The *criminal* lawyer.'

'*Criminal* lawyer, eh?' Jean-Pierre was unappeased. 'Well, don't commit your crimes in my restaurant. If you want "mashed spuds", I suggest you move down to the working-men's caff at the end of the street.'

'That's a very helpful suggestion.' I was, as you see, trying to be as pleasant as possible.

'You might get a few bangers while you're about it. And a bottle of OK sauce. That suit your delicate palate, would it?'

'Very well indeed! I'm not a great one for wafer-thin slices of anything.'

'You don't look it. Now, let's get this straight. People who come into my restaurant damn well eat as I tell them to!'

'And I'm sure you win them all over with your irresistible charm.' I gave him the retort courteous. As the chef seemed about to explode, Hilda weighed in with a well-meaning 'I'm sure my husband doesn't mean to be rude. It's just, well, we don't dine out very often. And this is such a delightful room, isn't it?'

'Your husband?' Jean-Pierre looked at She Who Must Be Obeyed with deep pity. 'You have all my sympathy, you unfortunate woman. Let me tell you, Mr Rumpole, this is La Maison Jean-Pierre. I have three stars in the Michelin. I have thrown out an Arabian king because he ordered filet mignon well cooked. I have sent film stars away in tears because they dared to mention Thousand Island dressing. I am Jean-Pierre O'Higgins, the greatest culinary genius now working in England!'

I must confess that during this speech from the patron I found my attention straying. The other diners, as is the way with the English at the trough, were clearly straining their ears to catch every detail of the row while ostentatiously concentrating on their plates. The pale, bespectacled girl making up the bills behind the desk in the corner seemed to have no such inhibitions. She was staring across the room and looking at me, I thought, as though I had thoroughly deserved the O'Higgins rebuke. And then I saw two waiters approach Erskine-Brown's table with domed dishes, which they laid on the table with due solemnity.

'And let me tell you,' Jean-Pierre's oration continued, 'I started my career with salads at La Grande Bouffe in Lyons under the great Ducasse. I was *rôtisseur* in Le Crillon, Boston. I have run this restaurant for twenty years and I have never, let me tell you, in my whole career, served up a mashed spud!'

The climax of his speech was dramatic but not nearly as startling as the events which took place at Erskine-Brown's table. To the count of '*Un, deux, trois!*' the waiters removed the silver covers and from under the one in front of Tricia Benbow sprang a small, alarmed brown mouse, perfectly visible by the light of a table candle, which had presumably been nibbling at the *poésie*. At this, the elegant lady solicitor uttered a piercing scream and leapt on to her chair. There she stood, with her skirt held down to as near her knees as possible, screaming in an ever-rising crescendo towards some ultimate climax. Meanwhile, the stricken Claude looked just as a man who'd planned to have a quiet dinner with a lady and wanted to attract no one's attention would look under such circumstances.

'Please, Tricia,' I could hear his plaintive whisper, 'don't scream! People are noticing us.'

'I say, old darling,' I couldn't help saying to that three-star man

O'Higgins, 'they had a mouse on that table. Is it the *spécialité de la maison?*'

A few days later, at breakfast in the mansion flat, glancing through the post (mainly bills and begging letters from Her Majesty, who seemed to be pushed for a couple of quid and would be greatly obliged if I'd let her have a little tax money on account), I saw a glossy brochure for a hotel in the Lake District. Although in the homeland of my favourite poet, Le Château Duddon, 'Lakeland's Paradise of Gracious Living', didn't sound like old Wordsworth's cup of tea, despite the 'king-sized four-poster in the Samuel Taylor Coleridge suite'.

'Cousin Everard wants to take me up there for a break.' Hilda, who was clearing away, removed a half-drunk cup of tea from my hand.

'A break from what?' I was mystified.

'From you, Rumpole. Don't you think I need it? After that disastrous evening at La Maison?'

'Was it a disaster? I quite enjoyed it. England's greatest chef laboured and gave birth to a ridiculous mouse. People'd pay good money to see a trick like that.'

'*You* were the disaster, Rumpole,' she said, as she consigned my last piece of toast to the tidy-bin. 'You were unforgivable. Mashed spuds! Why ever did you use such a vulgar expression?'

'Hilda,' I protested, I thought, reasonably, 'I have heard some fairly fruity language round the courts in the course of a long life of crime. But I've never heard it suggested that the words "mashed spuds" would bring a blush to the cheek of the tenderest virgin.'

'Don't try to be funny, Rumpole. You upset that brilliant chef, Mr O'Higgins. You deeply upset Cousin Everard!'

'Well' – I had to put the case for the defence – 'Everard kept on suggesting I didn't make enough to feed you properly. Typical commercial lawyer. Criminal law is about life, liberty and the pursuit of happiness. Commercial law is about money. That's what I think, anyway.'

Hilda looked at me, weighed up the evidence and summed up,

not entirely in my favour. 'I don't think you made that terrible fuss because of what you thought about commercial law,' she said. 'You did it because you have to be a "character", don't you? Wherever you go. Well, I don't know if I'm going to be able to put up with your "character" much longer.'

I don't know why but what she said made me feel, quite suddenly and in a most unusual way, uncertain of myself. What was Hilda talking about exactly? I asked for further and better particulars.

'You have to be one all the time, don't you?' She was clearly getting into her stride. 'With your cigar ash and steak and kidney and Pommeroy's Ordinary Red and your arguments. Always arguments! Why do you have to go on arguing, Rumpole?'

'Arguing! It's been my life, Hilda,' I tried to explain.

'Well, it's not mine! Not any more. Cousin Everard doesn't argue in public. He is quiet and polite.'

'If you like that sort of thing.' The subject of Cousin Everard was starting to pall on me.

'Yes, Rumpole. Yes, I do. That's why I agreed to go on this trip.'

'Trip?'

'Everard and I are going to tour all the restaurants in England with stars. We're going to Bath and York and Devizes. And you can stay here and eat all the mashed spuds you want.'

'What?' I hadn't up till then taken Le Château Duddon entirely seriously. 'You really mean it?'

'Oh, yes. I think so. The living is hardly gracious here, is it?'

On the way to my place of work I spent an uncomfortable quarter of an hour thinking over what She Who Must Be Obeyed had said about me having to be a 'character'. It seemed an unfair charge. I drink Château Thames Embankment because it's all I can afford. It keeps me regular and blots out certain painful memories, such as a bad day in court in front of Judge Graves, an old darling who undoubtedly passes iced water every time he goes to the gents. I enjoy the fragrance of a small cigar. I relish an argument. This is the way of life I have chosen. I don't have to do any of these things in order to be a character. Do I?

I was jerked out of this unaccustomed introspection on my arrival in the clerk's room at chambers. Henry, our clerk, was striking bargains with solicitors over the telephone while Dianne sat in front of her typewriter, her head bowed over a lengthy and elaborate manicure. Uncle Tom, our oldest inhabitant, who hasn't had a brief in court since anyone can remember, was working hard at improving his putting skills with an old mashie-niblick and a clutch of golf balls, the hole being represented by the waste-paper basket laid on its side. Almost as soon as I got into this familiar environment I was comforted by the sight of a man who seemed to be in far deeper trouble than I was. Claude Erskine-Brown came up to me in a manner that I can only describe as furtive.

'Rumpole,' he said, 'as you may know, Philly is away in Cardiff doing a long fraud.'

'Your wife,' I congratulated the man, 'goes from strength to strength.'

'What I mean is, Rumpole' – Claude's voice sank below the level of Henry's telephone calls – 'you may have noticed me the other night. In La Maison Jean-Pierre.'

'Noticed you, Claude? Of course not! You were only in the company of a lady who stood on a chair and screamed like a banshee with toothache. No one could have possibly noticed you.' I did my best to comfort the man.

'It was purely a business arrangement,' he reassured me.

'Pretty rum way of conducting business.'

'The lady was Miss Tricia Benbow. My instructing solicitor in the VAT case,' he told me, as though that explained everything.

'Claude, I have had some experience of the law and it's a good plan, when entertaining solicitors in order to tout for briefs, *not* to introduce mice into their *plats du jour*.'

The telephone by Dianne's typewriter rang. She blew on her nail lacquer and answered it, as Claude's voice rose in anguished protest. 'Good heavens. You don't think I did *that*, do you, Rumpole? The whole thing was a disaster! An absolute tragedy! Which may have appalling consequences . . .'

'Your wife on the phone, Mr Erskine-Brown,' Dianne interrupted him and Claude went to answer the call with all the eager cheerfulness of a French aristocrat who is told the tumbrel is at the door. As he was telling his wife he hoped things were going splendidly in Cardiff, and that he rarely went out in the evenings, in fact usually settled down to a scrambled egg in front of the telly, there was a sound of rushing water without and our head of chambers joined us.

'Something extremely serious has happened.' Sam Ballard, QC made the announcement as though war had broken out. He is a pallid sort of person who usually looks as though he has just bitten into a sour apple. His hair, I have to tell you, seems to be slicked down with some kind of pomade.

'Someone nicked the nail-brush in the chambers loo?' I suggested helpfully.

'How did you guess?' He turned on me, amazed, as though I had the gift of second sight.

'It corresponds to your idea of something serious. Also I notice such things.'

'Odd that you should know immediately what I was talking about, Rumpole.' By now Ballard's amazement had turned to deep suspicion.

'Not guilty, my Lord,' I assured him. 'Didn't you have a meeting of your God-bothering society here last week?'

'The Lawyers As Christians committee. We met here. What of it?'

'"Cleanliness is next to godliness." Isn't that their motto? The devout are notable nail-brush nickers.' As I said this, I watched Erskine-Brown lay the telephone to rest and leave the room with the air of a man who has merely postponed the evil hour. Ballard was still on the subject of serious crime in the facilities.

'It's of vital importance in any place of work, Henry,' he batted on, 'that the highest standards of hygiene are maintained! Now I've been instructed by the City Health Authority in an important case, it would be extremely embarrassing to me personally if my chambers were found wanting in the matter of a nail-brush.'

'Well, don't look at me, Mr Ballard.' Henry was not taking this lecture well.

'I am accusing nobody.' Ballard sounded unconvincing. 'But look to it, Henry. Please, look to it.'

Then our head of chambers left us. Feeling my usual reluctance to start work, I asked Uncle Tom, as something of an expert in these matters, if it would be fair to call me a 'character'.

'A what, Rumpole?'

'A "character", Uncle Tom.'

'Oh, they had one of those in old Sniffy Greengrass's chambers in Lamb Court,' Uncle Tom remembered. 'Fellow called Dalrymple. Lived in an absolutely filthy flat over a chemist's shop in Chancery Lane and used to lead a cat round the Temple on a long piece of pink tape. "Old Dalrymple's a character," they used to say, and the other fellows in chambers were rather proud of him.'

'I don't do anything like that, do I?' I asked for reassurance.

'I hope not,' Uncle Tom was kind enough to say. 'This Dalrymple finally went across the road to do an undefended divorce. In his pyjamas! I believe they had to lock him up. I wouldn't say you were a "character", Rumpole. Not yet, anyway.'

'Thank you, Uncle Tom. Perhaps you could mention that to She Who Must?'

And then the day took a distinct turn for the better. Henry put down his phone after yet another call and my heart leapt up when I heard that Mr Bernard, my favourite instructing solicitor (because he keeps quiet, does what he's told and hardly ever tells me about his bad back), was coming over and was anxious to instruct me in a new case which was 'not on the legal aid'. As I left the room to go about this business, I had one final question for Uncle Tom. 'That fellow Dalrymple. He didn't play golf in the clerk's room did he?'

'Good heavens, no.' Uncle Tom seemed amused at my ignorance of the world. 'He was a character, do you see? He'd hardly do anything normal.'

Mr Bernard, balding, pin striped, with a greying moustache and a kindly eye, through all our triumphs and disasters remained imperturbable. No confession made by any client, however bizarre, seemed to surprise him, nor had any revelation of evil shocked him. He lived through our days of murder, mayhem and fraud as though he were listening to *Gardeners' Question Time*. He was interested in growing roses and in his daughter's nursing career. He spent his holidays in remote spots like Bangkok and the Seychelles. He always went away, he told me, 'on a package' and returned with considerable relief. I was always pleased to see Mr Bernard, but that day he seemed to have brought me something far from my usual line of country.

'My client, Mr Rumpole, first consulted me because his marriage was on the rocks, not to put too fine a point on it.'

'It happens, Mr Bernard. Many marriages are seldom off them.'

'Particularly so if, as in this case, the wife's of foreign extraction. It's long been my experience, Mr Rumpole, that you can't beat foreign wives for being vengeful. In this case, extremely vengeful.'

'Hell hath no fury, Mr Bernard?' I suggested.

'Exactly, Mr Rumpole. You've put your finger on the nub of the case. As you would say yourself.'

'I haven't done a matrimonial for years. My divorce may be a little rusty,' I told him modestly.

'Oh, we're not asking you to do the divorce. We're sending that to Mr Tite-Smith in Crown Office Row.'

Oh, well, I thought, with only a slight pang of disappointment, good luck to little Tite-Smith.

'The matrimonial is not my client's only problem,' Mr Bernard told me.

' "When sorrows come," Mr Bernard, "they come not single spies, But in battalions!" Your chap got something else on his plate, has he?'

'On his plate!' The phrase seemed to cause my solicitor some amusement. 'That's very apt, that is. And apter than you know, Mr Rumpole.'

'Don't keep me in suspense! Who is this mysterious client?'

'I wasn't to divulge the name, Mr Rumpole, in case you should refuse to act for him. He thought you might've taken against him, so he's coming to appeal to you in person. I asked Henry if he'd show him up as soon as he arrived.'

And, dead on cue, Dianne knocked on my door, threw it open

and announced, 'Mr O'Higgins.' The large man, dressed now in a deafening checked tweed jacket and a green turtle-necked sweater, looking less like a chef than an Irish horse coper, advanced on me with a broad grin and his hand extended in a greeting, which was in strong contrast to our last encounter.

'I rely on you to save me, Mr Rumpole,' he boomed. 'You're the man to do it, sir. The great criminal defender!'

'Oh? I thought *I* was the criminal in your restaurant,' I reminded him.

'I have to tell you, Mr Rumpole, your courage took my breath away! Do you know what he did, Mr Bernard? Do you know what this little fellow here had the pluck to do?' He seemed determined to impress my solicitor with an account of my daring in the face of adversity. 'He only ordered mashed spuds in La Maison Jean-Pierre. A risk no one else has taken in all the time I've been *maître de cuisine*.'

'It didn't seem to be particularly heroic,' I told Bernard, but O'Higgins would have none of that.

'I tell you, Mr Bernard' – he moved very close to my solicitor and towered over him – 'a man who could do that to Jean-Pierre couldn't be intimidated by all the judges of the Queen's Bench. What do you say then, Mr Horace Rumpole? Will you take me on?'

I didn't answer him immediately but sat at my desk, lit a small cigar and looked at him critically. 'I don't know yet.'

'Is it my personality that puts you off?' My prospective client folded himself into my armchair, with one leg draped over an arm. He grinned even more broadly, displaying a judiciously placed gold tooth. 'Do you find me objectionable?'

'Mr O'Higgins.' I decided to give judgement at length. 'I think your restaurant pretentious and your portions skimpy. Your customers eat in a dim, religious atmosphere which seems to be more like evensong than a good night out. You appear to be a self-opinionated and self-satisfied bully. I have known many murderers who could teach you a lesson in courtesy. However, Mr Bernard tells me that you are prepared to pay my fee and, in accordance with the great traditions of the Bar, I am on hire to even the most unattractive customer.'

There was a silence and I wondered if the inflammable restaurateur were about to rise and hit me. But he turned to Bernard with even greater enthusiasm. 'Just listen to that! How's that for eloquence? We picked the right one here, Mr Bernard!'

'Well, now. I gather you're in some sort of trouble. Apart from your marriage, that is.' I unscrewed my pen and prepared to take a note.

'This has nothing to do with my marriage.' But then he frowned unhappily. 'Anyway, I don't think it has.'

'You haven't done away with this vengeful wife of yours?' Was I to be presented with a murder?

'I should have, long ago,' Jean-Pierre admitted. 'But no. Simone is still alive and suing. Isn't that right, Mr Bernard?'

'It is, Mr O'Higgins,' Bernard assured him gloomily. 'It is indeed. But this is something quite different. My client, Mr Rumpole, is being charged under the Food and Hygiene Regulations 1970 for offences relating to dirty and dangerous practices at La Maison. I have received a telephone call from the environmental health officer.'

It was then, I'm afraid, that I started to laugh. I named the guilty party. 'The mouse!'

'Got it in one.' Jean-Pierre didn't seem inclined to join in the joke.

'The "wee, sleekit, cow'rin, tim'rous beastie",' I quoted at him. 'How delightful! We'll elect for trial before a jury. If we can't get you off, Mr O'Higgins, at least we'll give them a little harmless entertainment.'

Of course it wasn't really funny. A mouse in the wrong place, like too many milk bottles on a doorstep, might be a sign of passions stretched beyond control.

I have always found it useful, before forming a view about a case, to inspect the scene of the crime. Accordingly I visited La Maison Jean-Pierre one evening to study the ritual serving of dinner.

Mr Bernard and I stood in a corner of the kitchen at La Maison Jean-Pierre with our client. We were interested in the two waiters who had attended table eight, the site of the Erskine-Brown assignation. The senior of the two was Gaston, the station waiter, who had four tables under his command. 'Gaston Leblanc,' Jean-Pierre told us, as he identified the small, fat, cheerful, middle-aged man who trotted between the tables. 'Been with me for ever. Works all the hours God gave to keep a sick wife and their kid at university. Does all sorts of other jobs in the daytime. I don't enquire too closely. Georges Pitou, the head waiter, takes the orders, of course, and leaves a copy of the note on the table.'

We saw Georges move, in a stately fashion, into the kitchen and hand the order for table eight to a young cook in a white hat, who stuck it up on the kitchen wall with a magnet. This was Ian, the sous-chef. Jean-Pierre had 'discovered' him in a Scottish hotel and wanted to encourage his talent. That night the bustle in the kitchen was muted, and as I looked through the circular window into the dining-room I saw that most of the white-clothed tables were standing empty, like small icebergs in a desolate polar region. When the prosecution had been announced, there had been a headline in the *Evening Standard* which read GUESS WHO'S COMING TO DINNER? MOUSE SERVED IN TOP LONDON RESTAURANT and since then attendances at La Maison had dropped off sharply.

The runner between Gaston's station and the kitchen was the commis waiter, Alphonse Pascal, a painfully thin, dark-eyed young man with a falling lock of hair who looked like the hero of some nineteenth-century French novel, interesting and doomed. 'As a matter of fact,' Jean-Pierre told us, 'Alphonse is full of ambition. He's starting at the bottom and wants to work his way up to running a hotel. Been with me for about a year.'

We watched as Ian put the two orders for table eight on the serving-table. In due course Alphonse came into the kitchen and called out, 'Number eight!'

'Ready, frog-face,' Ian told him politely, and Alphonse came back with, '*Merci*, idiot.'

'Are they friends?' I asked my client.

'Not really. They're both much too fond of Mary.'

'Mary?'

'Mary Skelton. The English girl who makes up the bills in the restaurant.'

I looked again through the circular window and saw the unmemorable girl, her head bent over her calculator. She seemed an unlikely subject for such rivalry. I saw Alphonse pass her with a tray, carrying two domed dishes and, although he looked in her direction, she didn't glance up from her work. Alphonse then took the dishes to the serving-table at Gaston's station. Gaston looked under one dome to check its contents and then the plates were put on the table. Gaston mouthed an inaudible *'Un, deux, trois!'*, the domes were lifted before the diners and not a mouse stirred.

'On the night in question,' Bernard reminded me, 'Gaston says in his statement that he looked under the dome on the gentleman's plate.'

'And saw no side order of mouse,' I remembered.

'Exactly! So he gave the other to Alphonse, who took it to the lady.'

'And then . . . Hysterics!'

'And then the reputation of England's greatest *maître de cuisine* crumbled to dust!' Jean-Pierre spoke as though announcing a national disaster.

'Nonsense!' I did my best to cheer him up. 'You're forgetting the reputation of Horace Rumpole.'

'You think we've got a defence?' my client asked eagerly. 'I mean, now that you've looked at the kitchen?'

'Can't think of one for the moment,' I admitted, 'but I expect we'll cook up something in the end.'

Unencouraged, Jean-Pierre looked out into the dining-room, muttered, 'I'd better go and keep those lonely people company,' and left us. I watched him pass the desk, where Mary looked up and smiled and I thought, however brutal he was with his customers, at least Jean-Pierre's staff seemed to find him a tolerable employer. And then, to my surprise, I saw him approach the couple at table eight, grinning in a most ingratiating manner, and stand chatting and bowing as though they could have ordered doner kebab and chips and that would have been perfectly all right by him.

'You know,' I said to Mr Bernard, 'it's quite extraordinary, the power that can be wielded by one of the smaller rodents.'

'You mean it's wrecked his business?'

'No. More amazing than that. It's forced Jean-Pierre O'Higgins to be polite to his clientele.'

After my second visit to La Maison events began to unfold at breakneck speed. First our head of chambers, Soapy Sam Ballard, made it known to me that the brief he had accepted on behalf of the Health Authority, and of which he had boasted so flagrantly during the nail-brush incident, was in fact the prosecution of J.-P. O'Higgins for the serious crime of being in charge of a rodent-infested restaurant. Then She Who Must Be Obeyed, true to her word, packed her grip and went off on a gastronomic tour with the man from Saskatoon. I was left to enjoy a lonely high-calorie break-fast, with no fear of criticism over the matter of a fourth sausage, in the Taste-Ee-Bite Café, Fleet Street. Seated there one morning, enjoying the company of *The Times* crossword, I happened to over-hear Mizz Liz Probert, the dedicated young radical barrister in our chambers, talking to her close friend, David Inchcape, whom she had persuaded us to take on in a somewhat devious manner – a barrister as young but, I think, at heart, a touch less radical than Mizz Liz herself.

'You don't really *care*, do you, Dave?' she was saying.

'Of course, I care. I care about you, Liz. Deeply.' He reached out over their plates of muesli and cups of decaff to grasp her fingers.

'That's just physical.'

'Well. Not just physical. I don't suppose it's *just*. Mainly physical, perhaps.'

'No one cares about old people.'

'But you're not old people, Liz. Thank God!'

'You see. You don't care about them. My dad was saying there's old people dying in tower blocks every day. Nobody knows about it for weeks, until they decompose!'

And I saw Dave release her hand and say, 'Please, Liz. I *am* having my breakfast.'

'You see! You don't want to know. It's just something you don't want to hear about. It's the same with battery hens.'

'What's the same about battery hens?'

'No one wants to know. That's all.'

'But surely, Liz, battery hens don't get lonely.'

'Perhaps they do. There's an awful lot of loneliness about.' She looked in my direction. 'Get off to court then, if you have to. But do *think* about it, Dave.' Then she got up, crossed to my table, and asked what I was doing. I was having my breakfast, I assured her, and not doing my yoga meditation.

'Do you always have breakfast alone, Rumpole?' She spoke, in the tones of a deeply supportive social worker, as she sat down opposite me.

'It's not always possible. Much easier now, of course.'

'Now. Why *now* exactly?' She looked seriously concerned.

'Well. Now my wife's left me,' I told her cheerfully.

'Hilda!' Mizz Probert was shocked, being a conventional girl at heart.

'As you would say, Mizz Liz, she is no longer sharing a one-on-one relationship with me. In any meaningful way.'

'Where does that leave you, Rumpole?'

'Alone. To enjoy my breakfast and contemplate the crossword puzzle.'

'Where's Hilda gone?'

'Oh, in search of gracious living with her cousin Everard from Saskatoon. A fellow with about as many jokes in him as the Dow Jones Average.'

'You mean, she's gone off with another man?' Liz seemed unable to believe that infidelity was not confined to the young.

'That's about the size of it.'

'But, Rumpole. *Why?*'

'Because he's rich enough to afford very small portions of food.'

'So you're living by yourself? You must be terribly lonely.'

' "Society is all but rude," ' I assured her, ' "To this delicious solitude." '

There was a pause and then Liz took a deep breath and offered her assistance. 'You know, Rumpole, Dave and I have founded the YRL, Young Radical Lawyers. We don't only mean to reform the legal system, although that's part of it, of course. We're going to take on social work as well. We could always get someone to call and take a look at your flat every morning.'

'To make sure it's still there?'

'Well, no, Rumpole. As a matter of fact, to make sure you are.'

Those who are alone have great opportunities for eavesdropping, and Liz and Dave weren't the only members of our chambers I heard engaged in a heart-to-heart that day. Before I took the journey back to the She-less flat, I dropped into Pommeroy's and was enjoying the ham roll and bottle of Château Thames Embankment which would constitute my dinner, seated in one of the high-backed, pew-like stalls Jack Pommeroy has installed, presumably to give the joint a vaguely medieval appearance and attract the tourists. From behind my back I heard the voices of our head of chambers and Claude Erskine-Brown, who was saying, in his most ingratiating tones, 'Ballard. I want to have a word with you about the case you've got against La Maison Jean-Pierre.'

To this, Ballard, in thoughtful tones, replied unexpectedly, 'A strong chain! It's the only answer.' Which didn't seem to follow.

'It was just my terrible luck, of course,' Erskine-Brown complained, 'that it should happen at my table. I mean, I'm a pretty well-known member of the Bar. Naturally I don't want my name connected with, well, a rather ridiculous incident.'

'Fellows in chambers aren't going to like it.' Ballard was not yet with him. 'They'll say it's a restriction on their liberty. Rumpole, no doubt, will have a great deal to say about Magna Carta. But the only answer is to get a new nail-brush and chain it up. Can I have your support in taking strong measures?'

'Of course you can, Ballard. I'll be right behind you on this one.' The creeping Claude seemed only too anxious to please. 'And in this case you're doing, I don't suppose you'll have to call the couple who actually *got* the mouse?'

'The couple?' There was a pause while Ballard searched his memory. 'The mouse was served – appalling lack of hygiene in the workplace – to a table booked by a Mr Claude Erskine-Brown and guest. Of course he'll be a vital witness.' And then the penny dropped. He stared at Claude and said firmly, '*You'll* be a vital witness.'

'But if I'm a witness of any sort, my name'll get into the papers and Philly will know I was having dinner.'

'Why on earth *shouldn't* she know you were having dinner?' Ballard was reasoning with the man. 'Most people have dinner. Nothing to be ashamed of. Get a grip on yourself, Erskine-Brown.'

'Ballard. Sam.' Claude was trying the appeal to friendship. 'You're a married man. You should understand.'

'Of course I'm married. And Marguerite and I have dinner. On a regular basis.'

'But I wasn't having dinner with Philly.' Claude explained the matter carefully. 'I was having dinner with an instructing solicitor.'

'That was your guest?'

'Yes.'

'A solicitor?'

'Of course.'

Ballard seemed to have thought the matter over carefully, but he was still puzzled when he replied, remembering his instructions. 'He apparently leapt on to a chair, held down his skirt and screamed three times!'

'Ballard! The solicitor was Tricia Benbow. You don't imagine I'd spend a hundred and something quid on feeding the face of Mr Bernard, do you?'

There was another longish pause, during which I imagined Claude in considerable suspense, and then our head of chambers spoke again. 'Tricia Benbow?' he asked.

'Yes.'

'Is that the one with the long blonde hair and rings?'

'That's the one.'

'And your wife knew nothing of this?'

'And must never know!' For some reason not clear to me, Claude seemed to think he'd won his case, for he now sounded grateful. 'Thank you, Ballard. Thanks awfully, Sam. I can count on you to keep my name out of this. I'll do the same for you, old boy. Any day of the week.'

'That won't be necessary.' Ballard's tone was not encouraging, although Claude said, 'No? Well, thanks, anyway.'

'It *will* be necessary, however, for you to give evidence for the prosecution.' Soapy Sam Ballard pronounced sentence and Claude yelped, 'Have a heart, Sam!'

'Don't you "Sam" me.' Ballard was clearly in a mood to notice the decline of civilization as we know it. 'It's all part of the same thing, isn't it? Sharp practice over the nail-brush. Failure to assist the authorities in an important prosecution. You'd better prepare yourself for court, Erskine-Brown. And to be cross-examined by Rumpole for the defence. Do your duty! And take the consequences.'

A moment later I saw Ballard leaving for home and his wife, Marguerite, who, you will remember, once held the position of matron at the Old Bailey. No doubt he would chatter to her of nail-brushes and barristers unwilling to tell the whole truth. I carried my bottle of plonk round to Claude's stall in order to console the fellow.

'So,' I said, 'you lost your case.'

'What a bastard!' I have never seen Claude so pale.

'You made a big mistake, old darling. It's no good appealing to the warm humanity of a fellow who believes in chaining up nail-brushes.'

So the intrusive mouse continued to play havoc with the passions of a number of people, and I prepared myself for its day in court. I told Mr Bernard to instruct Ferdinand Isaac Gerald Newton, known in the trade as 'Fig' Newton, a lugubrious scarecrow of a man who is, without doubt, our most effective private investigator, to keep a watchful eye on the staff of La Maison. And then I decided to call in at the establishment on my way home one evening, not only to get a few more facts from my client but because I was becoming bored with Pommeroy's ham sandwiches.

Before I left chambers an event occurred which caused me deep satisfaction. I made for the downstairs lavatory, and although the door was open, I found it occupied by Uncle Tom, who was busily engaged at the basin washing his collection of golf balls and scrubbing each one to a gleaming whiteness with a nail-brush. He had been putting each one, when cleaned, into a biscuit tin and as I entered he dropped the nail-brush in also.

'Uncle Tom!' – I recognized the article at once – 'that's the chambers nail-brush! Soapy Sam's having kittens about it.'

'Oh, dear. Is it, really? I must have taken it without remembering. I'll leave it on the basin.'

But I persuaded him to let me have it for safe-keeping, saying I longed to see Ballard's little face light up with joy when it was restored to him.

When I arrived at La Maison the disputes seemed to have become a great deal more dramatic than even in Equity Court. The place was not yet open for dinner, but I was let in as the restaurant's legal adviser and I heard raised voices and sounds of a struggle from the kitchen. Pushing the door open, I found Jean-Pierre in the act of forcibly removing a knife from the hands of Ian, the sous-chef, at whom an excited Alphonse Pascal, his lock of black hair falling into his eyes, was shouting abuse in French. My arrival created a diversion in which both men calmed down and Jean-Pierre passed judgement on them.

'Bloody lunatics!' he said. 'Haven't they done this place enough harm already? They have to start slaughtering each other. Behave yourselves. *Soyez sages!* And what can I do for *you*, Mr Rumpole?'

'Perhaps we could have a little chat,' I suggested as the tumult died down. 'I thought I'd call in. My wife's away, you see, and I haven't done much about dinner.'

'Then what would you like?'

'Oh, anything. Just a snack.'

'Some pâté, perhaps? And a bottle of champagne?' I thought he'd never ask.

When we were seated at a table in a corner of the empty restaurant, the patron told me more about the quarrel. 'They were fighting again over Mary Skelton.'

I looked across at the desk, where the unmemorable girl was getting out her calculator and preparing for her evening's work. 'She doesn't look the type, exactly,' I suggested.

'Perhaps,' Jean-Pierre speculated, 'she has a warm heart? My wife Simone looks the type, but she's got a heart like an ice-cube.'

'Your wife. The vengeful woman?' I remembered what Mr Bernard had told me.

'Why should she be vengeful to me, Mr Rumpole? When I'm a particularly tolerant and easy-going type of individual?'

At which point a couple of middle-aged Americans, who had strayed in off the street, appeared at the door of the restaurant and asked Jean-Pierre if he were serving dinner. 'At six-thirty? No! And we don't do teas, either.' He shouted across at them, in a momentary return to his old ways, 'Cretins!'

'Of course,' I told him, 'you're a very *parfait*, gentle cook.'

'A great artist needs admiration. He needs almost incessant praise.'

'And with Simone,' I suggested, 'the admiration flowed like cement?'

'You've got it. Had some experience of wives, have you?'

'You might say, a lifetime's experience. Do you mind?' I poured myself another glass of unwonted champagne.

'No, no, of course. And your wife doesn't understand you?'

'Oh, I'm afraid she does. That's the worrying thing about it. She blames me for being a "character".'

'They'd blame you for anything. Come to divorce, has it?'

'Not quite reached your stage, Mr O'Higgins.' I looked round the restaurant. 'So, I suppose you have to keep these tables full to pay Simone her alimony.'

'Not exactly. You see, she'll own half La Maison.' That hadn't been entirely clear to me and I asked him to explain.

'When we started off, I was a young man. All I wanted to do was to get up early, go to Smithfield and Billingsgate, feel the lobsters and smell the fresh scallops, create new dishes and dream of sauces. Simone was the one with the business sense. Well, she's French, so she insisted on us getting married in France.'

'Was that wrong?'

'Oh, no. It was absolutely right, for Simone. Because they have a damned thing there called "community of property". I had to agree to give her half of everything if we ever broke up. You know about the law, of course.'

'Well, not everything about it.' Community of property, I must confess, came as news to me. 'I always found knowing the law a bit of a handicap for a barrister.'

'Simone knew all about it. She had her beady eye on the future.' He emptied his glass and then looked at me pleadingly. 'You're going to get us out of this little trouble, aren't you, Mr Rumpole? This affair of the mouse?'

'Oh, the mouse!' I did my best to reassure him. 'The mouse seems to be the least of your worries.'

Soon Jean-Pierre had to go back to his kitchen. On his way, he stopped at the cash desk and said something to the girl, Mary. She looked up at him with, I thought, unqualified adoration. He patted her arm and went back to his sauces, having reassured her, I suppose, about the quarrel that had been going on in her honour.

I did justice to the rest of the champagne and pâté de foie and started off for home. In the restaurant entrance hall I saw the lady who minded the cloaks take a suitcase from Gaston Leblanc, who had just arrived out of breath and wearing a mackintosh. Although large, the suitcase seemed very light and he asked her to look after it.

Several evenings later I was lying on my couch in the living-room of the mansion flat, a small cigar between my fingers and a glass of Château Fleet Street on the floor beside me. I was in vacant or in pensive mood as I heard a ring at the front doorbell. I started up, afraid that the delights of *haute cuisine* had palled for Hilda, and then I remembered that She would undoubtedly have come armed with a latchkey. I approached the front door, puzzled at the sound of young and excited voices without, combined with loud music. I got the door open and found myself face to face with Liz Probert, Dave Inchcape and five or six other junior hacks, all wearing sweatshirts with a picture of a wig and YOUNG RADICAL LAWYERS written on them. Dianne was also there in trousers and a glittery top, escorted by my clerk, Henry, wearing jeans and doing his best to appear young and swinging. The party was carrying various bottles and an article we know well down the Bailey (because it so often appears in lists of stolen property) as a ghetto blaster. It was from this contraption that the loud music emerged.

'It's a surprise party!' Mizz Liz Probert announced with considerable pride. 'We've come to cheer you up in your great loneliness.'

Nothing I could say would stem the well-meaning invasion. Within minutes the staid precincts of Froxbury Mansions were transformed into the sort of disco which is patronized by under-thirties on a package to the Costa del Sol. Bizarre drinks, such as rum and blackcurrant juice or advocaat and lemonade, were being mixed in what remained of our tumblers, supplemented by tooth-mugs from the bathroom. Scarves dimmed the lights, the ghetto blaster blasted ceaselessly and dancers gyrated in a self-absorbed manner, apparently oblivious of each other. Only Henry and Dianne, practising a more old-fashioned ritual, clung together, almost motionless, and carried on a lively conversation with me as I stood on the outskirts of the revelry, drinking the best of the wine they had brought and trying to look tolerantly convivial.

'We heard as how Mrs Rumpole has done a bunk, sir.' Dianne looked sympathetic, to which Henry added sourly, 'Some people have all the luck!'

'Why? Where's your wife tonight, Henry?' I asked my clerk. The cross he has to bear is that his spouse has pursued an ambitious career in local government so that, whereas she is now the Mayor of Bexleyheath, he is officially her Mayoress.

'My wife's at a dinner of South London mayors in the Mansion House, Mr Rumpole. No consorts allowed, thank God!' Henry told me.

'Which is why we're both on the loose tonight. Makes you feel young again, doesn't it, Mr Rumpole?' Dianne asked me as she danced minimally.

'Well, not particularly young, as a matter of fact.' The music yawned between me and my guests as an unbridgeable generation gap. And then one of the more intense of the young lady radicals approached me, as a senior member of the Bar, to ask what the hell the Lord Chief Justice knew about being pregnant and on probation at the moment your boyfriend's arrested for dope. 'Very little,

I should imagine,' I had to tell her, and then, as the telephone was bleating pathetically beneath the din, I excused myself and moved to answer it. As I went, a YRL sweatshirt whirled past me; Liz, dancing energetically, had pulled it off and was gyrating in what appeared to be an ancient string-vest and a pair of jeans.

'Rumpole!' the voice of She Who Must Be Obeyed called to me, no doubt from the banks of Duddon. 'What on earth's going on there?'

'Oh, Hilda. Is it you?'

'Of course it's me.'

'Having a good time, are you? And did Cousin Everard enjoy his sliver of whatever it was?'

'Rumpole. What's that incredible noise?'

'Noise? Is there a noise? Oh, yes. I think I do hear music. Well . . .' Here I improvised, as I thought brilliantly. 'It's a play, that's what it is, a play on television. It's all about young people, hopping about in a curious fashion.'

'Don't talk rubbish!' Hilda, as you may guess, sounded far from convinced. 'You know you never watch plays on television.'

'Not usually, I grant you,' I admitted. 'But what else have I got to do when my wife has left me?'

Much later, it seemed a lifetime later, when the party was over, I settled down to read the latest addition to my brief in the O'Higgins case. It was a report from Fig Newton, who had been keeping observation on the workers at La Maison. One afternoon he followed Gaston Leblanc, who left his home in Ruislip with a large suitcase, with which he travelled to a smart address at Egerton Crescent in Knightsbridge. This house, which had a bunch of brightly coloured balloons tied to its front door, Fig kept under surveillance for some time. A number of small children arrived, escorted by nannies, and were let in by a manservant. Later, when all the children had been received, Fig, wrapped in his Burberry with his collar turned up against the rain, was able to move so he got a clear view into the sitting-room.

What he saw interested me greatly. The children were seated on the floor watching breathlessly as Gaston Leblanc, station waiter and part-time conjuror, dressed in a black robe ornamented with stars, entertained them by slowly extricating a live and kicking rabbit from a top hat.

For the trial of Jean-Pierre O'Higgins we drew the short straw in the shape of an Old Bailey judge aptly named Gerald Graves. Judge Graves and I have never exactly hit it off. He is a pale, long-faced, unsmiling fellow who probably lives on a diet of organic bran and carrot juice. He heard Ballard open the proceedings against La Maison with a pained expression, and looked at me over his half-glasses as though I were a saucepan that hadn't been washed up properly. He was the last person in the world to laugh a case out of court and I would have to manage that trick without him.

Soapy Sam Ballard began by describing the minor blemishes in the restaurant's kitchen. 'In this highly expensive, allegedly three-star establishment, the environmental health officer discovered cracked tiles, open waste-bins and gravy stains on the ceiling.'

'The ceiling, Mr Ballard?' the judge repeated in sepulchral tones.

'Alas, yes, my Lord. The ceiling.'

'Probably rather a tall cook,' I suggested, and was rewarded with a freezing look from the Bench.

'And there was a complete absence of nail-brushes in the kitchen handbasins.' Ballard touched on a subject dear to his heart. 'But wait, Members of the Jury, until you get to the –'

'Main course?' I suggested in another ill-received whisper and Ballard surged on '– the very heart of this most serious case. On the night of May the eighteenth, a common house mouse was served up at a customer's dinner table.'

'We are no doubt dealing here, Mr Ballard,' the judge intoned solemnly, 'with a defunct mouse?'

'Again, alas, no, my Lord. The mouse in question was alive.'

'And kicking,' I muttered. Staring vaguely round the court, my eye lit on the public gallery where I saw Mary Skelton, the quiet restaurant clerk, watching the proceedings attentively.

'Members of the Jury' – Ballard had reached his peroration – 'need one ask if a kitchen is in breach of the Food and Hygiene

Regulations if it serves up a living mouse? As proprietor of the restaurant, Mr O'Higgins is, say the prosecution, absolutely responsible. Whomsoever in his employ he seeks to blame, Members of the Jury, he must take the consequences. I will now call my first witness.'

'Who's that pompous imbecile?' Jean-Pierre O'Higgins was adding his two pennyworth, but I told him he wasn't in his restaurant now and to leave the insults to me. I was watching a fearful and embarrassed Claude Erskine-Brown climb into the witness-box and take the oath as though it were the last rites. When asked to give his full names he appealed to the judge.

'My Lord. May I write them down? There may be some publicity about this case.' He looked nervously at the assembled reporters.

'Aren't you a member of the Bar?' Judge Graves squinted at the witness over his half-glasses.

'Well, yes, my Lord,' Claude admitted reluctantly.

'That's nothing to be ashamed of – in most cases.' At which the judge aimed a look of distaste in my direction and then turned back to the witness. 'I think you'd better tell the jury who you are, in the usual way.'

'Claude . . .' The unfortunate fellow tried a husky whisper, only to get a testy 'Oh, do speak up!' from his Lordship. Whereupon, turning up the volume a couple of notches, the witness answered, 'Claude Leonard Erskine-Brown.' I hadn't known about the Leonard.

'On May the eighteenth were you dining at La Maison Jean-Pierre?' Ballard began his examination.

'Well, yes. Yes. I did just drop in.'

'For dinner?'

'Yes,' Claude had to admit.

'In the company of a young lady named Patricia Benbow?'

'Well. That is . . . Er . . . er.'

'Mr Erskine-Brown' – Judge Graves had no sympathy with this sudden speech impediment – 'it seems a fairly simple question to answer, even for a member of the Bar.'

'I was in Miss Benbow's company, my Lord,' Claude answered in despair.

'And when the main course was served were the plates covered?'

'Yes. They were.'

'And when the covers were lifted what happened?'

Into the expectant silence, Erskine-Brown said in a still, small voice, 'A mouse ran out.'

'Oh, do speak up!' Graves was running out of patience with the witness, who almost shouted back, 'A mouse ran out, my Lord!'

At this point Ballard said, 'Thank you, Mr Erskine-Brown,' and sat down, no doubt confident that the case was in the bag – or perhaps the trap. Then I rose to cross-examine.

'Mr Claude Leonard Erskine-Brown,' I weighed in, 'is Miss Benbow a solicitor?'

'Well. Yes . . .' Claude looked at me sadly, as though wanting to say, '*Et tu*, Rumpole?'

'And is your wife a well-known and highly regarded Queen's Counsel?'

Graves's face lit up at the mention of our delightful Portia. 'Mrs Erskine-Brown has sat here as a Recorder, Members of the Jury.' He smiled sickeningly at the twelve honest citizens.

'I'm obliged to your Lordship.' I bowed slightly and turned back to the witness. 'And is Miss Benbow instructed in an important forthcoming case, that is the Balham Mini-Cab Murder, in which she is intending to brief Mrs Erskine-Brown, QC?'

'Is – is she?' Never quick off the mark, Claude didn't yet realize that help was at hand.

'And were you taking her out to dinner so you might discuss the defence in that case, your wife being unfortunately detained in Cardiff?' I hoped that made my good intentions clear, even to a barrister.

'Was I?' Erskine-Brown was still not with me.

'Well, weren't you?' I was losing patience with the fellow.

'Oh, yes.' At last the penny dropped. 'Of course I was! I do remember now. Naturally. And I did it all to help Philly. To help my wife. Is that what you mean?' He ended up looking at me anxiously.

'Exactly.'

'Thank you, Mr Rumpole. Thank you very much.' Erskine-Brown's gratitude was pathetic. But the judge couldn't wait to get on to the exciting bits.

'Mr Rumpole,' he boomed mournfully, 'when are we coming to the mouse?'

'Oh, yes. I'm grateful to your Lordship for reminding me. Well. What sort of animal was it?'

'Oh, a very small mouse indeed.' Claude was now desperately anxious to help me. 'Hardly noticeable.'

'A very small mouse and hardly noticeable,' Graves repeated as he wrote it down and then raised his eyebrows, as though, when it came to mice, smallness was no excuse.

'And the first you saw of it was when it emerged from under a silver dish-cover? You couldn't swear it got there in the kitchen?'

'No, I couldn't.' Erskine-Brown was still eager to cooperate.

'Or if it was inserted in the dining-room by someone with access to the serving-table?'

'Oh, no, Mr Rumpole. You're perfectly right. Of course it might have been!' The witness's cooperation was almost embarrassing, so the judge chipped in with 'I take it you're not suggesting that this creature appeared from a dish of duck breast by some sort of miracle, are you, Mr Rumpole?'

'Not a miracle, my Lord. Perhaps a trick.'

'Isn't Mr Ballard perfectly right?' Graves, as was his wont, had joined the prosecution team. 'For the purposes of this offence it doesn't matter *how* it got there. A properly run restaurant should not serve up a mouse for dinner! The thing speaks for itself.'

'A talking mouse, my Lord? What an interesting conception!' I got a loud laugh from my client and even the jury joined in with a few friendly titters. I also got, of course, a stern rebuke from the Bench.

'Mr Rumpole!' – his Lordship's seriousness was particularly deadly – 'this is not a place of entertainment! You would do well to remember that this is a most serious case from your client's point of view. And I'm sure the jury will wish to give it the most weighty consideration. We will continue with it after luncheon. Shall we say, five past two, Members of the Jury?'

Mr Bernard and I went down to the pub, and after a light snack of shepherd's pie, washed down with a pint or two of Guinness, we hurried back into the *palais de justice* and there I found what I had hoped for. Mary Skelton was sitting quietly outside the court, waiting for the proceedings to resume. I lit a small cigar and took a seat with my instructing solicitor not far away from the girl. I raised my voice a little and said, 'You know what's always struck me about this case, Mr Bernard? There's no evidence of droppings or signs of mice in the kitchen. So someone put the mouse under the cover deliberately. Someone who wanted to ruin La Maison's business.'

'Mrs O'Higgins?' Bernard suggested.

'Certainly not! She'd want the place to be as prosperous as possible because she owned half of it. The guilty party is someone who wanted Simone to get nothing but half a failed eatery with a ruined reputation. So what did this someone do?'

'You tell me, Mr Rumpole.' Mr Bernard was an excellent straight man.

'Oh, broke a lot of little rules. Took away the nail-brushes and the lids of the tidy-bins. But a sensation was needed, something that'd hit the headlines. Luckily this someone knew a waiter who had a talent for sleight of hand and a spare-time job producing livestock out of hats.'

'Gaston Leblanc?' Bernard was with me.

'Exactly! He got the animal under the lid and gave it to Alphonse to present to the unfortunate Miss Tricia Benbow. Consequence: ruin for the restaurant and a rotten investment for the vengeful Simone. No doubt someone paid Gaston well to do it.'

I was silent then. I didn't look at the waiting girl, but I was sure she was looking at me. And then Bernard asked, 'Just who are we talking about, Mr Rumpole?'

'Well, now. Who had the best possible reason for hating Simone, and wanting her to get away with as little as possible?'

'Who?'

'Who but our client?' I told him. 'The great *maître de cuisine*, Jean-Pierre O'Higgins himself.'

'No!' I had never heard Mary Skelton speaking before. Her voice was clear and determined, with a slight North Country accent. 'Excuse me.' I turned to look at her as she stood up and came over to us. 'No, it's not true. Jean-Pierre knew nothing about it. It was my idea entirely. Why did *she* deserve to get anything out of us?'

I stood up, looked at my watch, and put on the wig that had been resting on the seat beside me. 'Well, back to court. Mr Bernard, take a statement from the lady, why don't you? We'll call her as a witness.'

While these events were going on down the Bailey, another kind of drama was being enacted in Froxbury Mansions. She Who Must Be Obeyed had returned from her trip with Cousin Everard, put on the kettle and surveyed the general disorder left by my surprise party with deep disapproval. In the sitting-room she fanned away the bar-room smell, drew the curtains, opened the windows and clicked her tongue at the sight of half-empty glasses and lipstick-stained fag ends. Then she noticed something white nestling under the sofa, pulled it out and saw that it was a Young Radical Lawyers sweatshirt, redolent of Mizz Liz Probert's understated yet feminine perfume.

Later in the day, when I was still on my hind legs performing before Mr Justice Graves and the jury, Liz Probert called at the mansion flat to collect the missing garment. Hilda had met Liz at occasional chambers parties but when she opened the door she was, I'm sure, stony-faced, and remained so as she led Mizz Probert into the sitting-room and restored to her the sweatshirt which the Young Radical Lawyer admitted she had taken off and left behind the night before. I have done my best to reconstruct the following dialogue, from the accounts given to me by the principal performers. I can't vouch for its total accuracy, but this is the gist, the meat, you understand. It began when Liz explained she had taken the sweatshirt off because she was dancing and it was quite hot.

'You were *dancing* with Rumpole?' Hilda was outraged. 'I knew he was up to something. As soon as my back was turned. I heard all that going on when I telephoned. Rocking and rolling all over the place. At his age!'

'Mrs Rumpole. Hilda . . .' Liz began to protest but only provoked a brisk 'Oh, please. Don't you "Hilda" me! Young Radical Lawyers, I suppose that means you're free and easy with other people's husbands!' At which point I regret to report that Liz Probert could scarcely contain her laughter and asked, 'You don't think I fancy Rumpole, do you?'

'I don't know why not.' Hilda has her moments of loyalty. 'Rumpole's a "character". Some people like that sort of thing.'

'Hilda. Look, please listen,' and Liz began to explain. 'Dave Inchcape and I and a whole lot of us came to give Rumpole a party. To cheer him up. Because he was lonely. He was missing you so terribly.'

'He was *what*?' She Who Must could scarcely believe her ears, Liz told me.

'Missing you,' the young radical repeated. 'I saw him at breakfast. He looked so sad. "She's left me," he said, "and gone off with her cousin Everard."'

'Rumpole said that?' Hilda no longer sounded displeased.

'And he seemed absolutely broken-hearted. He saw nothing ahead, I'm sure, but a lonely old age stretching out in front of him. Anyone could tell how much he cared about you. Dave noticed it as well. Please can I have my shirt back now?'

'Of course.' Hilda was now treating the girl as though she were the prodigal grandchild or some such thing. 'But, Liz . . .'

'What, Hilda?'

'Wouldn't you like me to put it through the wash for you before you take it home?'

Back in the Ludgate Circus verdict factory, Mary Skelton gave evidence along the lines I have already indicated and the time came for me to make my final speech. As I reached the last stretch I felt I was making some progress. No one in the jury-box was asleep, or suffering from terminal bronchitis, and a few of them looked distinctly sympathetic. The same couldn't be said, however, of the scorpion on the Bench.

'Ladies and Gentlemen of the Jury.' I gave it to them straight. 'Miss Mary Skelton, the cashier, was in love. She was in love with her boss, that larger-than-life cook and "character", Jean-Pierre O'Higgins. People do many strange things for love. They commit suicide or leave home or pine away sometimes. It was for love that Miss Mary Skelton caused a mouse to be served up in La Maison Jean-Pierre, after she had paid the station waiter liberally for performing the trick. She it was who wanted to ruin the business, so that my client's vengeful wife should get absolutely nothing out of it.'

'Mr Rumpole!' His Lordship was unable to contain his fury.

'And my client knew nothing whatever of this dire plot. He was entirely innocent.' I didn't want to let Graves interrupt my flow, but he came in at increased volume, 'Mr Rumpole! If a restaurant serves unhygienic food, the proprietor is guilty. In law it doesn't matter in the least how it got there. Ignorance by your client is no excuse. I presume you have some rudimentary knowledge of the law, Mr Rumpole?'

I wasn't going to tangle with Graves on legal matters. Instead I confined my remarks to the more reasonable jury, ignoring the judge. 'You're not concerned with the law, Members of the Jury,' I told them, 'you are concerned with justice!'

'That is a quite outrageous thing to say! On the admitted facts of this case, Mr O'Higgins is clearly guilty!' His Honour Judge Graves had decided, but the honest twelve would have to return the verdict and I spoke to them.

'A British judge has no power to direct a British jury to find a defendant guilty! I know that much at least.'

'I shall tell the jury that he is guilty in law, I warn you.' Graves's warning was in vain. I carried on regardless.

'His Lordship may tell you that to his heart's content. As a great Lord Chief Justice of England, a judge superior in rank to any in this court, once said, "It is the duty of the judge to tell you as a jury what to do, but you have the power to do exactly as you like." And what you do, Members of the Jury, is a matter entirely between God and your own consciences. Can you really find it in your consciences to condemn a man to ruin for a crime he didn't commit?' I looked straight at them. 'Can any of you? Can you?' I gripped the desk in front of me, apparently exhausted. 'You are the only judges of the facts in this case, Members of the Jury. My task is done. The future career of Jean-Pierre O'Higgins is in your hands, and in your hands alone.' And then I sat down, clearly deeply moved.

At last it was over. As we came out of the doors of the court, Jean-Pierre O'Higgins embraced me in a bear hug and was, I greatly feared, about to kiss me on both cheeks. Ballard gave me a look of pale disapproval. Clearly he thought I had broken all the rules by asking the jury to ignore the judge. Then a cheerful and rejuvenated Claude came bouncing up bleating, 'Rumpole, you were brilliant!'

'Oh yes,' I told him. 'I've still got a win or two in me yet.'

'Brilliant to get me off. All that nonsense about a brief for Philly.'

'Not nonsense, Leonard. I mean, Claude. I telephoned the fair Tricia and she's sending your wife the Balham Mini-Cab Murder. Are you suggesting that Rumpole would deceive the court?'

'Oh' – he was interested to know – 'am I getting a brief too?'

'She said nothing of that.'

'All the same, Rumpole' – he concealed his disappointment – 'thank you very much for getting me out of a scrape.'

'Say no more. My life is devoted to helping the criminal classes.'

As I left him and went upstairs to slip out of the fancy dress, I had one more task to perform. I walked past my locker and went on into the silks' dressing-room, where a very old QC was seated in the shadows snoozing over the *Daily Telegraph*. I had seen Ballard downstairs, discussing the hopelessness of an appeal with his solicitor, and it was the work of a minute to find his locker, feel in his jacket pocket and haul a large purse out of it. Making sure that the sleeping silk hadn't spotted me, I opened the purse, slipped in the nail-brush I had rescued from Uncle Tom's tin of golf balls, restored it to the pocket and made my escape undetected.

I was ambling back up Fleet Street when I heard the brisk step of Ballard behind me. He drew up alongside and returned to his favourite topic. 'There's nothing for it, Rumpole,' he said, 'I shall chain the next one up.'

'The next what?'

'The next nail-brush.'

'Isn't that a bit extreme?'

'If fellows, and ladies, in chambers can't be trusted,' Ballard said severely, 'I am left with absolutely no alternative. I hate to have to do it, but Henry is being sent out for a chain tomorrow.'

We had reached the newspaper stand at the entrance to the Temple and I loitered there. 'Lend us twenty Pee for the *Evening Standard*, Bollard. There might be another restaurant in trouble.'

'Why are you never provided with money?' Ballard thought it typical of my fecklessness. 'Oh, all right.' And then he put his hand in his pocket and pulled out the purse. Opening it, he was amazed to find his ten pees nestling under an ancient nail-brush. 'Our old nail-brush!' The reunion was quaintly moving. 'I'd recognize it anywhere. How on earth did it get in there?'

'Evidence gets in everywhere, old darling,' I told him. 'Just like mice.'

When I got home and unlocked the front door, I was greeted with the familiar cry of 'Is that you, Rumpole?'

'No,' I shouted back, 'it's not me. I'll be along later.'

'Come into the sitting-room and stop talking rubbish.'

I did as I was told and found the room swept and polished and that She, who was looking unnaturally cheerful, had bought flowers.

'Cousin Everard around, is he?' I felt, apprehensively, that the floral tributes were probably for him.

'He had to go back to Saskatoon. One of his clients got charged with fraud, apparently.' And then Hilda asked, unexpectedly, 'You knew I'd be back, didn't you, Rumpole?'

'Well, I *had* hoped . . .' I assured her.

'It seems you almost gave up hoping. You couldn't get along without me, could you?'

'Well, I had a bit of a stab at it,' I said in all honesty.

'No need for you to be brave any more. I'm back now. That nice Miss Liz Probert was saying you missed me terribly.'

'Oh, of course. Yes. Yes, I missed you.' And I added as quietly as possible, 'Life without a boss . . .'

'What did you say?'

'You were a great loss.'

'And Liz says you were dreadfully lonely. I was glad to hear that, Rumpole. You don't usually say much about your feelings.'

'Words don't come easily to me, Hilda,' I told her with transparent dishonesty.

'Now you're so happy to see me back, Rumpole, why don't you take me out for a little celebration? I seem to have got used to dining *à la carte*.'

Of course I agreed. I knew somewhere where we could get it on the house. So we ended up at a table for two in La Maison and discussed Hilda's absent relative as Alphonse made his way towards us with two covered dishes.

'The trouble with Cousin Everard,' Hilda confided in me, 'is he's not a "character".'

'Bit on the bland side?' I enquired politely.

'It seems that unless you're with a "character", life can get a little tedious at times,' Hilda admitted.

The silver domes were put in front of us, Alphonse called out, '*Un, deux, trois!*' and they were lifted to reveal what I had no difficulty in ordering that night: steak and kidney pud. Mashed spuds were brought to us on the side.

'Perhaps that's why I need you, Rumpole.' She Who Must Be Obeyed was in a philosophic mood that night. 'Because you're a "character". And you need me to tell you off for being one.'

Distinctly odd, I thought, are the reasons why people need each other. I looked towards the cashier's desk, where Jean-Pierre had his arm round the girl I had found so unmemorable. I raised a glass of the champagne he had brought us and drank to their very good health.

Rumpole and the Children of the Devil

Sometimes, when I have nothing better to occupy my mind, when I am sitting in the bath, for instance, or in the doctor's surgery having exhausted the entertainment value of last year's *Country Life*, or when I am in the corner of Pommeroy's Wine Bar waiting for some generous spirit in chambers, and there aren't many of them left, to come in and say, 'Care for a glass of Château Fleet Street, Rumpole?', I wonder what I would have done if I had been God. I mean, if I had been responsible for creating the world in the first place, would I have cobbled up a globe totally without the minus quantities we have grown used to, a place with no fatal diseases or traffic jams or Mr Justice Graves – and one or two others I could mention? Above all, would I have created a world entirely without evil? And, when I come to think rather further along these lines, it seems to me that a world without evil might possibly be a damned dull world – or an undamned dull world, perhaps I should say – and it would certainly be a world which would leave Rumpole without an occupation. It would also put the Old Bill and most of Her Majesty's judges, prosecutors, prison officers and screws on the breadline. So perhaps a world where everyone rushes about doing good to each other and everyone, including the aforesaid Graves, is filled with brotherly love, is not such a marvellous idea after all.

Brooding a little further on this business of evil, it occurs to me that the world is fairly equally divided between those who see it everywhere because they are always looking for it and those who hardly notice it at all. Of course, the mere fact that some people recognize devilment in the most everyday matters doesn't mean that it isn't there. I have known the first indication that evil was present, in various cases that I have been concerned with, to be a missing library ticket, a car tyre punctured or the wrong overcoat taken from the cloakroom of an expensive restaurant. At other times, the signs of evil are so blatant that they are impossible to ignore, as in the dramatic start to the case which I have come to think of as concerning the 'Children of the Devil'. They led to a serious and, at times, painful enquiry into the machinations of Satan in the Borough of Crockthorpe.

Crockthorpe is a large, sprawling, in many parts dejected, in others rather too cosy for comfort, area south of the Thames. Its inhabitants include people speaking many languages, many without jobs, many gainfully employed in legal and not so legal businesses – and the huge Timson clan, which must by now account for a sizeable chunk of the population. The Timsons, as those of you who have followed my legal career in detail will know, provide not only the bread and marge, the Vim and Brasso, but quite often the beef and butter of our life in Froxbury Mansions, Gloucester Road. A proportion of my intake of Château Thames Embankment, and my wife Hilda's gin and tonic, comes thanks to the tireless activities of the Timson family. They are such a large group, their crime rate is so high and their success rate so comparatively low, that they are perfect clients for an Old Bailey hack. They go in for theft, shop breaking and receiving stolen property but they have never produced a Master Crook. If you are looking for sensational crimes, the Timsons won't provide them or, it would be more accurate to say, they didn't until the day that Tracy Timson apparently made a pact with the devil.

The story began in the playground of Crockthorpe's Stafford Cripps Junior School. The building had not been much repaired since it was built in the heady days of the first post-war Labour government, and the playground had been kicked to pieces by generations of scuffling under-twelves. It was during the mid-morning break when the children were out fighting, ganging up on each other, or unhappy because they had no one to play with – among the most active, and about to pick a fight with a far larger black boy, was Dominic Molloy, angel-faced and Irish, who will figure in this narrative – when evil appeared.

Well, as I say, it was halfway through break and the headmistress, a certain Miss Appleyard, a woman in her early forties who would have been beautiful had not the stress of life in the Stafford Cripps

Junior aged her prematurely, was walking across the playground, trying to work out how to make fifty copies of *The Little Green Reading Book* go round two hundred pupils, when she heard the sound of concerted, eerie and high-pitched screaming coming from one of the doors that led on to the playground.

Turning towards the sound of the outcry, Miss Appleyard saw a strange sight. A small posse of children, about nine of them, all girls and all screaming, came rushing out like a charge of miniature cavalry. Who they were was, at this moment, a mystery to the headmistress for each child wore a similar mask. Above the dresses and the jeans and pullovers hung the scarlet and black, grimacing and evil faces of nine devils.

At this sight even the bravest and most unruly children in the playground were taken aback, many retreated, some of the younger ones adding to the chorus of screams. Only young Dominic Molloy, it has to be said, stood his ground and viewed the scene that followed with amusement and contempt. He saw Miss Appleyard step forward fearlessly and, when the charge halted, she plucked off the devil's mask and revealed the small, heart-shaped face of the eight-year-old Tracy, almost the youngest, and now apparently the most devilish, of the Timson family.

Events thereafter took an even more sinister turn. At first the headmistress looked grim, confiscated the masks and ordered the children back to the classroom, but didn't speak to them again about the extraordinary demonstration. Unfortunately she laid the matter before the proper authority, which in this case was the Social Services and Welfare Department of Crockthorpe Council. So the wheels were set in motion that would end up with young Tracy Timson being taken into what is laughingly known as care, this being the punishment meted out to children who fail to conform to a conventional and rational society.

Childhood has, I regret to say, like much else, got worse since I was a boy. We had school bullies, we had headmasters who were apparently direct descendants of Captain Bligh of the *Bounty*, we had cold baths, inedible food and long hours in chapel on Sundays, but there was one compensation. No one had invented social workers.

Now British children, it seems, can expect the treatment we once thought was only meted out to the political opponents of the late unlamented Joseph Stalin. They must learn to dread the knock at the door, the tramp of the Old Bill up the stairs, and being snatched from their nearest and dearest by a member of the alleged caring professions.

The dreaded knock was to be heard at six-thirty one morning on the door of the semi in Morrison Close, where that young couple Cary and Rosemary (known as Roz) Timson lived with Tracy, their only child. There was a police car flashing its blue light outside the house and a woman police constable in uniform on the step. The knock was administered by a social worker named Mirabelle Jones, of whom we'll hear considerably more later. She was a perfectly pleasant-looking girl with well-tended hair who wore, whenever I saw her, a linen jacket and a calf-length skirt of some ethnic material. When she spoke she modulated her naturally posh tones into some semblance of a working-class accent, and she always referred to the parents of the children who came into her possession as Mum and Dad and spoke with friendliness and deep concern.

When the knock sounded, Tracy was asleep in the company of someone known as Barbie doll, which I have since discovered to be a miniature American person with a beehive hairdo and a large wardrobe. Cary Timson was pounding down the stairs in his pyjamas, unhappily convinced that the knock was in some way connected with the break-in at a shop in Gunston Avenue about which he had been repeatedly called in for questioning, although he had made it clear, on each occasion, that he knew absolutely bugger all about it.

By the time he had pulled open the door his wife, Roz, had appeared on the stairs behind him, so she was able to hear Mirabelle telling her husband, after the parties had identified each other, that she had 'come about young Tracy'. From the statements which I was able to read later it appears that the dialogue then went something like this. It began with a panic-stricken cry from Roz of 'Tracy? What about our Tracy? She's asleep upstairs. Isn't she asleep upstairs?'

'Are you Mum?' Mirabelle then asked.

'What do you mean, am I Mum? Course I'm Tracy's mum. What

do you want?' Roz clearly spoke with rising hysteria and Mirabelle's reply sounded, as always, reasonable.

'We want to look after your Tracy, Mum. We feel she needs rather special care. I'm sure you're both going to help us. We do rely on Mum and Dad to be *very* sensible.'

Roz was not deceived by the soothing tones and concerned smile. She got the awful message and the shock of it brought her coldly to her senses. 'You come to take Tracy away, haven't you?' And before the question was answered she shouted, 'You're not bloody taking her away!'

'We just want to do the very best for your little girl. That's all, Mum.' At which Mirabelle detached a dreaded and official-looking document from the clipboard she was carrying. 'We do have a court order. Now shall we go and wake Tracy up? Ever so gently.'

It would be unnecessarily painful to dwell on the scene that followed. Roz fought like a tigress for her young and had to be restrained, at first by her husband, who had learnt, as a juvenile, the penalty for assaulting the powers of justice, and then by the uni-formed officer who was called in from the car. The Timsons were told that they would be able to argue the case in court eventually, the woman police officer helped pack a few clothes for Tracy in a small case and, as the child was removed from the house, Mirabelle took the Barbie doll from her, explaining that it was bad for children in such circumstances to have too many things that reminded them of home. So young Tracy Timson was taken into custody and her parents came nearer to heartbreak than they ever had in their lives, even when Cary got a totally unexpected two years' for the theft of a clapped-out Volvo Estate from Safeway's car park. Throughout it all it's fair to say that Miss Mirabelle Jones behaved with the tact and consideration which made her such a star of the Social Services and such a dangerous witness in the Juvenile Court.

Tracy Timson was removed to a gloomy Victorian villa now known as the Lilacs, Crockthorpe Council Children's Home, where she will stay for the remainder of this story, and Mirabelle set out to interview what she called Tracy's peers, by which she meant the other kids Tracy was at school with, and, in the course of her activities, she called at another house in Morrison Close, this one being occupied by the father and mother of young Dominic Molloy. Now anyone who knows anything about the world we live in, anyone who keeps his or her ear to the ground and picks up as much information as possible about family rivalry in the Crockthorpe area, will know that the Molloys and the Timsons are chalk and cheese and as deadly rivals as the Montagues and the Capulets, the Guelphs and the Ghibellines, or York and Lancaster. The Molloys are an extended family; they are also villains, but of a more purposeful and efficient variety. To the Timsons' record of small-time thieving the Molloys added wounding, grievous bodily harm and an occasional murder. Now Mirabelle called on the eight-year-old Dominic Molloy and, after a preliminary consultation with him and his parents, he agreed to help her with her enquiries. This, in turn, led to a further interview in an office at the school with young Dominic which was immortalized on videotape.

I remember my first conference with Tracy's parents, because on that morning Hilda and I had a slight difference of opinion on the subject of the Scales of Justice Ball. This somewhat grizzly occasion is announced annually on a heavily embossed card which arrived, with the gas bill and various invitations to insure my life and go on Mediterranean cruises, on the Rumpole breakfast table.

I had launched this invitation towards the tidy-bin to join the tea-leaves and the eggshells when Hilda, whose eagle eye misses nothing, immediately retrieved it, shook various particles of food off it and challenged me with, 'And why are you throwing this away, Rumpole?'

'You don't want to go, Hilda.' I did my best to persuade her. 'Disgusting sight, Her Majesty's judges, creaking round in the foxtrot at the Savoy Hotel. You wouldn't enjoy it.'

'I suppose not, Rumpole. Not in the circumstances.'

'Not in what circumstances?'

'It's too humiliating.'

'I quite agree.' I saw her point at once. 'When Mr Justice Graves breaks into the veleta I hang my head in shame.'

'It's humiliating for me, Rumpole, when other chaps in chambers lead their wives out on to the floor.'

'Not a pretty sight, I have to agree, the waltzing Bollards, the pirouetting Erskine-Browns.'

'Why do you never lead me out on to the dance floor nowadays, Rumpole?' She asked me the question direct. 'I sometimes dream about it. We're at the Scales of Justice Ball. At the Savoy Hotel. And you lead me out on to the floor, as the first lady in chambers.'

'You are, Hilda,' I hastened to agree with her, 'you're quite definitely the senior . . .'

'But you never lead me out, Rumpole! We have to sit there, staring at each other across the table, while all around us couples are dancing the night away.'

'Hilda' – I decided to disclose my defence – 'I have, as you know, many talents, but I'm not Nijinsky. Anyway, we don't get much practice at dancing down the Old Bailey.'

'Oh, it doesn't matter. When is the ball? Marigold Featherstone told me but I can't quite remember.' I saw, with a sort of dread, that she was checking the food-stained invitation to answer her question. 'November the eighteenth! It just happens to be my birthday. Well, we'll stay at home, as usual. At least I won't have to sit and watch other happy people dancing together.' And now she applied the corner of a handkerchief to her eye.

'Please, Hilda,' I begged, 'not the waterworks!' At which she sniffed bravely and dismissed me from her presence.

'No, of course not. Go along now. You've got to get to work. Work's the only thing that matters to you. You'd rather defend a murderer than dance with your wife.'

'Well, yes. Perhaps,' I had to admit. 'Look, do cheer up, old thing. Please.' She gave me her last lament as I moved towards the door.

'Old, yes, I suppose. We're both too old for a party. And I'll just have to get used to the fact that I didn't marry a dancer.'

'Sorry, Hilda.'

So I left She Who Must Be Obeyed, sitting alone in the kitchen and looking, as I thought, genuinely unhappy. I had seen her miffed before. I had seen her outraged. I had seen her, all too frequently, intensely displeased at some item of Rumpole's behaviour which fell short of perfection. But I was unprepared for the sadness which seemed to have engulfed her. Had she spent her life imagining she was Ginger Rogers, and was she at last reconciled to the fact that I had neither the figure nor the top hat to play whatever his name was – Astaire? For a moment a sensation to which I am quite unused came over me. I felt inadequate. However, I pulled myself together and pointed myself in the direction of my chambers in the Temple, where I knew I had a conference with a couple of Timsons in what I imagined would be no more than a routine case of petty thievery.

I had acted for Cary before in a little matter of lead removed from the roof of Crockthorpe Methodist Church. He was tall and thin, and usually spoke in a slow, mocking way as though he found the whole of life slightly amusing. He didn't look amused now. His wife, Roz, was a solid girl in her mid twenties with broad cheek-bones and capable hands. In attendance was the faithful Mr Bernard, who, from time immemorial, has acted as the solicitor-general to the Timson family.

'They wouldn't let Tracy take even a doll. Not one of her Barbies. How do you think people could do that to a child?' Roz asked me when Mr Bernard had outlined the facts of the case. Her eyes were red and swollen and, as she sat in my client's chair, nervously twisting her wedding ring, she looked not much older than a child herself.

'Nicking your kid. That's what it's come to. Well, I'll allow us Timsons may have done a fair bit of mischief in our time. But no one in the family's ever stooped to that, Mr Rumpole.' And Cary Timson added for greater emphasis, 'People what nick kids get boiling cocoa poured on their heads, when they're inside like.'

'Cary worships that girl, Mr Rumpole,' Roz told me. 'No matter what they say.'

'Take a look at these' – her husband was already pulling out his wallet – 'and you'll see the reason why.' So the brightly coloured snaps were laid proudly on my desk and I saw the three of them on a Spanish beach, at a theme park or on days out in the country. The mother and father held their child aloft, in the manner of successful athletes with a golden prize, triumphantly and with unmistakable delight.

'Bloody marvellous, isn't it?' Cary's gentle mocking had turned to genuine anger. 'Eight years old and our Trace needs a brief.'

'You'll get Tracy back for us, won't you, Mr Rumpole?' I thought Roz must have given birth to this much-loved daughter when she was about seventeen. 'She'll be that unhappy.'

'You seen the photos, Mr Rumpole.' And Cary asked, 'Does she have the look of a villain?'

'I'd say not a hardened criminal,' I had to admit.

'What's her crime, Mr Rumpole? That's what Roz and I wants to know. It's not as though she nicked things ever.'

'Well, not really –' And Roz admitted, 'She'll take a Jaffa cake when I'm not looking, or a few sweets occasionally.'

'Our Tracy's too young for any serious nicking.' Her father was sure of it. 'What you reckon she done, Mr Rumpole? What they got on her charge-sheet?'

'Childhood itself seems a crime to some people.' It's a point that has often struck me.

'We can't seem to get any sense out of that Miss Jones.' Roz looked helpless.

'Jones?'

'Officer in charge of case. Tracy's social worker.'

'One of the "caring" community.' I was sure of it.

'All she'll say is that she's making further enquiries,' Mr Bernard told me.

'I never discovered what I'd done when they banged me up in a draughty great boarding-school at the age of eight.' I looked back down the long corridor of years and began to reminisce.

'Hear that, Roz?' Cary turned to his wife. 'They banged up Mr Rumpole when he was a kid.'

'Did they, Mr Rumpole? Did they really?'

But before I could give them further and better particulars of the bird I had done at Linklaters, that downmarket public school I attended on the Norfolk coast, Mr Bernard brought us back to the fantastic facts of the case and the nature of the charges against Tracy. 'I've been talking to the solicitor for the local authority,' he reported, 'and their case is that the juvenile Timson has been indulging in devil-worship, hellish rituals and satanic rights.'

It might be convenient if I were to give you an account of that filmed interview with Dominic Molloy which, as I have told you, we finally saw at the trial. Before that, Mr Bernard had acquired a transcript of this dramatic scene, so we were, by bits and pieces, made aware of the bizarre charges against young Tracy, a case which began to look as though it should be transferred from Crockthorpe Juvenile Court to Seville to be decided by hooded inquisitors in the darkest days of the Spanish Inquisition.

The scene was set in the headmistress's office in Stafford Cripps Junior. Mirabelle Jones, at her most reassuring, sat smiling on one side of the desk, while young Dominic Molloy, beaming with self-importance, played the starring role on the other.

'You remember the children wearing those horrid masks at school, do you, Dominic?' Mirabelle kicked off the proceedings.

'They scared me!' Dominic gave a realistic shudder.

'I'm sure they did.' The social worker made a note, gave the camera – no doubt installed in the corner of the room – the benefit of her smile and then returned to the work in hand.

'Did you see who was leading those children?'

'In the end I did.'

'Who was it?'

'Trace.'

'Tracy Timson?'

'Yes.'

'Your mum said you went round to Tracy Timson's a few times. After school, was that?'

'Yes. After school like.'

'And then you said you went somewhere else. Where else, exactly?'

'Where they put people.'

'A churchyard. Was it a churchyard?' Mirabelle gave us a classic example of a leading question. Dominic nodded approval and she made a note. 'The one in Crockthorpe Road, the church past the roundabout? St Elphick's?' Mirabelle suggested and Dominic nodded again. 'It was the churchyard. Was it dark?' Dominic nodded so eagerly that his whole body seemed to rock backwards and forwards and he was in danger of falling off his chair.

'After school and late. A month ago? So it was dark. Did a grown-up come with you? A man, perhaps. Did a man come with you?'

'He said we was to play a game.' Now Dominic had resorted to a kind of throaty whisper, guaranteed to make the flesh creep.

'What sort of game?'

'He put something on his face.'

'A mask?'

'Red and horns on it.'

'A devil's mask.' Mirabelle was scribbling enthusiastically. 'Is that right, Dominic? He wanted you to play at devils? This man did?'

'He said he was the devil. Yes.'

'He was to be the devil. And what were you supposed to be?'

Dominic didn't answer that, but sat as if afraid to move.

'Perhaps you were the devil's children?'

At this point Dominic's silence was more effective than any answer.

'What was the game you had to play?' Mirabelle tried another approach.

'Dance around.' The answer came in a whisper.

'Dance around. Now I want you to tell me, Dominic, when did you meet this man? At Tracy Timson's house? Is that where you met him?' More silence from Dominic, so Mirabelle tried again. 'Do you know who he was, Dominic?' At which Dominic nodded and looked round fearfully.

'Who was he, Dominic? You've been such a help to me so far. Can't you tell me who he was?'

'Tracy's dad.'

Everything changes and with ever-increasing rapidity. Human beings no longer sell tickets at the Temple tube station. Machines and not disillusioned waitresses dispense the so-called coffee in the Old Bailey canteen and, when I became aware that Dianne, our long-time typist and close personal friend to Henry, our clerk, had left the service, I feared and expected that she might be replaced by a robot. However, what I found behind the typewriter, when I blew into the clerk's room after a hard day's work on an actual bodily harm in Acton a few weeks after my conference with Tracy's parents, was nothing more mechanical than an unusually pretty and very young woman, wearing a skirt as short as a suspended sentence and a smile so ready that it seemed never to leave her features entirely but to be waiting around for the next opportunity to beam. Henry introduced her as Miss Clapton. 'Taken over from Dianne, Mr Rumpole, who has just got herself married. I don't know if you've heard the news.'

'Married? Henry, I'm sorry.'

'To a junior clerk in a bankruptcy set.' He spoke with considerable disgust. 'I told her she'd live to regret it.'

'Welcome to Equity Court, Miss Clapton,' I said. 'If you behave really well, you might get parole in about ten years.' She gave me the smile at full strength, but my attention was diverted by the sight of Mizz Liz Probert who had just picked up a brief from the mantelpiece and was looking at it with every sign of rapture. Liz, the daughter of Red Ron Probert, Labour leader on Crockthorpe Council, is the most radical member of our chambers. I greeted her with, 'Soft you now! The fair Mizz Probert! What are you fondling there, old thing?' Or words to that effect.

'What does it look like, Rumpole?'

'It looks suspiciously like a brief.'

'Got it in one!' Mizz Liz was in a perky mood that evening.

'Time marches on! My ex-pupil has begun to acquire briefs. What is it? Bad case of non-renewed dog licence?'

'A bit more serious than that. I'm for the Crockthorpe local authority, Rumpole.'

'I am suitably overawed.' I didn't ask whether the presence of Red Ron on the council had anything to do with this manna from heaven, and Mizz Liz went on to tell a familiar story.

'A little girl had to be taken into care. She's in terrible danger in the home. You know what it is – the father's got a criminal record.

As a matter of fact, it's a name that might be familiar to you. Timson.'

'So they took away a Timson child because the father's got form?' I asked innocently, hoping for further information.

'Not just that. Something rather awful was going on. Devil-worship! The family were deeply into it. Quite seriously. It's a shocking case.'

'Is it really? Tell me, do you believe in the devil?'

'Of course I don't, Rumpole. Don't be so ridiculous! Anyway, that's hardly the point.'

'Isn't it? It interests me, though. You see, I'm likely to be against you in the Juvenile Court.'

'You, Rumpole! On the side of the devil?' Mizz Probert seemed genuinely shocked.

'Why not? They tell me he has the best lines.'

'Defending devil-worshippers, in a *children's* case! That's really not on, is it, Rumpole?'

'I really can't think of anyone I wouldn't defend. That's what I believe in. I was just on my way to Pommeroy's. Mizz Liz, old thing, will you join me in a stiffener?'

'I don't really think we should be seen drinking together, not now I'm appearing for the local authority.'

'For the local authority, of course!' I gave her a respectful bow on leaving. 'A great power in the land! Even if they do rather interfere with the joy of living.'

No sooner had I got to Pommeroy's Wine Bar and chalked up the first glass of Jack Pommeroy's Very Ordinary when Claude Erskine-Brown of our chambers came into view in a state of considerable excitement about the new typist. 'An enormous asset, don't you think? Dot will bring a flood of spring sunshine into our clerk's room.'

'Dot?' I was puzzled. 'What are you babbling about?'

'Her name's Dot, Rumpole. She told me that. I said it was a beautiful name.'

I didn't need to tell the fellow he was making a complete ass of himself; this was a fact too obvious to mention.

'I've told her she must come to me if she has any problems work-wise.' Claude is, of course, married to Phillida Erskine-Brown, QC, the attractive and highly competent Portia of our chambers. Perhaps it's because he has to play second fiddle to this powerful advocate that Claude is forever on the lookout for alternative company, a pursuit which brings little but embarrassment to himself and those around him. I saw nothing but trouble arising from the appearance of this Dot upon the Erskine-Brown horizon, but now the fellow completely changed the subject and said, 'You know Charlie Wisbeach?'

'I've never heard of him.'

'Wisbeach, Bottomley, Perkins & Harris.' Erskine-Brown spoke in an awestruck whisper as though repeating a magic formula.

'Good God! Are they *all* here?'

'I rather think Claude's talking about my dad's firm.' This came from a plumpish but fairly personable young man who was in the offing, holding a bottle of champagne and a glass, which he now refilled and also gave a shower of bubbles to Erskine-Brown.

'Just the best firm in the City, Rumpole. Quality work. And Charlie here's come to the Bar. He wants a seat in chambers.' Erskine-Brown sounded remarkably keen on the idea, no doubt hoping for work from the firm of Wisbeach, Bottomley, Perkins & Harris.

'Oh, yes?' I sniffed danger. 'And where would he like it? There might be an inch or two available in the downstairs loo. Didn't we decide we were full up at the last chambers meeting?'

'I say, you must be old Rumpole!' Young Wisbeach was looking at me as though I were some extinct species still on show in the Natural History Museum.

'I'm afraid I've got very little choice in the matter,' I had to admit.

'You're not still practising, are you?' Charlie Wisbeach had the gall to ask.

'Not really. I suppose I've learnt how to do it by now.'

'Oh, but Claude Erskine-Brown told me you'd soon be retiring.'

'Did you, Claude? Did you tell young Charlie that?' I turned upon the treacherous Erskine-Brown the searchlight eyes and spoke in the pained tones of the born cross-examiner.

'Well, no. Not exactly, Rumpole.' The man fumbled for words. 'Well, of course, I just assumed you'd be retiring sometime.'

'Don't count on it, Erskine-Brown. Don't you ever count on it!'

'And Claude told me that when you retired, old chap, there might be a bit of space in your chambers.' The usurper Wisbeach apparently found the situation amusing. 'A pretty enormous space is what I think he said. Didn't you, Claude?'

'Well no, Charlie. No . . . Not *quite*.' Erskine-Brown's embarrassment proved his guilt.

'It sounds like an extremely humorous conversation.' I gave them both the look contemptuous.

'Charlie has a pretty impressive CV, Rumpole.' Erskine-Brown tried to change the subject as his new-found friend gave him another slurp.

'See what?'

'Curriculum vitae. Eton . . .'

'Oh. Good at that as well, is he? I thought it was mainly drinkin'.'

'Claude's probably referring to the old school.' Wisbeach could not, of course, grasp the Rumpole joke.

'Oh, Eton! Well, I've no doubt you'll rise above the handicaps of a deprived childhood. In somebody else's chambers.'

'As a matter of fact Claude showed me *your* room.' Wisbeach gave the damning evidence. 'Very attractive accommodation.'

'You did *what*, Claude?'

'Charlie and I . . . Well, we . . . called in to see you. But you were doing that long arson in Snaresbrook.'

'Historic spot, your room!' Wisbeach told me as though I'd never seen the place before. 'Fine views over the churchyard. Don't you look straight down at Dr Johnson's tomb?'

'It's Oliver Goldsmith's, as it so happens.' Eton seemed to have done little for the man's store of essential knowledge.

'No, Johnson's!' You can't tell an old Etonian anything.

'Goldsmith,' I repeated, with the last of my patience.

'Want to bet?'

'Not particularly.'

'Your old room needs a good deal of decorating, of course. And some decent furniture. But the idea is, we might share. While you're still practising, Rumpole.'

'That's not an idea. It's a bad dream.' I directed my rejection of the offer at Erskine-Brown, who started up a babble of 'Rumpole! Think of the work that Wisbeach could send us!'.

'And I would like to let it be known that *I* still have work of my own to do, and I do it best alone. As a free spirit! Wrongs are still to be righted.' Here I drained my plonk to the dregs and stood up, umbrella in hand. 'Mr Justice Graves is still putting the boot in. Chief Inspector Brush is still referring to his unreliable notebook. And an eight-year-old Timson has been banged up against her will, not in Eton College like you, Master Charlie, but in the tender care of the Crockthorpe local authority. The child is suspected of devil-worship. Can you believe it? An offence which I thought went out with the burning of witches.'

'Is that your case, Rumpole?' Erskine-Brown looked deeply interested.

'Indeed, yes. And I have a formidable opponent. None other than Mizz Liz Probert, with the full might of the local authority behind her. So, while there are such challenges to be overcome, let me tell you, Claude, and you, Charlie Whatsit, Rumpole shall never sheath the sword. Never!'

So I left the bar with my umbrella held aloft like the weapon of a crusader, and the effect of this exit was only slightly marred by my colliding with a couple of trainee solicitors who were blocking the fairway. As I apologized and lowered the umbrella I could distinctly hear the appalling Wisbeach say, 'Funny old buffer!'

In all my long experience down the Bailey and in lesser courts I have not known a villain as slithery and treacherous as Claude Erskine-Brown proved on that occasion. As soon as he could liberate himself from the cuckoo he intended to place in my nest, he dashed up to Equity Court in search of our head of chambers, Samuel Ballard, QC. Henry, who was working late on long-delayed fee notes, told him that Soapy Sam was at a service with his peer group, the

Lawyers As Christians Society, in Temple Church. Undeterred, Claude set off to disturb the holy and devoutly religious Soapy at prayer. It was, he told a mystified Henry as he departed, just the place to communicate the news he had in mind.

I am accustomed to mix with all sorts of dubious characters in pursuit of evidence and, when I bought a glass of Pommeroy's for an LAC (member of the Lawyers As Christians Society), I received an astonishing account of Claude's entry into evensong. Pushing his way down the pew he arrived beside our head of chambers, who had risen to his feet to an organ accompaniment and was about to give vent to a hymn. Attending worshippers were able to hear dialogue along the following lines.

'Erskine-Brown. Have you joined us?' Ballard was surprised.

'Of course I've joined LACS. Subscription's in the post. But I had to tell you about Rumpole, as a matter of urgency.'

'Please, Erskine-Brown. This is no place to be talking about such matters as Rumpole.'

'*Devil-worshippers*. Rumpole's in with devil-worshippers,' Claude said in a voice calculated to make our leader's flesh creep.

However, at this moment, the hymn-singing began and Ballard burst out with:

> 'God moves in a mysterious way
> His wonders to perform;
> He plants his footsteps in the sea,
> And rides upon the storm.'

Betraying a certain talent for improvisation, my informant told me that he distinctly heard Claude Erskine-Brown join in with:

> 'Rumpole in his mischievous way
> Has taken on a case
> About some devil-worshippers.
> He's had them in your place!
> Your chambers, I mean.'

At which point Ballard apparently turned and looked at the conniving Claude with deep and horrified concern.

It was a time when everyone seemed intent on investigating the alleged satanic cult. Mirabelle Jones continued to make films for showing before the Juvenile Court and this time she interviewed Tracy Timson in a room, also equipped with a camera and recording apparatus, in the children's home.

Mirabelle arrived, equipped with dolls, not glamorous pin-up girls, but a somewhat drab and unsexy family consisting of a Mum and Dad, Grandpa and Grandma, who looked like solemn New England farmworkers. Tracy was ordered to play with this group, and when, without any real interest in the matter, she managed to get Grandpa lying on top of Mum, Miss Jones sucked in her breath and made a note which she underlined heavily.

Later, Tracy was shown a book in which there was a picture of a devil with a forked tail, who looked like an opera singer about to undertake Mephistopheles in *Faust*. The questioning, as recorded in the transcript, then went along these lines.

'You know who he is, don't you, Tracy?' Mirabelle was being particularly compassionate as she asked this.

'No.'

'He's the devil. You know about devils, don't you?' And she added, still smiling, 'You put on a devil's mask at school, didn't you, Tracy?'

'I might have done.' Tracy made an admission.

'So what do you think of the devil, then?'

'He looks funny.' Tracy was smiling, which I thought, in all the circumstances, was remarkably brave of her.

'Funny?'

'He's got a tail. The tail's funny.'

'Who first told you about the devil, Tracy?'

'I don't know,' the child answered, but the persistent inquisitor was not to be put off so easily.

'Oh, you must know. Did you hear about the devil at home? Was that it? Did Dad tell you about the devil?'

Tracy shook her head. Mirabelle Jones sighed and tried again.

'Does that picture of the devil remind you of anyone, Tracy?' Still getting no answer, Mirabelle resorted to a leading question, as was her way in these interviews. 'Do you think it looks like your dad at all?'

In search of an answer to Miss Jones's unanswered question, I summoned Cary and Roz to my presence once again. When they arrived, escorted by the faithful Bernard, I put the matter as bluntly as I knew how. At the mention of evil, Tracy's mother merely looked puzzled. 'The devil? Tracy don't know nothing about the devil.'

'Of course not!' Cary's denial was immediate. 'It's not as if we went to church, Mr Rumpole.'

'You've never heard of such a suggestion before?' I looked hard at Tracy's father. 'The devil. Satan. Beelzebub. Are you saying the Timson family knows nothing of such matters?'

'Nothing at all, Mr Rumpole.'

'When they came that morning . . .'

'When they came to get our Tracy?' Roz's eyes filled with tears as she relived the moment.

'Yes. When they came for that. What did you *think* was going on exactly?' I asked Cary the question.

'I thought they come about that shop that got done over, Wedges, down Gunston Avenue. They've had me down the nick time and time again about it.'

'And it wasn't you?'

'Straight up, Mr Rumpole. Would I deceive you?'

'It has been known, but I'll believe you. Do you know who did it?' I asked Cary.

'No, Mr Rumpole. No, I won't grass. That I won't do. I've had enough trouble being accused of grassing on Gareth Molloy when he was sent down for the Tobler Road supermarket job.'

'The Timsons and the Molloys are deadly enemies. How could you know what they were up to?'

'My mate Barry Peacock was driving for them on that occasion. They thought I knew something and grassed to Chief Inspector Brush. Would I do a thing like that?'

'No, I don't suppose you would. So you thought the Old Bill were just there about ordinary, legitimate crime. You had no worries about Tracy?'

'She's a good girl, Mr Rumpole. Always has been,' Roz was quick to remind me.

'Always cheerful, isn't she, Roz?' Her husband added to the evidence of character. 'I enjoys her company.'

'So where the devil do these ideas come from? Sorry, perhaps I shouldn't've said that . . . You know Dominic Molloy told the social worker you taught a lot of children satanic rituals.'

'You ever believed a Molloy, have you, Mr Rumpole, in court or out of it?' Cary Timson had a good point there, but I rather doubted if I could convince the Juvenile Court of the wisdom learnt at the Old Bailey.

When our conference was over I showed my visitors out and I thought I saw, peering from a slightly open doorway at the end of the corridor, the face of Erskine-Brown, as horrified and intent as a passerby who suddenly notices that, on the other side of the street, a witches' coven is holding its annual beano. The door shut as soon as I clocked him and Claude vanished within. Twenty minutes later I received a visit from Soapy Sam Ballard, QC, our so-called head of chambers. I don't believe that these events were unconnected. As soon as he got in, Ballard sniffed the air as though detecting the scent of brimstone and said, 'You've had them in here, Rumpole?'

'Had who in here, Bollard?'

'Those who owe allegiance to the Evil One.'

'You mean the Mr Justice Graves fan club? No. They haven't been near the place.'

'Rumpole! You know perfectly well who I mean.'

'Oh, yes. Of course.' I decided to humour the fellow. 'They were all here. Lucifer, Beelzebub, Belial. All present and correct.

'High on a throne of royal state, which far
Outshone the wealth of Ormus and of Ind,
Or where the gorgeous East with richest hand
Showers on her kings barbaric pearl and gold,
Satan exalted sat, by merit raised

To that bad eminence; and from despair
Thus high uplifted beyond hope.

'Grow up, Bollard! I am representing an eight-year-old child who's been torn from the bosom of her family and banged up without trial. You see here Rumpole, the protector of the innocent.'

'The protector of devil-worshippers!' Ballard said.

'Those too. If necessary.' I sat down at the desk and picked up the papers in a somewhat tedious affray.

'Rumpole. Every decent chambers has to draw the line somewhere.'

'Does it?'

'There are certain cases, certain clients even, which are simply, well, not acceptable.'

'Oh, I do agree.'

'Do you?'

'Oh, yes. I agree entirely.'

'Well, then. I'm glad to hear it.' Soapy Sam looked as gratified as a cleric hearing a deathbed confession from a lifelong heathen.

'Didn't I catch sight of you prosecuting an accountant for unpaid VAT?' I asked the puzzled QC. 'Some cases are simply unacceptable. Far too dull to be touched by a decent barrister with a bargepole. Don't you agree, old darling?'

'Rumpole, there's something I meant to raise with you.' The saintly Sam was growing distinctly ratty.

'Then buck up and raise it, I'm busy.' I returned to the affray.

'Young Charlie Wisbeach wants to come into these chambers. He'd bring us a great deal of high-class, *commercial* work from his father's firm. Unfortunately we have no room for him at the moment.'

'Has he thought of a cardboard box in Middle Temple Lane?' I thought this a helpful suggestion; Bollard didn't agree.

'This is neither the time nor the place for one of your jokes, Rumpole. You have a tenancy here and tenancies can be brought to an end. Especially if the tenant in question is carrying on a practice not in the best traditions of 3 Equity Court. There is something in this room which makes me feel uneasy.'

'Oh, I do so agree. Perhaps you'll be leaving shortly.'

'I'm giving you fair warning, Rumpole. I expect you to think it over.' At which our leader made for the door and I called after him, 'Oh, before you go, Bollard, why don't you look up "exorcism" in the *Yellow Pages*? I believe there's an unfrocked bishop in Stepney who'll quote you a very reasonable price. And if you call again, don't forget the holy water!'

But the man had gone and I was left alone to wonder exactly what devilment Cary Timson had been up to.

I have, or at a proper moment I will have, a confession to make. At this time I was presenting She Who Must Be Obeyed with a mystery which she no doubt found baffling, although I'm afraid a probable solution presented itself to her mind far too soon. I had reason to telephone a Miss Tatiana Fern and, not wishing to do so with Hilda's knowledge, and as the lady in question left her house early, I called when I thought She was still asleep. I now suspect Hilda was listening in on the bedroom extension, although she lay motionless and with her eyes closed when I came back to bed. Later I discovered that when Hilda went off to shop in Harrods she spotted me coming out of Knightsbridge tube station, a place far removed from the Temple and the Old Bailey, and sleuthed me to a house in Mowbray Crescent which she saw me enter when the front door was opened by the aforesaid Tatiana Fern. So it came about that She met Marigold, Mr Justice Featherstone's outspoken wife, and together they formed the opinion that Rumpole was up to no good whatsoever.

Of course, She didn't tackle me openly about this, but I could sense what was in the wind when she started up a conversation about the male libido at breakfast one morning. It followed from something she had read in her *Daily Telegraph*.

'They're doing it again, Rumpole.'

'Who are?'

'Men.'

'Ah.'

'Causing trouble in the workplace.'

'Yes. I suppose so.'

'Brushing up against their secretaries. Unnecessarily. I suppose that's something you approve of, Rumpole?'

'I haven't got a secretary, Hilda. I've got a clerk called Henry. I've never felt the slightest temptation to brush up against Henry.' And that answer you might have thought would finish the matter, but Hilda had more information from the *Telegraph* to impart.

'They put it all down to glands. Men've got too much something in their glands. That's a fine excuse, isn't it?'

'Never tried it.' But I thought it over. 'I suppose I might: "My client intends to rely on the glandular defence, my Lord."'

'It wouldn't wash.' Hilda was positive. 'When I was a child we were taught to believe in the devil.'

'I'm sure you were.'

'He tempts people. Particularly men.'

'I thought it was Eve.'

'What?'

'I thought it was Eve he tempted first.'

'That's you all over, Rumpole.'

'Is it?'

'Blame it all on a woman! That's men all over.'

'Hilda, there's nothing I'd like more than to sit here with you all day, discussing theology. But I've got to get to work.' I was making my preparations for departure when She said darkly, 'Enjoy your lunch-hour!'

'What did you say?'

'I said, "I hope you enjoy your lunch-hour," Rumpole.'

'Well, I probably shall. It's Thursday. Steak pie day at the pub in Ludgate Circus. I shall look forward to that.'

'And a few other little treats besides, I should imagine.'

Hilda was immersed in her newspaper again when I left her. I knew then that, no matter what explanation I had given, She Who Must Be Obeyed had come to the firm conclusion that I was up to something devilish.

It's a strange fact that it was not until nearly the end of the three-score years and ten allotted to me by the psalmist that I was first called upon to perform in a Juvenile Court. It was, as I was soon to discover, a place in which the law as we know and occasionally love it had very little place. It was also a soulless chamber in Crockthorpe's already chipped and crumbling glass and concrete courthouse complex. Tracy's three judges – a large motherly-looking magistrate as chairwoman, flanked by a small, bright-eyed Sikh justice in a sari, and a lean and anxious headmaster – sat with their clerk, young, officious and bespectacled, to keep them in order. The defence team, Rumpole and the indispensable Bernard, together with the prosecutor, Mizz Liz Probert, and a person from the council solicitor's office, sat at another long table opposite the justices. Miss Mirabelle Jones, armed with a ponderous file, was comfortably ensconced in the witness chair and a large television set was playing that hit video, the interview with Dominic Molloy.

We had got to the familiar dialogue which started with Mirabelle's question: 'He wanted you to play at devils? This man did?'

'He said he was the devil. Yes,' the picture of the boy Dominic alleged.

'He was to be the devil. And what were you supposed to be? Perhaps you were the devil's children?'

At which point Rumpole ruined the entertainment by rearing to his hind legs and making an objection, a process which in this court seemed as unusual and unwelcome as a guest lifting his soup plate to his mouth and slurping the contents at a state banquet at Buckingham Palace. When I said I was objecting, the clerk switched off the telly with obvious reluctance.

'That was a leading question by the social worker,' I said, although the fact would have been obvious to the most superficial reader of *Potted Rules of Evidence*. 'It and the answer are entirely inadmissible, as your clerk will no doubt tell you.' And I added, in an extremely audible whisper to Bernard, 'If he knows his business.'

'Mr Rumpole' – the chairwoman gave me her most motherly smile – 'Miss Mirabelle Jones is an extremely experienced social worker. We think we can rely on her to put her questions in the proper manner.'

'I was just venturing to point out that on this occasion she put her question in an entirely improper manner,' I told her, 'Madam.'

'My Bench will see the film out to the end, Mr Rumpole. You'll have a chance to make any points later.' The clerk gave his decision in a manner which caused me to whisper to Mr Bernard, 'Her Master's Voice.' I hope they all heard, but to make myself clear I said to Madam Chair, 'My point is that you shouldn't be seeing this film at all.'

'We are going to continue with it now, Mr Rumpole.' The learned clerk switched on the video again. Miss Jones appeared to ask, 'What was the game you had to play?' And Dominic answered, 'Dance around.'

'Dance around.' Mirabelle Jones's shadow repeated in case we had missed the point. 'Now I want you to tell me, Dominic, when did you meet this man? At Tracy Timson's house? Is that where you met him?'

'It's a leading question!' I said aloud, but the performance continued and Mirabelle asked, 'Do you know who he was?' And on the screen Dominic nodded politely.

'Who was he?' Mirabelle asked and Dominic replied, 'Tracy's dad.'

As the video was switched off, I was on my feet again. 'You're not going to allow that evidence?' I couldn't believe it. 'Pure hearsay! What a child who isn't called as a witness said to Miss Jones here, a child we've had no opportunity of cross-examining said, is nothing but hearsay. Absolutely worthless.'

'Madam Chairwoman.' Mizz Probert rose politely beside me.

'Yes, Miss Probert.' Liz got an even more motherly smile; she was the favourite child and Rumpole the black sheep of the family.

'Mr Rumpole is used to practising at the Old Bailey –'

'And has managed to acquire a nodding acquaintance of the law of evidence,' I added.

'And of course *this* court is not bound by strict rules of evidence. Where the welfare of a child is concerned, you're not tied down by a lot of legal quibbles about hearsay.'

'Quibbles, Mizz Probert? Did I hear you say quibbles?' My right-eous indignation was only half simulated.

'You are free,' Liz told the tribunal, 'with the able assistance of Miss Mirabelle Jones, to get at the truth of this matter.'

'My learned friend was my pupil.' I was, I must confess, more than a little hurt. 'I spent months, a year of my life, in bringing her up with some rudimentary knowledge of the law. And when she says that the rule against hearsay is a legal quibble . . .'

'Mr Rumpole, I don't think my Bench wants to waste time on a legal argument.' The clerk of the court breathed heavily on his glasses and polished them briskly.

'Do they not? Indeed!' I was launched on an impassioned protest and no one was going to stop me. 'So does it come to this? Down at the Old Bailey, that backward and primitive place, no villain can be sent down to chokey as a result of a leading question, or a bit of gossip in the saloon bar, or what a child said to a social worker and wasn't even cross-examined. But little Tracy Timson, eight years old, can be banged up for an indefinite period, snatched from the family that loves her, without the protection the law affords to the most violent bank robber! Is that the proposition that Mizz Liz Probert is putting before the court? And which apparently finds favour in the so-called legal mind of the court official who keeps jumping up like a jack-in-the-box to tell you what to do?'

Even as I spoke the clerk, having shined up his spectacles to his total satisfaction, was whispering to his well-upholstered chair.

'Mr Rumpole, my Bench would like to get on with the evidence. Speeches will come later,' the chairwoman handed down her clerk's decision.

'They will, Madam. They most certainly will,' I promised. And then, as I sat down, profoundly discontented, Liz presumed to teach me my business.

'Let me give you a tip, Rumpole,' she whispered. 'I should keep off the law if I were you. They don't like it around here.'

While I was recovering from this lesson given to me by my ex-pupil, our chairwoman was addressing Mirabelle as though she were a mixture of Mother Teresa and Princess Anne. 'Miss Jones,' she purred, 'we're grateful for the thoroughness with which you've gone into this difficult case on behalf of the local authority.'

'Oh, thank you so much, Madam Chair.'

'And we've seen the interview you carried out with Tracy on the video film. Was there anything about that interview which you thought especially significant?'

'It was when I showed her the picture of the devil,' Mirabelle answered. 'She wasn't frightened at all. In fact she laughed. I thought . . .'

'Is there any point in my telling you that what this witness thought isn't evidence?' I sent up a cry of protest.

'Carry on, Miss Jones. If you'd be so kind.' Madam Chair decided to ignore the Rumpole interruption.

'I thought it was because it reminded her of someone she knew pretty well. Someone like Dad.' Mirabelle put in the boot with considerable delicacy.

'Someone like Dad. Yes.' Our chair was now making a careful note, likely to be fatal to Tracy's hopes of liberty. 'Have you any questions, Mr Rumpole?'

So I rose to cross-examine. It's no easy task to attack a personable young woman from one of the caring professions, but this Mirabelle Jones was, so far as my case was concerned, a killer. I decided that there was only one way to approach her and that was to go in with all guns firing. 'Miss Jones' – I loosed the first salvo – 'you are, I take it, against cruelty to children?'

'Of course. That goes without saying.'

'Does it? Can you think of a more cruel act, to a little child, than coming at dawn with the Old Bill and snatching it away from its mother and father, without even a Barbara doll for consolation?'

'Barbie doll, Mr Rumpole,' Roz whispered urgently.

'What?'

'It's a Barbie doll, Mrs Timson says,' Mr Bernard instructed me on what didn't seem to be the most vital point in the case.

'Very well, Barbie doll.' And I returned to the attack on Mirabelle. 'Without that, or a single toy?'

'We don't want the children to be distracted.'

'By thoughts of home?'

'Well, yes.'

'You wanted Tracy to concentrate on your dotty idea of devil-worship!' I put it bluntly.

'It wasn't a dotty idea, Mr Rumpole, and I had to act quickly. Tracy had to be removed from the presence of evil.'

'Evil? What do you mean by that exactly?' The witness hesitated, momentarily at a loss for a suitable definition in a rational age, and Mizz Liz Probert rose to the rescue.

'You ought to know, Mr Rumpole. Haven't you had plenty of experience of that down at the Old Bailey?'

'Oh, well played, Mizz Probert!' I congratulated her loudly. 'Your pupilling days are over. Now, Miss Mirabelle Jones' – I returned to my real opponent – 'let's come down, if we may, from the world of legend and hearsay and gossip and fantasy, to what we call, down at the Old Bailey, hard facts. You know that my client, Mr Cary Timson, is a small-time thief and a minor villain?'

'I have given the Bench the list of Dad's criminal convictions, yes.' Mirabelle looked obligingly into her file.

'It's not the sort of record, is it, Mr Rumpole, that you might expect a good father to have?' The chair smiled as she invited me to agree but I declined to do so.

'Oh, I don't know,' I said. 'Are only the most law-abiding citizens meant to have children? Are we about to remove their offspring from share-pushers, insider dealers and politicians who don't tell the truth? If we did, even this tireless local authority would run out of children's homes to bang them up in.'

'Speeches come later, Mr Rumpole.' The loquacious clerk could keep silent no longer.

'They will,' I promised him. 'Cary Timson is a humble member of the Clan Timson, that vast family of South London villains. Now, remind us of the name of that imaginative little boy you interviewed on prime-time television.'

'Dominic Molloy.' Mirabelle knew it by heart.

'Molloy, yes. And, as we've been told so often, you are an extremely experienced social worker.'

'I think so.'

'With a vast knowledge of the social life in this part of South London?'

'I get to know a good deal. Yes, of course I do.'

'Of course. So it will come as no surprise to you if I suggest that the Molloys are a large family of villains of a slightly more dangerous nature than the Timsons.'

'I didn't know that. But if you say so . . .'

'Oh, I do say so. Did you meet Dominic's mother, Mrs Peggy Molloy?'

'Oh, yes. I had a good old chat with Mum. Over a cuppa.' The Bench and Mirabelle exchanged smiles.

'And over a cuppa did she tell you that her husband, Gareth, Dominic's dad, was in Wandsworth as a result of the Tobler Road supermarket affair?'

'Mr Rumpole. My Bench is wondering if this is entirely relevant.' The clerk had been whispering to the chair and handed the words down from on high.

'Then let your Bench keep quiet and listen,' I told him. 'It'll soon find out. So what's the answer, Miss Jones? Did you know that?'

'I didn't know that Dominic's dad was in prison.' Miss Jones adopted something of a light, insouciant tone.

'And that he suspected Tracy's dad, as you would call him, Cary Timson, of having been the police informer who put him there?'

'Did he?' The witness seemed to find all this talk of adult crime somewhat tedious.

'Oh, yes. And I shall be calling hearsay evidence to prove it. Miss Jones, are you telling this Bench that you, an experienced social worker, didn't bother to find out about the deep hatred that exists between the Molloys and the Timsons, stretching back over generations of villainy to the dark days when Crockthorpe was a village and the local villains swung at the crossroads?'

'I have nothing about that in my file,' Mirabelle told us, as though that made all such evidence completely unimportant.

'Nothing in your file. And your file hasn't considered the possibility that young Dominic Molloy might have been encouraged to put

215

an innocent little girl of a rival family "in the frame", as we're inclined to call it down the Old Bailey?'

'It seems rather far-fetched to me.' Mirabelle gave me her most superior smile.

'Far-fetched, Miss Jones, to you who believe in devil-worship?'

'I believe in evil influences on children.' Mirabelle chose her words carefully. 'Yes.'

'Then let us just examine that. Your superstitions were first excited by the fact that a number of children appeared in the play-ground of Crockthorpe Junior wearing masks?'

'Devil's masks. Yes.'

'Yet the only one you took into so-called care was Tracy Timson?'

'She was the ringleader. I discovered that Tracy had brought the masks to school in the kitbag with her lunch and her reading books.'

'Did you ask her where she got them from?'

'I did. Of course, she wouldn't tell me.' Mirabelle smiled and I knew a possible reason for Tracy's silence. Even if Cary had been indulging in satanic rituals his daughter would never have grassed on him.

'I assumed it was from her father.' Mirabelle inserted her elegant boot once more.

'Miss Mirabelle Jones. Let's hope that at some point we'll get to a little reliable evidence, and that this case doesn't rely entirely on your assumptions.'

The lunch-break came none too soon and Mr Bernard and I went in search of a convenient watering-hole. The Jolly Grocer was to Pom-meroy's Wine Bar what the Crockthorpe Court was to the Old Bailey. It was a large, bleak pub and the lounge bar was resonant with the bleeping of computer games and the sound of muzak. Pommeroy's claret may be at the bottom end of the market, but I suspected that the Jolly Grocer's red would be pure paint stripper. I refreshed myself on a couple of bottles of Guinness and a pork pie, which was only a little better than minced rubber encased in cardboard, and then we started the short walk back to the Crock-thorpe *palais de justice*.

On the way I let Bernard know my view of the proceedings so far. 'It's all very well to accuse the deeply caring Miss Mirabelle Jones of guessing,' I told him, 'but we've got to tell the old darlings on the Bench, bonny Bernard, where the hell the masks came from.'

'Our client, Mr Cary Timson . . .'

'You mean "Dad"?'

'Yes. He denies all knowledge.'

'Does he?' And then, quite suddenly, I came to a halt. I found myself outside a shop called Wedges Carnival and Novelty Stores. The window was full of games, fancy-dress, hats, crackers, Hallowe'en costumes, Father Christmas costumes, masks and other equipment for parties and general merrymaking. It was while I was gazing with a wild surmise at these goods on display that I said to Mr Bernard, in the somewhat awestruck tone of a watcher of the skies when a new planet swims into his ken, 'Well, he would, wouldn't he? The honour of the Timsons.'

'What do you mean, Mr Rumpole?'

'What's the name of this street? Is it by any chance . . . ?'

It was. My instructing solicitor, looking up at a street sign, said, 'Gunston Avenue.'

'Who robbed Wedges?' We had arrived back at the courthouse with ten minutes in hand and I found Cary Timson smoking a last fag on the gravel outside the main entrance. His wife was with him and I lost no time in asking the vital question.

'Mr Rumpole' – Tracy's dad looked round and lowered his voice – 'you know I can't –'

'Grass? It's the code of the Timsons, isn't it? Well, let me tell you, Cary. There's something even more important than your precious code.'

'I don't know it, then.'

'Oh, yes, you do. You know it perfectly well. Get that wallet out, why don't you? Look at the photographs you were so pleased to show me. Look at them, Cary!'

Cary took out his wallet and looked obediently at the pictures of the much-loved Tracy.

'Is she less important than honour among thieves?' I asked them both. Roz looked at her husband, her jaw set and her eyes full of determination. I knew then what the answer to my question would have to be.

The afternoon's proceedings dragged on without any new drama, and although Cary had told me what I needed to know I hadn't yet got his leave to use the information. The extended Timson family would have to be consulted. When the day's work was done I took the tube back to the Temple and, with my alcohol content having sunk to a dangerous low, I went at once to Pommeroy's for first aid.

Then I was unfortunate enough to meet my proposed cuckoo, the old Etonian Charlie Wisbeach, who, being not entirely responsible for his actions, was administering champagne to a toothy and Sloaney girl solicitor called, if I can bring myself to remember the occasion when she instructed me in a robbery and forgot to summon the vital witness, Miss Arabella Munday. Wisbeach greeted me with a raucous cry of 'Rumpole, old man! Glass of Bolly?'

'Why? What are you celebrating?' I did my best to sound icy; all the same I possessed myself of a glass, which he filled unsteadily.

'Ballard asked me in for a chat. It seems there may be a vacancy in your chambers, Rumpole.'

'Wherever Ballard is there's always a vacancy. What do you mean exactly?'

'Pity you blotted your copybook.'

'My what?'

'Not very clever of you, was it? Defending devil-worshippers with such a remarkably devout head of chambers. It seems I may soon be occupying your room, old man, looking down on Temple Church and Oliver Goldsmith's tomb.'

I looked at the slightly swaying Wisbeach for a long time and then, as I sized up the enemy, a kind of plot began to form itself in my mind. 'Dr Johnson's,' I corrected the man again.

'You told me it was Oliver Goldsmith's.'

'No, I told you it was Dr Johnson's.'

'Goldsmith's.'

'Johnson's.'

'You want to bet?' Charlie Wisbeach's face moved uncomfortably close to mine. 'Does old roly-poly Rumpole want to put his money where his mouth is, does he?'

'Ten quid says it's Johnson.'

'I'm going to give you odds.' Charlie was clearly an experienced gambler. 'Three to one against Johnson. Olly Goldsmith evens. Twenty to one the field. Since I'm taking over the room we'll check on it tomorrow.'

'Why not now?' I challenged him.

'What?'

'Why not check on it now?' I repeated. 'Thirty quid in my pocket and I can take a taxi home.'

'Ten quid down and you'll walk. All right, then. Come on, Arabella. Bring the bottle, old girl.'

As they left Pommeroy's, I hung behind and then went to the telephone on the wall by the gents. I had seen the light in Ballard's window when I came up from Temple station. He usually worked late, partly because he was a slow study so far as even the simplest brief was concerned and partly, I believe, because of a natural reluctance to go home to his wife, Marguerite, a trained nurse, who had once been the Old Bailey's merciless matron. I put in a quick telephone call to Soapy Sam and advised him to look out of his window in about five minutes' time and pay particular attention to any goings on in the Temple churchyard. Then I went to view the proceedings from a safe distance.

What I saw, and what Sam Ballard saw from his grandstand view, was Charlie Wisbeach holding a bottle and a blonde. He gave a triumphant cry of 'Oliver Goldsmith!' and then mounted the tomb as though it were a hunter and, alternately swigging from the bottle and kissing Miss Arabella Munday, he laughed loudly at his triumph over Rumpole. It was a satanic sound so far as our head of chambers was concerned, and this appalling graveyard ritual convinced him that Charlie Wisbeach, who no doubt spent his spare moments reciting the Lord's Prayer backwards, was a quite unsuitable candidate for a place in a Christian chambers such as 3 Equity Court.

★

That night important events were also taking place in my client's home in Morrison Close, Crockthorpe. Numerous Timsons were assembled in the front room, assisted by minor villains and their wives. Cary's uncle Fred, the undisputed head of the family, was there, as was Uncle Dennis, who should long ago have retired from a life of crime to his holiday home on the Costa del Sol. I have done my best to reconstruct the debate from the account given to me by Roz. After a general family discussion and exchange of news, Uncle Fred gave his opinion of the Wedges job. 'Bloody joke shop. I always said it was a bad idea, robbing a joke shop.'

'There was always money left in the till overnight. Our info told us that. And the security was hopeless. Through the back door, like.' Uncle Dennis explained the thinking behind the enterprise.

'What you want to leave the stuff round my place for?' Cary was naturally aggrieved because the booty had, it transpired, included a box of satanic masks to which, as they were left in her father's garage, young Tracy had easy access. 'You should have known how dangerous them things were, what with young kids and social workers about.'

'Well, Fred's was under constant surveillance,' Uncle Dennis explained. 'As was mine. And seeing as you and Roz was away on Monday . . .'

'Oh, thank you very much!' Cary was sarcastic.

'And Den knowing where you kept your garage key . . .' Uncle Fred was doing his best to protect Uncle Dennis from charges of carelessness.

'Lucky the Bill never thought of looking there,' Cary pointed out.

'I meant to come back for the stuff sometime. It was a bit of a trivial matter. It slipped my memory, quite honestly.' Uncle Dennis was notoriously forgetful, once having left his Fisherman's Diary containing his name and address at the scene of a crime.

'Well, it wasn't no trivial matter for our Tracy.'

'No, I knows, Roz. Sorry about that.'

'Look, Den,' Cary started, 'we're not asking you to put your hands up to Chief Inspector Brush . . .'

'Yes, we are, Cary.' Roz was in deadly earnest. 'That's just what we're asking. You got to do it for our Tracy.'

'Hang about a bit.' Uncle Dennis looked alarmed. 'Who says we got to?'

And then Roz told him, 'Mr Rumpole.'

So the next morning Dennis Timson gave evidence in the Juvenile Court. Although I had been careful to explain his criminal record, he looked, in his comfortable tweed jacket and cavalry twill trousers, the sort of chap that might star on *Gardeners' Question Time* and I could see that Madam Chair took quite a shine to him. After some preliminaries we got to the heart of the matter.

'I was after the money, really,' Dennis told the Bench. 'But I suppose I got a bit greedy, like. I just shoved a few of those boxes in the back of the vehicle. Then I didn't want to take them round to my place, so I left them in Cary's garage.'

'Why did you do that?' I asked.

'Well, young Cary didn't have anything to do with the Wedges job, so I thought they'd be safe enough there. Of course, I was under considerable pressure of work at that time, and it slipped my mind to tell Cary and Roz about it.'

'Did you see what was in any of those cases?'

'I had a little look-in. Seemed like a lot of carnival masks. That sort of rubbish.'

'So young Tracy getting hold of the devil's masks was just the usual Timson cock-up, was it?'

'What did you say, Mr Rumpole?' The chairwoman wasn't quite sure she could believe her ears.

'It was a stock-up, for Christmas, Madam Chair,' I explained. 'Oh, one more thing, Mr Dennis Timson. Do you know why young Dominic Molloy has accused Tracy and her father of fiendish rituals in a churchyard?'

'Course I do.' Uncle Den had no doubt. 'Peggy Molloy told Barry Peacock's wife and Barry's wife told my Doris down the Needle Arms last Thursday.'

'We can't possibly have this evidence!' Liz Probert rose to object. Perhaps she'd caught the habit from me.

'Oh, really, Mizz Probert?' I looked at her in amazement. 'And why ever not?'

'What Barry's wife told Mrs Timson is pure hearsay.' Mizz Probert was certain of it.

'Of course it is.' And I gave her back her own argument. 'And pure hearsay is totally acceptable in the Juvenile Court. Where the interest of the child is at stake we are not bound by legal quibbles. I agree, Madam Chair, with every word which has fallen from your respected and highly learned clerk. Now then, Mr Timson, what did you hear exactly?'

'Gareth thought Cary had grassed on him over the Tobler Road supermarket job. So they got young Dominic to put the frame round Tracy and her dad.'

'So what you are telling us, Mr Timson, is that this little boy's evidence was a pure invention.' At last Madam Chair seemed to have got the message.

Uncle Dennis gave her the most charming and friendliest of smiles as he said, 'Well, you can't trust the Molloys, can you, my Lady? Everyone knows they're a right family of villains.'

There comes a time in many cases when the wind changes, the tide turns and you're either blown on to the rocks or make safe harbour. Uncle Dennis's evidence changed the weather, and after it I noticed that Madam Chair no longer returned Miss Mirabelle Jones's increasingly anxious smile, Mizz Probert's final address was listened to in stony silence and I was startled to hear a distinct 'thank you' from the Bench as I sat down. After a short period of retirement the powers that were to shape young Tracy Timson's future announced that they were dissatisfied by the evidence of any satanic rituals and she was, accordingly, to be released from custody forthwith. Before this judgment was over, the tears which Roz had fought to control since the dawn raid were released and, at her moment of joy, she cried helplessly.

I couldn't resist it. I got into Mr Bernard's car and followed the Timson Cortina to the children's home. We waited until we saw the mother and father emerge from that gaunt building, each holding one of their daughter's hands. As they came down the steps to the street they swung her in the air between them, and when they got into the car they were laughing. Miss Mirabelle Jones, who had brought the order for release, stood in the doorway of the Lilacs and watched without expression, and then Tracy's legal team drove away to do other cases with less gratifying results.

When I got home, after a conference in an obtaining credit by fraud and a modest celebration at Pommeroy's Wine Bar, Hilda was not in the best of moods. When I told her that I brought glad tidings all She said was, 'You seem full of yourself, Rumpole. Been having a good time, have you?'

'A great time! Managed to extricate young Tracy Timson from the clutches of the caring society and she's back in the bosom of her family. And I'll be getting another brief defending Dennis Timson on a charge of stealing from Wedges Carnival Novelties. Well, I expect I'll think of something.'

I poured myself a glass of wine to lighten the atmosphere and Hilda said, somewhat darkly, 'You never wanted to be a judge, did you, Rumpole?'

'Judging people? Condemning them? No, that's not my line, exactly. Anyway, judges are meant to keep quiet in court.'

'And they're much more restricted, aren't they?' It may have sounded an innocent question on a matter of general interest, but her voice was full of menace.

'Restricted?' I repeated, playing for time.

'Stuck in court all day, in the public eye and on their best behaviour. They have far less scope than you to indulge in other activities . . .'

'Activities, Hilda?'

'Oh, yes. Perhaps it's about time we really talked for once, Rumpole. Is there something that you feel you ought to tell me?'

'Well. Yes, Hilda. Yes. As a matter of fact there is.' I had in fact done something which I found it strangely embarrassing to mention.

'I suppose you've had time to think up some ridiculous defence.'

'Oh, no. I plead guilty. There are no mitigating circumstances.'

'Rumpole! How could you?' The court was clearly not going to be moved by any plea for clemency.

'Temporary insanity. But I did it at enormous expense.'

'You had to pay!' It would scarcely be an exaggeration to say that Hilda snorted.

'Well. They don't give these things away for nothing.'

'I imagine not!'

'One hundred smackers. But it *is* your birthday next week.'

'Rumpole! I can't think what my birthday's got to do with it.' At least I had managed to puzzle her a little.

'Everything, Hilda. I've just bought us two tickets for the Scales of Justice Ball. Now, what was it *you* wanted us to talk about?'

All I can say is that Hilda looked extremely confused. It was as though Mr Injustice Graves was just about to pass a stiff sentence of chokey and had received a message that, as it was the Queen's birthday, there would be a general amnesty for all prisoners.

'Well,' she said, 'not at the moment. Perhaps some other time.' And she rescued the lamb chops from the oven with the air of a woman suddenly and unexpectedly deprived of a well-justified and satisfactory outburst of rage.

Matters were not altogether resolved when we found ourselves at a table by the dance floor in the Savoy Hotel in the company of Sam Ballard and his wife, Marguerite, who always, even in a ball gown, seemed to carry with her a slight odour of antiseptic and sensible soap. Also present were Marigold Featherstone, wife of a judge whose foot was never far from his mouth, Claude Erskine-Brown and Liz Probert with her partner, co-mortgagee and fellow member of 3 Equity Court, young Dave Inchcape.

'Too bad Guthrie's sitting at Newcastle!' Claude commiserated with Marigold Featherstone on the absence of her husband and told her, 'Philly's in Swansea. Prosecuting the Leisure Centre Murder.'

'Never mind, Claude.'

And Marguerite Ballard added menacingly, 'I'll dance with you.'

'Oh, yes, Erskine-Brown' – her husband was smiling – 'you have my full permission to shake a foot with my wife.'

'Oh, well. Yes. Thank you very much. I say, I thought Charlie Wisbeach and his girlfriend were going to join us?' Claude seemed unreasonably disappointed.

'No, Erskine-Brown.' The Ballard lips were even more pursed than usual. 'Young Wisbeach won't be joining us. Not at the ball. And certainly not in chambers.'

'Oh, really? I thought it was more or less fixed.'

'I think, Claude, it's become more or less unstuck,' I disillusioned him. In the ensuing chatter I could hear Marigold Featherstone indulging in some whispered dialogue with my wife which went something like this.

'Have you faced him with it yet, Hilda?'

'I was just going to do it when he told me we were coming here. He behaved well for once.'

'They do that, occasionally. Don't let it put you off.'

Further whispers were drowned as Erskine-Brown said to Ballard in a loud and challenging tone, 'May I ask you why Charlie Wisbeach isn't joining us, after all?'

'Not on this otherwise happy occasion, Erskine-Brown. I can only say . . . Practices.'

'Well, of course he practises. In the commercial court.' And Claude turned to me, full of suspicion. 'Do you know anything about this, Rumpole?'

'Me? Know anything? Nothing whatever.' I certainly wasn't prepared to incriminate myself.

'I have told Wisbeach we simply have no accommodation. I do not regard him as a suitable candidate to share Rumpole's room. It will be far better for everyone if we never refer to the matter again.' So our head of chambers disposed of the case of *Rumpole v. Wisbeach* and the band played an old number from the days of my youth called 'Smoke Gets in Your Eyes'.

'Now, as head of chambers' – Ballard claimed his alleged rights – 'I think I should lead my wife out on to the floor.'

'No. No, Ballard. With all due respect' – I rose to my feet – 'as the longest-serving chambers wife, She, that is Mrs Rumpole, should be led out first. Care for a dance, Hilda?'

'Rumpole! Are you sure you can manage it?' Hilda was astonished.

'Perfectly confident, thank you.' And, without a moment's hesitation, I applied one hand to her waist, seized her hand with the other, and steered her fearlessly out on to the parquet, where, though I say it myself, I propelled my partner for life in strict time to the music. I even indulged in a little fancy footwork as we cornered in front of a table full of solicitors.

'You're *chasséing*, Rumpole!' She was astounded.

'Oh, yes. I do that quite a lot nowadays.'

'Wherever did you learn?'

'To be quite honest with you . . .'

'If you're capable of such a thing.' She had not been altogether won over.

'From a Miss Tatiana Fern. I looked her up in the *Yellow Pages*. One-time Southern Counties Ballroom Champion. I took a few lessons.'

'*Where* did you take lessons?'

'Place called Mowbray Crescent.'

'Somewhere off Sloane Street?'

'Hilda! You knew?'

'Oh, don't ever think you can do anything I don't know about.' At which point the Ballards passed us, not dancing in perfect harmony. 'You're really quite nippy on your feet, Rumpole. Marguerite Ballard's looking absolutely green with envy.' And then, after a long period of severity, she actually smiled at me. 'You are an old devil, Rumpole!' she said.

Rumpole on Trial

I have often wondered how my career as an Old Bailey hack would terminate. Would I drop dead at the triumphant end of my most moving final speech? 'Ladies and Gentlemen of the Jury, my task is done. I have said my say. This trial has been but a few days out of your life, but for me it is the *whole* of my life. And that life I leave, with the utmost confidence, in your hands,' and then keel over and out. 'Rumpole snuffs it in court'; the news would run like wild fire round the Inns of Court and I would challenge any jury to dare to convict after that forensic trick had been played upon them. Or will I die in an apoplexy after a particularly heated disagreement with Mr Injustice Graves, or Sir Oliver Oliphant? One thing I'm sure of, I shall not drift into retirement and spend my days hanging around Froxbury Mansions in a dressing-gown, nor shall I ever repair to the Golden Gate Retirement Home, Weston-super-Mare, and sit in the sun lounge retelling the extraordinary case of the Judge's Elbow, or the Miracle in the Ecclesiastical Court which saved a vicar from an unfrocking. No, my conclusion had better come swiftly, and Rumpole's career should end with a bang rather than a whimper. When thinking of the alternatives available, I never expected I would finish by being kicked out of the Bar, dismissed for unprofessional conduct and drummed out of the monstrous regiment of learned friends. And yet this conclusion became a distinct possibility on that dreadful day when, apparently, even I went too far and brought that weighty edifice, the legal establishment, crashing down upon my head.

The day dawned grey and wet after I had been kept awake most of the night by a raging toothache. I rang my dentist, Mr Lionel Leering, a practitioner whose company I manage to shun until the pain becomes unbearable, and he agreed to meet me at his Harley

Street rooms at nine o'clock, so giving me time to get to the Old Bailey, where I was engaged in a particularly tricky case. So picture me at the start of what was undoubtedly the worst in a long career of difficult days, stretched out on the chair of pain and terror beside the bubbling spittoon. Mr Leering, the smooth, grey-haired master of the drill, who seemed perpetually tanned from a trip to his holiday home in Ibiza, was fiddling about inside my mouth while subliminal baroque music tinkled on the cassette player and the blonde nurse looked on with well-simulated concern.

'Busy day ahead of you, Mr Rumpole?' Mr Leering was keeping up the bright chatter. 'Open just a little wider for me, will you? What sort of terrible crime are you on today then?'

'Ans . . . lorter,' I did my best to tell him.

'My daughter?' Leering purred with satisfaction. 'How kind of you to remember. Well, Jessica's just done her A-levels and she's off to Florence doing the history of art. You should hear her on the quattrocento. Knows a great deal more than I ever did. And of course, being blonde, the Italians are mad about her.'

'I said . . . Ans . . . lorter. Down the Ole . . . Ailey,' I tried to explain before he started the drill.

'My old lady? Oh, you mean Yolande. I'm not sure she'd be too keen on being called that. She's better now. Gone in for acupuncture. What were you saying?'

'An . . . cord . . . Tong . . .'

'Your tongue? Not hurting you, am I?'

'An . . . supposed . . . Illed is ife.'

'Something she did to her back,' Leering explained patiently. 'Playing golf. Golf covers a multitude of sins. Particularly for the women of Hampstead Garden Suburb.'

'Ell on the ender . . .'

The drill had stopped now, and he pulled the cotton wool rolls away from my gums. My effort to tell him about my life and work had obviously gone for nothing because he asked politely, 'Send her what? Your love? Yolande'll be tickled to death. Of course, she's never met you. But she'll still be tickled to death. Rinse now, will you? Now what were we talking about?'

'Manslaughter,' I told him once again as I spat out pink and chemicated fluid.

'Oh, no. Not really? Yolande can be extremely irritating at times. What woman can't? But I'm not actually tempted to bash her across the head.'

'No' – I was showing remarkable patience with this slow-witted dentist – 'I said I'm doing a case at the Old Bailey. My client's a man called Tong. Accused of manslaughter. Killed his wife, Mrs Tong. She fell down and her head hit the fender.'

'Oh, really? How fascinating.' Now he knew what I was talking about, Mr Leering had lost all interest in my case. 'I've just done a temporary stopping. That should see you through the day. But ring me up if you're in any trouble.'

'I think it's going to take a great deal more than a temporary stopping to see me through today,' I said as I got out of the chair and struggled into the well-worn black jacket. 'I'm before Mr Justice "Ollie" Oliphant.'

As I was walking towards the Old Bailey I felt a familiar stab of pain, warning me that the stopping might be extremely temporary. As I was going through the revolving doors, Mizz Liz Probert came flying in behind me, sent the door spinning, collided into my back, then went dashing up the stairs, calling, 'Sorry, Rumpole!' and vanished.

'Sorry, Rumpole!' I grumbled to myself. Mizz Probert cannons into you, nearly sends your brief flying and all she does is call out 'Sorry, Rumpole!' on the trot. Everyone, it seemed to me, said 'Sorry, Rumpole!' and didn't mean a word of it. They were sorry for sending my clients to chokey, sorry for not showing me all the prosecution statements, sorry for standing on my foot in the Underground, and now, no doubt, sorry for stealing my bands. For I had reached the robing-room and, while climbing into the fancy-dress, searched for the little white hanging tabs that ornament a legal hack's neck and, lo and behold, these precious bands had been nicked. I looked down the robing-room in desperation and saw young Dave Inchcape, Mizz Liz Probert's lover and co-mortgagee, carefully tie a snow-white pair of crisp linen bands around his winged collar. I approached him in a hostile manner.

'Inchcape' – I lost no time in coming to the point – 'have you pinched my bands?'

'Sorry, Rumpole?' He pretended to know nothing of the matter.

'You have!' I regarded the case as proved. 'Honestly, Inchcape. Nowadays the barristers' robing-room is little better than a den of thieves!'

'These are my bands, Rumpole. There are some bands over there on the table. Slightly soiled. They're probably yours.'

'Slightly soiled? Sorry, Rumpole! Sorry, whoever they belonged to,' and I put them on. 'The bloody man's presumably got mine, anyway.'

When I got down, correctly if sordidly decorated about the throat, to Ollie Oliphant's Court One I found Claude Erskine-Brown all tricked out as an artificial silk and his junior, Mizz She Who Cannons Into You Probert.

'I want to ask you, Rumpole,' Claude said in his newly acquired QC's voice, 'about calling your client.'

'Mr Tong.'

'Yes. Are you calling him?'

'I call him Mr Tong because that's his name.'

'I mean,' he said with exaggerated patience, as though explaining the law to a white wig, 'are you going to put him in the witness-box? You don't have to, you know. You see, I've been asked to do a murder in Lewes. One does have so many demands on one's time in silk. So if you're not going to call Mr Tong, I thought, well, perhaps we might finish today.'

While he was drooling on, I was looking closely at the man's neck. Then I came out with the accusation direct. 'Are those my bands you're wearing?' I took hold of the suspect tabs, lifted them and examined them closely. 'They look like my bands. They *are* my bands! What's that written on them?'

'C.E.B. stands for Claude Erskine-Brown.' This was apparently his defence.

'When did you write that?'

'Oh really, Rumpole! We don't even share the same robing-room now I'm in silk. How could I have got at your bands? Just tell me, are you calling your client?'

I wasn't satisfied with his explanation, but the usher was hurrying us in as the judge was straining at the leash. I pushed my way into court, telling Erskine-Brown nothing of my plans.

I knew what I'd like to call my client. I'd like to call him a grade A, hundred-per-cent pain in the neck. In any team chosen to bore for England he would have been first in to bat. He was a retired civil servant and his hair, face, business suit and spectacles were of a uniform grey. When he spoke, he did so in a dreary monotone and never used one word when twenty would suffice. The only unexpected thing about him was that he ever got involved in the colourful crime of manslaughter. I had considered a long time before deciding to call Mr Tong as a witness in his own defence. I knew he would bore the jury to distraction and no doubt drive that North Country comedian Mr Justice Oliphant into an apoplexy. However, Mrs Tong had been found dead from a head wound in the sitting-room of their semi-detached house in Rickmansworth, and I felt her husband was called upon to provide some sort of an explanation.

You will have gathered that things hadn't gone well from the start of that day for Rumpole, and matters didn't improve when my client Tong stepped into the witness-box, raised the Testament on high and gave us what appeared to be a shortened version of the oath. 'I swear by,' he said, carefully omitting any reference to the deity, 'that the evidence I shall give shall be the truth, the whole truth and nothing but the truth.'

'Mr Rumpole. Your client has left something out of the oath.' Mr Justice Oliphant might not have been a great lawyer but at least he knew the oath by heart.

'So I noticed, my Lord.'

'Well, see to it, Mr Rumpole. Use your common sense.'

'Mr Tong,' I asked the witness, 'who is it you swear by?'

'One I wouldn't drag down to the level of this place, my Lord.'

'What's he mean, Mr Rumpole? Drag down to the level of this court? What's he mean by that?' The judge's common sense was giving way to uncommon anger.

'I suppose he means that the Almighty might not wish to be seen in Court Number One at the Old Bailey,' I suggested.

'Not wish to be seen? I never heard of such a thing!'

'Mr Tong has some rather original ideas about theology, my Lord.' I did my best to deter further conversation on the subject. 'I'm sure he would go into the matter at considerable length if your Lordship were interested.'

'I'm not, Mr Rumpole, not interested in the least.' And here his Lordship turned on the witness with 'Are you saying, Mr . . . What's your name again?'

'Tong, my Lord. Henry Sebastian Tong.'

'Are you saying my court isn't good enough for God? Is that what you're saying?'

'I am saying that this court, my Lord, is a place of sin and worldliness and we should not involve a Certain Being in these proceedings. May I remind you of the Book of Ezekiel: "And it shall be unto them a false divination in their sight, to them that have sworn oaths." '

'Don't let's worry about the Book of Ezekiel.' This work clearly wasn't Ollie Oliphant's bedtime reading. 'Mr Rumpole, can't you control your client?'

'Unfortunately not, my Lord.'

'When I was a young lad, the first thing we learnt at the Bar was to control our clients.' The judge was back on more familiar territory. 'It's a great pity you weren't brought up in a good old commonsensical chambers in Leeds, Mr Rumpole.'

'I suppose I might have acquired some of your Lordship's charm and polish,' I said respectfully.

'Let's use our common sense about this, shall we? Mr Tong, do you understand what it is to tell the truth?'

'I have always told the truth. During my thirty years in the ministry.'

'Ministry?' The judge turned to me in some alarm. 'Is your client a man of the cloth, Mr Rumpole?'

'I think he's referring to the Ministry of Agriculture and Fisheries, where he was a clerk for many years.'

'Are you going to tell the truth?' The judge addressed my client in a common-sense shout.

'Yes.' Mr Tong even managed to make a monosyllable sound boring.

'There you are, Mr Rumpole!' The judge was triumphant. 'That's the way to do it. Now, let's get on with it, shall we?'

'I assure your Lordship, I can't wait. Ouch!' The tooth Mr Leering had said would see me through the day disagreed with a sharp stab of pain. I put a hand to my cheek and muttered to my instructing solicitor, the faithful Mr Bernard, 'It's the temporary stopping.'

'Stopping? Why are you stopping, Mr Rumpole?' The judge was deeply suspicious.

Now I knew what hell was, examining a prize bore before Ollie Oliphant with a raging toothache. All the same, I soldiered on and asked Tong, 'Were you married to the late Sarah Tong?'

'We had met in the Min of Ag and Fish, where Sarah Pennington, as she then was, held a post in the typing pool. We were adjacent, as I well remember, on one occasion for the hot meal in the canteen.'

'I don't want to hurry you.'

'You hurry him, Mr Rumpole.'

'Let's come to your marriage,' I begged the witness.

'The thirteenth of March 1950, at the Church of St Joseph and All Angels, in what was then the village of Pinner.' Mr Tong supplied all the details. 'The weather, as I remember it, was particularly inclement. Dark skies and a late snow flurry.'

'Don't let's worry about the weather.' Ollie was using his common sense and longing to get on with it.

'I took it as a portent, my Lord, of storms to come.'

'Could you just describe your married life to the jury?' I tried a shortcut.

'I can only, with the greatest respect and due deference, adopt the words of the psalmist. No doubt they are well known to his Lordship?'

'I shouldn't bet on it, Mr Tong,' I warned him, and, ignoring Ollie's apparent displeasure, added, 'Perhaps you could just remind us what the Good Book says?'

' "It is better to dwell in a corner of the housetop, than with a brawling woman in a wide house," ' Mr Tong recited. ' "It is better to dwell in the wilderness than with a contentious and angry woman." '

★

So my client's evidence wound on, accompanied by toothache and an angry judge, and I felt that I had finally fallen out of love with the art of advocacy. I didn't want to have to worry about Mr Tong or the precise circumstances in which Mrs Tong had been released from this world. I wanted to sit down, to shut up and to close my eyes in peace. She Who Must Be Obeyed had something of the same idea. She wanted me to become a judge. Without taking me into her confidence, she met Marigold Featherstone, the judge's wife, for coffee in Harrods for the purpose of furthering her plan. 'Rumpole gets so terribly tired at night,' Hilda said in the Silver Grill, and Marigold, with a heavy sigh, agreed.

'So does Guthrie. At night he's as flat as a pancake. Is Rumpole flat as a pancake too?'

'Well, not exactly.' Hilda told me she wasn't sure of the exact meaning of this phrase. 'But he's so irritable these days. So edgy, and then he's had this trouble with his teeth. If only he could have a job *sitting down*.'

'You mean, like a clerk or something?'

'Something like a judge.'

'Really?' Marigold was astonished at the idea.

'Oh, I don't mean a Red Judge,' Hilda explained. 'Not a really posh judge like Guthrie. But an ordinary sort of circus judge. And Guthrie does know such important people. You said he's always calling in at the Lord Chancellor's office.'

'Only when he's in trouble,' Marigold said grimly. 'But I suppose I might ask if he could put in a word about your Horace.'

'Oh, Marigold. Would you?'

'Why not? I'll wake the old fellow up and tell him.'

As it happened, my possible escape from the agonies of the Bar was not by such an honourable way out as that sought by Hilda in the Silver Grill. The route began to appear as Mr Tong staggered slowly towards the high point of his evidence. We had enjoyed numerous quotations from the Old Testament. We had been treated to a blow-by-blow account of a quarrel between him and his wife during a holiday in Clacton-on-Sea and many other such incidents. We had learnt a great deal more about the Ministry of Agriculture and Fisheries than we ever needed to know. And then Ollie, driven beyond endurance, said, 'For God's sake –'

'My Lord?' Mr Tong looked deeply pained.

'All right, for all our sakes. When are we going to come to the facts of this manslaughter?'

So I asked the witness, 'Now, Mr Tong, on the night this *accident* took place.'

'Accident! That's a matter for the jury to decide!' Ollie exploded. 'Why do you call it an accident?'

'Why did your Lordship call it manslaughter? Isn't that a matter for the jury to decide?'

'Did I say that?' the judge asked. 'Did I say that, Mr Erskine-Brown?'

'Yes, you did,' I told him before Claude could stagger to his feet. 'I wondered if your Lordship had joined the prosecution team, or was it a single-handed effort to prejudice the jury?'

There was a terrible silence and I suppose I should never have said it. Mr Bernard hid his head in shame, Erskine-Brown looked disapproving and Liz appeared deeply worried. The judge controlled himself with difficulty and then spoke in quiet but dangerous tones. 'Mr Rumpole, that was a quite intolerable thing to say.'

'My Lord. That was a quite intolerable thing to do.' I was determined to fight on.

'I may have had a momentary slip of the tongue.' It seemed that the judge was about to retreat, but I had no intention of allowing him to do so gracefully. 'Or,' I said, 'your Lordship's well-known common sense may have deserted you.'

There was another sharp intake of breath from the attendant legal hacks and then the judge kindly let me know what was in his mind. 'Mr Rumpole. I think you should be warned. One of these days you may go too far and behaviour such as yours can have certain consequences. Now, can we get on?'

'Certainly. I didn't wish to interrupt the flow of your Lordship's rebuke.' So I started my uphill task with the witness again. 'Mr Tong, on the night in question, did you and Mrs Tong quarrel?'

'As per usual, my Lord.'

'What was the subject of the quarrel?'

'She accused me of being overly familiar with a near neighbour. This was a certain Mrs Grabowitz, my Lord, a lady of Polish extraction, whose deceased husband had, by a curious coincidence, been a colleague of mine – it's a small world, isn't it? – in the Min of Ag and Fish.'

'Mr Tong, ignore the neighbour's deceased husband, if you'd be so kind. What did your wife do?'

'She ran at me, my Lord, with her nails poised, as though to scratch me across the face, as it was often her habit so to do. However, as ill-luck would have it, the runner in front of the gas fire slipped beneath her feet on the highly polished flooring and she fell. As she did so, the back of her head made contact with the raised tiling in front of our hearth, my Lord, and she received the injuries which ultimately caused her to pass over.'

'Mr Rumpole, is that the explanation of this lady's death you wish to leave to the jury?' the judge asked with some contempt.

'Certainly, my Lord. Does your Lordship wish to prejudge the issue and are we about to hear a little premature adjudication?'

'Mr Rumpole! I have warned you twice, I shall not warn you again. I'm looking at the clock.'

'So I'd noticed.'

'We'll break off now. Back at ten past two, Members of the Jury.' And then Ollie turned to my client and gave him the solemn warning which might help me into retirement. 'I understand you're on bail, Mr Tong, and you're in the middle of giving your evidence. It's vitally important that you speak to no one about your case during the lunchtime adjournment. And no one must speak to you, particularly your legal advisers. Is that thoroughly understood, Mr Rumpole?'

'Naturally, my Lord,' I assured him. 'I do know the rules.'

'I hope you do, Mr Rumpole. I sincerely hope you do.'

The events of that lunch-hour achieved a historic importance. After a modest meal of beanshoot sandwiches in the Nuthouse Vegetarian Restaurant down by the Bank (Claude was on a regime calculated to make him more sylph-like and sexually desirable), he returned to the Old Bailey and was walking up to the silks' robing-room when he saw, through an archway, the defendant Tong seated and silent. Approaching nearer, he heard the following words (Claude was good enough to make a careful note of them at the time) shouted by Rumpole in a voice of extreme irritation.

'Listen to me,' my speech, which Claude knew to be legal advice to the client, began. 'Is this damn thing going to last for ever? Well, for God's sake, get on with it! You're driving me mad. Talk. That's all you do, you boring old fart. Just get on with it. I've got enough trouble with the judge without you causing me all this agony. Get it out. That's all. Short and snappy. Put us out of our misery. Get it out and then shut up!'

As I say, Claude took a careful note of these words but said nothing to me about them when I emerged from behind the archway. When we got back to court I asked my client a few more questions, which he answered with astounding brevity.

'Mr Tong. Did you ever intend to do your wife the slightest harm?'
'No.'
'Did you strike her?'
'No.'
'Or assault her in any way?'
'No.'
'Just wait there, will you?' – I sat down with considerable relief – 'In case Mr Erskine-Brown can think of anything to ask you.' Claude did have something to ask, and his first question came as something of a surprise to me.

'You've become very monosyllabic since lunch, haven't you, Mr Tong?'

'Perhaps it's something he ate,' I murmured to my confidant, Bernard.

'No' – Erskine-Brown wouldn't have this – 'it's nothing you ate, is it, as your learned counsel suggests? It's something Mr Rumpole said to you.'

'*Said* to him?' Ollie Oliphant registered profound shock. 'When are you suggesting Mr Rumpole spoke to him?'

'Oh, during the luncheon adjournment, my Lord.' Claude dropped the bombshell casually.

'Mr Rumpole!' Ollie gasped with horror. 'Mr Erskine-Brown, did I not give a solemn warning that no one was to speak to Mr Tong and he was to speak to no one during the adjournment?'

'You did, my Lord,' Claude confirmed it. 'That was why I was so surprised when I heard Mr Rumpole doing it.'

'You heard Mr Rumpole speaking to the defendant Tong?'

'I'm afraid so, my Lord.'

Again Bernard winced in agony, and there were varying reactions of shock and disgust all round. I didn't improve the situation by muttering loudly, 'Oh, come off it, Claude.'

'And what did Mr Rumpole say?' The judge wanted all the gory details.

'He told Mr Tong he did nothing but talk. And he was to get on with it and he was to get it out and make it snappy. Oh, yes, he said he was a boring old fart.'

'A boring old what, Mr Erskine-Brown?'

'Fart, my Lord.'

'And he's not the only one around here either,' I informed Mr Bernard.

If the judge heard this he ignored it. He went on in tones of the deepest disapproval to ask Claude, 'And, since that conversation, you say that the defendant Tong has been monosyllabic. In other words, he is obeying Mr Rumpole's quite improperly given instructions?'

'Precisely what I am suggesting, my Lord.' Claude was delighted to agree.

'Well, now, Mr Rumpole.' The judge stared balefully at me. 'What've you got to say to Mr Erskine-Brown's accusation?'

Suddenly a great weariness came over me. For once in my long life I couldn't be bothered to argue and this legal storm in a lunch-hour bored me as much as my client's evidence. I was tired of Tong, tired of judges, tired of learned friends, tired of toothache, tired of life. I rose wearily to my feet and said, 'Nothing, my Lord.'

'Nothing?' Mr Justice Oliphant couldn't believe it.

'Absolutely nothing.'

'So you don't deny that all Mr Erskine-Brown has told the court is true?'

'I neither accept it nor deny it. It's a contemptible suggestion, made by an advocate incapable of conducting a proper cross-examination. Further than that I don't feel called upon to comment. So far as I know I am not on trial.'

'Not at the moment,' said the judge. 'I cannot answer for the Bar Council.'

'Then I suggest we concentrate on the trial of Mr Tong and forget mine, my Lord.' That was my final word on the matter.

When we did concentrate on the trial it went extremely speedily. Mr Tong remained monosyllabic, our speeches were brief, the judge, all passion spent by the drama of the lunch-hour, summed up briefly and by half past five the jury were back with an acquittal. Shortly after that many of the characters important to this story had assembled in Pommeroy's Wine Bar.

Although he was buying her a drink, Liz Probert made no attempt to disguise her disapproval of the conduct of her learned leader, as she told me after these events had taken place. 'Why did you have to do that, Claude?' she asked in a severe manner. 'Why did you have to put that lunchtime conversation to Tong?'

'Rather brilliant, I thought,' he answered with some self-satisfaction and offered to split a half-bottle of his favourite Pouilly-Fumé with her. 'It got the judge on my side immediately.'

'And got the jury on Rumpole's side. His client was acquitted, I don't know if you remember.'

'Well, win a few, lose a few,' Claude said airily. 'That's par for the course, if you're a busy silk.'

'I mean, why did you do that to Rumpole?'

'Well, that was fair, wasn't it? He shouldn't have talked to his client when he was still in the box. It's just not on!'

'Are you sure he did?' Liz asked.

'I heard him with my own ears. You don't think I'd lie, do you?'

'Well, it has been known. Didn't you lie to your wife, about taking me to the opera?' Liz had no compunction about opening old wounds.

'That was love. Everyone lies when they're in love.'

'Don't ever tell me you're in love with me again. I shan't believe a single word of it. Did you really mean to get Rumpole disbarred?'

'Rumpole disbarred?' Even Claude sounded shaken by the idea. 'It's not possible.'

'Of course it's possible. Didn't you hear Ollie Oliphant?'

'That was just North Country bluff. I mean, they couldn't do a thing like that, could they? Not to Rumpole.'

'If you ask me, that's what they've been longing to do to Rumpole for years,' Liz told him. 'Now you've given them just the excuse they need.'

'Who needs?'

'The establishment, Claude! They'll use you, you know, then they'll throw you out on the scrapheap. That's what they do to spies.'

'My God!' Erskine-Brown was looking at her with considerable admiration. 'You're beautiful when you're angry!'

At which point Mizz Probert left him, having seen me alone, staring gloomily into a large brandy. Claude was surrounded by thirsty barristers, eager for news of the great Rumpole–Oliphant battle.

Before I got into conversation with Liz, who sat herself down at my table with a look of maddening pity on her face, I have to confess that I had been watching our clerk, Henry, at a distant table. He had bought a strange-looking white concoction for Dot Clapton, and was now sitting gazing at her in a way which made me feel that this was no longer a rehearsal for the Bexleyheath Thespians but a real-life drama which might lead to embarrassing and even disastrous results. I didn't manage to earwig all the dialogue, but I learnt enough to enable me to fill in the gaps later.

'You can't imagine what it was like, Dot, when my wife was mayor.' Henry was complaining, as he so often did, about his spouse's civic duties.

'Bet you were proud of her.' Dot seemed to be missing the point.

'Proud of her! What happened to my self-respect in those days when I was constantly referred to as the lady mayoress?'

'Poor old Henry!' Dot couldn't help laughing.

'Poor old Henry, yes. At council meetings I had to sit in the gallery known as the hen pen. I was sat there with the wives.'

'Things a bit better now, are they?' Dot was still hugely entertained.

'Now Eileen's reverted to alderperson? Very minimally, Dot. She's on this slimming regime now. What shall I go back to? Lettuce salad and cottage cheese – you know, that white stuff. Tastes of soap. No drink, of course. Nothing alcoholic. You reckon you could go another Snowball?'

'I'm all right, thanks.' I saw Dot cover her glass with her hand.

'I know you are, Dot,' Henry agreed enthusiastically. 'You most certainly are all right. The trouble, is, Eileen and I haven't exactly got a relationship. Not like *we've* got a relationship.'

'Well, she doesn't work with you, does she? Not on the fee notes,' Dot asked, reasonably enough.

'She doesn't work with me at all and, well, I don't feel close to her. Not as I feel close to you, Dot.'

'Well, don't get that close,' Dot warned him. 'I saw Mr Erskine-Brown give a glance in this direction.'

'Mr Erskine-Brown? He's always chasing after young girls. Makes himself ridiculous.' Henry's voice was full of contempt.

'I *had* noticed.'

'I'm not like that, Dot. I like to talk, you know, one on one. Have a relationship. May I ask you a very personal question?'

'No harm in asking.' She sounded less than fascinated.

'Do you like me, Dot? I mean, do you like me for myself?'

'Well, I don't like you for anyone else.' Dot laughed again. 'You're a very nice sort of person. Speak as you find.'

And then Henry asked anxiously, 'Am I a big part of your life?'

'Course you are!' She was still amused.

'Thank you, Dot! Thank you very much. That's all I need to know.' Henry stood up, grateful and excited. 'That deserves another Snowball!'

I saw him set out for the bar in a determined fashion, so now Dot was speaking to his back, trying to explain herself. 'I mean, you're my boss, aren't you? That's a big part of my life.'

Things had reached this somewhat tricky stage in the Dot–Henry relationship by the time Liz came and sat with me and demanded my full attention with a call to arms. 'Rumpole,' she said, 'you've got to fight it. Every inch of the way!'

'Fight what?'

'Your case. It's the establishment against Rumpole.'

'My dear Mizz Liz, there isn't any case.'

'It's a question of free speech.'

'Is it?'

'Your freedom to speak to your client during the lunch-hour. You're an issue of civil rights now, Rumpole.'

'Oh, am I? I don't think I want to be that.'

And then she looked at my glass and said, as though it were a sad sign of decline, 'You're drinking brandy!'

'Dutch courage,' I explained.

'Oh, Rumpole, that's not like you. You've never been afraid of judges.'

'Judges? Oh, no, as I always taught you, Mizz Liz, fearlessness is the first essential in an advocate. I can cope with judges. It's the other chaps that give me the jim-jams.'

'Which other chaps, Rumpole?'

'Dentists!' I took a large swig of brandy and shivered.

Time cures many things and in quite a short time old smoothy-chops Leering had the nagging tooth out of my head and I felt slightly better-tempered. Time, however, merely encouraged the growth of the great dispute and brought me nearer to an event that I'd never imagined possible, the trial of Rumpole.

You must understand that we legal hacks are divided into Inns, known as Inns of Court. These Inns are ruled by the benchers, judges and senior barristers, who elect each other to the office rather in the manner of the council which ruled Venice during the Middle Ages. The benchers of my Inn, known as the Outer Temple, do themselves extremely proud and, once elected, pay very little for lunch in the Outer Temple Hall, and enjoy a good many ceremonial dinners, Grand Nights, Guest Nights and other such occasions, when they climb into a white tie and tails, enter the dining-hall with bishops and generals on their arms, and then retire to the Parliament Room for fruit, nuts, port, brandy, Muscat de Beaumes de Venise and Romeo y Julieta cigars. There they discuss the hardships of judicial life and the sad decline in public morality and, occasionally, swap such jokes as might deprave and corrupt those likely to hear them.

On this particular Guest Night Mr Justice Graves, as Treasurer of the Inn, was presiding over the festivities. Ollie Oliphant was also present, as was a tall, handsome, only slightly overweight QC called Montague Varian, who was later to act as my prosecutor. Sam Ballard, the alleged head of our chambers and recently elected bencher, was there, delighted and somewhat overawed by his new honour. It was Ballard who told me the drift of the after-dinner conversation in the Parliament Room, an account which I have filled up with invention founded on a hard-won knowledge of the characters concerned. Among the guests present were a Lady Mendip, a sensible grey-haired headmistress, and the Bishop of Bayswater. It was to this cleric that Graves explained one of the quainter customs of the Outer Temple dining process.

'My dear Bishop, you may have heard a porter ringing a handbell before dinner. That's a custom we've kept up since the Middle Ages. The purpose is to summon in such of our students as may be fishing in the Fleet river.'

'Oh, I like that. I like that *very* much.' The bishop was full of enthusiasm for the Middle Ages. 'We regard it as rather a charming eccentricity.' Graves was smiling but his words immediately brought out the worst in Oliphant.

'I've had enough of eccentricity lately,' he said. 'And I don't regard it as a bit charming.'

'Ah, Oliver, I heard you'd been having a bit of trouble with Rumpole.' Graves turned the conversation to the scandal of the moment.

'You've got to admit, Rumpole's a genuine eccentric!' Montague Varian seemed to find me amusing.

'Genuine?' Oliphant cracked a nut mercilessly. 'Where I come from we know what genuine is. There's nothing more genuine than a good old Yorkshire pudding that's risen in the oven, all fluffy and crisp outside.'

At which a voice piped up from the end of the table singing a

Northern folk song with incomprehensible words, 'On Ilkley Moor baht'at!' This was Arthur Nottley, the junior bencher, a thin, rather elegant fellow whose weary manner marked a deep and genuine cynicism. He often said he only stayed on at the Bar to keep his basset hound in the way to which it had become accustomed. Now he had not only insulted the Great Yorkshire Bore, but had broken one of the rules of the Inn, so Graves rebuked him.

'Master Junior, we don't sing on Guest Nights in this Inn. Only on the Night of Grand Revelry.'

'I'm sorry, Master Treasurer.' Nottley did his best to sound apologetic.

'Please remember that. Yes, Oliver? You were saying?'

'It's all theatrical,' Oliphant grumbled. 'Those old clothes to make himself look poor and down-at-heel, put on to get a sympathy vote from the jury. That terrible old bit of waistcoat with cigar ash and gravy stains.'

'It's no more than a façade of a waistcoat,' Varian agreed. 'A sort of dickie!'

'The old Lord Chief would never hear argument from a man he suspected of wearing a backless waistcoat.' Oliphant quoted a precedent. 'Do you remember him telling Freddy Ringwood, "It gives me little pleasure to listen to an argument from a gentleman in light trousers"? You could say the same for Rumpole's waistcoat. When he waves his arms about you can see his shirt.'

'You're telling me, Oliver!' Graves added to the horror, 'Unfortunately I've seen more than that.'

'Of course, we do have Rumpole in chambers.' Ballard, I'm sure, felt he had to apologize for me. 'Unfortunately. I inherited him.'

'Come with the furniture, did he?' Varian laughed.

'Oh, *I'd* never have let him in,' the loyal Ballard assured them. 'And I must tell you, I've tried to raise the matter of his waistcoat on many occasions, but I can't get him to listen.'

'Well, there you go, you see.' And Graves apologized to the cleric, 'But we're boring the bishop.'

'Not at all. It's fascinating.' The Bishop of Bayswater was enjoying the fun. 'This Rumpole you've been talking about. I gather he's a bit of a character.'

'You could say he's definitely got form.' Varian made a legal joke.

'Previous convictions that means, Bishop,' Graves explained for the benefit of the cloth.

'We get them in our business,' the bishop told them. 'Priests who try to be characters. They've usually come to it late in life. Preach eccentric sermons, mention Saddam Hussein in their prayers, pay undue attention to the poor of North Bayswater and never bother to drop in for a cup of tea with the perfectly decent old ladies in the South. Blame the government for all the sins of mankind in the faint hope of getting their mugs on television. "Oh, please God," that's my nightly prayer, "save me from characters."'

Varian passed him the Madeira and when he had refilled his glass the bishop continued: 'Give me a plain, undistinguished parish priest, a chap who can marry them, bury them and still do a decent Armistice Day service for the Veterans Association.'

'Or a chap who'll put his case, keep a civil tongue in his head and not complain when you pot his client,' Oliphant agreed.

'By the way,' Graves asked, 'what did Freddy Ringwood *do* in the end? Was it that business with his girl pupil? The one who tried to slit her wrists in the women's robing-room at the Old Bailey?'

'No, I don't think that was it. Didn't he cash a rubber cheque in the circuit mess?' Arthur Nottley remembered.

'That was cleared. No' – Varian put them right – 'old Freddy's trouble was that he spoke to his client while he was in the middle of giving evidence.'

'It sounds familiar!' Ollie Oliphant said with relish. 'And in Rumpole's case there was also the matter of the abusive language he used to me on the Bench. Not that I mind for myself. I can use my common sense about that, I hope. But when you're sitting representing Her Majesty the Queen it amounts to *lèse majesté*.'

'High treason, Oliver?' suggested Graves languidly. 'There's a strong rumour going round the Sheridan Club that Rumpole called you a boring old fart.'

At which Arthur Nottley whispered to our leader, 'Probably the only true words spoken in the case!' and Ballard did his best to look disapproving at such impertinence.

'I know what he said.' Oliphant was overcome with terrible common sense. 'It was the clearest contempt of court. That's why I felt it was my public duty to report the matter to the Bar Council.'

'And they're also saying' – Varian was always marvellously well informed – 'that Rumpole's case has been put over to a disciplinary tribunal.'

'And may the Lord have mercy on his soul,' Graves intoned. 'Rumpole on trial! You must admit, it's rather an amusing idea.'

The news was bad and it had better be broken to She Who Must Be Obeyed as soon as possible. I had every reason to believe that when she heard it, the consequent eruption of just wrath against the tactless bloody-mindedness of Rumpole would register on the Richter scale as far away as Aldgate East and West Hampstead. So it was in the tentative and somewhat nervous way that a parent on Guy Fawkes night lights the blue touch-paper and stands well back that I said to Hilda one evening when we were seated in front of the gas fire, 'Old thing, I've got something to tell you.'

'And I've got something to tell *you*, Rumpole.' She was drinking coffee and toying with the *Telegraph* crossword and seemed in an unexpectedly good mood.

All the same, I had to confess, 'I think I've about finished with this game.'

'What game is that, Rumpole?'

'Standing up and bowing, saying, "If your Lordship pleases, In my very humble submission, With the very greatest respect, my Lord" to some old fool no one has any respect for at all.'

'That's the point, Rumpole! You shouldn't have to stand up any more, or bow to anyone.'

'Those days are over, Hilda. Definitely over!'

'I *quite* agree.'

I was delighted to find her so easily persuaded. 'I shall let them go through their absurd rigmarole and then they can do their worst.'

'And you'll spend the rest of your days sitting,' Hilda said. I thought that was rather an odd way of putting it, but I was glad of her support and explained my present position in greater detail.

'So be it!' I told her. 'If that's all they have to say to me after a lifetime of trying to see that some sort of justice is done to a long line of errant human beings, good luck to them. If that's my only reward for trying to open their eyes and understand that there are a great many people in this world who weren't at Winchester with them, and have no desire to take port with the benchers of the Outer Temple, let them get on with it. "From this time forth I never will speak word!" '

'I'm sure that's best, Rumpole, except for your summings-up.'

'My what?' I no longer followed her drift.

'Your summings-up to the jury, Rumpole. You can do those sitting down, can't you?'

'Hilda,' I asked patiently, 'what *are* you talking about?'

'I know what *you're* talking about. I had a word with Marigold Featherstone, in Harrods.'

'Does *she* know already?' News of Rumpole's disgrace had, of course, spread like wildfire.

'Well, not everything. But she was going to see Guthrie did something about it.'

'Nothing he can do.' I had to shatter her hopes. 'Nothing anyone can do, now.'

'You mean, they told you?' She looked more delighted than ever.

'Told me what?'

'You're going to be a judge?'

'No, my dear old thing. I'm not going to be a judge. I'm not even going to be a barrister. I'm up before the Disciplinary Tribunal, Hilda. They're going to kick me out.'

She looked at me in silence and I steeled myself for the big bang, but to my amazement she asked, quite quietly, 'Rumpole, what is it? You've got yourself into some sort of trouble?'

'That's the understatement of the year.'

'Is it another woman?' Hilda's mind dwelt continually on sex.

'Not really. It's another man. A North Country comedian who

gave me more of his down-to-earth common sense than I could put up with.'

'Sir Oliver Oliphant?' She knew her way round the judiciary. 'You weren't rude to him, were you, Rumpole?'

'In all the circumstances, I think I behaved with remarkable courtesy,' I assured her.

'That means you were rude to him.' She was not born yesterday. 'I once poured him a cup of tea at the Outer Temple garden party.'

'What made you forget the arsenic?'

'He's probably not so bad when you get to know him.'

'When you get to know him,' I assured her, 'he's much, much worse.'

'What else have you done, Rumpole? You may as well tell me now.'

'They say I spoke to my client at lunchtime. I am alleged to have told him not to bore us all to death.'

'Was it a woman client?' She looked, for a moment, prepared to explode, but I reassured her.

'Decidedly not! It was a retired civil servant called Henry Sebastian Tong.'

'And when is this tribunal?' She was starting to sound determined, as though war had broken out and she was prepared to fight to the finish.

'Shortly. I shall treat it with the contempt it deserves,' I told her, 'and when it's all over I shall rest:

> 'For the sword outwears its sheath,
> And the soul wears out the breast,
> And the heart must pause to breathe,
> And love itself have rest.'

The sound of the words brought me some comfort, although I wasn't sure they were entirely appropriate. And then she brought back my worst fears by saying, 'I shall stand by you, Rumpole, at whatever cost. I shall stand by you, through thick and thin.'

*

Perhaps I should explain the obscure legal process that has to be gone through in the unfrocking, or should I say unwigging, of a barrister. The Bar Council may be said to be the guardian of our morality, there to see we don't indulge in serious crimes or conduct unbecoming to a legal hack, such as assaulting the officer in charge of the case, dealing in dangerous substances round the corridors of the Old Bailey or speaking to our clients in the lunch-hour. Mr Justice Ollie Oliphant had made a complaint to that body and a committee had decided to send me for trial before a High Court judge, three practising barristers and a lay assessor, one of the great and the good who could be relied upon to uphold the traditions of the Bar and not ask awkward questions or give any trouble to the presiding judge. It was the prospect of She Who Must Be Obeyed pleading my cause as a character witness before this august tribunal which made my blood run cold.

There was another offer of support which I thought was far more likely to do me harm than good. I was, a few weeks later, alone in Pommeroy's Wine Bar, contemplating the tail-end of a bottle of Château Fleet Street and putting off the moment when I would have to return home to Hilda's sighs of sympathy and the often-repeated, unanswerable question, 'How *could* you have done such a thing, Rumpole? After all your years of experience', to which would no doubt be added the information that her daddy would never have spoken to a client in the lunch-hour, or at any other time come to that, when I heard a familiar voice calling my name and I looked up to see my old friend Fred Timson, head of the great South London family of villains from which a large part of my income is derived. Naturally I asked him to pull up a chair, pour out a glass and was he in some sort of trouble?

'Not me. I heard you was, Mr Rumpole. I want you to regard me as your legal adviser.'

When I explained that the indispensable Mr Bernard was already filling that post at my trial he said, 'Bernard has put me entirely in the picture, he having called on my cousin Kevin's second-hand car lot as he was interested in a black Rover, only fifty thousand on the clock and the property of a late undertaker. We chewed the fat to a considerable extent over your case, Mr Rumpole, and I have to inform you, my own view is that you'll walk it. We'll get you out, sir, without a stain on your character.'

'Oh, really, Fred' – I already felt some foreboding – 'and how will you manage that?'

'It so happened' – he started on a long story – 'that Cary and Chas Timson, being interested spectators in the trial of Chas's brother-in-law Benny Panton on the Crockthorpe post office job, was in the Old Bailey on that very day! And they kept your client Tongue – or whatever his name was –'

'Tong.'

'Yes, they kept Mr Tong in view throughout the lunch-hour, both of them remaining in the precincts as, owing to a family celebration the night before, they didn't fancy their dinner. And they can say, with the utmost certainty, Mr Rumpole, that you did not speak one word to your client throughout the lunchtime adjournment! So the good news is, two cast-iron alibi witnesses. I have informed Mr Bernard accordingly, and you are bound to walk!'

I don't know what Fred expected but all I could do was to look at him in silent wonder and, at last, say, 'Very interesting.'

'We thought you'd be glad to know about it.' He seemed surprised at my not hugging him with delight.

'How did they recognize Mr Tong?'

'Oh, they asked who you was defending, being interested in your movements as the regular family brief. And the usher pointed this Tong out to the witnesses.'

'Really? And who was the judge in the robbery trial they were attending?'

'They told me that! Old Penal Parsloe, I'm sure that was him.'

'Mr Justice Parsloe is now Lord Justice Parsloe, sitting in the Court of Appeal,' I had to break the bad news to him. 'He hasn't been down the Bailey for at least two years. I'm afraid your ingenious defence wouldn't work, Fred, even if I intended to deny the charges.'

'Well, what judge was it, then, Mr Rumpole?'

'Never mind, Fred.' I had to discourage his talent for invention. 'It's the thought that counts.'

When I left Pommeroy's a good deal later, bound for Temple tube station, I had an even stranger encounter and a promise of further embarrassment at my trial. As I came down Middle Temple Lane on to the Embankment and turned right towards the station, I saw the figure of Claude Erskine-Brown approaching with his robe bag slung over his shoulder, no doubt whistling the big number from *Götterdämmerung*, perhaps kept late by some jury unable to make up its mind. Claude had been the cause of all my troubles and I had no desire to bandy words with the fellow, so I turned back and started to retrace my steps in an easterly direction. Who should I see then but Ollie Oliphant issuing from Middle Temple Lane, smoking a cigar and looking like a man who has been enjoying a good dinner. Quick as a shot I dived into such traffic as there was and crossed the road to the Embankment, where I stood, close to the wall, looking down into the inky water of the Thames, with my back well turned to the two points of danger behind me.

I hadn't been standing there very long, sniffing the night air and hoping I had got shot of my two opponents, when an unwelcome hand grasped my arm and I heard a panic-stricken voice say, 'Don't do it, Rumpole!'

'Do what?'

'Take the easy way out.'

'Bollard!' I said, for it was our head of chambers behaving in this extraordinary fashion. 'Let go of me, will you?'

At this, Ballard did relax his grip and stood looking at me with deep and intolerable compassion as he intoned, 'However serious the crime, all sinners may be forgiven. And remember, there are those that are standing by you, your devoted wife – and me! I have taken up the burden of your defence.'

'Well, put it down, Bollard! I have nothing whatever to say to those ridiculous charges.'

'I mean, I am acting for you, at your trial.' I then felt a genuine, if momentary, desire to hurl myself into the river, but he was preaching on. 'I think I can save you, Rumpole, if you truly repent.'

'What *is* this?' I couldn't believe my ears. 'A legal conference or a prayer meeting?'

'Good question, Rumpole! The two are never far apart. You may achieve salvation, if you will say, after me, you have erred and strayed like a lost sheep.'

'*Me?* Say that to Ollie Oliphant?' Had Bollard taken complete leave of his few remaining senses?

'Repentance, Rumpole. It's the only way.'

'Never!'

'I don't ask it for myself, Rumpole, even though I'm standing by you.'

'Well, stop standing by me, will you? I'm on my way to the Underground.' And I started to move away from the man at a fairly brisk pace.

'I ask it for that fine woman who has devoted her life to you. A somewhat unworthy cause, perhaps. But she is devoted. Rumpole, I ask it for Hilda!'

What I didn't know at that point was that Hilda was being more active in my defence than I was. She had called at our chambers and, while I was fulfilling a previous engagement in Snaresbrook Crown Court, she had burst into Ballard's room unannounced, rousing him from some solitary religious observance or an afternoon sleep brought on by over-indulgence in beanshoot sandwiches at the vegetarian snack bar, and told him that I was in a little difficulty. Ballard's view, when he had recovered consciousness, was that I was in fact in deep trouble and he had prayed long and earnestly about the matter.

'I hope you're going to do something a little more practical than pray!' Hilda, as you may have noticed, can be quite sharp on occasions. She went on to tell Soapy Sam that she had called at the Bar Council, indeed there was no door she wouldn't open in my cause, and had been told that what Rumpole needed was a QC to defend him, and if he did his own case in the way he carried on down the Bailey 'he'd be sunk'.

'That seems to be sound advice, Mrs Rumpole.'

'I said there was no difficulty in getting a QC of standing and that Rumpole's head of chambers would be delighted to act for him.'

'You mean' – there was, I'm sure, a note of fear in Ballard's voice – 'you want me to take on Rumpole as a *client*?'

'I want you to stand by him, Sam, as I am doing, and as any decent head of chambers would for a tenant in trouble.'

'But he's got to apologize to Mr Justice Oliphant, fully and sincerely. How on earth am I going to persuade Rumpole to do that?' Ballard no doubt felt like someone called upon to cleanse the Augean stables, knowing perfectly well that he'd never be a Hercules.

'Leave that to me. I'll do the persuading. You just think of how you'd put it nice and politely to the judge.' Hilda was giving the instructions to counsel, but Ballard was still daunted.

'Rumpole as a client,' he muttered. 'God give me strength!'

'Don't worry, Sam. If God won't, I certainly will.'

After this encounter Ballard dined in his newfound splendour as a bencher and after dinner he found himself sitting next to none other than the complaining Judge Ollie Oliphant, who was in no hurry to return to his bachelor flat in Temple Gardens. Seeking to avoid a great deal of hard and thankless work before the Disciplinary Tribunal, Soapy Sam started to soften up his Lordship, who seemed astonished to hear that he was defending Rumpole.

'I am acting in the great tradition of the Bar, Judge,' Soapy Sam excused himself by saying. 'Of course we are bound to represent the most hopeless client, in the most disagreeable case.'

'Hopeless. I'm glad you see that. Shows you've got a bit of common sense.'

'Might you take' – Ballard was at his most obsequious – 'in your great wisdom and humanity, which is a byword at the Old Bailey; you are known, I believe, as "the Quality of Mercy" down there – a merciful view if there were to be a contrite apology?'

'Rumpole'd rather be disbarred than apologize to me.' Oliphant was probably right.

'But if he would?'

'If he would, it'd cause him more genuine pain and grief than anything else in the world.' And then the judge, thinking it over, was heard to make some sort of gurgling noise that might have passed for a chuckle. 'I'd enjoy seeing that, I really would. I'd love to see Horace Rumpole grovel. That might be punishment enough. It would be up to the tribunal, of course.'

'Of course. But your attitude, Judge, would have such an influence, given the great respect you're held in at the Bar. Well, thank you. Thank you very much.'

It was after that bit of crawling over the dessert that I spotted Oliphant coming out of Middle Temple Lane and Ballard imagined he'd saved me from ending my legal career in the cold and inhospitable waters of the Thames.

It soon became clear to me that my supporters expected me to appear as a penitent before Mr Justice Oliphant. This was the requirement of She Who Must Be Obeyed, who pointed out the awful consequences of my refusal to bow the knee. 'How could I bear it, Rumpole?' she said one evening when the nine o'clock news had failed to entertain us. 'I remember Daddy at the Bar and how everyone respected him. How could I bear to be the wife of a disbarred barrister? How could I meet any of the fellows in chambers and hear them say, as I turned away, "Of course, you remember old Rumpole. Kicked out for unprofessional conduct."'

Of course I saw her point. I sighed heavily and asked her what she wanted me to do.

'Take Sam Ballard's advice. We've all told you, apologize to Sir Oliver Oliphant.'

'All right, Hilda, you win.' I hope I said it convincingly, but down towards the carpet, beside the arm of my chair, I had my fingers crossed.

Hilda and I were not the only couple whose views were not entirely at one in that uneasy period before my trial. During a quiet moment in the clerk's room, Henry came out with some startling news for Dot.

'Well, I told Eileen last night. It was an evening when she wasn't out at the Drainage Inquiry and I told my wife quite frankly what we decided.'

'What did we decide?' Dot asked nervously.

'Like, what you told me. I'm a big part of your life.'

'Did I say that?'

'You know you did. We can't hide it, can we, Dot? We're going to make a future together.'

'You told your wife that?' Dot was now seriously worried.

'She understood what I was on about. Eileen understands I got to have this one chance of happiness, while I'm still young enough to enjoy it.'

'Did you say "young enough", Henry?'

'So, we're beginning a new life together. That all right, Dot?'

Before she could answer him, the telephone rang and the clerk's room began to fill with solicitors and learned friends in search of briefs. Henry seemed to regard the matter as closed and Dot didn't dare to reopen it, at least until after my trial was over and a historic meeting took place.

During the daytime, when the nuts and fruit and Madeira were put away and the tables were arranged in a more threatening and judicial manner, my trial began in the Outer Temple Parliament Room. It was all, I'm sure, intended to be pleasant and informal: I wasn't guarded in a dock but sat in a comfortable chair beside my legal advisers, Sam Ballard, QC, Liz Probert, his junior, and Mr Bernard, my instructing solicitor. However, all friendly feelings were banished by the look on the face of the presiding judge; I had drawn the short straw in the shape of Mr Justice Graves – or Gravestone, as I preferred to call him – who looked as though he was sick to the stomach at the thought of a barrister accused of such appalling crimes, but if someone had to be he was relieved, on the whole, that it was only Horace Rumpole.

Claude gave evidence in a highly embarrassed way of what he'd heard and I instructed Ballard not to ask him any questions. This came as a relief to him as he couldn't think of any questions to ask. And then Ollie Oliphant came puffing in, bald as an egg without his wig, wearing a dark suit and the artificial flower of some charity in his buttonhole. He was excused from taking the oath by Graves, who acted on the well-known theory that judges are incapable of fibbing, and he gave his account of all my sins and omissions to Montague Varian, QC, for the prosecution. As he did so, I examined the faces of my judges. Graves might have been carved out of yellowish marble; the lay assessor was Lady Mendip, the headmistress, and she looked as though she were hearing an account of disgusting words found chalked up on a blackboard. Of the three practising barristers sent to try me only Arthur Nottley smiled faintly, but then I had seen him smile through the most horrendous murder cases.

When Varian had finished, Ballard rose, with the greatest respect, to cross-examine. 'It's extremely courteous of you to agree to attend here in person, Judge.'

'And absolutely charming of you to lodge a complaint against me,' I murmured politely.

'Now my client wants you to know that he was suffering from a severe toothache on the day in question.' Ballard was wrong; I didn't particularly want the judge to know that. At any rate, Graves didn't think much of my temporary stopping as a defence.

'Mr Ballard,' he said, 'is toothache an excuse for speaking to a client during the luncheon-time adjournment? I should have thought Mr Rumpole would have been anxious to rest his mouth.'

'My Lord, I'm now dealing with the question of rudeness to the learned judge.'

'The boring old fart evidence,' I thought I heard Nottley whisper to his neighbouring barrister.

And then Ballard pulled a trick on me which I hadn't expected. 'I understand my client wishes to apologize to the learned judge in his own words,' he told the tribunal. No doubt he expected that, overcome by the solemnity of the occasion, I would run up the white flag and beg for mercy. He sat down and I did indeed rise to my feet and address Mr Justice Oliphant along these lines.

'My Lord,' I started formally, 'if it please your Lordship, I do realize there are certain things which should not be said or done in court, things that are utterly inexcusable and no doubt amount to contempt.'

As I said this, Graves leant forward and I saw, as I had never in court seen before, a faint smile on those gaunt features. 'Mr Rumpole, the tribunal is, I believe I can speak for us all, both surprised and gratified by this unusually apologetic attitude.' Here the quartet beside him nodded in agreement. 'I take it you're about to withdraw the inexcusable phrases.'

'Inexcusable, certainly,' I agreed. 'I was just about to put to Mr Justice Oliphant the inexcusable manner in which he sighs and rolls his eyes to heaven when he sums up the defence case.' And here I embarked on a mild imitation of Ollie Oliphant: '"Of course you can believe that if you like, Members of the Jury, but use your common sense, why don't you?" And what about describing my client's conduct as manslaughter during the evidence, which was the very fact the jury had to decide? If he's prepared to say sorry for that, then I'll apologize for pointing out his undoubted prejudice.'

Oliphant, who had slowly been coming to the boil, exploded at this point. 'Am I expected to sit here and endure a repetition of the quite intolerable . . .'

'No, no, my Lord!' Ballard fluttered to his feet. 'Of course not. Please, Mr Rumpole. If it please your Lordship, may I take instructions?' And when Graves said, 'I think you'd better,' my defender turned to me with, 'You said you'd apologize.'

'I'm prepared to *swap* apologies,' I whispered back.

'I heard that, Mr Ballard.' Graves was triumphant. 'As I think your client knows perfectly well, my hearing is exceptionally keen. I wonder what Mr Rumpole's excuse is for his extraordinary behaviour today. He isn't suffering from toothache now, is he?'

'My Lord, I will take further instructions.' This time he whispered, 'Rumpole! Hadn't you better have toothache?'

'No, I had it out.'

'I'm afraid, my Lord' – Ballard turned to Graves, disappointed – 'the answer is no. He had it out during the trial.'

'So, on this occasion, Mr Ballard, you can't even plead toothache as a defence?'

'I'm afraid not, my Lord.'

'Had it out . . . during the trial.' Graves was making a careful note, then he screwed the top back on his pen with the greatest care and said, 'We shall continue with this unhappy case tomorrow morning.'

'My Lord' – I rose to my feet again – 'may I make an application?'

'What is it, Mr Rumpole?' Graves asked warily, as well he might.

'I'm getting tired of Mr Ballard's attempts to get me to apologize, unilaterally. Would you ask *him* not to speak to his client over the adjournment?'

Graves had made a note of the historic fact that I had had my tooth out during the trial, and Liz had noted it down also. As she wrote she started to speculate, as I had taught her to do in the distant days when she was my pupil. As soon as the tribunal packed up business for the day she went back to chambers and persuaded Claude Erskine-Brown to take her down to the Old Bailey and show her the *locus in quo*, the scene where the ghastly crime of chattering to a client had been committed.

Bewildered, but no doubt filled with guilt at his treacherous behaviour to a fellow hack, Claude led her to the archway through which he had seen the tedious Tong listening to Rumpole's harangue.

'And where did you see Rumpole?'

'Well, he came out through the arch after he'd finished talking to his client.'

'But *while* he was speaking to his client.'

'Well, actually,' Claude had to admit, 'I didn't see him then, at all. I mean, I suppose he was hidden from my view, Liz.'

'I suppose he was.' At which she strode purposefully through the arch and saw what, perhaps, she had expected to find, a row of telephones on the wall, in a position which would also have been invisible to the earwigging Claude. They were half covered, it's true, with plastic hoods, but a man who didn't wish to crouch under these contrivances might stand freely with the connection pulled out to its full extent and speak to whoever he had chosen to abuse.

'So Rumpole might have been standing *here* when you were listening?' Liz had taken up her position by one of the phones.

'I suppose so.'

'And you heard him say words like, "Just get on with it. I've got enough trouble without you causing me all this agony. Get it out!"?'

'I told the tribunal that, don't you remember?' The true meaning of the words hadn't yet sunk into that vague repository of Wagnerian snatches and romantic longings, the Erskine-Brown mind. Liz, however, saw the truth in all its simplicity as she lifted a telephone, brushed it with her credit card in a way I could never manage, and was, in an instant, speaking to She Who Must Be Obeyed. Mizz Probert had two simple requests: could Hilda come down to the Temple tomorrow and what, please, was the name of Horace's dentist?

When the tribunal met next morning, my not so learned counsel announced that my case was to be placed in more competent hands. 'My learned junior Miss Probert,' Sam Ballard said, 'will call our next witness, but first she wishes to recall Mr Erskine-Brown.'

No one objected to this and Claude returned to the witness's chair to explain the position of the archway and the telephones, and the fact that he hadn't, indeed, seen me speaking to Tong. Montague Varian had no questions and my judges were left wondering what significance, if any, to attach to this new evidence. I was sure that it would make no difference to the result, but then Liz Probert uttered the dread words, 'I will now call Mr Lionel Leering.'

I had been at a crossroads; one way led on through a countryside too well known to me. I could journey on for ever round the courts, arguing cases, winning some, losing more and more perhaps in my few remaining years. The other road was the way of escape, and once Mr Leering gave his evidence that, I knew, would be closed to me. 'Don't do it,' I whispered my instructions to Mizz Probert. 'I'm not fighting this case.'

'Oh, Rumpole!' She turned and leant down to my level, her face shining with enthusiasm. 'I'm going to win! It's what you taught me to do. Don't spoil it for me now.'

I thought then of all the bloody-minded clients who had wrecked the cases in which I was about to chalk up a victory. It was her big moment and who was I to snatch it from her? I was tired, too tired to win, but also too tired to lose, so I gave her her head. 'Go on, then,' I told her, 'if you *have* to.'

With her nostrils dilated and the light of battle in her eyes, Mizz Liz Probert turned on her dental witness and proceeded to demolish the prosecution case.

'Do you carry on your practice in Harley Street, in London?'

'That is so. And may I say, I have a most important bridge to insert this morning. The patient is very much in the public eye.'

'Then I'll try and make this as painless as possible,' Liz assured him. 'Did you treat Mr Rumpole on the morning of May the sixteenth?'

'I did. He came early because he told me he was in the middle of a case at the Old Bailey. I think he was defending in a manslaughter. I gave him a temporary stopping, which I thought would keep him going.'

'Did it?'

'Apparently not. He rang me around lunchtime. He told me that his tooth was causing him pain and he was extremely angry. He raised his voice at me.'

'Can you remember what he said?'

'So far as I can recall he said something like, "I've got enough trouble with the judge without you causing me all this agony. Get it out!" and, "Put us out of our misery!" '

'What do you think he meant?'

'He wanted his tooth extracted.'

'Did you do it for him?'

'Yes, I stayed on late especially. I saw him at seven thirty that evening. He was more cheerful then, but a little unsteady on his feet. I believe he'd been drinking brandy to give himself Dutch courage.'

'I think that may well have been so,' Liz agreed.

Now the members of the tribunal were whispering together. Then the whispering stopped and Mr Justice Gravestone turned an ancient and fish-like eye on my prosecutor. 'If this evidence is correct, Mr Varian, and we remember the admission made by Mr Claude Erskine-Brown and the position of the telephones, and the fact that he never saw Mr Rumpole, then this allegation about speaking to his client falls to the ground, does it not?'

'I must concede that, my Lord.'

'Then all that remains are the offensive remarks to Mr Justice Oliphant.'

'Yes, my Lord.'

'Yes, well, I'm much obliged.' The fishy beam was turned on to the defence. 'This case now turns solely on whether your client is prepared to make a proper, unilateral apology to my brother Oliphant.'

'Indeed, my Lord.'

'Then we'll consider that matter, after a short adjournment.'

So we all did a good deal of bowing to each other and as I came out of the Parliament Room, who should I see but She Who Must Be Obeyed, who, for a reason then unknown to me, made a most surprising U-turn. 'Rumpole,' she said, 'I've been thinking things over and I think Oliphant treated you abominably. My view of the matter is that you shouldn't apologize at all!'

'Is that your view, Hilda?'

'Of course it is. I'm sure nothing will make you stop work, unless you're disbarred, and think how wonderful that will be for our marriage.'

'What *do* you mean?' But I'd already guessed, with a sort of dread, what she was driving at.

'If you can't consort with all those criminals, I'll have you at home all day! There's so many little jobs for you to do. Repaper the kitchen, get the parquet in the hallway polished. You'd be able to help me with the shopping every day. And we'd have my friends round to tea; Dodo Mackintosh complains she sees nothing of you.' There was considerably more in this vein, but Hilda had already said enough to make up my mind. When my judges were back, refreshed with coffee, biscuits and, in certain cases, a quick drag on a Silk Cut, Sam Ballard announced that I wished to make a statement, the die was cast and I tottered to my feet and spoke to the following effect.

'If your Lordship, and the members of the tribunal, please. I have, I hope, some knowledge of the human race in general and the judicial race in particular. I do realize that some of those elevated to the Bench are more vulnerable, more easily offended than others. Over my years at the Old Bailey, before your Lordship and his brother judges, I have had to grow a skin like a rhinoceros. Mr Justice Oliphant, I acknowledge, is a more retiring, shy and sensitive plant, and if anything I have said may have wounded him, I do most humbly, most sincerely apologize.' At this I bowed and whispered to Mizz Liz Probert, 'Will that do?'

What went on behind closed doors between my judges I can't say. Were some of them, was even the sea-green incorruptible Graves, a little tired of Ollie's down-to-earth North Country common sense; had they been sufficiently bored by him over port and walnuts to wish to deflate, just a little, that great self-satisfied balloon? Or did they stop short of depriving the Old Bailey monument of its few moments of worthwhile drama? Would they really have wanted to take all the fun out of the criminal law? I don't know the answer to these questions but in one rather athletic bound Rumpole was free, still to be audible in the Ludgate Circus *palais de justice*.

The next events of importance occurred at an ambitious chambers party held as a delayed celebration of the fact that Mrs Phillida Erskine-Brown, our Portia, was now elegantly perched on the High Court Bench and her husband, Claude, had received the lesser honour of being swathed in silk. This beano took place in Ballard's room and all the characters in Equity Court were there, together with their partners, as Mizz Liz would call them, and I had taken the opportunity of issuing a few further invitations on my own account.

One of the most dramatic events on this occasion was an encounter, by a table loaded with bottles and various delicacies, between Dot and a pleasant-looking woman in her forties who, between rapid inroads into a plate of tuna fish sandwiches, said that she was Henry's wife, Eileen, and wasn't Dot the new typist, because 'Henry's been telling me all about you'?

'I don't know why he does that. He has no call, really.' Dot was confused and embarrassed. 'Look, I'm sorry about what he told you.'

'Oh, don't be,' Eileen reassured her. 'It's a great relief to me. I was on this horrible slimming diet because I thought that's how Henry liked me, but now he says you want to make your life together. So, could you just whirl those cocktail sausages in my direction?'

'We're not going to make a life together and I don't know where he got the idea from at all. I mean, I like Henry. I think he's very sweet and serious, but in a boyfriend, I'd prefer something more muscular. Know what I mean?'

'You're not going to take him on?' Henry's wife sounded disappointed.

'I couldn't entertain the idea, with all due respect to your husband.'

'He'll have to stay where he is then.' Eileen lifted another small sausage on its toothpick. 'But I'm not going back on that horrible cottage cheese. Not for him, not for anyone.'

By now the party was starting to fill up and among the first to come was old Gravestone, to whom, I thought, I owed a very small debt of gratitude. I heard him tell Ballard how surprised he was that I'd invited him and he congratulated my so-called defender (and not my wife, who deserved all the credit) on having got me to apologize. Ballard lied outrageously and said, 'As head of these chambers, of course, I do have a little influence on Rumpole.'

Shortly after this, another of my invitees came puffing up the stairs and Ballard, apparently in a state of shock, stammered, 'Judge! You're here!' to Mr Justice Oliphant.

'Of course I'm here,' Ollie rebuked him. 'Use your common sense. Made Rumpole squirm, having to apologize, did it? Good, very good. That was all I needed.'

Later Mr Justice Featherstone arrived with Marigold and among all these judicial stars Eileen, the ex-mayor, had the briefest of heart to hearts with her husband. 'She doesn't want you, Henry,' she told him.

'Please!' Our clerk looked nervously round for earwiggers. 'How on earth can you say that?'

'Oh, she told me. No doubt about it. She goes for something more muscular, and I know exactly what she means.'

Oblivious of this domestic drama, the party surged on around them. Ballard told Mr Justice Featherstone that it had been a most worrying case and Guthrie said things might be even more worrying now that I'd won, and Claude asked me why I hadn't told him that I was talking to my dentist.

'Your suggestion was beneath contempt, Erskine-Brown. Besides which I rather fancied being disbarred at the time.'

'Rumpole!' The man was shocked. 'Why ever should you want that?'

' "For the sword outwears its sheath," ' I explained, ' "And the soul wears out the breast, And the heart must pause to breathe." – But not yet, Claude. Not quite yet.'

At last Henry managed to corner Dot, while Claude set off in a bee-line for the personable Eileen. The first thing Henry did was to apologize. 'I never wanted her to come, Dot, but she insisted. It must have been terribly embarrassing for you.'

'She's ever so nice, isn't she? You're a very lucky bloke, Henry.'

'Having you, you mean?' He still nursed a flicker of hope.

'No' – she blew out the flame – 'having a wife who's prepared to eat cottage cheese for you.'

Marigold said to Hilda, 'I hear Rumpole's not sitting as a judge. In fact I heard he was nearly made to sit at home permanently.' Marguerite Ballard, ex-matron down at the Old Bailey, told Mr Justice Oliphant that 'his naughty tummy was rather running away with him'. I told Liz that she had been utterly ruthless in pursuit of victory and she asked if I had forgiven her for saving my legal life.

'I think so. But who fed Hilda that line about having me at home all day?'

'What are you talking about, Rumpole?' She Who Must joined us.

'Oh, I was just saying to Liz, of course it'd be very nice if we could spend all day together, Hilda. I mean, *that* wasn't what led me to apologize.'

'That's the trouble with barristers.' She gave me one of her piercing looks. 'You can't believe a word they say.'

Before I could think of any convincing defence to Hilda's indictment, the last of my personally invited guests arrived. This was Fred Timson, wearing a dark suit with a striped tie and looking more than ever like a senior member of the old Serious Crimes Squad. I found him a drink, put it into his hand and told him how glad I was he could find time for us.

'What a do, eh?' He looked round appreciatively. 'Judges and sparkling wine! Here's to your very good health, Mr Rumpole.'

'No, Fred,' I told him, 'I'm going to drink to yours.' Whereupon I banged a glass against the table, called for silence and proposed a toast. 'Listen, everybody. I want to introduce you to Fred Timson, head of a noted family of South London villains, minor thieves and receivers of stolen property. No violence in his record. That right, Fred?'

'Quite right, Mr Rumpole.' Fred confirmed the absence of violence and then I made public what had long been my secret thoughts on the relationship between the Timsons and the law.

'This should appeal to you, my Lords, Ladies and Gentlemen. Fred lives his life on strict monetarist principles. He doesn't believe in the closed shop; he thinks that shops should be open all night, preferably by jemmy. He believes firmly in the marketplace, because that's where you can dispose of articles that dropped off the back of a lorry. But without Fred and his like, we should all be out of work. There would be no judges, none of Her Majesty's counsel, learned in the law, no coppers and no humble Old Bailey hacks. So charge your glasses, fill us up, Henry, and I would ask you to drink to Fred Timson and the criminals of England!'

I raised my glass but the faces around me registered varying degrees of disapproval and concern. Ballard bleated, 'Rumpole!', Hilda gave out a censorious 'Really, Rumpole!', Featherstone J. said, 'He's off again,' and Mr Justice Oliphant decided that if this wasn't unprofessional conduct he didn't know what was. Only Liz, flushed with her success in court and a few quick glasses of the *méthode champenoise*, raised a fist and called out, 'Up the workers!'

'Oh, really!' Graves turned wearily to our head of chambers. 'Will Rumpole never learn?'

'I'm afraid never,' Ballard told him.

I was back at work again and life would continue much as ever at 3 Equity Court.

Rumpole and the Way through the Woods

There are times, I have to admit, when even the glowing flame of Rumpole sinks to a mere flicker. It had been a bad day. I had finished a case before old Gravestone, a long slog against a hostile judge, an officer in charge of the case who seemed to regard the truth as an inconvenient obstacle to the smooth and efficient running of the Criminal Investigation Department, and a client whose unendurable cockiness and self-regard rapidly lost all hearts in the jury. It had been a hard slog which would have seemed as nothing if it had ended in an acquittal. It had not been so rewarded and, when I said goodbye to my client in the cells, carefully failing to remind him that he might be away for a long time, he said, 'What's the matter with you, Mr Rumpole? Losing your touch, are you? They was saying in the Scrubs, isn't it about time you hung up the old wig and took retirement?' Every bone in my body seemed to ache as I stumbled into Pommeroy's where the Château Thames Embankment tasted more than ever of mildew and Claude Erskine-Brown cornered me in order to describe, at interminable length, the triumph he had enjoyed in a rent application. Leaving for home early, I had to stand up in the tube all the way back. Returning to the world from the bowels of Gloucester Road station, I struggled towards Froxbury Mansions with the faltering determination of a dying Bedouin crawling towards an oasis. All I wanted was my armchair beside the gas fire, a better bottle of the very ordinary claret, and a little peace in which to watch other people in trouble on the television. It was not to be.

When I entered the living-room the lights were off and I heard the sound of heavy and laboured breathing. My first thought was that She had fallen asleep by the gas fire, but I could hear the clatter of saucepans from the kitchen. I sniffed the air and received the usual whiff of furniture polish and cabbage being boiled into submission. But, added to this brew, was a not particularly exotic perfume, acrid and pervasive, which might, if bottled extravagantly, have been marketed as wet dog. Then the heavy breathing turned into the sort of dark and distant rumble which precedes the arrival of an Underground train. I snapped on the light and there it was: long legged, overweight and sprawled in my armchair. It was awake now, staring at me with wide-open, moist black eyes. I put out a hand to shift the intruder and the sound of the approaching train increased in volume until it became a snarl, and the animal revealed sharp and unexpectedly white pointed teeth. 'Hilda,' I called for help from a usually reliable source, 'there's a stray dog in the living-room.'

'That's not a stray dog. That's Sir Lancelot.' I turned round and She was standing in the doorway, looking with disapproval not at the trespasser but at me.

'What on earth do you mean, Sir Lancelot?'

'That's your name, isn't it, darling?' She approached the animal with a broad smile. 'Although sometimes we call you Lance for short, don't we?' To these eager questions the dog returned no answer at all, although it did, I was relieved to see, put away its teeth.

'Whatever its name is, shall we call the police?'

'Why?'

'To have it removed.'

'Have you *removed*, Sir Lancelot? What a silly husband I've got, haven't I?' In this, the dog and my wife seemed to be of the same mind. It settled itself into my chair and she tickled it, in a familiar fashion, under the chin.

'Better be careful. It's got a nasty snarl.'

'He only snarls if you do something to annoy him. Was Rumpole doing something to annoy you, Lance?'

'I was trying to budge it off my chair,' I told her quickly, before the dog could get a word in.

'You like Rumpole's chair, don't you, Lance? You feel at home there, don't you, darling?' I was starting to feel left out of the conversation until she said, 'I think we might make that his chair, don't you, Rumpole? Just until he settles in.'

'Settles in? What do you mean, settles in? What's this, a home of rest for stray animals?'

'Lance isn't a stray. Didn't I tell you? I meant to tell you. Sir Lance-lot is Dodo Mackintosh's knight in shining armour. Aren't you, darling?' Darling was, of course, the dog.

'You mean he's come up from Cornwall?' I looked at the hound with new respect. Perhaps he was one of those animals they make films about, that set off on their own to travel vast distances. 'Hadn't we better ring Dodo to come and fetch him?'

'Don't be silly, Rumpole.' Hilda had put on one of her heroically patient voices. 'Dodo brought Lancelot up here this afternoon. She left him on her way to the airport.'

'And what time's she getting back from the airport? I suppose I can wait until after supper to sit in my chair.'

'She's going to Brittany to stay with Pegsy Throng who was jolly good at dancing and used to be at school with us. Of course, she couldn't take Sir Lancelot because of the quarantine business.'

'And how long is Pegsy Throng entertaining Dodo?' I could feel my heart sinking.

'Just the three weeks, Rumpole. Not long enough, really. Dodo did ask if I thought you'd mind and I told her, of course not, Lance will be company for both of us. Come and have supper now, and after that you can take him out on the lead to do his little bit of business. It'll be a chance for you two to get to know each other.'

Sleep was postponed that night as I stood in the rain beside a lamppost with the intruder. Sir Lancelot leapt to the extent of his lead, as though determined to choke himself, wrenching my arm almost out of its socket, as he barked savagely at every passing dog. Looking down at him, I decided that I never saw a hound I hated more, and yet it was Sir Lancelot that brought me a case which was one of the most curious and sensational of my career.

'What on earth are we doing here, Hilda?' Here was a stretch of countryside, blurred by a sifting March rain so, looking towards the horizon, it was hard to tell at which precise point the soggy earth became the sodden sky.

'Breathe in the country air, Rumpole. Besides which, Sir Lancelot couldn't spend all his time cooped up in a flat. He had to have a couple of days' breather in the Cotswolds. It'll do you both good.'

'Couldn't Sir Lancelot have gone for a run in the Cotswolds on his own?'

'Try not to be silly, Rumpole.'

The dog was behaving in an eccentric manner, making wild forays into the undergrowth as though it had found something to chase and, ending up with nothing, it came trotting back to the path quite unconscious of its own stupidity. It was, I thought, an animal with absolutely no sense of humour.

'Why on earth does your friend Dodo Mackintosh call that gloomy hound Sir Lancelot?'

'After Sir Lancelot of the Lake, of course. One of the knights of the Table Round. Dodo's got a very romantic nature. Come along, Lance. *There's* a good boy. Enjoying your run in the country, are you?'

'Lance,' I told her firmly, 'or, rather, *Launce* is the chap who had a dog called Crab in *Two Gentlemen of Verona*. Crab got under the duke's table with some "gentlemanlike dogs" and after "a pissing while" a terrible smell emerged. Launce took responsibility for it and was whipped.'

'Do be quiet, Rumpole! You always look for the seamy side of everything.' At which point, Lance, in another senseless burst of energy, leapt a stile and started chasing sheep.

'Can't you keep that dog under control?' The voice came from a man in a cap, crossing the field towards us, with a golden labrador trotting in an obedient manner at his side. Hilda and I, having climbed the stile and called Lance, with increasing hopelessness, were set out on a course towards him.

'I'm afraid we can't,' I apologized from a distance. 'The animal won't listen to reason.'

'What did you say its name was?'

'Sir Lancelot,' Hilda boasted.

'Of the Lake. To give him his full title,' I added, trying to make the best of our lamentable attachment.

'Sir Lancelot! Here, boy!' the man in the cap called in a commanding tone and gave a piercing whistle. Whereupon Dodo's dog stood still, shook itself, came to its senses and, much to the relief of the sheep, joined our group. At which, the man in the cap turned, looked me in the face for the first time and said, 'By God, it's Horace Rumpole!'

'Rollo Eyles!'

'And this is your good lady?'

I resisted the temptation to say, 'No, it's my wife.' Rollo was telling Hilda about our roots in history. He had been the prosecution junior in the Penge Bungalow affair, arguably the classic murder of our time and undoubtedly the greatest moment of triumph in the Rumpole career.

Until they heard my first devastating cross-examination of the police surgeon, legal hacks in the Penge Bungalow case treated me as an inexperienced white-wig who shouldn't be allowed out on a careless driving. A notable exception was young Rollo Eyles, then a jovial, schoolboyish young man, born, like me, without any feelings of reverence. He was a mimic, and we would meet after court in Pommeroy's to drown our anxiety, and Rollo would do his impressions of the judge, the prosecuting silk and the dry, charnel-house voice of Professor Ackerman, master of the morgues. In the middle of his legal career Rollo inherited an estate, and a good deal of money, from an uncle, and left the busy world of the Old Bailey for, it appeared, these damp fields where he was a farmer, Master of Foxhounds and Chairman of the Bench.

For a while he wrote to me at Christmas, letters in neat handwriting, full of jokes. After a while, I forgot to answer them and our friendship waned. Now he said, 'Why don't you come up to the house and we'll all have a strong drink.' Rollo Eyles always had a sensible solution to the most desperate case. Sir Lancelot, realizing he had met a man he couldn't trifle with, came and joined us with unusual docility.

It was over a large whisky in front of a log fire that I told Rollo where we were staying. Our hotel was a plastic and concrete nightmare of a building conveniently situated for the trading estate outside the nearest town. It had all the joys of piped music in the coffee shop, towels in a thinness contest with the lavatory paper, and waitresses who'd undergone lengthy training in the art of not allowing their eyes to be caught. It was the only place we could find where we were allowed, after slipping a bribe larger than the legal aid fee for a guilty plea to the hall porter, to secretly have Sir Lancelot in the bathroom. There, he was due to spend a restless night on a couple of wafer-thin blankets. Having heard this sad story, Rollo offered us dinner and a bed for the night; Lancelot could be kennelled with the gentlemanlike dogs. Our host said he was looking forward to hearing the latest gossip from the Old Bailey and, in return, we could have the pleasure of seeing the hunt move off from his front drive before we went back to London.

The rain had stopped during the night and the March morning was cold and sunny. Sir Lancelot was shivering with excitement, as if delightedly aware that something, at some time, was going to be killed; although I doubted if, during his peaceful cohabitation with Dodo Mackintosh in Lamorna Cove, he had ever met foxhunters before. However, he leapt into the air, pirouetted at the end of his lead, barked at the horses and did his best to give the impression that he was entirely used to the country sports of gentlemanlike dogs. So there I was, eating small slices of pork pie and drinking port which tasted, on that crisp morning, delicious. Hilda, wearing an old mac and a tweed hat which she'd apparently bought for just such an occasion, was doing her best to look as though, if her horse hadn't gone lame or suffered some such technical fault, she'd've been up and mounted among our dinner companions of the night before.

I looked up with my mouth full of pork pie to join in Hilda's smiles at these new acquaintances who had merged with the children on ponies, the overweight farmers, the smart garage owners and the followers on foot. Rollo was there, sitting in the saddle as though it was his favourite armchair, talking to a whipper-in, or hunt servant, or whatever the red-coated officials may be called. Mrs Rollo – Dorothea – was there, the relic of a great beauty, still slim and upright, her calm face cracked with lines like the earth on a dried-up river bed, her auburn hair streaked with grey, bundled into a hairnet and covered with a peaked velvet cap. I also recognized Tricia Fothergill, who had clung on to the childish way she mispronounced her name, together with the good looks of an attractive child, into her thirties. She was involved in a lengthy divorce and had, during dinner, bombarded me with questions about family law for which I had no ready answer. And there, raising his glass of port to me from the immense height of a yellow-eyed horse, sitting with his legs stuck out like wings, was the old fellow who had been introduced to us as Johnny Logan and who knew the most intimate details of the private lives of all sporting persons living in the Cotswolds. Rollo Eyles, in the absence of any interesting anecdotes from the Central Criminal Court, clearly relied on him for entertaining gossip. 'Roll 'em in the aisles, that's what I call him,' Logan whispered to me at dinner. 'Our host's extremely attractive to women. Of course, he'll never leave Dorothea.'

Now, at the meet in front of Wayleave Manor, Logan said, 'Seen our charming visitors at the end of the drive? You might go and have a look at them, Horace. They're the antis.'

Dorothea Eyles was leaning down from her horse to chat to Hilda in the nicest possible way, so I took Lancelot for a stroll so I could see all sides of the hunting experience. A van was parked just where the driveway met the road. On it there were placards posted with such messages as STOP ANIMAL MURDER, HUNT THE FOXHUNTERS and so on. There was a small group standing drinking coffee. At that time they seemed as cheerful and excited as the foxhunters, looking forward as eagerly to a day's sport. There was a man with a shaven head and earrings, but also a woman in a tweed skirt who looked like a middle-aged schoolmistress. There was a girl whose hair was clipped like a sergeant-major back and sides, with one long, purple lock left in the middle. The others were less colourful – ordinary people such as I would have seen shopping in Safeway's and there, I thought, probably buying cellophane-packed joints and pounds of bacon. The tallest was a young man who remained profoundly serious in spite of the excited laughter around him. He was wearing jeans and a crimson shirt which made him stand out as clearly, against the green fields, as the huntsmen he had come to revile.

There was the sound of a horn. The dogs poured down the drive with their tails waving like flags. Then came Rollo, followed by the riders. The antis put down their sandwiches, lowered their mugs of coffee and shouted out such complimentary remarks as 'Murdering bastards', 'Get your rocks off watching little furry animals pulled to pieces, do you?' and 'How would you like to be hunted and thrown to the dogs this afternoon, darling?' – an invitation to Tricia.

Then Dorothea came riding slowly, to find the Crimson Shirt was barring her path, his arms spread out as though prepared to meet his death under a ton of horseflesh. A dialogue then took place which I was to have occasion to remember.

'You love killing things, don't you?' from the Crimson Shirt.

'Not particularly. Mostly, I enjoy the ride.'

'Why do you kill animals?'

'Perhaps because they kill other animals.'

'Do you ever think that something might kill you one fine afternoon?'

'Quite often.' Dorothea looked down at him. 'A lot of people die, out hunting. A nice quick death. I hope I'll be so lucky.'

'You might get killed this afternoon.'

'Anyone might.'

'It doesn't worry you?'

'Not in the least.'

'It's only what you deserve.'

'Do you think so?' Looking down from her horse, I thought she suddenly seemed thin and insubstantial as a ghost, her lined face very pale. Then she pulled a silver flask from her jacket pocket, unscrewed it and leant down to offer the Crimson Shirt a drink.

'What have you got in there?' he asked her.

'Fox's blood, of course.'

He looked up at her and said, 'You cruel bitch!'

'It's only whisky. You're very welcome.' He shook his head and the cobweb-faced lady took a long pull at the flask. Other riders had come up beside her and were listening, amused at first and then angry. There were shouts, conflicting protests, and the Crimson Shirt called out in the voice of doom, 'One of you is going to die for all the dead animals. Justice is sure to be done!'

I saw a whip raised at the back of the cavalcade but the Crimson Shirt had dropped his arm and moved to join his party by the van. Dorothea Eyles put away her flask, kicked her horse's sides and trotted with the posse after her. They were chattering together cheerfully, after what had then seemed no more than a routine confrontation between the hunters and the sabs – rather enjoyed by both sides.

The sound of the horn, the baying of the dogs and the clattering of horses had died away. The van, after a number of ineffectual coughs and splutters, started its engine and went. It was very quiet as Lancelot and I walked back down the drive to join Hilda, who was enjoying a final glass of port. We went into the house to wait for the taxi which would take us back to the station.

That evening we were at home at the mansion flat and I had been restored to my armchair. Lancelot, exhausted by the day's excitement, was asleep on the sofa, breathing heavily and, no doubt, dreaming of imaginary hunts. The news item was on the television after a war in Africa and an earthquake in Japan. There were stock pictures of hunters and sabs. Then came the news that Dorothea Eyles, out hunting and galloping down a woodland track, had ridden into a high wire stretched tight between two trees. Her neck was broken and she was dead when some ramblers found her. An anti-hunt demonstrator named Dennis Pearson was helping the local police with their enquiries.

Rollo Eyles had returned to my life, suffered a terrible tragedy and immediately disappeared again. Of course I telephoned but his recorded voice always told me he was not available. I left messages of sorrow and concern but the calls were never answered, and neither were the letters I wrote to him. Tragedy too often causes embarrassment and we didn't visit Rollo in the Cotswolds. Tragedy vanishes quickly, swept on by the tide of horrible events in the world, and I began to think less often of Dorothea Eyles and her ghastly ride to death. Rollo joined the unseen battalion of people whom I liked but never saw.

'Rumpole! I have heard reports of your extraordinary behaviour!'

'Don't believe everything you hear in reports.'

'Erskine-Brown has told me that Henry told him . . .'

'I object! Hearsay evidence! Totally inadmissible.'

'Well well. I have had a direct account from Henry himself.'

'Not under oath, and certainly not subject to cross-examination!'

'You were seen entering the downstairs toilet facility with a bowl.'

'What's *that* meant to prove? I might have been rinsing out my dentures. Or uttering prayers to a water god to whose rites I have been recently converted. What on earth's it got to do with Henry, anyway? Or you, for that matter, Bollard?'

'Having filled your bowl with water, you were seen to carry it to your room.'

'It would be inappropriate to say prayers to the water god in the downstairs toilet facilities.'

'Come now, Rumpole, don't fence with me.' Soapy Sam Ballard was using one of the oldest and corniest of legal phrases, long fallen into disuse in the noble art of cross-examination, and I allowed myself a dismissive yawn. It wasn't the brightest period of my long and eventful practice at the bar. Since our visit to the Cotswolds, and its terrible outcome, briefs had been notable by their absence. I came into chambers every day and searched my mantelpiece in vain for a new murder, or at least a taking away without the owner's consent. My wig gathered dust in my locker down the Bailey; the ushers must have forgotten me and I looked back with nostalgia on the days when I had laboured long and lost before Mr Injustice Gravestone. At least something was happening then. Now the suffocating boredom of inactivity was made worse by the arrival of an outraged head of chambers in my room, complaining of my conduct with something so totally inoffensive as a bowl of water.

'You might as well confess, Rumpole.' Ballard's eye was lit with a gleam of triumph. 'There was one single word written in large letters on that chipped enamel bowl.'

'Water?'

'No, Rumpole. Henry's evidence was quite clear on this point. What was written was the word DOG.'

'So what?'

'What do you mean, so what?'

'Plenty of people wash their socks in bowls with DOG written on them.'

Before Ballard could meet this point, there was that low but threatening murmur, like the sound heralding the dark and distant approach of a tube train, from behind my desk.

'What was that noise, Rumpole?'

'Low-flying aircraft?' I suggested, hopefully. But at this point the accused, like so many of my clients, ruined his chances by putting in a public appearance. Sir Lancelot, looking extra large, black and threatening, emerged like his more famous namesake – with lips curled, dog teeth bared – eager to do battle in the lists. There was no contest. At the sight of the champion, even before the first snarl, Sir Soapy Sam, well-known coward and poltroon of the Table Round, started an ignominious retreat towards the door, crying in terror, 'Get that animal out of here at once!'

'No!' I relied on my constitutional rights. 'Not until the matter has been properly decided by a full chambers meeting.'

'I shall call one,' Ballard piped in desperation, 'as a matter of urgency.' And then he scooted out and slammed the door behind him.

The fact of the matter was that Hilda had been out a lot recently at bridge lessons and coffee mornings, and I, lonely and unoccupied in chambers, started in a curious way to relish the company of a hound who looked as gloomy as I felt. On the whole, the dog was not demanding. Like many judges, Lancelot fought, nearly all the time, a losing battle against approaching sleep. Water from the downstairs loo, and the dog biscuits I brought in my briefcase, satisfied his simple wants. The sound of regular breathing from somewhere by my feet was company for me as I spent the day with *The Times* crossword.

The chambers meeting was long and tense. At first the case for the prosecution looked strong. Henry sent a message to say that he undertook to clerk for a barristers' chambers and not a kennel. He added that the sight of Sir Lancelot peering round my open door and baring his teeth had frightened away old Tim Daker of Daker, Winterbotham & Guildenstern, before he'd even delivered a brief. Erskine-Brown questioned the paternity of Sir Lancelot and when I said labrador loudly, he replied, 'Possibly a labrador who'd had hanky-panky with a dubious Jack Russell.' He ended up by asking in a dramatic fashion if we really wanted a mongrel taking up residence in 3 Equity Court. This brought a fiery reply from Mizz Liz Probert who said that animals had the same rights to our light, heat, comforts and presumably law reports, as male barristers. She personally could remember the days, not long past, when she, as a practising woman, was treated as though she were a so-called labrador of doubtful parentage. Gender awareness was no longer enough. In Mizz Probert's considered opinion we needed species awareness as well. She saw no reason, in the interests of open government and tolerance of minorities, why a living being should be denied entrance to our chambers simply because it had four legs instead of two. 'Of course,' Mizz Probert concluded, looking at Erskine-Brown in a way which forced him to reconsider his position, 'if we were to support the pinstriped chauvinists who hated mongrels and women, we should be alienating the Sisterhood of Radical Lawyers, devoted to animal rights.'

I took up her last point in my speech for the defence and did so in a way calculated to make Soapy Sam's flesh creep. I had seen something of animal rights enthusiasts. Did we really want their van parked outside chambers all day and most of the night? Did Ballard want a shorn-headed enthusiast with earrings shouting, 'Get your rocks off shutting out innocent dogs, do you?' Could we risk a platoon of grey-haired, middle-class dog-lovers staging a sit-in outside our front door every time we wanted to go to court? After this, the evidence of a member of chambers, to the effect that dogs made him sneeze, seemed to carry very little weight. The result of our deliberations was, of course, leaked and a paragraph appeared in next day's Londoner's Diary in the *Evening Standard*:

Should dogs be called to the Bar? The present showing of the legal profession might suggest that they could only be an improvement on the human intake. Indeed, a few Rottweilers on the Bench might help reduce the crime rate. The question was hotly debated in the chambers of Samuel Ballard, QC when claret-tippling Old Bailey character Horace Rumpole argued for the admittance of a pooch, extravagantly named Sir Lancelot. Rumpole won his case but then he's long been known as a champion of the underdog.

It was a pyrrhic victory. Dodo came back from holiday a week later and reclaimed Sir Lancelot. She was delighted he had been mentioned in the newspapers but furious he was called a pooch.

Sir Lancelot's trial had a more important result, however. Henry told me that a Mr Garfield of Garfield, Thornley & Strumm had telephoned and, having heard that I was a stalwart battler for animal rights, was going to brief me for a hunt saboteur charged with murder. I was relieved that my period of inactivity was over, but filled with alarm at the thought of having to tell Hilda that I had agreed to appear for the man accused of killing Dorothea Eyles.

Mr Garfield, my instructing solicitor, was a thin, colourless man with a pronounced Adam's apple. He had the rough, slightly muddy skin of the dedicated vegetarian. The case was to be tried at Gloucester Crown Court and we sat in the interview room in the prison, a Victorian erection much rebuilt, on the outskirts of the town. Across the plastic table-top our client sat smiling in a way which seemed to show that he was either sublimely self-confident or drugged. He was a young man, perhaps in his late twenties, with a long nose, prominent eyes and neat brown hair. The last time I had seen him he was wearing a crimson shirt and telling the hunt in general, and Dorothea Eyles in particular, that one of them was going to die for all the dead animals. Garfield introduced him to me as Den; my instructing solicitor was Gavin to my client. I had the feeling they had known each other for some time and later discovered that they sat together on a committee concerned with animal rights.

'Gavin tells me you fought for a dog and won?' Den looked at me with approval. Was that to be my work in the future, I wondered. Not white-collar crime but leather-collar crime, perhaps?

'More than that,' I told him. 'I'm ready to fight for you and win the case.'

'I'm not important. It's the cause that's important.'

'The cause?'

'Den feels deeply about animals,' Gavin interpreted.

'I understand that. I was there, you know. Watching the hunt move off. I'd better warn you I heard what you said, so it's going to be a little difficult if you deny it.'

'I said it,' Den told me proudly. 'I said every word of it. We're going to win, you know.'

'Win the case?'

'I meant the war against the animal murderers. Did you see the looks on their faces? They were going out to enjoy themselves.'

I remembered the words of the historian Lord Macaulay: 'The Puritan hated bear-baiting, not because it gave pain to the bear, but because it gave pleasure to the spectators.' But I wasn't going to be drawn into a debate about foxhunting when I was there to deal with my first murder case for a long time, too long a time, and I fully intended to win it. I rummaged in my papers and produced the first, the most important witness statement, the evidence to be given by Patricia Fothergill of Cherry Trees near Wayleave in the county of Gloucester.

'I'd better warn you that I met this lady at dinner.'

'I don't mind where you met her, Mr Rumpole.'

'I'm glad you take that view but I had to tell you. All right, Tricia – that's what she calls herself – Tricia is going to say that she saw a man in a red shirt in the driveway of the Eyles's house, Wayleave Manor. She heard you shout at Mrs Eyles. Well, we all know about that. Now comes the interesting bit. At about one o'clock in the afternoon of the day before the meet she'd been out for a hack and was riding home past Fallows Wood – that's where Dorothea Eyles met her death. She says she saw a man in a red shirt coming out of the wood, carrying what looked like a coil of wire: "I didn't think much of it at the time. I suppose I thought he had to do with the telephone or the electricity or something. There was a moment when I saw him quite clearly and I'm sure he was the same man I saw at the meet, shouting at Dorothea." We can challenge that identification. It was far away, she was on a horse, how many men wear red shirts – all that sort of thing . . .'

'I'm sure you will destroy her, Mr Rumpole.' Gavin was trying to be helpful.

'I'll do my best.' I hunted for another statement. 'I'm just looking . . . Here it is! Detective Constable Armstead searched the van you came in and found part of a coil of wire of exactly the same make and thickness as that which was stretched across the path and between the trees in Fallows Wood.' I looked at my client and my solicitor. Neither had, apparently, anything to say. 'Who drives the van?'

'Roy Netherborn. It's his van,' Gavin volunteered.

'Is he the hairless gentleman with the earrings?'

'That's the one.'

'And did Mr Netherborn pack the things in the van? The tools and so on?'

'He did, didn't he, Den?' Gavin had been answering the questions. When he was asked one, Dennis Pearson was silent.

'Had you taken wire with you before?'

'We'd discussed it,' Den admitted. 'There'd been some talk of using it to trip up the horses.'

'Did you know there was wire in the van that day?' I asked Den the question direct, but Gavin intervened, 'I don't think you did, did you?'

Den said nothing but shook his head.

'Did you know that exactly the same wire was used as a death-trap in Fallows Wood?'

'Den didn't know that. No.' Gavin was positive.

'When did you arrive in Wayleave village? And *that's* a question for Mr Dennis Pearson,' I invited.

'We came up the morning before. We were staying with Janet Freebody who lives in the village. Janet's a schoolteacher.'

'And chair of our activist committee.' Gavin was finding it difficult to keep quiet.

'Where was the van parked?'

'In front of Janet's house.'

'From what time?'

'About midday.'

'You hadn't taken a trip in it to Fallows Wood before then?'

'Den tells me he hadn't.' Once again, Gavin took on the answering.

'Was the van kept locked?'

'Supposed to be. Roy's a bit careless about this, isn't he, Den?'

'Roy's careless about everything,' Den agreed.

There were a lot more questions that required answering, but I didn't want them all answered by way of the protective Gavin Garfield.

'There's one other thing I should tell you,' I said as I gathered up my papers. 'I know Rollo Eyles. I met him when he was at the Bar. And I was staying with him the night before . . . Well, the night before the fatal accident. I'll have to tell him I'm defending the man accused of murdering his wife. If you don't want me to defend you, you know that, of course, I shall understand.' I was giving them a chance to sack me even before my precious murder case had begun. I kept my fingers crossed under the table.

'I'd like you to carry on with the case, Mr Rumpole,' Den was now speaking for himself. 'Seeing what you did for that dog, I don't think I'll cause you much trouble.'

'Oh, why's that?'

'Well, you see . . .' Dennis Pearson was still smiling pleasantly, imperturbably.

Gavin looked at him anxiously and started off, 'Den . . .'

But my client interrupted him, 'You see, I did it.'

'You knew he was going to do that?' Gavin was driving me from the prison to Gloucester station in a car littered with bits of comics, old toys, empty crisp packets and crumpled orange juice cartons with the straws still stuck in them. I supposed that, in his pale, vegetarian way, he had fathered many children.

'I had an idea. Yes,' Gavin admitted it. 'What do we do now?'

'We're entitled to cross-examine the prosecution witnesses and see if they prove the case. We can't call Dennis to deny the charge, so, if the prosecution holds up, we'll have to plead guilty at half-time.'

'Is that what you'd advise him to do?'

'I'd advise him to tell us the truth.'

'Why do you say that?'

'Because I don't believe he is.'

I wanted to work on the case away from the garrulous Gavin and the uncommunicative Den. I thought that they lurked somewhere between the world of human communication and the secret and silent kingdom of animals, and I didn't feel either of them would be much help. The case seemed to me to raise certain awkward and interesting questions, not to say a matter of legal ethics and private morality which was, not to put too fine a point upon it, devilishly tricky to cope with.

As I sat in chambers I decided it was better for a legal hack like me to stop worrying about such things as ideas of proper or improper behaviour and concentrate on the facts. I lit a small cigar and opened a volume of police photographs. As I did so, I stooped for a moment to pat the head of the gloomy Lancelot, who had become my close companion, and then realized he was gone, ferreting for disgusting morsels, no doubt, at the edge of the sea while Dodo Mackintosh sat at her easel and perpetrated a feeble watercolour. I felt completely alone in the defence of Den Pearson, who didn't even want to be defended.

I hurried past the mortuary shots of Dorothea and her fatal injuries, and got to a picture of a path through trees. It was a narrow strip hardly wide enough for two people to pass in comfort, so the beech trees on either side were not much more than six feet apart. A closer shot showed the wire, then still stretched between nails driven into the trees. The track was muddy, with patches of grass and the bare earth. I picked up a magnifying glass and looked at the photo carefully. Then I rang little Marcus Pitcher, who, I had discovered, was to be in charge of the prosecution. 'Listen, old darling,' I said, when I got his chirrup on the line, 'what about you and me organizing a visit to the *locus in quo*?' When he asked me what I meant, I said, 'There was once a road through the woods.'

'A day out in the country?' Marcus sounded agreeable. 'Why ever not. I'll drive you.'

My learned friend was a small man with a round face, slightly protruding teeth and large, horn-rimmed glasses, so that he looked like an agreeable mouse, although he could be a cunning little performer in court. Marcus owned a bulky old Jaguar and had to sit up very straight to peer out of the windscreen. In the back seat a white bull-terrier sat, pink-eyed and asthmatic, looking at me as though she wondered why I'd come to ruin the day out.

'Meet Bernadette,' Marcus introduced us. 'As soon as she heard about the trip to the Cotswolds, she had to come. Hope you don't mind.'

'Not at all. In fact I might have brought my own dog, but Lancelot's away at the moment.'

At the scene of the crime Bernadette went bounding off into the undergrowth, while Marcus, his solicitor from the DPP's office, and I stood with the detective inspector in charge of the case. D. I. Palmer was a courteous officer who lacked the tendency of the Metropolitan force to imitate the coppers they've seen on television. He led us to the spot where death had taken place. The wire and nails had been removed to be exhibited in the case, and the hoof marks had been rubbed out by the rain.

' "There was once a road through the woods," ' I told the inspector, ' "Before they planted the trees./It is underneath the coppice and heath,/And the thin anemones . . ." But this one isn't, is it, Inspector?'

'I'm not quite sure that I follow you, Mr Rumpole.'

'This road hasn't disappeared so that

> 'Only the keeper sees
> That, where the ring-dove broods,
> And the badgers roll at ease,
> There was once a road through the woods.'

'It's a footpath here as I understand it, Mr Rumpole.' The DI was ever helpful. 'Mr Eyles is very good about keeping open the footpaths on his land.' It did seem that the edges of the path had been trimmed and the brambles cut back.

'Is the footpath used a lot? Did you ever find that out, Inspector?'

'Ramblers use it. It was ramblers that found Mrs Eyles. A shocking experience for them.'

'It must have been. Don't know why they call it rambling, do you? We used to call it going for a walk. So people don't ride down here much?'

'I wouldn't think a lot. You'd have to be a good horseman to jump that.'

We had come to a stile at the end of the narrow track. Beside it there was a green signpost showing that the footpath continued across the middle of a broad field dotted with sheep. The stile had a single pole to hold on to and a wide step set at right angles to the top bar. I supposed it would have been a difficult jump but I saw a scar in the wood. Could that have been the mark of a hoof that had just managed it?

Marcus Pitcher called Bernadette and she came lolloping over the brambles and started to root about in the long grass at the side of the stile.

'You gents seen all you want?' the DI asked us.

Marcus was satisfied. I wasn't. I thought that if we waited we might learn something else about that cold, sunny day in March when Dorothea died as quickly as she'd said she'd always wanted to. And then I was rewarded. Bernadette pulled some weighty object out of the grass, carried it in her mouth and laid it, as a tribute, at the feet of Marcus Pitcher. I said I'd like a note made of exactly where we found the horseshoe.

'I don't see what it can possibly prove.' Marcus was doubtful. 'It might have been dropped from any horse at any time.'

'Let's just make a note,' I asked. 'We'll think about what it proves later.'

So the polite inspector took charge of the horseshoe and he, Marcus and Bernadette moved on across the field on their way back to the road. I sat on the stile to recover my breath and looked into the darkness of the wood. What was it at night? A sort of killing field – owls swooping on mice, foxes after small birds – a place of unexpected noises and sudden death? Was it a site for killing people or killing animals? I remembered Dorothea, old and elegant, handing down with a smile to Den what she said was a flask of fox's blood. I thought about the hunters and the antis shouting at each other and Den's yell: 'One of you is going to die for all the dead animals.' And I tried to see Dorothea, elated, excited, galloping down the narrow path and her sudden, unlooked-for near-decapitation. From somewhere in the shadows under the trees, I seemed to hear the sound of hoofs and I remembered more of Kipling, a grumpy old darling but with a marvellous sense of rhythm. I chanted to myself:

> 'You will hear the beat of a horse's feet,
> And the swish of a skirt in the dew,
> Steadily cantering through
> The misty solitudes,
> As though they perfectly knew
> The old lost road through the woods.
> But there is no road through the woods.'

But there was no swish of a skirt. It was Rollo Eyles who came cantering down the track, reined in his horse and sat looking down on me as I sat on his stile.

'Horace! *You* here? I heard the police were in the wood.'

I looked up at him. He was getting near my age but healthier and certainly thinner than me. He was not a tall man, but he sat up very straight in the saddle. His reins were loose and his hands relaxed; his horse snorted but hardly moved. He wore a cap instead of a hard riding-hat, regardless of danger, and an old tweed jacket. His voice was surprisingly deep and there was little grey in the hair that showed.

'I was having a look at the scene of the crime.' Then I told him, as I had to, 'I'm defending the man who's supposed to have killed your wife.'

'Not the man who killed her?'

'We won't know that until the jury get back. Do you mind?'

'That he killed Dorothea?'

'No. That I'm defending him.'

'You have to defend even the most disgusting clients, don't you?' His voice never lost its friendliness and there was no hint of anger. 'It's in the best traditions of the Bar.'

'That's right. I'm an old taxi.'

'Well, I wish you luck. Who's your judge?'

'We're likely to get stuck with Jamie MacBain.'

' "I was not born yesterday, y'know, Mr Rumpole. I think I'm astute enough to see through *that* argument!" ' Rollo had lost none of his talents as a mimic and did a very creditable imitation of Mr Justice MacBain's carefully preserved Scottish accent. 'Why don't you come down to the house for a whisky and splash?' he asked in his own voice.

'I can't. They'll be waiting for me in the car. You're sure you don't mind me taking on the case?'

'Why should I mind? You've got to do your job. I've no doubt justice will be done.'

I climbed over the stile, then walked away. When I looked back, he wasn't going to jump but turned the horse and trotted back the way he had come. He had said justice would be done but I wasn't entirely sure of it.

I kept all of this to myself and said nothing to She Who Must Be Obeyed, although I knew well enough that the time would come when I'd certainly have to tell her. As the trial of Dennis Pearson drew nearer, I decided that the truth could no longer be avoided and chose breakfast time as, when the expected hostilities broke out, I could retreat hastily down the tube and off to chambers and so escape prolonged exposure to the cannonade.

'By the way,' I said casually over the last piece of toast, 'I'll probably be staying down in the Gloucester direction before the end of the month.'

'Has Rollo Eyles invited us again?'

'Well, not exactly.'

'Why exactly, then?' With Hilda you can never get away with leaving uncomfortable facts in a comforting blur.

'I've got a trial.'

'What sort of a trial?'

'A rather important murder as it so happens. You'll be glad to know, Hilda, that when it comes to the big stuff, the questions of life and death, the cry is still "Send for Rumpole!"'

'Who got murdered?'

The question had been asked casually, but I knew the moment of truth had come. 'Well, someone you've met, as a matter of fact.'

'Who?'

My toast was finished. I took a last gulp of coffee, ready for the off. 'Dorothea Eyles.'

'You're defending that horrible little hunt saboteur?'

'Well, he's not so little. Quite tall actually.'

'You're defending the man who murdered the wife of your friend?'

'I suppose someone has to.'

'Well! It's no wonder you haven't got any friends, Rumpole.'

Was it true? Hadn't I any friends? Enemies, yes. Acquaintances. Opponents down the Bailey. Fellow members of chambers. But *friends*? Bonny Bernard? Fred Timson? Well, I suppose we only met for work. Who was my real friend? I could only think of one. 'I got on fairly well with the dog Lancelot. Of course he's no longer with us.'

'Just as well. If you defend people who kill your friends' wives, you're hardly fit company for a decent dog.' You have to admit that when Hilda comes to a view she doesn't mince words on the matter.

'We don't know if he killed her. He's only accused of killing her.'

'No hair and earrings? You only had to take a look at him to know he was capable of anything!'

'They didn't arrest the one with no hair,' I told her. 'I'm defending another one.'

'It doesn't matter. I expect they're all much of a muchness. Can you imagine what Rollo's going to say when he finds out what you're doing?'

'I know what he thinks.'

'What?'

'That it's in the best tradition of the Bar to defend anyone, however revolting.'

'How do you know that's what he thinks?'

'Because that's what he said when I told him.'

'You told him?'

'Yes.'

'I must say, Rumpole, you've got a nerve!'

'Courage is the essential quality of an advocate.'

'And I suppose it's the essential quality of an advocate to be on the side of the lowest, most contemptible of human beings?'

'To put their case for them? Yes.'

'Even if they're guilty?'

'That hasn't been proved.'

'But you don't know he's not.'

'I think I do.'

'Why?'

'Because of what he told me.'

'He told you he wasn't guilty?'

'No, he told me he *was*. But, you see, I didn't believe him.'

'He told you he was guilty and you're still defending him? Is that in the best traditions of the Bar?'

'Only just,' I had to admit.

'Rumpole!' She Who Must Be Obeyed gave me one of her unbending looks and delivered judgement. 'I suppose that, if someone murdered *me*, you would defend them?'

There was no answer to that so I looked at my watch. 'Must go. Urgent conference in chambers. I won't be late home. Is it one of your bridge evenings?' I asked the question, but answer came there none. I knew that for that day, and for many days to come, as far as She Who Must Be Obeyed was concerned, the mansion flat in Froxbury Mansions would be locked in the icy silence of the tomb.

During the last weeks before the trial Hilda was true to her vow of silence and the mansion flat offered all the light-hearted badinage of life in a Trappist order. Luckily I was busy and even welcomed the chance of a chat with Gavin Garfield whom, although I had excluded him from my visit to the Cotswolds, I now set to work. I told him his first job was to get statements from the other saboteurs in the van, and when he protested that we'd never get so far as calling evidence in view of what Den had told us, I said we must be prepared for all eventualities. So Gavin took statements, not hurriedly, but with a surprising thoroughness, and in time certain hard facts emerged.

What surprised me was the age and respectability of the saboteurs. Shaven-headed Roy Netherborn was forty and worked in the accounts department of a paper cup factory. He had toyed with the idea of being a schoolmaster and had met Janet Freebody, who was a couple of years older, at a teacher training college. Janet owned the cottage in Wayleave where the platoon of fearless saboteurs had put up for the night. She taught at a comprehensive school in the nearby town where we had fled from the dreaded hotel. Angela Ridgeway, the girl with the purple lock, was a researcher for BBC Wales. Sebastian Fells and Judy Caspar were live-in partners and worked together in a Kensington bookshop, and Dennis Pearson, thirty-five, taught sociology at a university which had risen from the ashes of a polytechnic. They all, except Janet, lived in London and were on the committee of a society of animal rights activists.

Janet had kept Roy informed about the meet at Rollo Eyles's house, and they had taken days off during her half-term when the meet was at Wayleave. The sabbing was to be made the occasion of a holiday outing and a night spent in the country. When they had got their rucksacks and sleeping-bags out of the van, Roy, Angela, Sebastian and Judy retired to the pub in Wayleave where real ale was obtainable and they used it to wash down vegetable pasties and salads until closing-time at three. Janet Freebody had things to do in the cottage, exercise books to correct and dinner to think about, so she didn't join the party in the pub. Neither did Den. He said he wanted to go for a walk and so set off, according to Roy, apparently to commune, in a solitary fashion, with nature. This meant that he was alone and unaccounted for at one o'clock when Tricia was going to swear on her oath that she saw him coming out of Fallows Wood with a coil of wire.

Other facts of interest: Fallows Wood was only about ten minutes from Wayleave. Roy couldn't remember there being any wire in the

van when they set out from London; it was true that they had discussed using wire to trip up horses, but he had never bought any and
was surprised when the police searched the van and found the coil
there. It was also true that the van was always in a mess, and probably the hammer found in it was his. Den had brought a kitbag with
his stuff in it and Roy couldn't swear it didn't contain wire. Den was
usually a quiet sort of bloke, Roy said, but he did go mad when he
saw people out to kill animals: 'Dennis always said that the movement was too milk and watery towards hunting, and that what was
needed was some great gesture which would really bring us into the
news and prove our sincerity – like when the girl fell under a lorry
that was taking sheep to the airport.' I made a mental note not to ask
any sort of question likely to produce that last piece of evidence and
came to the conclusion that Roy, despite his willingness to give Gavin
a statement, wasn't entirely friendly to my client, Dennis Pearson.

The placards, a small plantation at the meet, had become a forest
outside the court in Gloucester. Buses, bicycles, vans, cars in varying degrees of disrepair, had brought them, held up now by a crowd
which burst, as I elbowed my way towards the courthouse door,
into a resounding cheer for Rumpole. I didn't remember any such
ovation when I entered the Old Bailey on other occasions. In the
robing-room I found Bernadette asleep in a chair and little Marcus
Pitcher tying a pair of white bands around his neck in front of a mirror. 'See you've got your friends from rent-a-crowd here this morning,
Rumpole.' He was not in the best of tempers, our demonstrators
having apparently booed Bernadette for having thrown in her lot
with a barrister who prosecuted the friends of animals.

I wondered how long their cheers for me would last when I went
into court, only to put my hands up and plead guilty. My client,
however, remained singularly determined: 'When we plead guilty,
they'll cheer. It'll be a triumph for the movement. Can't you understand that, Mr Rumpole? We shall be seen to have condemned a
murderer to death!'

The approach of life imprisonment seemed to have concentrated
Den's mind wonderfully. He was no longer the silent and enigmatic
sufferer. His eyes were lit up and he was as excited as when he'd

shouted his threats at the faded beauty on the horse. 'I want you to tell them I'm guilty, first thing. As soon as we get in there. I want you to tell them that I punished her.'

'No, you don't want that. Does he, Mr Garfield?' Gavin, sitting beside me in the cell under the court, looked like a man who had entirely lost control of the situation. 'I suppose if that's what Den has decided . . .' His voice, never strong, died away and he shrugged hopelessly.

'I *have* decided finally' – Den was standing, elated by his decision – 'in the interests of our movement.' For a moment he reminded me of an actor I had seen in an old film, appearing as Sydney Carton on his way to the guillotine, saying, 'It's a far, far better thing I do, than I have ever done.'

'You're not going to do the movement much good by pleading guilty straight away,' I told him.

'What do you mean?'

'A guilty plea at the outset? The whole thing'll be over in twenty minutes. The animal murderers, as you call them, won't even have to go into the witness-box, let alone face cross-examination by Rumpole. Will anyone know the details of the hunt? Certainly not. Do you want publicity for your cause? Plead guilty now and you will be lucky to get a single paragraph on page two. At least, let's get the front page for a day or so.' I wasn't being entirely frank with my client. The murder was serious and horrible enough to get the front pages in a world hungry for bad news at breakfast, even if we were to plead guilty without delay. But I needed time. In time, I still hoped, I would get Den to tell me the truth.

'I don't know.' My client sat down then as though suddenly tired. 'What would you do, Gavin?'

'I think' – Gavin shrugged off all responsibility – 'you should be guided by Mr Rumpole.'

'All right' – Den was prepared to compromise – 'we'll go for the publicity.'

'Dennis Pearson, you are accused in this indictment of the murder of Dorothea Eyles on the sixteenth of March at Fallows Wood,

Wayleave, in the county of Gloucester. Do you plead guilty or not guilty?'

'My Lord, Members of the Jury' – Den, as I had feared, was about to orate. 'This woman, Dorothea Eyles, was guilty of the murder of countless living creatures, not for her gain but simply for sadistic pleasure and idle enjoyment. My Lord, if anything killed her, it was natural justice!'

'Now then, Mr – ' Mr Justice James MacBain consulted his papers to make sure who he was trying. 'Mr Pearson. You've got a gentleman in a wig sitting there, a Mr Rumpole, who's paid to make the speeches for you. It's not your business to make speeches now or at any time during this case. Now, you've been asked a simple question: are you guilty or not guilty?'

'She is the guilty one, my Lord. This woman who revelled in the death of innocent creatures.'

'Mr Rumpole, are you not astute enough to control you client?'

'It's not an easy task, my Lord.' I staggered to my feet.

'Your first job is to control your client. That's what I learnt as a pupil. Make the client keep it short.'

'Well, if you don't want a long speech from the dock, my Lord, I suggest you enter a plea of not guilty and then my learned friend, Mr Marcus Pitcher, can get on with opening his case.'

'Mr Rumpole, I was not born yesterday!' Jamie MacBain was stating the obvious. It was many years since he had first seen the light in some remote corner of the Highlands. He was a large man whose hair, once ginger, had turned to grey, and who sat slumped in his chair like one of those colourless beanbags people use to sit on in their Hampstead homes. He had small, pursed lips and a perpetually discontented expression. 'And when I want your advice on how to conduct these proceedings, I shall ask you for it. Mr Moberly!' This was a whispered summons to the clerk of the court, who rose obediently and, after a brief *sotto voce* conversation, sat down again as the judge turned to the jury.

'Members of the Jury, you and I weren't born yesterday and I think we're astute enough to get over this little technical difficulty. Now we don't want Mr Pearson, the accused man here, to start giving us a lecture, do we? So what we're going to do is to take it he's pleading not guilty and then ask Mr Marcus Pitcher to get on with it and open the prosecution case. You see, there's no great mystery about the law. We can solve most of the problems if we apply a wee bit of worldly wisdom.'

I suppose I could have got up on my hind legs and said, 'Delighted to have been of service to your Lordship,' or, 'If you're ever in a hole, send for me.' But I didn't want to start a quarrel so early in the case. I sat quietly while little Marcus went through most of the facts. The jury of twelve honest Gloucestershire citizens looked stolid, middle-aged and not particularly friendly to the animal rights protesters who filled the public gallery to overflowing. I imagined they had grown up with the hunt and felt no particular hostility to the Boxing Day meet and horses streaming across the frosty countryside. They had looked embarrassed by Dennis's speech from the dock, and flattered when Jamie MacBain shared his lifetime's experience with them. Like him, they hadn't been born yesterday, and worldly wisdom, together with their dogs and their rose gardens, was no doubt among their proudest possessions. As I listened to my little learned friend's opening, I thought he was talking to a jury which, whatever plea had been entered, was beginning to feel sure that Den was as guilty as he was anxious to appear.

The first witness was the rambler, a cashier from a local bank who, out for a walk with his wife and daughter, had been met with the ghastly spectacle of an elderly woman almost decapitated and fallen among the brambles of Fallows Wood.

'Where was the horse?' was all I asked him in cross-examination.

'The horse?'

'Yes. Did you see her horse by any chance?'

'I think there was a horse there, some distance away, and all saddled up. I think it was just eating grass or something. I didn't stay long. I wanted to get my wife and Sandra away and phone the police.'

'Of course. I understand. Thank you very much, Mr Ovington.'

'Is that all you want to ask, Mr Rumpole?' Jamie MacBain looked at me in an unfriendly fashion.

'Yes, my Lord.'

'I don't think that question and answer has added much to our understanding of this case, Members of the Jury. I'd be glad if the defence would not waste the time of the court. Yes. Who is your next witness, Mr Marcus Pitcher?'

I restrained myself and sat down in silence 'like patience on a monument'. But my question *had* added something: Dorothea's riderless horse hadn't galloped on and jumped the stile. We learnt more from Bob Andrews, a hunt servant who, when the hunt was stopped, went back to the wood to recover Dorothea's horse, which had been detained by the police. I risked Jamie's displeasure by questioning Andrews for a little longer.

'When you got to the wood, had Mrs Eyles's body been removed?'

'It was covered. I think it was just being taken away on a stretcher. I knew the ambulance was in the road. The police were taking photographs.'

'The police were taking photographs – and where was Mrs Eyles's horse?'

'I think a police officer was holding her.'

'Can you remember, had Mrs Eyles's horse lost a shoe?'

'Not that I noticed. I looked her over when I took her from the policeman. He seemed a bit scared, holding her.'

'I'm not surprised. Horses can be a little alarming.'

'Can be. If you're not used to them.'

There were a few smiles from the jury at this; not because it was funny but as a relief from the agony of hearing the details of Dorothea Eyles's injuries. The jury, I thought, rather liked Bob Andrews, while the animal rights enthusiasts in the public gallery looked down on him with unmitigated hatred and contempt.

'Mr Andrews,' I went on, while Mr Justice MacPain (as I had come to think of him) gave a somewhat exaggerated performance of a long-suffering judge, bravely enduring terminal boredom, 'tell me a little about the hunt that day. You were riding near to Mr Eyles?'

'Up with the master. Yes.'

'Did your hunt go near Fallows Wood?'

'Not really. No.'

'What was the nearest you got to that wood?'

'Well, they found in Plashy Bottom. Down there they got a scent. Then we were off in the other direction entirely.'

'How far is Plashy Bottom from Fallows Wood?'

'About half a mile . . . I'd think about that.'

'Did you see Mrs Eyles leave the hunt and ride up towards the wood?'

'Well, they'd got going then. I wouldn't have looked round to see the riders behind me.'

'Did you see anyone else – Miss Tricia Fothergill, for instance – leave the hunt and ride up towards Fallows Wood?'

'I didn't, no.'

'He's told us he wasn't looking at the riders behind him, Mr Rumpole.' Jamie managed to sound like a saint holding on to his patience by the skin of his teeth.

'Then let me ask you a question you *can* answer. It's clear, isn't it, that the hunt never went through Fallows Wood that day?'

'That's right.'

'So, it follows that in order to come into collision with that wire, Mrs Eyles had to make a considerable detour?'

'That's surely a matter for argument, Mr Rumpole.' Jamie MacBain did his best to scupper the question so I asked another one, very quickly.

'Do you know why she should make such a detour?'

'I haven't got any idea, no.'

'Thank you, Mr Andrews.' And I sat down before the judge could recover his breath.

Johnny Logan replaced the whipper-in. He was wearing a dark suit and some sort of regimental tie; his creased and brown walnut face grinned over a collar which seemed several sizes too large for him. He treated the judge with a mixture of amusement and contempt, as though Jamie were some alien being who could never understand the hunting community of the Cotswolds. Logan said he had heard most of the dialogue between the sabs and the hunters in the driveway of Wayleave Manor. He also told the jury that he had seen the saboteurs' van at various points during the day, and heard similar abuse from them as he rode by.

'You never saw the saboteurs' van near Fallows Wood?' I asked when it was my turn.

'We never went near Fallows Wood as far as I can remember.'

'Then let you and I agree about that. Now, will you tell me this? Did you ever see Mrs Eyles leave the hunt and ride off in a different direction?'

'No, I never saw that. I'm not saying she didn't do it. We were pretty spread out. I'd seen a couple of jumps I didn't like the look of, so I'd gone round and I was behind quite a lot of the others.'

'Gone round, had you?' Jamie MacBain, about to make a note, looked confused.

'Quite a lot of barbed wire about. I don't think you'd have fancied jumping that, my Lord,' Johnny Logan added with a certain amount of mock servility.

'Never mind what I'd've fancied. Just answer the questions you get asked. That's all you're required to do.' It was clear that the judge and the witness had struck up an immediate lack of rapport.

'Did you see anyone else leave the hunt?'

'I don't think so. Well, you mean at *any* time?'

'At any time when you were out hunting, yes.'

'Well, I think Tricia Fothergill left. But that was at the very end, just before the police arrived and told us that Mrs Eyles had been – well, had met with an accident.'

'So that must have been after Mrs Eyles's death?' The judge made the deduction.

'You've got it, my Lord,' Johnny Logan congratulated him in such a patronizing fashion that I almost felt sorry for the astute Scot.

'Why did she leave then, do you remember?'

'I'm not sure. Her horse was wrong in some way, I think.'

'Just one more thing, Mr Logan.'

'Oh, anything you like.' Johnny showed his contempt for us all.

'It would be right to say, wouldn't it, that Mr Rollo Eyles was devoted to his wife?'

'He would certainly never have left her. Is that what you mean?'

'That's exactly what I mean. Thank you very much.'

As I was about to sit down, the judge said, 'And what were the jury meant to make of that last question and answer?'

'They may make of it what they will, my Lord, when they are in full possession of the facts of this interesting but tragic case.' At which point I lowered my head in an ornate eighteenth-century bow and sat down with as much dignity as I could muster.

'Work at the Bar!' little Marcus said. 'Sometimes I think I'd rather be digging roads.'

'Only one thing to be said for work at the Bar,' I tended to agree, 'is that it's better than no work at the Bar.'

It was the lunch adjournment and the three of us – Marcus, Bernadette and I – were in a dark corner of the Carpenters Arms, not far from the court. There they did a perfectly reasonable bangers and mash. Marcus and I had big glasses of Guinness and Bernadette took hers from a bowl on the floor. The little prosecutor said he was looking forward to going for a holiday with a Chancery barrister called Clarissa Clavering on the Isle of Elba. 'I'd been living for the day, but now it seems likely I'll have to cancel.'

'Why on earth?'

'I can't find anyone to leave Bernadette with. Clarissa only likes cats. And I do love her, Rumpole! Love Clarissa, I mean. She has a lot of sheer animal magnetism for a girl in the Chancery Division.'

'Couldn't you put her in a kennel? Bernadette, I mean.'

'I couldn't do that.' Marcus looked as though I'd invited him to murder his mother. 'Much as I fancy Clarissa, I couldn't possibly do that.'

'Then, there's nothing else for it . . .'

'Nothing else for it.' His little mouse-like face was creased with lines of sorrow. My heart went out to the fellow. 'Except cancel the holiday. I won't blame Bernadette, of course. It's not *her* fault. But . . .'

'It's a pity to miss so much animal magnetism?'

'You've said it, Rumpole. You've said it exactly.'

When we arrived back at the court, there was a certain amount of confusion among the demonstrators. They started with the clear intention of cheering me and Bernadette, who, even if she was part of the prosecution team, was, after all, an animal. They knew they should boo and revile young Marcus, the disappointed lover. Finally, when they saw that I, as well as Bernadette, was on friendly terms with the forces of evil and the prosecutors of sabs, they decided to boo us all.

In the entrance hall the prospective witnesses sat waiting. I saw Tricia Fothergill as smartly turned out as a pony at a show, with gleaming hair, shiny shoes and glistening legs. She was prepared for court in a black suit and her hands were folded in her lap. On the other side of the hall sat the prospective witnesses for the defence: purple-haired Angela Ridgeway, Sebastian and Judy from the bookshop, and shaven-headed Roy Netherborn. Janet, the schoolteacher, sat next to Roy, but I noticed that they didn't speak to each other but sat gazing, as though hypnotized, silently into space. Then, as I was wigged and gowned by now, I crossed the entrance hall towards the court. Roy got up and walked towards me slowly, heavily and with something very like menace. 'What the hell's the idea,' he muttered in a low voice, full of hate, 'of you getting into bed with the prosecution barrister?'

'Little Marcus and I are learned friends,' I told him, 'against each other one day and on the same side the next. We went out to lunch because his dog Bernadette felt in need of a drink. And I didn't get into bed with him. I left that to his girlfriend Clarissa of the Chancery Division. Any more questions?'

'Yes. Haven't you got any genuine beliefs?'

'As few as possible. Genuine beliefs seem to end up in death threats and stopping other people living as they choose. I do have one genuine belief, however.'

'Oh, do you? And what's that when it's at home?'

'Preventing the conviction of the innocent. So, if you will allow me to get on with my job . . .' I moved away from him then, and he stood watching me go, his fists clenched and his knuckles whitening.

*

Tricia had given her evidence-in-chief clearly, with a nice mixture of sadness, brightness and an eagerness to help. The jury had taken to her and Jamie MacBain seemed no less smitten than little Marcus was with Clarissa, although there was a great gulf fixed between them and she called him my Lord, and he called her Miss Fothergill in a voice which can best be described as a caressing, although still judicial, purr. She looked, as she stood in the witness-box and answered vivaciously, prettier than I had remembered. Her nose was a little turned up, her front teeth a little protruding, but her eyes were bright and her smile beguiling.

'Tricia Fothergill, you say your name is?' I rose, after Marcus had finished with her, doing my best to break the spell woven by the most damaging prosecution witness. 'Why not Patricia?'

'Because I couldn't say Patricia when I was a little girl. So I stayed Tricia, even when I went away to school.'

'Which, I'm sure, wasn't long ago. Don't you agree, Members of the Jury?' the judge purred and a few weaker spirits in the jury box gave a mild giggle. Tricia Fothergill, in Jamie's view, it seemed, *had* been born yesterday.

'I'll call you Miss Fothergill, if I may, if that's your grown-up name. Or is it? Were you once married?'

'Yes.'

'And your husband's name is . . . ?'

'Charing.'

'Cheering, did you say?'

'No, Charing.'

'Are you going deaf, Mr Rumpole?' the judge raised his voice to me as though at the severely afflicted.

'Not quite yet, my Lord.' I turned to this witness. 'Are you divorced from this Mr Charing?'

'Not quite yet, Mr Rumpole,' the witness answered with a smile and won a laugh from the jury. The judge's pursed lips were stretched into a smile, and the inert beanbag was shaken up and repositioned in his chair. 'The divorce hasn't gone through,' Tricia explained when order was restored.

'Yet you call yourself Miss Fothergill?'

'It was such an unhappy relationship. I wanted to make a clean break.'

'Surely you can understand that, Mr Rumpole?' Jamie was giving the witness his full and unqualified support.

'And have you now found a new and happier relationship?'

Little Marcus, the mouse that roared, rose to object, but the learned judge needed no persuading. 'That was an entirely irrelevant and embarrassing question, Mr Rumpole. Please be more careful in the future.'

'I hope we shall all be careful,' I said, 'in our efforts to discover the truth. So I understand you live alone, Miss Fothergill, in Cherry Trees in the village of Wayleave?'

'That is another entirely improper question. What does it matter whether this young lady lives alone or not?' This time the judge was doing Marcus's objections for him. 'We'd be greatly obliged, Mr Rumpole, if you'd move on to something relevant.'

'I'll move on to something very relevant. Do you say you saw a man coming out of Fallows Wood carrying wire on the day before the hunt?'

'That's right.'

'What time was it?'

'One o'clock.'

'How do you know?'

'I'd just looked at my watch. I was out for a hack and had to be home before two because my lawyer was ringing me. I saw it was only one and I decided to do the long round through Plashy Bottom. Then I saw the man coming out of the wood, with the coil of wire.'

'When you saw the man with the wire, you were alone?'

'Yes.'

'No one else saw him at that time?'

'Not so far as I know.'

'You say you thought he might have been working for Telecom or the electricity company? Did you see a van from any of those companies?'

'No.'

'Or the van the saboteurs came in?'

'I didn't see the van then, no. Of course it might have been parked on the road.'

'Or it might still have been parked in the village. As far as you know.'

'As far as I know.'

'You saw a man the next day, shouting at Mrs Eyles?'

'That was the same man. Yes.'

'Why didn't you warn everyone in the hunt that you'd seen that man coming out of the wood, carrying wire?'

'I suppose I just didn't put two and two together at the time. It was only when I heard Dorothea had been killed by a wire . . .'

'You put two and two together then?' The judge was ever helpful to his favourite witness.

'Yes, my Lord. And I was going to say that, in all the excitement of starting out with the hunt, I may have forgotten what I saw, just for a little while.'

'I don't suppose Mr Rumpole knows much about the excitement of the hunt.' Jamie MacBain was wreathed in smiles and seemed almost on the point of laying a finger alongside his nose.

I didn't join in the obedient titters from the jury, or the shocked intake of breath from the faces in the public gallery. I started the long and unrewarding task of chipping away at Tricia's identification. How far had she been away from the wood? Was the sun in her eyes? How fast was her horse moving at the time? As is the way with such questioning, the more the witness was attacked the more positive she became.

'On your way back to your house in Wayleave, on the day before the hunt, did you pass Janet Freebody's cottage?'

'Yes, I had to pass that way.' Tricia made it clear that she wouldn't go near anything of Janet Freebody's unless it were absolutely necessary.

'Did you see the sabs' van parked outside Miss Freebody's cottage?'

'I think I did. I can't honestly remember.'

'Was it locked?'

'How would she know that, Mr Rumpole?' Jamie put his oar in.

'Perhaps you tried the door.'

'I certainly didn't! I was just riding past.'

'Let me ask you something else. Mr Logan has told us that you left the hunt shortly before the police arrived with the news of Mrs Eyles's death. There was something wrong with your horse. What was it?'

'Oh, Trumpeter had lost a shoe,' Tricia said as casually as possible. 'It must have happened earlier, but I hadn't noticed it. I noticed it then and I had to take him home.'

It was a moment when I felt a tingle of excitement, as though, after a long search in deep and muddy waters, we had struck some hard edge of the truth. 'Miss Fothergill,' I asked her, 'were you riding with Mrs Eyles in Fallows Wood on the day she met her death?'

The jury were looking at Tricia, suddenly interested. Even Jamie MacBain didn't rush to her assistance.

'No, of course I wasn't.' She turned to the judge with a small, incredulous giggle which meant 'What a silly question'.

'My Lord. I call on my learned friend to admit that a horseshoe was found by Inspector Palmer near to the stile in Fallows Wood.'

'Perfectly true, my Lord,' Marcus admitted. 'It was found some weeks after Mrs Eyles died.'

'So it might have been dropped by one of any number of horses at any unknown time?' Jamie was delighted to point out. 'Isn't that so, Miss Fothergill?' Tricia was pleased to agree and repeated that she had never ridden through Fallows Wood that day. I was coming to the end of my questions.

'When your divorce proceedings are over, Miss Fothergill, are you going to embark on another marriage?' I asked and waited for the protest. It came. Little Marcus drew himself up to his full height and objected. Jamie agreed entirely and said that he wouldn't allow any question about the witness's private life. So my conversation with Tricia ended, finally silenced by the judge's ruling.

At the end of the afternoon I came out of court frustrated, despondent, seeing nothing in front of me but a pathetic guilty plea. Gavin hurried away to see Den in the cells and I heard an urgent voice saying, 'Mr Rumpole! I've got to talk to you.' I looked around and there was Janet Freebody, showing every sign of desperation.

I saw Roy and a representative group of the sabs watching us, as well as the hunters who were leaving the court. I said I'd meet her in the Carpenters Arms round the corner in half an hour.

'It's kind of you to see me. So kind.' I realized I had never looked closely at Janet Freebody before, but just filed her away in my mind as a grey-haired schoolmistress in a tweed skirt. It was true that her hair was grey and her skirt was tweed but her eyes were blue, her eyelids finely moulded and her long, serious face beautiful as the faces on grave madonnas or serious angels in old paintings. At that moment her cheeks were pink and her hands, caressing her glass of gin and tonic, were long-fingered and elegant.

'What is it you want to tell me?'

She didn't answer directly, but asked me a question. 'Wasn't it at one o'clock that Dennis was meant to be coming out of that wood, carrying wire?'

'That's what Tricia said.'

'Well, he wasn't. I know where he was.'

'Where?'

'In bed with me.'

I looked at her and said, 'Thank you for telling me.'

'I know I've got to tell that in court. Den's going to be furious.' And then it all came out, shyly at first, nervously, and then with increasing confidence. She'd had an affair with shaven-headed Roy, who was jealous of Den and now in a perpetually bad temper. She and Dennis had waited until the others went out to the pub to go upstairs, where, it seemed, the solemn Den forgot his duty to the animals in his love for the schoolmistress. Meanwhile, the saboteurs' van was unlocked and unattended outside Janet's front gate.

'You can't go on pretending.'

'Pretending what?'

'Pretending you're guilty, just to help animals. I doubt very much whether the animals are going to be grateful to you. In fact they'll hardly notice. Like Launce's dog, Crab. Do you know *The Two Gentlemen of Verona*?'

'How do they come into the case?'

'They don't. They're in a play. And so is Launce. And so is his dog, Crab. When Crab farts at the duke's dinner party, Launce takes the blame for it and is whipped out of the room. Launce also sat in the stocks for puddings Crab stole and stood in the pillory for geese Crab killed. How did Crab reward him? Simply by lifting his leg and peeing against Madam Silvia's skirt. That's how much Crab appreciated Launce's extraordinary sacrifice.'

There was a silence and then Dennis said, 'Mr Rumpole.'

'Yes, Den.'

'I am not quite following the drift of your argument.'

'It's just that Launce led an unrewarding life trying to take the blame for other people's crimes. Don't be a martyr! And don't pretend to be a murderer.'

'I'm not.'

'Of course you are. And what do you think it's going to get you? A vote of thanks from all the foxes in Gloucestershire?'

'I don't know what you're saying, Mr Rumpole.'

'I'm saying, come out of some fairy-story world full of kind little furry animals and horrible humans and tell the truth for a change.'

'What's the truth?'

'That you didn't kill anyone. All right, you can shout bloodthirsty threats and work yourself into a fury against toffs on horses. But I don't believe you'd really hurt a fly. Particularly not a fly.'

It was early in the morning, before Jamie MacBain had disposed of bacon and eggs in his lodgings, and I was alone with my client in the cells. I hadn't bothered to tell Gavin about this dawn meeting, and he would have been distressed, I'm sure, at Dennis's look of pain.

'I'm thinking of the cause.'

'The cause that can't accept that we're all hunters, more or less?'

'And I told you I was guilty.'

'You told me a lie. That was always obvious.'

'Why? Why was it obvious?'

'Because you had no way of knowing that Dorothea Eyles was going to leave the hunt and gallop between the trees in Fallows Wood.'

'You can't prove it.' For a moment Den was lit up with the light of battle.

'Prove what?'

'That I'm innocent.'

'Really! Of all the cockeyed clients. I've had some dotty ones but never one that didn't want to be proved innocent before.' It was early in the morning and the hotel had only been serving the continental breakfast. I'm afraid that my temper was short and I didn't mince my words. 'I can prove you didn't carry wire out of the wood at one o'clock on the day before the murder.'

'How?'

'Because you were doing something far more sensible. You were making love to Janet Freebody.'

There was a silence. Den looked down at his large hands, folded on his lap. Then he looked up again and said, 'Janet's not going to say that, surely?'

'Yes, she is. She's going to brave the story in the *Sun* and the giggles in her class at the comprehensive, and she's going to say it loud and clear.'

'I'm not going to let her.'

'You can't stop her.'

'Why not?'

'Because you're going to tell the truth also. And because you're going to fight this case to the bitter end. With a little help from me, you might even win.'

'Why should I fight it?' Den looked back at his hands, avoiding my eye. 'You give me one good reason.'

So then I gave him one very good reason indeed. 'You can't tell the story,' I warned Den. 'It can't be proved and you'd be sued for libel. But I promise to tell them what I know.' Later, when I had finished with Den, I went into the robing-room to slip into the fancy-dress and there I confronted little Marcus, combing his mouse-coloured hair. 'My learned friend,' I told him, 'I'm serving an alibi notice on you. Only one witness. You'll be a sweetheart and tell darling old Jamie that you don't want an adjournment or anything awkward like that. I can rely on you, can't I, Marcus?'

'Why on earth' – Marcus looked like a very determined mouse that morning – 'should you think that you can rely on me?'

'Because,' I told him, with some confidence, 'if you behave well, Hilda and my good self might see our way to looking after Bernadette while you're away in the Chancery Division.'

'That' – little Marcus turned back to the mirror and the careful arrangement of his hair – 'puts an entirely different complexion on the matter.'

'What is the single most important fact about this case, Members of the Jury? The fact which I ask you to take with you into your room and put first and last in your deliberations. It's just this: Mrs Eyles met her death half a mile from any point where the hunt had been. If Dennis Pearson intended to kill her, how did he lure her away to that remote woodland path? Did he offer her a date or an assignation? Did he promise to give her the winner of the two-thirty at Cheltenham? Or did he say, "Just gallop along the track in Fallows Wood and you'll probably be killed by a bit of tight wire I stretched there yesterday lunchtime"? How did he organize not only that she should be killed, but that she should go so far out of her way to meet her death? It was impossible to organize it, was it not, Members of the Jury? Doesn't that mean that you must have doubts about Dennis Pearson's guilt?

'Remember, he was seen at various places during the hunt, with the other saboteurs, shouting his usual abuse at the riders. So whoever went off and lured Dorothea Eyles to her death, it certainly wasn't him. And remember this, if he's guilty, the whole hunt would have had to come down that track, and the first to be killed wouldn't have been Mrs Eyles but the Master of Foxhounds himself, or one of the hunt servants. The prosecution haven't even tried to explain these mysteries and, unless they can explain them, you cannot be certain of guilt.'

Little Marcus was reading a guidebook on Elba and Jamie MacBean was feigning sleep, but the jury was listening, attentive and, I thought, even interested. The abrupt manner in which the judge had put an end to my cross-examination of Tricia had, I suspected, aroused their curiosity. What was it that the judge didn't wish them to know? There are moments when an objection sustained can be almost as good as evidence.

And then Janet Freebody turned out to be a dream witness. When Jamie asked her, in what he hoped were withering tones, if she was in the habit of having sexual intercourse with men at lunchtime, she answered, with the smallest of smiles, 'Only when my feelings overcome me, my Lord. And I am dreadfully in love.' The judge was silent, the jury liked her, and little Marcus closed his eyes and no doubt thought of Clarissa. I needn't go through all the points I made in my final speech, brilliant as they were. They will have become obvious to my readers who have studied my cross-examination. Jamie summed up for a conviction which, as the jury were not entirely on his side, was a considerable help to us. They were out for an hour and a half, but when they came back they looked straight at my client and said not guilty. The judge then threatened to have those cheering in the gallery committed to prison for contempt; however astute he was, and however long ago he'd been born, he had failed to achieve a conviction.

When I said goodbye to Dennis he was hardly overcome with gratitude. He said, 'You prevented me from striking a real blow for animal rights, Mr Rumpole. I came prepared to suffer.'

'I'm sorry,' I said, 'Janet Freebody ruined your suffering for you. And I think she's prepared to give you something a good deal more valuable than a martyr's crown.'

Months later, on the occasion of a long-suffering member of our chambers becoming a metropolitan magistrate, he gave his fellow legal hacks dinner at the Sheridan Club. She Who Must was not of the party, having gone off on yet another visit to Dodo and the dog Lancelot on the Cornish Riviera. As I sat trying not to drop off during one of Ballard's lively discussions of the chambers telephone bill, I saw, softly lit by candlelight, Rollo Eyles and Tricia Fothergill dining together at a distant table. I remembered a promise unfulfilled, a duty yet undone. I excused myself and went over to join them.

'Horace! Have a seat. What's going on over there? A chambers dinner? This is the claret we choose on the wine committee. Not too bad.' Rollo was almost too welcoming. Tricia, on the other hand, looked studiously at her plate.

'So' – Rollo was signalling to the waiter to bring me a glass – 'you won another murder?'

'Yes.'

'I suppose the jury thought another of those revolting antis did it.'

'I don't suppose we'll ever know exactly what they thought.'

'By the way, Horace' – Rollo looked at me, one eyebrow raised quizzically – 'I thought you'd like to know. Tricia and I are going to get married.'

'I thought you would be.'

For the first time Tricia raised her eyes from her plate. 'Did you?'

'Oh, yes. Rollo would never have left his wife, while she was alive. Thank you.' The waiter had brought a glass and Rollo filled it. 'You know my client, Dennis Pearson, was going to take the blame for the crime. He thought, in some strange way, that it might help the animals. He only agreed to fight because, if he was acquitted, the real murderer might still be discovered.'

'The real murderer?' I still didn't believe that Rollo knew the truth. Tricia knew it and I wanted Tricia to be sure I knew it too.

'What made Dorothea ride through Fallows Wood?' I looked at Tricia. 'I think you were riding with her in the hunt and you said something, probably something about Rollo, which made her want to know more. But you rode away and she followed you. When you got on to the track between the trees, you knew where the wire was and you ducked. Dorothea was galloping behind and knew nothing. It was a very quick death. You carried on and jumped the stile, where your horse lost a shoe.'

'You're drunk!' Rollo had stopped smiling.

'Not yet!' I took a gulp of his wine.

Tricia said, 'But I saw the man with the wire.'

'At least we proved you were lying about that. The only person who went into the wood with wire was you. And when you'd done the job, you dumped the coil in the sabs' van. You knew one of them could be relied on to threaten the riders. Dennis said exactly what was required of him.'

'Tricia?' Rollo looked at her, expecting her furious denial. He was disappointed.

'You repeat one word of that ridiculous story, Rumpole' – he was angry now – 'and I'll bloody sue you.'

'I don't think you will. I don't think she'll let you.'

'What are you going to do?' Tricia was suddenly businesslike, matter of fact.

'Do? I'm not going to do anything. I don't know who could prove it. Anyway, I'm not the police, or the prosecuting authority. What you do is for you two to decide. But I promised the man you wanted to convict that I'd let you know I knew. And now I've kept my promise.'

I drained my glass, got up and left their table. As I went, I saw Rollo put his hand on Tricia's and hold it there. Did he not believe in her crime, or was he prepared to live with it? I don't know and I can't possibly guess. I had left the world of the hunters and those who hunted them, and I never saw Rollo or his new wife again, although Hilda did tell me that their wedding had been recorded in the *Daily Telegraph*.

When I got back to our table I sat in silence for a while beside Mrs Justice Erskine-Brown, Phillida Trant that was, the Portia of our chambers.

'What are you thinking about, Rumpole?' Portia asked me.

'With all due respect to your Ladyship, I was thinking that a criminal trial is a very blunt implement for digging out the truth.'

Some weeks later Ballard entered my room when I was busy noting up an affray in Streatham High Street.

'I'm sending you a memo about the telephone bill, Rumpole.'

'Good. I shall look forward to that.'

'Very well. I'll send it to you then.' Apparently in search of another topic of conversation, the man sniffed the air. 'No dogs in here now, are there?'

'Certainly not.'

'I well remember the time when you had a dog in here.'

'No longer.'

'And we had to call a chambers meeting on the subject!'

'That was some while ago.'

'And you assure me you now have got no dog here, of any sort?'

'Close the door behind you, Bollard, when you go.'

As he left, the volume was turned up on the sound of heavy breathing. Bernadette was sleeping peacefully behind my desk.

Rumpole and the Angel of Death

I have, from time to time in these memoirs, had some harsh things to say about judges, utterances of mine which may, I'm afraid, have caused a degree of resentment among their assembled Lordships who like nothing less than being judged. To say that their profession makes them an easy prey to the terrible disease of judgeitis, a mysterious virus causing an often fatal degree of intolerance, pomposity and self-regard, is merely to state the obvious. Being continually bowed to and asked 'If your Lordship pleases?' is likely to unhinge the best-balanced legal brain; and I have never thought that those who were entirely sane would undertake the thankless task of judging their fellow human beings anyway. However, the exception to the above rule was old Chippy Chippenham, who managed to hold down the job of a senior circuit judge, entitled to try murder cases somewhere in the wilds of Kent, and remain, whenever I had the luck to appear before him, not only sensible but quite remarkably polite.

Chippy had been a soldier before he was called to the Bar. He had a pink, outdoors sort of face, a small scourer of a grey moustache and bright eyes which made him look younger than he must have been. When I appeared before him I would invariably get a note from him saying, 'Horace, how about a jar when all this nonsense is over?' I would call round to his room and he would open a bottle of average claret (considerably better, that is, than my usual Château Thames Embankment), and we would discuss old times, which usually meant recalling the fatuous speeches of some more than usually tedious prosecutor.

In court Chippy sat quietly. He summed up shortly and perfectly fairly (that I *did* object to – a fair summing-up is most likely to get the customer convicted). His sentences erred, if at all, on the side of clemency and were never accompanied by any sort of sermon or homily on the repulsive nature of the accused. I once defended a perfectly likeable old countryman, a gamekeeper turned poacher from somewhere south of Sevenoaks, who, on hearing that his wife was dying from a painful and inoperable cancer, took down his gun and shot her through the head. 'Deciding who will live and who will die,' Chippy told him, having more or less ordered the jury to find manslaughter, 'is a task Almighty God approaches only with caution,' and he gave my rustic client a conditional discharge, presumably on the condition that he didn't shoot any more wives.

The last time I appeared before Chippy he had changed. He found it difficult to remember the name of the fraudster in the dock and whether he'd dealt in spurious loft conversions or non-existent caravans. He shouted at the usher for not supplying him with pencils when a box was on his desk, and quite forgot to invite me round for a jar. Later, I heard he had retired and gone to live with some relatives in London. Later still, such are the revenges brought in by the whirligig of time, he appeared in the curious case of *R. v. Dr Elizabeth Ireton*, as the victim of an alleged murder.

The Angel of Death no doubt appears in many guises. She may not always be palely beautiful and shrouded in black. In the particularly tricky case which called on my considerable skills and had a somewhat surprising result, the fell spirit appeared as a dumpy, grey-haired, bespectacled lady who wore sensible shoes, a shapeless tweed skirt, a dun-coloured cardigan and a cheerful smile. This last was hard to explain considering her position of peril in Number One Court at the Bailey. She was a Dr Elizabeth Ireton, known to her many patients and admirers as 'Dr Betty', and she carried on her practice from a chaotic surgery in Notting Hill Gate.

I'll admit I was rather distracted that breakfast time in the kitchen of our so-called mansion flat in the Gloucester Road. I was trying to gain as much strength as possible from a couple of eggs on a fried slice, pick up a smattering of the events of the day from the wireless and make notes in the case of Dr Ireton, with whom I had a conference booked for five o'clock. My usual calm detachment about that case was unsettled by the discovery that the corpse in question was that of Judge Chippy with whom I had shared so many a friendly jar. There was little time to spare before I had to set off for a banal matter of receiving a huge consignment of frozen oven-ready Thai dinners in Snaresbrook.

Accordingly, I stuffed the papers in my battered briefcase, placed my pen in the top pocket and submerged my dirty plate and cutlery in the washing-up bowl, in accordance with the law formulated by She Who Must Be Obeyed.

'Rumpole!' The voice of authority was particularly sharp that morning. 'Have you the remotest idea what you have done?'

'A remote idea, Hilda. I have prepared for work. I am going out into the harsh, unsympathetic world of a Crown Court for the sole purpose of keeping this leaky old mansion flat afloat and well stocked with Fairy Liquid and suchlike luxuries . . .'

'Is this the way you usually prepare for work?'

'By consuming a light cooked breakfast and doing a bit of last-minute homework? How else?'

'And I suppose you intend to appear in court with the butter knife sticking out of your top pocket, having thrown your fountain-pen into the sink.'

A glance at my top pocket told me that She Who Must Be Obeyed, forever eagle-eyed, had sized up the situation pretty accurately. 'A moment of confusion,' I agreed. 'My mind was on more serious subjects. Particularly it was on a Dr Ireton, up on a charge of wilful murder.'

'Dr Betty?' As usual Hilda was about four steps ahead of me. 'She's the most wonderful person. Truly wonderful!'

'You're not thinking of her as Quack By Appointment to the Rumpole household?' I asked with some apprehension. 'She's accused of doing in his Honour Charles Chippy Chippenham, a circuit judge for whom I had an unusual affection.'

'She didn't do it, Rumpole!'

'My dear old thing, I'm sure you know best.'

'I was at school with her. She was a house monitor and we all simply adored her. I promised you'd get her off.'

'Hilda, I know you have enormous respect for me as a courtroom genius, but your good Dr Betty was apparently a leading light in Lethe, a society to promote the joys of euthanasia . . .'

'It's not a question of your being a genius, Rumpole. It's just that I told Betty Ireton that you'd have me to answer to if you didn't win her case. I know quite well she believes passionately' – and here I saw Hilda watching me closely as I dried the fountain-pen – 'that life shouldn't be needlessly prolonged. Not, at any rate, after old people have completely lost their senses.'

The case of the frozen Thai dinners wound remorselessly on and was finally adjourned to the next day. When I got back to chambers I found my room inhabited by a tallish, thinnish man in a blue suit with hair just over his ears and the sort of moustache once worn by South American revolutionaries and now sported by those who travel the Home Counties trying to flog double-glazing to the natives. He had soft, brown eyes, a wristwatch with a heavy metallic strap which gleamed in imitation of gold, and all around him hung a deafening odour of aftershave. This intruder appeared to be measuring my room, and the top of my desk, with a long, wavering, metal tape.

'At long last,' I said, as I unloaded the antique briefcase. 'Bollard's got the decorators in.'

'It's Horace Rumpole, isn't it? I'm Vince.'

'Vince?'

'Vince Blewitt.'

'Glad to know you, Mr Blewitt, but you can't start rubbing down now. I'm about to have a conference.' I was a little puzzled; we'd had the decorators in more than once in the last half-century and none of them had introduced themselves so eagerly.

'Rubbing down?' The man seemed mystified.

'Preparing to paint.'

'Oh, that!' Vince was laughing, showing off a line of teeth which would have graced a television advertisement. 'No, I'm not here regarding the paint. I'm just measuring your workspace so I can see if it makes sense in terms of your personal throughput in the organization's overall workload. That's what I'm regarding. And I have to tell you, Horace, I'm going to have a job justifying your area in terms of your contribution to overall chambers market profitability.'

'I have no idea what you're talking about.' I sat down wearily in the workspace area and lit a small cigar. 'And I'm not sure I want to. But I assume you're only passing through?'

'Hasn't Sam Ballard told you? My appointment was confirmed at the last chambers meeting.'

'I've given up chambers meetings,' I told him. 'I regard them as a serious health hazard.'

'I'm really going to enjoy this opportunity. That Dot Clapton. Am I going to enjoy working with her! Isn't she something else?'

'What *else* do you mean? She's our general typist and telephone answerer.'

'And much more. That girl's got a big future in front of her!' Here, the man laughed in a curiously humourless way. 'Oh, and there's another thought I'd like to share with you.'

'Please. Don't share anything else with me.'

'Looking at your own workload, Horace, what strikes me is this: you fight all your cases. They go on far too long. Of course you get daily refreshers, don't you?'

'Whenever I can.' All I could think of at that moment was how refreshing it would be to get this bugger Blewitt out of my room.

'But the brief fee for the first day has far more profitability?'

'If you're trying to say it's worth more money, the answer is yes.'

'So why not accept the brief and bargain for a plea, whatever you do? Then you'd be free to take another one the next day. And so on. Do I need to spell it out? That way you could increase market share on your personal achievement record.'

'And a lot of innocent people might end up in chokey. You say you've joined our chambers? Are you a lawyer?'

'Good heavens, no!' Blewitt seemed to find the suggestion mildly amusing. 'My experience was in business. Sam Ballard headhunted me from catering.'

'Catering, eh?' I looked at him closely. He had, I thought, a distinctly fishy appearance. 'Frozen Thai dinners come into it at all, did they?'

'From time to time. Do you have an interest in oriental cuisine, Horace?'

'None at all. But I do have an interest in my conference in a murder case which is just about to arrive.'

'Likely to be a plea?' Blewitt appeared hopeful.

'Over my dead body.'

'Well, make sure it's a maximum contributor to chambers cashflow.'

'That's quite impossible,' I told him. 'If I don't do this case free, gratis and for nothing, I shall get into serious trouble with She Who Must Be Obeyed.'

'Whoever's that?'

'Be so good as to leave me, Blewitt. I see you have a great deal to learn about life in Equity Court. Things you'd never pick up in catering.'

He left me then, and I thought I wasn't only landed with the defence of Dr Betty Ireton but the defence of our chambers against the death-dealing ministrations of Vincent Blewitt.

After our new legal administrator had left my presence, I refreshed my memory, from the papers in front of me, on the circumstances of old Chippy's death.

It seemed that he had a considerable private fortune passed down from some eighteenth-century Chippenham who had ransacked the Far East while working for the East India Company. He had lived with his wife, Connie, in a large Victorian house near Holland Park until she died of cancer. Chippy was heartbroken and began to show the early symptoms of the disease which led to his retirement from the Bench – Alzheimer's. This is a condition in which the mind atrophies, the patient becomes apparently infantile, incomprehensible and incontinent. Early symptoms are a certain vagueness and loss of memory (such as washing up your fountain-pen? Perish the thought!). After the complaint has taken hold, the victim remains physically healthy and may live on for many years to the distress, no doubt, of the relatives. Whether, although unable to express themselves in words, those with Alzheimer's may still enjoy moments of happiness must remain a mystery.

As he became increasingly helpless, Chippy's nephew Dickie and Dickie's wife, Ursula, moved in to look after him. They kept their ten-year-old son, Andrew, reasonably quiet and they devoted themselves to the old man. He was also cared for by a Nurse Pargeter, who came when the young Chippenhams went out in the evenings, and by Dr Betty, who, according to the witnesses' statements, got on like a house on fire with the old man.

In fact they were such good friends that Dr Betty used to call at least one or two times a week and sit with Chippy. They would drink a small whisky together and the old man had, in the doctor's presence, occasional moments of lucidity, when he would laugh at an old legal joke or weep like a child when remembering his wife. When she left, Dr Betty would, on her own admission, leave her patient a sleeping tablet, or even two, to see him through the night. So far, Dr Betty's behaviour couldn't be criticized, except for the fact that she thought it right to prescribe barbiturates. But, to be fair to her, she was told that these were the soporifics Chippy relied on in the days when he still had all his marbles.

One night the Chippenhams went out to dinner. Nurse Pargeter had been engaged with another patient and Dr Betty volunteered to sit with Chippy. (I couldn't help wondering if her kindness on that occasion included a release from this vale of tears.) When the Chippenhams arrived home Dr Betty told them that her patient was asleep and she left then. The old man died that night with a suddenness that the nurse, who found him in the morning, thought suspicious. In an autopsy his stomach was found to contain the residue of a massive overdose of the sleeping tablets Dr Betty had prescribed and also a considerable quantity of alcohol. Dr Betty was well known as a passionate supporter of euthanasia and she was charged with murder. She was given bail and her trial was due to start in three weeks' time.

'Of course I remember Hilda. She was such a quiet, shy girl at school.' I looked at Dr Betty, sitting in my client's chair in chambers, and came to the conclusion that here was a quite unreliable witness.

The suggestion of a quiet and shy Hilda was not, on the face of it, one that would satisfy the burden of proof.

'She told me that you don't think life should be needlessly prolonged in certain circumstances. Is that right?'

'Oh, yes.' The doctor, I judged, was in her late sixties but her smile was that of an innocent; her eyes behind her spectacles were shining with as girlish an enthusiasm as when she led her mustard-keen team out on to the hockey field. 'Death is such a lovely thing when you're feeling really poorly,' she said. 'I don't know why we don't all give it a hearty welcome.'

' "The grave's a fine and private place," ' I reminded her, ' "But none, I think, do there embrace." '

'How do we know, Mr Rumpole? How can we possibly know? Are you really sure there won't be any cuddles beyond the grave?'

'Cuddles? I hardly think so.'

'We're so prejudiced against the dead!' Dr Betty was almost giggling and her glasses were glinting. 'Rather like there used to be prejudice against women when I went in for medicine. There must be so many really nice dead people!'

'You believe in the afterlife?'

'Oh, I think so. But whatever sort of life goes on after death, I'd be out of a job there, wouldn't I? No one would need a doctor.'

'Or a barrister?' Or might there be some celestial tribunal at which a crafty advocate could get a sinner off hell? Plenty of briefs, of course, but my heart sank at the thought of eternal work before a jury of prejudiced saints. I decided to return to the business in hand. 'Do you think that sufferers from Alzheimer's disease are appropriate candidates for the Elysian Fields?'

'Of course they are! I'd fully decided to send old Chippy off there as soon as I judged the time was ripe.'

My heart sank further. The danger of having a conference with customers accused of murder is that they may tell you they did the deed and then, of course, the fight is over and you have no alternative but to stagger into court with your hands up. That's why, during such conferences, it's much wiser to discuss the Maastricht Treaty or Whither the Deutschmark? than to refer directly to the crude facts of the charge. It was my error to have done so and now I had to tell Dr Betty that she had as good as pleaded guilty.

'No, I haven't,' she told me, still, it seemed, in a merry mood. 'I'm not guilty of anything.'

'You're not?'

'Of course not! It's true I was prepared to release old Chippy from this unsatisfactory world, when the time came.'

'And it had come the night he died?'

'No, it certainly had not! He was still having lucid intervals. I would have done it eventually, but not then.' I meant to rob the bank, Guv, but not on that particular occasion: it didn't sound much of a defence, but I was determined to make the most of it.

'So do you think' – I threw Dr Betty a lifeline – 'Chippy might have got depressed during the night and committed suicide?'

'Of course not!' I'd never had a client who was so cheerfully anxious to sink herself. 'He was an old soldier. He always told me that he regarded suicide as cowardice in the face of the enemy. He'd have battled on against all odds, until I decided to sound the retreat.'

It hadn't been an easy day and to go straight home to Froxbury Mansions without a therapeutic visit to Pommeroy's Wine Bar would have been like facing an operation without an anaesthetic. So, because my alcohol content had sunk to a dangerous low, I pushed open the glass door and made for the bar. I saw, on top of a stool, a crumpled figure slumped in deepest gloom and attacking what I thought was far from his first gin and Dubonnet. Closer examination proved him to be our learned clerk.

'Cheer up, Henry,' I said, when I had called upon Jack Pommeroy to pour a large Château Fleet Street and mark it up on the slate. 'It may never happen!'

'It *has* happened, Mr Rumpole. And I could manage another of the same if you're ordering. Our new legal administrator has happened.'

'You mean the blighter Blewitt?'

'Tell me honestly, Mr Rumpole, have you ever seriously considered taking your own life?'

'No.' It was perfectly true. Even in the darkest days, even when I was put on trial for professional misconduct after a run-in with a hostile judge and when She Who Must Be Obeyed's disapproval of my way of life meant that there was not only an east wind blowing in Froxbury Mansions but a major hurricane, I could always find solace in a small cigar, a glass of Pommeroy's plonk, a stroll down to the Old Bailey in the autumn sunshine and the possibility of a new brief to test my forensic skills. 'I have never felt the slightest temptation to place my head in the gas oven.'

'Neither have I,' Henry told me and I congratulated him. 'We're all electric at home. But, I have to say, I'm tempted by a handful of aspirins.'

'Messy,' I told him. 'And, in my experience, not entirely dependable. But why this desperate remedy?'

'I have lost everything, Mr Rumpole.'

'Everything?'

'Everything I care about. Dot Clapton and I. Our relationship is over.'

'Really? I didn't think it ever began.'

'Too right, Mr Rumpole. Too very right!' Our clerk laughed bitterly. 'And my job has gone. What's my future? Staying at home . . .'

'In Bexleyheath?'

'Exactly. Helping out with a bit of shopping. Decorating the bathroom. And my wife will lose all respect for me as a breadwinner.'

'Your wife, the alderperson?'

'Chairman of Social Services. It gives her a lot of status.'

'You'll have a good deal of time for your amateur dramatics.'

'I have been offered the lead in *Laburnum Grove*. I turned it down.'

'But why, Henry?'

'Because I'm losing my job, and I've got no heart left for taking on a leading role!'

Further enquiry revealed what I should have known if I'd had more of a taste for chambers meetings. The skinflint Bollard had decided to get rid of a decent old-fashioned barrister's clerk who got a percentage of our takings and to appoint a legal administrator, at what I was to discover was a ludicrously high salary. 'Vince takes over at the end of the month,' Henry told me.

'Vince?'

'He asked me to call him Vince. He said that for us two to be on first-name terms would "ease the process". And what makes me so bitter, Mr Rumpole, is I think he's got his eye on our Dot.' Mizz Clapton is so casually beautiful that I thought she must have many eyes on her, but I didn't think it would cheer up our soon to be ex-clerk to tell him that. Instead I gave him my considered opinion on what I took to be the heart or nub of the matter.

'This man, Blewitt,' I said, 'appears to be a considerable blot on the landscape.'

'You're not joking, Mr Rumpole.'

'One that must be removed for the general health of chambers.'

'And of me in particular, Mr Rumpole, as your long-serving and faithful clerk.'

'Then all I can tell you, Henry, is that a way must be found.'

'Agreed, Mr Rumpole, but who is to find it?'

It seemed to me a somewhat dimwitted question, and one that Henry would never have asked had he been entirely sober. 'Who else,' I asked, purely rhetorically, 'but the learned counsel who found a defence in the Penge Bungalow affair, which looked, at first sight, even blacker than the case of the blot Blewitt – or even the predicament of Dr Betty Ireton?'

'Then I'll leave it to you, Mr Rumpole.'

'Many doubtful characters have said those very words, Henry, and not been disappointed.'

'And I could do with another gin and Dubonnet, sir. Seeing as you're in the chair.'

So Jack Pommeroy added to the figure on the slate and Henry seemed to cheer up considerably. 'I just heard a really ripe one in here, Mr Rumpole, from old Jo Castor who clerks Mr Digby Tappit in Crown Office Row. Do you know, sir, the one about the sleeveless woman?'

'I do not know it, Henry. But I suppose I very soon shall.'

As a matter of fact I never did. My much-threatened clerk began to tell me this ripe anecdote which had an extremely lengthy build-up. Long before the delayed climax I shut off, being lost in my own thoughts. Did old Chippy Chippenham die in the course of nature or was he pushed? If he had been, would he have felt as merciful to Dr Betty as he had to my rustic client who shot his sick wife?

Had one long, confused afternoon arrived when Chippy muttered to himself, 'I have been half in love with easeful Death'? The sound of the words gave me a lift only otherwise to be had from Pommeroy's plonk and I intoned privately and without interrupting Henry's flow:

> 'Now more than ever seems it rich to die,
> To cease upon the midnight with no pain,
> While thou art pouring forth thy soul abroad
> In such an ecstasy!'

Then Henry laughed loudly; his story had apparently reached its triumphant and no doubt obscene conclusion. I joined in for the sake of manners, but now I was thinking that I had to win the case of Blewitt as well as that of Dr Betty, and I had no idea how I was to emerge triumphant from either.

'We don't call this a memorial service. We call it a joyful thanksgiving for the life of his Honour Judge Chippenham.' So said the Reverend Edgedale, the Temple's resident cleric. Sitting at the back of the congregation, I thought that old Chippy wasn't in a position to mind much what we called it, and wondered if some of the villains he'd felt it necessary to send away to chokey would call it a joyful thanksgiving for his death. Chippy was dead, a word we all shy away from nowadays when almost anything else goes. What would Mizz Liz Probert have said? Old Chippy had become a non-living person. And then I thought how glowingly Dr Betty had talked about Chippy's present position, happily unaware of the length of the sermon – 'Chippy was the name he rejoiced in since his first term at Charterhouse, but you and I can hardly think of anyone with less of a chip on his shoulder' – and the increasing hardness of the pews. I looked around at the assembled mourners, Mr Injustice Graves, and various circuit judges and practising hacks who were no doubt wondering how soon they might expect a joyful thanksgiving for their own lives. I peered up at the stained-glass windows in the old round church built for the Knights Templar, who had gone off to die in the Crusades without the benefit of a memorial service, and then I fell into a light doze.

I was woken up by a peal on the organ and old persons stumbling across my knees, anxious to get out of the place which gave rise to uncomfortable thoughts of mortality. And, when we joined in the general rush for the light of day, I heard a gentle voice, 'Mr Rumpole, how delighted Uncle Chippy would have been that you could join us.'

I focused on a pleasant-looking, youngish woman, pushing back loose hair which strayed across her forehead. Beside her stood an equally pleasant, tall man in his forties. Both of them smiled as though their natural cheerfulness could survive even this sad occasion.

'Dick and Ursula Chippenham,' the tall man bent down considerately to inform me. 'Uncle Chippy was always talking about you. Said you could be a devilish tricky customer in court but he always enjoyed having you in for a jar when the battle was over.'

'Chippy was so fond of his jar. What we wanted was to ask all his real friends back to toast his memory,' Ursula told me. 'Do say you'll come!'

'I honestly don't think . . .' What I meant to say was that I already felt a little guilty for slipping into the memorial service of a man when I was defending his possible murderer. Could I, in all conscience, accept even one jar from his bereaved family?

'It's 31 Dettingen Road, Holland Park.' Dick Chippenham smiled down on me from a great height. 'Chippy would have been so delighted if you were there to say goodbye.'

As I say, I felt guilty but I also had a strong desire to see what we old-fashioned hacks call the *locus in quo* – the scene of the crime.

It was an English spring, that is to say, dark clouds pressed down on London and produced a doleful weeping of rain. I splurged out on a taxi from the Temple to Dettingen Road and spent some time in it while the approach to number 31 was blocked by a huge, masticating rubbish lorry which gave out strangled cries such as 'This vehicle is reversing!' as it tried to extricate itself from a jam of parked cars. Whistling dustmen were collecting bins from the front entrance of sedate, white-stuccoed houses, pouring their contents into the jaws of the curiously articulate lorry and then returning the empty bins, together with a small pile of black plastic bags, given, by courtesy of the council, to their owners. I paid the immobile taxi off and took a brisk walk in the sifting rain towards number 31. As I did so, I saw a solemn boy come down the steps of the house and, in a sudden, furtive motion, collect the black plastic bags from the top of the dustbin, stuff them under his school blazer and disappear into a side entrance of the house. I climbed up the front steps, rang the bell and was admitted by a butler-like person who I thought must have been specially hired for Chippy's send-off. Sounds of the usual high cocktail-party chatter with no particular note of grief in it were emerging from the sitting-room. The wake seemed to be a great deal more cheerful than the weather.

Ursula Chippenham bore down on me with a welcome glass of champagne. 'We're so glad you came.' She moved me into a corner and spoke confidentially, much more in sorrow than in anger. 'Dr Betty got on so terribly well with Chippy. We never thought for a moment that she'd do anything like that.'

'Perhaps she didn't.'

'Of course, Dick and I don't want anything terrible to happen to her.'

'Neither do I.'

'We know you'll do your very best for her. Chippy always said you were quite brilliant with a jury on a good day, when you didn't go over the top and start spouting bits of poetry at them.'

'That was very civil of him.'

'And, of course, Dr Betty and Chippy became best friends. Towards the end, that was.'

'I suppose you know that she was against . . . Well, prolonging life?' Or in favour of killing people, I suppose I would have said, if I were appearing for the prosecution.

'Of course. But I never dreamt she'd do anything . . . Well, without discussing it with the family. She seemed so utterly trustworthy! Of course we hadn't known her all that long. She only came to us when Chippy took against poor Dr Eames.'

'When was that exactly?'

'There are certain rules, Mr Rumpole. Certain traditions of the Bar which you might find it convenient to remember.' Chippy had said that to me in court when I asked a witness who happened to work in advertising if that didn't mean he'd taken up lying as a career. In his room afterwards he'd said, 'Horace, sometimes I wish you'd stop being such an *original* barrister.' 'Is trying to squeeze information out of a prosecution witness while consuming her champagne at a family wake in the best traditions of the Bar?' he would have asked. 'Probably not, my Lord,' I would have told Chippy, 'but aren't you curious to know exactly how you met your death?'

'Only about six months ago.' Ursula answered my question willingly. 'Eames is a bit politically correct, as a matter of fact. He kept telling Chippy that at least his illness meant that his place on the Bench was available to a member of an ethnic minority.'

'Not much of a bedside manner, this quack Eames?'

'Oh, I don't think Chippy minded that so much. It was when Eames said, "No more claret and no more whisky to help you to go to sleep, for the rest of your life," that the poor chap had to go.'

'Understandable.'

'Dick thought so too.'

'And how did you happen to hear of Dr Betty Ireton?'

'Some friends of mine in Cambridge Terrace said she was an absolute angel. Oh, there you are, Pargey! This is Nurse Pargeter, Mr Rumpole. Pargey was an angel to Chippy too.' The nurse who was wandering by had reddish hair, a long equine face and suddenly startled eyes. She wasn't in uniform, but was solemnly dressed in a plain black frock and white collar. I had already seen her, standing alone, taking care not to look at the other guests in case they turned and noticed her loneliness.

Ursula Chippenham drifted off to greet some late arrivals. 'Are you family?' the nurse asked in a surprisingly deep and unyielding voice, with a trace of a Scottish accent.

'No, I'm a barrister. An old friend of Chippy's . . .'

'Mr Rumpole? I think I've heard him mention you.'

'I'm glad. And then, of course, I have the unenviable task of defending Dr Betty Ireton. Mrs Chippenham says she got on rather well with the old boy.'

'Defend her?' Nurse Pargeter suddenly looked as relentless as John Knox about to denounce the monstrous regiment of women. 'She cannot be defended. I warned the Chippenhams against her. They can't say I didn't warn them. I told them all about that dreadful Lethe.'

'Everyone *can* be defended,' I corrected her as gently as possible. 'Of course whether the defence is successful is entirely another matter.'

'I prefer to remember the Ten Commandments on the subject.' Pargey was clearly of a religious persuasion.

Those nicknames, I thought – Pargey and Chippy – you might as well be in a school dormitory or at a gathering of very old actors.

'Oh, the Ten Commandments.' I tried not to sound dismissive of this ancient code of desert law. 'Not too closely observed nowadays, are they? I mean adultery's about the only subject that seems to interest the newspapers, and coveting other people's oxen and asses is called leaving everything to market forces. And, as for worshipping graven images, think of the prices some of them fetch at Sotheby's. As for Thou shalt not kill – well, some people think that the terminally ill should be helped out of their misery.'

'And some people happen to believe in the sanctity of life. And now, if you'll excuse me, Mr Rumpole, I have an important meeting to go to.'

As I watched her leave, I thought that I hadn't been a conspicuous success with Nurse Pargeter. Then a small boy piped up at my elbow, 'Would you like one of these, sir? I don't know what they are actually.' It was young Andrew Chippenham, with a plate of small brown envelope arrangements made of brittle pastry. I took one, bit into it and found, hardly to my delight, goat's cheese and some green, seaweed-like substance.

'You must be Andrew,' I said. The only genuine schoolboy around wasn't called Andy or Drew, or even Chippy, but kept his whole name, uncorrupted. 'And you go to Bolingbroke House?' I recognized the purple blazer with brass buttons. Bolingbroke was an expensive prep school in Kensington, which I thought must be so over-subscribed that the classrooms were used in a rota system and the unaccommodated pupils were sent out for walks in a crocodile formation, under the care of some bothered and junior teacher, round the streets of London. I had seen regiments of purple blazers marching dolefully as far as Gloucester Road; the exit from Bolingbroke House had a distinct look of the retreat from Moscow.

'How do you like being a waiter?' I asked Andrew, thinking it must be better than the daily urban trudge.

'Not much. I'd like to get back to my painting.'

'You're an artist?'

'Of course not.' He looked extremely serious. 'I mean painting my model aeroplanes.'

'How fascinating.' And then I lied as manfully as any unreliable witness. 'I was absolutely crazy about model aeroplanes when I was your age. Of course, that was a bit before Concorde.'

'Did you ever go in a Spitfire?' Andrew looked at me as though I had taken part in the Charge of the Light Brigade or was some old warrior from the dawn of time.

'Spitfires? I know all about Spitfires from my time in the RAF.' I forgot to tell him I was ground staff only. And then I said, 'I say, Andrew, I'd love to see your collection.' So he put down his plate of goat's cheese envelopes and we escaped from the party.

Andrew's room was on the third floor, at the back of the house. In the front, a door was open and I got a glimpse of a big, airy room with a bed stripped and the windows open. When I asked who slept there, he answered casually and without any particular emotion, 'That was Great-uncle Chippy's room. He's the one who died, you know.'

'I know. I suppose your parents' bedroom's on the floor below?' It wasn't the subtlest way of getting information.

'Oh, yes. I'm all alone up here now.' Andrew opened the door of his room which smelt strongly of glue and, I thought for a moment, was full of brightly coloured birds which, as I focused on them, became model aeroplanes swinging in the breeze from an open window. From what seemed to be every inch of the ceiling, a thread had been tied or tacked to hold up a fighter or an old-fashioned sea-plane in full flight.

'That's the sort of Spitfire you piloted,' Andrew said, to my silent embarrassment. 'And that's a Wellington bomber like you had in the war.' I did remember the planes returning, when they were lucky, with a rear-gunner dead or wounded and the stink of blood and fear when the doors were opened. I had been young then, unbearably young, and I banished the memory for more immediate concerns.

'Are these all the models you've made?' I asked Andrew. 'Or have you got lots more packed away in black bin bags?'

'Bin bags?' He was fiddling with a half-painted Concorde on his desk. 'Why do you say that?'

'You know, the plastic bags the dustmen leave after they've taken away the rubbish. Don't you collect them? A lot of boys do.'

'Collect plastic bags? What a funny thing to do.' Andrew had his head down and was still fiddling with his model. 'That wouldn't interest me, I'm afraid. I haven't got any plastic bags at all.'

Back in chambers that afternoon I found Dot Clapton alone in front of her typewriter, frowning as she looked over a brightly coloured brochure, on the cover of which a bikinied blonde was to be seen playing leapfrog with a younger, fitter version of Vincent Blewitt on a stretch of golden sand.

'I'm afraid Henry's just slipped out, Mr Rumpole. I don't know what it is. His heart doesn't seem to be in his work nowadays.' She looked up at me in genuine distress and I saw the perfectly oval face, sculptured eyelids and blonde curls that might have been painted by some such artistic old darling as Sandro Botticelli, and heard the accent which might have been learnt from the Timson family some-where south of Brixton. I didn't tell her that not only Henry's heart, but our learned clerk himself, might not be in his work very soon. Instead I asked, 'Thinking of going on holiday, Dot?'

She handed me the brochure in silence. On the front of it was emblazoned THE FIVE S HOLIDAYS: SEA, SUN, SAND, SINGLES AND SEX ON THE COSTA DEL SOL. WHY NOT GO FOR IT? 'Quite honestly, is that your idea of a holiday, Mr Rumpole?'

'It sounds,' I had to tell her, 'like my idea of hell.'

'I've got to agree with you. I mean, if I want burger and chips with a pint of lager, I might as well stay in Streatham.'

'Very sensible.'

'If I'm going to be on holiday, I want something a bit romantic.'

'I understand. Sand and sex are as unappealing as sand in the sandwiches?'

'My boyfriend's planning to take me to the castles down the Rhine. Of course, I don't want to upset him.'

'Upset your boyfriend?'

'No. Upset Mr Blewitt.'

'Upsetting Mr Blewitt – I have to say this, Dot – is my idea of a perfect summer holiday.'

'Oh, don't say that, Mr Rumpole.' Dot Clapton looked nervously round the room as though the blot might be concealed behind the arras. 'He is my boss now, isn't he?'

'Not *my* boss, Dot. No one's my boss, and particularly not Blewitt.'

'He's mine then. And he told me these singles holidays are a whole lot of fun.'

'Did he now?' I felt that there was something in this fragment of information which might be of great value.

'I don't know, though. Vince . . . Well, he asked me to call him Vince.'

'And you agreed?'

'I didn't have much choice. Does he honestly think I haven't got a boyfriend?'

'If he thinks that, Dot, he can't be capable of organizing a piss-up in a brewery, let alone a barristers' chambers.'

'Piss-up in a brewery!' Dot covered her mouth with her hand and giggled. 'How do you think of these things, Mr Rumpole?'

I didn't tell her that they'd been thought of and forgotten long before she was born, but took my leave of her, saying I was on my way to see Mr Ballard.

'Oh, he's busy.' Dot emerged from behind her hand. 'He said he wasn't to be disturbed.'

'Then it will be my pleasure and privilege to disturb him.'

'Have you "eaten on the insane root",' I asked the egregious Ballard, with what I hoped sounded like genuine concern, ' "That takes the reason prisoner"?'

'What *do* you mean, Rumpole?'

'I mean no one who has retained one single marble would dream of introducing the blight Blewitt into Equity Court.'

'I thought you'd come to me about that eventually.'

'Then you thought right.'

'If you had bothered to attend the chambers meeting you might have been privy to the selection of Vincent Blewitt.'

'I have only a few years of active life left to me,' I told the man with some dignity. 'And they are too precious to be wasted on chambers meetings. If I'd been there, I'd certainly have banned Blewitt.'

'Then you'd have been outvoted.'

'You mean those learned but idiotic friends decided to put their affairs in the hands of this second-rate, second-hand car salesman.'

'Catering.' Ballard smiled tolerantly.

'What?'

'Vincent Blewitt was in catering, not cars.'

'Then I wouldn't buy a second-hand cake off him.'

'Horace' – Soapy Sam Ballard rose and placed a considerate and totally unwelcome hand on my shoulder – 'we all know that you're a great old warhorse and that you've had a long, long career at the Bar. But you have to face it, my dear old Horace, you don't understand the modern world.'

'I understand it well enough to be able to tell a decent, honest, efficient, if rather over-amorous, clerk from the dubious flogger of suspect and probably mouldy canteen dinners.' I shrugged the unwelcome hand off my shoulder.

'The clerking system,' Ballard told me then, with a look of intolerable condescension, 'is out of date, Horace. We are moving towards the millennium.'

331

'You move towards it if you like. I prefer to stay where I am.'

'Why should we pay Henry a percentage when we can get an experienced businessman for a salary?'

'What sort of salary?'

'Vincent Blewitt was good enough to agree to a hundred, to be reviewed at the end of one year. The contract will be signed when the month's trial period is over.'

'A hundred pounds? Far too much!'

'A hundred thousand, Rumpole. It's far less than he would expect to earn in the private sector of industry.'

'Let him go back to the private sector then. If you want to be robbed, I could lend you one of the Timsons. They only deal in petty theft.'

'Vincent Blewitt has been very good to join us. At some personal financial sacrifice . . .'

'Did you check on what his screw was in the canteen?'

'I took his word for it.' Ballard looked only momentarily embarrassed.

'Famous last words of the fraudster's victim.'

'Vincent Blewitt isn't a fraudster, Rumpole. He's a businessman.'

'That's the polite word for it.'

'He says we must earn our keep by a rise in productivity.'

'How do you measure our productivity?'

'By the turnover in trials.'

'In your case, by the amazing turnover in defeats.' It was below the belt, I have to confess, but it didn't send Ballard staggering to the ropes. He came back, pluckily, I suppose. 'Business, Rumpole,' he told me, 'makes the world go round.' Later I discovered he'd got these words of wisdom from some ludicrous television advertisement.

'Rubbish. Justice might make the world go round. Or poetry. Or love. Or even God. *You* might think it's God, Bollard, as a founder member of the Lawyers As Christians Society.'

'As a Christian, Rumpole, I remember the parable of the talents. The Bible points out that you can't fight market forces.'

'Didn't the Bible also say something like blessed are the poor? Or do you wish it hadn't said that?'

'I've got no time to trade texts with you, Rumpole.' Soapy Sam looked nettled.

I was suddenly tired, half in love, perhaps for a moment, with easeful death. 'Oh, let's stop arguing. Get rid of the blot, confirm Henry in the job and we need say no more about it.'

'I'm sure you'll find Vincent Blewitt a great asset to chambers, Rumpole. He's a very human sort of person. He likes his joke, I understand. I'm sure you'll have plenty of laughs together.'

'If he stays . . .'

'He *is* staying . . .'

'Then I'll take a handful of pills, washed down with a glass of whisky, and cease upon the midnight with no pain.'

'If you wish to do that, Rumpole' – our learned head of chambers sat down at his desk and pretended to be busy with a set of papers – 'that is entirely a matter for you.'

That evening, before the news, Ballard's favourite commercial about business making the world go round came on. Later there were some pictures of a Pro-Life demonstration outside an abortion clinic in St John's Wood. Prominent among those present was a serious, long-faced woman with reddish hair. Nurse Pargey was waving a placard on which were written the words THOU SHALT NOT KILL.

'Alzheimer's isn't a killer in itself. Certainly the patient gets weaker and more forgetful. Helpless, in fact. But it would need something more to kill Chippy.'

'Like an overdose of sleeping pills, for instance?'

'Evidently that's what did it.' Dr Betty was one of those awkward clients, it seemed, who felt impelled to tell the truth. And what she went on to say wasn't particularly helpful. 'I might have given Chippy an overdose of something when the time came, but it hadn't come on the night he died. You must believe that, Horace.'

'Whether I believe it or not isn't exactly the point. What matters is whether the jury believe it.'

'That's for them to decide, isn't it?'

'I'm afraid it is.' At which moment there was a rapid knock on the door which immediately opened to admit Blewitt's head. He took a quick look at the assembled company and said, 'Sorry folks! Mustn't interrupt the workers' productivity. Speak to you later, Horace.' At which, as rare things will, he vanished.

'Who on earth was that extraordinary man?' For the first time Dr Betty looked shaken.

'A temporary visitor,' I told her. 'Nothing for you to worry about. Now tell me about the sleeping pills.'

'I gave him two.'

'And you saw him drink his whisky?'

'A small whisky and soda. Yes.'

'And then . . . ?'

'Well, I settled him down for the night.'

'Did he go to sleep?'

'He seemed tired and dreamy. He'd been quite contented that day, in fact. But incontinent, of course. Quite soon after he'd settled down, I heard the Chippenhams come home from their dinner party, so I went downstairs to meet them.'

'What happened to the bottle of pills?'

'Well, that was kept in the house so that the Chippenhams or Nurse Pargeter could give Chippy his pills when I wasn't there.'

'Kept where in the house?'

'I put them back in the bathroom cupboard.'

'Are there two bathrooms?'

'Yes. The one next to the judge's bedroom. You know the house?' Dr Betty looked surprised.

'I have a certain nodding acquaintance with it. And young Andrew?'

'His mother had sent him up to bed before they went out. But I'm afraid he hadn't gone to sleep.'

'How do you know that?'

'When I went to put the pills back in the bathroom, I saw his light on and his bedroom door open. He was still reading – or playing with his model aeroplanes more likely.'

'Quite likely, yes. Oh, one other thing. Had you ever spoken to Chippy about Lethe?'

'No, certainly not. I told you, Horace. The time had not come.'

'And was anyone else Chippy knew a member of Lethe? Any friends or his family?'

'Oh, no, I'm sure they weren't.'

'I think it might be just worth getting a statement from a Dr Eames.' I turned to Bonny Bernard, my instructing solicitor. 'Oh, and a few enquiries about the firm of Marcellus & Chippenham, house agents and surveyors.'

'David Eames?' Dr Betty looked doubtful.

'He treated Chippy before you came on the scene. He might know if he'd ever talked of suicide.'

Dr Betty once again spurned a line of defence. 'As I told you, I'm quite sure he never contemplated such a thing.'

'So if you didn't kill him, Dr Betty, who do you think did?'

She was looking at me, quite serious then, as she said, 'Well, that's not for me to say, is it?'

'Sorry to have intruded on your conference. Although it may be no bad thing for me to make spot checks on the human resource in the workplace.'

I had hardly recovered from the gloomy prospect of defending Dr Betty when the Blight was with me again. I sat, sunk in thought.

'Cheer up, Horace.' Vince's laugh was like a bath running out. 'It may never happen.' As he said that, I regretted having used the same fatuous words of encouragement to Henry, our condemned clerk. Most of the worst things in life are absolutely bound to happen, the trial of the cheerful doctor, for instance, or death itself.

'I wanted a word or two with you about formalizing staff holidays. You thinking of getting away to the sun yourself?'

'Hardly,' I told him, 'having glanced at the brochure you gave Dot Clapton.'

'Sea, sand and sex, Rumpole. You'd enjoy that. Very relaxing,' Vince gurgled.

'I'm hardly a single.'

'Well, send the wife on a tour of the Lake District or something, and you head off to the Costa del Sol. That's my advice. I mean, when you're invited to a gourmet dinner, why take a ham sandwich?'

I looked at Vincent Blewitt with a wild surmise. Was there no limit to the awfulness of the man? I could imagine no matrimonial situation, however grim, in which I could tell Hilda that she was a ham sandwich.

'I've rota'd Dot early July in the format,' Vince told me. 'I don't think she can wait to join me and assorted singles.'

I thought of telling him that Dot didn't even like the Costa del Sol. That she didn't think that sex and sand made a good mix. That she had a romantic nature and she wanted to drift past the castles on the Rhine listening to the Lorelei's mystic note. Some glimmering hope, a faint idea of a plan, led me to encourage the Blot. 'Considerable fun, these singles holidays, are they, Vincent?'

'You're not joking!' He had now sunk into my client's armchair and stuck out his legs in anticipation of delight. 'First day you get there, as soon as you've got checked in, it's down to the beach for games to break the ice.'

'Games?'

'I'll just tell you one. Whet your appetite.'

'Carry on.'

'The fellas get to blow up balloons inside the girls' bikini bottoms. And then the girls do it vice versa in our shorts. By the time we've played that, everyone's a swinger.'

I looked longingly at the door, thinking how restful the forthcoming murder trial would be, compared with a quiet chat with our legal administrator.

'It sounds very tasteful.'

'I think you've got the message. I'll rota you for a couple of weeks then. After Dot and I have left the Costa, of course. I never knew you were a swinger, Horace.'

'Oh, we all have our joys and desires.'

'Don't we just!' Vincent looked at me, I thought, with unusual respect. 'Heard any good ones lately?'

'Ones?'

'You know. Jokes. You've got hidden talents, Horace. I bet you know about rib-ticklers.'

'You mean' – I looked at him seriously – 'like the one about the sleeveless woman?'

'Isn't that a *great* story?' Happily Vincent knew this anecdote and he gurgled again. 'Laughed like a drain when I first heard it. Whoever told you that one, Horace?'

I looked him straight in the eye and lied with complete conviction, 'Oh, Sam told me that. It's just his type of humour.'

'Sam?' Vincent was puzzled.

'You know, our learned head of chambers, Soapy Sam Ballard.'

I have often noticed that before any big and important cause or matter – and no one could doubt the size and importance of *R. v. Dr Betty* – a kind of peace descends on my legal business. In other words, I hit a slump. I had nothing in court, not even the smallest spot of indecency at Uxbridge. I had no conferences booked and those scurrying about their business in the Temple, or waiting in the corridors of the Old Bailey, might well have come to the conclusion that old Rumpole had ceased upon the midnight hour with no pain. In fact I was docked in Froxbury Mansions with my ham – no, I will not be infected by Vince's vulgarity – with She Who Must Be Obeyed.

Needless to say, I had no wish to spend twenty-four hours a day closeted with Hilda, so I went on a number of errands to the newsagent in search of small cigars, to the off-licence at the other end of Gloucester Road to purchase plonk, stretch my legs and breathe in the petrol fumes.

I was walking, wrapped in thought, through Canning Place, when I saw the familiar sight of purple blazers marching towards me in strict battle formation, led by a sharp-faced young female wearing a tweed skirt and an anorak, who uttered words of command or turned to rebuke stragglers. I stood politely in the gutter to let them pass, raising my umbrella in a kind of salute when I saw, taking up the rearguard, Andrew Chippenham.

'Andrew!' I called out in my matiest tones 'How are you, old boy? Marching up with your regiment to lay siege to the Albert Hall, are you? Or on the hunt for bin bags?'

It was not at all, I'm sure you'll agree, an alarming sally. I intended to be friendly and jocular, but when he heard my voice young Andrew stopped, apparently frozen, his head down. He raised it slowly and what I saw was a small, serious boy frozen in terror. Before I could speak again, he had turned and run off after his vanishing crocodile.

I was finding this enforced home leave so tedious that, a few days later, I took a trip on the tube back to my chambers in the Temple, although I had no business engagements. I was sunk in the swing chair with my feet on the desktop workspace, trying to fathom out the depths of ingenuity to which the setter of *The Times* crossword puzzle might have sunk, when the Blot oozed through the door and defiled my carpet.

'I thought it might be rather appropriate,' he said in the sort of solemn voice people use when they're discussing funeral arrangements, 'if we gave a great party in chambers to mark Henry's career change.'

'What's that called?' I asked him. 'Easing the passing?'

'At least give him a smashing send-off.'

'I suppose he can live on that as his retirement pension.'

'I'm sure Henry has got a bit put by.'

'He hasn't got a job put by. I happen to know that.' And then some sort of a plan began to take shape in my mind. 'Why does it have to be a *great* party?'

'Because' – and then Vince looked at me in a horribly conspiratorial fashion as the penny dropped. 'Horace, you're not suggesting?'

'A bit of a singles do, why not?'

'Leave the ham sandwiches at home, eh?'

'Exactly!' I forced myself to say it, although it stuck in my throat.

'I mean, we'd ask Dot Clapton, wouldn't we?'

'Of course,' I reassured him.

'And some of the gorgeous bits that float around the Temple.'

'As many of them as you can cram in. We'll make it a real send-off for Henry.'

'Something he'll remember all his life.'

'Certainly.'

'Only one drawback, as far as I know.'

'What's that?'

'We'll have to ask permission from the head of chambers.' Vincent looked doubtful and disappointed.

'The head of chambers would be furious if he weren't included,' I assured him, and the gurgling laughter was turned on again.

'Of course. I remember what you told me about Sam Ballard. A bit of a swinger, didn't you indicate?'

'Bollard,' I said, remembering an old song of my middle age, ' "swings as the pendulum do". Put the whole proposition to him, Vincent. Put it in detail, not forgetting the balloons blown up in the trousers, and then watch his eyes light up.'

'We're in for a good time, then?'

'I think so. At very long last.'

After the Blot had left me, suitably encouraged, I went home on the Underground. Emerging from Gloucester Road station, I saw the formation of purple blazers bearing down on me remorselessly on what must have been the last route-march of the day. I stood aside to let them pass, but the CO halted the column and looked at me, through a pair of horn-rimmed spectacles, with obvious distaste. 'Are you the person who spoke to Chippenham the other day, down at the end of the line?' she asked me. 'The boys told me he had spoken to somebody strange.'

'It just so happened' – I decided to overlook the description – 'that I know the family.'

'Whether you do or you don't' – she frowned severely – 'he was clearly upset by what you said to him. It's most unusual for people to speak to my Bolingbrokers in the street. He was obviously shocked, the other boys said so. Ever since he met you, Chippenham's been away sick.'

'But I honestly didn't say anything,' I started to explain but, before I could finish the sentence, the word of command had been given and the column quick-marched away from me.

When I got back to the seclusion of the mansion flat (there were times when I felt that our chilly matrimonial home was more a mausoleum than a mansion), I found Hilda had gone to her bridge club and left a message for me to ring my instructing solicitor and 'make sure neither of you slip up on Dr Betty's case'. When I got through to Bonny Bernard, he had news which interested me greatly. The puritanical Dr Eames had, it seemed, returned to care for the Chippenham family and, in particular, he was looking after young Andrew, who was suffering from some sort of nervous illness and was off school. As a witness, Bernard told me, Dr Eames was of the talkative variety and seemed to have something he was strangely anxious to tell me. I hoped he would become even more talkative in the days before the trial.

I discovered that our case was to come before Mrs Justice Erskine-Brown, for so long the Portia of our chambers and its acknowledged beauty (even now, when she is Dame Phillida and swathed in the scarlet and ermine of a High Court judge, she is a figure that the unspeakable Vince might well have wanted to lure into a singles holiday on the Costa del Sand and Sex). I had known her since she had joined us as a tearful pupil; we had been together and against each other, and I had taught her enough to turn her into a formidable opponent, in more trials than I care to remember. She was brave, tenacious, charming and provocative as compared with her husband Claude who, upon his hind legs in any courtroom, could be counted upon to appear nervous, hesitant and unconvincing. I have a distinct fondness for Portia which I have reason to believe, because of the way she behaved during the many crises in Equity Court, is suitably returned. In short, we have a mutual regard, and I hoped she might feel some sympathy for a case which, in other hands, was likely to prove equally difficult for Dr Betty Ireton and Horace Rumpole. There, hopes were dashed quite early on in the proceedings.

'It may be argued on behalf of the defence . . .' The prosecutor was the beefy QC, Barrington McTear. He had played rugby football for Oxford and his courtroom tactics consisted of pushing, shoving, tackling low and covering his opponents, whenever possible, with mud. Although his name had a Highland ring to it, he spoke in an arrogant and earblasting Etonian accent and considered himself a cut above such middle-class, possibly overweight and certainly unsporty barristers as myself. For this reason I had privately christened him Cut Above McTear.

Cut Above had massive shoulders, a large, pink face and small, gold half-glasses. They perched on him as inappropriately as a thin, gold necklace on a ham. Now, in a voice that could have been heard from one end of a football field to the other, he repeated what he thought would be my defence for the purpose of bringing it sprawling to the ground in a particularly unpleasant tackle. 'Your Ladyship may well think that Mr Rumpole's defence will be "This old gentleman was on his way out anyway, so Dr Ireton committed an act of mercy and not an act of murder" . . .'

'Such a defence will receive very little sympathy in this court, Mr McTear.' Portia was clearly not in a mood to fuss about the quality of mercy. 'Murder is murder until Parliament chooses to pass a law permitting euthanasia.'

'Oh, I do so entirely agree with your Ladyship,' Cut Above informed the Bench and probably those assembled in the corridor and nearby courts, 'so it will be interesting to discover if Mr Rumpole has a defence.'

'May I remind my learned friend' – I climbed to my feet and spoke, I think with admirable courtesy – 'that a prosecutor's job is to prove the charge and not to speculate about the nature of the defence. If he wishes any further advice on how to conduct his case, I shall be available during the adjournment.'

'I hardly need advice on prosecuting from Mr Rumpole, who hasn't done any of it!' Cut Above bellowed.

'Gentlemen' – Portia's quiet call to order was always effective – 'perhaps we should get on with the evidence. No doubt we shall hear from Mr Rumpole in the fullness of time.'

So Cut Above turned to tell the jury that they would find the evidence he was about to call entirely persuasive and leading to the inevitable verdict of guilty on Dr Ireton. A glance at Hilda, who had come to support her friend and make sure that I secured her deliverance from the dock, was enough to tell me that She Who Must Be Obeyed didn't think much of my performance so far.

Dick Chippenham was the sort of witness that Cut Above could understand and respect. They probably went to the same tailor and played the same games at the same sort of schools and universities. Dick even spoke in Cut Above's sort of voice, although with the volume turned down considerably. When he had finished his examination Cut Above said, 'I'm afraid I'll have to trouble you to wait there for a few minutes more,' as though there was an unfortunate deputation from the peasantry to trouble him, but it needn't detain him long.

'Mr Chippenham, I'm sure all of us at the Bar wish to sympathize with you in your bereavement.'

'Thank you.' I glanced at the jury. They clearly liked my opening gambit, one that Cut Above hadn't troubled himself to think of.

'I have only a few questions. Up to six months before he died, your uncle was attended by Dr Eames?'

'That is so.'

'But, rightly or wrongly, your uncle took against Dr Eames?'

'I'm afraid so.'

'That doctor not being convinced of the therapeutic effects of whisky and claret?'

I got a ripple of laughter from the jury and a smile of assurance from the witness. 'I believe that was the reason.'

'So you then engaged Dr Ireton. Why did you choose her?'

'She was a local doctor who had treated one of my wife's friends.'

'At the time when you transferred to Dr Ireton, did you know that she was a member of Lethe, a pro-euthanasia society?'

'Mr Rumpole admits that she was a member of Lethe.' Cut Above sprang to attention. 'I hope the jury have noticed this admission by the defence,' he bellowed.

'I'm sure you can't have helped noticing that,' I told the jury. 'And I'm sure that, during any further speeches from my learned friend, earplugs will be provided for those not already hard of hearing.'

'Mr Rumpole!' Portia rebuked me from the Bench. 'This is a serious case and I wish to see it is tried seriously.'

'An admirable ambition, my Lady,' I told her. 'And tried quietly too, I hope.' And then I turned to the witness before Cut Above could trumpet any sort of protest.

'When you and your wife got back from the dinner party, it was about eleven o'clock?'

'Yes.'

'And apart from your uncle, the only people in the house were Dr Betty Ireton and your son?'

'That's right. Dr Betty met us in the hall and she said she'd given Chippy his pills and a drink of whisky.'

'At that time, would your uncle have remembered whether he'd taken his pills or not?'

'He probably would have remembered. Dr Betty said she'd given him his pills as usual.'

'When you got upstairs, you went in to see your uncle?'

'We did.'

'Was he asleep?'

'Yes.'

'Was he still breathing?'

'I'm sure he was. Otherwise we'd have called for help immediately.'

'You noticed the bottle of whisky. Was it empty?'

'It must have been, but I can't say I noticed it then.'

'So perhaps it wasn't empty?'

'I can't say for sure, but I suppose it must have been.'

'You can't say for sure. And the bottle of pills had been put away in the bathroom?'

'Yes, I believe it had . . . My wife will tell you.'

'So you can't be sure how many pills were left when you last saw your uncle alive?'

'In the morning I saw the bottle of pills empty.'

'And in the morning your uncle was dead?'

'Yes, he was.'

'Thank you very much, Mr Chippenham.' I sat down with what I hoped was a good deal more show of satisfaction than I felt.

'Dr Betty said she thinks you and that deafening McTear person are behaving like a couple of small boys in the school playground.'

I thought it was perhaps unfortunate that Dr Betty was allowed bail if she was going to abuse her freedom by criticizing my forensic skills. 'She only sees what happens on the surface. Tactics, Hilda. She's no idea of the plans that are forming at the back of my mind.'

'Have you any idea of them either, Rumpole? Be honest. Or have you forgotten that, in the way you forgot to turn out the bathroom light when you'd finished shaving?'

It was breakfast time once again in Froxbury Mansions. I felt a longing to get away from the sharp cut-and-thrust of domestic argument and be off to the gentler world of the Old Bailey. Hilda pressed home her advantage. 'I hope you realize that I am personally committed to your winning this case, Rumpole. I have given my word to Dr Betty.'

Then you'd better ask for it back again, was what I might have said, but lacked the bottle. Instead I told Hilda that Dr Eames was going to give us a full statement which I thought might be helpful. At which, I gathered up my traps, ready to hotfoot it down to the Old Bailey canteen where I had a date with the industrious Bernard.

'You certainly need help from somewhere, Rumpole. And, I don't know if you noticed, you've left me your briefcase and taken my *Daily Telegraph.*' As I made the changeover, She said, 'We've learnt a lot lately, haven't we, about the onset of Alzheimer's disease?'

Dr David Eames was a rare bird, a doctor who liked talking to lawyers. He was tall, bony, with large, capable hands and a lock of fair hair that fell over his eyes, and a serious, enthusiastic way of speaking as though he hadn't yet lost his boyish faith in human nature, the National Health Service and the practise of medicine. I don't usually have much feeling for those who seek to deprive their fellow beings of their claret, but I felt a strange liking for this youthful quack who seemed only anxious to discover the truth about the fatal events which had taken place that night in Dettingen Road.

As we sat with Bernard in the Old Bailey canteen, with coffee from a machine, and went through the medical evidence, I noticed he was strangely excited, as though he had something to communicate but was not sure when, or if indeed ever, to communicate it.

'I'm right in thinking Alzheimer's is not a killer in itself, although those who contract it usually die within ten years?'

'That's right,' Eames agreed. 'They contract bronchitis or have a stroke, or perhaps they just lose their wish to live.'

'There's no evidence of bronchitis or a stroke here?'

'Apparently not.'

'So it seems likely that death was hurried on in some way?'

There was a silence, then Dr Eames said, 'I think that must follow.'

'My old friend and opponent, Dr Ackerman of the morgue, the Home Office pathologist, estimates death as between ten p.m. and one a.m.'

'I read that.'

'At any rate, he was dead by seven-thirty a.m. when Nurse Pargeter came to look after him. Dick Chippenham says that Chippy was alive and sleeping well at around eleven the night before. If Dr Betty had just given him an overdose . . .'

'The pills might not have taken their effect until some time later.'

'I was afraid you'd say that.' I took a gulp from the machine's coffee, which is pretty indistinguishable from the machine's tea, or the machine's soup if it comes to that. 'When you stopped being the Chippenhams' doctor . . .'

'When I was sacked, you mean?'

'If you like. Had you had a row with Chippy? I mean, did *he* sack you?'

'Not really. As far as I remember, it was Mr Chippenham who told me his uncle wanted me to go.'

'There was no question of you having had a row with Chippy about drinking whisky?'

'No. I can't remember anything like that.' The doctor looked puzzled and I felt curiously encouraged and lit a small cigar.

'Tell me, Doctor, did you know Nurse Pargeter?'

'Only too well.'

'And did you like her?'

'Pro-Life nurses can be a menace. They seem to think of themselves as avenging angels.'

'And she didn't care for Dr Betty?'

'She hated her! I think she thought of her as a potential murderess.'

I wondered if that might be helpful. Then I said, 'One more thing, Dr Eames, now that I've got you here . . .'

'What are you up to *now*, Rumpole? Talking to potential witnesses?

Is that in the best tradition of the Bar?' Wasn't Stentor some old Greek military man whose voice, on the battlefield, was louder than fifty men together? No doubt his direct descendant was the stentorian Cut Above, who now stood with his wig in his hand, his thick hair interrupted by a little tonsure of baldness so that he looked like a muscular monk.

'I am consulting with an expert witness. A doctor of medicine,' I told Cut Above. 'And for counsel to see expert witnesses is certainly in the best tradition of the Bar.'

'I'm warning you. Just watch it, Rumpole. Watch it extremely carefully. I don't want to have to report you to her lovely Ladyship for unprofessional conduct.' My opponent gave a bellow of laughter which rattled the coffee cups and passed on with his myrmidons, a junior barrister and a wiry little scrum-half from the DPP's office.

'Who's that appalling bully?' Dr Eames appeared shocked.

'Cut Above, QC, counsel for the prosecution.'

'I've known surgeons like that. Full of themselves and care nothing for the patient. Doesn't he want me to talk to you?' I think it was Cut Above's appearance and interruption which persuaded Dr Eames to tell me all he eventually did.

'Probably not. I want to talk to you, though. Aren't you treating young Andrew? He seemed a charming boy!'

'I'm not sure what's the matter with him. Some sort of nervous trouble. Something's worrying him terribly.' Dr Eames also looked worried.

'I spoke to him in the street, and a schoolmistress ticked me off for it. But that couldn't have had anything to do with his illness, could it?'

'I'm afraid you reminded him of something.' I felt a prickle of excitement. Dr Eames was about to reveal some evidence of great importance.

'What exactly?'

'I think I know. It was something you'd said before, when you came to the house. It reminded him of his dream.'

At a nearby table Cut Above was yelling orders to his junior. If

Dr Eames hadn't taken such an instant dislike to my opponent he might never have told me about young Andrew's dream.

Without doubt, the jury took strongly to Ursula Chippenham and I have to say that I also liked her. Standing in the box with her honey-coloured hair a little untidy, a scarf floating about her neck, her gentle voice sounding touchingly brave, yet clearly audible, she was the perfect prosecution witness. She showed no hatred of Dr Betty; she spoke glowingly of her care and friendship for the old judge; and she was only saddened by what the doctor's principles had led her to do. 'I'm quite sure that Dr Betty was only doing what she thought was right and merciful,' she said. Having got this perfect, and unhappily convincing, answer, even Cut Above had the good sense to shut up and sit down.

If I'd wanted to lose Dr Betty's case I'd've gone in to the attack on Ursula with my guns blazing. Of course I didn't. I started by roaring as gently as any sucking dove, showing the jury how much more polite and considerate I could be than Cut Above at his most gentlemanly.

'Mrs Chippenham, I hope it won't offend you if I call the deceased judge, Chippy?'

'Not at all, Mr Rumpole.' Ursula's smile could win all hearts. 'We both knew and loved him, I know. I'm sure he would have liked us to call him that.'

'And that's how he was affectionately known at the Bar,' Portia added to the warmth of the occasion.

'And Chippy was extremely ill?'

'Yes, he was.'

'And, entirely to your credit, you and your husband looked after him? With medical help?'

'We did our best. Yes.'

'He was unlikely to recover?'

'He wasn't going to recover. I don't think there's a cure for Alzheimer's.'

'Can we come to the time when Dr Betty started to treat Chippy? Was Nurse Pargeter coming in then?'

'Yes, she was.'

'And Nurse Pargeter strongly disapproved of Dr Betty's support for legalizing euthanasia?'

'She warned us about Dr Betty, yes.'

'And you discussed the matter with your husband?'

'Oh, yes. We thought about it very carefully. And then I had a talk about it with Dr Betty.'

'Did you?' I looked mildly, ever so mildly, surprised. 'Was your husband present?'

'No, I didn't want it to be too formal. We just chatted over coffee, and Dr Betty promised me she wouldn't give Chippy . . . Well, give him anything to stop keeping him alive, without discussing it with the family.'

I looked around at the dock where Dr Betty was shaking her head decisively. So I was put in the embarrassing position of having to call the witness a liar.

'Mrs Chippenham, I have to remind you that you said nothing about this conversation with Dr Betty in your original statement to the police.'

'Didn't I? I'm afraid I was upset and rather flustered at that time.' Ursula turned to the judge, 'I do hope you can understand?'

'Of course,' Portia understood, 'but can I just ask you this, Mrs Chippenham? If Dr Ireton had come to you and recommended ending Chippy's life what would you have said?'

'Neither Dick nor I would have agreed to it. Not in any circumstances. We may not go to church very much, but we do believe that life is sacred.'

' "We do believe that life is sacred," ' Portia repeated as she wrote the words down, and we all waited in respectful silence. 'Yes, Mr Rumpole?'

'We've heard that it was Nurse Pargeter who found Chippy dead.'

'Yes, she called for me and I joined her.'

'And it was Nurse Pargeter who reported the circumstances of Chippy's death to the police?'

'She insisted on doing so.'

'And you agreed?'

'I think I was too upset to agree or disagree.'

'I see. Now, that morning, when the nurse found Chippy dead, the whisky bottle was almost empty and the bottle of sleeping pills empty. You don't know how that came about?'

'I assumed that Dr Betty gave Chippy the overdose and the whisky.'

'You assumed that because she's a well-known supporter of euthanasia?'

'Well, yes, I suppose so.' Ursula frowned a little then and looked puzzled, but as attractive as ever.

'Because she believes in euthanasia, she's the most likely suspect?'

'Isn't that obvious, Mr Rumpole?' Portia answered the question for the witness.

'And because she was the most likely suspect, is that why you decided to ask her to look after Chippy?' I asked Ursula the first hostile question with my usual charm.

'I'm not sure I understand what you mean?' Ursula smiled in a puzzled sort of way at the jury, and they looked entirely sympathetic.

'I'm not sure I understand either.' Portia sounded distinctly unfriendly to counsel for the defence.

'I'll come back to it later, if I may. Mrs Chippenham, we've got a copy of Chippy's will. Nurse Pargeter does quite well out of it, doesn't she? She gets a substantial legacy.'

'Twenty thousand pounds. She did a great deal for Chippy.'

'And let me ask you this. Your husband's in business as an estate agent, is he not?'

'Marcellus & Chippenham, yes.'

'It's going through a pretty difficult time, isn't it?'

'I think the housing market is having a lot of difficulty, yes.'

'As we all know, Mr Rumpole.' The Erskine-Browns were trying to get rid of a house in Islington and move into central London, so the learned judge spoke from the heart.

'Let's say that the freehold of the house in Dettingen Road and the residue of Chippy's estate might solve a good many of your problems. Isn't that right?'

The jury looked at me as though I had suggested that Mother Teresa was only in it for the money and Ursula gave exactly the right answer. 'We were both extremely grateful for what Chippy decided to do for us.' Then she spoilt it a little by adding, 'When he made that will, he understood it perfectly.'

'And I am sure he was conscious of all you and your husband were doing for *him*?' Portia was firmly on Ursula's side.

'Thank you, my Lady.' Ursula didn't bob a curtsey, but it seemed, for a moment, as if she was tempted to do so.

'Mrs Chippenham, you know the way the Lethe organization recommends helping sufferers out of this wicked world?'

'I'm afraid I don't.'

'Are you sure? Didn't Nurse Pargeter give you a pamphlet like this when she was trying to persuade you not to engage Dr Betty?' I handed her the Lethe pamphlet which Bonny Bernard had got me and it was made Defence Exhibit One. Then I asked the witness to turn to page three where a recipe for easeful death was set out. I read it aloud: ' "The method recommended is a large dose of sleeping pills which are readily obtainable on prescription and a strong alcoholic drink such as whisky or brandy. When the patient is asleep, a long plastic bin-liner is placed over the head and pulled over the shoulders. Being deprived of air, the sleep is gentle, painless and permanent." Did you read that when Nurse Pargeter gave you the pamphlet?'

There was a silence and the courtroom seemed to have become suddenly chilly. Then Ursula answered, more quietly than before, 'I may have glanced at it.'

'*You* may have glanced at it. But I suggest that someone in your house remembered it quite clearly when old Chippy was helped out of this troubled world.'

Of course there was an immediate hullabaloo. Cut Above trumpeted that there was no basis at all for that perfectly outrageous suggestion, and Portia, in more measured tones, asked me to make it clear what my suggestion was. I said I was perfectly prepared to do so.

'I suggest someone woke Chippy up, around midnight. He hadn't remembered taking his pills, of course, so he was given a liberal overdose, washed down with a large whisky. One of the long black bin-liners that your dustmen provide so generously was then made use of.'

Ursula was silent, but counsel for the prosecution wasn't. 'I hope, my Lady, that Mr Rumpole will be calling evidence to support this extraordinary charge?'

I didn't answer him, but asked the witness, 'Your son Andrew hasn't been well lately?'

'I'm afraid not.' Ursula recovered her voice, thinking I'd passed to another subject.

'Mr Rumpole' – Portia was clearly displeased – 'the court would also like to know if you are going to call evidence to support the charge you have made.'

'I'm happy to deal with that, my Lady, when I've asked a few more questions.' I turned back to the witness. 'Is Dr Eames treating young Andrew?'

'Yes, Dr Eames has come back to us.'

'Is Andrew's illness of a nervous nature? I mean, has he become worried about something?'

'I don't know. He's had sick headaches and we've kept him out of school. Dr Eames isn't sure what the trouble is exactly.'

'Is Andrew worried by something he might have seen the night Chippy died? Remember, he sleeps with his door open and Chippy's room is immediately opposite. He saw something that night which has worried him ever since. Perhaps that's why he collects the plastic bags from the dustbins and hides them away. Is it because he knows bin bags can cause accidents?'

Ursula's voice slid upwards and became shrill as she asked, 'You say he saw . . . What did he see?'

'He thought it was a dream. But it wasn't a dream, was it?'

'My Lady, are we really being asked to sit here while Mr Rumpole trots out the dreams of a ten-year-old child?' Cut Above boomed, but I interrupted his cannonade.

'I'm not discussing dreams! I'm discussing facts. And the fact is' – I turned to Ursula – 'that you were coming out of Chippy's room that night, perhaps to take the empty bottle of pills back to the bathroom. It was then Andrew saw Chippy propped up on the pillows.

Shrouded, Mrs Chippenham. Suffocated, Mrs Chippenham, with a black plastic bag pulled down over his head.'

The court was cold now, and silent. Ursula looked at the judge who said nothing, and at the jury who said nothing either. Her beauty had gone as she became desperate, like a trapped animal. I saw Hilda watching and she appeared triumphant. I saw Dr Betty lean forward as though concerned for a patient who had taken a turn for the worse. When Ursula spoke, her voice was hoarse and hopeless. She said, 'You're not going to bring Andrew here to say that about the plastic bag, are you?'

I hated my job then. Chippy was dying anyway, so why should either Dr Betty, or this suffering woman, be cursed for ever by his death? I felt tired and longed to shut up and sit down, but if I had to choose between Ursula and Dr Betty, I knew I had to protect my client. So I took in a deep breath and said, 'That entirely depends, Mrs Chippenham, on whether you're going to tell us the truth.'

To her credit she didn't hesitate. She was determined to spare her son, so she turned to Portia and said quietly, 'I don't think he suffered and he would have died anyway. When I thought of doing it, I got Dr Ireton to treat Chippy so she would be blamed. That's all I have got to say.' Then she stood, stunned, like the victim of an accident, as though she didn't yet understand the consequences of any of the things she'd done or said.

When I came out of court, I felt no elation. Cut Above, almost, for him, pianissimo, had offered no further evidence after Ursula's admission, and the case was over very quickly. I had notched a win, but I felt no triumph. I saw the inspector in charge of the case talking to Dick and Ursula, and when I thought of their future, and Andrew's, I hated what I had done. The merciful tide of forgetfulness which engulfs disastrous days in court, sinking them in fresh briefs and newer troubles, would be slow to come. Then I saw Hilda embrace Dr Betty and give her one of She Who Must Be Obeyed's rare kisses. My wife turned to me with a look of approval which was also rare; it was as though I were some sort of domestic appliance, a food blender perhaps, or an electric blanket, she had lent to an old friend and which, for once, worked satisfactorily. They asked me to join them for coffee and went away as happy as they must have been when young Betty Ireton led the school team to another victory. Bonny Bernard went about his business and I stood alone, outside the empty court.

'Rumpole, a word with you, if you please, in a matter of urgency.'

Soapy Sam Ballard had paused, wigged and gowned, in full flight to another court. He looked pale and agitated to such an extent that I was about to greet him with a quotation I thought might be appropriate: 'The devil damn thee black, thou cream-fac'd loon! Where gott'st thou that goose look?' Before I could speak, however, Soapy Sam started to burble. 'Bad news, I'm afraid. Very bad news indeed. We shall not be entering into a contract of service with Vincent Blewitt.'

I managed to restrain my tears. 'But Bollard,' I protested, 'didn't you think he was the very man for the job?'

'I did. Until he came to me with an idea for a chambers party. Did you know anything about this, Rumpole?' The man was suddenly suspicious.

'He told me he wanted to give Henry some kind of a send-off. I thought it was rather generous of him.'

'But did he tell you exactly what sort of send-off he had in mind?'

'A chambers party, I think he said. I can't remember the details.'

'He described it as a singles party. At first, I thought he was suggesting tennis.'

'A natural assumption.'

'And then he asked me to leave my ham sandwich at home – I wondered what on earth the man was talking about. I mean, it's never been my custom to bring any sort of sandwich to a chambers party. Your wife's friend, Dodo Mackintosh, usually provides the nibbles.'

'Have you any idea, Ballard' – I looked suitably mystified – 'what he meant?'

'I have now. He was talking about my wife, Marguerite.'

'Marguerite, who once held the responsible position of matron at the Old Bailey?'

'That is exactly whom he meant.'

'Who was known, even to the Red Judges, as 'Matey'?

'Marguerite got on very well with the judiciary. She treated many of them.'

'Can I believe my ears? Vincent Blewitt called your Marguerite a ham sandwich?' I was incredulous.

'I can't imagine what she would have to say if she ever got wind of it.'

'All hell would break loose?'

'Indeed it would!' Ballard nodded sadly and went on, 'He said we'd all have more fun if I left her at home. And the same applied to your Hilda.'

'Ballard, I can see why you're concerned.' I sounded most reasonable. 'It was a serious error of judgement on Blewitt's part, but if that was the only thing . . .'

'It was not the only thing, Rumpole.'

'You mean there's worse to come?'

'Considerably worse!' Ballard looked around nervously to make sure he wasn't overheard. 'He suggested that the party should start . . . I don't know how to tell you this, Rumpole.'

'Just take it slowly. I understand that it must be distressing.'

'It is, Rumpole. It certainly is. He thought the party should start . . .' Soapy Sam paused and then the words came tumbling out. '. . . By the male members of chambers and the girl guests blowing up balloons inside each other's underclothes. Rumpole, can you imagine what Marguerite would have said to that?'

'I thought Marguerite was to be left at home.'

'There is that, of course. But he wanted Mrs Justice Erskine-Brown to come. What would she have said if Blewitt had approached her with a balloon?'

'She'd have jailed him for contempt.'

'Quite right too! And then to top it all . . .'

'He topped that?'

'He said he knew I liked a good story, and wasn't that a great joke about the sleeveless woman?'

'What on earth was he talking about?' I looked suitably mystified.

'I have no idea. Do you know any story about a sleeveless woman?'

'Certainly not!' I replied with absolute truth.

'So then he told me about a legless nun. It was clearly obscene but I'm afraid, Rumpole, the point escaped me.'

'Probably just as well.'

'I'm afraid I shall have to tell chambers. I'm informing you first as a senior member. We shall not be employing Vincent Blewitt or indeed any legal administrator in the foreseeable future.'

'It will be a disappointment, perhaps. But I'm sure we'll all understand.'

'Henry may have had his faults, Rumpole. But he calls me sir and not Sam. And I don't believe he knows any jokes at all.'

'Of course not. No, indeed.'

The case of *R. v. Ireton* had not, so far as I was concerned, ended happily. *Rumpole v. Blewitt*, on the other hand, was an undoubted victory. Win a few, lose a few. That is all you can say about life at the Bar.

Henry decided, in his considerable relief, that he should have a chambers party to celebrate his not leaving. All the wives came. Hilda's old schoolfriend Dodo Mackintosh provided the cheesy bits and, perhaps because he had a vague idea of what I had been able to do for him, our clerk laid on a couple of dozen of the Château Thames Embankment of which I drank fairly deep. The day after this jamboree, I was detained in bed with a ferocious headache and a distinct unsteadiness in the leg department.

In a brief period of troubled sleep about midday, I heard voices from the living-room and then the door opened quietly and the Angel of Death was at my bedside. 'Mr Rumpole,' she smiled and her glasses twinkled, 'I hear you're not feeling very well this morning.'

'Really?' I muttered with sudden alarm. 'Whatever gave you that idea? I'm feeling on top of the world, in absolutely' – and here I winced at a sudden stabbing pain across the temples – 'tiptop condition.'

'And Hilda tells me the dear old mind's not what it was?' Dr Betty smiled understandingly. 'The butter knife in the top pocket, is that what she told me? Dear Mr Rumpole, do remember I'm here to help you. There's no need for you to suffer. The way out is always open, and I can steer you gently and quite painlessly towards it.'

'I'm afraid I must ask you to leave now,' I told the Angel of Death. 'Got to get up. Late for work already. As I told you, I never felt better. Full of beans, Dr Betty, and raring to go.'

God knows how I ever managed to climb into the striped trousers, or button the collar, but when I was decently clad I hotfooted it for the Temple. There, I sat in my room suffering, my head in my hands, determined at all costs to keep myself alive.

Rumpole and the Old Familiar Faces

In the varied ups and downs, the thrills and spills in the life of an Old Bailey hack, one thing stands as stone. Your ex-customers will never want to see you again. Even if you've steered them through the rocks of the prosecution case and brought them out to the calm waters of a not guilty verdict, they won't plan further meetings, host reunion dinners or even send you a card on your birthday. If they catch a glimpse of you on the Underground or across a crowded wine bar, they will bury their faces in their newspapers or look studiously in the opposite direction.

This is understandable. Days in court probably represent a period of time they'd rather forget and, as a rule, I'm not especially keen to renew an old acquaintance when a face I once saw in the Old Bailey dock reappears at a Scales of Justice dinner or the Inns of Court garden party. Reminiscences of the past are best avoided and what is required is a quick look and a quiet turn away. There have been times, however, when recognizing a face seen in trouble has greatly assisted me in the solution of some legal problem, and carried me to triumph in a difficult case. Such occasions have been rare, but like number 13 buses, two of them turned up in short order round a Christmas which I remember as being one of the oddest, but certainly the most rewarding, I ever spent.

'A traditional British pantomime. There's nothing to beat it!'

'You go to the pantomime, Rumpole?' Claude Erskine-Brown asked with unexpected interest.

'I did when I was a boy. It made a lasting impression on me.'

'Pantomime?' The American judge who was our fellow guest round the Erskine-Brown dinner table was clearly a stranger to such delights. 'Is that some kind of mime show? Lot of feeling imaginary walls and no one saying anything?'

'Not at all. You take some good old story, like Robin Hood.'

'Robin Hood's the star?'

'Well, yes. He's played by some strapping girl who slaps her thighs and says lines like "Cheer up, Babes in the Wood, Robin's not far away."'

'You mean there's cross-dressing?' The American visitor was puzzled.

'Well, if you want to call it that. And Robin's mother is played by a red-nosed comic.'

'A female comic?'

'No. A male one.'

'It sounds sexually interesting. We have clubs for that sort of thing in Pittsburgh.'

'There's nothing sexual about it,' I assured him. 'The Dame's a comic character who gets the audience singing.'

'Singing?'

'The words come down on a sort of giant song-sheet,' I explained. 'And she, who is really a he, gets the audience to sing along.'

Emboldened by Erskine-Brown's claret (smoother on the tongue but with less of a kick than Château Thames Embankment), I broke into a stanza of the song I was introduced to by Robin Hood's masculine mother.

> 'I may be just a nipper,
> But I've always loved a kipper . . .
> And so does my loving wife.
> If you've got a girl just slip her
> A loving golden kipper
> And she'll be yours for life.'

'Is that all?' The transatlantic judge still seemed puzzled.

'All I can remember.'

'I think you're wrong, Mr Rumpole.'

'What?'

'I think you're wrong and those lines do indeed have some sexual significance.' And the judge fell silent, contemplating the unusual acts suggested.

'I see they're doing *Aladdin* at the Tufnell Park Empire. Do you think the twins might enjoy it, Rumpole?'

The speaker was Mrs Justice Erskine-Brown (Phillida Trant as she was in happier days when I called her the Portia of our chambers), still possessed of a beauty that would break the hearts of the toughest prosecutors and make old lags swoon with lust even as she passed a stiff custodial sentence. The twins she spoke of were Tristan and Isolde, so named by her opera-loving husband, Claude, who was now bending Hilda's ear on the subject of Covent Garden's latest *Ring* cycle.

'I think the twins would adore it. Just the thing to cure the Wagnerian death-wish and bring them into a world of sanity.'

'Sanity?' The visiting judge sounded doubtful. 'With old guys dressed up as mothers?'

'I promise you, they'll love every minute of it.' And then I made another promise that sounded rash even as I spoke the words. 'I know I would. I'll take them myself.'

'Thank you, Rumpole.' Phillida spoke in her gentlest judicial voice, but I knew my fate was sealed. 'We'll keep you to that.'

'It'll have to be after Christmas,' Hilda said. 'We've been invited up to Norfolk for the holiday.'

As she said the word 'Norfolk', a cold, sneeping wind seemed to cut through the central heating of the Erskine-Browns' Islington dining-room and I felt a warning shiver.

I have no rooted objection to Christmas Day, but I must say it's an occasion when time tends to hang particularly heavily on the hands. From the early-morning alarm call of carols piping on Radio Four to the closing headlines and a restless, liverish sleep, the day can seem as long as a fraud on the Post Office tried before Mr Injustice Graves.

It takes less than no time for me to unwrap the tie which I will seldom wear, and for Hilda to receive the annual bottle of lavender water which she lays down rather than puts to immediate use. The highlights after that are the Queen's speech, when I lay bets with myself as to whether Hilda will stand to attention when the television plays the national anthem, and the thawed-out Safeway's bird followed by port (an annual gift from my faithful solicitor, Bonny Bernard) and pudding. I suppose what I have against Christmas Day is that the courts are all shut and no one is being tried for anything.

That Christmas, Hilda had decided on a complete change of routine. She announced it in a circuitous fashion by saying, one late November evening, 'I was at school with Poppy Longstaff.'

'What's that got to do with it?' I knew the answer to this question, of course. Hilda's old school has this in common with polar expeditions, natural disasters and the last war: those who have lived through it are bound together for life and can always call on each other for mutual assistance.

'Poppy's Eric is rector of Coldsands. And for some reason or other he seems to want to meet you, Rumpole.'

'Meet me?'

'That's what she said.'

'So does that mean I have to spend Christmas in the Arctic Circle and miss our festivities?'

'It's not the Arctic Circle. It's Norfolk, Rumpole. And our festivities aren't all that festive. So, yes. You have to go.' It was a judgment from which there was no possible appeal.

My first impression of Coldsands was of a gaunt church tower, presumably of great age, pointing an accusing finger to heaven from a cluster of houses on the edge of a sullen, gun-metal sea. My second was one of intense cold. As soon as we got out of the taxi, we were slapped around the face by a wind which must have started in freezing Siberia and gained nothing in the way of warmth on its journey across the plains of Europe.

'In the bleak mid-winter / Frosty winds made moan . . .' wrote that sad old darling, Christina Rossetti. Frosty winds had made considerable moan round the rectory at Coldsands, owing to the doors that stopped about an inch short of the stone floors and the windows which never shut properly, causing the curtains to billow like the sails of a ship at sea.

We were greeted cheerfully by Poppy. Hilda's friend had one of those round, childishly pretty faces often seen on seriously fat women, and she seemed to keep going on incessant cups of hot, sweet tea and a number of cardigans. If she moved like an enormous tent, her husband, Eric, was a slender wraith of a man with a high aquiline nose, two flapping wings of grey hair on the sides of his face and a vague air of perpetual anxiety, broken now and then by high and unexpected laughter. He made cruciform gestures, as though remembering the rubric 'Spectacles, testicles, wallet and watch' and forgetting where these important articles were kept.

'Eric,' his wife explained, 'is having terrible trouble with the church tower.'

'Oh dear.' Hilda shot me a look of stern disapproval, which I knew meant that it would be more polite if I abandoned my overcoat while tea was being served. 'How worrying for you, Eric.'

The Rev. Eric went into a long, excited and high-pitched speech. The gist of this was that the tower, although of rare beauty, had not been much restored since the Saxons built it and the Normans added the finishing touches. Fifty thousand pounds was needed for essential repairs, and the thermometer, erected for the appeal outside the church, was stuck at a low hundred and twenty, the result of an emergency jumble sale.

'You particularly wanted Horace to come this Christmas?' Hilda asked the man of God with the air of someone anxious to solve a baffling mystery. 'I wonder why that was.'

'Yes. I wonder!' Eric looked startled. 'I wonder why on earth I wanted to ask Horace. I don't believe he's got fifty thousand smackers in his back pocket!' At this, he shook with laughter.

'There,' I told him, 'your lack of faith is entirely justified.' I wasn't exactly enjoying Coldsands Rectory, but I was a little miffed that the reverend couldn't remember why he'd asked me there in the first place.

'We had hoped that Donald Compton would help us out,' Poppy told us. 'I mean, he wouldn't notice fifty thousand. But he took exception to what Eric said at the Remembrance Day service.'

'Armistice Day in the village,' Eric's grey wings of hair trembled as he nodded in delighted affirmation, 'and I prayed for dead German soldiers. It seemed only fair.'

'Fair perhaps, darling. But hardly tactful,' his wife told him. 'Donald Compton thought it was distinctly unpatriotic. He's bought the Old Manor House,' she explained to Hilda. From then on the conversation turned exclusively to this Compton and was carried on in the tones of awe and muted wonder in which people always talk about the very rich. Compton, it seemed, after a difficult start in England, had gone to Canada where, during a ten-year stay, he laid the foundations of his fortune. His much younger wife was quite charming, probably Canadian, and not in the least stand-offish. He had built the village hall, the cricket pavilion and a tennis court for the school. Only Eric's unfortunate sympathy for the German dead had caused his bounty to stop short at the church tower.

'I've done hours of hard knee work,' the rector told us, 'begging the Lord to soften Mr Compton's heart towards our tower. No result so far, I fear.'

Apart from this one lapse, the charming Donald Compton seemed to be the perfect English squire and country gent. I would see him in church on Christmas morning, and we had also been invited for drinks before lunch at the manor. The Reverend Eric and the smiling Poppy made it sound as though the Pope and the Archbishop of Canterbury would be out with the carol singers and we'd been invited to drop in for high tea at Windsor Castle. I also prayed for a yule log blazing at the manor so that I could, in the true spirit of Christmas, thaw out gradually.

'Now, as a sign of Christmas fellowship, will you all stand and shake hands with those in front and behind you?' Eric, in full canonicals, standing on the steps in front of the altar, made the suggestion as though he had just thought of the idea. I stood reluctantly. I had found myself a place in church near to a huge, friendly, gently humming, occasionally belching radiator and I was clinging to it and stroking it as though it were a newfound mistress (not that I have much experience of new-, or even old-found mistresses). The man who turned to me from the front row seemed to be equally reluctant. He was, as Hilda had pointed out excitedly, the great Donald Compton in person: a man of middle height with silver hair, dressed in a tweed suit and with a tan which it must have been expensive to preserve at Christmas. He had soft brown eyes which looked, almost at once, away from me as, with a touch of his dry fingers, he was gone and I was left for the rest of the service with no more than a well-tailored back and the sound of an uncertain tenor voice joining in the hymns.

I turned to the row behind to shake hands with an elderly woman who had madness in her eyes and whispered conspiratorially to me, 'You cold, dear? Like to borrow my gloves? We're used to a bit of chill weather round these parts.' I declined politely and went back to hugging the radiator, and as I did so a sort of happiness stole over me. To start with, the church was beautiful, with a high timbered roof and walls of weathered stone, peppered with marble tributes to dead inhabitants of the manor. It was decorated with holly and mistletoe, a tree glowed and there were candles over a crib. I thought how many generations of Coldsands villagers, their eyes bright and faces flushed with the wind, had belted out the hymns. I also thought how depressed the great Donald Compton – who had put on little gold half-glasses to read the prophecy from Isaiah: 'For unto us a child is born, unto us a son is given: and the government shall be upon his shoulder: and his name shall be called "Wonderful"' – would feel if Jesus's instruction to sell all and give it to the poor should ever be taken literally.

And then I wondered why it was that, as he touched my fingers and turned away, I felt that I had lived through that precise moment before.

There was, in fact, a huge log fire crackling and throwing a dancing light on the marble floor of the circular entrance hall, with its great staircase leading up into private shadows. The cream of Coldsands was being entertained to champagne and canapés by the new lord of the manor. The decibels rose as the champagne went down and the little group began to sound like an army of tourists in the Sistine Chapel, noisy, excited and wonderstruck.

'They must be all his ancestors.' Hilda was looking at the pictures and, in particular, at a general in a scarlet coat on a horse prancing in front of some distant battle.

My mouth was full of cream cheese enveloped in smoked salmon. I swallowed it and said, 'Oh, I shouldn't think so. After all, he only bought the house recently.'

'But I expect he brought his family portraits here from some-where else.'

'You mean, he had them under the bed in his old bachelor flat in Wimbledon and now he's hung them round an acre or two of walls?'

'Do try and be serious, Rumpole, you're not nearly as funny as you think you are. Just look at the family resemblance. I'm abso-lutely certain that all of these are old Comptons.'

And it was when she said that that I remembered everything perfectly clearly.

He was with his wife. She was wearing a black velvet dress and had long, golden hair that sparkled in the firelight. They were talking to a bald, pink-faced man and his short and dumpy wife, and they were all laughing. Compton's laughter stopped as he saw me coming towards him. He said, 'I don't think we've met.'

'Yes,' I replied. 'We shook hands briefly in church this morning. My name's Rumpole and I'm staying with the Longstaffs. But didn't we meet somewhere else?'

'Good old Eric! We have our differences, of course, but he's a saintly man. This is my wife, Lorelei, and Colonel and Maudy Jacobs. I expect you'd like to see the library, wouldn't you, Rumpole? I'm sure you're interested in ancient history. Will you all excuse us?'

It was two words from Hilda that had done it: 'old' and 'Comp-ton'. I knew then what I should have remembered when we touched hands in the pews, that Old Compton is a street in Soho, and that was perhaps why Riccardo (known as Dicko) Perducci had adopted the name. And I had received that very same handshake, a slight touch and a quick turn away when I said goodbye to him in the cells under the Old Bailey and left him to start seven years for blackmail. The trial had ended, I now remembered, just before a long-distant Christmas.

The Perducci territory had been, in those days, not rolling Norfolk acres but a number of Soho strip clubs and clip joints. Girls would stand in front of these last-named resorts and beckon the lonely, the desperate and the unwary in. Sometimes they would escape after paying twenty pounds for a watery cocktail. Unlucky, affluent and important customers might even get sex, carefully recorded by microphones and cameras to produce material which was used for systematic and highly profitable blackmail. The victim in Dicko's case was an obscure and not much loved circus judge; so it was regarded as particularly serious by the prosecuting authority.

When I mitigated for Dicko, I stressed the lack of direct evidence against him. He was a shadowy figure who kept himself well in the background and was known as a legend rather than a familiar face round Soho. 'That only shows what a big wheel he was,' Judge Bullingham, who was unfortunately trying the case, bellowed unsympathetically. In desperation I tried the approach of Christmas on him. 'Crimes forgiven, sins remitted, mercy triumphant, such was the message of the story that began in Bethlehem,' I told the court, at which the Mad Bull snorted that, as far as he could remember, that story ended in a criminal trial and a stiff sentence on at least one thief.

'I suppose something like this was going to happen sooner or later.' We were standing in the library, in front of a comforting fire and among leather-bound books, which I strongly suspected had been bought by the yard. The new, like the old, Dicko was soft-eyed, quietly spoken, almost unnaturally calm; the perfect man behind the scenes of a blackmailing operation or a country estate.

'Not necessarily,' I told him. 'It's just that my wife has so many old schoolfriends and Poppy Longstaff is one of them. Well now, you seem to have done pretty well for yourself. Solid citizens still misconducting themselves round Old Compton Street, are they?'

'I wouldn't know. I gave all that up and went into the property business.'

'Really? Where did you do that? Canada?'

'I never saw Canada.' He shook his head. 'Garwick Prison. Up-and-coming area in the Home Counties. The screws there were ready and willing to do the deals on the outside. I paid them embarrassingly small commissions.'

'How long were you there?'

'Four years. By the time I came out I'd got my first million.'

'Well, then I did you a good turn, losing your case. A bit of luck His Honour Judge Bullingham didn't believe in the remission of sins.'

'You think I got what I deserved?'

I stretched my hands to the fire. I could hear the cocktail chatter from the marble hall of the eighteenth-century manor. 'Treat every man according to his deserts and who shall escape whipping?' I quoted *Hamlet* at him.

'Then I can trust you, Rumpole? The Lord Chancellor's going to put me on the local Bench.'

'The Lord Chancellor lives in a world of his own.'

'You don't think I'd do well as a magistrate?'

'I suppose you'd speak from personal experience of crime. And have some respect for the quality of mercy.'

'I've got no time for that, Rumpole.' His voice became quieter but harder, the brown eyes lost their softness: that, I thought, was how he must have looked when one of his clip-joint girls was caught with the punters' cash stuffed in her tights. 'It's about time we cracked down on crime. Well now, can I trust you not to go out there and spread the word about the last time we met?'

'That depends.'

'On what?'

'How well you have understood the Christmas message.'

'Which is?'

'Perhaps, generosity.'

'I see. So you want your bung?'

'Oh, not me, Dicko. I've been paid, inadequately, by legal aid. But there's an impoverished church tower in urgent need of resuscitation.'

'That Eric Longstaff, our rector – he's not a patriot!'

'And are you?'

'I do a good deal of work locally for the British Legion.'

'And I'm sure, next Poppy Day, they'll appreciate what you've done for the church tower.'

He looked at me for a long minute in silence, and I thought that if this scene had been taking place in a back room in Soho there might, quite soon, have been the flash of a knife. Instead, his hand went to an inside pocket, but it produced nothing more lethal than a cheque book.

'While you're in a giving mood,' I said, 'the rectory's in desperate need of central heating.'

'This is bloody blackmail!' Dicko Perducci, now known as Donald Compton, said.

'Well,' I told him, 'you should know.'

Christmas was over. The year turned, stirred itself and opened its eyes on a bleak January. Crimes were committed, arrests were made and the courtrooms were filled, once again, with the sound of argument. I went down to the Old Bailey on a trifling matter of fixing the date of a trial before Mrs Justice Erskine-Brown. As I was leaving, the usher came and told me that the judge wanted to see me in her private room on a matter of urgency.

Such summonses always fill me with apprehension and a vague feeling of guilt. What had I done? Got the date of the trial hopelessly muddled? Addressed the court with my trousers carelessly unzipped? I was relieved when the learned Phillida greeted me warmly and even offered me a glass of sherry, poured from her own personal decanter. 'It was so kind of you to offer, Rumpole,' she said unexpectedly.

'Offer what?' I was puzzled.

'You told us how much you adored the traditional British pantomime.'

'So I did.' For a happy moment I imagined Her Ladyship as

Principal Boy, her shapely legs encased in black tights, her neat little wig slightly askew, slapping her thigh and calling out, in bell-like tones, 'Cheer up, Rumpole, Portia's not far away.'

'The twins are looking forward to it enormously.'

'Looking forward to what?'

'*Aladdin* at the Tufnell Park Empire. I've got the tickets for the nineteenth of Jan. You do remember promising to take them, don't you?'

'Well, of course.' What else might I have said after the fifth glass of the Erskine-Brown St Emillion? 'I'd love to be of the party. And will old Claude be buying us a dinner afterwards?'

'I really don't think you should go round calling people "old", Rumpole.' Phillida now looked miffed, and I downed the sherry before she took it into her head to deprive me of it. 'Claude's got us tickets for Pavarotti. *L'Elisir d'Amore*. You might buy the children a burger after the show. Oh, and it's not far from us on the tube. It really was sweet of you to invite them.'

At which she smiled at me and refilled my glass in a way which made it clear she was not prepared to hear further argument.

It all turned out better than I could have hoped. Tristan and Isolde, unlike their Wagnerian namesakes, were cheerful, reasonably polite and seemed only too anxious to dissociate themselves, as far as possible, from the old fart who was escorting them. At every available opportunity they would touch me for cash and then scamper off to buy ice cream, chocolates, sandwiches or Sprite. I was left in reasonable peace to enjoy the performance.

And enjoy it I did. Aladdin was a personable young woman with an upturned nose, a voice which could have been used to wake up patients coming round from their anaesthetics, and memorable thighs. Uncle Abanazer was played, Isolde told me, by an actor known as a social worker with domestic problems in a long-running television series. Wishy and Washy did sing to electric guitars (deafeningly amplified) but Widow Twankey, played by a certain Jim Diamond, was all a Dame should be, a nimble little cockney, fitted up with a sizeable false bosom, a flaming red wig, sweeping eyelashes and scarlet lips. Never have I heard the immortal line, 'Where's that naughty boy Aladdin got to?' better delivered. I joined in loudly (Tristan and Isolde sat silent and embarrassed) when the Widow and Aladdin conducted us in the singing of 'Please Don't Pinch My Tomatoes'. It was, in fact and in fairness, all a traditional pantomime should be, and yet I had a vague feeling that something was wrong, an element was missing. But, as the cast came down a white staircase in glittering costumes to enthusiastic applause, it seemed the sort of pantomime I'd grown up with, and which Tristan and Isolde should be content to inherit.

After so much excitement I felt in need of a stiff brandy and soda, but the eatery the children had selected for their evening's entertainment had apparently gone teetotal and alcohol was not on the menu. Once they were confronted by their mammoth burgers and fries I made my excuses, said I'd be back in a moment, and slipped into the nearby pub which was, I noticed, opposite the stage door of the Empire.

As the life-giving draught was being poured I found myself standing next to Washy and Uncle Abanazer, now out of costume, who were discussing Jim the Dame. 'Very unfriendly tonight,' Washy said. 'Locked himself in his dressing-room before the show and won't join us for a drink.'

'Perhaps he's had a bust-up with Molly?'

'Unlikely. Molly and Jim never had a cross word.'

'Lucky she's never found out he's been polishing Aladdin's wonderful lamp,' Abanazer said, and they both laughed.

And as I asked the girl behind the bar to refill my glass, in which the tide had sunk to a dangerous low, I heard them laugh again about the Widow Twankey's voluminous bosom. 'Strapped-on polystyrene,' Abanazer was saying. 'Almost bruises me when I dance with her. Funny thing, tonight it was quite soft.'

'Perhaps she borrowed one from a blow-up woman?' Washy was laughing as I gulped my brandy and legged it back to the hamburgers. In the dark passage outside the stage door I saw a small, nimble figure in hurried retreat: Jim Diamond, who for some reason hadn't wanted to join the boys at the bar.

After I had restored the children to the Erskine-Browns' au pair, I sat in the tube on my way back to Gloucester Road and read the programme. Jim Diamond, it seemed, had started his life in industry before taking up show business. He had a busy career in clubs and turned down appearances on television. ' "I only enjoy the living show," Jim says. "I want to have the audience where I can see them." ' His photograph, without the exaggerated female make-up, showed a pale, thin-nosed, in some way disagreeable little man with a lip curled either in scorn or triumph. I wondered how such an unfriendly looking character could become an ebullient and warm-hearted Widow. Stripped of his make-up, there was something about this comic's unsmiling face which brought back memories of another meeting in totally different circumstances. It was the second time within a few weeks that I had found an old familiar face cast in a new and unexpected part.

The idea, the memory I couldn't quite grasp, preyed on my mind until I was tucked up in bed. Then, as Hilda's latest historical romance dropped from her weary fingers, when she turned her back on me and switched out the light, I saw the face again quite clearly but in a different setting. Not Diamond, not Sparkler, but Sparksman, a logical progression. Widow Twankey had been played by Harry Sparksman, a man who trained as a professional entertainer, if my memory was correct, not in clubs, but in Her Majesty's prisons. It was, it seemed, an interesting career change, but I thought no more of it at the time and, once satisfied with my identification, I fell asleep.

'The boy couldn't have done it, Mr Rumpole. Not a complicated bloody great job to that extent. His only way of getting at a safe was to dig it out of the wall and remove it bodily. He did that in a Barkingside boutique and what he found in it hardly covered the petrol. Young Denis couldn't have got into the Croydon supermarket peter. No one in our family could.'

Uncle Fred, the experienced and cautious head of the Timson

clan, had no regard for the safe-breaking talent of Denis, his nephew and, on the whole, an unskilled recruit in the Timson enterprise. The Croydon supermarket job had been highly complicated and expertly carried out and had yielded, to its perpetrators, thousands of pounds. Peanuts Molloy was arrested as one of the lookouts, after falling and twisting an ankle when chased by a nightwatchman during the getaway. He said he didn't know any of the skilled operators who had engaged him, except Denis Timson who, he alleged, was in general charge of the operation. Denis alone silenced the burglar alarm and deftly penetrated the lock on the safe with an oxyacetylene blowtorch.

It had to be remembered, though, that the clan Molloy had been sworn enemies of the Timson family from time immemorial. Peanuts's story sounded implausible when I met Denis Timson in the Brixton Prison interview room. A puzzled 25-year-old with a shaven head and a poor attempt at a moustache, he seemed more upset by his uncle Fred's low opinion of him than the danger of a conviction and subsequent prolonged absence from the family.

Denis's case was to come up for committal at the South London Magistrates' Court before 'Skimpy' Simpson, whose lack of success at the Bar had driven him to a job as a stipendiary beak. His nickname had been earned by the fact that he had not, within living memory, been known to splash out on a round of drinks in Pommeroy's Wine Bar.

In the usual course of events, there is no future in fighting proceedings which are only there to commit the customer to trial. I had resolved to attend solely to pour a little well-deserved contempt on the evidence of Peanuts Molloy. As I started to prepare the case, I made a note of the date of the Croydon supermarket break-in. As soon as I had done so, I consulted my diary. I turned the virgin pages as yet unstained by notes of trials, ideas for cross-examinations, splodges of tea or spilled glasses of Pommeroy's Very Ordinary. It was as I had thought. While some virtuoso was at work on the Croydon safe, I was enjoying *Aladdin* in the company of Tristan and Isolde.

★

'Detective Inspector Grimble. Would you agree that whoever blew the safe in the Croydon supermarket did an extraordinarily skilful job?'

'Mr Rumpole, are we meant to congratulate your client on his professional skill?'

God moves in a mysterious way, and it wasn't Skimpy Simpson's fault that he was born with thin lips and a voice which sounded like the rusty hinge of a rusty gate swinging in the wind. I decided to ignore him and concentrate on a friendly chat with DI Grimble, a large, comfortable, ginger-haired officer. We had lived together, over the years, with the clan Timson and their misdoings. He was known to them as a decent and fair-minded cop, as disapproving of the younger, Panda-racing, evidence-massaging intake to the Force as they were of the lack of discretion and criminal skills which marked the younger Timsons.

'I mean the thieves were well informed. They knew that there would be a week's money in the safe.'

'They knew that, yes.'

'And was there a complex burglar-alarm system? You couldn't put it out of action simply by cutting wires, could you?'

'Cutting the wires would have set it off.'

'So putting the burglar alarm out of action would have required special skills?'

'It would have done.'

'Putting it out of action also stopped a clock in the office. So we know that occurred at eight forty-five?'

'We know that. Yes.'

'And at nine twenty young Molloy was caught as he fell, running to a getaway car.'

'That is so.'

'So this heavy safe was burnt open in a little over half an hour?'

'I fail to see the relevance of that, Mr Rumpole.' Skimpy was getting restless.

'I'm sure the officer does. That shows a very high degree of technical skill, doesn't it, Detective Inspector?'

'I'd agree with that.'

'Exercised by a highly experienced peterman?'

'Who is this Mr Peterman?' Skimpy was puzzled. 'We haven't heard of him before.'

'Not Mr Peterman.' I marvelled at the ignorance of the basic facts of life displayed by the magistrate. 'A man expert at blowing safes, known to the trade as "peters",' I told him and turned back to DI Grimble. 'So we're agreed that this was a highly expert piece of work?'

'It must have been done by someone who knew his job pretty well. Yes.'

'Denis Timson's record shows convictions for shoplifting, bag-snatching and stealing a radio from an unlocked car. In all of these simple enterprises, he managed to get caught.'

'Your client's criminal record!' Skimpy looked happy for the first time. 'You're allowing that to go into evidence, are you, Mr Rumpole?'

'Certainly, sir.' I explained the obvious point. 'Because there's absolutely no indication he was capable of blowing a safe in record time, or silencing a complicated burglar alarm, is there, Detective Inspector?'

'No. There's nothing to show anything like that in his record . . .'

'Mr Rumpole,' Skimpy was looking at the clock; was he in danger of missing his usual train back home to Haywards Heath? 'Where's all this heading?'

'Back a good many years,' I told him, 'to the Sweet-Home Building Society job at Carshalton. When Harry Sparksman blew a safe so quietly that even the dogs slept through it.'

'You were in that case, weren't you, Mr Rumpole?' Inspector Grimble was pleased to remember. 'Sparksman got five years.'

'Not one of your great successes.' Skimpy was also delighted. 'Perhaps you wasted the court's time with unnecessary questions. Have you anything else to ask this officer?'

'Not till the Old Bailey, sir. I may have thought of a few more by then.'

With great satisfaction, Skimpy committed Dennis Timson, a minor villain who would have had difficulty changing a fuse, let alone blowing a safe, for trial at the Central Criminal Court.

★

'Funny you mentioned Harry Sparksman. Do you know, the same thought occurred to me. An expert like him could've done that job in the time.'

'Great minds think alike,' I assured DI Grimble. We were washing away the memory of an hour or two before Skimpy with two pints of nourishing stout in the pub opposite the beak's court. 'You know Harry took up a new career?' I needn't have asked the question. DI Grimble had a groupie's encyclopaedic knowledge of the criminal stars.

'Oh yes. Now a comic called Jim Diamond. Got up a concert party in the nick. Apparently gave him a taste for show business.'

'I did hear,' I took Grimble into my confidence, 'that he made a comeback for the Croydon job.' It had been a throwaway line from Uncle Fred Timson – 'I heard talk they got Harry back out of retirement' – but it was a thought worth examining.

'I heard the same. So we did a bit of checking. But Sparksman, known as Diamond, has got a cast-iron alibi.'

'Are you sure?'

'The time when the Croydon job was done, he was performing in a pantomime. On stage nearly all the evening, it seems, playing the Dame.'

'*Aladdin*,' I said, 'at the Tufnell Park Empire. It might just be worth your while to go into that alibi a little more thoroughly. I'd suggest you have a private word with Mrs Molly Diamond. It's just possible she may have noticed his attraction to Aladdin's lamp.'

'Now then, Mr Rumpole,' Grimble was wiping the froth from his lips with a neatly folded handkerchief, 'you mustn't tell me how to do my job.'

'I'm only trying to serve,' I managed to look pained, 'the interests of justice!'

'You mean, the interests of your client?'

'Sometimes they're the same thing,' I told him, but I had to admit it wasn't often.

As it happened, the truth emerged without Detective Inspector Grimble having to do much of a job. Harry had, in fact, fallen victim to a tip-tilted nose and memorable thighs; he'd left home and moved into Aladdin's Kensal Rise flat. Molly, taking a terrible revenge, blew his alibi wide open. She had watched many rehearsals and knew every word, every gag, every nudge, wink and shrill complaint of the Dame's part. She had played it to perfection to give her husband an alibi while he went back to his old job in Croydon. It all went perfectly, even though Uncle Abanazer, dancing with her, had felt an unexpected softness.

I had known, instinctively, that something was very wrong. It had, however, taken some time for me to realize what I had really seen that night at the Tufnell Park Empire. It was nothing less than an outrage to a Great British tradition. The Widow Twankey was a woman.

DI Grimble made his arrest and the case against Denis Timson was dropped by the Crown Prosecution Service. As spring came to the Temple gardens, Hilda opened a letter in the other case which turned on the recognition of old, familiar faces and read it out to me.

'The repointing's going well on the tower and we hope to have it finished by Easter,' Poppy Longstaff had written. 'And I have to tell you, Hilda, the oil-fired heating has changed our lives. Eric says it's like living in the tropics. Cooking supper last night, I had to peel off at least one of my cardigans.' She Who Must Be Obeyed put down the letter from her old school-friend and said, thoughtfully, '*Noblesse Oblige.*'

'What was that, Hilda?'

'I could tell at once that Donald Compton was a true gentleman. The sort that does good by stealth. Of course, poor old Eric thought he'd never get the tower mended, but I somehow felt that Donald wouldn't fail him. It was noblesse.'

'Perhaps it was,' I conceded, 'but in this case the noblesse was Rumpole's.'

'Rumpole! What on earth do you mean? You hardly paid to have the church tower repointed, did you?'

'In one sense, yes.'

'I can't believe that. After all the years it took you to have the bathroom decorated. What on earth do you mean about *your noblesse?*'

'It'd take too long to explain, old darling. Besides, I've got a conference in chambers. Tricky case of receiving stolen surgical appliances. I suppose,' I added doubtfully, 'it may lead, at some time in the distant future, to an act of charity.'

Easter came, the work on the tower was successfully completed, and I was walking back to chambers after a gruelling day down the Bailey when I saw, wafting through the Temple cloisters, the unlikely apparition of the Rev. Eric Longstaff. He chirruped a greeting and said he'd come up to consult some legal brains on the proper investment of what remained of the Church Restoration Fund. 'I'm so profoundly grateful,' he told me, 'that I decided to invite you down to the rectory last Christmas.'

'*You* decided?'

'Of course I did.'

'I thought your wife Poppy extended the invitation to She . . .'

'Oh yes. But I thought of the idea. It was the result of a good deal of hard knee-work and guidance from above. I knew you were the right man for the job.'

'What job?'

'The Compton job.'

What was this? The rector was speaking like an old con. The Coldsands caper? 'What *can* you mean?'

'I just mean that I knew you'd defended Donald Compton. In a previous existence.'

'How on earth did you know that?'

Eric drew himself up to his full, willowy height. 'I'm not a prison visitor for nothing,' he said proudly, 'so I thought you were just the chap to put the fear of God into him. You were the very person to put the squeeze on the lord of the manor.'

'Put the squeeze on him?' Words were beginning to fail me.

'That was the idea. It came to me as a result of knee-work.'

'So you brought us down to that freezing rectory just so I could blackmail the local benefactor?'

'Didn't it turn out well!'

'May the Lord forgive you.'

'He's very forgiving.'

'Next time,' I spoke to the man of God severely, 'the church can do its blackmailing for itself.'

'Oh, we're quite used to that.' The rector smiled at me in what I thought was a lofty manner. 'Particularly around Christmas.'

Rumpole Rests His Case

'Members of the jury. This case has occupied only ten days of your lives. In a week or two you will have forgotten every detail about the dead budgerigar, the torn-up photograph of Sean Connery, the mouldering poached egg on toast behind the sitting-room curtain and the mysterious cry (was it a call for help, as the prosecution invite you to believe, or the delighted shriek produced by a moment of sexual ecstasy?) which could be heard issuing from 42B Mandela Buildings on that sultry and fatal night of July the twenty-third. All this has been but a part, a fleeting moment perhaps, of your lives, but for the woman I represent, the woman who has endured every scrap of innuendo, scandal and abuse the almighty Crown Prosecution Service can dredge up, with the vast resources of the state at their disposal, for her this case represents the whole of her future life. That and nothing less than that is at stake in this trial. And it is her life I now leave, Members of the Jury, in your hands, confident that she will hear from your foreman, in the fullness of time, the words that will give the remainder of her life back to her: "Not guilty!" So I thank you for listening to me, Members of the Jury. I rest my case.'

The sweetest moment of an advocate's life comes when he sits down after his final speech, legs tired of standing, shirt damp with honest sweat, mouth dried up with words. He sits back and a great weight slides off his shoulders. There's absolutely nothing more that he can do. All the decisions, the unanswered questions, the responsibility for banging up a fellow human being, have now shifted to the judge and the jury. The defence has rested and the Old Bailey hack can rest with it.

As I sat, relaxed, and placed my neck comfortably against the wooden rail behind me, I removed the wig, scratched my head for comfort, and put it on again. As I rested, I looked for a moment at

His Honour Judge Bullingham, an Old Bailey judge now promoted to trying murders. To call them trials is perhaps to flatter the learned judge, who conducts the proceedings as though the Old Bailey were a somewhat prejudiced and summary offshoot of the Spanish Inquisition. One of my first jobs as a defending counsel in the present case was to taunt and tempt, by many daring passes of the cape and neat side-steps in the sand, the bellowing and red-eyed bull to come out as such a tireless fighter on behalf of the prosecution that the jury began to see him as I did. They might, perhaps, acquit my client because an ill-tempered judge was making it so desperately clear that he wanted her convicted.

But who had killed the budgerigar, a bird which, it seemed, had stood equally high in the regard of both the husband and the wife? It was as I toyed with this question, in an increasingly detached sort of way, that I closed my eyes and found not darkness but a sudden flood of bright golden light into which the familiar furnishings of Court Number One at the Old Bailey seemed to have melted away and vanished. Then I saw a small black dot which, rushing towards me like a shooting star, grew rapidly into the face of His Honour Judge Bullingham, who filled the landscape wearing the complacent expression of a man about to pass a sentence of life imprisonment. Then I heard a voice, deeper and more alarming than that of any clerk of the court I had ever heard before, saying, 'Have you reached a verdict on which you all agree?' 'We have,' some faint voice answered. 'Do you find the defendant Rumpole guilty or not guilty?' But before the answer could be given, the great light faded, and Bullingham's face melted away with it. There was a stab of pain in my chest, night fell and I became, I suppose, unconscious.

Undoubtedly, this was a dramatic way of ending a closing speech. Mrs Ballard, known round the Bailey as 'Matey', was soon on the scene, as I understand it loosening my collar and pulling off my wig. The prosecutor rose to ask His Honour what steps he wished to take in view of the complete collapse of Mr Rumpole.

'He's not dead. I'm sure of that.' Bullingham declined to accept the evidence. 'He's tried that one on me before.' This was strictly true, when, many years before, the stubborn old Bull dug his heels in and refused an adjournment, so I had to feign death as the only legal loophole left if I wanted to delay the proceedings. I put on, as I thought, a pretty good performance on that occasion. But this was no gesture of theatrical advocacy. Matey made the appropriate telephone call. An ambulance, howling with delight, was enjoying its usual dangerous driving round Ludgate Circus. Strong men in uniform, impeded by offers of incompetent help from the prosecution team no doubt thankful to see the back of me, rolled me out of my usual seat and on to a stretcher. So I left court (was it for the last time?) feet first.

'I know what this is,' I thought as I looked upon the vision of hell. My chest was still crunching with pain. There was a freezing draught blowing scraps of torn-up and discarded paper across the lino, and a strong smell composed of equal parts rubber and disinfectant. I saw some shadowy figures, a mother with a child on her lap, a white-faced girl with staring eyes and a scarlet mouth, and old man, his tattered coat tied with string, who seemed to have abandoned all hope and was muttering to himself, a patient Chinese couple, the woman holding up a hand swathed in a bloodstained bandage. They all sat beneath a notice which read: 'Warning. The average waiting time here is four and a half hours.' It seemed a relatively short period measured against eternity. If this place wasn't hell, I thought, it was, at least, some purgatorial anteroom.

When I had opened my eyes I had found myself staring at the ceiling, yellow plaster mysteriously stained, a globe surrounding a light in which, it seemed, all the neighbourhood insects had come to die. Then I realized, with a sudden pang, that I was lying on some particularly hard surface. It felt like metal and plastic and I was more or less covered with a blanket. Then a vision appeared, a beautiful Indian girl with a clipboard, wearing a white coat and a look of heavenly confusion. Perhaps this wasn't hell after all.

'Hello, Mr Robinson. Are you quite comfortable?'

'No.' I still had, so it seemed, retained the gift of speech.

'No, you're not comfortable?'

'No, and I'm not Mr Robinson either.'

'Oh. So that's all right then.' She made a tick somewhere on her clipboard and vanished. I missed her but could no longer worry. I stirred with discomfort and went back to sleep.

When I woke up again, it must have been much later. The windows which once let in faint daylight were now black. The old man who had once sat quietly was now wandering round the room, muttering complaints and, from time to time, shouting, 'Vengeance is mine!' or 'Up the Arsenal!' There was a clattering as of a milk cart parking, and a formidable machine was wheeled up beside me, a thing of dials and trailing wires steered by a young man this time, also in a white coat. He had a large chin, gingery hair and an expression of thinly disguised panic. He also had another clipboard which he consulted.

'Ted Robinson?'

'No.'

'Collapsed in the workplace?'

'If you call the Old Bailey a workplace. Which I certainly never do.'

'All the same, you collapsed, didn't you?'

He'd got me there. 'Yes,' I had to admit. 'I collapsed completely.'

'All right, Mr Robinson. I'll just get you wired up.'

'But I'm really not . . .'

'You'll make it much easier for both of us if you don't talk. Just lie still and relax.'

I lay still as wires were fixed to me. I watched a line on a flickering screen which seemed to be on a perpetual downward curve. The stranger in the white coat was also watching. In the end the machine handed him a scrap of paper.

'Rest. A time in bed,' he told me. 'That's the best we can do for you.'

'But I haven't got a bed.'

'Neither have we.' He began to laugh, holding on to my arm as though he wanted me to join in the joke. 'Neither have we.' He repeated the phrase, as though to squeeze the last drops of laughter out of it. 'I expect someone, sometime, will do something about it. In the meantime, your job is to rest. Have you got that, Mr Rumpole?'

'You know my name?'

'Of course I do. We've got it written down. I don't know why you kept calling yourself Robinson all the time.'

No doubt the man worked unsociable hours. He wandered away from me in a sort of daze. Everything became terribly silent and, once again, I fell asleep despite the crunching pain.

My sleep was not undisturbed. Half awake and only a little conscious, I felt that I was on the move. I opened my eyes for a moment and saw the ceiling of a long passage gliding past. Then gates clanged. Was I at last going the way of too many of my customers? Was I being banged up? It was a possibility I chose to ignore until I felt myself rolled over again. I caught a glimpse of a kindly black face, the brilliant white teeth and hands pulling, in a determined way, at what was left of my clothing. Then I was alone again in the darkness, and I heard, like the waves of a distant sea, the sounds of low incessant snores, and the expulsion of breath was like the rattle of small stones on the beach as the waves retreat.

'I didn't bring you grapes, Rumpole. I thought you wouldn't want grapes.'

'No interest in grapes.' My voice, as I heard it, came out in a hoarse whisper, a ghostly shadow of the rich courtroom baritone which had charmed juries and rattled the smoothest bent copper telling the smoothest lies. 'I'm only interested in grapes when they've been trodden underfoot, carefully fermented and bottled for use in Pommeroy's Wine Bar.'

'Don't talk so much. That's a lesson you'll have to learn from now on, Rumpole.'

I looked at Hilda. She had smartened herself up for this hospital visit, wearing her earrings, a new silk blouse and smelling a great deal more strongly than usual of her Violetta Eau de Toilette.

'I thought you wouldn't want flowers, Rumpole.'

'No. You're right, Hilda, I wouldn't want flowers.' Plenty of time for flowers, I thought, later.

'Flowers always look so sick in a hospital.'

'That's right, of course. Most of us do!'

Conversation between myself and She Who Must Be Obeyed

was flowing like cement. It wasn't that we were embarrassed by the presence of other men on the ward. The snorer, the tooth-grinder, the serial urinator had headphones glued to their ears, their heads nodding gently to the beat of the easy listening. The young man who had lost a kidney held the hand of his visiting girlfriend; they only spoke occasionally and in whispers. The other youngish man, perhaps in his thirties, brown-haired with soft, appealing eyes and a perpetually puzzled expression, lay in the bed next to mine. His was a face I recognized from newspapers and the television, and I knew his name was David Stoker and that he had been operated on as a result of gunshot wounds.

'Let this be a lesson to you, Rumpole,' Hilda went on remorselessly. 'You've got to give it all up.'

This was how she spoke to me at home and she made no effort to moderate her tone, although the much-bandaged Stoker was well within earshot.

'Give what up, Hilda? I don't really mind giving up anything, so long as it's not small cigars or Pommeroy's Very Ordinary or the Bar.'

'That's the one!'

'Which one?'

'The Bar. That's what you've got to give up. Well, after this business it's perfectly obvious you can't go on with it. All these criminals you're so fond of defending will just have to go off to prison quietly, and about time too, if you want my opinion, Rumpole.'

'Of course I want your opinion, Hilda. But . . .'

'No "but" about it. I've spoken to the doctor here.'

'That was nice of you. How is he?'

'He's perfectly well, Rumpole. Which is more than can be said about you. It's your heart. You've put too great a strain on it. You do understand that, don't you?'

'Is that what he said?'

'His very words.'

'He called me Robinson.' I thought of the most likely explanation for this ridiculous verdict. 'He's seriously overworked. I don't think, Hilda, you should attach the slightest importance to his evidence.'

'That woman you were defending when you passed out. Your last case, Rumpole. The woman who stabbed her husband. You got her off.'

'I know,' I said. 'They let me read the Sunday papers. The jury found she didn't mean to stab him. She held the knife to keep him away and he stumbled and fell on it. That's what the jury believed.'

'What you persuaded them to believe.'

'I have a certain skill, as an advocate.'

'A skill that'll finish you off, Rumpole, if you don't give it up entirely.'

'Anyway, he wasn't a particularly nice man. He wrung her budgerigar's neck.'

'Oh, well, then I suppose he deserved it.' She was easily persuaded. 'But now you've given it all up, you'll be able to enjoy life.'

'Enjoy life doing what?'

'Well, you can rest. Help around the flat. I've always thought we ought to go in for window boxes. If you make a good recovery you could help me with the shopping.' I couldn't think of a weaker incentive for a return to health. But I didn't say so. A silence fell between us and then she said, 'I bumped into Chappy Bowers the other day.'

'Who?' The name meant little to me at first.

'You must remember Chappy. He was in Daddy's chambers when you joined. He didn't get much work. It was rather sad. He said he just couldn't bear spinning improbable stories for ungrateful people.'

'Then he clearly had absolutely no talent for the law.'

'He went into the City and did a number of jobs. Then he fell on his feet. They made him secretary of his local golf club. Chappy Bowers loves his golf.'

'And where did you bump into him – on the thirteenth green?'

'Don't be silly, Rumpole. He rang me up when he read about your collapse in the *Evening Standard*. He agrees with me that you must have a complete rest. It's the only answer.'

'Has he got any medical qualifications, this Chappy person?'

'Not that I know of, but he's truly understanding, and, what's more, he's asked me out for dinner.'

'Where to – the club house?'

'Of course not. He knows this little place in Soho. Very intimate and excellent cooking. He's told me I'll adore Chez Achille . . . Good heavens!'

This last breathed, barely whispered exclamation arose from Hilda's observation of the bed next to mine. David Stoker had been called for an X-ray. He couldn't immediately get up and go. A thin chain, about eight-foot long, was cuffed to his wrist and the wrist of an overweight screw who, dressed informally in a sweater and track-suit trousers, sat at the end of David Stoker's bed, easy listening also fastened to his ears. The screw rose and this mini-chaingang left us.

'He's in chains, Rumpole!' Hilda couldn't get over it. 'That patient is in chains!'

'That's right.' I did my best to reassure her. 'He's not dangerous. It's just that he had his operation while awaiting trial and the prison hospital's full up. He's got a bit of previous form, I know. Apart from that he's not a bad sort of young fellow.'

'Good heavens!' Hilda repeated her prayer. 'What's he waiting trial for?'

'House-breaking by night, I think it is. Armed with a pistol.'

She looked at me then, and said, more in sorrow than in anger, 'You just can't keep away from them, can you, Rumpole? The criminal classes. You just can't keep away from them at all.'

'Mr Rumpole.' The voice in the darkness came from the chained man in the bed beside me. 'Was that your wife, Mr Rumpole?'

'What did you think?'

'Well, I hardly thought it was your girlfriend.' He laughed softly but I didn't join in his laughter. 'She's a member of the public, isn't she? All members of the public hate me for what they think I've done.'

'What have you done, exactly?'

'Only got shot up so badly I had to have two hours on the operating table. Only got pumped as full of lead as a fucking pencil. And for getting that done to me, I'll probably get four years. That's what they tell me my brief's thinking of, four to five he reckons. That's my youth gone, all that's left of it.'

'Who's this brief you speak of?'

'It's a Mr Erskine-Brown QC. He's a senior man.'

'QC? I've always thought those letters stand for "Queer Customer". If you've got Claude defending you, you might as well plead guilty. He'll probably do you a very nice plea in mitigation.' As soon as I'd said that I regretted it. It wasn't worthy of me. The onset of death, I thought, brings out the worst in you.

'I'm joking of course,' I told him. 'Claude Erskine-Brown is a man of considerable experience.' And I restrained myself from adding, 'Of opera.'

There was silence then. At last my neighbour spoke in a smaller voice. 'I always heard you were a fighter, Mr Rumpole.'

'Where did you hear that?'

'Round the Scrubs. When I was in there. They were talking about it.'

'You've got a bit of previous, haven't you?'

'Quite a bit, to be honest. I was a bad lad in my younger years. Before I decided to straighten myself out.'

'Why don't you two shut the fuck up.' It was the snorer, to whom I owed quite a few sleepless nights, sending us a message from the other side of the ward.

I had read enough, when I was alive and kicking, in the newspaper accounts of the shooting at Badgershide Wood to recall David Stoker's past, both as instigator and victim of the affair, and to be able to inform Hilda of my neighbour's problem. The next day he opened his locker and brought out a bundle of press cuttings, copies of the indictment and statements of evidence, so I was able to sit up in bed and read the details of the events which had led my neighbour to the operating table and would take him to my familiar hunting ground at the Old Bailey and, in all probability, to a long term of imprisonment.

Badgershide Wood, from what I found out about it, did its best to claim that it was still a country village, an island in the suburban sprawl that stretched from the north-west of London towards the Chiltern Hills. It had a small Norman church, a main street, two pubs, four antiques shops, a hairdressing salon called Snippers and a Thai restaurant. In the middle of the village, larger and more imposing than the church, was a Georgian house which had been the home of the Dunkerton family for generations. The present heir, Major Ben Dunkerton, was the hero who had peppered Stoker with shots and confined him to bed in chains.

Major Ben Dunkerton, who succeeded in behaving like an eccentric but amiable country squire in what had, in fact, become a suburb of London, did a great deal to preserve Badgershide Wood's claim to be a rural community. He was old enough to have joined the army in the last years of the war and had been honourably wounded after D-Day as a very young officer. He stayed on in the army until he took over the family business and became the chairman of a local firm of estate agents. During his long retirement he was a favourite customer at the Badger's Arms, had a kind word for everyone in the village street and penetrated more deeply into the countryside to shoot with his old friends. He fished in Scotland and, although childless and a long-time widower, gave a lavish party for all the Badgershide Wood children at Christmas. He was spoken of with great affection as a thoroughly good chap, one who enjoyed his malt whisky and still, God bless him, had an eye for the girls.

Major Dunkerton's account of the night of the fifth of March was a simple one. He'd gone upstairs to get ready for bed when he heard sounds of breaking glass and something knocked over in the kitchen. He kept a shotgun upstairs, since there had been a number of cases of armed robbery in well-known country houses. He loaded the shotgun and went downstairs, calling first at the kitchen, where he saw a pane of glass broken, a window forced open and crockery smashed. Someone had undoubtedly crawled in through the window. The light had been left on.

Then he crossed the hall to the library, which was also lit. The door was open and he could see someone standing by his desk, a man he had no difficulty in identifying as Stoker. As the intruder turned, the major saw he had what looked like an old army pistol in his hand. Before Stoker could shoot, the major fired the shotgun and he fell, as the major thought at first, dead. Before he could fully examine the fallen body, there was a loud knocking at the front door. It was Doctor Jefferson who, on his way to his home next door, had heard the shot and, when the major opened the door to him, saw what at first sight he also thought was a dead body.

The police and the ambulance were called. When it was discovered that the shots hadn't killed Stoker, the major was, to quote Doctor Jefferson, 'in a terrible state of anxiety as to whether the wretched robber was going to live or die'. What was clear from the newspaper cuttings, however, was that the great British public couldn't care less about the fate of my neighbour in the ward, and Major Ben Dunkerton was a national hero. His right to defend his house against an armed intruder was trumpeted. MAJOR'S HOUSE HIS CASTLE; HE GOT HIS SHOT IN FIRST; 76-YEAR-OLD MAJOR SHOOTS FOR HIS LIFE; ARMED THUGS BETTER NOT MESS WITH MAJOR BEN: such were the headlines in all the papers.

The major was charged with unlawful wounding, grievous bodily harm and a firearms offence. It was clear that the press regarded his trial as a short preliminary before a triumphant acquittal and the receipt of a George Medal for bravery. Stoker, the armed robber, however, was sure to be sent to prison for a sizeable chunk of the foreseeable future, once he was well enough to leave hospital.

Stoker's statement told a very different story – and one which, in contrast to Major Ben's clear account, seemed hard to swallow. His childhood had been perfectly happy. The only child of an insurance salesman and a devoted mother, he had done well at school and seemed set for a decent job, a first home on a mortgage and holidays on the Costa Brava. He was only seventeen, however, when, in the course of a night's clubbing, he fell in with a group of boys a year or two older, who had graduated from nicking car radios and snatching unattended handbags to house-breaking. 'It's the excitement, Mr Rumpole,' Stoker told me during one of our many conversations. 'There's no drug, no drink you can take like it. Standing in someone else's place when you know anything you fancy is yours to pick up, and them snoring upstairs. All right, it's dangerous. That's what's exciting about it. Dangerous but so easy, sometimes I had a hard job not to laugh out loud.' By the time he was twenty-five, Stoker had half a dozen convictions and got four years.

It was in prison that he began to write a wry, unselfpitying account of life in the nick and the memories of a house-breaker, which led, apparently, to his reform. His book was serialized in a Sunday paper. He became, in the public eye, the statutory reformed con, the hard man gone soft, who appeared on television chat shows, took part in *Any Questions* and was rung up to comment yet again on the latest Criminal Justice Act introduced by New Labour. So, instead of coming out of prison with a few pounds and an irresistible temptation to return to crime, Stoker had a flat in now fashionable Hackney and a steady income from his writing and as an adviser to a spate of British gangster films. He was held up as an example of how prison can work and how a long dose of it produces a reformed citizen wanting to appear on *Newsnight*. Such hopes were dashed by the appearance of David Stoker, not answering the questions of the day but armed and having broken into an elderly stranger's house by night.

As I say, Stoker's explanation would have seemed way beyond the bounds of probability, even in the gangster films on which he gave advice. There was a girl named Dawn, once the girlfriend of one of his burgling mates, whom he had always fancied. They had met again by chance in a club round Notting Hill Gate and she had told him that she had tired of London and had a flat in a town near Badgershide Wood, where she had satisfied a long-held ambition to open a hairdressing salon. Now she had a thriving business offering up-to-the-minute hairdos to a large catchment area. So far so bad. Stoker's knowledge of the village, and the presence of a large and robbable house, was now explained.

From there on his story got stranger. He had, he said, met Major Ben Dunkerton before. Dawn was busy with a customer and he had gone for a walk in the woods, where an elderly man with a tweed cap and a walking stick came up to him and said he recognized him from the television.

'I've seen you around the village from time to time,' the major said. 'Attractive place, isn't it?' And he added, with a particular emphasis, 'I'm sure it must have many attractions for you.'

Then he went on to be extremely complimentary to Stoker on his reform and his literary skills. 'Wouldn't your book make a tremendously exciting film?' the major asked him, before mentioning a hugely famous, although also elderly, film director whom he said he had known 'since our National Service days', who would love to meet David. And so a meeting was arranged for one of the few nights when the director would be touching down in Badgershide Wood between Los Angeles and his current location in Morocco.

'Have to be a bit late, I'm afraid. Sam is having dinner with the money people. But he'll be back at my house around ten thirty, if you'd like to call in for a nightcap?'

Stoker said he took all this in, including the major's improbable demand for secrecy.

'Sam would hate there to be any sort of publicity about meeting you before a deal's done. So if you could keep quiet about all this, to everyone?'

'Of course.'

'Better not even tell your friend the hairdresser. You know how quickly these stories get about.'

'All right, I won't tell her. I'm going back to London tonight anyway.'

'So why not drive straight to my house tomorrow evening? You can park round the back. Not a word to anybody.'

Not unnaturally, Stoker was surprised at the complexity of these arrangements. 'Why are you doing all this for me?'

'Because I think, from what I've heard and read about you,' the major told him, 'you're a decent lad that's doing his best to go straight, and I want to encourage you.'

Stoker put it down to being so used to obeying orders and having everything arranged for him in prison that he obeyed the major's curious instructions. He drove down the next evening, straight from his flat in Hackney. He got to the major's house at ten twenty-five, parked behind it and walked round to ring at the front door.

Before he could touch the bell the door was opened by the smiling major, who showed him into the study, a book-lined room. On the desk, carefully laid out on the blotter between the paperweight and a letter-opener, lay an old service revolver.

'Used to be mine in my army days. I brought it home when I was demobbed. I know you're interested in guns.'

'I never went tooled up,' Stoker said he assured the major.

'Just feel it. Perfect balance, hasn't it? For an outdated weapon.'

Again obedient, Stoker picked up the pistol, felt its weight as directed and put it down as quickly as possible. 'I know Sam will want guns in his picture,' the major said. 'By the way he's just gone upstairs for something. I'll go and hurry him up.'

The major left then, but returned almost immediately. What happened next was, according to Stoker, quite inexplicable. As he turned to face the door, his host lifted a shotgun and fired. Stoker remembered a blow like a kick from a horse, a sudden and terrible pain, and then darkness – until he came to, bumping in the back of an ambulance in such agony that he wished he'd never woken up.

One other fact emerged from the mass of papers he'd handed me. Sam, the famous film director, was nowhere near England on the date of the shooting and, when asked, denied all knowledge of Badgershide or Major Dunkerton. All this proved was that either David Stoker or the major was lying prodigiously. That was no help to either of them.

'Long time, Rumpole, such a very long time no see.'

When I first put on the whitest of white wigs, having joined the chambers of C. H. Wystan, my wife Hilda's 'Daddy', there was, if I recollect, a rather chubby, smiling-for-no-reason young barrister, reduced to inarticulate jelly by appearing in court for something really taxing, like fixing a date for a hearing. His career in the law had been short and unimpressive, but Chappy Bowers, as he rather liked to be known, had, as the climax of an apparently harmless and uneventful life, 'bumped into' Hilda after ringing her up because he'd heard of my collapse in court. Unexpected and uninvited, he turned up and sat himself down in my visitor's chair just when my mind was full of strange and far more interesting business at Badgershide Wood. He still managed to look boyish in his grey-haired age. His face was round and chubby, his eyes blue and anxious to please and he had, over the years, become no more articulate.

'When we were, er . . . in chambers together, I – well, what I mean is we – were both of us, what's the word? Umm . . . smitten by Hilda Wystan.'

'I suppose we were.' I didn't want to tell him that, from my point of view, I sometimes felt that the smiting had gone on for a lifetime.

'What I really came to, well . . . I mean, umm, what I came to . . . well, really, and in all honest truth, Rumpole, to say was that if anything should happen to you. And it's a big "if".'

'No, it's not.' I couldn't help correcting him. 'It's not a big "if" at all. I collapsed in court with a dicky ticker. I'm confined in the hospital block and have no idea when I'll get out of it. Any day, to be honest with you, I might lose my grasp of the twig.'

'Well, if that . . . Well if . . . Which umm – we profoundly . . . Well, not profoundly. What's the word?'

'Sincerely?'

'That's it, Rumpole! Trust you, old fellow. You always knew the right word. Sincerely.'

'That's the word you use when you don't mean what you're saying.'

'No? Not really? No! I do mean this. Of . . . umm. Of course I do. If, again I say *if*, you should drop off the . . . What was it, Rumpole?'

'Twig?' I suggested.

'Yes, if you should drop off the twig, Hilda knows she'd always have someone to look after her.'

'You mean her friend Dodo Mackintosh?'

'No, Rumpole.' Now the words came out in a rush. 'I honestly mean me.'

'You'd look after Hilda, if I turned up my toes?'

'It would be an honour and a privilege.'

'Then all I can say, Chappy, old darling, for the sake of your health and sanity, is I'd better make an astonishing recovery.'

Conversation dried up then, until Chappy leant towards me and said in a penetrating whisper, 'That fellow in the next bed – looks, well . . . umm, chained up.'

'That's because he *is* chained up,' I explained. 'It's what they do to you nowadays if you get shot.'

When Chappy had gone back to his golf club, apparently unshaken in his desire to take care of She Who Must Be Obeyed, I asked Ted, the screw, to put the headphones on again for another

dose of Petula Clark and asked the wounded suspect just a few more
questions.

'You parked your car round the back of the house. Did you notice
a kitchen window open?'

'It was quite dark.'

'A window broken?'

'I didn't notice.'

'Did *you* break a window?'

'I told you, I came in by the front door.'

'You say the major was there waiting. He opened it for you.'

'He must have seen my car arrive.'

'You told me that.'

After that I gave my full attention to the evidence of the scene of
crime officer, with particular relation to finger-prints.

'Henry.' I was on the ward telephone to my clerk.

'Mr Rumpole! We heard you were taken really bad, sir. It's good
to hear you're still with us, as you might say.'

'As you might say, Henry, if you were in a particularly tactless mood.
Never mind. It's wonderful to hear your voice. Just like old times.'

'It's not about work, is it, sir? Mrs Rumpole rang to say we weren't
to worry you about work. She said you'd be resting from now on. It
made me feel envious. Not much rest round Equity Court. Not for
a clerk, there isn't.'

'It's not about my work. Actually, it's about someone else's work.
Mr Erskine-Brown's got an attempted robbery case called Stoker.'

'The Badgershide Wood job? I'm afraid it's going to clash with a
civil he's got. Personal injury with real money to it. Claude's leading
Mizz Probert in the crime.'

'Henry.'

'Yes, sir?'

'Remind me to order the drinks in Pommeroy's if you let them
clash. And go for the civil.'

'That's what I had in mind. But why exactly?'

'Who knows? I might be leading Mizz Liz in the Badgershide
shooting business. Stranger things have happened.'

'You think Mrs Rumpole would allow it, sir . . . ?'

'We'll wait and see if we've got any sort of defence. Oh, and get Bonny Bernard to give me a ring here, will you? The Princess Margaret ward. You have to sell your soul here to make an outside call.'

The system was that a telephone was wheeled to the side of your bed as though it was a cardiogram machine or materials for a blanket bath. If there was a call for you, it came after a short interval. If you wanted to make a call you had to wait a considerable time for the instrument, and also provide money to cover its cost. I had to pay out to call Henry, so I was relieved when Bonny Bernard's voice was wheeled towards me, with a selection of pills as an after-breakfast treat.

'You had a brief in a sensational shoot-out in an old-age pensioner's home and you sent it to Erskine-Brown?' I accused the man.

'I was planning it for you. But then we heard you'd left the Bar.'

'The Bar? I never left it. Left life perhaps, but the Bar? Never! Now listen, my old darling. It's very possible that Claude Queer Customer may not be able to do this case owing to the pressures of civil work in the personal injuries department.'

'So we'll have to look elsewhere, then.'

'You may not have to look very far. The future depends, to a certain extent, on the evidence of the heart. All I ask is that you don't rush into any decisions. And there's one thing you can do.' I gave Bonny Bernard certain instructions and then I asked him if he'd like to speak to his client. 'He happens to be here beside me.'

'Mr Rumpole,' Bernard's question came in a horrified whisper, 'you're not in the nick, are you?'

'Don't worry, old darling. He's in hospital.'

I covered the mouthpiece and called to my neighbour, 'Would you like to speak to your solicitor?'

'No point, is there? He came to see me before you got here. Then he sent me all these papers. I could see it in his face. He didn't believe a word I said.'

'We'll talk to you later,' I told Bernard, 'when we've decided if there's a possible defence.'

'Can't you remember, Mr Rumpole, you're meant to rest . . .' My old friend started some form of protest and I put the phone down gently.

It happened a few mornings later when Stoker needed some minor surgery. He was wheeled away chained to his trolley and accompanied by his shadow, Ted, the ever-present screw. I saw another visitor enter the ward, a thin, hawk-like figure in a crumpled mackintosh, carrying, like an angel in a painting, a stiff, upright bunch of white lilies as though to deck the top of a coffin. He sat in my visitor's chair, removed his hat, and Esmeralda, the cheerful Jamaican nurse we were always glad to see, relieved him of his flowers, promising to put them in water.

'Would you rather have had grapes, Mr Rumpole?'

'Grapes, lilies, it's all the same to me,' I told him. 'It's you I wanted to see, Fig. You're going to provide the key to my present problem.'

'Your heart?'

Did Ferdinand Isaac Gerald (known to us as Fig) Newton believe that I credited him with medical skills?

'Of course not. My heart can look after itself. It would, however, be greatly encouraged by a solution to the mystery of the Badgershide Wood shooting.'

'Is it a mystery, Mr Rumpole? In my paper it's just a decent citizen defending himself and his property.'

'Perhaps your paper doesn't know the half of it.'

'No? You may be right, Mr Rumpole. What's the other half, then?'

'That's exactly what I want you to find out. Hang around Badgershide Wood with your ears open. Find out all you can about the eccentric major. Oh and there's a girl called Dawn something who works at Snippers the hairdressers.'

'You want her kept under twenty-four-hour observation? I'm afraid we're in for some inclement weather.' Fig sniffed gloomily, as though in anticipation of the cold he was likely to catch.

'Don't just observe her. Meet her. Take her off to the Thai restaurant. Make her like you. Say that if she tells us all she knows, it just might help her wounded lover escape a lengthy sentence. Mention my name if you have to. Say that Rumpole is relying on her. No, better still, tell her that a hospital patient in chains thinks of her constantly.'

'I brought you a few grapes, Rumpole.'

'That was very thoughtful of you, Hilda.'

'Don't eat them all at once. They looked nice in the shop.' She Who Must pulled off a couple and chewed them thoughtfully. 'Not bad at all. Nice and juicy. Well now, Rumpole.' She looked at me with an eye born to command. 'I want you to make a complete recovery.'

'Anything you say, Hilda.' I had no intention of arguing with her. 'Your fancy man was here.'

'My what?'

'Your fellow. Your little bit on the side,' I might have said. Instead I stuck to 'Your friend Chappy Bowers. The one who took you out to a candlelit dinner. I hope you enjoyed it.'

'I did *not* enjoy it, Rumpole!'

'Veal escalope on the tough side, was it? Nasty collapse of the soufflé at . . . What was it called?'

'Chez Achille in Soho. The ladies' lavatory was down a long, damp staircase and far too near the kitchen, and I didn't find the tablecloth entirely clean.'

'And no candles?'

'Oh yes. There was a nasty guttering thing in an old wine bottle. The waiter was extremely familiar with Chappy and said, "Another of your girlfriends, Mr Bowers?" before we even got a glance at the menu.'

'Wasn't that rather a compliment?' The waiter, I thought, was laying it on with a trowel by putting Hilda in the 'girlfriend' category.

'Not to be called a girlfriend of Chappy's. I imagine they're a lot of old trouts.'

'Oh yes,' I nodded. 'Of course that's what they probably are.'

'I wouldn't want to be the "girlfriend", Rumpole, of any man who added up his bill.'

'Did Chappy do that?'

'Worse than that. They gave us each, Rumpole, a "selection of vegetables" on two small plates.'

'That was bad news?'

'I wasn't greatly impressed. We had a few bullet-hard potatoes, some green beans that were also undercooked, and three undersized carrots. Well, Chappy actually asked for a reduction because we hadn't eaten the potatoes.'

'On the tight side, as I remember. Always fumbled for his money when it was his turn at Pommeroy's.'

'He is the sort of man, Rumpole, who would check up on a woman's shopping list.'

I knew a great deal of the Rumpoles' income was frittered away on such luxuries as Ajax, kitchen rolls and saucepan scourers, but I would never have intruded on the sanctity of Hilda's list.

'So I want you to recover, Rumpole,' she went on. 'You may have your faults, but you don't argue about the selection of vegetables. So, what I'm trying to tell you is, I simply couldn't put up with a person like Chappy Bowers. I want you back round the house.'

'That is very encouraging, Hilda.'

'I hope you will agree to give up work entirely. That's the only way you're going to get well. It's so good your being here, where you can't spend your time worrying about crimes.'

I glanced at the prisoner in the next bed. He lowered the *Daily Beacon* slightly and closed one eye in a discreet wink.

I took the opportunity to discuss the major with the customers in the Badger's Arms as well as the staff at the local garage and the owners of at least two of the antiques shops. On all sides he's spoken of as a hero who was acting in self-defence and to protect his property. There is no sympathy whatsoever for the client.

Fig Newton's reports never concealed the bad news, for which he has a particular relish. He went on:

The major is admired as an amiable eccentric. 'His own man,' the landlord of the Badger's Arms told me. 'One of the old school. Friendly with everyone, likes his drop of Scotch and always got an eye for the ladies.' It's the landlord's opinion that the client, when he entered the major's house, got exactly what he deserved. Several of the regulars in the Badger's Arms and the landlord said they had seen the client, whom they recognized from his photograph in the papers, on his visits to Snippers the hairdressers.

I myself called at Snippers on the pretext of a hair wash and trim, as the place is advertised as 'unisex'. Dawn Maresfield was engaged with another client and I was attended to by a 'trainee stylist'. I did, however, get the chance of a word with Miss Maresfield, and when I told her we were acting in the interests of David Stoker, she agreed to meet me after work. We fixed a rendezvous in the Pizza Palace of the Parallelogram Shopping Mall, about eight miles from Badgershide Wood. Her reason for choosing this venue was, she said, that 'people were talking'.

At my meeting with Miss Maresfield, I formed a favourable impression of her and think that, if the time should ever come, she'd make a good witness. She said she was very disappointed with David, who she thought had gone back to his old criminal ways and ruined his life. She was, however, extremely worried about his condition and, when pressed, said she would see him again, and I feel she retains her affection for him.

Her attitude to the major was in marked contrast to the view of him held by all the other witnesses. When I first mentioned him she sighed heavily and said, 'Don't talk about *him*.' When I told her that he was what I wanted her to talk about, she said he'd been a pest, a nuisance, a bit of a joke at times, and at times a menace. I asked if that meant he had taken a fancy to her, and she said she would have described it as 'besotted'. He'd sent her flowers, presents, bits of jewellery that had belonged to his family which didn't suit her and she had no use for. She said she'd been out with him once or twice but she'd got tired of moving his hand off her knee. 'He even tried to stick his tongue down my throat in the car and would have if I hadn't clenched my teeth on him. At his age it is just ridiculous.' His letters to her became 'just disgusting', so she stopped opening them. Quite recently he'd telephoned her at work and told her he knew she'd marry him if it wasn't for that 'bloody little crook' he'd seen her with. She thought that when he said that he was probably drunk, because she'd never told him about Stoker and, as far as she knew, they'd never met. She never told Stoker about the major's advances as she was afraid he'd go up to the big house and make a scene, which would do her no good: she relied on the major's many friends of both sexes to get their hair styled at Snippers.

I don't know how much this helps and I am not clear at the moment what further steps I can take. I therefore await further instructions and I enclose my account, which includes travel expenses and a reasonable sum for entertaining at the Badger's Arms and the Pizza Palace in the Parallelogram Shopping Mall.

(signed) F. I. G. Newton. Member of the National Institute of Enquiry Agents

I put down Fig's report and yes, I thought, we're ready for trial. I had a great deal to say and I could hardly wait for an opportunity to say it.

It was late, almost midnight, when I began my final speech. I made it to a jury which included the snorer, the tooth-grinder and the serial urinator, who stayed in his bed during the greater part of it. I was sufficiently confident of my case to allow Ted, the screw on duty, to remove his earphones and listen from the public gallery. Quietly and, I believe, with perfect fairness, I outlined the prosecution case, the facts which had appeared in all the newspapers, the story of an outraged householder who was merely upholding the sacred principle that an Englishman's home is his castle.

'Now I come,' I spoke even more quietly, causing the jury to listen attentively as I lured them into taking another and totally different view of the facts, 'to the case for the defence of David Stoker. The defence is not made easier by the fact that it is well known that he had committed offences in the past, indeed he has written about them and spoken about them on television. We are not trying him for his past offences, and you must be even more vigilant to see that he is not now, because of his past, convicted of a crime he didn't commit.

'The first thing that puzzled me was the report of the scene of crime officer who was in charge of taking fingerprints. There were, of course there were, Mr Stoker's fingerprints on the old army pistol on the library table, but, extraordinarily enough, members of the jury, *nowhere else*. In the light of that, let us consider how he got into the house.

'You will remember the kitchen window, broken and forced, things knocked over by the kitchen sink, clear signs that someone had climbed in that way. But none of Mr Stoker's fingerprints! Many of the major's fingerprints, of course – that was to be expected, in his kitchen. But what is suggested here? That Mr Stoker wore gloves? No gloves were found on him or anywhere near the scene of the crime. And remember, he was taken straight from the library floor to hospital. Do you think he climbed in through the kitchen window and then carefully wiped all the surfaces on which he might have left his prints? Can you picture that happening, Members of the Jury? Is it within the realms of probability? Let us take this matter a little further. There were none of Mr Stoker's prints by the front door, none on the bell push, none at all. Does that, or does it not, Members of the Jury, support the suggestion that the major heard Mr Stoker's car arrive and park at the back of the house, so he opened the front door to him? Was Mr Stoker a visitor the major was expecting? Could it be, could it just possibly be, he was a visitor the major had invited? The major has said he never saw Mr Stoker before in his life. Can you really believe that, if he opened the door before Mr Stoker had even rung the bell? Let us see, shall we, if we can find the facts that might account for this.

'Mr Stoker undoubtedly visited Badgershide Wood on a number of occasions to see his girlfriend, Dawn Maresfield, who worked in the hairdresser's shop. He stayed with her in her flat, which was in the town a few miles away, but you've heard that he sometimes drove her to work and picked her up again in his car. Now I have to give you a rather different picture of the lovable and eccentric major. He was seriously sexually obsessed with Dawn, and you'll forgive me if I take up a little more of your time by reading an account of a conversation Miss Maresfield had with a highly reputable private detective, a Mr Ferdinand Isaac Gerald Newton.' (Here Fig Newton's evidence was read to the jury.)

'What picture have you in your minds now, Members of the Jury, of Major Ben Dunkerton? Is it not of an old man sexually obsessed with a young woman almost to the point of insanity? So obsessed that he starts to give her the family jewellery, which she doesn't want, and writes her letters so embarrassingly obscene that she stops reading them. But does he get more and more deeply convinced that she might, at last, be tempted by his house and his wealth and agree to be his mistress, perhaps his wife? Only one thing, he was deluded enough to think, stood in his way. She has a lover, much younger and considerably more attractive than the elderly major, and moreover a man with a criminal past whom she feels she can keep on the straight and narrow path of virtue. Does it need a great effort of your imagination, Members of the Jury, to understand how the major managed to convince himself that, if only her lover was removed, Miss Dawn Maresfield might become available to him?

'How did he set about it? He had, we all have, read cases in the papers of householders shooting at intruders and earning public approval. Did this outrageous plan begin to form in the obsessed, in the by now mentally unbalanced, old man's mind? We all have to grow old, Members of the Jury, but we may hope to come to terms with the limitations of old age and not, in a vain effort to recover some of the joys of youth, commit desperate and criminal acts. So let us look again at the evidence and see if we can see behind the carefully calculated pretence and discover exactly what Major Ben Dunkerton did out of frustrated love and irrational jealousy.

'First he met Mr Stoker when he was walking in the woods. You may think that he had Mr Stoker under observation for some time and his plan to obliterate his rival had been carefully worked out. You'll remember he asked Mr Stoker about the attraction of Badgershide Wood, a question which might well have had a reference to the charms of Dawn. He then invented a story about a famous film director wanting to meet Mr Stoker, a ploy which had no point except to lure my client to the major's house after ten thirty on a particular night. He risked this pack of lies because he didn't expect David to live to tell the tale.

'What did the major do on the night of the visit, Members of the

401

Jury? Consider this as a possibility with me. Did he break his kitchen window? Did he, carefully and deliberately, create evidence of a break-in? Then, when he heard the car, did he open his front door and welcome in the man he was prepared to kill?

'It all went quite easily. He took Mr Stoker into the library, and showed him the old army pistol he had brought home from the war and never bothered to get a licence for. He told Mr Stoker to handle the weapon, so his fingerprints might be left on it. And then, Members of the Jury, he left the room to fetch his shotgun.

'None of us can know, not one of us should ever know, what it feels like to commit a murder. Was the major afraid, or triumphant, or filled with nervous excitement? What it was that caused his shotgun to go off too soon we shall never know. Did his old finger press the trigger before he'd taken aim? Did he see Mr Stoker duck down behind the table and try to follow him like a moving bird? All we know is that he shot his rival for Dawn's affection, but, happily, he didn't kill him. His victim is here, in the bed beside me, still alive to tell you his story.

'Did this happen, Members of the Jury? Is that an account which fits all the facts of this case? If you think it's true you will, of course, acquit. But if you only think it might very well be true, if as a thoughtful and fair-minded jury you cannot reject the possibility, then you must also acquit because the prosecution won't have satisfied you beyond reasonable doubt.

'Members of the Jury, this case has only occupied a short part of your lives. Perhaps an hour of late-night entertainment to take the place of the telly or the headphones. You will soon forget all about Badgershide Wood, and Snippers hairdresser's, and the conversation in the Pizza Palace. But for David Stoker, whom I represent, this case represents the whole of his life. Is he to go free, or is he to be forced, by the devilish plot of a mad old man, back to his misspent younger life of prison and crime? It is his life I now leave, Members of the Jury, in your hands, confident that he will hear from you, in the fullness of time, those blessed words "Not guilty" which, more effectively than any surgery, will give life back to David Stoker.'

Then with a great flood of relief, I lay back on the pillows and closed my eyes. My final speech was over and I could do no more. The decision now had to be taken by other beds. It was the best moment of an anxious trial. As I lay resting, I heard the sound of distant voices. Verdicts came from the snorer, the tooth-grinder and many others. 'Not guilty,' they said, and 'Not guilty' they all voted. Even Ted, the screw, at the end of the chain piped up with 'I don't reckon David did it.' So the trial in the Princess Margaret ward was over.

Would I ever do the case down the Bailey? Would I ever repeat that closing speech to a real jury, up and dressed, in a real jury box? I felt sleep drifting over me, dulling my senses and darkening my world. Should I ever . . . Who knows? For the moment all I can say is, 'The defence rests.'

Rumpole and the Primrose Path

The regular meeting of the barristers who inhabit my old chambers in Equity Court took place, one afternoon, in an atmosphere of particular solemnity. Among those present was a character entirely new to them, a certain Luci Gribble, whom our leader, in a momentary ambition to reach the status of 'entrepreneur', had taken on as director of marketing and administration.

Mizz Liz Probert, observing the scene, later described Luci (why she had taken to this preposterous spelling of the name of Wordsworth's great love was clear to nobody) as in her thirties, with a 'short bob', referring to hair which was not necessarily as blonde as it seemed, a thin nose, slightly hooded eyes and a determined chin. She wore a black trouser suit and bracelets clinked at her wrists. The meeting was apparently interrupted from time to time, as she gave swift instructions to the mobile phone she kept in her jacket pocket. She also wore high-heeled black boots which Liz Probert priced at not far short of three hundred pounds.

'I'm vitally concerned with the profile of Equity Court.' Luci had a slight northern accent and a way, Liz noticed, of raising her voice at the end of her sentence, so every statement sounded like a question. 'I take it that it's in the parameters of my job description to include the field of public relations and the all-important question of the company's – that is to say' (here Liz swears that Luci corrected herself reluctantly) 'the *chambers*' image. Correct, Chair?'

This was an undoubted question, but it seemed to be addressed to an article of furniture, one of that old dining-room set, now much mended and occasionally wobbly, which had been bequeathed to Equity Court in the will of C. H. Wystan, my wife Hilda's father and once head of our chambers. However, Soapy Sam Ballard, as our present head and so chairman of the meeting, appeared to follow the new arrival's drift.

'Of course that's your job, Luci.' Soapy Sam was on Christian-name terms with the woman who called him chair. 'To improve our image. That's why we hired you. After all, we don't want to be described as a group of old fuddy-duddies, do we?' Chair, who might be thought by some to fit the description perfectly, smiled round at the meeting.

'It's not so much the fuddy-duddy label that concerns me at the moment, although I shall be including that in a future presentation. It's the heartless thing that worries me.'

'Heartless?' Ballard was puzzled.

'The public image of barristers,' Luci told the meeting, 'equals money-grabbing fat cats, insincere defenders of clients who are obviously guilty, chauvinists and outdated wig-wearing shysters.'

'Did you say "shysters"?' Claude Erskine-Brown, usually mild mannered, ever timid in court, easily doused by a robust opponent or an impatient judge, rose in his seat (once again this is the evidence of Liz Probert) and uttered a furious protest. 'I insist you withdraw that word "shyster".'

'No need for that, Erskine-Brown.' Ballard was being gently judicial. 'Luci is merely talking us through the public perception.'

'You put it, Chair, succinctly and to the point.' Once again, Luci was grateful to the furniture.

'Oh, well. If it's only the public perception.' Erskine-Brown sank back in his seat, apparently mollified.

'What we have to demonstrate is that barristers have outsize hearts. There is no section of the community, and we can prove this by statistics, which cares more deeply, gives more liberally to charity, signs more letters to *The Times*, and shows its concern for the public good by pointing out more frequent defects in the railway system, than the old-fashioned, tried-and-trusted British barrister.'

'You can prove anything by statistics.' Erskine-Brown was still out, in a small way, to cause trouble.

'Exactly so.' Luci seemed unexpectedly delighted. 'So we have chosen our statistics with great care, and we shall use them to the best possible advantage. But I'm not talking statistics here. I'm talking of the situation, sad as I'm sure we all agree it may be, which gives us the opportunity to show that we *do* care.' Luci paused and seemed, for a moment, moved with deep emotion. 'So much so that we should all join in a very public display of heartfelt thanks.'

'Heartfelt thanks for what?' Erskine-Brown was mystified. 'Surely not our legal aid fees?'

At this point, Luci produced copies of a statement she invited Erskine-Brown to circulate. When Liz Probert got it, she found that it read:

We wish to give heartfelt thanks for the life of one of our number. An ordinary, workaday barrister. An old warhorse. One who didn't profess to legal brilliance, but one who cared deeply and whom we loved as a fellow member of number 3 Equity Court.

'By this act we shall show that barristers have hearts,' Luci summed up the situation.

'By what act is that, exactly?' Erskine-Brown was still far from clear.

'The memorial service. In the Temple Church for the late Horace Rumpole, barrister at law. Chair, I'm sure we can rely on you for a few remarks, giving thanks for a life of quiet and devoted service.'

It later emerged that at this stage of the chambers meeting Liz Probert, undoubtedly the most sensible member of the gathering, suggested that a discussion of a memorial service was a little premature in view of the fact that there had as yet been no announcement of Rumpole's death. Erskine-Brown told her that he had spoken to She Who Must Be Obeyed, who was, he said, 'putting a brave face on it', but admitted that I had been removed from the hospital to which I had been rushed after a dramatic failure in the ticker department, brought about by an unusually brutal encounter with Judge Bullingham, to the Primrose Path Home in Sussex, and would not be back in chambers for a very long time indeed. In that case, Liz suggested, all talk of a memorial service might be postponed indefinitely.

'Put our programme on hold?' Luci was clearly disappointed. 'It'd be a pity not to continue with the planning stage. Naturally, Mrs Rumpole's hoping for the best, but let's face it, at his age

Rumpole's actuarial chances of survival are approximate to a nega-
tive-risk situation –'

'And one knows, doesn't one,' Erskine-Brown asked, 'what places
like the Primrose Path are like? They call themselves "homes", but
the reality is they are –'

'What do you think they are?' Liz Probert was cynical enough to
ask. 'Houses of ill fame? Gambling dens? Five-star hotels?'

'They are places,' Erskine-Brown was looking at her, she said,
more in sorrow than in anger, 'where people are sent to end their
days in peace. They call themselves "convalescent homes" to reassure
the relatives. But the truth of it is that not many people come out of
them alive.'

'We'll need to put together a programme.' Ballard was seriously
worried. 'And we can hardly ask Mrs Rumpole for her help. As yet.'

'I have an aunt in Godalming.' Erskine-Brown seemed unnaturally proud of the fact. 'I can call in on Rumpole when I go down to
see her next.'

'And I'm sure your visit, Erskine-Brown,' Ballard said, 'will be a
welcome treat for Rumpole.'

As usual, our head of chambers had got it completely wrong.

So now Claude and I were together in my room in the Primrose
Path Home, somewhere on the sleepy side of Sussex. It was a place
of unremitting cleanliness, and so tidy that I was homesick for
the unwashed ashtray, resting place for the butt ends of small cigars,
the pile of unreturned briefs, the dusty, yellowing accounts of
ancient crimes (for which those found guilty must have now completed their sentences), outdated copies of Archbold on *Criminal
Law and Procedure*, and the Old English Law Reports, bound in
crumbling leather and gathering dust, as was the collapsing umbrella
left by some long-forgotten client. On the mantelpiece I kept a few
souvenirs of my notable cases: the bullet found embedded in the
radiogram in the Penge Bungalow affair, the china mug inscribed to
a 'Perfect Dad' from which Leonard Peterson had drunk his last,
arsenic-flavoured cup of tea, and the sheet music of 'In a Monastery
Garden', which Mrs Florence Davenport had been playing as she

awaited the news of her husband's death after his brakes had been partially severed by her lover.

By contrast, the Primrose Path Home was uncomfortably tidy. The atmosphere was heavy with the smell of furniture polish, chemical air fresheners and disinfectant. There was a constant hum of hoovering and the staff seemed to handle everything, including the patients, with rubber gloves.

'What's your favourite music, Rumpole?'

'Music, Erskine-Brown?'

'Schubert trio? Mozart concerto? We know you're absurdly prejudiced against Wagner. What about "When I was a little page" from Verdi's *Falstaff*?'

'I never was a little page! Don't babble, Erskine-Brown.'

'Or Elgar? Typically English, Elgar.'

'When I sing to myself, which is only very occasionally –' Poor old Claude seemed, for no particular reason, to be in some distress, and I was doing my best to help him out.

'Yes. Yes!' His nose twitched with excitement. 'Tell me, Rumpole. When you sing to yourself, what do you sing?'

'Sometimes "Pop Goes the Weasel". Occasionally "Knock'd 'em in the Old Kent Road". More often than not a ballad of the war years, "We're going to hang out the washing on the Siegfried Line". You remember that, don't you?'

'No, Rumpole, I'm afraid I don't.' Erskine-Brown's nose twitched again, though this time it was a sign of displeasure. He tried another tack. 'Tell me, Rumpole. Talking of the war years, did you ever serve your country overseas?'

'Oh yes,' I told Claude, in answer to his ridiculous question. 'I flew Spitfires in the war. I shot down the Red Baron and was the first British pilot to enter Berlin.'

Claude looked at me sadly and said, 'I only ask because Ballard wants material for his speech.'

'His speech about me?' I was puzzled.

'About your life. To give thanks for your existence.'

It sounded extremely improbable. 'Ballard's going to do that?'

'We shall celebrate you, Rumpole.'

'You mean –' I was hoping against all the probabilities that they were contemplating some sort of party '– a chambers piss-up in Pommeroy's Wine Bar? Drinks on the Soapy Sam Memorial Fund?'

'Not exactly that, Rumpole.' Claude glanced, nervously I thought, at his watch. 'I'd better be getting back. I've got a rating appeal tomorrow.'

'I envy you, Erskine-Brown. You seem to lead a life of perpetual excitement.'

'Oh, there's just one more thing.' The man was already on his feet. 'Do you have a favourite prayer?'

'Why do you ask?'

'To help us, Rumpole, to celebrate your life.'

'Then I pray to God to be left alone. So I can get out of here as quickly as possible. It's all far too clean for my liking.'

'I'm sure you're quite comfortable here, Rumpole.' Erskine-Brown gave me a smile of faint encouragement. 'And I know they'll look after you extremely well. For as long as you have left.'

At which he stood up and stole silently out of the room with the guilty look of a man leaving a funeral early.

When Erskine-Brown had gone, I watched morning television. A group of people had been assembled, having, it seemed, only one thing in common. They had each had sexual intercourse with someone who turned out to be a close relative. This incident in their lives, which many people might wish to keep discreetly under wraps, led them to speak out at length, as cheerfully as though they were discussing gardening or cookery, to the huge audience of the unemployed, the pensioned-off and the helpless in hospitals. As their eager, confiding faces filled the screen I began to doze off – the best way, I had found, of enjoying life at the Primrose Path Home.

Whoever had christened this place of eternal rest the Primrose Path betrayed insufficient knowledge of English literature. According to Ophelia in *Hamlet*, it's the path of dalliance – and any dalliance in the home was confined strictly to the television. The porter in *Macbeth*, however, said that the primrose way led 'to the everlasting bonfire'. This may have been a more accurate description. The inhabitants of the rooms down the corridor were given to disappearing quietly during the night and leaving the Primrose Path, I felt sure, for the nearest crematorium.

I woke up, it seemed hours later, to my untouched lunch, a tray mainly loaded with a plethora of paper napkins, much unwelcome salad and a glass of orange juice. I was searching for a mouthful of edible cheese under the stationery when I caught a sound, unusual, even unknown, in the Primrose Path. A woman was sobbing. People died there, but you heard no cries of agony, no angry slamming of doors or wailing of relatives. The sobs I heard were restrained, but they were undeniably heartfelt. I abandoned my lunch, switched off the television and moved, as quietly as I could manage it, into the corridor.

At the end of the passage, with its linoleum shining like polished shoes, a woman was sobbing as she watered a bowl of hyacinths. She was, perhaps, in her late forties, her chestnut hair fading a little, but with high cheekbones, usually amused eyes and a generous mouth. She was Nurse Albright, my favourite member of staff, known to me as 'Dotty Dorothy', owing to her habit of occasionally promising to dust off my aura by polishing the surrounding air. She also brought me an assortment of roots, herbs and leaves, which, if added to my tea, she promised, would soon make me fit to run a mile, spend a day defending in a murder trial and learn to tango at evening classes. She was, above all, cheerful and unfailingly kind, and we would sing together songs we both loved, songs I had kept from the prying ears of Erskine-Brown, such as 'Night and Day', 'That Old Black Magic' and 'Bewitched, Bothered and Bewildered', which I had danced to in a far-distant time, before Hilda's and my foxtrotting days were over.

Dotty Dorothy's singing, her use of herbs and strange roots, and, on many occasions, her kindness got her into frequent trouble with her boss, Sister Sheila Bradwell, who ruled the Primrose Path with the kind of enlightened and liberal principles which guided Captain Bligh when he was in charge of the *Bounty*. Sister Sheila recognized no superior being, except for one called Nanki-Poo, an evil-tempered, spoilt and domineering Pekinese whom I had seen the Sister kiss, fondle, feed with chocolate biscuits and generally spoil in a way she would never treat a patient. Like many of the inhabitants of the Primrose Path, Nanki-Poo suffered a degree of incontinence which littered the garden and added some significance to his name. He would also, when out walking, sit down if a leaf attached itself to his trailing hair, and yelp until a nurse came and relieved him of the encumbrance.

It was the sudden appearance of the powerful Sister Sheila, with or without her pet, that Nurse Dotty Albright feared as we stood chatting in the corridor.

'Get back into your room, Mr Rumpole,' Dotty swallowed a sob and wiped an eye on the back of her hand, 'before Sister spots you.'

'Never mind about Sister Sheila.' I had grown impervious to the icy disapproval of the head girl. 'Tell me what's the matter.'

'A terrible night, Mr Rumpole. It's been the most ghastly night ever at the Primrose Path.'

'Tell me what happened.'

'Poor Mr Fairweather . . . He passed away during the night. They took him away. It was my night off and they took him away without even telling me.'

I had caught a glimpse of Fairweather – Freddy, Dotty often called him – a short, beady-eyed, bald-headed, broad-shouldered man in a dressing-gown being pushed in a wheelchair to his room down the corridor. He was recovering, Dotty told me, from a massive heart attack, but she brought him roots and herbal remedies and he made jokes and flirtatious suggestions. Freddy and I, she assured me, were her two favourite patients.

'Can you imagine that?' Dotty said as she took out a crumpled handkerchief and blew her nose gently. 'Sister let them take him without even a chance of saying goodbye. Freddy would have hated that. He was full of rude suggestions, of course he was. He was a bit of a Jack the lad, we know that, even in his condition of health. But underneath all that, he had the most perfect manners. Even if he'd gone, even if it was too late, he'd have liked me to be there to hold his hand and say goodbye before he passed away. But *she* wouldn't have that. *She* has to know best, always.'

As Dotty went on talking, it appeared that the sad death of Freddy

Fairweather wasn't the only disaster of that long, eventful night. A certain Michael Masklyn, high up on the list of unpopular patients, had, in Dotty's words, 'done a runner' and strayed from the Primrose Path under the cover of darkness. Masklyn was an unknown quantity; he seemed to have few friends and no visitors except an older woman who had visited him once and, as their voices were raised in a quarrel, was heard to vow never to come near him again. He'd been transferred from a hospital which had, as might be expected, run out of beds, and found a place in the Primrose Path under some sort of government scheme. He had, Dotty assured me, a vile temper, was thankful for nothing, and had once thrown a glass containing his urine sample at the head of a trainee nurse who would do no harm to anybody.

'I never thought he was well enough to get out of here.' Dotty had stopped crying now and her voice was full of anger. 'Sister's security's just hopeless. His clothes were in his room, just as yours are, and Gavin was fast asleep at his desk downstairs. So Mr Masklyn just walked off and left us. I hate to say this to you, Mr Rumpole, but there's just no organization in this place. No organization at all. It's all rules and no practice. Not the place for either of us really, is it?'

Strangely enough, after that sad and eventful evening, the Primrose Path became, in some elusive and quiet way, more interesting. I tried to discuss the break-out of Michael Masklyn with Sister Sheila, but was met with pursed lips and the shortest of possible answers.

'He was an impossible patient,' Sheila Bradwell told me. 'In one way we were glad to get rid of him. But of course we had our duty of care. You can't keep an eye on everyone twenty-four hours a day.'

'Do the police know he's gone missing?' I felt a stirring of the old need to cross-examine the witness.

'We reported it, naturally, Mr Rumpole, if you're so interested. There was no sign of him at his last known address.'

'Did he have a family?'

'Someone he said was his sister came once. No one's been able to track her down either.'

'My friend Dotty says his door was locked in the morning when she came on duty.'

'Your friend Nurse Albright says a lot of things we don't have to take too much notice of. Of course the door wasn't locked at night. We locked it in the morning, until the police came to see if there were any clues to where he'd gone. You don't want the evidence disturbed. You know all about that, don't you, Mr Rumpole?'

'I suppose I do. All the same, it must have been a terrible night for you. I was sorry to hear about Mr Fairweather.'

Sister Sheila Bradwell stood looking at me, a straight-backed, straight-haired woman, born to command. I thought I saw in her eyes not sorrow for the passing of another patient, but a faint amusement at the fact that I had bothered to raise the subject.

'These things happen, Mr Rumpole, at a place like this. They're very sad, but they happen all the time. We've got used to it, of course. And we deal with it as kindly as possible, whatever your friend Nurse Albright may say about the matter.'

'She said she was very fond of Mr Fairweather. He was kind to her, and she enjoyed looking after him.'

'And did your friend tell you that dear old Mr Fairweather had also said he'd left her money in his will?' Sister Bradwell was smiling as she said that, and it came as something of a shock. After being clearly disapproved of for asking impertinent questions, it suddenly seemed as though I was being drawn into an argument from which, for the moment, I retreated.

'She never said anything like that. Only that she was upset because he died so suddenly.'

'Well, it's nothing for you to worry about, Mr Rumpole, is it? You can concentrate on getting a good rest. Shall I switch your telly on for you?'

'Please don't.'

'Very well then, Mr Rumpole. And if you take my advice, you'll steer very clear of your friend's herbal remedies. Some of them may have unfortunate results.'

★

In the days that followed, Dotty seemed unusually busy, but late one afternoon, as I woke from a light doze, I found her sitting by my bed with a surprise present. It was half a bottle of claret she had managed to get opened in an off-licence and smuggled in under her mac. We shared a toothglassful of a wine in the same humble class as Château Thames Embankment, but none the less welcome to a palate starved of alcohol. So the old friendly Dotty was back, but quieter and sadder, and I didn't dare suggest even a muted rendition of 'Bewitched, Bothered and Bewildered'.

'They don't want me to go to the funeral,' she said.

'Who doesn't want you to? The family?'

'No, Sister Sheila. And Freddy's special doctor. Freddy wouldn't see anyone else.'

The common run of patients, myself included, were attended to by one of the local GPs. However, the Primrose Path was visited almost daily by a tall, elegantly dressed man in a well-cut suit who moved down the corridor in a deafening smell of aftershave, always escorted by Sister Sheila and referred to by the staff, in tones of considerable awe, as Doctor Lucas.

'I've never got on with that Lucas. Well, they won't even tell me where the funeral's going to be.'

'They won't?'

'They said it was Freddy's special wish. He hated funerals . . .'

'Well, none of us like them. Particularly our own.'

'So he didn't want anyone to be there. That was his last wish, they told me. And, of course, he wanted to be cremated.'

The primrose way, I thought, to the everlasting bonfire.

'You know what happened? Doctor Lucas and Sister Sheila were with him when he died. They rang the undertaker, they said, and they had him taken away at once. During the night. As though . . . Freddy was something to be ashamed of.'

'You miss him, don't you?'

'Poor old darling. Sometimes he said he was in love.' She put a hand into the pocket of her uniform and pulled out a photograph, a bald-headed, suntanned, bright-eyed elderly man with a nose which looked as though it had, at some distant time in his life, been broken in hostility or sport. He was sitting up in bed, smiling, with his arm round Nurse Dotty. It had been taken, Dotty told me, by trainee Nurse Jones, and they had all been laughing a good deal at the time.

'Sister Sheila said something.' I hesitated before I asked the question. 'Was he going to leave you money in his will?'

'Oh, he told everyone that.' She was smiling now. 'Not that I ever really expected anything, of course. But it just showed how well we got on. He said he didn't have much of a family left to provide for.'

We talked a little more, and she told me that Freddy had a business somewhere in the north of England and he 'wasn't short of a bob or two', and then she asked for my legal advice, adding, 'Do you mind if I pay you with this glass of wine?'

'That makes it as profitable as a conference on legal aid,' I told her.

'I'm going to find out about Freddy's funeral. When I've found out, I'm going to it. I don't care what Sister Sheila has to say about it. I'm entitled to do that, aren't I?'

'I'm sure,' I gave her my best legal opinion, 'you're entitled to go to any funeral you choose. I'd even invite you to mine.'

'Don't be silly.' She smiled and, for an unexpected moment of delight, held my hand. 'That's not going to happen. And we're not going to stay here much longer, are we? Either of us. The Primrose Path's really just not our sort of place.'

'Not our sort of place.' Dotty's words, together with her account of the ease with which the awkward customer Masklyn had escaped from the Primrose Path, fired my enthusiasm. I waited for a night when Dotty was not only off duty but had gone to stay with her sister in Haywards Heath. I made sure that she couldn't be blamed by the Obergruppenführer for my having gone missing from the list of inmates. And I wanted to avoid any lengthy argument with the Primrose Path (whose bill had been paid to the end of this month) or my wife, Hilda, which might prolong my term of imprisonment.

The clothes I was wearing when my ticker overreacted so dramatically to the strain put upon it by an appearance before the raging Judge Bullingham had come with me to hospital and from there to the Primrose Path. They were hanging in a cupboard in my room, so I was able to change the pyjamas for my regulation uniform of black jacket and waistcoat, a pair of striped trousers supported by braces, a white shirt with detachable collar, and dark socks with, by this time, dusty and unpolished black shoes. I had kept charge of my wallet, which had four ten-pound notes and a travel pass in it, so I was soon prepared for the dash to freedom. I paused only to scribble a note for Dotty, which contained simply my four-line version of an old song:

> The way you feel my pulse
> The way you test my pee
> The memory of much else
> They can't take that away from me.

I wasn't particularly proud of rhyming 'pulse' with 'else', but time was pressing and I had a journey to make. I signed the message 'Love Rumpole', put the dressing-gown back on over my clothes and moved out stealthily towards the staircase.

The gods who look after the elderly trying to escape the clutches of the medical profession were on my side. That night a poll was being taken on television to decide the Sexiest Footballer of the Year, an event which had aroused far more interest than any recent election. So the television sets were humming in the rooms, and the nurses had withdrawn to their staff room to watch. The desk in the hallway was, more often than not, manned by Gavin, a quiet and serious young man to whom a shaven head and an over-large brown jumper gave a curiously monkish appearance. He was studying somewhere, but turned up for nights at the Primrose Path, where he read until dawn. His attendance was irregular, and, as on the night that Michael Masklyn walked free, he was away from his desk. I slid back bolts, undid chains and passed out into the night.

Somewhere in the back streets of the town I discarded the dressing-gown, tossing it over a hedge into somebody's front garden as a surprise present. I found a spotted bow-tie in a jacket pocket and fixed it under my collar. Accoutred as though for the Old Bailey,

I presented myself at the railway station, where the last train to Victoria was, happily, half an hour late.

My first call in London was to Equity Court. Our chambers were silent and empty, the clerk's room was fuller than ever of screens and other mechanical devices and I searched in vain for briefs directed to me. I went into my room, which seemed on first glance to be depressingly tidy. However, the eagle eyes of the tidier-up had missed a half-full packet of small cigars at the back of a drawer. I lit one, puffed out a perfect smoke ring, and then I noticed a glossy little folder, which looked like the advertisement for a country hotel or a tour of the Lake District, except that the cover bore the words 'Equity Court Chambers' with the truncated address 'bestofthebar. com'. There was an unappealing photograph captioned 'Samuel Ballard QC, chair and head of chambers' standing in the doorway as though to tempt in passing trade.

Inside, on the first page, was a list of our chambers' members. My eye was immediately drawn to one entry, 'Horace Rumpole, BA Oxon', against which someone had written with a felt-tip pen, 'Deceased?' I immediately lifted the telephone and called my home in Froxbury Mansions.

'Rumpole, is that you?' Hilda sounded as though I had woken her from a deep sleep.

'Yes. It's me, Rumpole. And not Rumpole deceased either. It's Rumpole alive and kicking.'

'Isn't it way past bedtime in the Primrose Path?'

'I don't care what bedtime is in the Primrose Path. I'm not in the Primrose Path any more. I've put the Primrose Path far behind me. I'm in chambers.'

'You're in chambers? Whatever are you doing in chambers? Go back to the nursing home at once!' Hilda's orders were clear and to be disobeyed at my peril. I took the risk.

'Certainly not. I'm coming home to Gloucester Road. And I don't need nursing any more.'

It would be untrue to say that there was – at first, anyway – a hero's welcome for the returning Rumpole. There were no flowers, cheers or celebratory bottles opened. There was the expected denunciation of the defendant Rumpole as selfish, ungrateful, irresponsible, opinionated, wilful and, not to put too fine a point upon it, a pain in the neck to all who had to deal with him. But behind these stiff sentences, I got the strange and unusual feeling that Hilda was fairly pleased to see me alive and kicking and to discover that I had, so far as could be seen, passed out of the Valley of the Shadow of Death and had come back home, no doubt to give trouble, probably to fail to cooperate with her best-laid schemes, but at least not gone for ever.

I have to admit that our married life has not been altogether plain sailing. There have been many occasions when the icy winds of Hilda's disapproval have blown round Froxbury Mansions. There have been moments when the journey home from the Temple felt like a trip up to the front line during a war which seemed to have no discernible ending. But, in all fairness, I have to say that her behaviour in the matter of the Rumpole Memorial Service was beyond reproach. She told me of the impending visit of the two QCs, and when Ballard let her know, over the telephone, that they planned a 'fitting tribute to Rumpole's life', she guessed what they were after and even suffered, she admitted with apparent surprise, a curious feeling of loss. She had telephoned the Primrose Path and spoken to Sister Sheila, who was able to tell her, much to her relief, that 'Mr Rumpole was being as awkward as ever!' Now that I appeared to be back in the land of the living, she was prepared to fall in with my masterplan and enable me to eavesdrop, as the two leading pomposities of our chambers unfolded their plans to mark the end of Rumpole's life on earth.

Accordingly, I was shut away in the kitchen when Ballard and Erskine-Brown arrived. Hilda left the sitting-room door ajar, and I moved into the hall to enjoy the conversation recorded here.

'We're sure you would like to join us in offering up thanks for the gift of Rumpole's life, Mrs Rumpole,' Soapy Sam started in hushed and respectful tones.

'A gift?' She Who Must Be Obeyed sounded doubtful. 'Not a free gift, certainly. It had to be paid for with a certain amount of irritation.'

'That,' Ballard had to concede, 'is strictly true. But one has to admit that Horace achieved a noticeable position in the courts. Notwithstanding the fact that he remained a member of the Junior Bar.'

'Albeit a rather elderly member of the Junior Bar,' Claude had to remind Hilda.

'It's true that he never took a silk gown *or* joined us in the front row. The Lord Chancellor never made him a QC,' Ballard admitted.

'His face didn't fit,' Claude put it somewhat brutally, I thought, 'with the establishment.'

'All the same, many of the cases he did brought him –' Ballard hesitated and Claude supplied the word:

'Notoriety.'

'So we want to arrange a memorial service. In the Temple Church.'

It was at this point that She Who Must Be Obeyed offered a short, incredulous laugh. 'You mean a memorial service for *Rumpole?*'

'That, Mrs Rumpole, Hilda if I may,' Ballard seemed relieved that the conversation had, at last, achieved a certain clarity, 'is exactly what we mean.'

'We're sure that you, of course, Hilda, and Rumpole's family and friends would wish to join us in this act of celebration.'

'Friends?' Hilda sounded doubtful and added, I thought unkindly, 'Rumpole has friends?'

'Some friends, surely. From all sections of society.'

'You mean you're going to invite that terrible tribe of South London criminals?' I thought this ungrateful of Hilda. The Timsons' addiction to ordinary decent crime had kept us in groceries, including huge quantities of furniture polish, washing-up liquid and scouring pads, and had frequently paid the bill at the butcher's and several times redecorated the bathroom over the long years of our married life.

'I hardly think,' Claude hastened to reassure her, 'that the Timsons would fit in with the congregation at the Temple Church.'

'I'm sure there will be many people,' Ballard was smiling at She Who Must, 'who aren't members of the criminal fraternity and who'll want to give Rumpole a really good send-off.'

It was at this point that I entered the room, carrying a bottle of Château Thames Embankment and glasses. 'Thank you for that kind thought, Ballard,' I greeted him. 'And now you're both here, perhaps we will all drink to Rumpole revived.'

Hamlet, happening to bump into his father's ghost on the battlements, couldn't have looked more surprised than my learned friends.

The return to life was slow and, in many ways, painful. At first there was a mere trickle of briefs. Bonny Bernard, my favourite solicitor, had given up hope of my return and sent a common theft charge against two members of the Timson clan to Hoskins in our chambers. I'm only too well aware of the fact that Hoskins has innumerable daughters to support, but I had to make sure that the Timsons knew I was no longer dead, and had to finance a wife with a passion for cleaning materials, as well as the life-giving properties of Pommeroy's Very Ordinary claret.

I was sitting in my room in chambers, wondering if I would ever work again, when our clerk, Henry, put through a phone call and I heard, to my delight, the cheerful voice of Nurse Dotty, although on this memorable occasion the cheerfulness seemed forced and with an undertone of deep anxiety. After the usual enquiries about whether or not I was still alive, and the news that she was doing freelance and temporary nursing and had taken a small flat in Kilburn, she said, with a small and unconvincing laugh, 'I had a visit from the police.'

'You had a burglary?'

'No. They wanted me to help them with their enquiries.'

I felt a chill wind blowing. People who help the police with their enquiries often end up in serious trouble.

'Enquiries about what?'

'Poor old Freddy Fairweather's death. They suggest I call in at the station and bring my solicitor. And I haven't really got a solicitor.'

'Then I'll get you one. Where are you? I'll ring you back.'

This was clearly a job for my old friend Bonny Bernard. I called him to remind him that I was, in spite of all the evidence to the contrary, up for work, and put him in touch with Dotty. A few days later, they called in at my chambers to report the result of an extraordinary conversation which had taken place with Detective Inspector

Maundy and Detective Sergeant Thorndike in a nick not too far from the Primrose Path Home.

'They were a decent enough couple of officers,' Bernard told me. 'But they soon made their suspicions clear to me and the client.'

'Suspicions of what?'

'Murder.'

I looked at Dotty, all her smiles gone to be replaced with a bewildered, incredulous terror. I did my best to make light of the moment. 'You haven't done in Sister Sheila?'

'They're investigating the death of one of the patients,' Bernard said. 'A Mr Frederick Fairweather.'

'Freddy! As though I'd do anything to hurt him. We were friends. You know that. Just as we were, Mr Rumpole.'

'And what's she supposed to have done to Fairweather?'

'Digitalis.' Bernard looked at his notes.

'Foxgloves?' I remembered Dotty's collection of herbal remedies.

'It's used to stabilize the action of the heart.' Words began to pour out of Dotty. 'They asked me about the access I had to digitalis, they seemed to think that I had a huge collection of pills and potions . . .'

'Well, you had, hadn't you?'

'Herbal remedies, you know that. And, of course, I had digitalis, but I'd enter every dose I had to give a patient – and I never treated Freddy with it at all.'

'So what do they suggest?' I asked Bernard.

'That they have evidence my client used a whole lot of digitalis without entering it or keeping a note,' he told me. 'And that she was seen coming out of Fairweather's room an hour before he died. She also boasted she was going to benefit from the deceased's will.'

'It's all completely ridiculous!' Dotty could contain herself no longer. 'I went to bed early and never left my room until I went on duty next day. I didn't care a scrap about Freddy's will. I only wanted him to get better, that was all I wanted. Nothing would have made me harm him, nothing in the world!'

She was crying, I remembered, as she watered a bowl of hyacinths after Freddy Fairweather died. She was crying again now, but angrily, dabbing at her eyes with the clutched ball of a handkerchief.

'That doctor. Lucas, was it? He must have entered the cause of death?' I asked Bernard.

'The cause of death was a heart attack. The deceased had heart problems. But Lucas told the inspector that what he saw might also have been brought about by an overdose of digitalis.'

I made a note and then asked Dotty, 'You told me you were going to Freddy's cremation. Did you go?'

'It was very strange. I rang the undertakers that used to come to the Primrose Path, but they knew nothing about Freddy. Then I rang the crematorium and I got a date. It was terrible, Mr Rumpole, just terrible. There was no one there. Absolutely no one at all. Sheila had said Freddy didn't want anyone to see him go, but I couldn't believe it. I was alone, in that horrible place . . . I think they were waiting for someone to come. I don't know who they thought I was. One of the family, even a wife, perhaps. I told them I was his nurse and they said they might as well begin. There was some sort of music. I suppose they had it left over from someone else's funeral, but there was no one to say anything. Not a word. Not a prayer. And there was just me to watch the coffin slide away behind the curtains. Apart from me – he went quite alone.' She dabbed her eyes again and then looked up at me. A look full of unanswered questions.

'Did you tell the police that?'

'No. I just answered their questions.'

'And is there anything else you want to tell me?'

'Only that I'm angry. So angry.'

'Because you know who's been talking to the police?'

'Of course. Sister Sheila!'

'You think it's Sheila?'

'Who else could it be?'

'They told us, Mr Rumpole,' Bonny Bernard, of course, had no experience of the mysteries of the Primrose Path Home, 'that they'd be making further enquiries. Of course, we don't know what they'll find out.'

'Perhaps they'll find out,' I told my client Dotty, 'why Sister Sheila would have gone to them with a story like that.'

*

I was, of course, torn. I believed that Nurse Dotty was wholly innocent and would remain innocent even if proven guilty. Nothing
would give me greater pleasure than pricking this bubble of so-called
evidence and unworthy suspicion, and teaching the jury to love
Nurse Dotty as much as they doubted the thin-lipped and hard-faced
Sister who had given evidence for the prosecution. And yet, the more
I thought about it, the more there seemed something unconvincing
about the whole story, from the escape of the man Masklyn to
the tenuous accusation about an overdose of digitalis. The trial, if
there was to be a trial, might answer none of these questions. Well,
that was often the case with trials. And I needed a sensational case at
the Old Bailey, didn't I, to resurrect Rumpole's fading career? Then I
felt a pang of guilt. Did I want Dotty to suffer just so that I could,
after all these years, do something almost as sensational in court as
the case of the Penge Bungalow Murders? The Primrose Path Crime
would be sure to hit the headlines.

It was while I was turning these matters over in my mind that my
room was invaded by a pungent but not unpleasant perfume, and a
tall, blonde woman in a black trouser suit came with it. She spoke
in a surprisingly deep voice with more than a hint of a Yorkshire
accent.

'Got a minute? It's about time we had a word. I'm Luci Gribble.
Luci with an "i". I'm your new director of marketing and administration. Sorry I haven't had a window before.'

A window? What was the woman talking about? Was she shut in
some airless oubliette in the chambers cellarage? By now she had
made herself comfortable in my client's chair.

'I never had an *old* director of marketing,' I had to tell her. 'So I
don't know why I should need a new one.' I had, of course, heard
complaints from our clerk, Henry, who regarded Luci with deep
suspicion as one likely to butt into his drinks with solicitors and seriously deplete his clerk's fees.

'I'm here to look after your image,' Luci told me.

'I know what that means.' I'd heard it all before. 'It means you
think I should get a new hat.'

'Not at all! The hat's perfect! And the striped pants, and the cigar ash down the waistcoat. They all suit your image perfectly. Don't change a thing!'

I suppose I should have found that reassuring, but somehow I didn't.

'I believe,' I told her, 'you were behind the idea of a church service to celebrate my death.'

'To celebrate your life, Horace. That's what we were going to celebrate. Of course, that's on hold. For the time being.'

'I'm glad to hear it.'

'I understand you're going through a bit of a sticky period, practice wise.'

'Sticky?'

'Bit of a lull? A serious shortfall in briefs?'

'Not at all.' I had on my desk the instructions Bonny Bernard had sent me in the matter of Nurse Dotty and I fingered the papers proudly. 'I've just been instructed in a rather sensational murder case.'

'Really?' Luci showed a polite interest. 'Who got murdered?'

'Probably no one. My client's a nurse. It's suggested she murdered a patient called Freddy Fairweather in the Primrose Path Home. A place,' I had to add, 'from which I was extremely glad to escape.'

What Luci said then astonished me. She only seemed mildly surprised. 'Not Freddy Fairweather of Primrose?'

'The Primrose *Path*,' I reminded her.

'I don't know anything about the "Path". The Freddy Fairweather I worked for was Primrose Personal Pensions. He was an IFA – independent financial adviser. Invested anyone's money in what he called a "gilt-edged pension scheme". On the whole, about as gilt-edged as a bouncing cheque. Which is why we parted company. Do you say he's dead?'

'I'm afraid so, and without a memorial service. If he's the same Freddy Fairweather, of course.'

'Short, square shoulders? No hair and a broken nose? He could turn on the charm, Freddy could. Had a bit of a chip on his shoulder as he'd left school at fifteen and never been to university like the rest of the Chamber of Commerce. Of course, if he's been murdered, you never met him, did you, Horace?'

'I might have done, strangely enough. You say you worked for him. Where exactly?'

'You know Leeds, Horace?'

'I'm afraid I have only a sketchy knowledge of Leeds.'

'That's where I started in marketing. I was marketing for Freddy. I won't say they were the best days of my life. I left because I didn't like the way the place was run. And I couldn't stand the company doctor, a quack who was meant to examine the pensioners. Objectionable's not the word.'

'His name wasn't Lucas, was it?'

'Sydney Lucas! That was him! But as for Freddy, he might have cut a few business corners but I wouldn't have wanted to see him murdered.'

I looked at her then, her black-trousered legs crossed, shiny boots pointed, an alien being in the dusty world of Equity Court. I lit a small cigar and, rather to my surprise, she made no protest. I blew out smoke and said, 'I'd be very much obliged if you'd tell me everything you know about the late Freddy Fairweather.'

'All right then. But would you mind passing me one of those whiffs?'

I did so, and we sat smoking and talking together, and what the new director of marketing told me was of considerable interest.

It was time to call in old favours. I had entered Pommeroy's Wine Bar in order to arrange overdraft facilities until the legal aid cheques came dribbling in (my recuperation at the Primrose Path had not only provided the tempting possibility of a brief in a sensational murder case, but exhausted a cashed-in insurance policy). I stood at the bar waiting for a lugubrious figure, who wore, however pleasant the weather, an elderly mackintosh and the expression of a man suffering from a cold who forever feels a drip forming at the end of his nose. This was, of course, the invaluable sleuth Ferdinand Isaac Gerald Newton, known throughout the legal profession as 'Fig', who, since adultery no longer had any legal significance, had taken to crime, in which field his investigations were often more thorough, and far more useful, than those carried out by the police.

'Hello, Mr Rumpole.' There was no hint of welcome in Fig's voice; his emotions were hidden under his perpetual raincoat. 'I heard you passed over.'

'I've come back to haunt you, Fig. And also to remind you of the interesting and profitable work I've put your way over many years.'

'Interesting, Mr Rumpole. Rather less profitable. I wouldn't say any of them paid out above the average. What've you got in mind?'

I invested in a bottle of Château Thames Embankment (I'm afraid it was of an indifferent year and not long enough in bottle) and sat Fig down at a quiet table in the corner of the bar. Then I told him all I knew, and all Luci, the marketing director, had told me, about Freddy Fairweather and the Primrose Path, which had led, in his case so suddenly, 'to the everlasting bonfire'. Then I gave him the list I'd made of all the required information. Fig looked at it doubtfully, like a man invited to swallow peculiarly nasty medicine.

'Are you suggesting, Mr Rumpole, that I do all this as some sort of favour?'

'We'll try and meet your reasonable expenses. I can't promise you much more at the moment.'

There's no point in recording that Fig looked disappointed, his expression was one of perpetual disappointment, but it's enough to say that he didn't jump at my offer.

'Time's money, Mr Rumpole. If you can give me one good reason –'

'All right, Fig,' I said, 'I'll give you a good reason. I'm just back from a near-death experience. Business is slow, not to say boring. An excellent, charming and entirely innocent woman has been accused of a murder. It may all come to nothing, in a way I hope so, but meanwhile the case is shrouded in mystery and I need your help. And if I can't solve it I might as well turn up my toes and hang up my wig.'

It was a long speech, but heartfelt. As I refreshed myself with a gulp of Pommeroy's Very Ordinary, I saw something suspiciously like a smile pass over Fig's far-from-cheerful face.

'Don't do that, Mr Rumpole,' he said. 'When do we start?'

I also had more work for Bonny Bernard. After I had reminded him of at least three considerable victories which we had achieved

together in the Ludgate Circus *palais de justice*, I was able to persuade him to pursue enquiries at Somerset House and, through a
local firm, in the Leeds area, the costs of which might be attributed
to Dotty's legal aid if her trial ever occurred. I also got him to agree
to open informal discussions with that apparently decent and reasonable officer, Detective Inspector Maundy of the Sussex Police.

So south and north my messengers set forth in search of information, and I had nothing much to do but sit in my room awaiting
results. I was busily engaged in lighting a small cigar while wrestling
with *The Times* crossword puzzle when my phone rang and I heard
the voice of Dotty, still troubled, but a little calmer than when I had
last seen her. No, she hadn't been summoned to another interview
with the forces of law and order. She had, however, had a call from
the Primrose Path.

'You heard from Sister Sheila?'

'No. From Gavin. You remember Gavin? The quiet boy, university student. He used to be on the desk at nights. Always had his head
in a book.'

'Or else he wasn't there much. He wasn't on guard to prevent the
escape of Michael Masklyn. Or, come to that, mine.'

'We used to get on rather well. He seemed a lonely sort of boy.
We used to make coffee and talk when I was on nights and nothing
much was happening. We argued about God and sex and fidelity
and Eminem. All those things that students talk about. It made me
feel quite young again. I think he liked me.'

'I'm not at all surprised. Did you talk about the night they took
away Freddy Fairweather?'

'He told me, long ago, he was away on some sort of course when
that happened. No. This call was about his degree. He's due to get
it soon from the University of North Sussex. He asked me to go and
watch. I was rather flattered.'

'What's he qualified in? Golf-course Management? Window
Dressing? Spiritual Furniture Arrangement? Aren't they the sort of
things you get degrees in nowadays?' I may have sounded cynical;
I hadn't yet become fully reconciled to the world I had returned to.

'Nothing like that. Theology.'

I was thinking hard then, about the Primrose Path and young Gavin, occasionally present at the desk downstairs, doing his best to discover how to justify the ways of God to Man. I had advice for Dotty.

'Then I think you should go to the degree ceremony. Definitely. Get a good seat and keep your eyes open.'

And at long last I was ready to return along the Primrose Path. It was an afternoon in early spring, with the trees covered in a green mist of young shoots and pale sunshine on the garden of the home, where a patient or two had been pushed out in wheelchairs to snooze away the few afternoons that were left to them. The front door was open and I stepped into the familiar smell of furniture polish, disinfectant and an air freshener in which the scent of early flowers and budding leaves had been strongly sterilized. I thought, again, how easy it was to get in and out of the Primrose Path without attracting any particular attention. I stood for a minute alone in the hallway, thinking about the eventful night which had led to Dotty's tears, and then a young nurse, one I had not seen before, asked my name and said that Sister Sheila was expecting me in her office.

She didn't move from behind her desk when I came in and her face was set in a frown of stern disapproval, her lips closed as tight as tweezers, so I felt as though I had absconded from some place of conviction and been brought back under escort to face the consequences. Nanki-Poo, a hairy heap in his basket, slept through most of our interview, only occasionally opening an eye and uttering a small snort of disapproval.

'I suppose you've come to apologize for the way you left us, slinking away like a thief in the night. It merely goes to show that you are still seriously unwell, Mr Rumpole. By the way, there is a bill for extras which you left unpaid.'

I was sitting in a chair opposite her, my hat on the floor, as she pushed a piece of paper towards me.

'I haven't come here to apologize, exactly. I've come here to discuss one of your patients. Frederick Fairweather.'

She gave a short sigh, a quick formal acknowledgement of another death at the Primrose Path. 'Mr Fairweather sadly died, Mr Rumpole, as I believe you know. He had trouble with his heart, as you have. Now, is there anything else you want to say to me?'

So that was her evidence in chief and, as in a courtroom, I was about to cross-examine the witness. I felt a stir of the old excitement, setting out on a series of questions which just might, possibly, expose the truth. I wasn't in court, of course, and what I was about to do was calculated only to avoid the trial of Dotty on the unsubstantial charge against her. Greater love, I thought, has no man than this, that he give up a defence brief at the Old Bailey for a friend.

'I wonder if you could help me. There are a few little things I'd like to ask about Freddy.' The art of cross-examining, I have always believed, is not the art of examining crossly, and I started in my politest, gentlest and most respectful tone of voice. Lull the witness into a false sense of security was my way, and ask questions she has to agree to before you spring the surprises. 'Mr Fairweather had a company selling private pensions up in Leeds, hadn't he?'

'That was his business, was it? Then you know more than I do.' Sheila was expressionless, and now Nanki-Poo snorted.

'Oh, I doubt that. And his business was called Primrose Personal Pensions, wasn't it? And this is the Primrose Path Home.'

'A pure coincidence.' Sister Sheila was, for the first time, on the defensive.

'Really? There are a lot of coincidences, aren't there, about that eventful night? But let's stick to his business for a moment. Didn't he buy this home as an investment about ten years ago? That was when you'd started to run it, and you got to know him rather well. Isn't that the truth of the matter?'

'I really don't see why I should sit here answering questions about the home's private business. That is absolutely no concern of yours, Mr Rumpole.'

'I'm afraid it *is* my business, Mrs Fairweather.'

There was a silence then. A heavy stillness, during which the dog made no sound and Sister Sheila moved not at all. She sat looking at her undrunk cup of coffee, and the plate on which four chocolate biscuits lay in a neat pattern. Then she managed to whisper, 'What did you call me?'

'By your name. You married Freddy last year, didn't you, at a Leeds Register Office? He was the divorced husband of Barbara Elizabeth Threadwell, by whom he had one son, Gavin. A quiet boy who got into university to read theology and is occasionally on duty at the desk in the hallway. I suppose you got Freddy to marry you as part of the deal.'

'Deal?' The witness was now making the mistake of asking *me* questions. 'What sort of a deal are you suggesting?'

So I told her. 'Primrose Personal Pensions is in serious trouble, isn't it? The pensions just aren't there any more. The poor devils who subscribed to Primrose have no comfortable income to look forward to. God knows what'll happen to them. They'll be sleeping in doorways and dying on the National Health because the truth of the matter is that Freddy trousered their money. Then he had nowhere to hide, except a quiet nursing home run by his wife, where he could be treated by his company doctor, who would issue endless chits assuring the world and the Fraud Squad that Freddy was far too ill to come to court.'

Had I been advising Sister Sheila at that moment, she would have refused to answer further questions on the grounds that they might incriminate her. Without the advantages of my advice, she tried to discover the strength of the evidence against her.

'Mr Rumpole, are you telling me you knew Mr Fairweather well?'

'Since I left here I've got to know him very well indeed.'

'You must be seriously ill, Mr Rumpole.' A faint smile appeared on Sister Sheila's face, a smile of derision. 'Since you left here Mr Fairweather has, as you well know, been dead.'

'Are you sure?'

'Sure?' She spoke as though there was no possible doubt about the matter. 'Of course I'm sure.'

'It would have been what he wanted.' I seemed to surprise her.

'You think he wanted to die?' The smile was overtaken by a brief, mirthless laugh. 'People who come here don't *want* to die, Mr Rumpole.'

'Not everyone has the Fraud Squad and the Pensions Watchdog breathing down their necks. Not everyone has filched thousands of pensioners' money. The time was coming when Dr Lucas's chits and Freddy's shelter in the Primrose Path might not have been enough. There was only one place left for him to hide in. Death.'

'Are you suggesting my patient committed suicide?'

'Of course not. Freddy wouldn't give up as easily as that. His way out, and I think you know this as well as I do, was a death which was as much a fake as his pensions.'

'That's a most outrageous suggestion!' Sister Sheila, as so many witnesses do when they strike a sticky patch, fell back on righteous indignation. 'My lawyers will make sure you pay for it. And never repeat it.'

'Oh, I think your lawyers will have more important business on their hands. I'm sure Freddy's death was discussed, but not planned exactly. No one could have planned the great opportunity of that night. It was more by luck, wasn't it, than good management?'

'Mr Rumpole,' Sister Sheila gave a magnificent display of patience with a questioner in an advanced stage of senile decay, 'Mr Fairweather died of heart failure. Confirmed by Doctor Lucas. His body was cremated, an event which was witnessed by your friend, Nurse Albright, who says he promised her something in his will.'

'Let me first deal with that.' I fed her tightly controlled fury by smiling tolerantly as I counted off the points on my fingers. 'Doctor Lucas had spent years as the official medical adviser to a fraudulent pension company. Like you, I'm sure he expected to share in the spoils. You did your best to keep the date and place of Freddy's funeral a secret, but Dotty made her own enquiries. It's true she saw a coffin slide into the everlasting bonfire, but whose coffin was it, exactly?'

'Freddy's, of course.' By now the witness was standing, furious, all pretence that we were just discussing another unfortunate patient gone. 'Who else could it have been?'

'A man called Masklyn?' I suggested. 'A transfer from a crowded hospital. A man no one knew much about. No apparent friends. No traceable relatives. He left the hospital that night. Was it, perhaps, the night *he* happened to die? I'm not saying you and Lucas killed him. I don't think you did, I just think his death was a stroke of luck.

It meant that one of you could tell the undertaker that the dead man's name was Frederick Fairweather.

'And now, do you want to know why I've gone to the trouble of finding all this out? Because you got in a panic when you thought Dotty was asking too many questions and finding out too much about that dubious event in the crematorium. So what did you do? You decided Dotty would lose her credibility if she was a murder suspect and not a reliable witness. So you spun the police some ridiculous story about too much digitalis, as though she would have killed Freddy because he'd promised to remember her in his will! I'm sure he liked her. But there wasn't any will, any more than there was any fatal heart attack. When you next see Freddy, give him my regards and ask him if he's enjoying his death.'

I got up to go then, and the room, which had seemed so still, was suddenly full of movement. Nanki-Poo jumped out of his basket and started to bark, a high-pitched, irritable yelp like a particularly difficult patient complaining hysterically. At the same time, the door opened and Doctor Sydney Lucas stood in my way. He was looking at me in what I took to be a distinctly unfriendly fashion.

'He's mad!' I heard Sister Sheila tell him. 'He's come back to us and he's seriously insane. He's been talking nonsense to me about poor Freddy.'

Doctor Lucas filled the doorway, considerably younger, taller and a great deal stronger than I am.

'Excuse me' was all I could think of to say. 'Detective Inspector Maundy of the local Force is waiting for me outside. He'll be very worried if I don't emerge. I did warn him that I might have some difficulty leaving . . .'

Whatever they had done to help a crooked businessman disappear from the face of the earth, however outrageous and reckless that plan had been, and however dishonest the doctor's conduct, the mention of the local constabulary made him step away from the door. I walked past him and out into air no longer freshened by chemicals. A cloud had covered the sun, there was a stirring of wind and I felt heavy drops of rain. Wheelchairs were being hurriedly pushed into shelter. I walked away from the Primrose Path for the last time and towards the forces of law and order. I was prepared to make a statement.

The University of North Sussex is not an old foundation. The main hall is a modern glass and concrete building, in front of which stands a large piece of abstract statuary built, so far as I could see, of flattened and twisted girders and bits and pieces of motionless machinery. But inside the steeply raked amphitheatre the chancellor, professors and lecturers were decked out in pink and scarlet gowns with slung-back medieval hoods.

I sat with Dotty among the parents, behind the rows of students. A cleric in a purple gown, the head of the theology department, was calling out names, and the chairman of the local waste-disposal company, earlier granted an Honorary Doctorate of Literature, handed out the scrolls. Gavin, in his clean white shirt and rarely worn suit, looked younger than ever, hardly more than a schoolboy. As he waited his turn in the queue, his eyes were searching the audience. When he saw Dotty he gave her a small, grateful wave and a smile. Then his name was called and he stepped forward.

'Look now,' I gave Dotty an urgent instruction. 'Look at the entrances.'

She turned and I turned with her. High above us, at the top of the raked seats, there were three doorways. He was standing in the middle one. He must have just moved to where he could see his son, far below him, get his degree. He stood there, a small, broad-shouldered, square figure with a broken nose. It was a moment of pride he had not been able to resist and, as a great chancer, why shouldn't he have taken this risk to see Gavin get what he had never had – a university degree? Gavin shook hands with the waste-disposal magnate and went off with his scroll. Freddy Fairweather turned away, meaning to disappear again into the world of the dead. But he was stopped by Fig Newton and DS Thorndike, who had been waiting for him at my suggestion.

So the case of the Primrose Path never got me a brief. Neither Sister Sheila nor Doctor Sydney Lucas, when arraigned for their various offences, thought of employing Rumpole to defend them. Freddy Fairweather ended up in an open prison, from which he may expect an early release owing to the unexpected onset of Alzheimer's disease. Gavin has taken holy orders and returned to Leeds. I still meet Dotty, from time to time, for tea in the Waldorf Hotel, where we sing, quietly but with pleasure, the old standards together.

The day after Freddy Fairweather was arrested, Henry brought a brief into my room. 'Good news at last, Mr Rumpole,' he said. '*R. v. Denis Timson*. Receiving stolen DVDs. It should be interesting. You won't get cases like that from our so-called marketing director.' But I have to say, it was to the marketing director I owed my greatest debt of gratitude when I came back to the land of the living and solved the mystery of the Primrose Path Home.

Rumpole Redeemed

'By the way, Rumpole, have you been keeping up with your exercises at the Lysander Club?' The cross-examination started, as the best do, in a quiet and casual manner; but I sniffed danger.

'Of course,' I answered boldly and then, to cover myself, added, 'whenever I get the chance.'

'So what is it that stops you going regularly?'

'Pressure of work.' I kept it vague, but hoped that would settle the matter.

'Oh yes?' Hilda sounded unconvinced. 'I thought I heard you complain about the shortage of work lately, the rare appearance of briefs. And yet Dermot Fletcher tells me he never sees you on the bicycle!'

I quietly cursed the grey-haired sports commentator whose small boy had become Hilda's favourite person. Weren't there football matches, had cricket been abandoned so that this man could spend his life noticing my absence from the stationary bicycle?

'I get round to the Lysander whenever I can.' It was time to call my best evidence. 'If you look at the book you'll see I'm signed in.'

'I have looked at the book. And I've seen you signed in by Luci Gribble. Perhaps you'd be good enough to tell me how many times you went to the club with Luci?'

'Off and on. Look, I'd better be getting down to chambers. See what's around. I believe Henry's got me a dangerous driving.'

'Don't prevaricate, Rumpole.' It was a word Hilda's father had liked to use in court; I suppose he sometimes took it home with him. At least she didn't say, 'Don't fence with me!' 'I have spoken to Luci Gribble.'

That was it, then. I stood and watched my defence collapse like a tent in a tornado.

'I have spoken to Luci Gribble,' Hilda repeated, 'and she had to admit that on most of the occasions when you asked her to sign you in, you didn't join her. You were notably absent, Rumpole, but no doubt shortening your life overdosing on red wine in that favourite wine bar of yours.'

'Can I change my plea?' I took a quick legal decision. 'Guilty.'

'Of course you are. What can we do about you, Rumpole?' she sighed heavily. My case was clearly hopeless.

'I can only say,' I started to mitigate, 'I do find bicycling nowhere to Caribbean music, even with an occasional word from your friend the sports commentator, deeply boring.'

'Boring? Oh, I'm so sorry.' Hilda had now adopted the retort contemptuous. 'I'm sorry I can't provide a few murders, or a bank robbery, or a nice long fraud to keep you entertained, Rumpole. You can't live entirely for pleasure. You've got to put up with a bit of boredom occasionally, if you want to keep yourself alive. So it's entirely up to you. I can no longer take any responsibility for you.'

At which she left the kitchen where breakfast, together with much else, was over. Shortly after that I heard the sound of angry hoovering from the sitting-room. My case of non-compliance with exercise requirements was clearly lost and I was free to go.

Aware that a chill wind of disapproval would be blowing round Froxbury Mansions that evening, I delayed my homeward journey by a brief visit to the wine bar Hilda had condemned in her judgement. I wandered into Pommeroy's as lonely as a cloud, and was accompanied only by a single glass of Château Fleet Street when I heard a brisk, upper-crust voice at my elbow. 'Rumpole! I want to invite you to lunch.'

'Then invite, old darling.'

I gave Archie Prosser full permission to feed me, regardless of expense. The newest arrival in our chambers in Equity Court, Prosser was a distant relative of Lord someone or other, an obscure link which predisposed She Who Must Be Obeyed slightly in his favour. Soapy Sam Ballard had introduced him into chambers as a sparkling wit, one likely to set Pommeroy's Wine Bar in a roar, but I hadn't yet heard him utter any line, or produce any thought worth including in a slim volume to be entitled *The Wit and Wisdom of*

Archie Prosser. He was, however, an inoffensive soul who had been cooperative when he prosecuted me in the case of the female Fagin of the Underground. He was also, as he was continuously reminding me, a member of the Sheridan Club, a somewhat gloomy and ill-lit institution which does, as Archie was fond of telling us all, an excellent liver and bacon, which, if preceded by nine oysters in the half shell and followed by a summer pudding well covered with cream, the whole to be washed down with some rare vintage never even heard of in Pommeroy's, might make Archie seem an agreeable companion for lunch and the smoking of an unusually large cigar. In return, I could reward him with a few of my jokes which had, like the wine, improved with age.

'Delighted,' I told him. 'Any time next week would suit me. I think I may have what Luci Gribble would call a window of opportunity. There's been a rise in the law-abiding rate. I think it's hitting everybody.'

Not much of a joke, I agree, and Archie took it without a smile. Instead he gave me a look of deep and maddening concern. 'I bet you're glad of the rest, aren't you, Rumpole?'

At this my patience snapped. 'No,' I told him. 'I'm not in the least glad of the rest. I'm bored to tears by the rest. I've had quite enough rest to last until my final day on earth, which I intend to spend wearing a wig and arguing. I just wanted to point out that, as luck would have it, I've got one of Luci's windows next week and I'd be delighted to fill it with a lengthy lunch at your club.'

'You mean the Sheridan?'

'Of course I mean the Sheridan.'

'Talking of which,' Archie told me, 'I'm going to put Bernard up for membership. I think he'd appreciate that, don't you?'

'Bonny Bernard? You're speaking of my favourite solicitor. I feel sure he would. And I'm equally sure I'd enjoy lunch with you there. Very kind of you, Archie.'

'I'm afraid I wasn't thinking exactly in terms of the Sheridan.'

'All right, if you insist. Where were you thinking in terms of?' I imagined Archie Prosser's ideas had gone upmarket. 'The Ritz?'

'Not exactly, Rumpole.' The unpredictable Archie seemed to be shaking with some particular private joke. 'I was thinking more in terms of Worsfield Prison.'

We lived in a time when the government was cracking down on everything. Every week, it seemed, brought a new list of things which were to be cracked down on: single mothers who didn't make sure their children went into school, noisy neighbours, graffiti artists and mobile-phone stealers were to be cracked down on with particular severity. What was noticeable was that very little was cracked up. There was a total absence of government announcements offering a free glass of Guinness on the National Health and wishing everyone a good time. The cracking down had become so universal that I didn't know when I would wake up to discover that Château Thames Embankment, small cigars and legal jokes more than three years old were being cracked down on, and that I was on my way to Worsfield and not just for lunch.

Another dearly held belief of the puritan masters of what claimed to be a deeply caring political party was that prison was a universal panacea. Like a magic potion which could relieve headaches, tonsillitis, yellow fever and broken legs, prison could do you nothing but good. The result of all this cracking down and locking up was that the prison population had risen to record levels, the nicks were bursting at the seams, the mad and bad were packed in with the merely muddled. In the face of this wave of overcrowding the Bunyan Society (named after a devout and imprisoned author) stood like Canute. It published facts and figures, protesting at the incarceration of fifteen-year-olds, the absence of education, the failure to stop reoffending and the sad story of a women's prison without a visitors' lavatory, where friends and relatives were instructed to pee in the car-park hedge. Ministers received these reports politely, perhaps even read them, and continued to crack down as before. The Bunyan Society's reply was to arrange, so Archie Prosser told me, a lunch in Worsfield Prison, outside London, where the great and the good could show their solidarity with those of my customers whom even the Rumpole magic touch couldn't save from custody.

'Now I'm on the Committee of the Bunyan Society.' Archie Prosser announced the fact with some satisfaction, feeling no doubt that he'd joined the great and the good. 'I suggested we should have a representative of the old-fashioned criminal defender present at our prison lunch. You'll be at home, Rumpole. I'm sure you'll know lots of the people there.'

'Yes,' I agreed and there was, I'm afraid, a mournful note in my voice, 'I most probably will.'

'This way! Would you mind looking this way?'

'Over here. Over on your right for the *Daily Post*.'

'Look at me now. No – me, not him. All right. That's lovely!'

These were voices behind flashes of light as I approached, in drizzling rain, the castellated mini towers that flanked the gates of Worsfield Prison. When the flashes were no longer blinding me I saw, among the men with cameras, the shadowy figure of Luci Gribble, our chambers director of marketing, wearing a white belted mackintosh and a smile of achievement.

'Well done, Horace! That's a great photo opportunity!'

I was about to say 'Opportunity for what?' when one of the photographers asked her, 'Who the hell was he?'

'Counsel for the defence,' Luci told him. 'Just an ordinary, everyday criminal barrister. An old workhorse paying a visit to his clients. Not a leader, perhaps, but one of the trusted foot soldiers of our chambers at Equity Court. No, not Rumbold. Rumpole. R–U–M . . .'

Times have changed. When I joined our chambers, in Hilda's father's time, you would have been threatened with dismissal and heavily fined if you'd allowed your photograph to appear in a newspaper. Now we were being packaged and advertised like cornflakes. There was no chance of arguing about it with Luci. It was lunchtime and the old workhorse was in search of its nosebag. I rang a bell set into the stonework and a screw appeared with a bunch of jangling keys attached. 'Name, please?' he said, consulting a list. I had never felt more anonymous.

The menu featured grey mince, watery mashed potatoes, digestive biscuits and a blue plastic mug of tepid water. The tables were set out in a main assembly area, and at each one, a member of the great and the good shared the feast with representatives of the small and the iffy. I sat between two thieves, one about to be set loose once more on the fallible locks and vulnerable window fastenings of the outside world. The other, once of the same persuasion, was so redeemed that he now worked for the Bunyan Society, gave lectures to gatherings of sociologists, students of criminology and interested police officers, and had sold his autobiography, *Set a Thief*, to a publisher. His name, proudly announced on the Bunyan Society label pinned to his jacket, was Brian Skidmore. He was a pale-faced fellow, probably in his early forties, with a high, aquiline nose which gave him the inappropriate look of a medieval cleric, and a case of premature baldness which added to the monkish nature of his appearance. He introduced the soon-to-be-released prisoner. 'This is Chirpy Molloy. I don't know if you've ever bumped into him round the courts, Mr Rumpole.' Brian sounded like a schoolteacher introducing the most hopeless but likeable member of the class.

'You were never my brief, were you, Mr Rumpole?' I could see why he was called Chirpy. He was small, round-faced, plump, and his smile, half challenging, half defensive, must have stayed with him since he was a bright-eyed, tousle-headed child always responsible for the broken window, the fight in the playground or the missing contribution for the school outing.

'I never had that pleasure.' I bit into a digestive biscuit; it went badly with the mince.

'Me being a Molloy, and you always appearing on behalf of the Timsons.'

He was speaking of one of the great divides. The Montagues and the Capulets were friendly neighbours compared to the Timsons and the Molloys. This particular Molloy, however, was held even by the Timsons to be a perfectly straightforward and strictly non-violent villain, who appeared to his pub acquaintances and to the juries who were called on to try him to be a cheerful cockney chappie who could take the rough with the smooth, the benefit of the doubt with the guilty verdict, and the big blowouts in a Marbella holiday hotel with the grey mince and biscuits in Worsfield.

'We Molloys generally use Mr Arkwright in Queen Alexandra's Buildings. You heard of him?'

'Of course I know Percy Arkwright. I believe, as a defender, he's a great help to the prosecution.' I shouldn't have said it, but grey mince does bring out the worst in people.

'You mean I'd be better off with you, Mr Rumpole?'

'Perhaps. If you consult Mr Bernard, solicitor of Camberwell, he'd lead you to me.'

'I'd say I'll remember that for next time,' Chirpy was now looking extra cheerful, 'but there's not going to be a next time. I'm sure of that.'

'Chirpy has decided to go straight, Mr Rumpole.' Brian Skidmore was once again the schoolteacher, announcing, in an amused sort of way, that one of his less talented pupils was planning to build, in the carpentry lesson, a light aircraft capable of transatlantic flight.

'To be honest, I got a girlfriend, and she doesn't like me being away in prison, Mr Rumpole. She's always on about it. She says she gets lonely nights. I've got to listen to her. I'm going to get a job round her father's Videos R Us and that'll be the end of it.'

'You mean you're going to buy your own aftershave from now on, Chirpy?' Brian was gently mocking.

Now I remembered what the Timsons had told me, with considerable amusement, about Chirpy Molloy. He was devoted to personal hygiene. He chose fairly small but expensive houses to break into, places belonging to owners who were known to be away on holiday. After collecting whatever valuables he could find, he invariably treated himself to a long and luxurious session in the bathroom. He sprinkled bath salts from glass jars into deep, hot water. He made considerable use of the Imperial Leather soap and applied the loofah. He borrowed the electric razor, slapped on the stinging perfume of Pour Les Hommes or Machisimo by Peruque. He didn't spare the hand cream or the all-over body lotion. Then he would dress again in his working clothes and, having wiped off all possible fingerprints, make a dignified exit through a back door. The bathroom, after he left it, looked as though it had been hit by a typhoon. He needn't have bothered about the fingerprints, the laughing Timsons told me, he might as well have left his name and address on the hall table.

'It's a wise decision,' I was telling Chirpy. 'If you've got a good job and a good girlfriend you certainly don't need me!'

'Quiet, Rumpole.' Archie Prosser gave me orders from the next table. 'The Home Secretary is about to say a few words.' And he added, as though to remind me of one of the highlights of my long life, 'You *have* met her. Don't you remember?'

Of course I remembered 'Bunty' Heygate, the elegant but earnest minister in the Home Office. I had met her with Archie in the Sheridan Club when I was engaged in the case of Doctor Nabi, an asylum seeker. She had been arguing that such colourful customs as cutting off hands, or stoning women to death for adultery, were traditional in certain countries, and that it would be racist to denounce them, and unreasonable to protect those who were in flight from them. Such views must have found favour with the government, as Bunty had, in the latest reshuffle, been promoted to Home Secretary, in which office she had forsaken her nickname and announced that she would, from now on, be known as Brenda.

So there she was in all her glory, smiling with an even deeper self-satisfaction now she was a secretary of state. She still looked, however, like an enormously successful schoolgirl who had suddenly found herself promoted to headmistress. The page-boy haircut was neat and burnished, she was wearing a bottle-green suit, and her high-heeled, pointed-toed shoes clicked across the stone floor as she found the most favourable speaking position. Above her, galleries of cells rose like a great circle in a theatre; a net was stretched beneath the top one to catch any long-term convicts who might be tempted to take a quick way out. Brenda Heygate's clear, untroubled voice carried easily, not only to the furthest visitor but to the lifers far above her.

'It's a great pleasure to be here,' she said, 'and to share with so many of you this excellent prison meal.' Was mine the only muted groan? 'I have to say, on behalf of all of us in government, and in particular those of us in the Home Office, that we are profoundly grateful to the Bunyan Society for (here she seemed to have some trouble remembering exactly what it was she was grateful to the Bunyan Society for, so she retreated, as soon as possible, to her familiar territory) – for the very useful work it has done, and, of course, for organizing this get-together. Now, I'm sure we'll all have read in today's papers I have made an important announcement.' The inmates looked at her blankly, being unlikely to have read Home Office pronouncements, and the great and the good supporters of the Bunyan Society let out a disappointed sigh. 'We have, as you know, greatly improved the safety on our streets and reduced the crime rate since the opposition party were in power and old people were in genuine fear of taking a short walk down to the corner shop. However, there is one area in which the crime rate is, unfortunately, rising, and this is what I have called "short-break burglary". This is when criminals find that the householder is taking, shall we say, a short break in Paris, or perhaps Barcelona, or enjoying a longer break during school holidays, and take advantage.' (Here I glanced at Chirpy Molloy, who was looking modestly down at his plate as the Home Secretary discussed his special subject.) 'We have issued a Home Office warning to everyone going away for a holiday not to advertise the fact by cancelling, shall we say, the milk, or the daily papers. A sensible idea would be to donate your milk and papers to a friendly neighbour during a holiday period. Meanwhile, I give you all fair warning that I mean to crack down heavily on short-break burglaries, the maximum sentence for which will be seven years, which I hope to see applied in appropriate cases. Unlike the previous party in power, we intend to wake up the judiciary, who seem to find it a little difficult to move with the times, and make them crack down appropriately.

'Finally, I'd like to say that, at this excellent lunch, we have, thanks to the Bunyan Society, a remarkable proof of what we have always said – that prison can work and does work in many cases. I'm going to ask Brian Skidmore to say a few words to you.' It seemed to have been the usual story. 'Brian came from a broken home and lacked the role model of a father figure.' Here it was the turn of Brian Skidmore to look down modestly at his plate. 'He turned to minor crime as a youth, and then got into more serious trouble, but it was here at Worsfield that a few words from the governor made the great change in his life. Now, as I'm sure you know, he works full time for the Bunyan Society and has kept completely out of trouble. Inmates of Worsfield and their guests, will you all welcome Brian Skidmore! Come along Brian, don't be shy!'

Although he said, 'Excuse me, Mr Rumpole. I never wanted anything like this,' Brian didn't seem in the least shy. In a surprisingly short time he was up beside the Home Secretary and was greeted, as an ex-prisoner, by warmer applause from the great and the good.

'I'm not used to this,' he said. 'This is worse than a prison sentence, having to speak. All I can say is I have to thank a lot of people. First of all, Mr Frank Dalton, when he was governor. I was up on a charge for something, and he said, "Why don't we see you in chapel, Skidmore? There's something we get to learn there. Do you know what that is?" Well, of course I didn't know whatever he was talking about, and when I heard what they read out from the Bible I wasn't any the wiser. The words were "The redemption of their soul is precious." I didn't know what redemption was in those days, but I do now. Because Mr Dalton explained it. We could all get off the crime if we tried hard enough. With a bit of help we could. So he arranged to put me in touch with the Bunyan Society. They were visiting here at the time, and they gave me a job, making the tea, mostly. And now I'm under manager in charge of events. So thanks for coming and a special vote of thanks, for agreeing to fit us into her busy schedule, to the Home Secretary.'

At which the crackers-down and the cracked-down-on applauded. The party was breaking up when Archie Prosser suddenly said the word 'Applethorpe!' and started pushing his way between the departing guests towards a distant table, where a small, slightly wizened prisoner was thoughtfully picking his teeth.

Meanwhile, Chirpy had gone smiling back to his cell. 'He'll never make it, you know.' The redeemed Brian Skidmore had come back to our table and was watching Chirpy's retreat with pity and some amusement.

'Never make what?' I asked him.

'Never go straight. Not poor old Chirpy. He'll leave here with no money and probably no job. No one to look after him.'

'What about the girlfriend? And her father's Videos R Us?'

'She hasn't bothered to wait for him. That's what I heard in the chat round here. Of course, Chirpy doesn't know that yet. He'll be the last to know. So I doubt the job's still open. He'll drift back to the Molloys and you know what that means.'

'I'm not sure that I do know exactly.'

'I'm afraid he'll be looking for a house where the milk's been cancelled because they've all gone on holiday.'

'You think Chirpy Molloy's incapable of redemption?'

'We can hope for the best.' Brian put on the serious expression he had used for his speech. 'We can always hope. But we've got to face the facts, Mr Rumpole. This is it. The facts have to be faced.'

I moved on then, towards freedom and, in the fullness of time, a glass with better stuff than tepid water in it. Archie Prosser joined me at the prison gates. 'Who the hell was Applethorpe?' I asked him.

'Poor chap.' Archie looked serious. 'I was at school with him. In here waiting to be sentenced for thirty-two cases of indecent exposure. Come to think of it, he was head boy.'

Since my abandonment of the stationary bicycle, and Hilda's discovery of the fraudulent entries in the Lysander Club's records, home life in Gloucester Road began to feel like an extended visit to the Worsfield nick. No cries of welcome greeted me when I returned to the mansion flat, no sighs of regret when I left it after a hurried breakfast. Archie had made me a member of the Bunyan Society and I took refuge in some of its meetings, where I got to know the committee and was greeted warmly by the reformed Brian Skidmore. He told me that Chirpy Molloy had been released, but there was no news as yet of his having slid back into a life of crime.

I was in my chambers room, wondering when, if ever, a brief in a sensational new case would arrive, when Claude Erskine-Brown stole in, looked down the passage as though he feared listeners, and carefully closed the door.

'Rumpole, I don't know if you've heard any rumours?'

'Rumours? Of course I've heard rumours. Where do you think life in chambers would be without rumours?'

'Well, if you've heard any, don't believe them.'

'Why ever not? I usually believe rumours. But so far as politicians are concerned, I never believe anything until it's been officially denied.'

'Politicians?' Claude looked startled and afraid. 'Did you say politicians, Rumpole?'

'That's what I said.'

'So then you've heard.' He sat down in my client's chair in an attitude of despondent resignation.

'Heard what, exactly, Erskine-Brown?'

'About me and – well – her. I knew it would leak out eventually.'

Here, I thought, we go again. Claude Erskine-Brown, unlike the blessed Brian Skidmore, appeared irredeemable. Love provided as irresistible a temptation to him as crime did to such weak-minded characters as Chirpy Molloy. The only difference was that Erskine-Brown's infidelities, unlike Chirpy's burglaries, tended to remain in the world of dreams. As I was taught by my old, blind law tutor at Keble College, a crime requires a guilty act with a guilty intent. Dear old Claude had the guilty intent most of the time; it was the guilty act he found hard to pull off.

'There's only one thing I do beg of you, Rumpole. And I know I can count on you, because of our long friendship over the years.'

'You want a bit of free legal aid?'

'Not that. No. It hasn't come to that. It's just if you hear my name mentioned in connection with a well-known politician . . .'

I began to run them over in my mind. The Prime Minister? Leader of the Opposition? What on earth had come over poor old Claude? He couldn't resist, of course, supplying the answer. 'If you hear my name mentioned in connection with, for instance, the Home Secretary, just say you know there's absolutely nothing in it.'

'Erskine-Brown! *Not* the Home Secretary?' I couldn't believe it.

'You don't know her, Rumpole?'

'Indeed I do. She's a woman who believes that we shouldn't

blame countries who stone women to death and she's very keen on cracking down on people. You want to be careful she doesn't crack down on you, Claude.'

The man in my armchair assumed a far-away 'if only' expression. Then came a low murmur. 'I had the privilege of sitting next to her at a dinner in the Law Society. We really hit it off. She told me she found me a witty and sympathetic companion.'

'Mrs Justice Erskine-Brown – that is to say Lady Phillida – she was at this dinner party, was she?'

'Oh no. Philly was away on circuit somewhere.'

'So the Home Secretary had you to herself?'

'Almost entirely. She talked to the man on the other side, of course, but not for very long. I walked her to her car and she kissed me, Rumpole. I was kissed by a secretary of state. And I kissed her back!'

'I suppose I ought to congratulate you.'

'It's the power, I suppose. There's a sort of potent sexuality about her.'

'I can't honestly say I noticed.'

'I've always thought she was terribly attractive in photographs, of course. But in the flesh! Well, now it's happened, we might meet at the opera. Or a quiet dinner in a restaurant.'

'The possibilities are endless.'

'That's right, Rumpole! Of course, we'll have to be extremely careful. So do, please, just remember, this conversation never happened.' At which Claude left my client's chair and slunk off, on whatever business he had in hand.

It was a few days after this that an unfortunate event occurred at the home of Adele Alexander, the well-known actress, near Sloane Square. While she was away on a holiday in Majorca, her house, Number 5 Granville Road, was broken into and valuable jewellery was stolen. The remarkable thing, according to the police, was that the thief had enjoyed all the benefits of the bathroom: wet towels were left on the floor and a prodigious amount of bath salts and various lotions had been made use of.

I heard no rumours of Erskine-Brown's burgeoning love affair with the Home Secretary; but the member of the Timson family I was defending for dangerous driving told me that, as I had suspected, Chirpy Molloy had been arrested exactly a month after his release from Worsfield. 'It's the bath he can't resist,' young Les Timson told me. 'That's what's his undoing. That and the toilet requisites.' Clearly the doctrine of redemption didn't apply to Chirpy Molloy.

The period which followed the arrest of Chirpy Molloy for serial burglary and stolen jewellery was not, as I have already indicated, a golden age in the life of Rumpole. The sentence passed on me at home was clearly a long one and there was no hope of parole, or indeed any clear indication of when, or even if, I might expect a release. It would be an exaggeration to say that Hilda was silent when we were alone together, but she was, for most of the time, monosyllabic. Her longest speech, often repeated to the accompaniment of heavy sighs and upward glances, as though calling on the gods to witness her patience in the face of such outrageous persecution, was 'Of course, if you're looking for an early death, Rumpole, and can't be bothered to look after your health in any way, that's entirely up to you. Just don't expect *me* to do anything about it. That's all.' Having said this, she would leave to look after little Tom Fletcher, a child who no doubt exercised obediently, performing hand stands and vaulting over the furniture, so ensuring many long and healthy years to come. My dinner, as often as not, had not been left in the oven.

I tried various ploys. I attempted washing up, but She examined the plates and glasses critically, under a strong light, and then washed them up all over again. I tried a legal joke or two, but got an even heavier sigh and 'Please, Rumpole, not *that* one again.' I brought her the latest gossip, the strange misunderstanding over Judge Bullingham's wig, the unfortunate e-mail Soapy Sam Ballard sent to our director of marketing, but failed to capture Hilda's interest. The only thing I felt unable to concede was to return to the misery of the exercise bicycle in the Lysander Health Club. The day of the treadmill was, I had made up my mind, over. So I opted for what almost amounted to solitary confinement in Froxbury Mansions.

To make matters worse, briefs, which in happier times had fallen as thick as autumn leaves in my space on the clerk's room mantelpiece, were still as rare as swallows in winter. Every morning, when I strolled into chambers and asked Henry if there was anything much in the diary, he would say, 'Very little on at the moment, Mr Rumpole. I expect you'll be glad of the rest.' So I would retreat to my room to light a small cigar, struggle with *The Times* crossword or consider the possibility of writing my memoirs.

On one eventful morning, however, as I wandered into the clerk's room and glanced at the mantelpiece, I saw a brief clearly marked by the firm of Bernard and Tillbury of Coldharbour Lane, Camberwell. I knew that Bonny Bernard wouldn't think of briefing anyone else in chambers and I was interested to see whom the Queen, as the prosecuting party in all criminal trials, was after this time. The title of the case was none other than *R. v. Molloy*. Henry was out of the room on some mission of his own, so I grabbed the brief and carried it off to study at my leisure.

An hour later, I had not only read it but made a note of all the facts, together with a list of questions to be asked when we saw our client, no doubt a great deal less chirpy. After this welcome work, I lit a small cigar, leant back and blew what I flatter myself was a perfect smoke ring at the ceiling. The case seemed so obvious, the violation of the victim's bathroom so completely in character, that it was going to be difficult to think of a defence. And yet, I thought, and yet . . . I was lost in the sessions of sweet silent thought when the door burst open and I was rudely interrupted.

'So, Rumpole!' Archie Prosser seemed full of righteous indignation, as though he'd caught me red-handed pinching the small change for the coffee contributions. 'You've got the brief!'

'Yes, Archie,' I told him politely. 'Thanks to you.'

'What do you mean, "thanks to me"?'

'You took me to that ghastly lunch. That's when I met Chirpy Molloy. He said he'd remember me the next time he was in trouble. Well, it seems he's back in trouble extremely soon.'

'I have no idea what the defendant Molloy may or may not have said to you. All I know is that what you have there is *my* brief.'

'Your what?'

'Brief.'

'Don't babble, Archie. This case comes from my old friend Bonny Bernard.'

'My instructing solicitor.'

'*Yours?*' I couldn't believe it.

'You might take the trouble to look at the name on the front of those papers.'

I turned them over. It was true. I had read the name of the case and the solicitors, but now I saw in the small print the inexcusable name of the learned friend, Mr Archibald Prosser.

'Bonny Bernard,' I was struggling with the enormity of the idea, 'is briefing *you*?'

'He thought perhaps he should cast his net a little wider.'

'And pick up some rather odd fish,' was what I didn't say.

'Anyway, it's a pretty hopeless case.' Archie sat down in a more forgiving mood. 'Absolutely no defence, so far as I can see. Fellow couldn't resist using the bathroom. So he left his signature.'

'He told me he was going straight this time.'

'They all say that, don't they?'

'You don't believe in the possibility of redemption?'

'For people like Molloy, with a string of convictions as long as your arm? Hardly.'

I was putting back the papers, having decided to surrender them with as much gallantry as possible. 'I'll leave you my note. There are one or two things you might consider. Was it pretty widely known, for instance, that this actress was in the habit of leaving jewellery around when she went on holiday?'

'Presumably it was. That's why Molloy picked the place.'

'Isn't it odd that he should be so well informed? He'd only just got out of prison.'

'They learn a lot in those places, don't they?'

'Perhaps. Still it's worth a thought. Oh, and there's a witness statement in there, from the woman in the house that backs on to Number 5.'

'The judge's wife?' It was indeed Lady Sloper, the wife of the well-known Mr Justice 'Beetle' Sloper, who had got up in the small hours to close a bedroom window. Looking down the moonlit garden of Number 5, she could see, in the clear moonlight, a man come out of the back door. He must have heard her close the window, because he looked up and she got a view of his face. Then she saw him walk away, into the shadows by the garden wall.

'It's a prosecution statement,' Archie explained. 'Freddy Mares-field, who's prosecuting, was good enough to let me see it. They're not calling her, and I shan't be calling her either.'

'Why not? The description she gives doesn't sound in the least like Chirpy Molloy.'

'It was night time . . .'

'Bright moonlight.'

'All the same, she never got a clear view. Freddy would make mincemeat of her in cross-examination. And one doesn't really like to trouble a judge's wife unless it's absolutely necessary.'

'When it comes to a criminal defence,' I thought it worthwhile to tell Archie Prosser his business, 'it usually pays to trouble everyone as much as possible.'

I had one more question. 'By the way,' I said as Archie reached the door, 'did you ever get round to proposing Bonny Bernard for the Sheridan Club?'

'Oh yes, I did.' Archie clearly didn't get the full implications of my question. 'And he was extremely grateful.'

'Obviously!' My tone was bitter and my brow furrowed with rage, but I let Archie go.

> Just for a handful of silver he left us
> Just for a riband to stick in his coat . . .

He was sitting there, Bonny Bernard, in Pommeroy's Wine Bar, drinking with his partner in the law and, no doubt, in this instance, in crime, the almost anonymous Tillbury; drinking and eating cheese biscuits as though he hadn't been guilty of one of the most appalling acts of treachery in the history of the Bar.

'Oh, hello, Mr Rumpole, you're really looking well.' Bonny Bernard spoke as though all was well with the world and he had nothing on his conscience. The unnecessary Tillbury chipped in with 'Very well indeed, Mr Rumpole. Still at it, are you?'

'I am still at it!' I told them. 'I am still carrying on a practice to the best of my poor ability in Equity Court. All briefs received there marked Mr H. Rumpole will be attended to swiftly and to my usual high standard. But as for you, Bonny Bernard, I'm sorry to have wasted on you the lines written by the poet Browning to the Great Wordsworth, whom he thought a traitor to the cause of human freedom when he sold out and became a civil servant.'

'Really? I didn't know that.' Bernard didn't seem to understand the relevance of the lines to his own conduct. I pointed it out.

'I'm not suggesting you did it for a handful of silver, Bernard. Perhaps it had more to do with being put up as a member of the Sheridan Club.'

'Oh, yes.' Bernard persisted in behaving as though he had nothing to be ashamed of. 'Your Mr Prosser was kind enough to propose me.'

'So you were kind enough to slip him a brief by way of returning the favour? Do I need to tell you how the poet Browning went on? "He alone sinks to the rear and the slaves!" A slave, I am suggesting, Bernard, to the magnificent prize of becoming a member of a dusty old club. I tell you what. I'll get you into the Bunyan Society. You'll probably recognize Hypocrisy, born in the land of Vainglory.'

'Why don't you sit down, Mr Rumpole?' The unremarkable Tillbury seemed anxious to make peace. 'Can I offer you a drop of the red?'

I sat then, not yet placated, but my outburst had left me thirsty. 'When I think,' I said to Bernard as Tillbury trotted off to the bar, 'of all we've been through together – the business of the Tap End of the Bath murder, the case I called "The Angel of Death". And what about the Children of the Devil, or the Puzzling Murder in the Case of Toby Johnson . . . ?'

'Please, Mr Rumpole, don't go on . . .' Bonny Bernard was, I was glad to see, visibly moved, but I couldn't resist a final turn of the screw. 'And how am I rewarded? My work is transferred to Archie Prosser!'

'Quite honestly, Mr Rumpole, we didn't think you'd want to be bothered.'

Tillbury had arrived with my wine. I downed it and, as usual, the Château Thames Embankment had a calming effect on me. 'I met Chirpy Molloy in prison. His girlfriend's devoted. He means to take up a life of honest toil in her dad's Videos R Us shop in Lewisham. He instructs you that he never went near Sloane Square on the night in question and his girlfriend, Lorraine Hickson, provides him with an alibi. If all that's true, Chirpy Molloy is a candidate for redemption. Do you really think I wouldn't be bothered about his case?'

'It seems so open and shut. Nothing much to be done except go through the motions.'

'Seems, Bonny Bernard? I know not seems.' I had given him Browning and John Bunyan. I gave him Hamlet, and all he had given me was a glass of Pommeroy's Very Ordinary in return for a lost brief. 'There are one or two things I might do to help.'

'Things, Mr Rumpole?' Bernard looked vaguely alarmed. 'What sort of things, exactly?'

'Oh, important things. I'm sure Mr Prosser will find them extremely helpful.'

With that I downed a second glass of wine and left Bonny Bernard, who looked as though he were afraid that the trial he'd thought of as 'open and shut' might, with Rumpole on the case, be unexpectedly worrying.

My visit to Worsfield nick had other results, apart from my meeting with Chirpy Molloy, the prisoner who might or might not have reached a state of redemption. I got a taxi – a sudden, unexpected call to do a plea at London Sessions – and found it to be driven by Vince Timson, one member of the extended family who had, at least for most of the time, a legitimate occupation.

'Great to see you at liberty, Mr Rumpole,' he said. 'Last we saw of you was a picture in the papers when you was entering Worsfield Prison. All the family was upset by that. They really was. "Poor old Mr Rumpole," they said. "They got him at last." Short sentence, was it?'

'Short, but quite unpleasant,' I told him. 'They gave me lunch.'

But I was also given complimentary membership of the Bunyan Society and got a calendar of forthcoming events. The next bash was drinks on the terrace of the House of Lords, when the great and the good, released from lunch in the nick, would be bribed by glasses of champagne and finger food to sign cheques to help the cause of prison reform.

Sunlight glittered on the river and warmed the stone walls of Parliament. The champagne frosted the glasses and the Members, relaxing away from the company of the prisoners the Bunyan Society existed to care for, talked in low, agreeable voices, laughed moderately, nibbled at sausages on sticks or gently introduced fragments of celery into avocado dip. I had brought a guest, none other than Lady Sloper, wife of the Beetle Judge.

'My husband tells me that when you're in a case, Rumpole, he always expects some sort of trouble,' she had told me when I rang her up.

'No sort of trouble now,' I assured her. 'It's just that the Bunyan Society is terribly keen to have you at their drinks party. They've heard you're fantastically interested in prisons.'

'Well, not all that interested, actually. Beetle keeps putting people into them, of course. But my thing's Albanian orphans.'

'Of course it is.' I had tried to sound as though Lady Sloper's work with Albanian orphans was almost the sole topic of conversation round the Old Bailey. 'But if they get here, they quite often end up in prison. For all the wrong reasons, of course. Do say "yes", Lady Sloper. As I say, the Bunyan Society is really desperate to have you.'

'Are they, indeed? And where did you say this party was?'

'Very pleasant surroundings. The terrace of the House of Lords.'

'Really? Well, I do enjoy a party.' Was this a woman, I wondered, who would go anywhere for a samosa and a glass of champagne? 'I don't really see why not.' Lady Sloper, who, reasonably early on, gave me permission to call her Marjorie, was a small, bright-eyed woman, who made good use of the champagne and was licking her fingers after a particularly succulent samosa when she spotted another judge. 'There's Phillida Erskine-Brown. Beetle really rates her.'

'I think we all do,' I agreed. Across the gently grazing heads I saw the one-time Portia of our chambers with her QC husband in tow. He was occupying himself by gazing at the other end of the terrace, where the Home Secretary, today in flaming orange with matching earrings, was being chatted up by the top brass of the Bunyan Society. 'Beetle says Phillida Erskine-Brown's top notch on crime, she doesn't stand for any nonsense from you lot saying it's all down to bad parenting or insufficient weaning or whatever.'

'Just as well,' I hastened to agree with Marjorie. 'There's so much of it about nowadays.'

'You mean insufficient weaning?'

'No, I mean crime.' The time had come to bring matters to a head. 'It's everywhere, isn't it? You even saw it from your bedroom window.'

'Well, I saw a man come out of the back door of the house opposite and go off across the garden. Of course, I was the only one who saw it. Beetle was away on circuit.'

'I suppose if he hadn't been he'd have rushed out and collared the fellow.'

'Certainly not. He'd have dug in under the duvet. You obviously don't know my husband.'

'We all have a great deal of respect for Beetle.' I thought it was the right thing to say.

'Oh well, I'm sure he'd be very grateful to you for that.' Marjorie's affection for the judicial insect fell, it was clear, some degrees short of total adulation.

'You seem to have had a pretty good view of the burglar.'

'You're not defending him, are you?' She looked at me now with some distrust.

'No, not at all,' I reassured her. 'I just happened to read your statement in some papers that got delivered to me by mistake.'

'The prosecution aren't going to call me.' You bet they aren't, I might have said to her, because your description doesn't fit the customer they've decided has, on past performances, got to be guilty. 'Beetle's terribly relieved. He said I'd probably be given a ghastly time by "someone like Rumpole", I have to tell you.' She seemed to find the situation enormously amusing. 'That's exactly what he said.'

'Well, he was wrong,' I promised her. 'I'd have given you the warmest possible welcome. I'd have congratulated you on the clarity of your evidence and your powers of observation. In fact, I'd probably have made you my star witness. That is, if I were doing the case.'

'So it's lucky you aren't,' she told me, 'because I'm not being called at all.'

'Yes, of course. Lucky for someone, anyway.' I looked up the terrace to where the colourful Home Secretary had moved away from the governing group of the Bunyan Society. I took Marjorie up to them. I have to say, I bypassed the mustard-keen director, Katey Kershaw; I merely nodded at the chairman, Sir James Loveridge. I aimed, with Beetle's wife in tow, straight for the president of the Bunyan, together with the well-heeled Labour peer who had paid for the champagne and canapés. They were being held in no doubt fascinating conversation on prisons and prisoners by the reformed con, Brian Skidmore. I broke, I'm afraid rudely, into their gently murmured conversation to greet Brian. 'You were dead right about Chirpy Molloy,' I congratulated him. 'He couldn't go straight for a month or two. He's right back in the nick on another charge of burglary, with use of bathroom to be taken into consideration.'

Brian smiled knowingly and introduced me to the president and Lord Crane, the society's benefactor. 'We were talking about an inmate Mr Rumpole met when he had lunch with us in Worsfield.' He brought the top brass up to date with the Molloy affair. 'He's a serial burglar who breaks into people's homes when they're away on holiday and gives himself a bath and uses all the toiletries.'

'What you might call a clean break.' Lord Crane made what had to be the day's worst joke, causing the president to smile indulgently and Brian Skidmore to utter a short yelp of laughter.

'That's a good one, my Lord. A very good one. On a more serious note, though, I knew this chap Molloy hadn't got the strength of character to resist going back to his old ways. Everything's against you when you come out of prison. No money. No job. You meet all the old friends you did crime with . . . It's a hard struggle. I found that. And it needs strength of character.'

'You managed it though, didn't you, Brian?' The president of the Bunyan was smiling proudly.

'Yes, sir, I managed it. But as I say, it wasn't easy. Of course, I had a lot of help from the Bunyan. And I had faith.'

'Religious faith?' Lord Crane sounded doubtful, as though he wasn't sure what particular brand of faith might be under discussion.

'It's what the Bible tells us, isn't it? Whatever sins we might have done – we're all capable of redemption.'

'Pity Chirpy Molloy wasn't,' I agreed with Brian. 'Oh, I'm so sorry, I forgot to introduce Lady Sloper.' I made the introductions and added, 'By the way, she and the judge live just behind the house where Chirpy did his last break-in. She was telling me that she saw a man emerge from the back door. Two o'clock in the morning under a full moon. Isn't that right, Lady Sloper?'

But it was hard to get Marjorie's full attention. She had for some time been staring at Brian Skidmore. She was looking, wondering, and I remembered the description of the man she had seen by moonlight, in the statement no one had particularly wanted to be used. A tall man, she had said, with a pronounced nose and a bald dome of a head, which shone hairless in the moonlight. She had seen him clearly until he vanished into the shadows by the garden wall.

Then she answered my question. 'Yes,' she said, 'that's right.'

At this there was a flash of light; behind it, in the shadows, Luci was holding her newly acquired digital camera on which, so she had assured me, she could already see the picture she had taken. Brian

Skidmore, the perfect ex-prisoner, however, was having none of it. He snatched Luci's camera from her and stamped on it. 'No photographs!' he shouted, startling the quietly murmuring and grazing guests. 'Didn't anyone tell you? No photographs allowed!' So he left the party, and indeed the Bunyan Society, only to be found, without much difficulty, when he was required to help the police with their enquiries.

In the weeks that followed, I had ample opportunity to consider the doctrine of redemption, as I sat, smoking too many small cigars, not fully employed with briefs calculated to interrupt my train of thought. I did, however, receive several visitors who, in their various ways, threw some light on the subject under consideration. The first of these was Claude Erskine-Brown, who subsided into my client's chair and looked at me with the despairing eyes of a man who can't decide between drowning and an overdose of sleeping pills as the easiest way out of this cruel world.

'Well, Rumpole,' he said, 'it finally happened. At the Bunyan Society do in the House of Lords. You were there, weren't you?'

'Certainly I was there. But what do you mean by "it"?'

'I was speaking,' he said bitterly, 'of the woman who calls herself Home Secretary. She was there, you know.'

'Yes, I know. I saw her. But what I'm groping for, Erskine-Brown, is are you suggesting some sort of consummation?'

'Hardly.' He gave a short laugh which might have been reasonably described as mirthless.

'I thought not. I didn't notice you and the secretary of state in any sort of clinch behind the potted plants.'

'Of course you didn't. I was there with Philly.'

'Yes, I noticed that. You and the learned judge.'

'And that woman, Brenda Heygate, came up to us.'

'Smiling?'

'Smiling at Philly. And engaging her in conversation. In fact, she wanted my wife to chair a committee to decide if people should be able to trace the sperm donors who might have fathered them. Yes, Rumpole,' Erskine-Brown's tone became increasingly bitter. 'Sperm donors! That's what they were discussing. Then Philly said to her, "Of course, you know my husband." So this Heygate woman looked at me and do you know what she said?'

'No. Tell me. The suspense is killing me.'

' "No, we've never met." '

'Is that what she said?'

'That's exactly what she said. "No, we've never met." And she held out her hand for me to shake. I had kissed her, Rumpole! I had seen her to her car and I had kissed her!'

'On the lips?' I was trying to get the picture.

'Partially on the lips. And in part on her cheek. She appeared to enjoy it.'

'I'm sure she did.'

'And now she's saying, "No, we've never met." '

'Perhaps,' I did my best to give him a crumb of comfort, 'she was lying. Wanting to hide her considerable passion.'

'Please! I know you're trying to be kind, Rumpole. She had simply and genuinely forgotten my existence.'

'No doubt she had a good deal on her mind. Affairs of state and all that cracking down.'

'What would affairs of state matter, if she'd been genuinely in love?'

'I see your point. So what it comes to is – the affair's over?'

'If it ever started.'

'And you can spend more time with your family,' I told him. 'You've been redeemed.'

'I've been what?'

'Redeemed. You might have committed all sorts of sins with the Home Secretary. But now you're a reformed character. You have been granted redemption without even asking for it. Count yourself lucky, Erskine-Brown.'

'If that's redemption,' Claude was lifting himself wearily from my client's chair, 'I'm not sure I care for it at all.'

Some days later, Henry put through a call from my former solicitor, Bonny Bernard. I was delighted to hear him sound as ridden with guilt as any major sinner entering the confessional.

'We've done all you suggested, Mr Rumpole.'

'Good. I'm glad to hear it.' My voice, I hoped, was chilly and the tone curt.

'I've seen Lady Sloper and beefed up her statement. And we're investigating the fingerprint business.'

'Is that all?' I was preparing myself to think of a suitable penance, such as fifty contested careless drivings in the Uxbridge Magistrates' Court, but then the persistent Bernard sprang a surprise.

'I'm sending you a brief, Mr Rumpole.'

'Oh, are you really?' I kept the chill in my voice. 'What is it? Bad case of unrenewed telly licence?'

'No. A murder.'

'Is it indeed?' I couldn't help the voice warming up a little.

'The unusual thing is,' Bernard started to elaborate, 'the death occurred in a home for the blind and partially sighted.'

'Who's on trial?' I couldn't help asking for further particulars. 'One of the staff?'

'No, actually it's one of the patients. And I think she might have a defence.'

'Send it round then.' A dreadful thought occurred to me. 'I suppose you'll be taking in a leader?'

'No, Mr Rumpole.' My solicitor was admirably clear on this point. 'We thought you'd be better doing this one on your own.'

'Bonny Bernard!' I was then able to tell him, 'I have good news for you. You are a solicitor redeemed.'

I had scarcely slid the tape off the brief in the murder the reformed Bonny Bernard had sent me when, after a brisk knock, Luci Gribble entered the room with a cup of steaming instant. 'That bloody lunatic at the Bunyan,' she said, 'absolutely wrecked my camera. And I was getting some good pics for the Chambers Bulletin.'

'I know.' I was sympathetic. 'He didn't like the sight of his own face.'

I sipped instant, lit a small cigar, but Luci, instead of going, took her place, as so many customers with a guilty secret do, in my client's chair.

'Rumpole,' she said, 'I'm sorry I shopped you like that.'

'Like what, exactly?'

'Well, telling your wife I hadn't noticed you on the exercise bike when I signed you in. I'm afraid I got you into trouble.'

'Trouble? Oh, hardly at all,' I assured her. 'I've been about as welcome in Froxbury Mansions as mice in the larder or a nasty patch of rising damp on the bedroom walls since you grassed about the Lysander Club. That's all. I've had to learn to live with it.'

'I said I'm sorry.'

'That's all right. You told the truth. Some people find doing that an irresistible temptation.'

'But don't worry. I know exactly how you can make up for your shameful neglect of bicycling duty.'

'What are you suggesting?' I was, I have to confess, wary of the director of marketing's plans for my future. When it comes to dealing with marriage, the cure is often worse than the disease.

'All you have to do is to remember the date next Thursday.'

'Why?' I was mystified. 'What is the date next Thursday?'

'Just look it up and remember it. That's all. By the way, I've booked a table for the two of you at the Myrtle restaurant.'

'You mean . . .' Some distant memory began to trouble my mind.

'Yes. I do mean. It's your wedding anniversary and you're going to take She Who Must Be Obeyed out to dinner.'

'People all talked about Chirpy Molloy leaving his signature on the bathrooms of the houses he burgled. Well, if I know one thing about signatures, it is that they get forged. With all his contacts, the Blessed Saint Brian Skidmore knew all about the jewellery scattered around that house in the Sloane Square area. So he decided to do a job which seemed to have Chirpy's signature written large upon it.'

'Rumpole . . .'

'They were so sure it was Chirpy's work that they didn't bother to look for fingerprints. But when they started looking, they found Brian's on a bottle of Machisimo. He wasn't as careful as Chirpy, you see, and, of course, he never thought anyone would suspect the reformed con with a steady job in the Bunyan Society. He just didn't take enough care.'

'Rumpole, they're taking such a long time with my steak. Do you think they're slaughtering the animal?'

'It's an odd thing about redemption. It seems to come to the most improbable people. Chirpy, it seems, really was redeemed. He'd got his new job and his new girlfriend, and I think he really means to give up invading other people's bathrooms. But the Sainted Brian, exhibit A in the case for prison as a cure for crime, turns out not to have been redeemed at all. Not only did he want to get his fingers on Adele Alexander's baubles, he tried to get a reformed con to do his bird for him.'

'Rumpole, that asparagus wasn't cooked properly. It was hard as nails and had flakes of cheese all over it. It wasn't right, Rumpole. I should have complained at the time.'

'It might have all worked if I hadn't picked up the brief sent to Archie Prosser in a moment of treachery. Well, at least I could organize things so that Prosser could win the case. A somewhat rare event, as I understand it, in the life of our newest arrival in chambers!'

'Rumpole! Do we have to spend the evening discussing your cases?'

There was a distinct edge to Hilda's voice as she said that. I decided to drop the subject of the forged burglaries.

'No, of course we don't. I mean, why should we discuss my cases? Quite certainly not! By the way, what would you like to discuss?'

'What about – the reason we're here. Dining out. Is that because you're trying to redeem yourself, Rumpole?'

'Yes.' I had to tell her the truth. 'That's what I'm trying to do.'

The Myrtle was packed out as usual that evening; only the networking skills of Luci Gribble had won us a table. Against the dark wood of the walls, over the snowy white tablecloths, the faces, vaguely familiar from Hilda's tabloid and the telly, recognized each other, gave faint little cries of greeting, and then turned their attention back to their plates. Waiters in long white aprons sniffed corks, removed dripping champagne bottles from their buckets or set out plates. It was all far removed from lunch at the Worsfield nick, where this story began. I poured the unaccustomed vintage claret into our glasses and raised mine.

'Happy wedding anniversary.' I touched her glass with mine and took a gulp.

'You remembered?' She Who Must looked as though she didn't believe a word of it.

Again I decided to surprise her with the truth. 'Well, I have to say no, I didn't remember. At least not until Luci reminded me.'

'I told her you never remember.'

'Well, that may be true, as a general rule. But on this occasion Luci told me, and then I remembered it quite clearly.'

'You'd make a hopeless witness, Rumpole.'

'Do you really think so?'

'No one would believe your evidence for a moment.'

'I'm not in the business of giving evidence,' I told her. 'I'm in the business of asking questions.'

'Ask me then.'

'Do I really have to go on bicycling nowhere?'

'You're not going to, are you, whatever I say?'

'No.'

'All right then. I just wanted to keep you going for a little while longer. I can't think why it is, but I don't want to lose you, Rumpole.'

This was so astonishing that it sent me imagining a world without She Who Must Be Obeyed. What would it be like? I seemed to see a great emptiness. A world without difficult cases, as bland, perhaps, as a world without crime or the possibility of redemption. I was about to say something along these lines when the waiter arrived and slid her main course dexterously in front of Hilda. She switched her attention from me to the waiter.

'I hope it's as I like it,' she said. 'By the way, I think I should tell you, the asparagus was not right.'

'Not right?' The waiter was Australian and took Hilda's complaint with a cheerful smile.

'To begin with it was hard as nails. I almost broke my teeth on it.'

'That's right! Al dente.'

'Well, we can do without the al dente, thank you. And someone had put bits of cheese on it.'

'Parmesan.'

'Exactly! So you admit it. You don't put cheese on asparagus. It wasn't right, you know. I'd like you to know that, because we're quite likely to be back at the same time next year.'

Rumpole and the Christmas Break

I

'We must be constantly on guard. Night and day. Vigilance is essential. I'm sure you would agree, wouldn't you, Luci?'

Soapy Sam Ballard, our always nervous head of chambers, addressed the meeting as though the forces of evil were already beating on the doors of 3 Equity Court, and weapons of mass destruction had laid waste to the dining hall, condemning us to a long winter of cold meat and sandwiches. As usual, he longed for confirmation and turned to our recently appointed director of marketing and administration, who was now responsible for the chambers image.

'Quite right, Chair.' Luci's North Country voice sounded quietly amused, as though she didn't take the alarming state of the world quite as seriously as Ballard did.

'Thank you for your contribution, Luci.' Soapy Sam, it seemed, thought she might have gone a little further, such as recommending that Securicor mount a twenty-four-hour guard on the head of chambers. Then he added, in a voice of doom, 'I have already asked our clerk to keep an extremely sharp eye on the sugar kept in the coffee cupboard.'

'Why did you do that?' I ventured to ask our leader. 'Has Claude been shovelling it in by the tablespoonful?'

Claude Erskine-Brown was one of the few barristers I have ever met who combined a passionate affection for Wagner's operas with a remarkably sweet tooth, continuously sucking wine gums in court and loading his coffee with heaped spoonfuls of sugar.

'It's not that, Rumpole.' Soapy Sam was getting petulant. 'It's anthrax.'

'What anthrax?'

'The sugar might be. There are undoubtedly people out there

465

who are out to get us, Rumpole. Haven't you been listening at all to government warnings?'

'I seem to remember them telling us one day that if we went down the tube we'd all be gassed, and the next day they said, "Sorry, we were only joking. Carry on going down the tube." '

'Rumpole! Do you take nothing seriously?'

'Some things,' I assured Soapy Sam. 'But not the government.'

'We are,' here Ballard ignored me as an apparently hopeless case, and addressed the meeting, 'especially vulnerable.'

'Why's that?' I was curious enough to ask.

'We represent the law, Rumpole. The centre of a civilized society. Naturally we'd be high on their hit list.'

'You mean the Houses of Parliament, Buckingham Palace and Number 3 Equity Court? I wonder, you may be right.'

'I propose to appoint a small chambers emergency committee consisting of myself, Claude Erskine-Brown and Archie Prosser. Please report to one of us if you notice anything unusual or out of the ordinary. I assume you have nothing to report, Rumpole?'

'Nothing much. I did notice a chap on the tube. A fellow of Middle Eastern appearance wearing a turban and a beard and muttering into a dictaphone. He got out at South Kensington. I don't suppose it's important.'

Just for a moment, I thought – indeed, I hoped – our head of chambers looked at me as though he believed what I had said, but then justifiable doubt overcame him.

'Very funny,' Ballard told the meeting. 'But then you can scarcely afford to be serious about the danger we're all in, can you, Rumpole? Considering you're defending one of these maniacs.'

'Rumpole would defend anyone,' said Archie Prosser – the newest arrival in our chambers – who had an ill-deserved reputation as a wit.

'If you mean anyone who's put on trial and tells me they're innocent, then the answer is yes.'

Nothing alarming happened on the tube on my way home that evening, except for the fact that, owing to a 'work to rule' by the drivers, the train gave up work at Victoria and I had to walk the rest of the way home to Froxbury Mansions in the Gloucester Road. The shops and their windows were full of glitter, artificial snow and wax models perched on sleighs wearing party dresses. Taped carols came tinkling out of Tesco's. The chambers meeting had been the last of the term, and the Old Bailey had interrupted its business for the season of peace and goodwill.

There was very little of either in the case which I had been doing in front of the aptly named Mr Justice Graves. Mind you, I would have had a fairly rough ride before the most reasonable of judges. Even some compassionate old darlings like Mr Justice 'Pussy' Proudfoot might have regarded my client with something like horror and been tempted to dismiss my speech to the jury as a hopeless attempt to prevent a certain conviction and a probable sentence of not less than thirty years. The murder we had been considering, when we were interrupted by Christmas, had been cold-blooded and merciless, and there was clear evidence that it had been the work of a religious fanatic.

The victim, Honoria Glossop, Professor of Comparative Religion at William Morris University in East London, had been the author of a number of books, including her latest, and last, publication, *Sanctified Killing – A History of Religious Warfare*. She had been severely critical of all acts of violence and aggression – including the Inquisition and the Crusades – committed in the name of God. She had also included a chapter on Islam which spoke scathingly of some ayatollahs and the cruelties committed by Islamic fundamentalists.

It was this chapter which had caused my client, a young student of computer technology at William Morris named Hussein Khan, to issue a private fatwa. He composed, on one of the university computers, a letter to Professor Glossop announcing that her blasphemous references to the religious leaders of his country deserved nothing less than death – which would inevitably catch up with her. Then he left the letter in her pigeonhole.

It took very little time for the authorship of the letter to be discovered. Hussein Khan was sent down from William Morris and began spending his time helping his family in the Star of Persia restaurant they ran in Golders Green. A week later, Professor Glossop, who had been working late in her office at the university, was found slumped across her desk, having been shot at close quarters by a bullet from a revolver of Czech origin, the sort of weapon which is readily and cheaply available in certain South London pubs. Beside her on the desk, now stained with her blood, was the letter containing the sentence of death.

Honoria and her husband, Richard 'Ricky' Glossop, lived in what the estate agents would describe as 'a three-million pound town house in the Boltons'. The professor had, it seemed, inherited a great deal of money from a family business in the Midlands, which allowed her to pursue her academic career and Ricky to devote his life to country sports without the need for gainful employment. He was clearly, from his photographs in the papers, an outstandingly handsome figure, perhaps five or six years younger than his wife. After her murder, he received, and everyone felt deserved, huge public sympathy. He and Honoria had met when they were both guests on a yacht touring the Greek islands, and she had chosen him and his good looks in preference to all the available professors and academic authors she knew. In spite of their differences in age and interests, they seemed to have lived happily together for ten years until, so the prosecution said, death overtook Honoria Glossop in the person of my now universally hated client.

Such was the case I was engaged in at the Old Bailey in the run-up to Christmas. There were no tidings of great joy to report. The cards were stacked dead against me, and at every stage it looked like I was losing, trumped by a judge who regarded defence barristers as flies on the tasty dish of justice.

Mr Justice Graves, known to me only as 'the Old Gravestone', had a deep, sepulchral voice and the general appearance of a man waking up with an upset stomach on a wet weekend. He had clearly come to the conclusion that the world was full of irredeemable sinners. The nearest thing to a smile I had seen on the face of the Old Gravestone was the look of grim delight he had displayed when, after a difficult case, the jury had come back with the guilty verdict he had clearly longed for.

So, as you can imagine, the atmosphere in Court Number One at the Old Bailey during the trial of the Queen against Hussein Khan was about as warm as the South Pole during a blizzard. The Queen may have adopted a fairly detached attitude towards my client, but the judge certainly hadn't.

The prosecution was in the not altogether capable hands of Soapy Sam Ballard, which was why he had practically named me as a founding member of Al Qaeda at our chambers meeting. His junior was the newcomer Archie Prosser.

These two might not have been the most deadly optimists I had ever had to face during my long career at the Bar, but a first-year law student with a lowish IQ would, I thought, have had little difficulty in securing a conviction against the young student who had managed to become one of the most hated men in England.

As he was brought up from the cells and placed in the dock between two prison officers, the jury took one brief, appalled look at him and then turned their eyes on what seemed to them to be the less offensive figure of Soapy Sam as he prepared to open his devastating case.

So I sat at my end of counsel's benches. The brief had been offered to several QCs ('Queer Customers' I always call them), but they had excused themselves as being too busy, or unwell, or going on holiday – any excuse to avoid being cast as leading counsel for the forces of evil. It was only, it seemed, Rumpole who stuck to the old-fashioned belief that the most outrageous sinner deserves to have his defence, if he had one, put fairly and squarely in front of a jury.

Mr Justice Gravestone didn't share my views. When Ballard rose he was greeted with something almost like a smile from the bench, and his most obvious comments were underlined by a judicious nod followed by a careful note underlined in the judicial notebook. Every time I rose to cross-examine a prosecution witness, however, Graves sighed heavily and laid down his pencil as though nothing of any significance was likely to emerge.

This happened when I had a few pertinent questions to ask the pathologist, my old friend Professor Arthur Ackerman, forensic scientist and master of the morgues. After he had given his evidence about the cause of death (pretty obvious), I started off.

'You say, Professor Ackerman, that the shot was fired at close quarters?'

'Yes, Mr Rumpole. Indeed it was.' Ackerman and I had been through so many bloodstained cases together that we chatted across the court like old friends.

'You told us,' I went on, 'that the bullet entered the deceased's neck – she was probably shot from behind – and that, among other things, the bullet severed an artery.'

'That is so.'

'So, as a result, blood spurted over the desk. We know it was on the letter. Would you have expected the person, whoever it was, who shot her at close quarters to have had some blood on his clothing?'

'I think that may well have happened.'

'Would you say it probably happened?'

'Probably. Yes.'

When I got this answer from the witness, I stood a while in silence, looking at the motionless judge.

'Is that all you have to ask, Mr Rumpole?'

'No, my Lord. I'm waiting so your Lordship has time to make note of the evidence. I see your Lordship's pencil is taking a rest!'

'I'm sure the jury has heard your questions, Mr Rumpole. And the answers.'

'I'm sure they have, and you will no doubt remind them of that during your summing up. So I'm sure your Lordship will wish to make a note.'

Gravestone, with an ill grace, picked up his pencil and made the shortest possible note. Then I asked Ackerman my last question.

'And I take it you know that the clothes my client wore that evening were minutely examined and no traces of any bloodstains were found?'

'My Lord, how can this witness know what was on Khan's clothing?' Soapy Sam objected.

'Quite right, Mr Ballard,' the judge was quick to agree. 'That was an outrageous question, Mr Rumpole. The jury will disregard it.'

It got no better. I rose, at the end of a long day in court, to cross-examine Superintendent Gregory, the perfectly decent officer in charge of the case.

'My client, Mr Khan, made no secret of the fact that he had written this threatening letter, did he, Superintendent Gregory?'

'He did not, my Lord,' Gregory answered with obvious satisfaction.

'In fact,' said Mr Justice Graves, searching among his notes, 'the witness Sadiq told us that your client boasted to him of the fact in the university canteen.'

There, at last, the Gravestone had overstepped the mark.

'He didn't say "boasted".'

Soapy Sam Ballard QC, the alleged head of our chambers, got up with his notebook at the ready.

'Sadiq said that Khan told him he had written the letter and, in answer to your Lordship, that "he seemed to feel no sort of guilt about it".'

'There you are, Mr Rumpole.' Graves also seemed to feel no sort of guilt. 'Doesn't that come to exactly the same thing?'

'Certainly not, my Lord. The word "boasted" was never used.'

'The jury may come to the conclusion that it amounted to boasting.'

'They may indeed, my Lord. But that's for them to decide, without directions from your Lordship.'

'Mr Rumpole,' here the judge adopted an expression of lofty pity, 'I realize you have many difficulties in this case. But perhaps we may proceed without further argument. Have you any more questions for this officer?'

'Just one, my Lord.' I turned to the superintendent. 'This letter was traced to one of the university word processors.'

'That is so, yes.'

'You would agree that my client took no steps at all to cover up the fact that he was the author of this outrageous threat.'

'He seems to have been quite open about it, yes.'

'That's hardly consistent with the behaviour of someone about to commit a brutal murder, is it?'

'I suppose it was a little surprising, yes,' Jack Gregory was fair enough to admit.

'Very surprising, isn't it? And of course by the time this murder took place, everyone knew he had written the letter. He'd been sent down for doing so.'

'That's right.'

The Gravestone intervened. 'Did it not occur to you, Superintendent Gregory, that being sent down might have provided an additional motive for the murder?'

The judge clearly thought he was on to something, and was deeply gratified when the superintendent answered, 'That might have been so, my Lord.'

'That might have been so,' Graves dictated to himself as he wrote the answer down. Then he thought of another point that might be of use to the hardly struggling prosecution. 'Of course, if a man thinks he's justified, for religious or moral reasons, in killing someone, he might have no inhibitions about boasting of the fact?'

I knew it. Soapy Sam must have known it, and the jury had better be told it. The judge had gone too far. I rose to my feet, as quickly as my weight and the passage of the years would allow, and uttered a sharp protest.

'My Lord, the prosecution is in the able hands of Samuel Ballard QC. I'm sure he can manage to present the case against my client without your Lordship's continued help and encouragement.'

This was followed by a terrible silence, the sort of stillness that precedes a storm.

'Mr Rumpole.' His Lordship's words were as warm as hailstones. 'That was a most outrageous remark.'

'It was a point I felt I should make,' I told him, 'in fairness to my client.'

'As I have said, I realize you have an extremely difficult case to argue, Mr Rumpole.' Once more Graves was reminding the jury that I was on a certain loser. 'But I cannot overlook your inappropriate and disrespectful attitude towards the court. I shall have to consider whether your conduct should be reported to the proper authority.'

After these dire remarks and a few more unimportant questions to the superintendent, Graves turned to the jury and reminded them that this no doubt painful and shocking case would be resumed after the Christmas break. He said this in the solemn and sympathetic tones of someone announcing the death of a dear friend or relative, then he wished them a 'Happy Christmas'.

The tube train home was packed and I stood, swaying uneasily, sandwiched between an eighteen-stone man in a donkey jacket with a heavy cold and an elderly woman with a pair of the sharpest elbows I have ever encountered on the Circle Line.

No doubt all of the other passengers had hard, perhaps unrewarding, lives but they didn't have to spend their days acting as a sort of human buffer between a possibly fatal fanatic and a hostile judge who certainly wanted to end the career of the inconveniently argumentative Rumpole. The train, apparently as exhausted as I felt, ground to a halt between Embankment and Westminster, and as the lights went out I'd almost decided to give up the Bar. Then the lights glowed again faintly and the train jerked on. I supposed I would have to go on as well – wouldn't I? – not being the sort of character who could retire to the country and plant strawberries.

When I reached the so-called Mansion Flat in the Gloucester Road I was, I have to say, not a little surprised by the warmth of the welcome I received. My formidable wife Hilda, known to me only as She Who Must Be Obeyed, said, 'Sit down, Rumpole. You look tired out.' And she lit the gas fire. A few minutes later, she brought me a glass of my usual refreshment – the Very Ordinary claret available from Pommeroy's Wine Bar in Fleet Street, a vintage known to me as Château Thames Embankment. I suspected that all this attention meant that she had some uncomfortable news to break and I was right.

'This year,' she told me, with the firmness of the Old Gravestone pronouncing judgment, 'I'm not going to do Christmas. It's getting too much for me.'

Christmas is not usually much of a 'do' in the Rumpole household. There is the usual exchange of presents; I get a tie and Hilda receives the statutory bottle of Violetta Eau de Toilette, which seems to be for laying down rather than immediate use. She cooks the turkey and I open the Château Thames Embankment, and so our Saviour's birth is celebrated.

'I have booked us this year,' Hilda announced, 'into Cherry Picker's Hall. You look in need of a rest, Rumpole.'

What was this place she spoke of? A retirement home? Sheltered accommodation? 'I'm in the middle of an important murder. I can't pack up and go into a home.'

'It's not a home, Rumpole. It's a country house hotel. In the Cotswolds. They're doing a special offer – four nights with full board. A children's party. Christmas lunch with crackers and a dance on Christmas Eve. It'll be something to look forward to.'

'I don't really think so. We haven't got any children and I don't want to dance at Christmas. So shall we say no to the Cherry Picker's?'

'Whether you dance or not is entirely up to you, Rumpole. But you can't say no because I've already booked it and paid the deposit. And I've collected your old dinner jacket from the cleaners.'

So I was unusually silent. Not for nothing is my wife entitled She Who Must Be Obeyed.

I was unusually silent on the way to the Cotswolds too, but as we approached this country house hotel, I felt that perhaps, after all, She Who Must Be Obeyed had made a wise decision and that the considerable financial outlay on the 'Budget Christmas Offer' might turn out, in spite of all my apprehensions, to be justified.

We took a taxi from the station. As we made our way down deep into the countryside, the sun was shining and the trees were throwing a dark pattern against a clear sky. We passed green fields where cows were munching and a stream trickling over rocks. A stray deer crossed the road in front of us and a single kite (at least, Hilda said it was a kite) wheeled across the sky. We had, it seemed, entered a better, more peaceful world far from the problems of terrorists, the bloodstained letter containing a sentence of death, the impossible client and the no less difficult judge I struggled with down at the Old Bailey. In spite of all my troubles, I felt a kind of contentment stealing over me.

Happily, the contentment only deepened as our taxi scrunched the gravel by the entrance to Cherry Picker's Hall. The old grey stones of the one-time manor house were gilded by the last of the winter sun. We were greeted warmly by a friendly manageress and our things were taken up to a comfortable room overlooking a wintry garden. Then, in no time at all, I was sitting by a blazing log fire in the residents' lounge, eating anchovy paste sandwiches with the prospect of a dark and alcoholic fruit cake to follow. Even my appalling client, Hussein Khan, might, I thought, if brought into such an environment, forget his calling as a messenger of terror and relax after dinner.

'It's wonderful to be away from the Old Bailey. I just had the most terrible quarrel with a particularly unlearned judge,' I told Hilda, who was reading a back number of *Country Life*.

'You keep quarrelling with judges, don't you? Why don't you take up fishing, Rumpole? Lazy days by a trout stream might help you forget all those squalid cases you do.' She had clearly got to the country sports section of the magazine.

'This quarrel went a bit further than usual. He threatened to report me for professional misconduct. I didn't like the way he kept telling the jury my client was guilty.'

'Well, isn't he guilty, Rumpole?' In all innocence, Hilda had asked the awkward question.

'Well. Quite possibly. But that's for the jury of twelve honest citizens to decide, not Mr Justice Gravestone.'

'Gravestone? Is that his name?'

'No. His name's Graves. I call him Gravestone.'

'You would, wouldn't you, Rumpole?'

'He speaks like a voice from the tomb. It's my personal belief that he urinates iced water!'

'Really, Rumpole. Do try not to be vulgar. So what did you say to Mr Justice Graves? You might as well tell me the truth.'

She was right, of course. The only way of appeasing She Who Must was to plead guilty and throw oneself on the mercy of the court. 'I told him to come down off the bench and join Soapy Sam Ballard on the prosecution team.'

'Rumpole, that was terribly rude of you!'

'Yes,' I said, with considerable satisfaction. 'It really was.'

'So no wonder he's cross with you.'

'Very cross indeed.' Once again I couldn't keep the note of triumph out of my voice.

'I should think he probably hates you, Rumpole.'

'I should think he probably does.'

'Well, you're safe here anyway. You can forget all about your precious Mr Justice Gravestone and just enjoy Christmas.'

She was, as usual, right. I stretched my legs towards the fire and took a gulp of Earl Grey and a large bite of rich, dark cake.

And then I heard a voice call out, a voice from the tomb.

'Rumpole!' it said. 'What an extraordinary coincidence. Are you here for Christmas? You and your good lady?'

I turned my head. I had not, alas, been mistaken. There he was, in person – Mr Justice Gravestone. He was wearing a tweed suit and some type of regimental or old school tie. His usually lugubrious features wore the sort of smile only previously stimulated by a long succession of guilty verdicts. And the next thing he said came as such a surprise that I almost choked on my slice of fruit cake.

'I say,' he said, and I promise you these were Gravestone's exact words, 'this is fun, isn't it?'

II

'I've often wondered what it would be like to be married to Rumpole.'

It was a lie, of course. I dare swear that the Honourable Gravestone never spent one minute of his time wondering what it would be like to be Mrs Rumpole. But there he was, having pulled up a chair, tucking into our anchovy paste sandwiches and smiling at She Who Must Be Obeyed with as much joy as if she had just returned twenty guilty verdicts – one of them being in the case of the Judge *versus* Rumpole.

'He can be a bit difficult at times, of course,' Hilda weighed in for the prosecution.

'A little difficult! That's putting it mildly, Mrs Rumpole. You can't imagine the trouble we have with him in court.'

To my considerable irritation, my wife and the judge were smiling together as though they were discussing, with tolerant amusement, the irrational behaviour of a difficult child.

'Of course we mustn't discuss the case before me at the moment,' Graves said.

'That ghastly terrorist.' Hilda had already reached a verdict.

'Exactly! We won't say a word about him.'

'Just as well,' Hilda agreed. 'We get far too much discussion of Rumpole's cases.'

'Really? Poor Mrs Rumpole.' The judge gave her a look of what I found to be quite sickening sympathy. 'Brings his work home with him, does he?'

'Oh, absolutely! He'll do anything in the world for some ghastly murderer or other, but can I get him to help me redecorate the bathroom?'

'You redecorate bathrooms?' The judge looked at Hilda with admiration as though she had just admitted to sailing round the world in a hot-air balloon. Then he turned to me. 'You're a lucky man, Rumpole!'

'He won't tell you that.' Hilda was clearly enjoying our Christmas break even more than she had expected. 'By the way, I hope he wasn't too rude to you in court.'

'I thought we weren't meant to discuss the case,' I tried to make an objection, which was entirely disregarded by my wife and the unlearned judge.

'Oh, that wasn't Rumpole being merely rude. It was Rumpole trying to impress his client by showing him how fearlessly he can stand up to judges. We're quite used to that.'

'He says,' Hilda still seemed to find the situation amusing, 'that you threatened to report him for professional misconduct. You really ought to be more careful, shouldn't you, Rumpole?'

'Oh, I said that,' Graves had the audacity to admit, 'just to give your husband a bit of a shock. He did go a little green, I thought, when I made the suggestion.'

'I did not go green!' By now I was losing patience with the judge Hilda was treating like a long-lost friend. 'I made a perfectly reasonable protest against a flagrant act of premature adjudication! You had obviously decided that my client is guilty and you were going to let the jury know it.'

'But isn't he guilty, Rumpole? Isn't that obvious?'

'Of course he's not guilty. He's completely innocent. And will remain so until the jury come back into court and convict him. And that is to be their decision. And what the judge wants will have absolutely nothing to do with it!'

I may have gone too far, but I felt strongly on the subject. Judge Graves, however, seemed completely impervious to my attack. He stood, still smiling, warming his tweed-covered backside at the fire and repeated, 'We really mustn't discuss the case we're involved in at the moment. Let's remember, it is Christmas.'

'Yes, Rumpole. It is Christmas.' Hilda had cast herself, it seemed, as Little Lady Echo to his Lordship.

'That's settled, then. Look, why don't I book a table for three at dinner?' The judge was still smiling. 'Wouldn't that be tremendous fun?'

'What a perfectly charming man Judge Graves is.'

These were words I never expected to hear spoken, but they contained the considered verdict of She Who Must Be Obeyed before we settled down for the first night of our Christmas holiday. The food at dinner had been simple but good. (The entrecôte steak had not been arranged in a little tower swamped by tomato coulis and there had been a complete absence of rocket and all the idiocy of smart restaurants.) The Gravestone was clearly on the most friendly of terms with Lorraine, the manageress, and he and Hilda enjoyed a lengthy conversation on the subject of fishing, which sport Graves practised and on which Hilda was expert after her study of the back number of *Country Life* in the residents' lounge.

Now and again I was asked why I didn't go out on a day's fishing with Hilda's newfound friend the judge, a question I found as easy to answer as 'Why don't you take part in the London Marathon wearing nothing but bikini bottoms and a wig?' For a greater part of the dinner I had sat, unusually silent, listening to the ceaseless chatter of the newfound friends, feeling as superfluous as a maiden aunt at a lovers' meeting.

Soon after telling me how charming she had found the Gravestone, Hilda sank into a deep and contented sleep. As the moonlight streamed in at the window and I heard the faraway hooting of an owl, I began to worry about the case we hadn't discussed at dinner.

I couldn't forget my first meeting in Brixton Prison with my client, Hussein Khan. Although undoubtedly the author of the fatal letter, he didn't seem, when I met him in the company of my faithful solicitor, Bonny Bernard, to be the sort who would strike terror into the heart of anyone. He was short and unsmiling with soft brown eyes, a quiet monotonous voice and unusually small hands. He wasn't only uncomplaining, he seemed to find it the most natural thing in the world that he should find himself locked up and facing the most serious of all charges. It was, he told us early in the interview, the will of Allah, and if Allah willed, who was he, a 22-year-old undergraduate in computer studies, to ask questions? I was, throughout the case, amazed at the combination, in my inexplicable client, of the most complicated knowledge of modern technology and the most primitive and merciless religious beliefs.

'I wrote the letter. Of course I did. It was not my decision that she should die. It was the will of God.'

'The will of God that a harmless woman should be shot for writing something critical in a book?'

'Die for blasphemy, yes.'

'And they say you were her executioner, that you carried out the sentence.'

'I didn't do that.' He was looking at me patiently, as though I still had much to learn about the faith of Hussein Khan. 'I knew that death would come to her in time. It came sooner than I had expected.'

So, was I defending a man who had issued a death threat which had then been obediently carried out by some person or persons unknown in the peaceful precincts of an East London university? It seemed an unlikely story, and I had not been looking forward to the murder trial which started at the Old Bailey during the run-up to Christmas.

At the heart of the case there was, I thought, a mystery. The letter, I knew, was clear evidence of Hussein's guilt, and yet there was no forensic evidence – no bloodstains on his clothing, no traces of his having fired a pistol with a silencer (there must have been a silencer, because no one in the building had heard a shot). This was evidence in Hussein's favour, but I had to remember that he had been in the university building when the murder had taken place, although he'd already been sent down for writing the letter.

As the owl hooted, Hilda breathed deeply. Sleep eluded me. I went through Hussein Khan's story again. He had received a phone call, he said, when he was at his parents' restaurant. (He had answered the phone himself, so there was no one to confirm the call.) It had been, it seemed, from a girl who said she was the senior tutor's secretary and that the tutor wanted to meet him in the university library at ten o'clock that evening to discuss his future.

He had arrived at the William Morris building at nine thirty and had told Mr Luttrell, the man at the main reception area, that he was there to meet the senior tutor at the library. He said that when he had arrived at the library, the tutor wasn't there and that he had waited for over an hour and then gone home, having never been near Honoria Glossop's office.

Of course the senior tutor and his secretary denied that either had made such a telephone call. The implication was that Hussein was lying through his teeth and that he had gone to the university because he had known that Professor Glossop worked in her office until late at night and he had intended to kill her.

At last I fell into a restless sleep. In my dreams I saw myself being prosecuted by Soapy Sam Ballard who was wearing a long beard and arguing for my conviction under sharia law.

I woke early to the first faint flush of daylight as a distant cock crowed. I got up, tiptoed across the room, and extracted from the bottom of my case the papers in *R. v. Khan*. I was looking for the answer to a problem as yet undefined, going through the prosecution statement again, and finding nothing very much.

I reminded myself that Mr Luttrell, at his reception desk, had seen Honoria and her husband arrive together and go to her office. Ricky Glossop had left not more than fifteen minutes later, and later still he had telephoned and couldn't get an answer from his wife. He had asked Luttrell to go to Honoria's office because she wasn't answering her phone. The receptionist had gone to her office and found her lying across her desk, her hand close to the bloodstained letter.

Next I read the statement from Honoria's secretary, Sue Blackmore, describing how she had found the letter in Honoria's university pigeonhole and taken it to Honoria at her home. Of Honoria's reaction on receiving it, Ms Blackmore commented, 'She didn't take the note all that seriously and wouldn't even tell the police.' Ricky Glossop had finally rung the anti-terrorist department in Scotland Yard and showed them the letter.

None of this was new. There was only one piece of evidence which I might have overlooked.

In the senior tutor's statement he said he had spoken to Honoria on the morning of the day she had died. She had told him that she couldn't be at a seminar that afternoon because she had 'an urgent appointment with Tony Hawkin'. Hawkin, as the senior tutor knew, was a solicitor who acted for the university, and had also acted for Honoria Glossop in a private capacity. The senior tutor had no idea why she had wanted to see her solicitor. He never saw his colleague alive again.

I was giving that last document some thought when Hilda stirred, opened an eye, and instructed me to ring for breakfast.

'You'll have to look after yourself today, Rumpole,' she told me. 'Gerald's going to take me fishing for grayling.'

'Gerald?' Was there some new man in Hilda's life who had turned up in the Cotswolds?

'You know. The charming judge you introduced me to last night.'

'You can't mean Gravestone?'

'Don't be ridiculous. Of course I mean Gerald Graves.'

'You're going fishing with him?'

'He's very kindly going to take me to a bit of river he shares with a friend.'

'How delightful.' I adopted the ironic tone. 'If you catch anything, bring it back for supper.'

'Oh, I'm not going to do any fishing. I'm simply going to watch Gerald from the bank. He's going to show me how he ties his flies.'

'How absolutely fascinating.'

She didn't seem to think she'd said anything at all amusing and began to lever herself briskly out of bed.

'Do ring up about that breakfast, Rumpole!' she said. 'I've got to get ready for Gerald.'

He may be Gerald to you, I thought, but he will always be the Old Gravestone to me.

After Hilda had gone to meet her newfound friend, I finished the bacon and eggs with sausage and fried slice – which I had ordered as an organic, low-calorie breakfast – and put a telephone call through to my faithful solicitor, Bonny Bernard. I found him at his home talking over a background of shrill and excited children eager for the next morning and the well-filled stockings.

'Mr Rumpole!' The man sounded shocked by my call. 'Don't you ever take a day off? It's Christmas Eve!'

'I know it's Christmas Eve. I know that perfectly well,' I told him. 'And my wife has gone fishing with our sepulchral judge, whom she calls "Gerald". Meanwhile, have you got any close friends or associates working at Hawkin's, the solicitor?'

'Barry Tuck used to be our legal executive – moved there about three years ago.'

'A cooperative sort of character is he, Tuck?'

'We got on very well. Yes.'

'Then get him to find out why Honoria Glossop went to see Tony Hawkin the afternoon before she was shot. It must have been something fairly urgent. She missed a seminar in order to go.'

'Is it important?'

'Probably not, but it just might be something we ought to know.'

'I hope you're enjoying your Christmas break, Mr Rumpole.'

'Quite enjoying it. I'd like it better without a certain member of the judiciary. Oh, and I've got a hard time ahead.'

'Working?'

'No,' I told my patient solicitor gloomily. 'Dancing.'

'Quick, quick, slow, Rumpole. That's better. Now chassé! Don't you remember, Rumpole? This is where you chassé.'

The truth was that I remembered little about it. It had been so long ago. How many years could it have been since Hilda and I had trodden across a dance floor? Yet here I was in a dinner jacket, which was now uncomfortably tight around the waist, doing my best to walk round this small area of polished parquet in time to the music with one arm around Hilda's satin-covered waist and my other hand gripping one of hers. Although for much of the time she was walking backwards, she was undoubtedly the one in command of the enterprise. I heard a voice singing, seemingly from far off, above the music of the five-piece band laid on for the hotel's dinner dance. It was a strange sound and one that I hadn't heard for what seemed many years – She Who Must Be Obeyed was singing. I looked towards my table, rather as someone lost at sea might look towards a distant shore, and I saw Mr Justice Gravestone smiling at us with approval.

'Well done, Hilda! And you came through that quite creditably, I thought, Rumpole. I mean, at least you managed to remain upright, although there were a few dodgy moments coming round that far corner.'

'That was when I told him chassé. Rumpole couldn't quite manage it.'

As they were both enjoying a laugh I realized that, during a long day by the river which had, it seemed, produced nothing more than two fish so small that they had had to be returned to their natural environment, Mrs Rumpole had become 'Hilda' to the judge, who had already become 'Gerald'.

'You know, when you retire, Rumpole,' the judge was sounding sympathetic in the most irritating kind of way, 'you could take dancing lessons.'

'There's so much Rumpole could do *if* he retired. I keep telling him,' was Hilda's contribution. 'He could have wonderful days like we had, Gerald. Outdoors, close to nature and fishing.'

'Catching two small grayling you had to put back in the water?' I was bold enough to ask. 'It would've been easier to pay a quick visit to the fishmonger's.'

'Catching fish is not the point of fishing,' Hilda told me.

Before I could ask her what the point of it was, the judge came up with a suggestion. 'When you retire, I could teach you fishing, Rumpole. We could have a few days out together.'

'Now, then. Isn't that kind of Gerald, Rumpole?' Hilda beamed and I had to mutter, 'Very kind,' although the judge's offer had made me more determined than ever to die with my wig on.

It was at this point that Lorraine, the manageress, came to the judge with a message. He read it quickly and then said, 'Poor old Leslie Mulliner. You know him, don't you, Rumpole? He sits in the Chancery Division.'

I had to confess I didn't know anyone who sat in the Chancery Division.

'He was going to join us here tomorrow but his wife's not well.'

'He said on the phone that you'd do the job for him tomorrow.' Lorraine seemed anxious.

'Yes, of course,' Graves hurried to reassure her. 'I'll stand in for him.'

Before I could get any further explanation of the 'job', the music had struck up a more contemporary note. Foxtrots were out, and with a cry of 'Come along, Hilda' Graves was strutting the dance floor, making curious rhythmic movements with his hands. And Hilda, walking free and unfastened from her partner, was also strutting and waving her arms, smiling with pleasure. It wasn't, I'm sure, the most up-to-date form of dancing, but it was, I suppose, a gesture from two sedate citizens who were doing their best to become, for a wine-filled moment on Christmas Eve, a couple of teenagers.

Christmas Day at Cherry Picker's Hall was uneventful. The judge suggested church, and I stood while he and Hilda bellowed out 'O come, all ye faithful . . .' Then we sat among the faithful under the Norman arches, beside the plaques and monuments to so many vanished rectors and country squires, looking out upon the holly around the pulpit and the flowers on the altar. I tried to understand, not for the first time, how a religious belief could become so perverted as to lead to death threats, terror and a harmless professor shot through the head.

We had lunch in a pub and then the judge announced he had work to do and left us.

After a long and satisfactory sleep, Hilda and I woke around tea-time and went to the residents' lounge. Long before we got to the door, we could hear the excited cries of children, and when we went in we saw them crowded round the Christmas tree. And there, stooping among the presents, was the expected figure in a red dressing gown (trimmed with white fur), wellington boots, a white beard and a long red hat. As he picked up a present and turned towards us, I felt that fate had played the greatest practical joke it could have thought up to enliven the festive season.

Standing in for his friend Mulliner from the Chancery Division, the sepulchral, unforgiving, prosecution-minded Mr Justice Gravestone, my old enemy, had become Father Christmas.

On Boxing Day, I rang a persistent, dogged, ever-useful private detective who, sickened by divorce, now specialized in the cleaner world of crime – Ferdinand Isaac Gerald Newton, known in legal circles as 'Fig' Newton. I told him that, as was the truth, my wife, Hilda, was planning a long country walk and lunch in a distant village with a judge whom I had spent a lifetime trying to avoid. And I asked him, if he had no previous engagements, if he'd like to sample the table d'hôte at Cherry Picker's Hall.

Fig Newton is a lugubrious character of indeterminate age, usually dressed in an old mackintosh and an even older hat, with a drip at the end of his nose caused by a seemingly perpetual cold – most likely caught while keeping observation in all weathers. But today he had shed his outer garments, his nose was dry, and he was tucking into the lamb cutlets with something approaching enthusiasm. 'Bit of a step up from your usual pub lunch, this, isn't it, Mr Rumpole?'

'It certainly is, Fig. We're splashing out this Christmas. Now this case I'm doing down the Bailey . . .'

'The terrorist?'

'Yes, the terrorist.'

'You're on to a loser with that one, Mr Rumpole.' Fig was gloomily relishing the fact.

'Most probably. All the same, there are a few stones I don't want to leave unturned.'

'Such as what?'

'Find out what you can about the Glossops.'

'The dead woman's family?'

'That's right. See what's known about their lives, hobbies, interests. That sort of thing. I need to get more of a picture of their lives together. Oh, and see if the senior tutor knows more about the Glossops. Pick up any gossip going around the university. I'll let you know if Bonny Bernard has found out why Honoria had a date with her solicitor.'

'So when do you want all this done by, Mr Rumpole?' Fig picked up a cutlet bone and chewed gloomily. 'Tomorrow morning, I suppose?'

'Oh, sooner than that if possible,' I told him.

It was not that I felt that the appalling Hussein Khan had a defence – in fact he might well turn out to have no defence at all. But something at the children's Christmas party had suggested a possibility to my mind.

That something was the sight of Mr Justice Graves standing in for someone else.

III

Christmas was over, and I wondered if the season of goodwill was over with it. The Christmas cards had left the mantelpiece, the holly and the mistletoe had been tidied away, we had exchanged green fields for Gloucester Road, and Cherry Picker's Hall was nothing but a memory. The judge was back on the bench to steer the case of R. v. *Khan* towards its inevitable guilty verdict.

The Christmas decorations were not all that had gone. Gerald the cheerful dinner guest, Gerald the energetic dancing partner of

She Who Must Be Obeyed, Gerald the fisherman and, in particular, Gerald as Santa Claus had all gone as well, leaving behind only the old thin-lipped, unsmiling Mr Justice Gravestone with the voice of doom, determined to make a difficult case harder than ever.

All the same there was something of a spring in the Rumpole step. This was not only the result of the Christmas break but also due to a suspicion that the case *R. v. Khan* might not be quite as horrifyingly simple as it had at first appeared.

As I crossed the hall on my way to Court Number One, I saw Ricky Glossop – the dashingly handsome husband of the murdered professor – with a pretty blonde girl whom I took to be Sue Blackmore, Honoria's secretary, who was due to give evidence about her employer's reception of the fatal letter. She seemed, so far as I could tell from a passing examination, to be a girl on the verge of a nervous breakdown. She lit a cigarette with trembling fingers, then almost immediately stamped it out. She kept looking, with a kind of desperation, towards the door of the court, and then turning, with a sob, to Ricky Glossop and choking out what I took to be some sort of complaint. He had laid a consoling hand on hers and was talking in the sort of low, exaggeratedly calm tone that a dentist uses when he says, 'This isn't going to hurt.'

The medical and police evidence had been disposed of before Christmas and now, in the rather strange order adopted by Soapy Sam Ballard for the prosecution, the only witnesses left were Arthur Luttrell (who manned the reception desk), Ricky Glossop and the nervous secretary.

Luttrell, the receptionist, was a smart, precise, self-important man with a sharp nose and a sandy moustache who clearly regarded his position as being at the centre of the university organization. He remembered Hussein Khan coming at nine thirty that evening, saying he had an appointment with the senior tutor, and going up to the library. At quarter to ten the Glossops had arrived. Ricky had gone with his wife to her office, but had left about fifteen minutes later. 'He stopped to speak to me on the way out,' Luttrell told Soapy Sam, 'which is why I remember it well.'

After that, the evening at William Morris University followed its horrible course. Around eleven o'clock, Hussein Khan left, complaining that he had wasted well over an hour, no senior tutor had come to talk to him, and that he was going back to his parents' restaurant in Golders Green. After that Ricky telephoned the reception desk saying that he couldn't get any reply from his wife's office and would Mr Luttrell please go and make sure she was all right. As we all know, Mr Luttrell went to the office, knocked, opened the door, and was met by the ghastly spectacle which was to bring us all together in Court Number One at the Old Bailey.

'Mr Rumpole.' The judge's tone in calling my name was as aloofly disapproving as though Christmas had never happened. 'All this evidence is agreed, isn't it? I don't suppose you'll find it necessary to trouble Mr Luttrell with any questions.'

'Just one or two, my Lord.'

'Oh, very well.' The judge sounded displeased. 'Just remember, we're under a public duty not to waste time.'

'I hope your Lordship isn't suggesting that an attempt to get to the truth is a waste of time.' And before the Old Gravestone could launch a counter-attack, I asked Mr Luttrell the first question.

'You say Mr Glossop spoke to you on the way out. Can you remember what he said?'

'I remember perfectly.' The receptionist looked personally insulted as though I doubted his word. 'He asked me if Hussein Khan was in the building.'

'He asked you that?'

'Yes, he did.'

'And what did you tell him?'

'I told him yes. I said Khan was in the library where he had an appointment with the senior tutor.'

I allowed a pause for this curious piece of evidence to sink into the minds of the jury. Graves, of course, filled in the gap by asking if that was my only question.

'Just one more, my Lord.'

Here the judge sighed heavily, but I ignored that.

'Are you telling this jury, Mr Luttrell, that Glossop discovered that

the man who had threatened his wife with death was in the building, then left without speaking to her again?'

I looked at the jury as I asked this and saw, for the first time in the
trial, a few faces looking puzzled.

Mr Luttrell, however, sounded unfazed.

'I've told you what he said. I can't tell you anything more.'

'He can't tell us anything more,' the judge repeated. 'So that
would seem to be the end of the matter, wouldn't it, Mr Rumpole?'

'Not quite the end,' I told him. 'I don't think it's quite the end of
the matter yet.'

This remark did nothing to improve my relations with his Lordship, who gave me a look from which all traces of the Christmas
spirit had been drained.

The jury may have had a moment of doubt during the receptionist's evidence, but when Ricky Glossop was put in the witness box,
their sympathy and concern for the good-looking, appealingly modest, and stricken husband was obvious. Graves supported them with
enthusiasm.

'This is clearly going to be a terrible ordeal for you, Mr Glossop,'
the judge said, looking at the witness with serious concern. 'Wouldn't
you like to sit down?'

'No thank you, my Lord. I prefer to stand,' Ricky said bravely.
The judge gave him the sort of look a commanding officer might
give to a young subaltern who'd volunteered to attack the enemy
position single-handed. 'Just let me know,' Graves insisted, 'if you
feel exhausted or overcome by any part of your evidence, and you
shall sit down immediately.'

'Thank you very much, my Lord. That *is* very kind of your Lordship.'

So, with the formalities of mutual admiration over, Ricky Glossop began to tell his story.

He had met Honoria some ten years before when they were both
cruising round the Greek islands. 'She knew all the classical legends
and the history of every place. I thought she'd never be bothered
with an undereducated slob like me.' Here he smiled modestly, and

the judge smiled back as a sign of disagreement. 'But luckily she put up with me. And, of course, I fell in love with her.'

'Of course?' Soapy Sam seemed to feel that this sentence called for some further explanation.

'She was extremely beautiful.'

'And she found you attractive?'

'She seemed to. God knows why.' This answer earned him smiles for his modesty.

'So you were married for ten years,' Ballard said. 'And you had no children.'

'No. Honoria couldn't have children. It was a great sadness to both of us.'

'And how would you describe your marriage up to the time your wife got this terrible letter?' Ballard was holding the letter out, at a distance, as though the paper itself might carry a fatal infection.

'We were very happy.'

'When she got the letter, how did she react to it?'

'She was very brave, my Lord,' Ricky told the judge. 'She said it had obviously been written by some nutcase and that she intended to ignore it.'

'She was extremely brave.' The judge spoke the words with admiration as he wrote them down.

So Ricky Glossop told his story. And when I – the representative, so it appeared, of his wife's murderer – rose to cross-examine, I felt a chill wind blowing through Number One Court.

'Mr Glossop, you said your marriage to your wife Honoria was a happy one?'

'As far as I was concerned it was very happy.' Here he smiled at the jury and some of them nodded back approvingly.

'Did you know that on the afternoon before she was murdered, your wife had consulted a solicitor, Mr Anthony Hawkin of Henshaw and Hawkin?'

'I didn't know that, no.'

'Can you guess why?'

'I'm afraid not. My wife had considerable financial interests under her father's will. It might have been about that.'

'You mean it might have been about money?'

'Yes.'

'Did you know that Anthony Hawkin is well known as an expert on divorce and family law?'

'I didn't know that either.'

'And you didn't know that your wife was considering proceedings for divorce?'

'I certainly didn't.'

I looked at the jury. They were now, I thought, at least interested. I remembered the frightened blonde girl I had seen outside the court and the hand he had put on hers as he had tried to comfort her.

'Was there any trouble between your wife and yourself because of her secretary, Sue Blackmore?'

'So far as I know, none whatever.'

'Mr Rumpole. I'm wondering, and I expect the jury may be wondering as well, what on earth these questions have to do with your client's trial for murder,' the judge interjected.

'Then wonder on,' I might have quoted Shakespeare to Graves, 'till truth make all things plain.' But I did not do that. I merely said, 'I'm putting these questions to test the credibility of this witness, my Lord.'

'And why, Mr Rumpole, are you attacking his credibility? Which part of this gentleman's evidence are you disputing?'

'If I may be allowed to cross-examine in the usual way, I hope it may become clear,' I said, and then I'm afraid I also said, 'even to your Lordship.'

At this, Gravestone gave me the look that meant, 'You just wait until we come to the summing up, and I'll tell the jury what I think of your attack on this charming husband.' But for the moment he remained as silent as a block of ice, so I soldiered on.

'Mr Glossop. Your wife's secretary delivered this threatening letter to her.'

'Yes. Honoria was working at home and Sue brought it over from her pigeonhole at the university.'

'You've told us that she was very brave, of course. That she had said it was probably from some nutcase and that she intended to ignore it. But you insisted on taking the letter to the police.'

'An extremely wise decision, if I may say so,' Graves took it upon himself to note.

'And I think you gave the story to the Press Association so that this death threat received wide publicity.'

'I thought Honoria would be safer if it was all out in the open. People would be on their guard.'

'Another wise decision, the members of the jury might think.' Graves was making sure the jury thought it.

'And when the letter was traced to my client, everyone knew that it was Hussein Khan who was the author of the letter?'

'He was dismissed from the university, so I suppose a lot of people knew, yes.'

'So, if anything were to have happened to your wife after that, if she were to have been attacked or killed, Hussein Khan would have been the most likely suspect?'

'I think that has been obvious throughout this trial.' Graves couldn't resist it.

'My Lord, I'd really much rather get the answers to my questions from the witness than receive them from your Lordship.' I went on quickly before the judge could get in his two pennies' worth. 'You took your wife to the university on that fatal night?'

'I often did. If I was going somewhere and she had work to do in her office, I'd drop her off and then collect her later on my way home.'

'But you didn't just drop her off, did you? You went inside the building with her. You took her up to her office?'

'Yes. We'd been talking about something in the car and we went on discussing it as I went up to her office with her.'

'He escorted her, Mr Rumpole,' the sepulchral voice boomed from the bench. 'A very gentlemanly thing to do.'

'Thank you, my Lord.' Ricky's smile was still full of charm.

'And what were you discussing?' I asked him. 'Was it divorce?'

'It certainly wasn't divorce. I can't remember what it was exactly.'

'Then perhaps you can remember this. How long did you stay in the office with your wife?'

'Perhaps five, maybe ten minutes. I can't remember exactly.'

'And when you left, was she still alive?'

There was a small silence.

The witness looked at me and seemed to catch his breath.

Then he gave us the invariably charming smile.

'Of course she was.'

'You spoke to Mr Luttrell at the reception area on your way out?'

'I did, yes.'

'He says you asked him if Hussein Khan was in the building?'

'Yes, I did.'

'Why did you do that?'

'I suppose I'd heard from someone that he might have been there.'

'And what did Mr Luttrell tell you?'

'He said that Khan was in the building, yes.'

'You knew that Hussein Khan's presence in that building was a potential danger to your wife.'

'I suppose I knew. Yes.'

'I suppose you did. And yet you left and drove off in your car without warning her?'

There was a longer silence then and Ricky's smile seemed to droop.

'I didn't go back to the office, no.'

'Why not, Mr Glossop? Why not warn her? Why didn't you see that Khan left before you went off?'

And then Ricky Glossop said something which changed the atmosphere in court in a moment, even silencing the judge.

'I suppose I was in a hurry. I was on my way to a party.'

After a suitable pause I asked, 'There was no lock on your wife's office door, was there?'

'There might have been. But she never locked it.'

'So you left her unprotected, with the man who had threatened her life still in the building, because you were on your way to a party?'

The smile came again, but it had no effect now on the jury.

'I think I heard he was with the senior tutor in the library. I suppose I thought that was safe.'

'Mr Glossop, were you not worried by the possibility that the senior tutor might leave first, leaving the man who threatened your wife still in the building with her?'

'I suppose I didn't think of that,' was all he could say.

I let the answer sink in and then turned to more dangerous and uncharted territory.

'I believe you're interested in various country sports.'

'That's right, my Lord.' The witness, seeming to feel the ground was now safer, smiled at the judge.

'You used to go shooting, I believe.'

'Well, I go shooting, Mr Rumpole.' A ghastly twitch of the lips was, from the bench, Graves's concession towards a smile. 'And I hope you're not accusing me of complicity in any sort of a crime?'

I let the jury have their sycophantic laugh, then went on to ask, 'Did you ever belong to a pistol shooting club, Mr Glossop?' Fig Newton, the private eye, had done his work well.

'When such clubs were legal, yes.'

'And do you still own a handgun?'

'Certainly not.' The witness seemed enraged. 'I wouldn't do anything that broke the law.'

I turned to look at the jury with my eyebrows raised, but for the moment the witness was saved by the bell as the judge announced that he could see by the clock that it was time we broke for lunch.

Before we parted, however, Soapy Sam got up to tell us that his next witness would be Mrs Glossop's secretary, Sue Blackmore, who would merely give evidence about the receipt of the letter and the deceased's reaction to it. Miss Blackmore was, apparently, likely to be a very nervous witness, and perhaps his learned friend Mr Rumpole would agree to her evidence being read.

Mr Rumpole did not agree. Mr Rumpole wanted Miss Sue Blackmore to be present in the flesh and he was ready to cross-examine her at length. And so we parted, expecting the trial of Hussein Khan for murder to start again at two o'clock.

But Khan's trial for murder didn't start again at two o'clock or at any other time. I was toying with a plate of steak and kidney pie and a pint of Guinness in the pub opposite the Old Bailey when I saw the furtive figure of Sam Ballard oozing through the crowd. He came to me obviously heavy with news.

'Rumpole! You don't drink at lunchtime, do you?'

'Yes. But not too much at lunchtime. Can I buy you a pint of stout?'

'Certainly not, Rumpole. Mineral water, if you have to. And could we move to that little table in the corner? This is news for your ears alone.'

After I had transported my lunch to a more secluded spot and supplied our head of chambers with mineral water, he brought me up to date on that lunch hour's developments.

'It's Sue, the secretary, Rumpole. When we told her that she'd have to go into the witness box, she panicked and asked to see Superintendent Gregory. By this time, she was in tears and, he told me, almost incomprehensible. However, Gregory managed to calm her down and she said she knew you'd get it out of her in the witness box, so she might as well confess that she was the one who had made the telephone call.'

'Which telephone call was that?'

Soapy Sam was demonstrating his usual talent for making a simple statement of fact utterly confusing.

'The telephone call to your client. Telling him to go and meet the senior tutor.'

'You mean . . . ?' The mists that had hung over the case of Khan the terrorist were beginning to clear. 'She pretended to be . . .'

'The senior tutor's secretary. Yes. The idea was to get Khan into the building while Glossop . . .'

'Murdered his wife?' I spoke the words that Ballard seemed reluctant to use.

'I think she's prepared to give evidence against him,' Soapy Sam said, looking thoughtfully towards future briefs. 'Well, she'll have to, unless she wants to go to prison as an accessory.'

'Has handsome Ricky heard the news yet?' I wondered.

'Mr Glossop has been detained. He's helping the police with their enquiries.'

So many people I know, who help the police with their enquiries, are in dire need of help themselves. 'So you'll agree to a verdict of not guilty of murder?' I asked Ballard, as though it was a request to pass the mustard.

'Perhaps. Eventually. And you'll agree to guilty of making death threats in a letter?'

'Oh, yes,' I admitted. 'We'll have to plead guilty to that.'

But there was no hurry. I could finish my steak and kidney and order another Guinness in peace.

'It started off,' I was telling Hilda over a glass of Château Thames Embankment that evening, 'as an act of terrorism, of mad, religious fanaticism, of what has become the new terror of our times. And it ends up as an old-fashioned murder by a man who wanted to dispose of his rich wife for her money and be free to marry a pretty young woman. It was a case, you might say, of Dr Crippen meeting Osama Bin Laden.'

'It's hard to say which is worse.' She Who Must Be Obeyed was thoughtful.

'Both of them,' I told her. 'Both of them are worse. But I suppose we understand Dr Crippen better. Only one thing we can be grateful for.'

'What's that, Rumpole?'

'The terrorist got a fair trial. And the whole truth came out in the end. The day when a suspected terrorist doesn't get a fair trial will be the day they've won the battle.'

I refilled our glasses, having delivered my own particular verdict on the terrible events of that night at William Morris University.

'Mind you,' I said, 'it was your friend Gerald Graves who put me on to the truth of the matter.'

'Oh, really.' Hilda sounded unusually cool on the subject of the judge.

'It was when he was playing Father Christmas. He was standing in for someone else. And I thought, what if the real murderer thought he'd stand in for someone else. Hussein Khan had uttered the death threat and was there to take the blame. All Ricky had to do was go to work quickly. So that's what he did – he committed murder in Hussein Khan's name. That death threat was a gift from heaven for him.'

One of our usual silences fell between us, and then Hilda said, 'I don't know why you call Mr Justice Graves my friend.'

'You got on so well at Christmas.'

'Well, yes we did. And then he said we must keep in touch. So I telephoned his clerk and the message came back that the judge was busy for months ahead but he hoped we might meet again eventually. I have to tell you, Rumpole, that precious judge of yours does not treat women well.'

I did my best. I tried to think of the Old Gravestone as a heart-breaker, a sort of Don Juan who picked women up and dropped them without mercy, but I failed miserably.

'I'm better off with you, Rumpole,' Hilda told me. 'I can always rely on you to be unreliable.'

Rumpole and the Brave New World

When he died in January 2009 John Mortimer had just begun writing a new Rumpole novel, Rumpole and the Brave New World. *This is the text he left.*

1

At my age I'm about as far from childhood as it's possible to be. I'm nearer toppling off the peg than joining in adolescent games, but there was one case which gave me an alarming and, I hope, interesting insight into the world of the youth of today.

It began when one of Hilda's innumerable relatives, her niece Cynthia, a student at Oxford, was taking part in a performance of the *Messiah* and sent an invitation to Hilda saying that she wished we would both come. Naturally I did my best to have an important legal fixture on the date specified, but work was as plentiful as Manhattan cocktails in the desert. When I told Hilda that my practice was more important than the concert she went down to my chambers and checked up with Henry, my clerk, in the most treacherous manner. I was therefore condemned to the oratorio. So I was to be found on that particular Thursday, not in Number One Court in the Old Bailey, or even before the Snaresbrook magistrates, but in the vast auditorium which is the Sheldonian Theatre in Oxford. It was there, many years ago, that I had taken my degree, kneeling and being bumped on the head with a Bible.

I remember my days at Keble College as peaceful and untroubled, and I can't say that I was taught anything that would help me to become known throughout the Temple as one of the deadliest cross-examiners in the trade. Instead, the tutors and lecturers wanted to discuss property laws, the more obscure provisions of banking acts and rights of way. Despite all this I did reasonably well in criminal law with the help of useful little text books such as *Murder in a Nutshell* and *All You Need to Know About Offences Against the Person*.

I did learn one important lesson. I had become addicted to the college sherry and, as a ridiculous and useless gesture, I boasted that I could drink a tankard full of it. I did so and fell to the ground and found the religious character who shared my rooms kneeling beside me in silent prayer. Since then I have resolutely refused sherry.

Looking back on it I am grateful for Hilda's persistence. If we hadn't gone to the concert I would have missed an occasion which led, through a tangle of possibilities, to one of the most curious and unusual crimes in the Rumpole history.

So there I was, wondering why old Handel or his scriptwriter couldn't say a thing once and let it go at that. Every line in the *Messiah* seemed to be repeated again and again. I looked around the crowded auditorium and was curious to see so many children assembled, all below undergraduate age. There was a certain amount of giggling and pinching between them, but on the whole they sat quietly until the music came to an end.

During the interval a woman came on to the stage and asked for further contributions to 'Music in Oxford'. 'I've only got folding money.' 'Of course you'll give them folding money, a ten-pound note will be adequate,' Hilda told me. So I pulled out my wallet and parted with the cash. I tell you this only because of what happened when we were leaving the hall.

We left through a crowded doorway. My attention was diverted by Hilda calling out, 'Cynthia's here, Rumpole. I've told her how proud you are of her.' I remember being bumped into as she spoke and I felt some movement under my jacket pocket, the home of the Rumpole wallet. I felt for it, and any hand that might have been on it was quickly withdrawn. I looked round at the faces of laughing children and solemn-music lovers and wondered why it was that almost everything in the Rumpole existence seemed to lead, in one way or another, to an experience of crime.

'Oxford is thought of as a city of dreaming spires, quiet quadrangles and lofty ceilinged dining halls.' Cynthia's friend Harriet, a good-looking, dark-haired woman in her forties, had joined us for supper at Browns restaurant, which Cynthia had recommended. Harriet then reminded us of the other Oxford.

'These kids have got stepfathers who beat them up or worse and mothers who are too drunk to notice it. They get moved around by the social services and don't know where they're going to be spending the next night. We do our best to help.'

'Harriet founded All in the Family. It's an organization to help these children. Take them out into the country,' Cynthia told me. 'I go with them whenever I can.'

'Some of them have never seen a horse and others seem surprised to learn that their school dinners were not born in a fridge but started life grazing in the fields,' Harriet explained. 'Taking them to the *Messiah* was all part of widening their horizons.'

'Their horizons seem to have become wide enough to include a quick dive for my wallet,' I reminded her.

'It's a slow business, Mr Rumpole, but we've got to keep trying.'

I looked at her with admiration. No doubt it was an impossible task to persuade a bunch of adolescents that a choral work in a strange language was more interesting than picking the odd pocket. I felt a sudden affinity with Harriet. Both of us spent our lives trying to win impossible cases. My thoughts on this subject were interrupted by a twangy-voiced, prematurely balding, eager man who had arrived in front of our table.

'Henry Dyson' – he announced his name as though confident I would know all about him – 'of Dyson Furbelow, local solicitors. I'll be sending you a brief. I hope you may be able to fit us into your busy practice.'

Flattery will get you anywhere, and I couldn't help warming to the strange solicitor.

'A murder perhaps?' I shouldn't have expected anything so sensational.

'I'm afraid not. I've got some important clients. You'll have heard of Lord Winsome, big house and estate up on the way to Kidlington? His boy, young Charlie, is being done for "dangerous". I told him you were the only man for the job. You are the only brief I have ever seen getting a client off a dangerous driving. You came down to the magistrates' court here in Oxford. I was waiting to come on in the next case and I was astonished at the way you did it.'

'That's very kind of you.' I took a gulp of Guinness and tried not to look too flattered. 'I'll do my best.' I couldn't resist a smile of satisfaction as I savoured my drink. Not only had my wallet been saved but it was apparently due for a refill.

2

Extract from the Memoir of Hilda Rumpole

You can say what you like about Rumpole's attainments, but I have to admit that he lacks a spiritual side to his nature. Everything has to be tested, carefully labelled and filed away in Rumpole's mind as valuable evidence. Sometimes I've had to ask myself whether Rumpole is really in touch with life's deeper mysteries and I have had to come reluctantly to the conclusion that he is not. All this became clearer to me when I met a new friend, Eustace Peveril, who guided me into deeper understanding of life's mysteries. I have written before about my friend Marsha's bridge club. It was there that I met Judge Bullingham, who, in the end, let me down and has transferred his affections to Phillida, now ridiculously known as Mrs Justice Erskine-Brown. As someone who lives life on the surface I have no doubt she is a very suitable companion to the judge, who I am sure has no experience of the inner life. A door was opened on to the secrets of existence when I played a successful hand of four no trumps with the man I shall always feel privileged to call Eustace. By a happy chance I had drawn him as a partner, and to say we got on well is an understatement. Eustace has suggested that we might have been brother and sister in some previous existence and I can't help feeling that he has hit the nail quite truthfully on the head.

Eustace might not be thought by everyone as handsome but he has the irresistible quality of someone who lives life on a higher plane. He is always impeccably well dressed and he laughingly tells me that he has to keep up appearances for the sake of his work, which I believe is something to do with mail-order tailoring.

When I'd taken the final trick in our no trumps victory, he looked at me with what I can only call amazement.

'Your aura, Hilda – I may call you Hilda, mayn't I? It's glistening so brightly I can hardly look at it.'

'Is it really?'

'Of course it is. It can only be seen in moments of triumph and by people who understand such things. Will you allow me to polish it a little? I've rarely seen anything quite so spectacular.'

With that he took a silk handkerchief out of his breast pocket and gently seemed to caress an area round my forehead. I began to feel some sort of vibration in the air around me. I saw Marsha looking at me in a curious sort of way but I took no notice of her. After a while Eustace folded his handkerchief, restored it to his pocket and left the bridge table in quest of Marsha's sandwiches. When he did so I felt a curious emptiness, an indescribable feeling of loss.

'You're an extraordinary woman,' he told me as he brought me back a plate. 'You live very near the secret heart of existence. Are you aware of that?'

'Not really,' I told him, 'not until we played that last hand together.'

'Then you must have got the feeling of a door opening. A door into an inner world. You must have felt that before.'

'I think so, when Rumpole's been particularly irritating.'

'Don't fight against it, Hilda. You have been picked out to be one of the chosen.'

'Chosen? For what?'

'The deeper understanding. There are a few of us who meet in my studio. They'd be terrifically honoured if you could join us for an evening of deeper living. Would you consider it?'

'I don't see why not.'

'We do our best to live through the trivialities of existence and get to the deeper understanding, then we go off to a little place in Chelsea for a light meal. Do you think your husband would understand it?'

'Not at all, but that won't stop me joining you.'

'They will be enormously grateful. They've never met anyone who lived so near the Great Truth as you seem to do. We'll make a date, Mrs Rumpole. You must shed your light in as many dark holes as possible.'

3

The Rumpole practice in those days could be described as 'jogging along'. The mantelpiece wasn't entirely empty of briefs but they were of an unexciting and predictable variety. There was the case of Harry Timson, whose usually peaceful course of breaking and entering had become revealed to the authorities. This was owing to information, he strongly suspected, that was supplied by his cousin Percy, when he'd found himself in trouble over a quantity of stolen fish dinners. Such disloyalty was rare among the Timsons and Harry was pained by his cousin's behaviour.

While I was thinking these matters over at dinner in the kitchen in Froxbury Mansions (a couple of chops and boiled potatoes), I noticed Hilda looking at me in a strange and thoughtful manner. After a while she got up with a tea towel in her hand and made polishing motions in the air around my head.

'What on earth?'

'It's your aura.' She Who Must was speaking entirely seriously. 'I have to keep your aura clean. You want your aura polished, don't you?'

'I might do if I knew what on earth you were talking about.'

'I'm sorry for you Rumpole, you have such a lot to learn about life.'

With that she sat down, apparently having got the aura satisfactorily dusted, and I wondered how far I could adjust myself to a world which was becoming more and more difficult to understand.